AlignIt
A Tale for a New Civilization

Rick Whitney

DEDICATION

I am indebted to many teachers, centers, teachings, and technologies
including those of Buddhism, Yoga, Tantra, Taoism, Sufism, and Christianity.
A listing would be most personal and long. I simply hold my hands together
and bow to each. Especially to Llewellyn.
May this book be a worthy expression of what I have learned
and serve the noblest of aims.

By the grace and mercy of the Absolute,
May this work convey
some readers toward a ferry
With a skillful ferryman
Heading for the other shore.

DISCLAIMERS

The views expressed in this book are those of the author, or the characters.
They're not official expressions of one group or another.

While the characters' family stories may be minimally autobiographical,
I deliberately explored needs, choices, and family patterns
different from my own.

CONTENTS

Part 1
Bayside Village Tour

Day 1: Sunday

1

Greg arrived in Oakland International before the landing wheels touched the runway; sitting next to him, Sara was still in Seattle. Deplaning with their five year old, Tara, was no different. But at the curb under the Arrivals sign, something began to shift. Despite plane, bus and taxi exhaust, the April afternoon was balmy and pleasant. Greg flagged a taxi, but it was taken. He checked the time on his mobile and grimaced. They arrived at 4:30. An hour late. Sara put down her bags, brushed her long brunette hair behind her left ear, flagged the next cab. It swerved to the curb and stopped.

The Taxi driver, an elder Indian man, hopped out and loaded the family's luggage into the trunk. He opened the back door, and Greg, Sara and Tara entered. The driver swung back around, got in and closed his door. Turning around, he asked in his Indian British, "Where are you going?"

"The Bridge Institute in Richmond," Greg said. He clicked his seat belt.

"The what?" the driver asked, puzzled.

"Bridge Institute."

The driver squinted, perplexed.

"Bayside Village? In Richmond?"

"Richmond I know. Do you have an address?"

"Yeah, hang on...." Greg reached into his side bag. "Here's a map," he said, handing it up.

The driver reached for his glasses in a dashboard compartment and studied the map. "Oh, the old RCC site," he said to himself. He pushed the glasses up to his head, turned back. "That is an old industrial park. Are you sure? Warehouses, light industrial, trucks, trains?"

"It's a new place on an old campus," Greg said confidently.

The driver shrugged his shoulders. "Okay." He handed the map back to Greg. Turning back around, he punched the coordinates into his GPS, put the car in gear and took off.

Greg and Sara peered out the windows as the scenes whizzed by. Oakland International Airport's long term parking, hangers, cheap hotels, chain restaurants. Tara sat between them with her new backpack on her lap. She studied the driver, the taxi meter, the radio with her young, attentive mind.

Sara slowly let go of her rush-project in Seattle. They had arrived in California, and Sara's thoughts were landing now, too. She slowly came to terms with the trip—the week for Bayside Village. "Industrial park?" She turned to Greg, flashing an ironic look.

"Don't fan my doubts. We're just checking it out." Greg ran his freckled fingers through a tuft of dirty blond hair over his forehead. "It's good for my relationship with Roger Barnes and the AlignIt board." He restated the obvious. Sara's challenge itself was restatement. Why wasn't Bayside Village compelling to her, he wondered. It was like so many daring ventures together in the past, but more promising. Where's her curiosity? "Anyway, I want you to meet Roger and Jenny."

Sara watched as they passed by the sprawl of buildings in the industrial corridor.

"I haven't been there lately," the driver said, looking into the rear view mirror. He looked back to the road ahead. "I used to take people there. But I think it has changed."

"The site was sold," Greg said. "It's been purchased by a group of philanthropists and made a techno-utopian village with a research institute." He rattled off surprising facts.

Sara looked at Greg, amazed by his knowledge. Had it gone that far?

The driver was silent, didn't respond. I said too much, Greg thought. He peered out the window, wondered what it looked like to Sara.

The driver looked again in the rear view mirror. "You are the first people I have taken there in...maybe six years."

Greg nodded.

The taxi sailed onto I-80 into a mighty river of cars, got caught in slow motion. Traffic backed up. The taxi crawled. Greg checked his mobile, turned to Sara. "We'll need time to freshen up."

The driver looked again in his rear view mirror. "What kind of research is it? Still the chemical research?"

"Philosophy and science," Greg said, surprised at the driver's interest. "I don't know about chemistry."

"Yes, they did industrial research there. Chemical manufacture. I took people there."

"Hmm," Greg said, not loud enough to hear above the road noise. "Now it's focused on what they call traditional science, or *sacred science*."

The driver looked back to the road and changed lanes. *That* was too much detail, Greg thought.

The driver looked back at Greg through the mirror. "Sacred science? Is it like yoga, Ayurveda?"

Greg was surprised again. "Yes, like that. And modern sciences. And philosophies that integrate traditional and modern sciences."

The driver looked down several long moments. Then up in the mirror. "I have a niece. She studies at College of Ayurveda, in Emeryville somewhere. She shows me her books and charts. That one I know. She helps me with diet and lifestyle."

"Really?" Greg said, interested. "Yes, Ayurveda is studied there, too, I think."

The car was silent several minutes.

"Daddy, are we there yet?" Tara asked.

"Soon, Honey. It's just down the road."

Tara flumped back and rested her blond head on Greg's shoulder.

Sara gave Tara's forehead an affectionate brush, then turned to Greg. "So where you met Roger? The semantic web conference last year in San Francisco?"

"Right. Where he unveiled AlignIt." Hadn't they gone over this?

"Okay." Sara recollected. "Consulting on AlignIt—I can see that for you. But moving us here, teaching at the Bridge Institute..." Sara trailed off, ruminating. Greg watched her head turn, following the scenery, wincing. She turned back. "Who are we meeting tonight?"

"Roger, for sure. And he'll introduce us to folks at the reception. I know a few other people from conference calls—programmers, business people, an attorney, other folks on the project team. My faculty interviews don't start till Tuesday, after the orientation."

Sara peered out her window on the left. She saw the traffic. Then a Bay view came up. "Look Tara," she said. "There's San Francisco. See all those tall buildings? And that's Alcatraz."

Tara looked. But her five year old mind didn't yet appreciate distant views of unknown places. What was San Francisco to her? But it caught Sara's attention. What would be here for Sara in the Bay Area? Much indeed, Greg thought. But she expected so little right now. Why was this visit so difficult for her?

"It just feels to me like we need to have our feet on the ground," Sara said. "I don't want us going off into ungrounded fantasy."

Here was that line again. But it lacked the conviction of prior weeks.

"There are contracting and expanding phases on the path," Greg said.

"I just think we need to be discriminating. I'm concerned about getting taken by ideas."

Greg looked out the window on his side as they passed beyond the Bay view on the left. Indeed, the scenery was not inviting. She promised an open mind. It was hard enough to keep up his own hopes about an unseen place while managing her misgivings as well. "Its not all contraction." He turned to her. "There are times of genuine expansion on the path where things can change, doors can open." Greg paused. The taxi moved ahead faster. Greg noticed the traffic clearing as they changed highways from 80 to 580 *en route* to Richmond. "When I look at my life over the past year, it feels I'm moving into an expanding phase. And Bayside Village could be part of that." He looked back to Sara. "Maybe things could open in your life, too."

"Maybe. We've been ground down so much."

"It hasn't been easy."

Finally the taxi took an off-ramp. Sara scanned the scenes—train tracks, tattered chain link fences, warehouses with graffiti. What a soulless place, she thought. Yet, beyond them, she noted open fields, wetlands, more Bay views. Maybe there was something here amidst the industrial corridor after all.

Greg leaned to Sara, pointed out her window. "There's the water front," he said with a playful grin. They looked sideways across empty lots to the San Francisco Bay. Greg bumped her gently with his elbow.

Sara rolled her eyes. "There's a romantic tour on a cargo ship." She smiled at him with a tinge of sarcasm.

The driver took an off ramp, zipped down a local road, and pulled up to a front gate with a sign reading, *Bayside Village*. "This is the old RCC site," the driver said. "Is this what you want?"

"Ah, *utopia*," Sara chided.

Greg glanced out the window at the signage, the address. "This is it." He leaned over and spoke reassuringly to Sara, "We're just exploring."

"What's utopia?" Tara asked.

The car pulled forward. Greg looked to Tara. How to explain in her terms? "Utopia is a special kind of place, a wonderful place where everything is just right. It has nice people, good food, and great toys."

The taxi approached a set of buildings on campus. "Is this utopia?" Tara asked.

Greg laughed. "I don't know. I think we'll meet nice people and eat good food."

"And see great toys," Sara said.

Ouch, Greg thought. She's edgy about this.

The driver pulled up to a beautifully landscaped reception area and parked there. Cars could go no further on the Bayside Village campus.

Sara looked with keen attention at the driveway. She noticed it was laid with attractively cut stones, bordered on both sides by garden beds lined artfully with patterned tiles.

She turned to Greg. "Well that's a nice touch."

"Mmm." Greg nodded, looking out. Feeling her bid for connection, he let go of the barb. He breathed, feeling now the pleasant April day without the planes, busses and taxis, away from exhaust, highways and warehouses. The reception area, at least, was attractive.

"This has really changed!" the driver said. He hopped out and opened the trunk. Greg got out and joined him. Sara stepped out and Tara followed, holding her backpack in front like a teddy bear.

The driver lifted the luggage out and set it down on the stone driveway before Greg, who handed him the cab fare and tip.

"Wow, wow, wow. This place has really changed!" the driver said, looking around at the colored tiles and the landscaping in native California plants. "This is remarkable."

"Its our first visit," Greg said.

"You should have seen it," the driver said. "I tell you. You would hardly recognize it. This looks beautiful compared to before."

"That's good to hear," Greg said. "I hope the rest of it is this nice. Hey, thanks for the ride. Have a great day."

"Thanks for the tip. Enjoy your sacred science, or whatever it is."

Greg did a double-take, hearing the driver reflect what they had come for. He pulled out the luggage handles of his suitcase, pulled forward.

Sara turned to Greg as they walked into the reception lobby for tours, bumped him affectionately on the shoulder. "Hey, sorry. I know its more than toys. I *will* have an open mind, okay?"

Greg nodded with a smile, accepting it. Tara foisted her backpack over her shoulders, and they headed in.

2

Greg checked in at the front desk. Sara spotted a table in the lobby with a scale model displayed under a Plexiglas cover. She took Tara over to it and picked her up for a view from above. There at a glance was the entire Bayside Village and its Bridge Institute. Trams and canal boats moved around the Village on tiny tracks, captivating Tara's attention by their very movement. Sara looked at the buildings, recalling the pictures she had seen online. The model was a preview, she thought. What would she explore—The Art Center, the Sensory Parlor Collective, the worker-owned Bath House? Despite the ride from the airport, the model at least looked decent enough. Maybe it is worth a trip, whatever enduring merits the place itself may have.

Greg and Sara wheeled their luggage past the reception desk, out a door and down a covered walkway through a courtyard to an adjoining visitor's lodge newly built in California Craftsman style. The perfume of blossoming white jasmine flowers on the vine-wrapped posts lining the walkway caught Greg's attention. This must be a new part. What was it like before? Finding room 14, Greg held his mobile to the door knob, heard the click. The door unlocked.

Sara walked in, wheeling her suitcase before the closet. Tara and Greg followed. Greg looked around. Modest, he thought, but clean. He caught a fresh, floral aroma. Not the hotel-clean smell of industrial products.

"Oh look," Sara said. There on the pillows of the bed a stuffed animal was nestled, positioned to face the door. She reached over to pick up the toy, a small bird. As Greg put his bags down on the bed, Sara read the tag aloud. "It says, 'For Tara. My name is Clappy. I'm a California Clapper Rail.' Oh, that's cute. Look, Tara. It's for you." Sara handed the bird to her.

"Oh, its so cute." Tara took it and hugged it tightly. "Can I keep it?"

"I think so."

"Daddy, it has toys here," Tara said. She ran her fingers down the bird's long beak and over its beaded eyes.

Greg nodded. "So it does." He grinned at Sara triumphantly. Confirmation, he said with his eyes. Sara smiled and playfully rolled her eyes.

Greg unzipped his suitcase on the bed. "A California Clapper Rail?"

"It's a water bird," Sara said. She unzipped hers.

Greg saw a tag attached to the bird. "Can I see?" he said. He reached down, held open the tag as Tara hugged the bird, and he read, "…like a small chicken with a long beak, found in the marsh lands…"

"A chicken?" Tara asked, surprised.

"*Like* a chicken," Greg said, "but it lives near the water."

Greg let go of the tag, removed shirts from his suitcase. "There are walking trails by the Bay. We can go see the birds and crabs and fish. Maybe we'll see a California Clapper Rail." Tara was silent. She walked Clappy across the bed.

"That was a nice gesture," Greg said to Sara. He pointed to Clappy. Sara smiled and nodded as she opened her second suitcase.

Greg opened up his brief case on a small table in the corner by a window. He laid out his schedule for the week. Interviews with faculty, consulting meetings, board meeting for AlignIt Commons. Then he turned, surveyed the room. The decor was unpretentious. No ostentatious furniture or amenities. He mentally compared it with past accommodations traveling as a university guest lecturer and company consultant. He preferred this, actually. It was simple, elegant. But the austerity unsettled him. What does the room say about the Bayside Village? It sure isn't the Hilton, he almost said aloud. What would his university colleagues think? And what was Sara making of this crazy venture? The opinions of others swirled in his mind momentarily. Yet he noticed that everything was placed artfully with apparent intention, decorated neatly with almost mathematical precision.

Sara walked to a monitor on the wall. She held her mobile in hand, flicked her thumb across the screen. "Do you want to upload our room preferences, or adjust room settings manually?"

"I don't know," Greg said. He hung his shirts in the closet.

"I'm thinking night temperature for Tara, dim lights, wake-up time…"

"Probably hotel family settings. It's easier for now."

Sara looked up to the wall monitor, touched it, navigated. Then something caught her eye. "Wow, look at the wallpaper! Those patterns!" She looked closely, studied its faint, intricate designs.

"Hmm," Greg said with a shirt in hand, looking to the wall. He walked up, near Sara. "It's so subtle. Looks like…computer chips, or…diagrams…" Greg trailed off. He couldn't identify the pattern.

"You don't see wallpaper anymore," Sara said. "Not like this, anyway. What are these designs?" she said to herself.

"Mommy, what's wallpaper?"

Sara stared inquisitively at the wall.

"Mommy?"

"Yes, Sweetie?" Sara turned with a start. "It's like pictures drawn onto big paper and glued to the wall. It makes the walls look pretty."

Tara looked a moment, working out the description, then returned to Clappy. Taking off her jacket, she made a bird nest on the bed.

Sara returned her gaze to the wall, entranced, tracing interconnecting lines with her eyes, struggling to register the design. "I haven't seen this pattern," she said softly to herself, bemused.

Sara is here now, Greg noted. He dug through his suitcase on the bed. Pants for tonight.

Then she whirled around and returned to the bed, taking out her evening dress. "What have you brought me to, my mysterious husband?" She glanced at him playfully. His blond hair. His freckled face and arms. His sharply drawn facial features, at once intense and sensitive.

My mysterious husband. That was her affectionate code. It meant something to her that he could never quite work out. He didn't seem so mysterious to himself. But if it meant something to her, well…

"Where have I brought you," he repeated, trailing off, looking down into his suitcase. "Apparently, to more than I realized—or less." He looked up at her, a twist of irony in his voice, yet hope glimmered in his eyes.

Sara flashed him another quick and knowing glance, suspecting his inner conflict. Greg met it with a half smile and subtle, gleaming eyes. She observed nuance, eyes of wonder held in check by something. His wonder, like a horse behind a gate. But what was the gate? She turned and hung clothes in the closet, took out her evening shoes.

Something caught her attention here, Greg thought, turning, looking back to the wallpaper. He returned to his suitcase, looked down for his socks.

"Oh," Sara said, suddenly. She walked back to the room monitor on the wall, touched the screen, touched her phone, selected, uploaded. "Okay, and how about ubiquitous preference recording?"

"Ubiquitous memory? For this room?" Greg looked up at her. "You're planning our return already?" He let the suggestion hang in the air.

"I'm just asking."

"Sure, why not?"

Sara selected it and returned to her suitcase. "I overheard you mentioning the Bayside Village Dollar at the desk," she said, walking to the closet. "Did you exchange money?"

"Yeah."

"How much?"

"A hundred."

"A hundred dollars? Greg....We don't have much right now. What are you thinking? What do you want to spend it on?"

"I don't know. Nothing in particular." Greg took out his underwear and arranged it neatly in the dresser. "I don't know all that's here yet. I just want to play and see how local currency works." He moved his folded clothes neatly into the drawers. "It's a long-time interest of mine. I figured fifty or seventy five for you since you'll have more free time." Sara returned to the bed. Greg reached into his pocket and pulled out two rolls of coins. He handed one to her.

She took the roll in hand and looked at it. Not sure what to do. "What if we don't spend it all? Can we change it back?"

"I don't know. Probably. But I think we'll spend it all."

Sara put the roll into her purse, still wrapped. "Can we be careful with money this week? I know the rooms are paid. But we also downloaded mobile meal trackers. We're paying for child care. We don't have reserves right now."

"I know. I don't mean to spend a lot. But we're here exploring. I don't want to be skimpy, either. This week is really important to me."

Sara nodded, acknowledging Greg's passion. She knew this week was important. She gave him that. Yet her frown remained. She didn't care to explore a lot, Greg thought. Not yet. He was ready for Bayside Village. She stood on the edge.

"Tara, do you want to see the coins?" Greg said. He sat down on the bed. Tara looked up from her play with Clappy. She walked around the bed to Greg, fascinated by a new object, another toy. Greg unwrapped the roll and released it. Gold-colored metal coins came loose in an organized tumble onto the bed spread. Greg and Tara picked them up, studied them. Greg held up one to inspect its elegant imprints. "Tara, look. Here's a clapper rail on this side. It's just like Clappy." She studied it. He then turned it over to a dungeness crab on the flip side. "Sara, take a look," Greg called.

Sara came from the closet. She stood by Greg a moment, leaning her thigh affectionately into his shoulder and looking. She glanced at Greg's coin as Tara rustled through the others on the bed. She took the coin in hand. "In Community We Trust," she read. She held the coin a moment, turned it around. "Hmm, different." She paused, held it up close, squinted. She inspected the crab, its legs, its claws. Then she handed it back. "We should get going on our walk before the reception."

Greg raked up the coins on the bed and put them into his pocket. As if ready to spend them now.

3

Greg studied the campus map in the Lodge courtyard's kiosk, charting a course for their first walk around Bayside Village. Sara adjusted her purse strap. "Let's head this way," he said. They started off down a path, taking in the campus before the welcome reception where they would meet Roger.

"Look!" Tara said, pointing to the right as they walked out of the courtyard. A tram half filled with people whizzed around the corner of the Lodge with hardly a sound. It looked like a San Francisco cable car, Greg recollected, but leaner, closer to the ground. They watched it zip blithely across the campus, speeding across an almost imperceptible track blended with the grounds and walking paths.

"Look at the patterns and colors," Sara said.

Greg trained his eyes on the car, and then it was gone.

"Quaint, touristy element," he said. "See? It's not all industrial."

"Okay, I see that," Sara said. "It's like we've entered a magical kingdom." She described to Greg the table in the lobby with the scale model.

Greg nodded, impressed. "We should ride the tram to get a big picture of the Village."

Ahead was the Village Plaza, and the late afternoon sun angled in from the Bay across the patchwork of greens, walking paths, and campus buildings. Sara noticed a woman and man walking together down the path towards them. Something caught her attention. A badge on their shirts? Were they guards or campus police? Or was it something about their manner? Each had clear, shining eyes of presence, each an air of attentiveness. They nearly passed. Sara noticed a slight bow to her and to Greg. Instinctively she returned the gesture, as though on retreat at a yoga ashram or Buddhist monastery. Hmm, she thought, registering the impression. Why this gesture from, what are they…guards? Something in her relaxed from the hurry of travel and came to attention. "What is this place? It gets more strange and marvelous with each step."

"Hmm," Greg said and nodded. "We don't have a lot of time," Greg said. "But I'd like to squeeze in a visit to the Plaza, at least. It's the main gathering place."

They headed toward the Plaza. An ornate metal gate looking like green copper crossed over the walkway. Sara looked up as she passed under it, then turned around to study a detail. She turned back. "I want to sketch that."

Greg smiled, nodded, recalling her yearning to return to art.

Ahead on a lawn, Bridge Institute students spread out in the late afternoon sun, some on towels, some sitting in groups, studying, discussing, drawing, eating. Now Greg relaxed, felt the agreeable April air.

One group played Asdaf, which Greg recognized as the game played with an aerodynamic disc, with game rules built from contemporary sacred science principles. The Village had a team. Greg read about it.

They passed a bench where a student group discussed a research project. One held measuring instruments, others had notebooks.

They spotted another student group in boots wading in a small canal feeding into the Bay. Two held water samples and the group was discussing.

"Looks like a class project," Sara said.

"I love this," Greg said. "This is a cool campus feeling! All these writers, artists, scientists, and philosophers meeting here—just like in the pictures."

They turned onto a wide lane. Sara pointed to a street sign and read, "Avenue of the Nations."

"I read that they have cultural street fairs on weekends and holidays."

As they passed through, the aromas of vegetables and spices wafted from a nearby kabob booth. Bursts of smoke jumped out as vegetables were turned and oil dripped into the fire and sizzled. They strolled past an eatery of small restaurant stalls with diverse cuisines and small stores selling global craft goods.

"It's like a mini world market," Sara said.

They strolled by street performers in the middle of the Avenue, interspersed amongst the booths, stalls, and people. They stopped momentarily and watched a troop of native American dancers. A portable sign nearby indicated Miwok, Pomo, and Ohlone nations in the Bay Area. Greg picked up Tara to observe the feathered outfits and low leg and hip movements.

Greg said, "I wonder if these groups are tapped for their knowledge of sacred science, or traditional knowledge." He contemplated the prospect of traditional knowledge captured and recorded in AlignIt, with consent.

They walked to the Plaza's midsection, a large grass and brick quadrangle filled with amazing sculptures and a central fountain based on sacred sciences, with shops and buildings around it.

"Did you see that the Village Plaza is known internationally for its Fountain Garden?" Sara said.

"No," Greg said.

"And its large scale works of public art."

"Oh, right," Greg said. "I did see that."

Greg realized now that Sara had looked further into Bayside Village than he expected. She knew about the fountains, statues and sculptures.

"People are sitting on them!" Greg said.

Sara nodded. "The design criteria specified functionality—even seating arrangements."

"That makes it a great place to hang out," Greg said, imagining himself living here, sitting there, conversing with students.

Sara pointed out a group of art students with pads sketching a sculpture, a globe of some kind.

Greg looked. "A three dimensional cosmology," he said. He began noticing what was catching Sara's attention.

The family walked on, stopping before a gorgeously landscaped section of the Plaza with flowering jasmine and bougainvillea bushes, opening out to a lush botanical garden leading beyond the Plaza. They stopped and read a sign about replanted native trees, bushes, grasses and flowers that flourished in the East Bay prior to industrialization. "Hmm," Greg said after reading. "They've restored the local ecology of the San Francisco Bay like it was before European settlements."

"Look," Sara said, pointing to the display. "There's Clappy." Greg picked up Tara to see the drawn image of the California Clapper Rail. Greg turned to Sara, summarized, "It's a bird population they're helping to revive, and Clappy is a sort of Village mascot."

"Wow," Sara said, continuing to read. "Botanical gardens, nurseries…Even marine science institutes, aquariums, and aviaries for native fish and marine mammal and bird populations. Wow, that's amazing."

Greg put Tara down and the family kept walking. Passing by a jasmine bush, Greg breathed in the wafting scent of the little white flowers. "Mmm," he moaned, swooning in its fragrance.

A yard to the side caught Greg's attention. He walked in, around raised garden beds, walls with pockets filled with soil and plants, and planter bricks with lips where flowers, leaves, and cacti poked out—the whole lot arranged in elegant patterns. Sara walked in with Tara, following Greg around the yard. He stopped to investigate a pocket wall, searching curiously for an internal watering system. He read a display sign together with Sara about the history of industrial pollution at the Bayside Village, current land reclamation projects, microremediation using mushrooms. "Hmm," he said, tucking away that bit of information. He moved on to walls made of planter bricks, wondering how water was fed to their lips. He looked to the ground, saw brown tarps covering patches of soil here and there. What kind of pollution, he wondered.

Looking around the yard, enclosed by bushes, Greg suddenly sensed a pattern, or hints of one at least. The raised beds and pocket walls were arranged not functionally, in rows or some other conventional order. They ended in angular patterns. And Greg saw curved beds and round barrels, placed in unexpected spots. And the planter walls were not parallel, but organized on some other basis, some parallel but most running in different directions. Bayside Village was a living laboratory of sacred science, after all, he thought, and this very possibly could be an exhibit with more than one purpose. Greg tried to look above the garden, tried for a greater vantage point, but could not see the whole. The pocket walls partially blocked his view. What was the pattern, he wondered.

Sara noticed Greg quiet, puzzled, studying. "What are you looking at?" she asked.

"The garden plan," Greg said without turning. "It seems like a pattern."

Pattern always caught Sara, and the suggestion made it immediately apparent to her. "Mmm." She liked this. She had been focused on Tara, but she had intuitively felt something different about this space as she followed Greg in, walked around the beds. Now giving it her full attention, she looked about, turning to the corners in turn. "Well, the yard is a trapezoid." She traced the rows of varying lengths, what they met, what new lines and arcs began there. Clearly, something here was different; this was no square garden of predictable rows. She mentally raced through traditional garden motifs, labyrinths, mazes. But not spotting quickly the design, she looked to the garden as a whole, jumped up a level in perspective, as it were, seeking shapes, energy flows. "Hmm," she said intrigued but mystified. She could register nothing familiar, and her mind kept busy at the task.

After some moments of failed pattern recognition, Greg sought to move on. Walking through another opening to the main path, they approached a rounded building. "Oh, the Bayside Village Play House," Greg said, perhaps to Tara. He read a poster by the entry way about tonight's performance. "…Taoist puppet plays with gods and goddesses, the Eight Immortals, and the ancestors." Whatever that would mean to her. But it interested him.

"Wow," Sara said. "That would be fun."

They stepped up to an open door, and traditional Chinese music streamed out from it. Sara noticed an attractive tile pattern on the steps, around the door—similar to the tiles in the driveway by the reception area. They briefly stepped in to watch a rehearsal from the lobby through open doors into the theater. Sara noticed immediately that the lobby featured an intricate wallpaper pattern—similar to that in the Lodge. Listening to music from the pit, Greg looked aside to a poster in the lobby, read about tonight's performance of the eight traditional sounds—stringed instruments, fiddles, flutes and pipes, a wooden box and stick, stone chimes, bronze bells and cymbals, a clay pot, a gourd reed mouth organ and an octagonal tambourine. He turned to the stage, watched marionettes. There, he saw the gods and sages of the Taoist pantheon. He recognized that they ritually enacted the great cosmic patterns, an epiphany of the divine in the world, the gods with the people. Greg picked up Tara to watch, and he stood there transfixed by the artistic integrity of the whole scene.

Exiting, Greg glanced at the marquis, noticed upcoming performances. Dramas and dances by Rudolf Steiner, George Gurdjieff, and other modern esoteric innovators.

They walked further down the Plaza to an attractive, French-style pavilion called the Philosophy Salon, a combination shop of philosophy books and artifacts, natural soda fountain and world tea emporium, with gourmet vegetarian sandwiches, soups and salads. They stepped inside. Ahead on the inside walls, Greg immediately spotted reproductions of classic paintings featuring Plato's Academy, Aristotle's Lyceum, and similar famous intellectual and spiritual symposia around the world—India, Asia, the Middle East.

They scanned the inside of the salon amidst the hum of lively conversation. "This is supposed to be modeled on the salons of the French Philosophes," Greg said to Sara. "But here, I guess, discussions focus on sacred sciences and philosophies." Sara nodded. "I'd love to hang out here," Greg said, imagining himself relocated to Bayside Village. "The cafes are apparently full of philosophical, spiritual, scientific, and cultural discussions." Sara nodded with interest.

Greg walked to the elegant glass cases at the counter, stocked with exotic health drinks and snacks designed to boost qualities of consciousness and restore balance to the body's systems. Delectable treats, all of them. "I'll have a sassafras soda, and a mango lassi for my girl." He turned to Sara. "Do you want something?"

Sara looked into the case, intrigued, then up to the artful menu boards above, spotting bottles of exotic drinks on a high shelf surrounding the entire salon. "I'll have that ginseng drink in the green bottle."

The attendant reached up, brought down the drink to the counter, then fetched the sassafras, the mangi lassi, brought them up to the counter.

Greg reached into his pocket, found some Bayside Village Dollars, slapped them down on the counter, heard the clink. He liked the feeling of the coin, the sound, the very idea. He handed the lassi to Tara, picked up the Sassafras and turned, moved aside for the next customer. Sara got the ginseng, twisted off the cap, sipped the potent brew. A punch of taste and power filled her mouth.

As they strolled out, Greg glanced at the people seated, and he listened for discussions. What kind of place is this? What people are here? He sipped his sassafras as he walked through the doorway. What is the character, the mood, the flavor, of this place?

Walking out, they passed a gazebo where ice cream was sold. Greg pointed to the French-style, wrought iron tables with marble tops.

The next building down was octagonal, an artful mix of Victorian and Ottoman-Turkish. "Oh, this is the reading club," Greg enthused. He stopped before a kiosk in front. "The Village Literary and Scientific Circle," he read aloud and then scanned the schedule of brown bag lunches, author readings, guest lectures, and discussions. "Hmm," he said. "I can join online, follow webinars, and read along from home. But it must be amazing to sit here and join a community of people studying and discussing sacred science."

Sara nodded, knowing his interest. She sipped her ginseng brew, then checked the time on her mobile. "We should head back and shower."

The family turned back toward the room on a paved path, bypassing further shops and cafes. There was more to see and Greg felt he could dally for days and find ever new fascinations. He pondered aloud, "What would a philosophy of science look like that took on recovery of sacred science?" He contemplated a moment. That was his question, he thought, his definitive question, the question he would take up for the week.

Sara had been pondering her own thoughts—of art, how to return, living the thread of artistic inspiration in her life. What would the Art Center be like?

"To restore some of these sciences," Greg said, "we have to work at the bigger questions in the history and philosophy of science. I might work on that—a philosophy of science focused on recovery of sacred science. Not just showing evidence that some sciences can work, and have worked. But also why they work, how they relate to modern sciences, and how to extend them." He paused. "As if that's original. The whole place here exists for that."

Sara nodded, noting his inspiration. "Just arriving here intoxicates you."

4

Back at the Lodge guest room, Sara turned to Tara. "Okay Sweetie, we're going to take a quick shower."

"No!" Tara protested. "I don't want to shower!" She grabbed Clappy from the bed, to keep her from the water.

"We'll make it short today, Honey."

"No," Tara protested again, tired from travel and yearning to play.

Sara walked into the bathroom to prepare the water. A moment later, she called, "Greg look!"

Greg turned from the dresser. "What?"

"Look at the tiles!"

He entered the bathroom. The fixtures were humble. But outlining the sink and tub were elegant tiles, muted and subtle, featuring intricate patterns complementing the wallpaper.

"Wow," Greg said, impressed. "Like we've seen around campus."

"What is this place?" Sara said in wonder.

"What, Mommy?" Tara said. She entered the bathroom.

"The pretty designs on the tiles," Sara replied.

Tara looked. "Oh," she said, expressionless, and walked back out to the bed where she put Clappy in a new nest she had made.

"What a strange combination," Greg said. "Its less than I expected… and yet more." He hesitated, smelling an unfamiliar fresh scent. He picked up the soap and towels, smelling them in turn, but couldn't identify the source. "Smells good in here," he said to himself, and walked out. Sara nodded, her eyes fixed on the tile designs.

While Sara bathed Tara, Greg picked up his mobile, touched the keypad, called and reached a voicemail. "Hello Mrs. Blocke. It's Greg Cobb. This is just a reminder that I'm on campus this week, and I'd like to meet with you over the faculty recruitment process. I still haven't heard from you about times. We're in room 14 in the Lodge, and you have my coordinates. I'll try to reach you in the morning when you're in. Thanks."

After everyone showered, Tara played with Clappy on the bed while Sara rustled in the closet for her new dress. In the bathroom, Greg squeezed pomegranate face cream into his hand and walked out rubbing his forehead. "Well, the accommodations are modest, but clean. There's a design integrity in the room." He thought Sara would pick up on that thought. He hesitated, rubbing the cream around his eyes. "I think that scent is in the soap. Its not quite floral—it almost smells like bark, or a root, or something."

"Mhmmm," Sara agreed. She stood in her underwear, looking over the new off-white hemp fabric dress in her hand. "I wonder if the Art Center here is behind this—the design, at least.... Now I'm curious," she said, looking up at Greg for a moment, and back down at her dress.

Sara had looked further into Bayside Village than Greg realized. He hadn't thought of the Art Center. She did.

Greg watched her a moment, her smooth skin. He rubbed cream on his nose, under his eyes, smelling the subtle, sweet fragrance. He watched her turn, look at the dress in her hand. Ever an elegant woman. Her long brunette hair, her fashionable but artsy taste, her toe ring. Always some little sign of non-conformity, some identification with exotic foreign cultures. And she had always some mysterious depth in her eyes when she made contact with his. So why didn't this place grab her interest like so many daring ventures they'd shared in the past? What is it about this place? Or would she warm to it? Was she now warming up? Did the short walk make a difference?

Sara slipped into her dress. "I'm not sure what to expect. I'm not as good at receptions and small talk—especially at your tech conferences."

"Yes you are."

"The philosophy ones are more interesting."

"Daddy, are we going to have ice cream?" Tara asked.

"I don't know, Honey. Maybe." Greg glanced at Tara's bird on the bed and smiled. "That's a wonderful nest you have there." He returned to the bathroom and looked in the mirror to comb his hair. "I think you'll find it's a different group of people here," he called out. "Its not like my other conferences. We have more in common here than just the techy stuff."

"I know. Love, can you zip my dress in the back?"

Greg turned from the bathroom mirror to Sara's bare back inside the white hemp dress. "Mmm," he said, gliding over and planting a kiss on the back of her neck. "Up or down?"

"*Up*, Sweetheart. We're going out, and we're starting to run late."

"Just checking," Greg said with a roll of frivolity in his voice. He zipped it up and turned back to the mirror to button his shirt and cuffs. "At least there's daily yoga," he said, consoling her. That was the big draw for her over the past weeks—the one thing he could count on to keep her interest.

Sara smoothed the dress around her figure. "Mmm," she said, lacking the resounding conviction Greg waited for. She picked at a thread near the edge. "What's that Sensory Parlor Collective?"

"I don't know."

"I saw it in our confirmation package last week. I might check it out."

Sensory Parlor Collective? Greg hadn't noticed it, he realized. She had.

That was interesting. What was it?

"And I brought sketch pads. I might do some pencil drawing while you're in meetings."

"Really?" Greg said with interest, walking across the room to the dresser, tucking his shirt in. "You haven't drawn like that in awhile. Seems like the industrial design world has gotten you away from it."

"I like my work." She slipped on her shoes. "I just need more time to draw."

"I know. But sketching again seems good for you." Greg picked up his wallet and mobile phone from the dresser, getting ready to leave. "Oh, I called Mrs. Blocke again."

Sara paused and gave Greg a reassuring look. "You'll reach her, Love. Don't worry." She picked up an evening sweater. "Are you ready?"

Greg slipped the mobile into his pocket. "Yeah."

"Tara, Sweetie, we're going now. Come put on your jacket."

Greg went to the closet, took his new dark black sport coat from a hanger. He put his arms through, adjusting the collar over his shoulders.

"Oooh, you look sharp," Sara said, pausing.

"Thanks." He straightened his lapel and stood up straighter. He looked up, his eyes twinkling, feeling himself handsome in Sara's beholding eyes.

"Mmm." She stepped up, grabbed his lapel gently. "Very sharp." She kissed him, let go.

"Ready Honey?" she asked Tara.

"Can I bring Clappy?" Tara asked, holding the bird tightly.

"Sure, bring Clappy," Greg said, affectionately brushing his hand on her blond head. "She'll be lonely here without us."

5

Outside the Lodge in the court yard, Greg studied the campus map in the kiosk again. "That's right. The Dining Commons is this way." He pointed to the right and the family started walking down a path to the Orientation's welcome reception.

The empty banquet room in the Dining Commons boasted large picture windows looking out across the lower campus toward the Siegel Marsh and the San Francisco Bay. The family was escorted by a wait staffer to a wall of windows, directed outside a set of double doors to the Bayside Village Welcome Reception on the patio. There, a jubilant hum of conversation animated the pleasant Spring air. The orange sun was descending into the mountains of Marin County across the Bay, near San

Francisco and the Golden Gate Bridge.

Greg scanned the patio and identified AlignIt creator Roger Barnes, an attractive man in his fifties, thin, tallish, trim-bearded, standing in a group of people. He held finger foods and talked. Greg walked in his direction. Sara and Tara followed behind.

Roger spotted them approaching. He turned, opened the circle and announced, "Ah, Greg Cobb! Here's our new ontologist…if we can entice him from Seattle." Roger and Greg shook hands firmly and exchanged warm glances. "And this must be his lovely wife, Sara," Roger said, extending his hand and beaming radiantly into her eyes.

Sara hadn't expected such warmth, such charisma.

"Yes, how do you do Roger?" Sara said.

"And this must be Tara," he said, bending down slightly to look into her eyes with a warm smile. "Welcome." He stood up again and looked to Greg and Sara. "I'm so glad you've all come to visit us."

"So, I finally meet the famous developer of AlignIt," Sara said in playful adulation, pulling her hair back behind her left ear, her friendly eyes flashing at Roger. "I've heard amazing things about you."

"I don't know about famous," Roger said modestly. "We hope AlignIt can be made a useful tool and deployed broadly, with the help of Greg, here." Roger patted him on the shoulder. "Anyway, must be you've heard good enough things, since you've joined us this week."

The first thing Sara noticed about Roger beyond her own projections was his compelling presence.

Roger turned closer to Sara with a twinkle in his squinted eyes. "But I wonder—will we need to work more on Greg, or you, to bring you guys here?"

Sara smiled at Roger's warm attention.

Such a beautiful woman, Greg thought.

"Ah, but I get ahead of myself. First, we must dine you." Roger swiveled. "Waiter!"

A young man, passing, stopped with his platter of *hors devours*. No doubt a student at the Bridge Institute, Greg thought. Sara took finger foods in hand with a napkin. Then Greg. Then Roger pointed, and the waiter bent down. Tara looked at the tray, surveyed the mouth-watering choices, took some finger foods.

Roger made introductions around the group. "I'd like you to meet Karen Mitchell, our Bayside Village's Director of Development." She was a sharply dressed woman, with a smart look and determined eyes. "She raises funds to shape our utopian projects," Roger said with a humorous air. "She also oversees our art and design initiatives," he said, looking especially to Sara, who felt some hint from Roger—but she wasn't sure to what end.

Karen shook hands. "Welcome to Bayside Village," she said to Sara first and then to Greg. She briefly discussed a current fundraising campaign, its theme. She was extroverted, purposeful, deliberate, attentive to interpersonal nuances.

"This is Randy Seton," Roger continued, "a professor of philosophy at the Bridge Institute, and our illustrious orientation tour guide—he'll give you the grand tour tomorrow." Randy was a tall, stocky, red-headed and bearded man, with a fun-loving, teddy bear smile. "In case you knew nothing at all about our global heritage of sacred sciences," Roger said, "Randy will initiate you to the inner mysteries—and much more."

"How do you do," Randy said, shaking hands with his gregarious demeanor and warm, welcoming presence.

"A man of my discipline," Greg said, shaking hands.

"I'm sure you could give some of the tour knowledgably yourself, if not Sara as well," Randy said, looking to both of them in turn.

Sara wondered how Randy knew of her interests.

"But," Randy said, "we hope you'll see a few new things you haven't seen before."

"I look forward to it," Greg said.

"Me too," Sara echoed. "I think tomorrow's tour will be one of the highlights for me."

"And this is Jackie Schrader, our Director of Technology Transfer," Roger said. Standing next to him, Jackie was petite, attractive, and sharp-eyed.

"Pleased to meet you," she said, shaking hands with Greg and Sara.

"I hear you've put a big emphasis on tech transfer here," Greg said.

"It's true," Jackie said, her eyes twinkling. "Even in the few short years of Bayside Village. Though its not just an emphasis. We're really modeling a new approach to it. Then we can transfer our model of tech transfer."

That was witty, Greg thought. Jackie was more reserved than Karen, he observed. Just as confident. But more intellectual perhaps, more articulate.

Roger turned to Jackie. "We were just brainstorming a different title for you, weren't we?"

Jackie nodded, turned to Greg. "It should be Technology Demonstration, Transfer and Scaling." She paused for effect. "But that's a mouthful," she said and laughed. "It's really an approach to stewarding the development and application of technology beyond mere intellectual property protection and licensing. We take our technologies further downstream to prime them for external uptake."

Greg nodded. "I was fascinated to learn of your novel AlignIt Commons structure based on principles of *ejido* and *usufruct*."

Sara listened carefully. She hadn't heard Greg mention these terms before.

"Yes," Jackie said, "that's a model unique to Roger's commons. We have other models. Its an experiment and appears to be successful." She looked to Roger, who nodded, agreeing, and turned back to Greg. "Bayside Village is kind of like a techno-utopia, a place where technologies are conceived and created to solve social and economic problems. Our experimenting with technology transfer is part of our endeavor to explore the potential of technology in service of a better society."

"Hmm," Greg said, nodding, contemplating.

"We do more than that here, of course," Jackie said. "And technologies are not always the best solutions. Sometimes, they're precisely the problem, or their application creates problems. But sometimes they help, and it particularly falls to my role here to explore technological, social and economic innovations that can help, rearchitecting society by small experiments that can be scaled up. This is aspirational, a stimulus for civilization building. We don't imagine we're creating utopia. We'll see how it goes."

"Mmm, fascinating!" Greg said, nodding, his eyes on fire with interest. Big ideas packed into few words, he thought. "I'm intrigued by this greater vision of tech transfer."

"I'm quite involved with Jackie, as you might guess," Roger said, "with the incubation of AlignIt right here in our Bayside Village Research Park and our membership-based commons. You'll hear more about it tomorrow, I think—right Randy?" Roger turned.

"Indeed," Randy said, "part of tomorrow's tour takes us through the Research Park, and we briefly pass through AlignIt and the AlignIt Commons."

"Great," Greg said, nodding. He noted Jackie's importance to Roger and to his own prospective consulting work with AlignIt.

Jackie excused herself to talk with another guest. Roger, Greg, and Randy discussed teaching at the Bridge Institute.

Karen turned to Sara. "Roger tells me you're an industrial designer."

"Yes," Sara replied, surprised but immediately confident and professional. "I work in a design firm in Seattle. We focus on print, package and web materials for the IT sector." Right on message, she thought, though she hadn't expected to be. This was Greg's work, her vacation.

"Roger sent me a link to your site a few months ago."

"He did?" A few months ago? Sara wondered. This trip was planned just last month. "My personal site or my firm's?"

"Both, actually. It's nice work."

"Thanks."

"My office has used an outside firm so far. And we're trying now to build this capacity in-house." Karen went on explaining the campaigns her office had organized. Sara wasn't sure where the focused conversation was headed, and why Karen provided such detail on a first meeting. But it felt important to attend carefully to her words, in case, Sara suspected, it was leading to something.

"Anyway," Karen finally said, "you have valuable marketing and design expertise. Will you have some time to talk the next few days about your background and capabilities?"

"Oh sure, that would be fine," Sara said, delighted and surprised. "I hadn't prepared a portfolio or anything."

"I looked over your online portfolio pretty thoroughly."

"Really? I'm impressed. Um, yeah. We're here for the week, but Roger has filled our schedule the next two days with the Orientation. But I'll make time for whenever you're free."

"Let me send you my card," Karen said and reached for her mobile. She found Sara's name and touched, touched, touched. Done.

She touched rather quickly, Sara observed, and she realized that Karen must have had it lined up already.

"Let me know a good free spot in your schedule. We can meet up and talk further."

"Great. Thanks," Sara said. Karen went on, mingling with others. Sara turned back to Greg and Roger. Her mind raced with unexpected purpose and a thousand new questions.

A moment later, an attractive and slender woman in her fifties with sandy blond hair approached the group. "And here is my lovely wife, Jenny" Roger said. "Jenn, this is Greg, Sara, and Tara."

"Oh, it's a pleasure," Jenny said, stepping into the circle and shaking hands with a radiant quality of presence. Greg noticed her quiet, introverted demeanor, which in no way held back the light welling up in her eyes. "Welcome to our Bayside Village. Roger has told me a lot about you, Greg, and I'm glad to finally meet you."

"Likewise," Greg said. "Roger has spoken about you as well. I'll be glad to get to know you on this trip."

"And I look forward to getting to know you, Sara," Jenny beamed.

"Thanks, me too," Sara said, opening like a flower. "It's so nice to have a home to visit while we're here."

"Good. So we're on for Tuesday dinner?" Jenny confirmed.

"Yeah," Greg said, nodding his head and looking to Sara, and then back. "We've kept our schedule clear for it."

Just then, a waiter passed by with a platter of chocolate cakes. Greg watched Sara take one and savor it and then smile intimately as she noticed him watching.

6

Roger spotted an older man walking by. Reaching out to touch his arm, Roger brought him into the circle. Greg noticed he was a tall, slender man in his sixties with silvery white hair. "Greg and Sara," Roger said, "I'd like you to meet Steve Bateson, President of both the Bayside Village and its Bridge Institute, and Professor in the History of Ideas."

Steve Bateson greeted Greg and Sara with expectant eyes. "Welcome to Bayside Village," he said with a dynamic, charismatic manner, extending his hand first to Greg and then to Sara. "And thank you for joining us the next few days."

"The next week," Roger emphasized. "This is Professor Greg Cobb, from University of Washington, and his wife Sara, and their daughter, Tara."

"Yes, of course, Greg," Bateson said, recollecting. "Well, good to meet you in person, and a very warm welcome to you. And to you, Sara. We're very happy you're visiting us."

"Thank you," Greg said, feeling the quality of Bateson's presence.

"It's a pleasure," Sara said.

"And we're meeting this week about the faculty position," Bateson said.

"Wednesday," Greg confirmed.

"Just about everything you see here was the dream of this man," Roger said, mainly to Sara, and patting Bateson on the shoulder. "What you see now resulted from his efforts to recruit and organize all of us toward achieving this goal."

"Many hands and hearts were joined to birth this new community," Bateson said. "And each person has brought their unique vision, gifts and talents." He turned to Greg. "As we hope you will."

Sara was surprised at Roger's and Steve's encouraging words to Greg. How had it gotten so serious so fast—the energy, rapport, and affiliation? It all rushed up to Sara with an urgency she hadn't expected. This couldn't be just a vacation for her, she realized. Something bigger is going on here.

Bateson made some overview comments about the Bayside Village, asked about University of Washington, and talked about a few common reference points in the field of his research. "So, I'll save my thunder for my Orientation welcome tomorrow and my Creative Writing with Utopias workshop on Tuesday. And then we're meeting privately Wednesday. Is there anything we can discuss now that would be of interest or useful to either of you?" Bateson looked invitingly to Sara.

Sara took the queue. "I don't know if we'll hear it in the Orientation, but if this is your dream, I'd love to hear how it came to you"

Good, she's engaging the place, Greg thought.

"No, it's not part of the Orientation," Randy said. "What do you think, Steve? Maybe it should be."

"It's not in the tour," Bateson said, surprised. He shrugged and nodded at Randy approvingly. "Maybe it's time to put it in." He leaned to Sara. "It's a personal story, I suppose." He took off his metal rim spectacles, held them in hand, produced a patch of felt from his pocket, and rubbed his lenses.

Greg picked up Tara and held her. Tara repositioned Clappy on his arm, facing outwards as an ornament. Greg chuckled to himself at the image he imagined Roger and Steve saw of him, with Clappy's beak sticking out. I hope this is included here, too, he thought.

Putting on his glasses again and looking to Sara, Bateson said, "The seed idea for The Bayside Village began a number of years ago at a dinner party with colleagues at my home. Each of us a scholar, each practicing diverse spiritual paths. We gathered socially many times to discuss our scholarly interests, academic institutions, and our spiritual lives and inquiries. On that evening, now a fateful one in hindsight, we discussed the interface between our scholarly disciplines and our spiritual paths. It was probably me who mused, wistfully," Bateson said, as he turned to Greg, massaging his jaw with his thumb and forefinger, "that it would be very nice if we could all teach in the same institution, lending each other support in our integration of scholarship and spiritual life."

Greg received the impression mindfully, digested it.

Roger's mobile phone rang. He pulled it from his pocket and viewed the caller ID. He decided to take it. He turned aside, answered. "Chris! Hey!....Yes, briefly—Greg Cobb has just arrived...." Roger motioned for Steve to continue and turned aside a bit more.

Hearing his name made Greg curious.

Roger continued and Greg could still hear him faintly above Bateson's continued overview. "For a call tomorrow?...Just you?....Sure. I'm free at 9:30....Before that? What's the purpose?....Yes, the AlignIt Commons Board materials were posted last week. You saw it, right?....A new item?....Mmm....Mhmm. Greg?....Mmm."

Greg heard his name again. He glanced at Roger, then turned back to Steve.

Roger finished: "Okay. Tomorrow morning at 6:00. Okay. Bye." He slipped his phone into his pocket, turned back to the group.

Jenny said to Sara, "This recreation of the university has been a long time interest of Steve's."

The hors devours platter passed by and Greg took a small item for Tara.

Steve nodded. "You see," he said, now leaning closer to Greg and Sara as Roger returned his attention, "I had contemplated for some years the kind of university I would like to teach in—a place where spiritual teachings and traditions were primary, like the great old universities in the East and West, but now it must be in a pluralistic society, in a respectful and integral way." Greg nodded his head as Bateson spoke, his eyes wide with heightened attention. He held Tara a bit tighter, perhaps, and noticed a crumb of hers drop onto his sleeve. "I knew that many great universities had existed in times past, in India and East Asia—great Buddhist monastic universities, Indian ashrams and maths—and in the West, in the ancient Greek world, the Islamic world, and Medieval Christian Europe."

Greg shifted his weight. "I've read your articles on these great schools as models for refocusing today's universities."

Sara realized now the strong affinity Greg felt for the place and people.

"Yes, good," Bateson said. "And you've seen the mountain of criticism, too, I suppose?"

Greg appreciated Steve's candor, his intellectual honesty. "Some, yes," he said. "Scholarly contributions and corrections are always welcome to me when they help sharpen a work. But the raw, destructive attacks—I'm not moved by it."

"Well, I've obviously provoked a stir in the zeitgeist," Bateson said. "But we're trying to build something here. We're not merely playing with ideas, movements, and fads. Anyway, many of those great schools were founded on a single religion, and many were only academic and contemplative. But I had envisioned a great school founded on an integral philosophy, but not less intense in focus because of it. I envisioned bringing together the depths of spiritual traditions with the best scholarship and scientific endeavors in respective fields. Also a school that would bring the fruits of its work to the world in applied arts and sciences for the public good, not leaving academia to elites in ivory towers. Roger's work in the History of Religions and his creation of AlignIt is a premier example of this public service, this transfer of technology."

The public good? Sara was liking this.

"Yes!" Greg said with passion. He felt his eyes lit, his energy tight and poised. "Jackie was just discussing this—technology transfer."

"Yup," Randy said. "And you'll see plenty of applications in development for the public good on the tour tomorrow."

"And in our meetings," Roger said to Greg, who nodded.

Bateson put his glasses on again. "After bearing my vision to my colleagues, one of them—Catherine, who is now on our distinguished faculty, teaching the Philosophy and Practice of Imagination, prodded us….She may be here tonight." Bateson looked across the patio and, not seeing her, turned back. "She deserves credit for instigating a group imagination that evening."

"I meet with Catherine on Tuesday," Greg interjected. "I'm deeply impressed by her work."

"Good, good," Bateson said. "Yes, she's a great friend, and a great teacher and scholar."

"And a wise elder," Jenny said, "and she'll be a great colleague."

Sara registered this collegial regard with profound respect. The way they affirm each other. And Jenny's affirmation of this woman, Catherine. How are they related, she wondered.

"Catherine midwifed the birth of Bayside Village," Bateson said.

Midwifed, Sara reflected. What an image of her role.

"Catherine suggested that evening," Bateson continued, "that we imagine we were given the task of creating such a university as I envisioned. Over a few hours and good food, we playfully dreamed what our new university would look like. How would each of our spiritual traditions inspire us to develop a new way of academic life? How would this institution form intellect and character and insight in its faculty and students? We played at this for several hours, becoming engrossed in vital discussion until late at night."

"Wow," Sara said almost under her breath, enthralled in the story.

"Then Catherine held us to task," Roger said.

Us?, Greg thought. Roger was part of it?

"Yes," Bateson replied. "She asked why wouldn't we create such a great university? We joked about the obstacles. But then our resolve quickened. One by one, we cast our lots for this project that fateful evening. Each of us decided to make a real effort to create what you now see before you as the Bayside Village and the Bridge Institute. Today our dream has grown into a small and growing faculty, more spiritual traditions than those represented around the table that first night, a number of dedicated philanthropists, and substantial businesses whose revenues are dedicated to a Trust that supports the Village."

"And," Roger added, "a few research-intensive companies and nonprofits in our Research Park working to extend our research findings into marvelous products, programs and services."

"Yes indeed," Bateson said. "So, while we don't all follow the same teachings, we do hold several aims in common."

"That's so inspiring!" Sara said. "You went from a dream to actually creating something so beautiful! It's important for me to hear how this all came together."

Something so beautiful? Greg reflected. Is Sara warming up to this? Or is that too much to say right now? My hope may be clouding my perception.

Roger noticed Sara's positive note, too, studying her to register her qualities, her manner.

"We should definitely work that story into our next tour," Randy said. "Sara, you've just made your first contribution to Bayside Village." Sara smiled. "Now if you'll excuse me, I'm going to welcome some folks who just arrived."

Randy shook Sara's hand, then Greg's. "Good meeting you," he said and then left.

Greg turned back to Bateson. "Do you feel satisfied that what you've created reflects your dream?"

"Very good question," Bateson replied, shifting his balance to his other leg, breathing in, thinking a moment. "Well, it's a work in progress, of course. And it will never finish. The Bayside Village as you see it now is the product of many people's visions, not just mine, and it is born from many people's dedicated labors. But overall, yes. I am satisfied that we are in the midst of creating a place fundamentally grounded in the gnosis of the heart, and growing out of that, a place that nourishes the study of the One and its waves of appearances all about us, in us, as us."

"It's interesting to hear you speak like that," Greg said. "Gnosis of the heart."

Bateson turned his head to Greg and looked over his spectacles, smiling subtly, knowingly. In a low voice, he said, "I heard about you from Roger, and talk like that is natural for me, too. Some of us call it marifa."

"I see," Greg said with an equally knowing smile. He glanced at Sara and back to Bateson. "Okay."

Sara's eyes dilated at this nuance.

Greg's heart was moved beyond words for a moment. This exchange promised enjoyment of a camaraderie far beyond his expectation.

"We do integrate science and spiritual training, as I had hoped," Bateson said. "And we do make our scholarly and technological developments broadly available through our Research Access Office."

"Headed by Jackie Schrader," Roger said.

"These and the Art Center are the focal points of our efforts at civilizational creativity," Jenny said.

Sara's eyes lit up on hearing Jenny mention the Art Center.

"Civilizational creativity," Greg said.

"Yes," Jenny nodded. "Creating new structures, new paradigms, new institutions, on a civilizational scale."

"Yes, and it's a daily challenge," Bateson said, "to attract, retain and then support the right people to keep the vision on course. And you can't imagine all the distractions that come our way to entice us into serving other aims."

Roger nodded his head distinctly in agreement.

What distractions, Greg wondered.

7

When Bateson left, Roger turned. "Let's find a table." He spotted one by the half-wall overlooking the path to the Bay where the two couples and Tara sat down. He signaled a waiter with an *hors d'evours* tray who came and gave out delicacies. Sara sat, and Tara climbed onto her lap while Sara helped her spear cheese cubes with toothpicks.

"So how was your trip?" Jenny asked.

"A bit delayed, unfortunately," Greg said. "But here we are. Considering everything we've come for, just being here is a daring venture."

"I like the accommodations," Sara said. She looked up from Tara's napkin. "The craftwork in the Lodge is really unexpected." Her eyes flared. "It's a delightful find."

"Yes," Jenny said. "There is quite a bit of craftwork around the Village. Given the history of this property, it elevates something in the feeling of the campus."

"It really adds something," Sara said. And she wondered what else there may be. "I admit to being put off by the old industrial corridor around the campus. As we drove up, I began suspecting this place was rather more dystopian than utopian." Sara rolled an olive back and forth on a napkin with her finger and then looked up to read Roger and Jenny. She's testing them, Greg thought. Roger nodded, raising his eyebrows. "Yet coming onto the Bayside Village campus surprised us both, I think," Sara said, looking to Greg. "Right?"

"Sure it did," Greg said. "We were admiring the wallpaper and tiles in our room. For a moment, I wondered they were based on an AlignIt entity relationship diagram."

Roger laughed. "The wall paper isn't from AlignIt, but it's an interesting thought—AlignIt ERD wall paper to fund AlignIt R&D….Not a bad idea. It's probably from something on campus, though."

"They're from the Bridge Institute's Art Center," Jenny said.

"I suspected," Sara said, and she wondered how Jenny knew.

"They've used the Village as their open studio," Jenny said. "Randy should say more about it tomorrow. You'll see a lot of nice craftwork around the buildings here."

"Are you an artist?" Sara asked Jenny.

"No. I'm on the board of the Art Center."

Sara nodded, raise her eyebrows. "Mmm." That could be a useful connection, she thought.

"Yes, Randy can tell you about the design work around campus," Roger said. "I can't even pretend to know all that he knows about this place."

Jenny turned to Sara as the sun slipped low to the mountains across the Bay. "How old is Tara?"

"How old are you, Sweetie?" Sara asked. Tara had just speared a cheese cube and filled her mouth. She held up five fingers.

"My, you're a big girl," Jenny said. "We'll have some very interesting activities for you this week. And who is your little friend, there?"

"Clappy," Tara said. "We found her in the room."

Greg watched, smiled.

A waiter brought a tray of cakes by the table. Sara took another two chocolate cakes onto a napkin, placed them on the table before her, then picked up one. She bit into the lush icing and cake. This left an itch of concern in Greg. Is she going back to that again? Is she that bothered by this place? But the conversation shifted, and Greg turned his attention to Roger.

"So, Neil Benson is coming after all," Roger said to Greg.

"Really?" Greg said, surprised, his eyes widening. He sat back in his chair.

"He hadn't confirmed when I called you last week, so I didn't mention it. I hoped he'd be here tonight. But he's meeting colleagues in Berkeley."

"Very interesting." Greg paused, pondering, and then looked at Roger. "I've seen him just once at a conference. I spoke with him only a few minutes." Greg took a deep breath. "He's an interesting character. Strong personality. Very, very sharp," Greg emphasized. "Well, that could raise the bar this week, eh?"

"Indeed. Or lower it—it could go either way. He's among the best, no doubt about it. But you know how it is. We're looking for a special kind of person who can hold the philosophical orientation as well, not just execute on the information architecture. As it happens, I have my eyes on someone else for software services—who combines technical expertise and inner qualities like you do. But you never know. We could be pleasantly surprised with Neil."

"I don't envy your recruitment challenge—for faculty, or even consulting on AlignIt," Greg said, shaking his head. "I suspect you're right about his disdain for AlignIt. I wonder why he came," Greg pondered aloud and paused.

"Its worth a lot just to have his feedback," Roger said. "We're not a cult of sacred science ideologues here. We stay on purpose, but we're fundamentally open. Anyway, we have a few other guests for Friday's AlignIt Commons Board meeting besides you and Neil. Other people you don't know yet. So you're not alone. We have a possible new board chair, a guy named Chris Mueller." Greg recalled the name Mueller, and Roger saw his eyes searching, his thought working. "He called a few minutes ago."

That was it, Greg thought, and he nodded.

"I'll introduce you on Friday," Roger said. "He's a venture advisor. He's been a resident entrepreneur at Hilltop Partners in Silicon Valley."

"Really, Hilltop?"

"Yeah. You know it?"

Greg nodded. "You know I've consulted for a few informatics and semantic web start ups in Seattle and the Valley."

"Right, so I thought you'd appreciate that."

"Very interesting." Greg nodded. "So if you're priming AlignIt for broad deployment as a tech platform, having a venture advisor already must feel pretty encouraging….You're fortunate to have someone like him on board."

"I think so," Roger said confidently but reservedly. "It shows AlignIt is going out into the world. Mueller's got a lot of connections with companies that could be potential new members of the AlignIt Commons. He knows a lot of people in the semantic web space. That's really valuable. Apparently, he meditates and does some inner work. But Mueller's world is unfamiliar to me, so…" Roger breathed in, "I hope we've got the right man."

"I'll look him up. Chris Mueller?"

"Yeah," Roger confirmed, and he spelled his last name. "I met him at the same conference where we met, actually. He then came to our last AlignIt Commons board meeting, and he'll try out guest chairing in Friday's meeting. So you'll meet him. And then, I'd especially like you to meet Thomas Finnegan, our archetypal image advisor, as we affectionately call him." Greg smiled faintly at the title. "He's an old friend of mine. He used to curate an archetypal image collection in San Francisco, and now he lives up near you in the Seattle area. I'm hopeful the two of you will hit it off. Thomas has deep knowledge of specific archetypal images, correlating to entities in our terms. And we're looking to you, of course, for hierarchy and relations."

"This'll be a good week," Greg said, relishing the anticipation of intellectual camaraderie like this in areas dearer to his heart than his current teaching schedule back home at University of Washington. He took a bite of a small vegetarian taco. Lime and chili burst upon the stage of his tongue. He chewed a moment. "Well, on the consulting side of your invitation, things are lining up with AlignIt."

"And how about the academic side—teaching at the Bridge Institute?"

"I'm still trying to connect up with Ms. Blocke in HR."

"Still?" Roger said, surprised and squinting his eyes.

"Still. I've called and emailed several times the last two weeks."

"I remember. And still nothing?"

"Her profile shows that she's in. But no reply."

"I'll help move that along. She's new and she's probably just getting things sorted out. We'll get it moving."

Jenny interrupted. "Roger. Sara studies Pythagorean forms in art and architecture."

"Really," Roger said with obvious interest, turning brightly to face Sara. "Pythagorean forms?"

"Well, I'm an amateur," Sara said humbly. "I'm an industrial designer. I just play with Pythagorean art after putting Tara to bed."

Why is she under-selling herself? Greg wondered.

"I'll have to show you what we've done with Pythagorean forms," Roger said. "Lining up geometric forms with corresponding numbers and musical notes. And these are linked again to images and attributes from the Orphic hymns, and so on. You may have some insights."

"I'd be delighted. I don't know how much help I'd be in sacred science."

"She's being modest," Greg said in Sara's defense. "She goes into the forms intuitively, and she keeps me on my toes!"

"Well, I do want to see your system," Sara said. "But from what I've seen looking over Greg's shoulder, it's annotated by scholars. I'll offer whatever I can."

"We do aim for experts, for masters in subjects," Roger said pointedly. He leaned forward. "Scholars may be masters. And we need scholarship. But we're looking for more than scholarship. We aim for mastery of the disciplines behind each system, not just research and publication. We seek people who can see into the essence of things, see directly the relations of things, discern the roles and functions of things."

"Well?" Greg looked at Sara.

"Okay," she said. "It does sound interesting."

"Show us what you know," Jenny said. "Did you bring samples?"

"I didn't think of it," Sara said. "I really planned this as Greg's conference. I kind of thought this was about software."

"Well it is about software, for Greg," Roger said. "But it's bigger."

Sara took up another chocolate cake as Roger spoke. She took a bite, pushed her tongue into the icing and rolled it around her mouth. Greg noticed this was her third piece, and he looked at her with some concern. But she didn't return the glance, knowing he noticed her and feeling conspicuous.

"It's about life," Roger continued, "about Reality with a capital 'R.' But by using software, we're representing entities and their properties and relations in just the same way as great art can. This is what we're doing by aggregating sacred science ontologies, and why we need this guy," Roger said, pointing to Greg, "to help us create an upper ontology for sacred sciences. Anyway, if you're open to it, let me show you what we've done with Pythagorean forms when you visit Tuesday night."

"Okay," Sara said openly. "Bayside Village and AlignIt just got bigger than I expected."

"I see," Roger said.

"Roger, maybe you should go over the schedule," Jenny prompted. The dusky sky had turned dark now, and the lamps had come on around the patio and down the walk leading to the Bay. "I think this little one needs some rest." Jenny rubbed the back of her forefinger gently on Tara's cheek, and Tara put her head down on Sara's shoulder in a shy but fond gesture.

"Right," Roger said. He pulled out his mobile and opened the schedule and map he sent to Greg and Sara. "We have a full plan for you this week," he said enthusiastically. "I hope I didn't pack it too tightly."

8

Back at the Lodge, Greg pulled out a picture book of the Buddhist Jataka Tales, a favorite of Tara's. With Sara on one side of the bed resting on pillows propped up, Greg on the other, and Tara in the middle, Greg read through the familiar story. Tara pointed to the pictures that usually fascinated her. At the story's end, Tara fought bed time at first. But she fell asleep in no time, exhausted from travel and social stimulation. Unusual treat, Greg thought. He picked her up with her new toy, Clappy, and walked slowly to the roll-away-bed brought in during the reception. He put her down gently and covered her with the blankets. Standing up straight, he glanced at her. "I hope she'll do okay with the Daycare tomorrow."

Tara turned over and hugged the pillow.

Sara got up and quietly arranged a few last items from her suitcase, setting up the room for the week. She pulled out her mobile, sat down on the bed, checked her work email. She replied to a query from a junior designer and one problem case.

Greg walked to the corner table, pulled books from his backpack. He organized a pile neatly on the table top, the largest below, the smallest on top. He touched the books with his finger to line them up exactly.

Sara looked up and spotted Greg in his ritual. "Well you're at home, aren't you?" She put her mobile on the night stand.

"Why do you say that?" he asked, turning.

Sara leaned back on the bed, making herself comfortable. "You've already built your pyramid."

Greg looked back at his book pile. "My pyramid?" He laughed, shook his head, and left it alone, joining her on the bed. He took a deep breath and stretched. "So, you seem energized," he said. "I thought by now you'd be telling me what a strange place this is, asking what I was thinking—to bring you to some ugly industrial complex boasting utopian ideals."

"Well, it was ugly—the ride here anyway," Sara said. "You have to admit that."

"It was."

Sara reached for her purse and pulled out her sketch book, putting it beside her mobile on the night stand. "But it's kind of attractive here—like, the design work." Sara looked up to the wallpaper again in amazement, staring off, collecting her thoughts. "I like Roger and Jenny," she said, looking back to Greg. "They're really good-hearted people. I felt resonant with them right away. And President Bateson seems a real leader."

"Mmm," Greg breathed.

"I can see why you like Roger. I was watching you talk with him—you really lit up. You two were in a flow."

"You were watching me?" Greg asked, surprised, as it often seemed to him that he was watching her.

"Mhmm." Sara nodded with a sweet smile. "I'm glad to see you that way again, actually. I know you've been struggling to find meaning in your work." She paused, looked at the floor, then back up at him. "It makes this trip more serious for me, you know." Sara trailed off. Greg nodded. "Then I think about our family, Tara's school, and my job—all the practical things about where we live ..." She decided not to repeat her litany. "But I really like Roger and Jenny. I felt an immediate affinity."

"Yeah, me too," Greg said. "I hadn't met Jenny before. She seems like a really solid, mature woman."

"She's deep! Quiet, but she speaks with authority."

"Yeah."

"And you said Roger and Jenny are on our path," Sara said.

Greg nodded. "Yeah. Not ours exactly."

"I was curious to see if they would bring it up. Maybe at their house."

"Yeah," Greg said, leaning back now. "I feel honored that they've invited us for dinner."

Sara rolled onto her side, closer to Greg. "I'm curious to see what could emerge from this....I feel a kinship with them, like we know each other more deeply than having just met, or at least like we have a common commitment and purpose."

"Well, I think we do," Greg said, sitting back against his pillows, still propped up from reading to Tara. "Look at AlignIt—it takes a certain kind of person to create that and keep a high standard for its development, technically and spiritually."

"I guess," Sara said. "I actually mean seeing them in person, seeing the quality of their presence and attention."

"Oh. Yeah, sure."

"And I had a great talk with Jenny on art. She's on the board of the Art Center."

"Really?"

"She actually plays a prominent role in several organizations here. She seems to be involved in everything."

"Interesting," Greg said. "I liked her, too. I want to learn more about her. Anyway, you seem more interested suddenly than I expected."

"Well, if we have a connection on the path….I know you told me a few times. I just forgot about it for some reason."

Greg nodded. He recollected images of the evening. Then he remembered. "Oh."

"Yeah?"

"I just want to check in about one thing. I noticed you had several cakes."

Sara felt herself recoil. "Yeah," she said blankly, feeling a shift in awareness and manner at the change in topic.

"I'm just concerned."

"I know." She looked down to the bed and smoothed a wrinkle in the covers. "It's not the same."

"Okay." Greg paused. "I just want to support you in any way I can."

"I know." She smoothed the covers with her hand, though nothing much was there. "I think I'm feeling stressed about coming here. I know this is very important to you. I know there are many things here that interest me, too. I just need to find my place here this week. I'm not going to slide into old stuff. Maybe it's just an instant reaction to arriving and trying to get my bearings."

"Okay," Greg said, not entirely assured, but knowing not to push. "Will you let me know if you need my support?"

"Of course." Sara smiled at Greg, inwardly confident this was history.

Greg reached over and put his arms around her. "You're so beautiful just the way you are." He kissed her on the cheek.

"Thanks," she said. Then in a sudden shift of energy and affect, her eyes shot wide open. "Oh, you know what? Do you remember Karen, the Director of Development?"

"Yeah," Greg said, sitting back again at the quick change in conversation.

"She offered me a job interview!"

"Really?" Greg burst out, surprised. "When?"

"Shhh." Sara put her finger to her lips and pointed to Tara, and then compensated by whispering, "When you were talking to Roger before we sat down."

"Oh yeah," Greg said, matching her whisper. "Well how did she know about you?"

"Apparently Roger set it up."

"Roger?" Greg said with obvious surprise. "How did Roger know?"

"He sent her links to my work. So she's seen it."

"Are you serious? How did he know about your work?"

"From you, probably. I guessed you had talked to him about it."

"Not really." Greg stopped, recollected. "I told him you do industrial design in the IT sector. I told him that if I take the position at the Bridge Institute, we'll need a way to come here as a family. I said you'd need to find work, and we'd need a school for Tara. But that's it." Greg stared off to the far wall. "Hmm. Maybe he found your work and set up an interview for you." He looked up again to Sara. "He must really like your work."

"Or he must really want you."

"Or both. I mean, you do really nice work. And your approach is no doubt one they'd appreciate here."

"I just didn't expect this at all," Sara said. "I'm thinking about how I can do an interview. Like, what do I wear, what work do I show, what do I say?"

Greg and Sara discussed the interview, the position, and how it might fit the picture of moving to the Village. Sara openly explored options in a kind of creative play until Greg felt it time to retire.

"Do you want to meditate?" Greg asked.

"Yeah." Sara hesitated. "Well, actually, let me first look up the Bayside Village again and see what images and messaging they have so far. Alright? Fifteen minutes?"

"Sure."

Sara sat down at the corner table, touched on her mobile, activated the screen projection, browsed the Bayside Village's visual design.

Greg joined her at the table, touched his mobile, activated both his screen and keyboard projections.

9

In the open space there at the corner table, with his mobile down flat, his screen projection up, and Sara by his side studying Bayside Village's visual identity, Greg looked into his screen projection. He recalled Technology Transfer Director Jackie Schrader's words, and for a moment his eyes focused beyond the screen to the wall, with its unfamiliar sacred science wallpaper. Where do utopian thinking and technology transfer meet? How could one inform the other? Greg's own research always seemed too abstract to amount to a new technology of any commercial merit or practical utility. Ontologies are in the background, operating at a level of abstraction. But what about possible work with Roger on AlignIt? That could amount to something. What kind of affiliate program is the AlignIt Commons, with its member companies developing practical applications of the AlignIt platform? Greg sat back, looked sideways across the room. How did *ejido* and *usufruct* principles play a role in the AlignIt Commons? What an interesting woman, Jackie. What other tech transfer novelties is she developing? Exploring utopian ideas must blow wide open the framework of conventional university approaches. Was tech transfer even contemplated in utopian classics?

Greg looked back to his screen view projected from his mobile, hovering in the air before him. He touched on a screen for AlignIt with his finger in the air, brought it to the front. He had kept it running in the background the past few months, seldom shut it down. What to look up now, while Sara surveyed Bayside Village's visual identity? His thoughts turned back to this daring venture—this visit to Bayside Village, the thought of moving here, the prospect of leaving his secure pathway to tenure back home at University of Washington. He had been feeling uneasy about such a crazy move, a zig-zag in his career, possible career suicide. Yet he felt a strong pull to such a place as this, a place to live so many of his values all at once, to live so many values shared with Sara right here in one place. The feeling of daring venture was strong. Opening AlignIt's Advanced Search window, he typed into the Attribute field the term *courage*. Just a quick, playful search while waiting. To delimit his search, Greg selected parameters:

> spiritual teachings, spiritual exercises, psychological exercises, poetry, quotes, mythology, folklore, gods, goddesses, saints, saint stories, animal fables, divine names, I Ching hexagrams, mandalas, yantras, physical exercises, diet

Then his eyes returned to the top and he scanned the list. That's too broad, he thought. What a hodge-podge. Nor had he delimited the search further by specifying spiritual or philosophical tradition, like Buddhism, Sufism, Yoga. But he could always narrow the search later, he thought. He named and saved his query, 'Courage—Broad Search', then tapped the Search button. 2,437 hits. Wow. That much in here already?

Greg scrolled down, searched the results returned, saw a link to *fortitude*. The brief text underneath referred to the wheels of Raymond Lully's logic engine in Ars Magna. Apparently AlignIt connected *courage* to Lully's *fortitude*.

Greg's thought went now to Lully. How interesting, he thought, that AlignIt would pull up Raymond Lully in this search, since he was just reading Lully's <u>Ars Magna</u> in preparation for this visit. Again he looked through the screen projection to the wall beyond, contemplating. Was this a synchronicity, the outer situation reflecting the inner state or question? But he shouldn't be surprised; of course Roger would include Raymond Lully's system in AlignIt's ontology, its mereology, its logic. Lully must be studied broadly here at Bayside Village, he thought, with a full museum of the history of sacred science named after him. Lully must be a big figure here. Greg clicked, opened to the Lullian wheel, saw it displayed before him, its Latin letters arranged about the circumference, qualities written underneath, and lines connecting the letters to one another across the circle in a star-like pattern.

Then he lamented—when will I have the time to study this, amidst family duties, teaching load, advising, writing grant proposals, preparing journal manuscripts—the duties just to live, to get by, to eek out a meager livelihood? Where is the time to study such works as <u>Ars Magna</u>? When can I get beyond the demands of the external environment, when can I contemplate what is truly of importance, or might be? How to really advance knowledge, how to explore? Wasn't an academic life supposed to be for this? Yet here I am now, in this week set apart, this week to explore. Now, at least, I have a little time.

Greg focused his eyes on the screen projection. He looked at the wheel with its Latin letters, B through K, found *fortitude* below the letter D, and clicked it. A little window popped up. Okay, its a definition: "Fortitude is a habit by which a strong heart acts courageously." Greg contemplated. His attention shuttled between the abstract principle fortitude and the need of his soul to contemplate and acquire this character quality he named courage. Courage to be here at Bayside Village, without expectation, openly exploring. Daring to be here, daring to see what arises without aversion or desire.

Greg clicked another screen, scanned it. Fortitude is associated with the alphabet letter D on the Lullian wheel. He went to D, saw the string of associations down from D. The chief quality is duration, and the text says, "Duration is what makes each quality durable." That's circular, he thought. How is that helpful? How does this system work, he wondered, looking at the diagram, the wheels, the Roman letters, the rules and principles. What's the logic here? He recalled previous readings, just weeks ago, days ago. The structure, movement and rules came to back him, vaguely. He looked at the string of associated figures, principles and rules. Contrariety is further down the chain under D, and it says, "a mutual resistance arising from divergent ends." Simple definition. Okay. Cross referencing another wheel, Greg noted that contrariety is linked by a triangle to difference and concord, connected with other alphabet letters, but contrariety itself is associated with fortitude, and with duration, and D. How? Contrariety entails natural instinct and appetite, hence motion. Mmm. He read an example. With another being, say a lion, I can experience difference, like the different species of lion and man, or concordance, like lion and man in the same genus. But lion and man can also fight; so contrariety entails privation and opposition. But how is contrariety related to this chain of associations from D? Perhaps duration and fortitude are qualities I can call up in myself when I face conditions like privation and opposition? God willing, I won't face privation and opposition here.

Greg looked again to the wheel, down the string of associations under D. Below contrariety, the rule for this letter D, for these qualities of duration and fortitude, is "Of what?" What does "Of what?" mean? Greg scrolled down, scanned the screen view. Ah, here, three classes—it means, where does something come from, what is it made of, to what or whom does it belong? So these are like origin questions, establishing an order in time, in ownership.

The subject of D is heaven, the third subject in the cosmic hierarchy, arranged around the wheel on the fourth circle, each hierarchic quality under its corresponding Latin letter—a hierarchy including God, angels, heaven, man, imagination, senses, vegetation, elements, and instruments. Hmm. Heaven. Greg looked up and down the string from D. Duration, fortitude, contrariety, the question "Of what," and heaven…. Scrolling the text, Greg read that in heaven, there is no contrariety, which means no appetite, no instinct, no motion. Hmm. In heaven, there is no contrariety. Then why are the two connected? Their very relation seems contrary! But in heaven, he read elsewhere, skipping down, there is beginning, efficient cause of what cascades down from heaven in the hierarchy. Which comes back to the origin question, "Of what?" Or, what causes what is created from heaven, from origin, from prior conditions or materials? Heaven is the prime mobile substance. What does that mean? Oy! This will take some time!

Greg skipped around, clicking here and there, hoping quick browsing would assemble enough loose impressions to amount to an insight. He clicked to Lully's table of seven columns, expandable to eighty four, which he perused a week ago after putting Tara to bed back at home. This table charts ascending and descending paths, he recalled, and horizontal paths across the table. Ascending paths go to antecedents of the present location, to qualities more general in nature; descending paths go to more consequent, particular things. And across—connections can be made across the columns, horizontal transformations across different types or elements or phases on the same level.

So here it is, very abstractly—metaphysics, ontology, cosmology. Right here in Lully's table of qualities, accessed in AlignIt as a working system. Wouldn't Lully have been impressed to see his wheels in motion, operable in AlignIt, side by side and interpenetrating with other ontologies! What a complete system it is, these Lullian wheels, but very abstract. And AlignIt, too—like reading data tables. AlignIt is a tech platform, an engine, an internet of bare qualities, relations and operating rules found across history, across the globe. But this is not an application layer. To grasp what AlignIt offers in any practical sense, one needs applications of these qualities, rules and principles in "real world" terms, "real world" applications. Which is why GameIt will help. And PlanIt. Games, schedulers, other tools and apps. Roger's AlignIt Commons is a good idea—to bring these apps together.

But Greg imagined he could go into AlignIt's raw tables and find his way without the apps. Just as he ventured into the naked cosmos, into bare ontologies ever present in life, with few reference points for esoteric work. Isn't all of life a pathway? Isn't the whole world the book of nature? And why shouldn't one trained to see find their way without books, charts, applications, all of them representations that simplify the vastness of knowledge in order to teach?

But how to travel these paths on Lully's table, and by what faculties, Greg wondered—pure intellectual contemplation, imagination? What had Lully intended? Greg hadn't read that far yet. He knew Lully himself was a mystic philosopher. Lully experienced revelation. The structure of <u>Ars Magna</u> came to him in a mountain hermitage on Mount Randa in Majorca in 1274, like Moses was given the law, like Mohammed was given Suras of the Quran, and Lully had only to write down what he saw. How to approach this Art, how to work it, how to see and know by it? Lully saw philosophy and theology as one, reason and faith as one. This was a sacred science, not a system of doctrines to take on belief and obedience. How, then, to approach the Lullian wheels and work them? Two things must be held together, it seemed—exploring the logic of the wheels with the intellect, and practicing an insight-based contemplation. Were other modes of cognition possible, whether Lully intended them or not?

Greg's eyes settled again on the screen view hovering in the air before him, on Lully's table of 9 columns filled with letters. Then he focused on the wall beyond it, and he fell into an imaginative play, working the paths with the eye of his heart, the eye of imagination, the eye of fire that pierces the husk of appearances.

Up the column he went on Lully's table, and down, like traversing a cosmic staircase. Then across to the right, across to the left. Walking around inside the table, traveling paths of letter combinations. But he hadn't memorized the letters, the qualities, the rules, and the principles. How could he practice the combinatory art? The letters first should be known by heart. Then one can travel.

Greg was just about to click back to the alphabet in <u>Ars Magna</u>.
"Ready?" Sara said. She deprojected her screen.
Greg felt jolted, but came back instantly from his contemplation, his
pathworking. "Yeah." He let go of the Art, touched off his screen and
keyboard projections, came back here, to the room.
Sara got up from the table, turned off the lights, and climbed into the
bed.
Greg followed, climbed in, and propped up the pillows for back
support, smelling a fresh scent in the bed sheets and pillow case.
Sara sat in half-lotus against her propped pillows, even though she
could keep a full lotus a short while. She stretched her spine to one side,
then the other, and made a faint guttural sound. "So much to digest today,"
she said.
"It is." Greg adjusted his clothes, pulled his legs into half-lotus—which
was all he could do. He closed his eyes, breathed in deeply, then out.
Sara breathed in, then let the day go in a long exhale.
Greg heard her slow, quiet breaths. How blessed I am, he thought.
In the dark, with the dim glow of light from the courtyard in the
curtain-drawn windows and a faint night light in the bathroom, Greg turned
his attention toward his heart. He found alignment with the deepest
longing of his soul and set his intention there. Thoughts and impressions
from the day buzzed around in his mind. But he kept to his wish to go
home, to be intimate with his Beloved, a wish like a light in his soul calling
another light and longing to meet, light upon light.

Day 2: Monday

10

Roger sat before the screen projection in his home office in the
neighborhood adjacent to the Bayside Village campus. The sun was just
rising, starting its burn through the San Francisco Bay's morning fog,
always heavier by the Richmond coastline. The first beams reached
through the window, lighting his bookshelf, throwing rays across his
treasures—the great books of world religions and their esoteric teachings.
He was finishing up an early web call with Chris Mueller, prospective
AlignIt Commons board chair from Hilltop Ventures, on Friday's board
meeting.
"So, I've been looking again at your market strategy," Mueller said. "I

have an idea to bring in more AlignIt Commons members and boost your research revenue."

"Oh," Roger said, interested, leaning in to the desk and hugging his tea cup.

"It requires opening up to more game companies," Mueller said with a voice that told Roger he knew it was controversial. "Gaming is a big application for AlignIt. I've made some good connections in gaming recently. And I want to have a candid discussion Friday about how royalties from more game companies can fund AlignIt, maybe even your speculative projects like your AlignIt Discovery Engine."

Two strange impressions mixed in Roger. What speculative projects? Roger thought to himself. Then he asked, "Game companies? Have you talked with Jeff Baker at GameIt?"

"Yeah, I've talked to him. I have a few ideas."

"He's licensed exclusively in the field of games."

"I know."

"Okay," Roger said. He paused, concern written in the lines of his face. He sat back. "I need to check in with Jeff, too, before we bring a conversation like that to a board meeting. This isn't a lot of advance notice."

"I know."

"And our agenda is packed with Greg Cobb and Neil Benson here as guest speakers."

"I realize that," Mueller said. "Sorry for the last-minute request. An opportunity opened up. That's how it is in Silicon Valley. You act quickly, seize opportunities."

"I appreciate that. Let me check with Jeff." Roger stood up with his tea, turned, thinking, and turned back. "And you said 'speculative projects'? The AlignIt Discovery Engine is well beyond speculative."

"Sure, sure. You've put a lot of time into it. But Roger," Mueller said with a mildly exasperated voice, then a pause, "at some point in the life cycle of a new venture, the technology side has to be consolidated and the business side has to mature. Sometimes you have critical windows of opportunity. I've managed scores of innovation projects, budgets, and timelines like yours. I know how businesses succeed—and fail. I'd like to talk with you about building up AlignIt's revenue stream, and look strategically at some of the non-revenue generating projects."

"Okay, I understand business cycles. But the high point of this meeting is to get the board's commitment on developing an upper ontology in AlignIt with Greg and rolling that out to AlignIt Commons members. We've gone over this."

"I realize that, yes. I've also read over the board materials and looked again at your financials. I find myself questioning the return on investment of bringing someone like Greg here at this time. I think we should hear him out, of course. But I think bringing him on now will consume a lot of resource while adding questionable value in the short run, when you have minimal cash flow."

Roger was perplexed at Mueller's unexpected turn, his sudden shift in strategy. And Greg is here already.

"Look, Roger, you already have two commercial licensees, Game It and PlanIt, among the Commons members, and they've created AlignIt-based applications. Right? So it's already working. And I have to say, parenthetically—their royalty payments on commercial sales are meager, and we may have to look at that, too. But my point is that if you spend more time developing the AlignIt platform, including your discovery engine project, I'm just concerned you'll miss critical revenue opportunities in present time." Mueller left a deliberate pause with a sigh. "Roger, I've seen a lot of technology projects come and go. If you keep tinkering with the AlignIt platform, like having Greg work on your upper ontology project, and building your discover engine, our current member companies will have to retool, and we'll make it harder for new companies to join. If you want my extensive experience from the Valley, I would strongly urge we focus your limited funds on marketing and licensing—signing on new members to the AlignIt Commons. More companies can come on right now and grow your royalty base. I've primed a few of them."

In the cool early morning before breakfast, when the sun's rays were just piercing the fog, Greg and Sara started out with Tara on the path to a yoga class. Not the class listed on today's Orientation schedule. This was the class held in the main room of the large, multi-path Temple, a building Greg noted would be on Randy's Orientation tour later in the morning. Sara wanted a taste of the deeper practice at Bayside Village, not the introductory sample offered for the Orientation. Of course she would, Greg thought, with a mix of pride at her capacity and hesitation at his.

Inside the temple, cushions and seats were pushed to the walls. The bare floor had a sheen from warm-colored, polished wood—an obvious sign the hall was built for movements as well. The walls were white with stained wood beams and large picture windows looking out to semi-wooded lawns. The ceiling exposed its beams, revealing a gradual A-frame roof. The atmosphere was warm, calm, and contemplative.

Greg and Sara spotted a rack of mats, blankets and cushions by the door and picked up one of each. Greg picked up extras for Tara. They walked to the middle of the room to lay out their mats alongside a few people already stretching.

Yoga would be one of Sara's refuges this week, Greg reflected. Accordingly, he assumed the designated parent role for this class. This gesture gave Sara freedom to go deep in practice. Then she could enjoy at least something from the week.

Greg made a place for Tara. "Here you go, Sweetie," he said quietly. He spoke in low tones matching the quiet ambiance. "You can do the yoga asanas with us if you want, or you can lie down quietly and use the pillow and blanket here. Do you want to stretch with us?" Tara nodded and moved onto the center of her mat. "We're not going to talk here when class starts, okay? You can use your whispering voice if you need to ask me something. Mommy and Daddy will be doing yoga. And we'll go to breakfast after yoga." Tara asked some questions that were aimed, Greg realized, at establishing boundaries in this new place—what if I get tired, how long is yoga, when is breakfast. Then Tara watched Greg and Sara warming up, and she imitated their stretches. Greg was aware of Tara's watching eyes, and gave an example of stretches she could follow.

The regular morning class would be Sara's choice, of course, Greg thought. He asked Sara as he moved into a forward bend, "You're sure this isn't Advanced?"

"It's Intermediate. Don't worry." She stepped into warrior pose, and Greg saw her toe ring as she put her left foot down on the mat. He liked this signature detail. Then he noticed her new yoga outfit. She didn't seek mainstream aerobic yoga, he thought proudly. The asanas meant more to her than keeping trim. Yoga was for moving meditation, for seeing.

"I think it's alright for you and Tara," she said.

A man looking like the teacher walked into the Temple. He seemed a mature man, maybe in his fifties, with short brown hair and hints of silver. He had a highly concentrated demeanor and commanding presence in his walk to the front where he put down some things.

Greg approached him. "Excuse me."

The teacher turned. Years of practice showed in the depths of his eyes, the defined features of his face.

"Hi. My wife and I are visiting for the Orientation. I wanted to ask if we can have our daughter in class with us here if she's quiet."

"Oh, this isn't the Orientation program," the teacher said.

"Yes, I realize," Greg said. "We're thinking of moving here, and my wife wants to try the regular sessions. And my daughter is used to sitting with us quietly, or else she lies down."

The teacher looked at Greg with warm eyes, studying him a moment with yogic sight. He looked to Sara and Tara, and then back to Greg. "This is a public class, and you're welcome. But it's Intermediate. Of course your daughter is welcome too, if she's quiet. She does yoga?"

"A little. She may start out and then lie down for the rest of the class."

"Some postures are beyond a child's level. If she's restless or wants to talk, one of you can take her outside."

"Okay," Greg said.

The teacher brought his hands to his chest, said "Namaste," and then turned around and unrolled his mat. Greg made the gesture and returned to his mat.

"Daddy, what did he say?" Tara whispered. Greg explained.

When the room was almost full, the teacher began in a calm, concentrated voice. "Take a seat at the front of your mat for *pranayama*, breathing exercises."

After a series of asanas, the teacher said, "Now let's take the *salamba sirasana*, the headstand pose." The teacher paused and gave time for students to take the posture. Greg and Sara put their heads into their hands locked together on the mat, walked their feet up close to their heads, and kicked their feet up into the air into the headstand pose. Tara sat and watched the adults.

"Hold the posture," the teacher called out as he walked amongst the students. "Try to stay in this position as long as you can." He paused after each bit of guidance, giving time for students to grasp and apply the instruction. "In this pose, bring your attention to your breath. Breath is essential in yoga—how you breathe, and your awareness of your breath. We breathe in *prana*, life energy." The teacher walked around the room correcting posture as he spoke periodically. "Just breathe naturally without forcing your breath. Just feel your breathing in and your breathing out." Again, the teacher gave time. Sara's posture was strong and firm. Greg wobbled.

"In Ayurveda, we talk about the *tridosha*, or the three constitutions— *vata*, *pitta*, and *kapha*." The teacher spoke in calm, measured tones, giving instruction while students held the headstand. "Each of us experiences the yoga asanas uniquely, according to our *dosha*, our constitution. The headstand is a good *vata*-balancing yoga asana. Its good for many *vata* ailments, including varicose veins, wrinkles, rheumatoid arthritis, and headaches." Again, the teacher gave time. Too much time, Greg thought, his legs waving in the air. Greg liked the feeling, felt his will active. But he struggled, his arms trembling from exertion, his face filling with blood, his cheeks quivering. This is Intermediate?

Roger walked across the Bridge Institute quadrangle to his faculty office in Avicenna Hall. He took out his mobile and clicked on Mrs. Blocke. Her number rang. No answer. He left a message. "Hi Amelia. Roger here. Monday morning about 7:45. You'll recall that I brought Professor Greg Cobb here this week for faculty interviews, and you said you'd meet with him to go over the process. I understand he's placed several calls and emails to you and hasn't heard back yet. I just want to make sure we nail down a time for him. I think you have his information.

But let me know if I can help in any way. Thanks." Roger ended the call. He approached Avicenna Hall on the quad. He gazed with pleasure on the sun's bright morning rays reaching across the dew-beaded quad.

11

After showering, Greg, Sara and Tara walked to the Bayside Village Dining Commons for breakfast. They pulled open a heavy wooden door, then a screen door that clacked shut behind them. Two unfamiliar beeps sounded from Greg's and Sara's mobile devices. Curious, Greg reached for his pocket.

"Oh, its the meal plan trackers I downloaded," Sara said.

Inside, they joined a long buffet line. "What an intimate dining room," Greg said. The Commons was abuzz with conversations over dining tables. He wondered how much of it was owing to the normal life of Bayside Village and Bridge Institute, and how much was a larger swell for the Orientation.

In line, Tara swung back and forth holding Sara's hands. Greg quickly checked his mobile for a message from Mrs. Blocke about interviewing. Nothing. For a moment, he felt concern. But it was still early. "I'm going to get coffee," he said. "Do you want one?"

"Yeah, thanks." Sara said.

Greg fetched two gourmet coffees from a self-serve and returned to the line, handing one to Sara and sipping his own. Steam rolled off the surface, curling away into the air. Moving slowly toward the buffet, Greg surveyed the architectural features of the room as he sipped. And he drank in the atmosphere. The Commons was built in a craftsman style, with open, exposed ceiling beams. Large picture windows punctuated wood-paneled walls bounded by wooden window frames. Other walls displayed art works which Greg took to be made on campus. He pointed them out to Sara, who had already noticed.

Greg and Sara picked up trays and plates when they reached the buffet, with Tara walking along between them. Greg turned back to the walls, studying the tile work accenting the wood frames. "Look at all the grain cereals!" Sara said, calling Greg's attention down to the food.

He turned back. "Wow." The display was extraordinary for its beauty and breadth. Dishes were labeled with ingredients, their origins, and their energetic qualities.

"It's a breakfast cornucopia," Sara said. "Miso soup? Enchiladas?" Greg and Sara surveyed the food and labels as they moved along. "This kitchari recipe is in our Ayurvedic cookbook—remember?"

"Mhmm," Greg said, scanning the ingredients on the recipe card.

They moved down the buffet line to the end. "No wonder it took so long," Sara said. "There's so much to see! Tara, do you see the silverware there?" Sara pointed ahead to the dispensary at the end of the line. "Can you get us three knives, three spoons, and three forks? And get napkins for all three of us." Tara went ahead with sudden purpose and picked out the utensils.

"Thank you, Sweetie," Greg said.

With trays in hand, Greg and Sara turned and faced the tables. Greg spotted the section marked off for orientation seating. "There it is," he said. Tara rejoined them. Greg led the family to an open spot at a table where a younger couple looking in their early twenties sat eating. "Mind if we join you?" Greg asked. The couple looked up at Greg, Sara and Tara and welcomed them as they sat down.

"Hi, I'm Greg."

"I'm Keith," the young man said.

"I'm Sara, and this is Tara." Sara leaned over and stirred Tara's kitchari to cool it. Steam escaped the bowl at the turns of her spoon.

"I'm Leah," the young woman said, almost under her breath.

"You're in the Orientation?" Greg asked.

"Yeah," Keith said. "I'm taking Leah so she can see Bayside Village. I've been here a few months, but I haven't actually done it myself yet."

"Are you students?" Greg asked.

Leah looked deferentially to Keith.

"We've recently graduated from Placid College in upstate New York," Keith explained. "I'm taking some time off, and I just moved recently to the Village. I'm taking a few courses at the Bridge Institute and thinking about my life direction."

"I live with friends near Placid College," Leah said, her head sinking into her shoulders as she gave a faint and shy smile. "I'm just visiting Keith for the Orientation—to see what this place is and what Keith is doing."

"Oh, and I'm here to figure out what he's doing," Sara said, pointing her thumb to Greg and looking to Leah with a feeling of kinship. Sara mixed nuts into Tara's yogurt.

"What I'm doing here," Greg clarified, "is interviewing for a faculty position."

"Wow, really!" Keith said. "What do you teach?"

"I teach philosophy at the University of Washington in Seattle. I also co-teach courses in ontology with faculty in computer science and life sciences."

"No way! My college major was philosophy and religion!" Keith replied emphatically. He spoke rapidly. "I'm really interested in philosophy. That's why I'm here right now, actually. But I'm not interested in university philosophy anymore—it's too mental for me. I want to live it. I want it to be part of my faith."

Faith? "Hmm. I understand, I think," Greg said. He peeled a banana for Tara. "I suppose that's why I'm visiting here, too—to see if we can live something more deeply. To help build this new research institute where people can integrate their ideals with their lives—or live their faith, as you say. Universities aren't always the most holistic environments for doing that."

The two couples talked about the Bayside Village, the Orientation ahead, and their backgrounds. Sara and Greg attended to Tara in turn, responding to her observations and questions.

Sara looked at her watch. "We should get Tara to the Day Care." Greg nodded. "Are you ready to go soon, Sweetie?" she asked Tara.

"No," Tara said, still eating.

"Are you thinking of moving here, too?" Sara asked Leah, buying time.

"Um, I don't know," Leah said, polite and agreeable. She seemed to contract. "I don't really understand what Bayside Village is or what Keith is doing here. I want to support him but I'm not really sure about all these teachings."

"I'm done, Mommy," Tara announced.

"I'm finished, too," Keith said.

"Me too," Leah said.

The two couples picked up their trays. Tara picked up hers carefully with Sara's guidance. Sara quickly removed the full cup of water to her own tray. Greg and Sara walked with Tara into the kitchen. Greg helped Tara separate her food scraps and napkins into the various bins for recycling, composting, and trash, and her silverware and plates in the proper wash bins.

Exiting the kitchen, Keith walked with Greg, who held Tara's hand, and he asked about philosophy.

Sara walked with Leah. "Are you a couple?" Sara asked quietly.

"I'm not sure right now," Leah admitted, with a face moving between polite smile and uncertain expression. "That's mostly why I'm here—to see what our future is."

Greg opened the Dining Commons door. The fog had burned off, and the early morning sun was beaming brightly. The sky was electric blue. Plants and flowers everywhere jumped with light. He turned to Keith and Leah. "We'll see you after we drop off Tara at the Daycare."

Greg and Sara walked with Tara down a path to the Bayside Village School and Daycare. Tara would spend her days there during the week while Greg and Sara toured the Village and had meetings.

"Wow!" Greg squinted at the sun's reflected light. He rolled up his sleeves as the air warmed. Turning to Sara, he said, "It's so clear today!"

"Look!" Tara said. A tram rolled by beside the path, its colors vibrant in the morning sun.

They found the Daycare on the main path—a quaint one-story cottage with a fenced in yard embraced by flowering bushes. Stepping inside the cottage door, they saw a mature, late-middle-aged woman seated at a low table with three young children working on an art project. The walls were painted in soft pastels. Light-colored fabrics gently graced the ceiling and walls. Quick glances revealed a room neatly organized with shelves and bins filled with natural and hand-made play objects and art supplies. A warm-colored rug with pillows lay to the side with a rocking chair. Swaths of fabrics and silks were neatly folded. Aprons were hung on hooks by a small kitchenette bar. Cups were neatly organized with children's names. And behind the mature woman, a young woman stood in the kitchenette with stools around her for children to stand up and cook.

"Welcome, come in," the elder woman said.

"Thanks. I'm Sara Cobb. We're here to drop off Tara for daycare. We're here all week for an orientation and interviews."

"Yes, you spoke with me on the phone," the mature one said. "I'm Claire Alpine. And this is Sally McKnight, my class helper." Sally stirred porridge at the stove top and waved, said hello.

"Hi, I'm Greg."

"Hello Greg, welcome," Claire said. "And this must be Tara." Claire turned toward her. "We heard you were coming to visit us. We've been waiting for you this morning. We're so glad you're here."

Tara held to Sara, studying the new situation.

"If you have a few moments before your activities," Claire said to Sara and Greg, "why don't you pull up a chair and chat while Tara settles in?" Greg checked the time on his mobile and nodded to Sara. They pulled up chairs, and Tara climbed onto Sara's lap.

"This is a lovely room," Sara said, looking around. "I wish I was going to stay here."

"You can think of this as part of your extended home for the week," Claire said. "This is a place to feel comfortable, safe, and curious—for the parents, too."

Claire gave an overview of the theory and method of their school. Greg and Sara were deeply moved by the philosophical resonance with the rest of Bayside Village.

After some moments, Greg checked his mobile, prompted Sara. It was time to go. Tara had warmed up to the Daycare. Greg and Sara left her in good hands.

Turning from the gate to the path, Sara said, "That's a lovely little place for Tara. It's kind of inspiring, actually. I feel reassured about her being there during the week."

"Me too," Greg said. "I hoped it would be as good as it sounded, and it seems like more."

"I like Claire and Sally," Sara said. "It feels like Tara's in good care." Greg nodded.

12

Greg and Sara walked up the path to the Bridge Institute quadrangle, beyond the Dining Commons, toward the auditorium for the orientation. On the quad, they entered the already full auditorium and took seats near the back. Greg surveyed the well-appointed room and looked over the heads of people. The room was filled with visitors like them, not the regulars who worked, studied and lived at Bayside Village. What kinds of people had come, Greg wondered, looking around? What would Sara see here?

Presently Director of Development Karen Mitchell, whom they met last night, walked to the lectern on stage.

"That's her," Sara said. "I might interview on Thursday." Greg raised his eyebrows, nodding, and listened to Karen with attention.

"Good morning," Karen said, leaning into the microphone. She paused. The room hushed. "I'd like to welcome you to The Bayside Village and to our graduate research program, The Bridge Institute. We're glad that all of you have come to visit us, learn with us, and inquire with us on this lovely April week in the San Francisco Bay Area. Many of you have come from across the United States, and we have a few international visitors from as far away as Germany, Turkey, and India. Welcome to all of you.

"We have a big line-up for you today and tomorrow. We've put together this orientation to give you the 'big picture' of The Bayside Village and how the Bridge Institute, our research institute, plays a role in it. Some of you will be interested in the Bayside Village's programs, focused on integrating spiritual life and scientific research. Some will be interested in the Bridge Institute's extension courses for the public, or our academic degree programs. You'll see a little of everything on the tour today. Tomorrow afternoon, we offer our famous public workshop, Creative Writing with Utopias, led by President Steve Bateson. And now, without further ado, let me introduce President Steve Bateson himself to formally welcome you."

To the sound of applause, Karen stepped aside from the lectern, clapped and waited for President Bateson.

Greg leaned to Sara amidst the clapping and whispered, "That could be you up there welcoming the President." Sara elbowed him playfully, but then held the thought, considering it.

President Bateson stood up from the audience and walked to the stage to shake Karen's hand. Last night Greg and Sara met him up close. Now, from this distance, Bateson's tall, slender form and silvery white hair became even more apparent. Greg recalled his vibrancy and presence and looked forward to hearing him. Karen left the stage and Bateson took the lectern.

"Good morning," President Steve Bateson said. "Welcome to Northern California, home of Silicon Valley, hi-tech, biotech, sourdough bread, Ghirardelli chocolate, Napa Valley wines, and now, the Bayside Village and its Bridge Institute. We hope you'll feel a warm reception from our community of faculty, students, and member organizations. I'll try to be brief since we have a very full tour awaiting you. Let me just say a few words about who we are and what we're up to in our marvelous experiment on the shore of the San Francisco Bay."

Bateson picked up his mobile device and clicked in the direction of the screen behind him. The screen lit up with an image of the Bayside Village logo and a presentation outline. Bateson continued talking as he clicked through slides on his mobile, with images of the Bayside Village and the Bridge Institute and his talking points.

"Visitors come to the Bayside Village and the Bridge Institute to find intellectual, artistic, social, physical, and spiritual growth. We encompass the arts, education, science, spiritual training and physical culture. Situated as we are in the San Francisco Bay Area, the Bayside Village and Bridge Institute are deeply engaged in the day-to-day world, bringing new ideas, research, and experiments to society for the good of all.

"Located near Berkeley, California, our 170-acre Bayside Village and Bridge Institute campus hosts educational, scientific, cultural, spiritual, and somatic events, including workshops, retreats, lectures, fairs, and festivals."

Bateson clicked through an array of images of Bayside Village and Bridge Institute and their buildings, people and activities, anchoring his presidential pitch in a display of existing, concrete programs.

"Our Institute is a pioneering educational setting: a graduate school rooted in historical academic disciplines while recovering threads of spiritual, emotional, social and physical training lost in modern Western civilization. We are proud to have developed the world's finest publication access system for the literature of sacred science, assembled a faculty of distinguished scholars, and established collaborative relationships with neighboring institutions like the University of California's distinguished ten-campus system, Stanford University, the Graduate Theological Union, and numerous independent graduate schools and research institutes. The proximity of the Bayside Village and the Bridge Institute to these nearby resources creates a dynamic intellectual community on our campus, drawing scholars, spiritual teachers, artists, and business leaders from around the world."

Greg rubbed his jaw with his fingers, imagining research at these great Bay Area universities through the Bridge Institute. He had faculty colleagues far flung at other venerable institutions. In case the Bridge Institute isn't substantial enough, he thought, at least he could collaborate with scholars at these fine nearby universities.

"The Bridge Institute conducts leading-edge research into disciplines of human development, philosophical inquiry, fundamental scientific research, and technology development left behind in most modern universities— including qualitative sciences of essences and attributes, and the study of human development beyond the limited range studied in the dominant Western medical paradigm, such as extended capacities for imagination, sensory perception, awareness, and attention."

Bateson clicked through screens with stunning photos of Bayside Village research projects, the labs, work on the field, profiles of its small but promising faculty, and a host of reseach results, including top publications, programs, products, and services.

"Since researchers tend to focus their inquiry where funding, reward, and recognition can be found, we have instituted a grant program and research prize to fund breakthrough research in the areas valued by the Bridge Institute, like sacred science and innovation in utopian thinking. In both its sponsorship and conduct of research, the Bridge Institute maintains a commitment to scientific rigor while exploring philosophical, spiritual, and scientific traditions and human capacities largely overlooked by mainstream Western science and philosophy."

Greg's eyes focused sharply on Bateson. But his attention went now to his imagination of funding sources available at the Bridge Institute. In the areas of his own research interests, little funding could be found. His deepest loves must always be pursued on the side, unfunded. And the standard grant announcements from federal and state agencies and foundations largely lay outside his interests; industry funding was usually more applied and related to business units, products and existing market opportunities. Hence the compromises of mainstream academic life. Here, though, funding was available for the esoteric subjects he cared deepest about. This fact burned in him. Imagine all I could do, he thought, if I only had the right climate and resources!

"Let me also draw your attention," Bateson said, "to our unique ecological environment here at the Bayside Village." Now, Bateson flashed images of the campus waterfront. "Our 170-acre property includes some of the most virgin marsh lands remaining on the Bay coastline. We have one of the few remaining shoreline areas of native coastal grasslands once covering the Bay Area. Monarch butterflies and raptors are drawn to the eucalyptus grove bordering our property to the northeast. Our coastal marsh and mudflats are habitats for a profusion of native flora and fauna, like crabs, muscles, and cord grass. On our walking paths, you may see the California Clapper Rail, now an endangered species like so many plants, fish, and animals of the San Francisco Bay." At the sight of the Clapper Rail on Bateson's slides, Greg and Sara glanced at each other, thinking of Tara's new stuffed animal, Clappy. "We've made this campus, rich in botanical and marine life and native beauty, into a critical learning laboratory for teaching and research. Ecological restoration is central to both the Bayside Village and the Bridge Institute's work in sacred science. We invite you to take walks and share this pristine beauty, catching a small glimpse of the San Francisco Bay as it was before the impacts of modern civilization."

Bateson paused, breathed deeply, looked out to his audience, his eyes passing from one side to the other.

"The Bridge Institute is rooted not only in great global traditions of classical learning but also in the most forward-looking visions of the future. We investigate utopian visions as possible models for contemporary projects and as social critiques of the worlds we live in. This is one of my own areas of research." Bateson now revealed images of great utopian art—of cities, towns and communes in Europe and America, some imagined by great visionaries, some built. Greg noticed Sara sit up, heard a groan of interest in her throat, saw her head cock forward. The utopian art captured her, he noted. The ideas captured him. "We study the great feats of human imagination in utopian classics, exploring some of the highest reaches of human social, political, economic, technological, educational, and spiritual organization. As we are working in an integral philosophy here, weaving strands of sacred knowledge and practice from diverse origins into a modern global civilization, utopian works offer us models of ideal Western and global forms for the importation of those gems of human learning and achievement from local cultures into a broader emerging global civilization."

Greg felt a thrill at the idea of utopias. But why? It wasn't among his studies in philosophy, except, perhaps, for Plato's Republic. His mind raced to synthesize the impressions registered from Bateson's words with the thrust of his own philosophical research. But why this sudden rush of interest in utopias? Was it a look at different histories of utopian thinking that roused him? Plato was an initiate in several mysteries, he knew. Was there a connection between ancient mystery schools and the spawning of great civilizations?

Bateson turned with special attention to the audience. "As you'll hear me say tomorrow in greater depth—those of you attending our utopia workshop—we study utopias here, but we do not claim to be one. This is an important point." He paused for emphasis. "Our study, imagination, and experiments with humanity's heritage of utopian expressions of highest human potential is a work in progress, not a destination. I have called this endeavor *utopianizing*—that is, being in the process of studying, evaluating, and establishing better human societies in light of utopian works, whether literary or artistic. But to do this work of *utopianizing*, we need to be familiar with our heritage of utopian visions. Thus the study of utopias forms part of the core curriculum at the Bridge Institute and it's one thrust of my research and that of several of my colleagues here."

So there must be a community of utopian scholars here, Greg pondered. This is part of the intellectual milieu. Is it related, somehow, to sacred sciences?

Bateson now projected religious symbols and ideological marks in rapid succession encompassing the many groups that had joined the Village's work. "While the Bridge Institute as a whole takes a stand for certain traditions of human inquiry, we are neither a spiritual association, nor a political action or social change group, nor an advocacy group for single causes as against a broader inquiry." He now showed portraits of conversations and conferences. "While we are a community of scholar-practitioners committed to spiritual training and traditions of investigative inquiry, we're not allied with any single spiritual system, ideology, method, association, or funding source. Working largely within a framework of integral philosophies like that found in Sri Aurobindo, we're a nexus of diverse traditions of inquiry into philosophy and the sciences. We cultivate a spirit of free inquiry, encouraging a diversity of perspectives on social, spiritual, and scientific matters. We respect multiple ways of knowing, and diverse means of demonstrating knowledge mastery and competency in its application. We bring discernment to our work, and we keep asking the hard questions rather than settling for easy dogmas, simplistic religious or scientific formulas, or expedient solutions."

Greg was awed at the scope of this vision, inspired by the possibilities. To work in a setting that honored what had always been self-evident to him, rather than pretending adherence to the materialistic modernist project...The possibility seemed real now, achievable. The door seemed to stand open to him.

Steve took off his glasses and leaned into the lectern toward the audience. "When I observe our distinguished faculty and diverse student body, some of the words that come to mind are..." Steve spoke slowly and thoughtfully, "creative, curious, intellectually rigorous, technologically innovative, socially conscious, mindful, and spiritually aspiring. Isaac Newton famously said, 'I could move the world if I had a place to stand.'

Many people are attracted to Bayside Village because they, too, want to make a positive difference in the world. At the Bayside Village, many have found a place to stand and move the world. It may be that our bold, utopianizing experiment becomes a place for you. We welcome you to join our endeavor, our inquiry, our investigation, our service to the world. I hope this brief introduction to our Bayside Village and its Bridge Institute gives you a well-rounded picture of our programs and offerings. If our vision inspires you, please feel a warm welcome to join our events, participate in our projects, inquire into our graduate studies and research programs, or find your place in any of the rich pathways available."

"Wow, he's articulate!" Greg said, leaning to Sara. She looked impressed. Still, Greg imagined her standing outside and looking in while he was already inside.

"And now," Bateson said, "your tour guide Randy Seton will take it from here. Enjoy your day, and I look forward to seeing you again tomorrow at the creative writing with utopias workshop."

The audience clapped. Randy stood up from the front row and turned to the audience, clapping himself while the audience clapped. Stockier than President Bateson or Roger Barnes, Randy stood confidently, gregariously, with a kindly smile. He seemed older than most of the people seen at Bayside Village so far. His red hair and beard showed signs of whitening. When the clapping subsided, Randy said, pointing to his right, "Follow me, and we'll head out these double doors."

The audience arose and gathered belongings. The volume of talk flared from a hum to a roar.

Entering the aisle, Keith and Leah met up with Greg and Sara again and exchanged greetings. Greg could feel Keith's interest in him, probably an affinity based on common study of religion and philosophy. "That was inspiring!" Keith said. At Keith's words, Leah's face gave an expectant and ready-to-respond glance to Greg and Sara, but her face showed no spark of her own inspiration. The group shuffled forward toward the large doors.

Keith asked Greg, "So what kinds of classes do you teach?"

"I specialize in ontology, a branch of metaphysics," Greg said. "I teach several classes in theoretical and applied ontology."

"What's ontology?" Keith asked. "I'm sure I've run across the word, but I've never really read about it or had a lecture in it."

"Ah. In philosophy," Greg said, "ontology is the study of being—of what things exist and how those things are related to other existing things." He stepped around a conversation in the aisle. "We investigate the structure, function, and properties of entities. Classically, ontology is a branch of metaphysics, and I teach it that way. But recently, ontology has also been used in computer science to model systems of existing things, or objects, in the real world, and to build representations of those real things that machines can read and translate. I teach ontology in this way, too, in computer science."

"Wow, that's pretty heavy," Keith said as they walked out the double doors with Sara and Leah following behind. Leah's face seemed unresponsive. Philosophy was Keith's thing. And she couldn't find connecting points in the passing conversations.

13

The group filed into a large atrium adjoining the auditorium. Glass walls stretched from floor to ceiling, facing the San Francisco Bay and mountainous Marin County. Showcases of pre-Bayside Village remnants and early promotional materials from the opening ceremony six years earlier surrounded the open area. The group studied these exhibits while the last people joined the tour from the auditorium. Sara's artistic eyes scanned as she entered the room.

"Ooh," Sara said. She stepped up to some posters of the Bayside Village covering the walls, studied the designs, looked for motifs. She registered images that may later serve in her interview with Karen.

Randy stopped at a table in the middle of the atrium before a scale model of the Bayside Village under a Plexiglas cover. Sara turned, recognized the table there as like the one she saw in the Lodge's lobby yesterday with Tara.

"Hello everyone," Randy said in a booming, warm-hearted voice. "I'm Randy Seton. I'm your tour guide for today. I'm a member of the Bridge Institute faculty, and I teach the Basic Course in Sacred Science here, part of our core curriculum. Bridge Institute tours are also part of my teaching of the Basic Course, and you'll see that many stops on our tour serve effectively as illustrations of sacred science.

"The model before us," Randy said, directing the group's attention to it, "shows our campus as it used to be. We purchased this site from Richmond Chemical Company, or RCC. In those days the site was used by its subsidiary, RCC Research, for R&D. RCC Research was also a satellite for storage, large projects, and unusual equipment. For instance, one of the chemical storage facilities is actually still located on site, right here…" He pointed to the building on the model. "The production is stopped now. But as I'll point out this afternoon, the residual of chemical dumping and spills remains on our grounds. And one of our mandates here is clean up. You may see patches of brown tarps roped off around campus. These are Bayside Village experiments in mycoremediation, using mushrooms to suck up and transform the chemicals leached into the ground over the years."

"Hmm," Greg said under his breath, recalling a side yard near the Plaza yesterday. Remediating the ground. Transforming the earth. Interesting metaphors for the larger work of the Bayside Village, perhaps.

"So how did this premier waterfront site get to be ours?" Randy asked. "Premier except for the residual pollution, that is. A few years ago during the global economic crisis, Richmond Chemical became financially distressed and divested several non-core assets and properties—before it went into bankruptcy and ultimately collapsed. This former RCC Research site is one of those divested assets. And through the generous assistance of a pool of donors and investors, we purchased this land from the receivership and reshaped it to what you see today—The Bayside Village.

"Now, let's move over to this table," Randy said pointing to another scale model under Plexiglas. He moved and the group reorganized itself. "So this is the Bayside Village today. And right now, we're standing here— at the Bridge Institute's Auditorium and Atrium." Randy pointed, tapped on the Plexiglas cover. People huddled closer to see. "This is one of the most public parts of the Bayside Village because of our public events, and the Atrium is where we start most of our tours. You'll see that these buildings form one side of a quadrangle, round which we have a class room building, library, museum, and Temple. The buildings on the quad make up the Bridge Institute, and we'll tour these momentarily. We'll tour the rest of Bayside Village after lunch. Any questions so far?" Randy queried.

An older woman, dressed smartly, said, "I understand that the Bayside Village receives delegations from city planning agencies, research institutes, and nonprofit organizations. Can you say something about what they come for and what you show them? Do they have this same tour?"

"Yes," Randy said, "we do receive many delegations—even international ministries of economic development. They come to see how we're living, learning, and experimenting. We host ambassadors, politicians, and international business leaders coming to study our attempts to solve social, political, economic, ecological, and spiritual problems. Receiving delegations is by design—it's part of our mission of creating demonstrations and facilitating change. We have a group dedicated to inviting and receiving delegations. We've organized workshops with our Bayside Village founders. Tomorrow's Creative Writing with Utopias workshop with President Steve Bateson is one variant of this theme, but developed more for the general public. Any more questions?" Randy queried. No one spoke up. "Okay. Feel free to stop me periodically."

"Yes, one question," a man said. He was slender, short, looking in his sixties, with an intense demeanor.

Greg recognized this was Neil Benson, information science guru, whom Roger said would be attending Friday's AlignIt Commons board meeting.

"Yes?" asked Randy.

"Does RCC Research still have a research presence on campus?"

"Ah, good question," Randy said. "For others who don't know that story, RCC Research was acquired by a venture capital firm specializing in workouts of distressed assets. Part of the property sale to us includes a lease back to RCC Research and a phased move out. So yes, RCC Research still has a small footprint here."

Neil spoke up again. "So there's still some robust RCC Research on site here? Do you know which groups remain?"

Greg eyed Neil with curiosity and interest. Why these questions? It's not his field.

"Not in detail," Randy admitted. "Mainly chemical engineering. And some health and safety people, given what they still have around in barrels. The reception office should have a list if you'd like to know precisely."

"I would," Neil said with an air of confidence, almost arrogance. "Do they collaborate with Bridge Institute researchers?"

"Yes," Randy said. "Actually, they do have a few research collaborations and internships on land reclamation and microremediation related the company's history on site."

"And do you know how long those chemical engineering groups are slated to remain here at RCC?"

"Again, this isn't the RCC site anymore. But the details of their lease back to Bayside Village and their phased move out—I'm not sure. Several more years, I believe. I can find out and get back to you."

"Thank you," Neil said presumptively.

"Any more questions?" Randy asked. The group was silent. Randy returned to his gregarious, tour-guide mode, focused again on the model. "So, this is the current plan for Bayside Village and the Bridge Institute. As you may have guessed, the model buildings made of clear, translucent material are those scheduled to be built but they don't exist yet. Our plan calls for another academic hall here for classrooms and lecture space," Randy said, pointing, "a library, a wet lab for biological and botanical sciences, and a marine science lab. Currently, these functions are housed in our main academic building, Avicenna Hall, which we'll visit this morning.

"Now, let me stop myself a moment to give a prefatory note about the term *sacred science*, which you heard already from President Bateson this morning." Randy stepped to a poster display of a schematic titled 'Sacred Science'. Greg now witnessed the professorial side of Randy. This is how the tour is used as a classroom, he reflected. "I'll continue using this term throughout our tour today. Briefly, 'sacred science' comes from the medieval Latin, *scientia sacra*. It means, essentially, an integral system of sciences grounded in a vaster cosmology and metaphysics than we find in modern science, where cosmology and metaphysics have been foreshortened to the empirically-verifiable, sense-perceivable universe. Many such sciences are integrated horizontally across domains and disciplines," Randy said, running his finger over the diagram in a vast sweep as he spoke, "and integrated vertically in great chains of emanations from nothingness," Randy pointed again, starting at the top and moving his hand down the chart, "down to divine unity, down to the grandest forces or beings, to human beings, on down to the smallest particles or forces of matter. You might also say sacred science is integrated across branches of philosophy, including metaphysics, ontology and cosmology."

Greg gazed with keen attention at the categories Randy glided over so easily. This is the work he wanted to join. How to drink it in so fast?

"What the term sacred science refers to, however, goes by many names in many traditions around the world and across time. As a convenience, and because we're located geographically in the West, we use the term sacred science, and we use it to refer to every science drawing upon a larger scheme of philosophy, cosmology and metaphysics like this."

"Randy?" a young man asked. He clutched his student backpack tighter to his shoulder.

"Yes?"

"So is this chart coming out of a specific philosophical system? It looks Indian or Chinese."

"No, and that's a good question." Randy shifted, made space for one of his favorite topics. Greg noted again the professor in Randy as he took the question. "As President Bateson alluded to in his welcome presentation, the Bayside Village doesn't promote a specific agenda or doctrine concerning sacred science, or even a particular tradition of it. This schema is deliberately broad, sufficient to encompass many systems. We welcome any serious, robust effort that is open and investigative. We do, however, take a stand on the need for the recovery and reintegration of sacred science into Western thought, indeed global civilization, particularly in modern scientific and philosophical disciplines. Not a romantic return to premodern civilization, bypassing the attainments of modernism, but a careful updating and integration. This is our mission."

A pure, fine feeling bubbled up in Greg. "This is my interest," he whispered passionately to Sara. She looked at him with knowing, loving eyes and smiled softly.

"So…we'll tour the Bridge Institute this morning and then the rest of the Bayside Village campus this afternoon. Now, let's move on, out of the Atrium, and we'll first visit the Temple."

"Oh, excuse me Randy," Sara said suddenly. Greg looked at her, surprised. "Are there more posters like this, of your opening ceremony and the beginnings of the Bayside Village and Bridge Institute?" She pointed to the walls behind and around the sacred science chart.

What's this sudden interest, Greg wondered. This engagement with the place? Her feelings about being here seem to be changing.

"Oh sure, we have lots of stuff," Randy said. "We produced a lot. It was a big splash."

"Where do you keep it?"

"We hold it in the Vault." Randy said, with a rolling, humorous tone.

Sara was intrigued. The Vault. Was it something special? Was it in the model, on a map somewhere? Or did his tone indicate a joke?

"Where's the Vault?" Sara asked.

"Oh, the Bayside Village archives, in the deep recesses of the Administration building."

Again, that humorous voice.

Sara nodded, etched the location in her memory.

The group filed out of the Atrium and down a sidewalk across a lawn. Greg caught up with the brusk questioner. "Neil?"

Neil Benson turned, surprised. "Yes?"

"I thought you'd be here. I'm Greg Cobb, Professor of Philosophy and Computer Science at the University of Washington."

Neil's eyes honed in on Greg. "Oh, Roger mentioned you." He said it with a different tone. Neil now had an academic peer. "Pleased to meet you," he said and paused.

"We met a few years back, actually," Greg said, "at the ACM annual meeting—a breakout session on knowledge representation."

"Hmm," Neil said, walking, evidently not recalling the meeting but impressed by the suggestion. "You thought I'd be here?"

"Yes, Roger mentioned you to me, too."

"So he asked you to attend this pep rally week, too, did he?"

Greg noted Neil's penetrating eyes and sardonic voice. "Pep rally?" Greg repeated with a chuckle.

"That's how it seems so far. The board asked my help in consulting for AlignIt. Apparently it wants AlignIt to have a service science component. But I'm not here for this Bayside Village stuff." Neil took a breath and in that moment seemed less penetrating, looking across the quad as he stepped outside, following the tour, and seemingly speaking now in a reflective tone. "I flew out here as a favor to a colleague," he said, confiding in Greg. "One of my former students is impressed with Roger. I haven't seen enough of Roger's work yet to judge it. But when the AlignIt board called, they asked me to attend this tour as well. So here I am." Neil looked back sharply at Greg. "I have little patience for utopian dreams and spiritual gurus. I'm quite ready to quit this side show and get on with the AlignIt meetings. Then we'll find out if AlignIt is rigorous or not."

"I see," Greg said, measuring his words. "Well, this orientation is all very interesting. I'm also waiting to see how intertwined the AlignIt project is with Bayside Village."

Roger picked up his mobile, clicked a pre-set number, and put the phone to his ear. He stood up from his desk on the second floor of Avicenna Hall, walked to his window, and looked out on the quadrangle.

"Jeff? Hey, it's Roger....I had a call with Chris Mueller this morning....Yeah, we did a run through of his guest chairing of Friday's AlignIt Commons board meeting.... Has Mueller ever talked with you about other game companies joining AlignIt Commons?....No? I didn't think so. We may have a little problem on our hands. What's the earliest you can meet?....This morning? Alright. How about 11:00? Yeah, I'll be in my AlignIt office there, so I'll just pop over next door. Alright, man. See you."

Roger held his mobile in hand. Looking out the window, he contemplated, considering Mueller's unexpected ideas, contemplating other courses of action he should take now.

14

The Orientation tour group walked a quarter way around the quadrangle. At the short end of the rectangular green stood a large Temple built in Craftsman style, but subtly interpolated with elements from non-Western sacred architectures—Asian, Indian, Middle Eastern. Randy stopped and collected people in front.

"Oh, that's where we did yoga this morning," Sara said to Greg. He nodded.

When the group reformed, Randy said, "Our Bridge Institute Temple is considered by some as the centerpoint of the Bayside Village. Here is a point of access between above and below, a place to honor our connection as humans with higher planes of existence all the way to Nothingness, a place where we bring down higher forces into our plane of existence. This is our first service. Of course, everywhere is such a place, with the right attention. But here we gather as a community—rather, as many communities. So the Temple symbolizes this and serves as the focal point of our common intention. For we do not have one great religion here, but many paths of inquiry and practice, each holding the same intention.

"Before we enter, let me draw your attention to our cornerstone, here," Randy said, pointing to the base of the building. He read:

Unite the pair so long disjoined.

Knowledge and vital piety.

"The inscription comes from a hymn of one of the great Protestant Christian reformers, Charles Wesley. His brother John Wesley founded the Methodist church in England, and Charles wrote a wealth of great hymns that brought word and song to the Methodist movement. This is from one of them. Now, let me point out that we've located the Bridge Institute Temple directly across the quad from our Bridge Institute Library there, at the other end," Randy pointed directly across the quad to Avicenna Hall. Eyes turned. "Right now, that building houses not only our library but also our class rooms. We're young, but we're growing. But this architectural relationship of the Temple across from the Library expresses the principle—uniting knowledge and vital piety."

Keith looked to Leah. "See, the faith is important here," he said. The evidence was there in the buildings. He felt eager to point out the Christian elements of Bayside Village, as if justifying to her why he had come. But by her look, Keith saw that Leah was unsure of it.

Randy continued. "In an old architectural style probably beginning in mosque complex design in the Islamic world and continuing into Europe in the High Middle Ages, libraries were placed across from houses of prayer and worship in a courtyard. This reminds us of the reciprocal relationship between contemplative inner study and the outer study of the cosmos. When exiting the place of prayer, mediation, and inner study in many great centers of learning, one faced the library. And when exiting the place of study, one faced the mosque or church. Here, our Bridge Institute Temple embodies half of this aphorism—the vital piety part. Vital spiritual aspiration is a crucial part of our community life and research at the Bridge Institute. This aphorism expresses the potential reciprocal relation between inner and outer study, the one informing the other. This is mirrored outwardly in placing the Temple across the quad from Avicenna Hall. At the Bridge Institute, we cultivate this respect for joining knowledge and spiritual life. Or knowledge of the world and knowledge of oneself. So there it is—unite the pair so long disjoined, knowledge and vital piety."

"I like that," Greg said.

"Yeah, that's interesting," Sara said. "I hadn't heard of that in art history."

"Now," Randy continued, "let's enter our main activity and meditation hall here in the front, facing Avicenna Hall." Randy walked the group up two steps to a covered veranda before the entrance to the Temple, and held open the doors as the group entered. The Temple interior had polished wood floors, arching wooden ceiling beams, white plaster walls, and large windows looking out to semi-wooded lawns on the sides.

Inside, Randy walked to the center of the empty space, turned around, and addressed the group. "This main room is used by many groups for meditation, movements, services, workshops and short retreats. It's an attractive room, and generally a quiet one. Most often the space is used for meditation, yoga, devotion, and teaching." The group looked around the simple but elegant space. Greg noticed cushions and folded chairs neatly stacked in unobtrusive, artful racks. The space itself was empty, as perhaps it ought to be. Not much to see in the room, but plenty to feel, he mused.

Randy turned and pointed to a set of double doors at the rear. "Down this hall, we have rooms used by diverse spiritual traditions. We've selected and invited groups to use our rooms—each group having some active study in sacred science, each one making a substantive contribution to the life of the Bayside Village." He walked to the double doors at the rear and stopped, holding them opening for the group to walk through. "You can peak in the windows of each door. Each space has a small office, shelves for ritual objects or books, a smaller meditation and meeting space, and room for teacher-student interviews. Most groups here also use the main hall. We also have smaller rooms to the side, here, for private or small group prayer, meditation, yoga or other practices."

"What groups are located here?" Sara asked.

Greg noticed Sara's interest.

"Right now," Randy said, "we have, in this room, a Tantric Indian group called Path of Ananda."

"They do the morning yoga?" Sara asked.

"They do. They have a yoga program here—mornings and evenings, and they also play an active role in menu planning and kitchen culture in the Bayside Village Dining Commons, shared with a few other groups. In fact, they're heavily involved with the meal planner tool, PlanIt, one of the technologies being incubated here, based on Roger Barnes' AlignIt which we'll see later this morning.

"And here, across the hall, is a Tibetan Buddhist group of the Nyingma order. The next room down the hall here is a Taoist group which also uses the main Temple room for Taoist Qigong practice. Across the hall from them is a room used by a Sufi group."

Greg and Sara made special efforts to look into windows of the closed door to the Sufi room, and then looked at each other with interest. "Is that Roger and Jenny's group?" Sara asked Greg.

He shrugged. "I don't know."

"Here in the middle of the hall," Randy said, "are two silent meditation rooms for use by anyone, anytime. They're always open from the outside door. The inside door locks when this building is locked.

"Down the hall at the end is a Christian Rosicrucian group. They share their space with an ecumenical group of Christians focused on Christian theurgical practice based on Pseudo Dionysus."

Keith looked into the windows of the closed doors. Leah joined him. The lights were off inside. Leah looked to Keith as if to say, "I can't see."

"Interesting," Keith whispered. "It's worth a trip back."

Greg's interest piqued. He said to Sara, "I'm meeting with someone on Wednesday related to this Christian group."

She nodded, looked into the darkened room. It was like peering into a secret mystery school.

"And across the hall from them," Randy continued, "is a Western esoteric group, the Builders, focused on theosophy, nature philosophy, alchemy, and hermeticism."

Randy led the group back to the Temple's main room and out the doors. Walking out, Greg saw Neil standing on the quad facing away from the Temple, talking on his mobile. He hadn't gone in, Greg realized. Neil turned, saw the tour, and slowly walked toward the group, still talking. Randy led the group a quarter way round the quadrangle to the Raymond Lully Museum.

Sara asked Greg as they walked, "Who is that guy you spoke with?"

"Oh," Greg said, changing his demeanor from awe-inspired tourist. "Neil Benson, professor of information science at University of Maryland. He's come for AlignIt. We have a few consulting meetings together with Roger, and then we're guest presenters at Friday's AlignIt Commons board meeting. I've seen him at a conference or two. He's quite an authority in service sciences."

"Not a very warm fellow," Sara whispered.

Greg nodded. "I guess not. He seems rather disaffected with the Institute's vision."

Before reaching the next building, Greg pulled out his mobile. "I'm going to try Mrs. Blocke again."

"She still hasn't returned your calls?"

"Not yet." Greg stopped outside, feeling the sun intense and penetrating. "Her assistant said she was in last week, and she'll be in this week. So I want to try her first thing this morning."

Greg punched the numbers. No answer. He left another message and then slipped his phone back into his pocket. He looked up where the sun beamed through the trees. "With my fair skin, I might need a hat if we're outside a lot. I burn fast."

Randy led the group up a step and inside the front double doors to the lobby of the Raymond Lully Museum.

"Oh, this I really want to see," Sara said to Greg.

"Me too."

Randy walked to a large, colorful mural facing the double doors and turned around to face the group, which formed a semi-circle around Randy and the mural. "This is the Bridge Institute's Raymond Lully Museum."

Sara looked past the mural to the fascinating exhibits beyond—art works, instruments, ritual objects, antique machines, odd miscellany.

"Here in the Raymond Lully Museum," Randy said, "we display visual works and tangible objects relating to sacred science. Our Museum exhibits help convey to our Bridge Institute community and visitors a grand visual impression of what sacred science looks like in its various embodiments."

"This is a great way to illustrate sacred science," Greg said to Keith. "It's a visual bonanza of the stuff I read."

Keith nodded. He grew ever fascinated with the world he imagined Greg inhabited.

"Today we'll just take a brief look at this mural. Tomorrow, I'm offering an extended museum tour as one of your Orientation electives."

Sara looked at Greg sadly. She wanted the whole tour now. "I'd like to do that tomorrow—the extended tour," she whispered.

He nodded. "Me too."

"The mural before us," Randy said, "presents a simplification of the vast panoply of sacred sciences. We created this mural for the lobby, at the start of the Museum tour, because it easily illustrates several principles of sacred sciences in a single glance.

"For now, the basic idea of many sacred sciences is that the world emanates or extends from nothingness into form in recognizable patterns of increasing complexity. These patterns can be discerned or discovered, such as in chains or threads of emanations." Randy pointed up and down the large mural as he spoke. "Some of the sciences established the relations between, for instance, planetary bodies and corresponding mineral elements on earth. Plato's Republic establishes these principles as the Ideal, above, and the real, below. His Timaeus has the demiurge mixing elements in a heavenly mixing bowl, and this is how worlds are made. Or the writer of the book of Hebrews of the Christian New Testament says, 'The church is an earthly copy of the heavenly temple'."

Greg was right at home. The Platonic cosmos was intimately familiar.

The mention of the verse from the book of Hebrews aroused Keith's interest. He looked to where Randy pointed, and he did, indeed, find the verse there on the wall. By a faint whisper, he caught Leah's attention and pointed it out to her. Together they read:

> They offer worship in a sanctuary that is a sketch and shadow of the heavenly one; for Moses, when he was about to erect the tent, was warned, "See that you make everything according to the pattern that was shown you on the mountain." (Hebrews 8:5)

Randy continued, "This principle is most famously summarized, for

Western sacred sciences, in the aphorism from the Emerald Tablet of Hermes Trismegistus, *As above, so below.* Various ancient schemas, like the Chaldean, the Neoplatonic, show orders of ascending and descending emanations. In this vertical scope, the sacred sciences concern everything, all of existence and non-existence—the Absolute, the uncreated or unmanifest realms, on down through the created or emanated world. By contrast, modern Western science has reduced its focus to the sense-perceivable universe—what Aristotle called *physis*—until recently, for example, when physics itself in the Twentieth century began penetrating physical existence, light, and energy to such a degree that the investigation begins returning to its basis, which seems empty again like the Absolute."

Hmm, Greg thought, listening astutely, impressed by Randy's capacity to deftly pull off a speech on metaphysical principles in sacred sciences. Randy was loquacious, no doubt about it. But articulate all the same.

Neil caught up to Greg and whispered, not so quietly, "Isn't there a reason modern science eschewed these medieval superstitions, or reduced them to measurable objects?"

A few people turned their heads at Neil's loud whispers.

Greg felt Neil trying to side with him, as though a compatriot in suffering an unsavory preamble to the real business of the trip—consulting on AlignIt. Greg smiled politely but didn't affirm Neil's sentiment.

"Secondly," Randy continued, "most sacred sciences presume, among other things, a correspondence theory—a theory that existing things and forces have inherent relationships to other things and forces, above or below them in vertical schemas, or beside them in horizontal ones." Randy pointed across the mural as he spoke. "Again, more details on the in-depth museum tour tomorrow. But traditionally, these relationships—both the vertical and the horizontal—are not understood to be merely socially constructed as part of human meaning-making; they're discovered and verified as facts in science and represented as such. We find expressions of their workings in historic works or art and technology like these in the Raymond Lully Museum, or contemporary technologies like Roger Barnes' AlignIt."

"Oh!" Greg breathed to Sara with exhilaration. "This is exactly why I'm interested in the Bridge Institute!" Sara nodded, acknowledging their shared interest.

"Which is why we don't study them today," Neil said to Greg, interrupting him, not hearing his rapturous expression to Sara. Greg looked at Neil, surprised. The juxtaposition jostled him. "Of course its meaning-making," Neil said. "This is primitive proto-science. They didn't recognize that what they thought they observed was really the imposition of their own constructs."

Greg smirked at Neil. That's a rather reactionary comment, Greg thought. And Neil's an esteemed, well-established academic in no need of reifying his worldview; this must have triggered him somehow. Nonetheless, Neil's chastising worked on Greg, bristling him, surfacing an inner tension in him about the academic integrity and reputation of the Bridge Institute. Would this be a good career move, a good place to relocate the family?

"If you join me here tomorrow morning," Randy said, turning to a promotional panel filled with images of featured exhibits, "we'll explore in depth a range of early sacred sciences, including exhibits in mathematics, astronomy, geography, medicine, pharmacology, optics, alchemy, animal physiology, and plant sciences. We'll look at arts and technologies developed within the context of early sacred sciences. It's a fascinating collection, and I encourage you to meet up with me tomorrow morning."

Randy turned and walked out, and the group exited.

"That's all?" Sara said to Greg, stepping out. "I want to see the exhibits."

"I'm up for the tour tomorrow." Greg looked out across the quadrangle. The bright mid-morning sun reached across the grassy lawn. Students walked around the other side of the quad. What were they studying, he wondered. Randy turned and led the group toward the building next door.

Sara turned to Greg as they walked. "I'm going to call Karen to schedule an interview." She stepped aside from the sidewalk and stopped, pulled out her mobile.

Greg stopped, too, letting tour participants pass by. "Right now?"

"Yeah, I want to make sure I get a time with her while we're here."

"Okay." Greg waited. Hmm. She's determined, he thought.

"You can go ahead. I can see Randy's going to that building." She touched the numbers. "I'll catch up. "

"Okay," Greg said. He turned and continued walking with the tail end of the tour.

Roger stood in his office on the second floor of Avicenna Hall, looked out the window. He searched on his mobile and then clicked on a number. He looked out his office window again and saw the orientation tour heading into the Research Access Office. The call went into voicemail.

"Hello Mrs. Blocke. It's Roger Barnes on Monday morning, April 4th at 10:15. I'm calling about Professor Greg Cobb from University of Washington. He's on campus this week, and I understand he's been trying to get an appointment with you. We really need to get this guy in to meet you and get things started. You'll recall we want to get him in on sabbatical this Fall or even have him join our faculty, if we're lucky. So we've got to get things moving. Maybe you've already scheduled with him. But if not, we need to get him in while he's here. Let me know if I can help with anything. Thanks."

Roger ended the call and slipped the mobile into his pocket. He took a deep breath, closed his eyes, breathed out. Eyes open, he looked through the window at the brilliant sun on the quad.

15

Randy led the group around the outside of the Raymond Lully Museum and into an attractive court yard off the Bridge Institute quadrangle. There, he approached a long, L-shaped, two-story building stretching away from the quad. It was obviously retrofitted from an earlier industrial building, prior to Bayside Village acquiring the property, into an elegant ecological design. A sign in front read Research Access Office.

Randy stopped in front of the building and held open the glass doors. The group walked into the lobby.

"This should be interesting," Neil said to Greg, catching up from behind. "I understand they have a pretty novel program here—some innovative ideas about industry-university partnership and tech transfer."

"So I hear," Greg said, stopping in the lobby as the group gathered. "I'm interested, too." He looked around at the reception atrium. He recalled from studying maps and buildings prior to arrival, and signs showed him now, too, that the Research Access Office was off to one side, and the leased spaces of the Bayside Village Research Park ran down and around the L-shaped corridor ahead. More than anything seen so far, this looked like a business space, an incubator for new businesses and projects, a place for business services to the community.

Neil turned in to Greg. "Did you hear that Roger's lining up Chris Mueller to sign on companies to his AlignIt Commons thing? You've heard of Mueller?"

"Yeah, I heard about Mueller. Where's he from, Hillside?"

"Hilltop Venture Partners. Yeah, that's a good choice. They've got a cadre of gaming, music, and media companies in their portfolio. Mueller's been CEO to some of them. Brought one to IPO. Cashed in pretty good on that one."

"Hilltop doesn't have any ontology or semantic web start ups, I don't think."

"Hell if I know. Yeah, I guess you're right. They don't do engines. Just application layers."

"It's probably good for the AlignIt Commons members," Greg said. "I'd like to see support for the AlignIt tech platform itself, though, before getting too excited. I don't have a lot of experience with VC-backed start ups, but I have seen a VC race ahead on application and skimp on platform."

"I guess ya gotta follow the money, right?" Neil said. "And if that's what Roger's doing, maybe he's a smart guy."

But that's just my area, Greg thought. Neil doesn't work at that level.

Sara entered the lobby, moved through the crowd of tour participants assembling, approached Greg. She smiled and gave a sharp, vibrant thumbs up sign to him about her call. "Thursday morning," she said.

"Cool!" Greg turned to Neil. "This is my wife, Sara. Sara, this is Neil Benson—one of the nation's foremost service science experts."

"Depends who you ask," Neil said with the polite self-deprecation of a figure who knew his own distinction. "Nice to meet you." Neil had a cordial streak, too, Greg observed. "He dragged you along here, did he?"

"Yeah, I guess." Sara smiled and flashed her eyes.

Such a pretty woman, Greg thought. So agile with men.

"I'm checking it out, too, for the week."

"Brave gal! I didn't bring my wife to this one. What field are you in?"

"Welcome to the Bridge Institute's Research Access Office," Randy boomed from one end of the large atrium, "and the Bayside Village Research Park—both of which are organized here in this building." Randy paused a moment while attention refocused on him.

Sara whispered to Neil, "Industrial design in IT—tell you more later." Neil raised his eyebrows and nodded, impressed.

"We just visited the Raymond Lully Museum," Randy began, "where we house historic examples of sacred sciences manifested in arts, technologies and artifacts. Now, in this building, we'll see examples of how the Bridge Institute is taking up this same impulse in our day. At the Bridge Institute, we study not only theories, texts and traditions, and we conduct not only basic lab research. We also develop applied science and technology. The Research Access Office to my right is responsible for facilitating the development, demonstration, transfer and scaling of our technologies, some of which are incubated in companies and projects right here in our Research Park."

Greg was impressed by these threads Randy wove to connect historic and contemporary examples of sacred science. AlignIt, he knew, was rooted in traditions of the past but stands in the present and future.

"Let's move down the hall to the first area," Randy said, corralling the group into a unified form. Randy turned around and faced the group, walking backwards. The group followed. He stopped in the hallway before a gallery space merged into an office space.

"These next few rooms showcase technologies being actively incubated right here at the Bridge Institute. These are just some of the practical expressions of contemporary sacred science." Randy turned to his right. "This gallery space before us, and the cluster of rooms and workspaces around it, feature visual portraits of a robust sacred science ontology platform called AlignIt."

"Ah, this is it," Sara said to Greg.

"Yes," Greg whispered, his eyes beaming interest.

"Finally," Neil said to Greg, who smiled again and nodded affirmatively, looking forward intently at images of entity relationship diagrams and logic engine rules on the wall. "Now we've come to something I can appreciate; a knowledge management system is the stuff of information science." Greg nodded again with interest, though contemplating the different philosophical pathways implied in Neil's notion of knowledge representation in a knowledge management system and his own notion of object representation in an ontology. Again, the paths may diverge. But this makes for good scholarly discourse.

Randy continued. "With today's database and web technology, AlignIt has built data tables that compile and expand on the tables, charts, lists and texts of earlier periods, substantially expanding our grasp of the heritage of humanity's traditional knowledge and sacred sciences." He stepped up to a poster displaying AlignIt tables. "Taking any given element or thing, AlignIt extends table columns exponentially to the right with everything from…well, let's see here," Randy said, looking closely at an expanded image of a database table structure, "oh, like…times of the day, musical notes, internal organs, limbs, fingers, sense organs, metals, stones, plants, herbs, flowers, yogic postures, Qigong postures, breathing exercises, medicines, holiday festivals, songs, epic tales forms of elimination like…what do we have here…urination, sweating, vomiting, bloodletting….You get the picture. Right? So the charts in this room simply show some of the AlignIt table structure.

"Imagine if ancient yogis or Taoists or Buddhists had computer database technology hundreds of years ago. What we can take away from this exhibit is that AlignIt is a contemporary tool of sacred science, the very type of web-based database that proves the principle of sacred sciences, except that AlignIt aggregates and integrates these traditional sciences we've seen so far on the tour, and many more, and extends them with contemporary investigations undertaken right here at the Bridge Institute and elsewhere. With contemporary technology, we can hold and relate a substantially greater volume of information, perform greater operations, and make research-based revisions."

Greg thought it a fair characterization, made for a lay audience.

"What the hell—fingers and toes?" Neil whispered, standing next to Greg, who grimaced and shrugged his shoulders. "AlignIt may be novel and robust," Neil said, "but it borders on the bizarre. I can't get my head around it."

"As for AlignIt's relationship structure with external parties," Randy said, "AlignIt is a technology platform owned by the Bridge Institute and project-managed by the Research Access Office here. Public access is provided for research, educational, and charitable use. Proprietary commercial rights are co-owned with members in a unique AlignIt Commons structure based on the legal principles of *ejido* and *usufruct*, but made available for commercial use exclusively to those members. There's a whole story in the legal principles, by the way, but we don't have time for it now."

Neil leaned to Greg. "Have you heard of Jackie Schrader, the Director? Of that Research Access Office?"

Greg turned, nodded. "I met her last night."

Neil raised his eyebrows, surprised that Greg, an aspiring but young professor, a newbie, would have met with her. "She's apparently cooked up a novel approach to tech transfer."

"So I hear," Greg said. "This AlignIt Commons structure is apparently a first of a kind."

Randy moved in closer to another part of the AlignIt gallery. "Here we have another expression of our technology development based on sacred science. AlignIt is not just a bigger database than was possible before the advent of computerized databases. It is also used to execute operations described in various sacred sciences. Many traditional operations have been described in literature, but they needed to be performed by an individual, painstakingly by hand. Now many of them can be performed computationally in AlignIt."

"Do you know this stuff? What operations does he mean?" Neil asked Greg.

"It means using a traditional system, and now AlignIt, to do things like diagnose, translate, identify, or show the pathway of a possible transformation."

Neil squinted his eyes, searching his memory for like instances from information science, informatics, knowledge representation, search engines.

"To use AlignIt or any of its applications optimally," Randy continued, "it helps to have an object for the AlignIt operations. You could use any object to start out—a cell strain, a human organ, a wave pattern. But using AlignIt directly is usually too abstract for most people, unless you're a researcher using it as a research tool, or developing an application.

"For most people, the obvious and personally relevant AlignIt object is you, yourself. So for general public access, the AlignIt team has created an application for individual users like you to create a master profile, called the AlignIt Profile, and to select to use this profile, at your option, with any of the family of AlignIt products and services. The profile is one type of home base, and it can be your main point of entry into any AlignIt applications. As you can see on the poster here, the AlignIt Profile has several features."

Randy turned to the poster on the wall, with images of AlignIt. He went down a bulleted list expounding the features. Greg listened with rapt attention, yet stepped back to observe other people's responses. For he knew well AlignIt's features. As prospective consultant, he sought now to observe how others approached it.

Sara listened keenly, knowing less than Greg, but interested for his sake. She had created her own AlignIt Profile, as Greg had, but she hadn't explored it much yet. She stood there listening, contemplating how she could use her profile.

Randy finished. "Okay," Neil said to Greg. "This is starting to get interesting." Greg nodded. Neil turned close, saying almost under his breath, "Weird, but interesting."

Randy moved to another gallery with its posters, signage, logos and large images of users. "Okay, that was AlignIt," he said. "Here we have another expression of our technology development rooted in sacred science. PlanIt is a collection of web-based calendaring programs drawing on the AlignIt technology platform. It uses astronomy and astrology including the Babylonian, Indian, Chinese, Islamic and Western systems. What you see displayed around you are applications of PlanIt based in sacred sciences, and traditional and modern scheduling needs. PlanIt is released in beta mode, and limited versions of these releases are available for free download. An interesting fact is that many offices at the Bridge Institute and the Bayside Village use PlanIt as a institutional calendaring and event planning tool."

Hmm, Greg thought, wondering how developed PlanIt was. He leaned to Neil. "I wonder if it does for work flow management."

"Work flow? It's freakin' astrology!"

Greg realized again the gulf between Neil's mainstream attitudes, where newspaper horoscopes would undoubtedly be Neil's reference point, and his own extensive study and contacts in this area. Not to say he endorsed it all. But these had been sciences.

"You'll notice," Randy said, "that the PlanIt name sounds like AlignIt, and that's because the two companies collaborate. PlanIt is built on the AlignIt technology platform and, in addition to its exclusive, field-of-use rights for commercial use of AlignIt in scheduling applications, under AlignIt Commons membership, PlanIt also has trademark rights to use the PlanIt and AlignIt names."

"So, apparently AlignIt is a community trademark available to AlignIt Commons members only," Greg said to Neil.

"Community trademark?" Neil said.

"Let me just point out the PlanIt features in these exhibits," Randy said, "and then you can look at your leisure."

Randy stepped up to a poster of PlanIt images and bulleted features. He went down the list, noting its personal planner and its planning tools for events, travel, meals, gardening, and spiritual practice, among other things.

"Hmm," Sara said after Randy went over the gardening tool, thinking of gardening back home in the yard with Tara.

When Randy described the tool for spiritual practice, Greg turned to Sara. "I'd like to get that."

"Me too!" Sara said. "And I like the meal planner and garden planner."

"As for the third party relationship structure PlanIt has worked out with AlignIt Commons," Randy said, "PlanIt is a private calendar and planning tool company; it's a member of the AlignIt Commons, and it has an exclusive, field-of-use right to AlignIt technology for calendaring."

Randy gave time for the group to peruse the PlanIt exhibits.

Neil asked Randy, on the side, "These tools are publicly available?"

"Partially," Randy said. "Subscribers pay for premium access."

"Do you know how PlanIt is being rolled out?"

"I don't," Randy said. "I'm not the business guy. What I can say is that there's a coordinated co-marketing effort with AlignIt Commons member companies, which organizes a distribution channel. But what else the PlanIt team is doing, I don't know."

"Alright, thanks." Neil stepped closer to Greg. "Did you hear that?"

"Publicly available?" Greg said.

"I was about to say I'd put my money on this one—except for the astrology bit. But with a front end application like this, at least you'll see some market interest. This company would be a great acquisition target for a social media company or an online social network."

Greg wondered if that's how it worked here—acquistions.

After a few moments, Randy moved down the corridor. "Let's move to GameIt," he said, "yet another embodiment of our technology development based on sacred science." The group reorganized around another area, this one having more developed displays, signage and logos. Greg canvassed the room. The walls were filled with fantastic game scenarios. Shimmering holographic game figures stood prominently in the middle of the room. A young man waved his hand through one, just to see if he could.

"GameIt," Randy said, "is an electronic gaming company with a game engine based on AlignIt, and featuring game worlds based on sacred sciences. All around us we're seeing displays from its gameworlds. You'll notice, again, that the GameIt name sounds like AlignIt. That's because GameIt employs the same AlignIt Commons technology and trademark strategy as PlanIt."

"This is very cool," Neil said to Greg. "And I can see now why Roger brought in Hilltop Ventures."

"If AlignIt can support applications like this…" Greg said, trailing off.

Randy stood next to visually stunning screens scrolling features sets of GameIt's portfolio of games now on the market. "GameIt specializes in game world creation," Randy continued, "based on sacred science principles and using AlignIt technology in a cloud-based setting. The games featured here come from the depths of the world's spiritual traditions. Many are training games for developing capacities in students or comprising initiation rites.

"Games show up prominently in traditional societies, just as sacred sciences do. In this context, games provide a means of conveying, in broad cosmological and metaphysical principles, the mythic templates of the creation of the world, the meaning of life, the struggle of human existence, and the journey of human development."

"Hmm," Sara thought. She hadn't ventured into games. This was fascinating territory.

"In the center of the room, we see a succession of holographic images from an immersive game program, the Mastery Series, now available in beta to early adopters. These projections are based on scenarios from Taoist martial tales, Tibetan Thanka and literature, Indian yantras and epic poems, Western Medieval and Renaissance stories, and early Modern Western esoteric lore. Gamers use headsets which read retinal movements, changes in the iris, and brainwaves to modulate responses to the game play. Gamers also use body suits and hand gloves with wearable sensors that read and translate body movements into the game avatar's movements."

"They've got the gear locked down," Neil said to Greg. "That's a key driver for any commercial game app." Greg nodded.

Randy again outlined the legal and intellectual property framework of the company. "GameIt also develops games for internal Bayside Village use in the Research Access Office and Village Security."

As a potential new faculty member at the Bridge Institute, Greg wondered what internal institutional applications had been developed. How could this help enhance organizational life, he wondered.

"I should also mention," Randy said, "that GameIt is the only example to date of a VC-funded company in the Bayside Village Research Park."

"Ah," Neil said, turning to Greg. "A VC picking up a company like this signals potential in this whole AlignIt thing."

"So," Randy said, "why don't you take a few moments to look through the game exhibits.

The tour participants spread through the exhibits examining brilliantly colorful game projections. Worlds sprawled out in thin air, scenes unfolded and shifted, characters shimmered—some moving, some responding dynamically to tour participants walking by.

"Randy, what are these games?" a man asked, standing near a table of board games and physical game pieces.

"Ah, I almost missed these," Randy said, speaking aloud to everyone. "This is a section of demonstrations GameIt created—they built already-created games drawn from the sacred sciences into its game engine platform. They're examples only; they're not available on the market. The GameIt folks used these to solicit seed funds. So we have, um, Chaturanga, from India, Enochian Chess, also called Rosicrucian Chess, the Glass Bead Game from one of Herman Hesse's novels, and the Platonic Riddle of Numbers found in the Plato's Timaeus and developed further by Eberhard Wortmann. Oh, and here's an early prototype of the Mayan Ball Game, now in final production mode. And I'll give an advertisement—The Mayan Ball Game will be demonstrated on Friday evening at our Floricanto event at the Dining Commons, if anyone here is still in town by then."

"Well, this is hot," Neil said to Greg. "Again, whatever AlignIt is, I'd put money on GameIt. There's some profit potential here"

"Oh, this one's based on The Name of the Rose," Greg said to Neil. "Have you read that? By Umberto Eco?"

"No," Neil said, glancing in the direction of Greg's attention. He looked at the display, recognized it. "Oh, I did see the movie. Long time ago. Murder mystery, wasn't it?"

"I guess. It remember its great medieval library and esoteric lore."

"Hmm," Neil said, unsure of that.

The contrast became conscious to Greg in a flash. It revealed him, he realized. And Neil stood bear before him, too. Yet Neil looked at Greg not disdainfully, but with a grin that hinted rather at acceptance. From that simple glimpse, Greg relaxed. There may be something growing between us, he felt.

The tour participants spent several minutes examining the GameIt exhibits, and then Randy addressed the group again. "Okay, folks. Tonight at our entertainment reception, you'll have the opportunity to sample several of these traditional sacred science games. You'll also have the opportunity, if you dare," Randy said, emphasizing these words in a spirit of fun and challenge, "to don the headgear and gloves and try your skills in the mysterious worlds of GameIt's Mastery Series." A few people chuckled at Randy's tone.

16

Roger stood up from his desk again, picked up his mobile and clicked on Jackie Schrader, head of Bridge Institute Research Access Office and the Bridge Institute Research Park. He paced his office, looking out the window to the quad in turns as he crossed the room.

"Jackie? Hey, it's Roger…. Lucky me to reach you. I had a surprising call with Chris Mueller this morning on a run through of Friday's AlignIt Commons board meeting. Do you have a few minutes to discuss?....So he talked about game companies in his network and said he wants to have a frank discussion on Friday about bringing them into the Commons….Right, I brought up GameIt's exclusive rights. He said he talked with Jeff about this. I just checked with Jeff, and he said Mueller never mentioned it….Yeah. I feel surprised and disappointed. It leaves me baffled, frankly. So I wanted to ask if you could have someone run through Mueller's file and see if we've missed something—in his conflict of interest forms, his curriculum vitae, his company list, anything else pertinent to this question….Great, thanks. And even if there's nothing, could you help me out with a broader search of his company connections, in case he hasn't disclosed everything?....Great.

"And then there's one other thing about Mueller—an unexpected philosophical divergence. He's urging me to focus on short term revenue gains by expanding the Commons to his game companies and then sideline the AlignIt development projects like the discovery engine….Yeah. He said he was questioning the business value of the upper ontology project and bringing Greg on board….Right, both boards are behind it—especially the AlignIt Scientific Advisory Board. I thought Mueller was, too…..Yes. So this is fair game for discussion—nothing overtly amiss here like with the possible conflicts of interest. And I do value his business advice. From one point of view, he has a good business rationale, for a typical VC-backed start up scenario. But I don't think this new approach matches the Commons' business model. And Mueller hasn't met Greg yet, hasn't talked with Jeff about his game companies like he said….Right, and he's bringing all of this to me right before the board meeting. Something doesn't feel quite right here….Great, thanks."

"Okay folks," Randy said, "let's move on, now, to Avicenna Hall, our first and only classroom building to date." Randy led the group out of the research park courtyard and back to the Bridge Institute quadrangle. There he turned right and led the group to the far end toward the largest building on the quad. In two stories, Avicenna Hall was attractive, modern, spread horizontally from one end of this short side of the quad to the other, with students crossing in front.

Randy turned around, walked backwards facing the group. "Because we just started up six years ago, Avicenna Hall now houses many other functions, beyond our library. It also houses our classrooms and wetlabs.

But this will change as other buildings go up.

Randy led the group into an attractive foyer at the long end of the Hall. He turned round again and walked backwards down the hallway, addressing the group. "As you saw on the Bayside Village model in the Atrium, this is our first main class room building so far. We have class rooms on your left and right." People slowed a bit, looking through windows and doors. "Faculty offices are at the end of the hall and upstairs. We also have reading rooms like this one to my right" he said, pointing to a door way with glass windows. "More class rooms and storage rooms are upstairs. Everything after this stair way and down to that section of faculty offices is temporary labs and study rooms."

Randy walked the group into a few empty class rooms and wet labs to give a feeling for the place. He then walked to the west wing where he held open the door to the graduate research library and the group filed in. The room was spacious and open, with great picture windows looking out to the quadrangle and the buildings around it. Greg gazed at the wooden tables, reading carrels, and couches, and the few stacks on the interior walls. It looked a nice enough place to study and conduct research. He made a mental note to log in and search the collection for works he would need.

"The Bridge Institute Graduate Research Library, as you may anticipate," Randy said, "features special collections in the sacred sciences, including natural sciences, history and philosophy of science, theosophy, humanities, and human sciences. We also house a number of non-circulating rare collections donated by individuals, including art collections and some rare objects.

Greg found himself wondering how the Bridge Institute Library would be expanded in Avicenna Hall when future buildings are completed.

"In conceiving the Library," Randy said, "we've rethought the ways people conduct research in the digital age. For instance, rather than focusing on maintaining special physical collections and the maintenance of physical assets, including book and manuscript repair services, except for rare books donated to us, we have instead focused on creating the library index for sacred sciences, and building a publication access service for rare materials not indexed or offered by most commercial Publication Access Plans. We make this service available beyond the Bridge Institute on a subscription basis, with the revenues reinvested in library infrastructure and research support for our sacred science index."

"A library index for sacred science," Greg repeated to himself audibly enough for Sara to hear. He cogitated a research angle he could take to it. Could it be tied in to ontology development for AlignIt, he wondered.

Randy walked out the library doors and into the hall in the center of the building, facing the front door to exit onto the quadrangle. Light conversation ensued as people filed into the hall. A woman asked, "Randy, who is Avicenna? Is this one of your founders, or a donor?"

"Oh, thank you for asking," Randy said. "Actually, Avicenna was a medieval philosopher, and he's one of our inspirations here at the Bridge Institute. And why have we chosen Avicenna Hall as a building name? Well, most of our buildings are named after great philosophers and scientists who drew upon the foundations of spiritual traditions in an integral manner."

Greg recalled that Randy taught the Basic Course in sacred science that incorporated the tour, using the campus for its teaching objects. Here was one—Avicenna. And here was Randy in his prime, as roving teacher.

"Avicenna," Randy said, "was a great medieval Persian scholar, medical doctor, scientist, philosopher and theologian who had a profound influence on the West. His name was Arabic, actually—Ibn Sina. But we know him by his Latinized name, Avicenna. His work influenced the rise of scholasticism in the medieval West, making a deep and lasting impact on Western thought. Thomas Aquinas was probably the most prominent Western figure to adopt and port Avicenna's work into Western form. We all know about Catholic schools and colleges named after Thomas Aquinas. But few of us know that Aquinas was influenced by the philosophy of Avicenna, who himself was regarded as a third Aristotle. You might know that Arab erudition reintroduced science and philosophy to a Europe beleaguered from its Dark Ages. But a good deal of Avicenna's work that did not come into the West was further developed in the Islamic world over the following centuries. So we have a lot still to learn from Avicenna. In any case, the Bridge Institute chose the name Avicenna for its first academic building because Avicenna served a bridging function that we value here—bridging Islamic and Western worlds, bridging ancient Greek science and philosophy with the then contemporary world of medieval philosophy and science. So we have our engraved plate and biography for him here in the front lobby."

"Tell me something," Neil whispered glibly to Greg. "Why does everyone here have to dig in to some old, dusty philosophy? Why can't they just develop something good and create a freakin' start-up company and go for some VC money? Jesus!"

Greg laughed quietly at Neil's now familiar style. Their sensitivities diverged, clearly. But Greg for some reason also felt a comforting camaraderie with Neil along the lines of his familiar university and consulting work. He hadn't expected this. And perhaps it was since Neil came to the Bayside Village on his own accord that Greg felt bold to match Neil's one-sided banter with his own. "Well just maybe," Greg said, "there's something in those old, dusty philosophies that makes the technology worth a damn." That was bold, Greg thought, feeling his young professional identity still forming. That was a step up, a match.

Neil didn't flinch. He seemed to welcome Greg's banter, Greg's right to his own view, though Greg was certain Neil wouldn't embrace it as his own. But here was the beginning, perhaps, of an honest dialogue.

Randy led the group out of Avicenna Hall and then stopped in front, turning around to face the group. Some paused inside to read the Avicenna plate, and Randy waited. When the group fully reformed outside, Randy continued. "You'll notice from the outside that a foundation stone of Avicenna Hall by the stairs here also has the engraved quote we saw at the Temple:

> *Unite the pair so long disjoined.*
> *Knowledge and vital piety.*

Now, let me again point out that we've located the Bridge Institute Graduate Research Library directly across the quad from our Bridge Institute Temple there, at the other end," Randy pointed directly across the quad to the Temple building, "as an expression of this principle—uniting knowledge and vital piety."

"I like that," Greg said. "joining knowledge with spiritual practice."

"Integrating head and heart," Sara said to Greg who nodded. "Oh, and did you notice the tile work in the library?"

"Oh yeah," Greg said, recollecting.

"Okay, folks," Randy said. "Our next stop before lunch is the Art Center, which takes us back to the side of the quad where we started.

17

Roger walked into the Research Park building on the Bridge Institute quadrangle, down the hall, into the GameIt office. In the lobby, vivid game images shimmered in holographic projections around the room, some interacting, reaching out, as Roger walked past them into Jeff's office.

"I'm glad you could meet so soon," Roger said, stepping inside.

"Of course," Jeff said. He stood. "Want a juice?"

"Sure."

They walked to the GameIt kitchenette. Jeff pulled two mango juices from the refrigerator, handed one to Roger.

Jeff leaned against a table. "So what's all this about?"

Jeff was a clean shaven Ph.D. in anthropology with a keen business sense. He was thoughtful about games and human development, sharp about his content, and committed to the Bayside Village mission. GameIt had a modest but decent venture capital investment, and Jeff had a trusting working relationship with his VC, Jack. But he fully embraced the slow, steady growth of the lifestyle company idea, and the values for which Roger and AlignIt Commons stood. Jeff's was a nuanced approach, and Roger appreciated it.

Roger stood by the sink and sighed. "So this morning I had a call with Chris Mueller."

"Right," Jeff said, twisting off the cap.

"About the AlignIt Commons board meeting on Friday. He told me he had talked to you about licenses for some of his game companies."

"No," Jeff said again. He looked at Roger. "Like I said, I didn't know he had game companies."

"Neither did I. He said he talked to you about this," Roger said, taking a swig of juice. "I was surprised, too."

"Hmm." Jeff recollected. "Well, when he attended his first board meeting about six months back, he did ask me a lot of questions afterwards about what GameIt is doing, what markets we're in, our future plans...which I felt were kind of intrusive, like more than he needed to know to do his homework as a prospective board member. I didn't give away our business plans, which he was kind of asking for. But he didn't say anything about game companies."

Roger turned to Jeff. "He said the funding situation changed for a few companies in his network, and he's priming them for AlignIt Commons."

"What kind of companies?" Jeff asked.

"He didn't say, exactly."

"Game companies?"

"Apparently."

"Damn." Jeff put his juice bottle on the table. "I hold the rights to gaming."

"I reminded him," Roger said. "And I said I needed to talk with you first. We can't just bring this conversation to the AlignIt Commons Board. But that's exactly where he wants me to focus the efforts of the AlignIt Commons. He said he'd talk with you." Roger turned to Jeff and leaned back against the counter. "He wants me to sign on more companies and drop our plans to develop an upper ontology with Greg. Leverage what's working now and don't mess with the tech platform. And he wants to focus more aggressively on marketing and licensing."

"And rake in a lot of profit for his game companies?"

"I think we should hear him out," Roger said. "But the board meeting is too soon. I think we should be prepared for some serious discussion and boundary setting." And perhaps more, Roger thought, but he wasn't ready to say it. It was extraordinary to have Mueller's interest and support for the

AlignIt Commons. Losing it would be a setback.

Jeff walked into the meeting room, and Roger followed. He pulled out a chair and sat down.

Roger sat on the other side. "Mueller's approach on the phone this morning didn't sit right with me. I didn't like what it could mean for the Commons. It would impact you and GameIt. It would interrupt the upper ontology with Greg. And it isn't the right strategy for the Commons."

"It feels like an end run around GameIt," Jeff said. "Maybe we need to backtrack on our due diligence and do some further discovery. If he's got game companies, we're missing some key intelligence."

"Yeah, maybe," Roger said. "He said they're new."

"New?" Jeff said. "Six months ago he was snooping into GameIt."

"I asked Jackie this morning if she could have someone run through his file again to check for any disclosures we may have missed. I also asked if she could help us in a broader search for company connections."

"Okay."

"So that's in progress," Roger said.

"We need to talk about actions," Jeff said. "This doesn't sound good." He paused, thinking. "I need to be clear, Roger—I don't want to compromise GameIt's exclusive field-of-use license to AlignIt. Even if he's talking about having a frank discussion. This is coming too fast without advance consideration, and he's circumventing me and GameIt."

"Of course. I know. I'm coming to you immediately. And we put the breaks on discussion at the meeting. He said he'd call you."

"You know I'm okay exploring co-exclusivity with other gaming companies, or differentiating fields of use if there are other markets that don't overlap mine. My VC, Jack, is willing to syndicate with other investors, too, in the right circumstances. You know this. But it's got to be people who share our vision, who have the integrity we've cultivated in the AlignIt Commons. And it's gotta be someone we trust."

"Of course," Roger said. "This isn't the way we do business in the Commons." He paused, took a sip of mango, put the bottle down, fingered the label with his thumb. "Mueller called the discovery engine my speculative project. Like it's a personal pet project. So he's also going after my vision of AlignIt. It made me suspect for the first time that he really doesn't get what AlignIt is about, nor the Commons."

"Well that can't feel good," Jeff said.

"It doesn't. It shocked me, and it's just catching up with me now." Roger paused, thinking. "He also wants to drop Greg out of the picture."

"That's not good. Where's Mueller coming from? I mean, what planet is he on, thinking he can come in and mess around like that at the last minute without establishing any trust and rapport?"

"I'm with you," Roger said. "Greg's not part of the team yet, but he, or someone like him, is central to what the AlignIt Scientific Advisory Board wants to do next. And you can't just yank people and strategy around for one person's special, short term interests—if that's what Mueller's trying to do."

Jeff nodded. "I haven't met Greg yet. We're meeting on Wednesday."

"You may see him tonight at the GameIt reception." Roger took another swig. "He's here now for the Bayside Village Orientation."

"Oh, right—I forgot he's here all week. I'll look for him tonight." Jeff paused a moment, sipped his juice, and put it down. "I've seen Mueller twice now. I have to say I'm not entirely comfortable with him—even before your call this morning. Just the way he interrogated me about GameIt. I'm not sure what's going on here, but I think we need to investigate it. I just want to give you an early warning that I'm not feeling comfortable."

"I hear you," Roger said. "We'll dig into this—fast. Something's clearly out of place." Roger sighed and stared off to a game design pinned to Jeff's wall. "Maybe I was caught off guard with some unchecked hopefulness. Maybe I let Mueller in too fast. Or maybe this is all very innocent and we just need to hear what Mueller's thinking."

Roger tapped his fingers in a pattern on the desk as he contemplated.

"Except that he hasn't been forthright with you or the Board," Jeff said. "There's a lack of transparency here. And changing strategy on you. And undermining Greg's role, maybe without sufficient investigation."

These thoughts disturbed Roger. He observed that they were harder to swallow than he had expected. He built his relationships on trust. Had Mueller violated his trust? Roger had hoped AlignIt would grow at a steady pace now, with Mueller's guidance and introductions. Had Mueller betrayed him?

"I think this is all I can do right now," Roger said. "I'm teaching in fifteen minutes."

18

Randy walked around the Plaza to the Bayside Village Art Center in a small complex of buildings in adobe Craftsman style built around an intricate pattern. He entered the courtyard, filled with exotic, native trees, bushes, flowers, and sculptures. Sara read signs as they walked by wildflower beds: California Poppies, Mission Bells, Western Houndstongue.

Greg realized by now that Sara had waited for the Art Center. He watched her keenly as they entered, saw her attention sparkle.

Turning around, Randy faced the group and spoke. "The Art Center was founded by William and Kate Blackford in Berkeley in temporary facilities just before the Bayside Village opened, and they relocated it here shortly after our opening ceremonies six years ago. The Art Center offers studio and classroom space, a gallery for shows and events, and a shop for the purchase of arts, crafts and art supplies. The Art Center also has an art materials purchasing and exchange cooperative made up of interested students, faculty and the local community. The idea of the cooperative is to purchase materials at a discount and to share or exchange unused or left over materials. Proceeds from the sale are dedicated to the Art Center."

"Hmm," Sara said, and Greg observed her keen attention.

"The buildings surrounding us here, and a few of the new buildings on campus, were designed by Bill and Kate. They feature a blend of California Craftsman style art and architecture with a post-modern adaptation of traditional Ottoman Turkish, Egyptian Mamluk, and Spanish Alhambra." Greg and Sara looked up to the buildings to pick out the architectural features of the facades Randy highlighted.

"Excuse me, Randy," Sara asked. "You said an art materials purchasing cooperative?"

"Right," Randy said. "Many organizations here at the Village work on a cooperative model, based in an organizational value of sharing. And the type of coop determines what is shared. For example, in our worker-owned coops the people who work in the business also own it, govern it, and share in the proceeds. Compare this to the conventional American corporate model where owners and share holders don't work in a business but take most of its profits. We have several coops on campus, like the Bath House in the Village Plaza and some researcher- and technician-owned coops in the Research Park. Bayside Village Properties is employee-owned. Here we have a purchasing coop, which means the coop members share in the purchasing, and the coop can get volume discounts and shares savings."

"Hmm," Sara said. Greg glanced at her, noted her interest.

"Our Bayside Village Community Housing is a housing coop," Randy said. "The Bayside Village School and Daycare is a parent-run coop."

"Hmm," Sara said. She turned to Greg and whispered, "I wonder what it's like participating in a parent coop." Greg raised his eyebrows, nodded.

Neil asked, "Why did you choose worker-owned cooperatives as opposed to, say, venture capital-backed start up companies?"

Greg listened with interest to Randy's reply.

"Because we've observed a higher degree of responsibility for the common good among employees of this type of business. The culture and incentive structure of coops is more suitable for cultivating the public spirit we're promoting at the Bayside Village. It's not that we avoid VC-backed start ups. GameIt has venture funding."

Neil squinted, contemplating. A VC-based GameIt he could understand. But these coops. Everything here was so alternative.

Randy turned, walked to a kiosk in the courtyard. "The Art Center studios are home to art students of the Bridge Institute working toward a Master of Fine Arts in Sacred Arts and Crafts."

"This I want to see!" Sara said, turning to Greg, who nodded and smiled at her. "Especially after seeing all the design around campus. I had no idea it was this extensive."

Randy continued. "Students come here from around the world to study in our unique program. The MFA curriculum is designed with a two-fold emphasis. The first is the disciplined study of sacred arts and crafts of times past, and it includes the study of art and craft of cultures around the world. This first emphasis includes both a practical knowledge of artisan skills and craftsmanship, and an academic knowledge of art history and theory. The second MFA emphasis is working toward an authentic, organic recovery of sacred arts and crafts for our time. By authentic, the Blackfords have in mind that students will not simply reproduce arts that belonged to a past era and another place, since art arises from context and responds to circumstances. It might be sacred art, but it isn't our sacred art. The idea here is to initiate a genuine sacred art for our time and global context based on inner study joined to outer study, and based on higher knowledge, but responsive to the themes, questions, needs, and knowledge of our time. For any of you who have read Bill and Kate's work, you'll know that I'm just scratching the surface. There's obviously more involved than that. I invite you to explore their writings and look further into the curriculum here."

Sara looked at Greg, surprised. "I had no idea the Art Center was so extensive! The last few months were so busy with work projects….There was so much to do before coming."

"I should have said more about it," Greg said. He realized the opportunity he missed. He hadn't anticipated Sara returning to the fine arts in such a way. Even now, he wasn't certain if this was a brief return or the beginning of a bigger shift for her. "Have you read the Blackfords?" Greg asked.

"No, but I will now."

Randy walked forward a bit and stood in front of the Drawing Studio. "Let me point out a few distinct features of the studios and traditions here. The drawing studio teaches basic skills in seeing, observing, and rendering. The instruction here is not focused on romantic subjectivity and impressionism. The students are training to see the world and represent it. Subjectivity is studied to the extent that the artists' point of view is part of the subject-object dance inherent in the very fact of art itself. We can't escape our situatedness as subjects, of course. But the emphasis here, unlike Western art of the last few hundred years, is not expression of the personal and subjective but to focus on seeing and rendering what is, what exists objectively, as free from mental obscurations as possible. It's rather Zen-like in that respect—seeing what is. Of course at some level, we're talking ultimately about bare attention, and the distance between artist, art and world is absorbed in a more complete consciousness. But I'll leave that to the art instruction.

"Now, the drawing studio trains students in something like scientific illustration. But the end goal is not illustration for text books or course materials, per se. Its a basic training in seeing and rendering objects of scientific investigation for use in other media, as we'll see in a moment. Of course, it's nice to acquire a practical skill set like scientific illustration in case students pursue text book illustration. Its one practical outcome for your resume. But we use the training for other purposes here."

Sara turned to the open door of the studio. A teacher inside was making rounds with students. Sara stood transfixed, drawn by an inward pull. Greg noticed. She wanted to step in and sit there. Sweet longing stirred in her. As the tour group standing around her stepped forward with Randy, Sara stood, immovable, peering into the studio. Greg stayed with her, and then Sara noticed him noticing her. "Part of me wants to go back to art school," she said. She met Greg's loving, supportive eyes—a look she realized she valued deeply. She smiled to him and moved on, and he followed, aware of her. Sara's attention was drawn inward to impressions stirred somehow by that single glance inside. She felt restless for something.

Randy walked to a permanent exhibit booth outside the Drawing Studio established as a visual aid for tours. "The MFA program is developing an entirely new book of patterns," he said, pointing to examples in the exhibit. "This pattern book project is grounded in two basic ideas. One is the use of new subject matter. For instance, while traditional pattern books used in the decorative arts use standardized floral and geometric patterns, the students here are encouraged to use a variety of new scientific imagery, including images of computer chip circuitry, human tissues and cells, marine plant and animal life, structures of new metals, structures of new chemical entities, images of planets and galaxies taken from earth-based, satellite and space ship telescopes, and more. In other words, the images chosen come from recently developed ways of observing nature that detect entities not observable even fifty years ago. So, part of the novelty of the pattern book project here lies in the imagery used. The students are also encouraged to draw local and regional natural subject matter as much as possible, such as plants, flowers, animals, fish, and rocks. The Blackfords aim to match art and place."

Sara listened with rapt attention, thinking through the implications of this fundamental shift in the art paradigm.

"Now, these images are not simply reproduced as though they were photographs," Randy said. "In the pattern book project, they're drawn into abstracted geometrical designs as can be found, for instance, in the traditional floral pattern books of past eras where the patterns were used in the production of textiles, wallpapers, ceramics, and tiles." Randy pointed to a new exhibit panel featuring decorative motifs applied to traditional textiles, ceramics and tiles. "And here we come to the second basic idea of our MFA." Randy directed the group's attention to yet another exhibit panel. "The mathematically abstracted patterns used as the framework or setting of the new images are based not on traditional Pythagorean and Euclidian geometry, but on these new mathematical discoveries and solutions only recently discovered and developed in the West during the last few centuries. For instance, in the examples here, we have…I have to look—I'm not a math guy." Randy turned and strained his eyes, reading the outdoor gallery legends: "toroidal rings, torus knots, moebius bands, and hyperbolic hexagons in this display case—just to give you an example." Randy turned back toward the tour group. "The details of new scientific images described earlier," he said, pointing back to the prior section of the exhibit, "are arranged in these new mathematical patterns," he said, pointing again to the contemporary math section. "The new mathematical patterns are used as a framework to arrange the details of new scientific images observed and recorded only in the last century or two. In other words, we've applied these new mathematical patterns to the traditional media used here, which we'll see in the next few studios. The groundwork for the other arts of the studio is laid solidly here in the Drawing Studio."

"Wow," Sara said to Greg, her eyes fixed on the displays before her. "And I was just playing with Pythagorean forms. This is a different league of art entirely!"

"Really?" Greg said, soliciting more from her.

"Yeah. This is humbling. You'd have to learn the mathematics somehow. Maybe they teach it."

Randy moved on a few steps in the courtyard and positioned himself before the Tile Studio. "You will have noticed the elegant tile work on many of our new Craftsman style adobe buildings around the Bayside Village and Bridge Institute. You can even see them on the buildings around us and in the fountains, gardens, and benches of the courtyard here. These are all created right here in the Tile Studio, which is becoming renowned throughout the artisan world.

"The historical impetus for this tile work is Mediterranean and Islamic art, particularly the latter with its emphasis on sacred geometry and abstract floral patterns. This art form then influenced the Mediterranean tile work found in Italy, Sicily and Spain and which traveled with missionaries to Latin America and California. In fact, we draw several craftspeople from these Middle Eastern and Mediterranean geographic areas—both instructors and students. Studying these early influences forms the historical study of tile work. You'll see many fine traditional tile patterns on display here in the Art Center that you won't find elsewhere in the Bayside Village or the Bridge Institute. What you will see throughout the new buildings of the Bayside Village and the Institute, are the new patterns I described earlier. Look especially in Avicenna Hall and the Bridge Institute Library, the Temple and the Dining Commons. These new tiles use patterns based on new mathematical discoveries like those toroidal rings, moebius bands, and so on," Randy said, pointing back, "and incorporate abstracted scientific illustrations based on recent observations, and local plants and animals, fitted to the new mathematical patterns. We call this the Bridge Tile."

"So that's what we've been seeing," Sara said to Greg. Then she said aloud to Randy, "I noticed that these new tiles are used in the bathrooms. They're even in our Lodge room."

"Yes, that's right," Randy replied. "For those of you who don't know, we have a Bayside Village Lodge on campus for guest lecturers and visiting and prospective faculty. And yes, the Lodge is built with Bridge Tiles. It also features textiles made from our Weaving Studio, wall paper made in our Wallpaper Arts Studio, and a few other arts, which we'll see momentarily."

"Did we also see these Bridge Tiles in the cafes here, like the ones in the Plaza?" a man on the tour asked.

"Yes," Randy answered. "We've included Bridge Tiles often in those places where visitors will see them most. They're also built into several fountains in the gardens and into the lobby and restrooms of the Bayside Village Playhouse, and our public and private hot tubs.

"Lastly, I'll say that orders are coming in from countries around the world—especially from the Mediterranean and Middle East where tiles are a well-accepted part of traditional architecture. We're also fortunate that demand for the Bridge Tiles is increasing right here in California, both in residential home design and for restaurants, parks, gardens, pools, spas— and even a new swimming pool. Stucco and tile design make for ecological building materials, too. To save trees the Bayside Village is trying to move away from using wood. We also receive delegations to the Bayside Village just to see the adobe style Craftsman buildings and the Bridge Tile. Even in the arts, we emphasize technology transfer, adoption, and impact."

Randy walked the group through the remaining studios. Sara looked again into the open door of the last studio, struggling to catch a feeling of being creative, being a fine artist. How to go back? But the door ajar afforded little view.

"So that concludes our morning tour of the Bridge Institute," Randy said.

"Let's get Tara," Sara said immediately.

19

Greg and Sara walked briskly away from the Bridge Institute quad to pick up Tara at the Bayside Village Daycare.

As they walked, Sara said, "I feel so inspired! I brought my sketch pad, and I thought I'd dabble in drawing again. But this is totally beyond what I expected!"

"Yeah, that Art Center blew me away!"

"Greg, this is amazing! You told me about it, I know. But I had no idea that so much was developing here around sacred arts."

"No, I'm surprised, too," Greg said. "Maybe I focused too narrowly on AlignIt in my planning. I didn't realize the arts were so big here."

"I definitely want to spend some of my time at the Art Center this week!"

A tram whizzed by merrily on a track that blended unobtrusively with the grass and walking paths.

"Hey, I'm just going to make a quick call to Mrs. Blocke," Greg said. He pulled out his mobile and dialed her again as he walked. It rang. No answer. He ended the call without a message.

Greg and Sara entered the Bayside Village School gate and walked in to the cottage. Tara was fully focused on drawing at an outdoor table under a vine-laden eave with other children. Greg walked up to see what she was doing and knelt beside her. "Hi, Sweetie."

"Daddy!" She got up and hugged him. Like she did on pick-ups from school back home. Dad was safety, home, security. Mom, too. But then, she turned back to her drawing project and showed him. That's a change, he thought. Unexpectedly so. Separation anxiety should be more pronounced in a new place. But something here draws her back to the table.

Sara stood talking with Sally, the assistant. "So what did Tara do today?" she asked.

Sally gave a report so Greg could hear it, too. "We told stories from around the world—from the Indian Panchatantra, the Persian Kalil and Dimna, Sufi stories and trickster tales, the Buddhist Jataka Tales, and the European Grimm's Tales."

"Oh, the Jataka Tales," Greg said to Tara.

"Yes," Sally said, "Occasionally, we have regular visiting story tellers from the Bayside Village come and share their stories. We may have a few this week. Then, we sang our daily and weekly songs," Sally said. "And we sang songs from around the world."

"Songs? That's wonderful," Sara said.

Sally nodded. "Right now we're learning songs in Japanese, Mandarin, Arabic, Spanish, and German. We learn songs in a different tongue than our own to stimulate the mouth, throat, and brain."

"Wow," Greg said, turning, listening carefully. He imagined the effect it would have on Tara during the week.

"We use songs, stories, and crafts as part of our daily and weekly rhythm," Sally said. "We bring in others from the Village to present stories, songs, crafts, and food."

Claire had finished with another parent and was listening to Sally. She came up next to Sara. "We learned rhymes together with movements in our morning circle. We learned tongue-twisters. We often provide rhymes, prayers, songs, and chants where each child has a place and participates. Sometimes we ring bells and play instruments. We also work on art projects with themes and materials from the world's spiritual traditions. Right now, we're working on mazes, mandalas, puzzles, and dolls. We also work on festivals and sacred traditions around holidays and festival times. So we have a rich abundance of activities. Sally and I cultivate our enactments with great skillfulness and deep devotion."

"Wow, this almost sounds richer than the adult activities!" Sara commented.

"Maybe," Claire said, laughing lightly. "In our daycare, we design activities to complement adult activities, where feasible, especially for workshops and conferences. There's a recursive design loop back to adult events, if the program leaders for adult activities are open to it. So the children's and adult's activities are often planned together to form a harmonious whole."

Hmm, that's intelligent, Greg thought.

A girl at the table asked for help cutting a pattern and Claire bent down, gave attention to her momentarily.

Sara commented to Greg, "Look how neat and orderly it is." Greg nodded. He looked to the outdoor bins under the porch awning by the table.

"We went on a little walk to the gardens just down the path," Sally said.

"That's good for the kids," Sara said.

"We use the gardens, waterfront, canals, and boats as part of our learning experience."

"Mmm," Sara said, nodding. "And she had a snack?"

"Yes, each day of the week, we have a different snack. This morning, we had oatmeal, almonds and peaches. We work with the rhythms of the day, the week and the seasons."

Sara nodded and stood silently a moment, observing Tara and the other children. She saw Greg kneeling quietly by Tara, just observing.

"Okay, Sweetie, it's time for lunch," Greg said. "Let's get up and go get our food."

Tara remained engrossed.

Greg waited a moment, then said more firmly, "Tara, come now, Honey. Everyone is going to lunch now."

Tara stood up, turned with her project in hand. "Mommy, look what I made. It's wallpaper. I drew flowers."

"That's beautiful, Tara," Sara said, stepping forward, taking the paper. She recalled Tara's discovery of wallpaper in the Lodge last night. It must have made an impression on her. "How did you remember the wallpaper?"

Greg stood, looked at the paper.

Tara shrugged. "I'm hungry."

20

Greg, Sara and Tara walked up the path to the Bayside Village Dining Commons. Greg opened the double wood-frame screen doors, which clacked shut behind them. The hall was astir with lively conversation over lunch.

After moving through the buffet line, Greg picked up his tray and turned around to Sara. "Do you see Neil?"

"No."

Holding his tray, Greg looked around the room, then the line. No sign of him. "I thought we could invite him to join us. But I don't see him."

"There's Keith and Leah," Sara said. "Want to join them again?"

"Sure."

Carrying trays, Greg and Sara walked up, with Tara following behind. "Mind if we join you again?" Sara asked.

"Sure," Keith said.

Greg set his tray down and pulled back his chair. When everyone settled in, Keith said, "We're just talking about what's inside the Raymond Lully Museum." He looked back to Leah, who seemed shy about the subject.

"I'm surprised," Leah said, "because Keith said there are Christian...sacred sciences...there." She seemed to struggle with a new term, hesitant to say it, as if speaking it meant owning it.

"Like Raymond Lully himself," Sara said, and took a bite of cheese melted on bread with basil, tomato.

"And a whole lot of people from the late medieval period up to probably the seventeenth century," Greg said.

"I was telling her about one section with exhibits on Christian arts and sciences," Keith said. "You'd see it on the tour tomorrow, if you're going to it."

"We are," Sara said.

Leah took up a glass, sipped, put it down. "It's kind of interesting to hear you say that the church pushed certain things away. I mean, of course it did, because of heresy. It feels kind of dangerous to me because exploring those things can lead to doubts and uncertainty and giving Satan a foothold in your mind to sow discord. But I'm also surprised that many people here seem polite and kind."

Keith looked to Greg and Sara. "We usually expect people in non-Christian religions to be fighting against the Christian faith."

"Why should people of other paths fight against Christianity," Greg asked disarmingly, "instead of work together in love toward the same aims?"

"I don't know," Leah said. But she was thinking because love can only come from God, and Christians are the only ones who know God, and everything else is a false god, and this is the problem with this strange Bayside Village place—it's filled with false gods, and Keith is straying into it and should come home now—to God, to Placid College, to her.

"Christians like we're used to don't study other religions," Keith said in a bold show of self-critique. "We study conservative Christian arguments against them, but not what they say in their own words. I took a whole class in apologetics."

That was thoughtful, Greg noted.

"It seems there are a lot of interesting people and ideas to learn from here," Sara said, spreading butter on Tara's toast.

"I don't really understand Bayside Village or what Keith is doing here," Leah said. She turned from Greg and Sara to Keith. "I want to support you but I'm not really sure about all these non-Christian religions, like in the Temple."

"I don't think the Bayside Village is non-Christian," Greg said. "I'm only visiting here, too, like you," he qualified, smiling kindly, showing rapport, "but there are a few Christian groups here. It's a very welcoming place."

Keith listened with sharpened interest. This struck a chord for him, as it became the central discussion point with Leah since she arrived last night.

"Well, I mean, it's not a Christian place," Leah continued, feeling both assertive in defense of her faith, as if it needed defending, and embarrassed now about conflict, because she didn't like to stand out or create conflict. And she felt out of her league.

"Hmm," Greg said. "I don't know how many Christians were among the founders of The Bayside Village, or how many run it. But if Bayside Village isn't a Christian place, per se, it might be a place for Christians—which is perhaps a different way to look at it."

Indeed, that was different, Keith thought. A place for Christians.

"I mean, there are yogis here, but its not only a yoga place," Greg said, "and there are Buddhists here, but it's not only a Buddhist place, there are Sufis here, but it's not only a Sufi place. But Buddhists, yogis, and Sufis have a place here just like Christians do."

Leah nodded hesitantly, cogitating, uncertain how to place this idea.

The mention of yogis, Sufis and Buddhists probably didn't help matters, Keith thought. But a place for Christians might help, whatever it meant. He felt a place here for himself.

When Sara had almost finished eating, she spotted something off to the corner. "Oh, what's that?"

Greg turned around in his seat. He saw a red rug, tables, small chairs, shelves, and toys. A small group of children was gathered around bean bag chairs, books, and a large black board where they drew and wrote with colored chalks. "Look at that! I didn't see it this morning."

"I didn't either," Sara said.

"We'll have to check it out when we're done."

"What is it?" Tara asked.

"It's a play area for kids," Greg said.

"Can we go?" Tara pleaded urgently.

"Yes, but let's finish our lunch first," Greg said, "then we'll go."

Tara finished and pleaded again, "Can we go play now?"

Greg turned to Sara. "I'm not done yet, but I can take her if you want sit longer."

"Okay."

Greg excused himself to Keith and Leah, got up with Tara, and walked to Kid's Corner. Two boys, a few years older than Tara, played with toy sea lions. Tara entered the area, enclosed by low shelves facing inward toward the corner and filled with toys, books, writing and drawing supplies, and natural and found objects. Tara scanned the collection.

After finishing her meal, Sara excused herself and approached Greg who was standing outside Kid's Corner, watching. She put her arm around him, leaned in to him intimately. "This is nice," she said. "Tara can play right here where we can see her, and we can enjoy our meals and relax."

Hmm, Greg thought, observing Sara's words; her sentence structure implies continuity of being here, he noted. "Yeah. This whole arrangement is well-conceived," he said. "The Day Care, Kids Corner. It's well built for kids here. I mean, look," Greg said, pointing to the floor. "Sea lions from the Bay, Clapper Rails, Dungeness crabs…This is amazing! I feel I can really let go here and not worry about you and Tara because its such a high quality, family-friendly environment."

"Mhmm." Sara acknowledged Greg's delight. She felt the security here, too. Maybe this space could hold them. Maybe they wouldn't get lost in utopian idealism, as she had feared several weeks back. She held these new thoughts in her heart, contemplating them silently.

Greg felt a difference between his enthusiasm and Sara's. She wasn't ready yet for a move to Bayside Village. Getting excited about art is one thing. This daring venture of his still left Sara uncertain for some reason. Greg couldn't yet fathom why.

21

After lunch and a family walk to the marshes, Greg and Sara returned Tara to Bayside Village Daycare. The orientation tour reconvened outside the Dining Commons at 1:30.

"Okay," Randy said, clapping his hands together once to call attention. "This morning, we toured the Bridge Institute. This afternoon, its the rest of Bayside Village."

"I just want to go back to the Art Center!" Sara pined to Greg.

"You don't want to skip the afternoon tour, I hope," Greg said. "After discovering the Art Center, who knows what further surprises we'll meet!"

"I know. I just love the Art Center."

Randy started down the path and the group followed. He turned around, walking backwards as he spoke aloud, facing the group. "The Bayside Village was built to bring our utopian visions into real, concrete demonstration projects. Then we try to transfer the projects to other locations and scale them up at a societal level, offering technical assistance and know-how. People have come together here from around the world to see what we do and get involved in our work."

An ornate metal gate looking like green copper crossed over the road. "You'll notice," Randy said, passing under it, "that our Bayside Village Gate is part of our logo."

Sara looked up as she passed under the gate, then turned around, stopped, and studied closely as she had yesterday on their first walk. She turned back, caught up with Greg. "I'm really going to come back and sketch that gate!"

Greg smiled, nodded.

Ahead on the lawn, Greg again saw students studying, discussing, drawing, and eating. And he marveled. "I love this," he said to Sara. "This has such a cool campus feeling!"

"We're approaching the Bayside Village Plaza," Randy said. "As you look around, you'll see that the Plaza is our main gathering place. Lots of people meet up here—writers, artists, actors, musicians, philosophers, scientists, intellectuals. Cafes here are buzzing with vital discussion. Bridge Institute projects are pursued here by students and faculty.

"In the afternoons, you'll find groups of students in boots wading in the canal, holding water samples and discussing. You'll see students out studying soil samples, working by the water front. The campus is our learning lab."

Randy walked to the Plaza's midsection where Greg and Sara had walked yesterday—the grass and brick quadrangle filled with amazing sculptures, with shops and buildings built around it and a central fountain.

Randy stopped, waiting for the group to catch up. "The Bayside Village Plaza is known internationally for its Fountain Garden and large scale works of public art."

"See?" Greg said to Sara. "More art surprises for you."

"I'm interested," Sara said, elbowing him playfully.

"The Plaza and Fountain Garden were the center of much attention just a few years ago," Randy said, "when we drew together international names in sculpture and public art in a fountain design contest based in sacred science design principles. The winning fountain, by artist Julian Dillon, was built in the center of the plaza. Besides the requirement to draw from sacred science principles, the design criteria included public utility for the plaza, such as seating arrangements, water fountains, garbage containers, recycle bins, and bulletin boards. These works are intended to nurture and support biotic life both in the immediate fountain and surrounding gardens, rather than merely consume resources."

Sara leaned to Greg, held her hand above her eyes shielding California's bright, dry sunlight. "I wonder what these design principles are."

Greg nodded, raised his eyebrows.

Then he spotted Neil walking down the path, catching up with the group and joining Greg and Sara.

"I didn't see you at lunch," Greg said. "I was hoping we could talk."

"I had lunch in Berkeley," Neil said, catching his breath. "Met some colleagues up there. We wrote a paper together a few years back and might do another."

Greg nodded.

"Randy?" a middle aged man said. "A few of us were wondering at lunch how the Bayside Village funds its projects. The stores I can understand, but the projects..."

"Right," Randy said. "We have a pretty special funding model. Many of our stores, services, and fee-bearing activities at the Bayside Village support our charitable activities as well as research at the Bridge Institute.

Revenues are held by the Bayside Village Charitable Trust, and proceeds from the sale of products, services, fees and events are allocated to the non-revenue-generating research and charitable projects."

"Interesting model," Greg said to Neil.

Neil's eyes squinted. "Yeah, I haven't heard of that." He scratched his neck, looked away.

Randy shaded his eyes from the sun. "Many of the Bayside Village's organizations and companies were deliberately created here by social entrepreneurs for dedication to the Village. Many of them were made operationally functional and profitable precisely to provide perpetual funding support to research and charitable projects."

Greg mused, rubbing his jaw with his finger and thumb. The notion of research funding from a charitable trust made up of dedicated business revenue fascinated him. Now, there's a way to fund novel research projects, he thought. How much funding might be dedicated to AlignIt to sustain his own work, he wondered—whether he consults for Roger only or moves to the Bridge Institute to teach? What funding might be available for Greg's other research interests?

Randy walked further down the Plaza to the Philosophy Salon, the attractive, French-style pavilion. "If you need refreshment, you can stop here at the Philosophy Salon, a combination shop of philosophy books and artifacts."

Greg observed Keith whispering to Leah about the Philosophy Salon, pointing to a gazebo outside selling ice cream, pointing to the French-style wrought iron tables with marble tops. It might be one of his favorite haunts, Greg imagined. Then he observed Leah clinging tightly to him, holding hands insecurely. Greg perceived that Leah was tuned in only to Keith, perhaps as a defense against the tour. He didn't know Keith or Leah, but he found himself wondering about Keith. Was this right for him?

"Some have critiqued the Salon as being too Western in scope," Randy said. "So the co-op owners have taken to highlighting the great meetings of Confucius, the Buddhist philosopher Nagarjuna, and the Indian philosopher and logician of the Nyaya school, Gautama. But the Salon is a place for everyone, East and West, philosopher or not. And I'd stop in to sample their fine French cheeses and pastries," Randy said, patting his rounded belly.

Standing in place, Randy pointed to the next building, octagonal in shape, Victorian and Ottoman-Turkish in style. "If you like reading clubs, you'll want to stop back to check the event schedule of the Village Literary and Scientific Circle. The model for our VLSC, as it's called, is one of America's oldest book clubs, the Chautauqua Scientific and Literary Circle, well known as CLSC. The book selection criteria at our VLSC is works of sacred science and sacred culture. VLSC also holds larger meetings and events in the Philosophy Salon and the Bridge Institute auditorium. Several works from the Bridge Institute curriculum are read here. Likewise many of the art pieces we'll see tomorrow in the Raymond Lully Museum have corresponding texts on the VLSC reading list."

"Hmm," Greg said aloud. The program integration inspired him, suggesting a larger framework than a random pastiche of interests.

"And I'll give a personal plug for one of my favorites at the VLSC—a reading circle of sacred science fiction—or SSF as it's known—that genre exploring the interface between science fiction and sacred science. We've read Mary Shelly's <u>Frankenstein</u> and Herbert Spencer's <u>Dune</u> as possible precursors welcomed into the SSF Hall of Fame, as well as a few fantasy works like Harold and Emily Masters' <u>The Epic of Zan and Arshan</u>. It's well known that science fiction inspires inventions and technologies. An author conceives an idea ahead of its time. Then scientists and technologists try to go out and make it. What I like about this SSF reading circle is how we deliberately use these works as a prompt for our scientific work. Not that inventions just pop out. But we do have a space to think, dream, and get inspired by these works."

"I definitely want to join," Greg said to Sara.

22

Jeff Baker closed the door of his GameIt office in the Research Park, alone now as Roger left to teach. Standing up, he called his venture capitalist investor on his mobile.

"Jack? Hi, its Jeff. Did you get my message?...Is this a good time?...Great....Yeah, I wanted to ask if you've learned anything more about Chris Mueller at Hilltop Ventures since Roger and I first mentioned him to you."

Jeff began to pace his office.

"Well, you know he's been starting to advise Roger and AlignIt Commons. He's been providing strategy and guidance and he's reviewed Roger's financials. And he's guest-chairing the AlignIt board meeting this Friday....Yeah. That's too fast?...That's what Roger felt, too. Okay. I'll pass that on...."

Jeff stopped pacing, looked out the window.

"Well, Mueller said a few things to Roger in a call this morning, prepping for Friday's AlignIt Commons Board meeting. It left Roger feeling disturbed....Apparently, Mueller may be trying to bring other game companies into the AlignIt Commons despite my exclusive license ....Yeah...Yeah, Roger's vigilant. He talked to me right away....No, we didn't know Mueller had them in his portfolio. We still don't, but we suspect based on what he said this morning. So that's one question—if you know anything more about his portfolio, where he's investing. Even just word on the street....Okay."

Jeff stared pacing again.

"And then, I guess I'd be interested in any read on him as a person....Yeah, his character, his reputation. Because not only is this portfolio question concerning, but he's also represented to Roger that he talked to me about his game companies, which he hasn't. And two more things about Mueller. He also wants Roger to abandon his foremost development strategy for AlignIt, you know—building out the upper ontology, and he wants him to just focus on marketing and licensing to build profit....Right, just licensing the platform as it is now....You might recall we're counting on AlignIt's new ontology as a strategic advantage for GameIt...It was in my 4th quarter report....And then, it feels to Roger, and me too, like Mueller's trying to slip in these changes at the last minute when the board materials were already posted, without the benefit of conversation ...Right, particularly in the AlignIt Commons, where that trust-based conversation and collaborative spirit is premium....Right....

Jeff pulled out his desk chair and sat down.

"So, since you have due diligence resources for the investment community that we don't have, and since you have your finger on the Silicon Valley pulse, I thought I'd ask....Okay, thanks....Well, anything you find could be of great help. The board meeting is Friday....Great, thanks!...Bye."

Jeff stared out the window, thinking. This was GameIt's first competitive threat. And it came in an unexpected way. He'd been on the look out for companies. But it's a VC moving into AlignIt Commons that brings the threat. He didn't even know Mueller's companies. He would have to handle this carefully.

Randy walked around the Plaza to the other side, near the pathway leading from the Dining Commons down to the marshes. He stopped at another building on the Plaza, an attractive adobe style club house with Bridge Tiles laid around its base and garden walls. The group gathered around Randy on the front lawn. "For the seniors among us—and I'm nearly one of them myself—the Academy of Elder Professionals, or AEP, is a unique member-based organization.

"I'm right behind him," Neil said. Greg glanced back at Neil, uncertain of his meaning. "The gettin' old thing," Neil clarified, seeing Greg's quizzical eyes. "I've looked into AEP. Not my content. But looks like a strong program."

"Ah," Greg said.

"The AEP embodies one of Bayside Village's key values," Randy said, "which is to knit people together from all phases of life in meaningful and mutually sustaining interactions. AEP draws its membership from active and engaged elders seeking to make a contribution. The AEP House, as it's called, serves as a meeting place, event and class organizer, social club, and a base of operations for a core of retired people. It helps match their interests and specialties with other organizations at the Village including Bridge Institute classes. Many seniors come here after a full family life or career, or a householder life, in the Indian sense. And they wish now to focus their full attention and labors on spiritual inquiry, service to the community and world, mentoring Bridge Institute students, collaborating in research projects, and for many, the return journey home—the spiritual path."

"Wow," Greg said to Sara, "your parents would love this."

"They would."

Greg again noticed Keith and Leah clumped together tightly, holding hands insecurely. It seemed to Greg that Leah was focused on Keith, shutting out the tour.

"We actively foster connections between AEP and other Bayside Village programs," Randy said. "For instance, AEP members get involved with children at the Bayside Village School and Daycare, serving as volunteer mentors, tutors, and even school board members. Other AEP members volunteer in the Bridge Institute as mentors, tutors, guest lecturers, researchers, research subjects, and administrators. Still others form new projects, organizations, or businesses."

"That's good," Neil said to Greg. "Back in DC, I'm involved in a group that mentors young entrepreneurs."

"Really?" Greg said. This detail expanded Greg's view of Neil—that he would devote his time to mentoring. Neil may be hard and bristly, but perhaps he had other admirable qualities.

"Bayside Village seeks to enhance the already existing intergenerational ties in families and communities," Randy said. "We encourage broad membership in AEP—from local residents, to parents of our employees, directors, faculty, grandparents of our Bayside Village School, to others already in our community. However, basic AEP membership, programs, and volunteer opportunities are open to all. So we also welcome seniors from elsewhere who may come to the Village from far away just to participate in AEP as a unique retirement experience. We offer guest elderhostels for extra fees. Since similar programs elsewhere might be limited to seniors with means, we offer scholarships and work-study opportunities for elders of lesser means."

"Hmm," Sara said to Greg. "I bet our parents would come visit us to participate in AEP. Or they could move in with us and then have this day program."

"Come here? You're imagining us here?" Greg reflected. This was a revealing statement.

"Just considering options," Sara replied. "It would be nice to live somewhere good for our parents, so we wouldn't be so far apart and see them only on holidays. I didn't really think of this before—a place we could live together."

"Yeah, I can see that."

Randy walked on to the building next door to AEP, and the group followed, reorganizing itself around him where he stopped. "Here we have the Bayside Village School and Daycare."

Sara moved over to Keith and Leah. "This is where we have Tara."

Greg scanned the tour group for Neil. But Neil had wandered down the path, talking on his mobile.

"Our vision for the school is to create a family-based community," Randy said. "At Bayside Village we support and nourish families. And our School and Daycare is designed to rebuild sacred culture for families." Greg and Sara looked at each other, visibly impressed. "When I say we're a family-based community, I mean that we recognize that parental involvement in the school and daycare is a critical element of the child's— and the family's—overall education. Many schools have high parental involvement. We don't mean just parents volunteering on a board or selling raffle tickets to raise money. So what distinguishes us? Bayside Village School and Daycare encourages parents to get involved intellectually, emotionally, and spiritually in the school and the educational process, not just socially and financially. We encourage parents to create rhythms in the home that match the child's environment at school. And teachers work with parents as much as with children. Parents often discover they need to undertake the journey of learning along with the children."

"That's like music to my ears," Sara said to Greg.

"Mine, too," Greg echoed.

"The school cultivates in our children those same values the Bayside Village promotes in society at large," Randy said, "including those in our demonstration projects. And you'll notice the school is right next to the Academy of Elder Professionals, so that we can easily bring together young and old, receive the service of elder volunteers, and provide a platform for intergenerational programs.

"Now," Randy said, "the school is part of our overall effort at the Bayside Village to rebuild sacred culture in the West. By *sacred culture*, we mean culture based on deep themes in spiritual traditions, as found in the arts, in stories, in craft, in sacred science, in philosophy and in psychology."

"I love this," Greg said to Sara. "This theme keeps coming up—

rebuilding sacred culture, recreating civilization."

Sara nodded. She listened, allowing herself to imagine more now than she had in the weeks leading up to the visit. Perhaps the school could be more than just a daycare. She still imagined the Village as an impractical dream of Greg's. But suppose she did get the visual design job with Karen? She could facilitate charettes for Bridge Institute projects. Suppose Greg took the faculty position? Suppose they enrolled Tara at this school?

23

Jackie Schrader stood up from her desk in the Research Access Office and walked to the room of a research and licensing officer. A man looked up from a contract he was reviewing.

"Hey Mark. So here's an interesting situation," Jackie said, walking in and sitting down in a chair by his desk. She explained Roger's concern with Chris Mueller, the need to identify Mueller's network.

"Do we have relationships with Mueller's companies?" Mark asked.

"Not that I'm aware of. So that's one question. I'd check all of our own records—anything Bayside Village or Bridge Institute have on him— gifts, contracts, industry visitors, any database records. I know Mueller himself has given one or two gifts to Roger and the Institute."

"We're looking for game companies, mainly?"

"Let's create a chart of all of his companies, tag them by type, and highlight game companies."

"Now let's head to the right," Randy said, "to the Ateneo de la Scientia Sacra." Randy walked down a path leading away from the Plaza and turned to a building set back from the path, amidst an old grove of eucalyptus trees. He waited for the group to reform, and it made a half circle around him, facing the building. The façade was decorated with motifs like stone carvings from ruins of ancient sites. Statues were artfully spaced in the yard, below the tree tops.

When the group had gathered, Randy started. "The Spanish word *Ateneo*, like the English *Atheneum*, means a cultural association, center, or club. The Ateneo de la Scientia Sacra is a cultural center founded by Jorge and Rosa Gonzales and devoted to recovering and promoting sacred sciences. Specifically, it focuses on ancient civilizations in Latin American countries—the Quiche Maya, Aztecas, and Incas. Where possible, it also draws on modern Latin American developments in sciences and philosophies supportive of sacred science in the Mayan, Aztec, and Incan traditions."

A young man, not older than his early thirties, presently walked out the front door, evidently seeing the gathered group, or else he was signaled by Randy's mobile. He approached Randy from behind and waited. Greg noticed he was fashionably dressed, alert, intense. Randy acknowledged him with a nod and continued.

"And before I introduce Mauricio Espado, the Ateneo's Director, let me just interrupt myself to draw your attention to the Floricanto Festival this Friday night. It's put on by the Ateneo, but held at the Dining Commons patio starting at 6:00 PM and running until midnight."

"Are we going to that?" Sara asked Greg as they stood.

"Yeah," Greg said. "It's on our schedule. Roger said it would be a fun event to wind up the week."

"I'd encourage you to attend if you're in the area," Randy continued. "It's an evening of food, music, dance, art, and poetry. Floricanto is Spanish for 'flower and song.' The word came into use during the Chicano movement in the 1960's and 70's when Chicano/Chicana poets took up a form of spoken song like that of the Aztecs. Since the Chicano movement, Floricanto events have celebrated Latino culture, mainly focused on readings by Chicano poets. Sometimes they feature live Latino music, dance, and Latin American foods. Here at the Bayside Village the Floricanto Festival follows the spiritual themes of the Ateneo de la Scientia Sacra which Mauricio will describe to you. If it is possible to recreate Mayan, Aztec, and Incan sacred rites today, in a way that is lively and relevant to our times but true to the original spiritual impulse, this Floricanto Festival aims to do it."

"Interesting," Sara said to Greg. "That's new to me."

Greg nodded.

"Okay, that's my announcement. Back to the Ateneo de la Scientia Sacra. It's my pleasure to introduce to you our new Director of the Ateneo, Dr. Mauricio Espado. He'll introduce you to the Ateneo and its work."

Randy stepped back.

"Right, so, thank you, Randy." Mauricio stepped forward, both casual and unassuming in gait but intense in demeanor. His deep-set eyes penetrated sharply. "Yes. So, before I begin, let me just point to the visuals here before us." He waved his hand out to the artifacts in the yard beneath the canopy of eucalyptus trees. "I think this gives us a way in. So, the facade here, and the small sculpture garden in front, are from contemporary artisan reproductions of Mayan, Aztec, and Incan carvings. Some of them are created right here in collaboration with the Bayside Village Art Center, using 3D printing. Some are imported carvings. Some of them are stone. Some are lighter material for portability—like for the Floricanto Festival, so we can move them around. If you've visited the great ruins of Mexico, Guatemala, or Peru, you've seen carvings like these in the pyramids and palatial compounds, especially the temples. This one," Mauricio said, pointing to a large, round disk, "is the *Haab*, an Aztec solar calendar with glyphs, each with a special meaning. These are artifacts of past sacred cultures. And they point to the possibility of recovering something, and taking it forward in our day. For instance, the model inscribed on the rock face here is also designed into PlanIt, one of the AlignIt Commons companies, which Randy no doubt showed you this morning. So this is our work at the Ateneo. Projects like this."

Greg noticed Sara listening intently, and he thought how wonderful it is that despite her uncertainty about Bayside Village, they at least had a common commitment to similar streams of ideas and aspirations.

Greg noticed Neil had wandered ahead down the path, talking on his mobile.

"Now a little background about our Ateneo de la Scientia Sacra," Espada continued. "Who are we, and what do we do? So, the Ateneo de la Scientia Sacra began when the Bayside Village began, six years ago. But it was really the creation of the founders, Jorge and Rosa Gonzales, several years before that. Jorge and Rosa were inspired by another Ateneo—let's not confuse the names—called the Ateneo de la Juventud which arose in Mexico in 1909 during the Mexican Revolution. The Ateneo de la Juventud was a cultural center and movement created by a group of young intellectuals disenchanted by the failure of liberal reforms based on European philosophy. The Mexican power structure at that time was fascinated with European philosophy, especially the French and German. Mexican progress had been viewed in this light and ignored what arose from within Mexico itself. But years of liberal reforms based on European positivist philosophy left Mexico in turmoil and social despair. So a group of young Mexican intellectuals turned away from philosophical materialism and positivism once associated with revolution and social change in Mexico and they met to articulate a new philosophy. Among them were noteworthy thinkers like Antonio Caso, Alfonso Reyes, Jose Vasconcelos, and Martin Luis Guzman. Together, they created the Ateneo de la Juventud to promote new ideas and culture. So Jorge and Rosa Gonzales here at Bayside Village followed this example, up to a point. Our Ateneo de la Scientia Sacra was created here at the Village to advance a different philosophical orientation that values the heritage of sacred rites in the Mayan, Aztec and Incan civilizations."

That's a novel comparison, Greg thought. What a peculiar pathway to expressing the Ateneo's work. Espado seems deeply rooted in a sense of Mexicanness, yet rooted in philosophy.

"Back to Mexico a hundred years ago," Espado continued. "The Ateneo de la Juventud mounted an attack on the old philosophies of materialism, the positivism of Comte and Spencer, and philosophical and biological determinism used to justify racism against indigenous peoples and Mestizos, or those of mixed European and indigenous blood. The Mexican philosopher Antonio Caso actually used positivism to serve this new end by advancing its doctrine of experience. He followed experience all the way to the actual experience of Mexicans, providing a new datum for philosophizing. In addition to this strategy, the Ateneo de la Juventud replaced a canon of positivist and materialist authors with the philosophical works of Immanuel Kant, Arthur Schopenhauer, and Henri Bergson. It was still European, you see, but one could argue it was more suitable for illuminating Mexican experience. So the Ateneo de la Juventud promoted changes in philosophical orientation. Now, back to our time, Jorge and Rosa Gonzales moved here to Bayside Village to pursue their aims of recovering sacred science of the Quiche Maya, Aztecas, and the Incas for our time. Specifically, Jorge identifies and promotes literature that values the recovery and development of Mayan, Aztec, and Incan traditions today."

Mauricio would be an interesting discussion partner in philosophy, Greg considered. He didn't recall seeing his name, or the Ateneo for that matter, in his preparations for this visit. Maybe just in passing. I should look up his curriculum vitae, Greg thought. Then he saw Sara turning to a statue. He imagined her keen eye was tracing its contours, registering its shape.

"Now back again in Mexico in the early twentieth century," Espado continued. "In addition to developing a new philosophy, the Ateneo de la Juventud made practical applications, successfully penetrating society with reform ideas and programs. They launched reforms in education and thought, fostering a new appreciation for the humanities. Jose Vasconcelos, a founding member of the Ateneo de la Juventud, took the Ateneo's revolutionary new philosophical ideas into education. The Ateneo de la Juventud formed a people's university called the Universidad Popular Mexicana to reach common working people with new ideas. It didn't grant degrees but it spread new ideas to those without access to the traditional university system. Back again to our time and place, Jorge and Rosa emphasize that the Ateneo de la Scientia Sacra should provide educational and cultural programs that broadly disseminate its work in recovery and development of sacred sciences in the Mayan, Aztec, and Incan civilizations. They have teamed up with the Bridge Institute's Extension program, the Village Literary and Scientific Circle, the School and Day Care, and Academy of Elder Professionals to offer primary and continuing education and lifelong learning programs. So our Ateneo is also a cultural and education platform. Our programs do indeed include political, social, and economic matters, but they're principally focused on recovery and promotion of the Mayan, Aztec, and Incan sacred sciences."

What a platform, Greg thought. It seems philosophically robust. How can I connect with this? Greg shifted his weight, and then the sun shone through the trees and blinded him. He stepped to a shaded spot.

"Unlike its historical predecessor, however," Espado said, "our Ateneo, and the Floricanto events like the one this Friday, create a ritual container— a concentrated space for practice, basically—and they recreate some of the ancient sacred rituals today, updating them for our time—without diminishing their power, we hope. They work intensively with the powerful paradigms found in the Mayan, Aztec and Incan sacred rites, like symbols, metaphors, and practices. A practicing group meets regularly, here in our space, to recreate these ancient rites for our day and do the practices. We keep the fire going, so to say. The public events are less intense, but in them you get a powerful taste of what these traditions can be when they're embraced and lived.

"So, that is basically all. You can find more about our programs, and please come join us, or give a donation, after the tour. Are there any questions about the Ateneo de la Scientia Sacra?"

"Yes," said a man in the group. "If I recall, Randy said earlier today that the term *scientia sacra* was used in the West at one time. Is there any relation to that use and this Ateneo de la Scientia Sacra?"

Mauricio looked to Randy, with eyebrows raised. Randy gestured with his open hand that Mauricio should take the inquiry. "Yes," Mauricio said, "so Thomas Aquinas is known for this term, *scientia sacra*. And of course, Thomas Aquinas is the principal exponent of scholasticism, which also was dominant in Mexico in its early history. But no, I don't believe there is a connection, if it means we are doing scholastic philosophy or theology. I don't think Jorge and Rosa use the work of Aquinas. Not directly, at least. The Bridge Institute has re-popularized the term *sacred science*, and many people here are using it now in a broader than Thomist way. Even Jorge and Rosa. But we are studying the sacred ways of the Maya, Aztecs and Incas, and we are doing it by investigation. For us, this is sacred science."

Mauricio paused, waiting for other questions. Then he began again, "But it is ironic, isn't it, that scholastic philosophy and theology, based on Aquinas, were dominant among the European conquerors and missionaries who invaded and largely destroyed these great civilizations. Yet they didn't appreciate the sacred science they encountered in what, to them, was 'the new world.' They destroyed the buildings and built churches over them. When they found golden objects and jewelry embodying the Aztec metaphysics and cosmology they didn't appreciate it or study it—they melted it and took it back to the King of Spain. Some Roman Catholic monks and friars were alarmed by this wholesale devastation, actually. They documented the culture as it was being destroyed. So it's not a black and white story, all good, all bad. But it amazes me that simply having a scholastic theology with the ideas of sacred science in it did not ensure the survival of sacred science—either in Europe or in lands it exploited." Mauricio waited, contemplating if he had any more to say.

Wow, Greg thought to himself. What bold exploration.

"Question for Randy," a student-aged woman said. "So, you have these area studies programs, like Latin American Studies, Native American, African American...Can you say more about equity and inclusion?"

Neil walked back from his call down the road and joined the group.

Interesting pattern, Greg thought—when he leaves and when he joins.

"Well yes," Randy said, "equity and inclusion are part of our values framework." Randy looked to Mauricio who nodded consentingly, and then Randy continued. "But not in the conventional sense of simply ensuring political fairness to diverse groups so that everyone can have a share of the resource pie, for instance. We do these programs mainly for the sake of cultural health. People live in cultures, and cultures need expression. And the wider American culture, like many dominant cultures, has excluded or marginalized the voices, arts, and sacred cultures of certain peoples. We think it is part of the health of a society to give place and voice to its own subcultures. We can't compensate here at Bayside Village for all the suppressions in American history, the genocide of Native American nations, the forced enslavement and transport of Africans to this continent, the theft of Mexican land, the internment of Japanese immigrants in California, and so on. But we try to do our part, as one village, to create a container for holding the subcultures in our midst—like including and celebrating diverse strands in the tapestry of Bayside Village. And we offer this model—of giving a place or creating a container—to others who might use it. In our time and our place, these particular cultures are important. In another time and place, different programs might arise. But we are exercising the value of cultural health by giving a place for the honoring and expressing of cultures, so that America's cultural unconscious, and its cultural shadow, do not grow too large and potentiated by dark forces."

"And," Mauricio interjected, "Bayside Village as a whole has also a value of preserving cultural heritage and recovering lost knowledge. Roger Barnes' AlignIt plays a role in that project."

"Hmm," Greg heard himself say.

"Yes," Randy immediately acknowledged. He looked to Mauricio, as if asking if he had any more.

Mauricio gave a quick and subtle shrug and looked out to the group. "Any more questions? No? Okay. Please return and visit us."

"Thank you, Mauricio," Randy said. "Yes, do return and explore the marvels of sacred science among the Mayan, Aztec, and Incan cultures.

Okay, folks, let's move on now to our next stop, The Sensory Parlor Collective."

24

Randy walked back to the Plaza to a long building with a sign in front reading, "The Sensory Parlor Collective." It was an older building, left over from the days before the land was purchased from Richmond Chemical Company to create Bayside Village. The building was not decorous, but it was now artfully surrounded by flowering eaves.

"This I want to see," Sara said. "I might do some activities here when you're in meetings."

"I hadn't looked into this," Greg admitted. He recalled his surprise last night when he commented to Sara that she would at least enjoy the yoga this week at the Village, and she said she may rather explore the Sensory Parlor Collective. He hadn't so much as seen it in the materials. She had noticed it and she was evidently planning on it.

Randy opened the door and escorted the group inside to the front lobby. Greg's eyes scanned the open spaces around him—Persian rugs, lounge chairs, large floor pillows, and elegant modern lights. What an unusual contrast to the building's exterior, he thought. And to the other exhibits.

A white-haired woman in her sixties, with a powerful presence, active attention, and artful dress, stood near Randy with deep, penetrating eyes.

"Elizabeth is the Director of our Sensory Parlor Collective," Randy said. "She keeps the parlors in top performance and creates a wonderful psychological and spiritual container for rich sensory experience. She's a fine human being. And she is wise in the ways of the senses," Randy said with a particular flair in his voice.

Elizabeth rolled her eyes and shook her head playfully. "And for full disclosure, Randy is my husband," Elizabeth announced loudly with stone-cold eyes, looking out intensely, and then laughed heartily with a resounding voice. "Welcome to our Sensory Parlor Collective," she said warmly. She spoke with a deep and cultivated voice, a commanding presence. "Usually I greet guests, bring them in the Parlor, ask them about their specifications, and establish a personalized Parlor experience. With open houses like today's, I'll guide everyone as a group through on our short tour. To start, let me just give a brief introduction to what we are.

"The Sensory Parlor Collective offers a tribute to our embodiment in physical existence. The Collective is a group of specialists in different sensory domains each of whom has stewardship over a parlor, one for each of the five senses. Each Sensory Parlor is organized here under one roof, arranged side by side down this hall, focused on producing expanded sensory awareness through the parlor experience. Some experiences provided in the parlors bring us back to such primal states that some visitors have described the experience as like returning to early childhood exploration of the surrounding physical world. At the same time, other aspects of the Parlor are so fundamentally reorienting to our ordinary, mainstream collective zeitgeist that people have experienced profound shifts in consciousness."

Greg had a flash of wondering what Keith was making of all this, and what poor Leah was to do with it. He turned slightly, unobtrusively, to watch them. Keith's young face was taut with attention, his eyes wide as the sky, as Elizabeth spoke. Leah was turned in toward Keith as if she couldn't bear to be here. God forbid, what would she do with the senses? What am I thinking, Greg wondered, suddenly coming to himself. What projection is this? What am I to do with the senses?

"The decor is exquisite," Elizabeth said, "because we want our guests to feel comfortable, relax, and go deep into their sensory experience—far beyond our culturally conditioned senses of embodiment, which is rather more like a limited set of accustomed postures and movements. We discover our own conditioned embodiments here and we try to expand beyond them. In addition to the sensory parlors, we have smaller rooms for individual and small group sensory meditations and exercises. We have a larger meeting room for special events, workshops, or trainings. Groups may come for private parties and special tours. This brings extra revenue to support the work of the Collective and it supports the Bayside Village and research at the Bridge Institute as well. And the Collective has a shop at the end of the row of parlors selling items related to each. Think of the Sensory Parlor Collective, overall, as a place for a quiet, interior experience of sensory awareness, deconditioning, and discovering freedom. Sometimes its also a social place, a meeting place, to share the expanded awareness of your sensory experience with others."

Sara contemplated what kind of resource this could be during the week. Yoga was familiar. But this was new. Enticingly new. What was all this about? How far could it open new doorways? And the social aspect— would Greg have time for it, too, in his tight schedule?

"Let me point out at the beginning," Elizabeth said, "and we can explore this further if you return, and I do hope you will—a Sensory Parlor is not a frivolity or an amusement. For many of us, this is an earnest and rigorous inquiry into the nature of sensation and its relationship to consciousness. Our work is drawn from spiritual and scientific traditions, and contemporary approaches to body work and somatics. We take this work seriously, and I invite you come back and explore it with us." Elizabeth paused a moment, as if looking for the next thing to say. Then she looked to Randy, and then back to the group. "Okay, I think that's all by way of introduction. So let's move on now to explore our sensory emporium." With that, Elizabeth strode down the hall.

"Here we have the Taste Parlor," Elizabeth said, stopping by a room, turning to the group.

Greg noticed what appeared like tasting stations organized around the room, with comfortable lounge chairs grouped in the center.

Elizabeth pointed out the different stations, giving examples. She passed around cardamom candies, or what seemed like candies—but they were different somehow. Greg took one, put it in his mouth, chewed. The spicy flavor burst upon the stage of his tongue and called him inward. The extraordinary possibilities of this taste parlor now dawned on him. And what would Sara do with it this week, he wondered.

"Now, the Taste Parlor is different from a culinary academy, or a food sampling event," Elizabeth said. "The focus here is on taste itself, not edible foods, per se. The atmosphere is deliberately quiet so that attention can be drawn inward to the experience of the taste sensation and to see where it takes us in our awareness. The tastes offered here are drawn from a wide variety of sources including world cuisines and global herbology and medicine. Samples are given on silver spoons at each booth and wiped with warm, moist cloths for the next taste sample. But taste samples go beyond food. We have taste samples of woods, metals, leaves, and grasses. For these non-edible items, a small swab made of recycled material is provided; after use, these are deposited into these receptacles for reuse." Elizabeth pointed to a few at tasting stations around the room. "Occasionally participants discuss the taste samples, such as what arises in their experience, how they feel in connection with the taste, what the taste means to them. They talk about composition, including spices or recipes. Our visitors can buy recipes. For your culinary delight, we also sell food sample packages in the store that you can take home for your own mini Taste Parlor. And for the children in your life, we have a Taste Parlor toy set, to encourage sensory awareness in our younger generations. The proceeds of these sales go to support the Sensory Parlor Collective and research at the Bridge Institute."

Sara whispered to Greg, "the toy set would be fun for Tara." Greg nodded, interested. Sara rustled in her purse for the roll of local currency coins, the BV Dollar, that Greg had given her yesterday after checking in at the Lodge. She hadn't planned to spend it, didn't know what to do with it. But what about a toy set? She felt the roll there in her purse, at the bottom.

Elizabeth moved down the hall and the group followed. "The next parlor in our Collective is the Touch Parlor, with articles of varying textures and makes to be touched or felt." Greg's eyes scanned the items as Elizabeth spoke, introducing the accoutrements. Again there was the same set up—stations and plush lounge chairs in the middle. "Here we have texture pads to explore rough, smooth, grainy, silky, and spongy surfaces." She moved around the stations. "Here we have oils to rub between the fingers. We have brushes with bristles of all kinds." She moved farther around. "Here we have fabrics of diverse kinds and textures. And here, techniques of judging excellence by touching with different parts of the body—feeling a fabric on the cheek, or the back of the neck, or the arm. There's a whole science and appreciation for this fine touch."

Greg mused at the wide world of objects he hadn't considered for this purpose, like seeds and other small objects to feel between the fingers.

"For the Touch Parlor," Elizabeth said, "you'll find special clothes, sheets, pillows, floors and floor products, furniture, and many other products that enable people to touch and feel differently. The proceeds of these sales go to support the Sensory Parlor Collective and research at the Bridge Institute."

Bed sheets, Sara imagined. What kinds? What would those feel like?

Elizabeth guided the group into the next room. "This is the Olfactory Parlor. On this wall, you can open bins and jars for a brief time to smell dried herbs, spices, flowers, fruits and vegetables, sea weeds, and many other items. On the counter to the left, scents are sprayed onto tabs of paper which you can smell and then recycle. A full range of scents is available, to touch all parts of our experience—not just the familiar fragrant aromas. In fact, for all the senses, we try to offer experiences that lie outside of our culture's familiar sensory range, to try to touch or evoke other types of consciousness. In particular, we've identified some very unusual scents, new scents unknown before the last twenty or thirty years, which tend to awaken quite unfamiliar parts of us. At the store, you can find the more familiar and pleasing scents for the home, the closet, the dresser, the office, the car—whatever you like. You'll find scented oils, candles, soaps, body lotions, incense, and incense burners.

"The Olfactory Parlor also specializes in events like traditional Japanese incense rituals, for refining and enjoying the sense of smell. And that's the focus of our next parlor."

"I love incense," Greg said to Sara.

Elizabeth moved to a small side room and the group followed. "Incense has long been used in India, China, Japan, and other countries, and its historically associated with spiritual traditions. For instance, in Buddhism, incense is offered to Buddha before rituals and chants. And it is said that at the level of a Buddha, everything is fragrant like incense. Everything. The dharma, or the teaching that leads to awakening, is also considered as incense. So consider this—we think of words as dharma, and dharma as words. Consider incense as dharma. The wafting fragrance rises up from the incense stick and reaches you as dharma."

"Hmm," Sara said aloud.

Greg looked at her curiously. The notion caught him, too, then. Imagine incense as dharma. How would one receive dharma teaching in the form of olfactory sensation?

"In Japan," Elizabeth continued, "incense was appreciated by the accomplished and by those in training along with arts like the tea ceremonies, flower arranging, poetry, and calligraphy. The Shogun practiced appreciation of incense at their gatherings and parties. And we have these incense poems from the classical text, Kokinshu." Elizabeth stepped closer to the wall where beautifully calligraphed poems were framed and mounted, next to artistic photographs of their subject matter. She read:

> The orange, fragrant
> Flowering in June
> Drifts on summer night breezes
> Remembering scented sleeves
> Of a lover long ago

Elizabeth waited as the poetic effect alighted on the hearts of tour participants. "Here's another:

> Where in the moon's light
> Do the plums blossom?
> Yet their fragrance guides you.

> This fragrance, ah—
>   enchants me more than colors—
> Whose scented sleeves have brushed
>   my tender garden blossoms?

Elizabeth paused, breathed in, spoke reflectively. "Beyond this lovely poetry, the incense masters left texts only on the external aspects of their rituals. They held their inner teachings secretly. Here at the Sensory Parlor Collective, though, we teach the characteristics of aromas and their psychological and spiritual aspects. We aim to open up old secrets, to explore the paths of masters. You're welcome to return at your leisure. Come join our classes, workshops and retreats on incense and scented oils. "

"Do you have anything in the Greek tradition?" Greg asked. "Like the ancient Mysteries and Neoplatonic schools?"

"I'm not familiar with those," Elizabeth said.

"Incense comes up frequently in the <u>Hymns to Orpheus</u> and in Iamblichus' <u>De Mysteries</u>, Greg said. "It's used theurgically."

Neil raised his eyebrows, mystified by Greg's contribution, yet impressed by it. How does an ontology scholar who consults to companies come to this kind of esoterica, he wondered.

"Maybe you could provide us with the references?" Randy suggested. "We focus on Japanese incense because we have Sensei Daisho as a Collective member who heads our Incense Parlor. But we'd like to learn of other traditions."

Greg nodded to Randy. Then he wondered about Neil's response, wondered if this expression of interest was to his detriment. Greg's many worlds of interest never came together before as they have now at Bayside Village. He had always remained safely hidden, one world never touching another. But here, where his worlds of interest met, how much should he open up like this? Here there can still be guests like Neil from Greg's mainstream academic world. How would Greg's interest in theurgic philosophy play in the world of information science, semantics, and ontology? Why is reputation such a concern to me, he wondered? Why do I focus so desperately on survival? How I'd like to shine in these areas dear to my heart!

Elizabeth guided the group into the next room. Again, the parlor was arranged by stations with plush chairs in the center. "Now we come to the Vision Parlor," Elizabeth said. "Modern Western civilization has focused far more on sight and sound than on the other senses, so we've needed to focus carefully on these next two parlors to ensure we are not simply carrying forward our conditioned approaches to these two senses. We're trying to open something new, not perpetuate the sleep of ordinary consciousness with familiar sensation."

Elizabeth gave an overview of the Vision Parlor stations and then focused on a new technology. "One of the prominent features of the Vision Parlor is the Color Light Box."

And there was Neil, Greg observed, zooming up next to him like a hawk. Greg guessed the business models and investment plans running in Neil's imagination.

"Guests can fit the light boxes around their heads to experience a profound color light show. Colors are projected from high quality LED lights, where the tints are slowly changed. The lights also change in brilliance from bright to dull. We also use strobe effects and black lights sparingly—very sparingly. Light stability fosters stable shifts in consciousness. As cultures have preferences for certain standard colors, even to the point of preferring certain tints, we employ a variety of colors—especially those less familiar to the modern Western eye. The object of this experience is not to be fascinated at the many colors, which after all may become boring, or lead to distraction, but to study the effect of color and colored light on consciousness, or how to entrain consciousness to certain frequencies. We're also after an experiential awareness of color, not just an intellectual apprehension of symbolic correspondences, like red means this, blue means that. Nor just an analysis of changes in brain chemistry from neuroscience. We invite guests to become aware of how viewing these colors affect their mood, feeling, and awareness. We also have exhibits here for studying the elements of art, such as color combinations, contrast, and sharpness. We've released a beta version of the Color Light Box for personal or small group use, and we expect these to be available for purchase in the next six months."

Greg looked to Neil and nodded, raising his eye brows. Here was another example of a technology with market potential. Neil nodded back, admitting he was impressed.

"And you've heard me say it before," Elizabeth said. "The proceeds of the sales come back into our Sensory Parlor Collective and fund further color light research at the Bridge Institute."

Elizabeth guided the group into the next room, the only one with doors. "Here we have the Audition Parlor, our last. The doors and sound proofing on this parlor's walls ensure that the sounds we make here don't disturb the guests of other parlors." Elizabeth went around the room, station by station. "Here we use a variety of exquisitely crafted bells. We listen to the striking and sustenance of the bell tone. We have bells from around the world—Japan, China, Russia. They're forged in the old ways and they produce amazing sounds. Here," she said, advancing to the next station, "we listen to the interiors of drums. We maintain a collection of instruments from around the world, focusing especially on those which produce sounds unfamiliar to the modern Western cultivated ear. We have a special collection of instruments, devices, and recorded sounds linked to the evocation of higher modes of consciousness in a wide variety of spiritual traditions. We also have a collection of recorded sounds, what in the 1960's was called *musique concrete.* We have on this wall several sets of headphones. We listen to recorded bird calls, bug sounds, under water sounds recorded in the Bay and Pacific Ocean, sounds of the earth's movements, like shifting plates, recorded sounds from space. We also have a number of electronic sounds. The objective here, as with each of these parlors, is to explore experientially the range of possible human consciousness, and to evoke shifts in awareness through a refined stimulation of the senses."

Greg noticed Keith whispering something to Leah and pointing to the headphones. This was the first time he expressed something to Leah in the Sensory Parlor Collective. Greg intuited that Keith was a sensitive soul whose type was attuned to music. Had Keith visited before? Had he wished to return with Leah? No matter. But somehow Greg surmised Keith was an auditory learner.

The group left the last parlor at the end of the hall before the store. Elizabeth collected the group there. "This ends the sequence of galleries making up the Sensory Parlor Collective. Does anyone have any final questions?"

"Elizabeth?" Sara asked. "Why are these called *parlors*? You also just said *galleries*. In some sense, you could almost see them as galleries, especially with the Vision Parlor. Is there a difference?"

"Right. Very good question," Elizabeth said. "And very perceptive." Elizabeth took a moment of thought, as if deciding how personal to go on this question. "I'll tell you that when I originally conceived this idea, I did use the word gallery."

Elizabeth seemed drawn to Sara, Greg intuited.

"I wanted something with the introspection of an art gallery," Elizabeth said, "but without its sense of spectacle. I wanted to break the subject-object dichotomy implied by a gallery—the sense of being an audience looking at an exhibit. An exhibit, you'll note, also implies something outward. But in the case of the sensory parlor, while we have external prompts as you've seen, our focus is on the interior sensory experience, on sensory awareness. When I take people through the parlors," Elizabeth said, turning toward the foregoing rooms down the hall, "we focus on the intimacy of this inner experience and the corresponding expansion of consciousness. This can be shared with other guests in the Sensory Parlor, if you've come as a group. A parlor is a somewhat private receiving room, where people are mutually engaged, often in talk or entertainment. I settled on the term parlor, actually, partly to pick up on its older use, and also to revive the term and use it in a slightly new way. So the idea of the sensory parlor is that people come into this contained space for a meaningful group experience of awakening the senses and correspondingly, expanding their consciousness. The relative privacy of the parlor creates a container of safety and social intimacy which is a good condition for exploring the depths of our sensory experience."

Sara nodded, contemplating the implications of *gallery* and *parlor* and how these notions may relate to presenting her fine art works.

"And now," Elizabeth said, "we've come to the Collective store, which is the last space in this long corridor making up the Sensory Parlor Collective. If you'd like to browse for some of the things we saw briefly on the walk through, please do. And I'll encourage you to return to the Sensory Parlor Collective at your leisure and give yourself the benefit of deep, immersive experience in each parlor."

"Thanks Elizabeth," Randy said, stepping forward and then turning to the group. "See? Wise woman." Randy winked at Elizabeth, who smiled.

"Okay folks," he said, "it's almost 3:00. We'll take a break now and resume our tour outside at 3:15."

Greg turned to Sara. "I need to check my email."

"Okay," Sara said. "Meet you back in a few minutes." Off she went quickly, determined, Greg observed. His attention now was bent toward answering student emails back at University of Washington. He reached into his pocket and pulled out his mobile, slowly walking outside to the Plaza.

Reaching a grassy spot, Greg first quickly scanned for Mrs. Blocke. No voicemail. No email. Greg called her again. It rang. No answer. He ended the call. He sent her a brief email before moving on to his students.

25

Mark walked across the Research Access Office to Jackie's open door. He knocked casually and walked in. "Hey, do you have a minute?"

"Sure," Jackie said, looking at her screen projection. "Just a second." Mark sat down. She typed a few things and then turned, looked up. "What's up?"

Mark pointed to her screen. "I sent you something."

"Already?"

"Yeah. I'm still compiling, but given the urgency I thought you'd like to see some preliminary findings."

"Okay." Jackie opened the document, scrolled, read.

"Mueller's on the boards of at least two game companies," Mark said. "And I found that he's recently joined the Online Games Network."

"The Online Games Network?"

"I'm a member. So when I found the two companies, I just looked there to corroborate my search. One of them, BlackDog, has a page, and it lists Mueller as a board member. So I clicked on his profile. He's a new member."

"A new member."

"Yeah. Of Online Games Network. He joined last month."

Jackie turned to the profile page. "That's a key data point. Not enough, but important."

"His profile says he's an investor. It doesn't say his firm, nor his investments. But it does suggest to me that he's positioning himself to game companies as an investor. And he's recently joined the Game Developer's Forum, too."

"Okay. This is interesting."

At 3:15, the orientation tour reconvened on a grassy lawn outside the Sensory Parlor Collective. "Now that we're all back," Randy said, "let's head this way to Bayside Village Community Housing."

Greg quickly pulled out his mobile again and checked as he walked. Still, no voicemail. No email. "Why isn't she getting back to me?" he asked aloud to himself.

"Who?" Sara asked.

Greg looked up. "Mrs. Blocke."

"Relax, Greg. Roger said he'd help move it along."

Randy stopped. "We'll jump on the Bayside Village Tram, here." A round, olive-green platform bed made of a contemporary hard rubber material was level with the ground and the track itself. "This will give us a little experience of futurism," Randy said with a jovial ring in his voice as he walked up to the track. "Imagine you're in a space age, science fiction film, and the answer to all of our transportation woes of the modern age has now been answered by this singular technology." Randy held up his mobile device triumphantly and clicked to call the tram.

The group stood around Randy, anticipating. A few people looked up and down the track in both directions.

"I'd say our robotic tram is one of the nicer, techy features of the Bayside Village," Randy said, buying time. "It links up all the areas of the Village very efficiently, which reduces the need for every family to own their own private electric vehicle. We've reduced the need for on-campus parking lots and traffic management. We've also increased campus safety by eliminating private on-campus vehicles. Anyway…the tram should be coming…."

Randy checked his mobile.

The group waited.

No tram.

"Nice track," Neil said. That was good for a few laughs. Randy continued. "Actually, the track and trams themselves are an information system, collecting data like…"

"Here it comes," a woman called out.

An empty tram approached from the right, the bell ringing as it approached. It looked stately as it slowed to a halt, with decorous features like a San Francisco cable car. But the tram was lighter, leaner, less bulky. Riding low to the ground, it seemed almost to hover over the grass. The connection of wheel to rail was so efficient that virtually no sound issued from the contact.

"Welcome to the Bayside Village Tram," a female voice exuded from the overhead speakers. "This is an on-call tram. If you are the requestor, please state your name and destination."

"Randy Seton, Bayside Village Community Housing," Randy answered, boarding first. "Party of twenty-two."

The computer voice spoke from the tram. "Hi, Randy and Orientation Tour. Trip confirmed. This is your on-call tram. Please board carefully and hold on to the hand rails." The tour participants boarded at ground level and seated.

Greg and Sara took a seat on the left side. Neil swung around to the seat ahead of them.

"Are you ready now?" the tram voice asked.

"Yes," Randy said.

The tram began to roll forward. "Your on-call tram will deliver you to your destination, Bayside Village Campus Housing, by the shortest available route," the tram voice said again. "At your prior instructions, this car will not stop for other passengers along the route."

The tram rolled along quietly at a swift pace, winding around the Village, transporting the group, driverlessly, out of the Plaza, past the Bayside Village School and around gardens and an animal farm toward Community Housing.

"Oh, I want to go there with Tara," Sara said to Greg as she turned and looked at the passing scene, her hair tossing in the wind in the window seat. Greg turned, following her gaze. She turned back again. "The animal farm," she said, seeing his question.

"Ah," he said.

Sara sat back, gazed up. Then she noticed the posts and ceiling of the tram. She pointed it out to Greg. He looked up, focused his eyes on the ceiling. Superficially the outlines of the decoration appeared as the art style of a San Francisco cable car. On closer inspection, Greg saw another instance of sacred art like they found at the Bayside Village Art Center. Behind the dominant design patterns were intricate webs of mathematical patterns of toroidal rings in-filled with little critters—frogs, crabs, quail, clapper rail, reeds, cord grass, and fish. "Wow," Greg said in a passionate whisper.

"What happens if you're not the requestor?" Neil asked loudly, above the wind passing through. Neil and Randy discussed tram route logistics. Greg watched, wondered at Neil's interest. Neil nodded at Randy's points.

As the wind blew past the tram, Greg leaned forward to Neil in the next row. "Analyzing service logistics?"

"Yes, yes," Neil said with a turn of his head and subtle smile.

The tram finally delivered the group to an enclave of two octagon townhouse buildings in meadows of high grass close to the wetlands. "Okay, let's step off here," Randy said. He walked the group to a courtyard, garden and playground.

Randy led the group to the courtyard of Bayside Village Community

Housing. Before the group stood a pair of four-story octagon residence halls sided with Berkeley Brown Shingle. Beyond them a field of tall grasses stretched to the wetlands of the San Francisco Bay.

Greg marveled. So this is it, he thought.

Randy pulled out his mobile and placed a quick call as he walked. "Bill?....Hi, we're just arriving in the courtyard…Okay." He put away his mobile.

Randy reached a three foot high wall layered in Bridge Tiles surrounding an attractive courtyard between the two residential complexes. He turned around to face the group. "This is the Bayside Village Community Housing. It offers residence mainly for Bridge Institute faculty, students, and staff, but also some Bayside Village special programs. Keeping with the original vision for the Bayside Village, Community Housing has been designed for communal living."

Sara braced herself. This was Greg's long-time interest. She noticed her reticence and recalled the open-minded posture she promised she'd take on the trip. But Sara just couldn't see herself living in a commune like Greg wanted to do—in Seattle or here. What about a family home with a yard? What about her art studio now that they've finally moved out of an apartment too small for it in Seattle?

"The buildings and grounds were designed with the assumption of community," Randy said. "Kitchen units are small and shared since most residents eat in the Bayside Village Dining Commons. Buildings share common living spaces, from study rooms, meeting rooms, and laundry facilities, to storage, tool sheds, and bike garage. So, private rooms and apartments are a little smaller than most modern American accommodations, which are designed for nuclear family households to be independent and self-sufficient."

Keith inched his way to Greg and Sara, holding Leah's hand. "I actually live here," he whispered. "It's really cool!"

"Really," Greg said, with interest. "I love intentional communities."

Sara smiled, but recoiled inwardly.

"The Bayside Village Community Housing was built up from scratch," Randy said, "after we acquired the campus property. Previously there was no housing here, in part owing to industrial zoning, and in part owing to the historical toxicity of the land from industrial dumping, which has largely been remediated. We're still working to clean it up. But thanks to these efforts, we obtained permits to build our Community Housing.

Greg scanned for Neil and saw him standing alone before a field of tall grass talking on his mobile. Interesting pattern, Greg thought again.

A middle-aged man with a trim beard and fashionable but quiet shirt and blue jeans exited a townhouse door inside the courtyard. He walked leisurely to the group, settling himself on the tiled half-wall bordering a garden just behind Randy, listening to his presentation. He looked out over the group, studying its members.

Greg watched the man, registering his manner. On a first impression, Greg trusted his unassuming yet cultivated presence, his deep eyes, his wise reserve and pleasant, relaxed smile.

Sara studied the Bridge Tiles on the wall where the man leaned— different from those seen elsewhere on campus.

Randy acknowledged the man with a nod and continued. "The construction of the housing units was funded through bond financing managed through our nonprofit company, Bayside Village Properties, which, unusually, is an employee-owned property management firm. And you'll notice in the courtyard here that the same tile work we found at the Art Center using the famous Bridge Tile," Randy said, turning to the wall, "is also used here. And while we can't go inside the houses at this time," Randy waved his hand to his left, "I will say that you'd find wall paper, textiles, and tile work used in the interior decoration as well. Anyway, some of the Institute faculty, students and staff live together here in residential community.

"In the neighborhood immediately north of the campus," Randy said, pointing farther to his left, "Bayside Village Properties has also acquired five housing units in a row for Institute faculty, students and staff. Those are larger units and residents there live a bit more independently, but they still live communally in a cohousing arrangement."

"That's where Roger and Jenny live," Greg said to Sara.

"Where?"

"In one of those off-campus houses. We'll see it tomorrow night."

Sara nodded.

"It's also the case," Randy said, "that faculty members, students and staff live in the surrounding cities of Berkeley, Albany, and El Cerrito, and so on. But for now, let's focus on our Bayside Village Community Housing, here."

Sara found herself wondering how the units looked inside. Were they decorated like the Lodge—the wallpaper, tiles, and other features? Curiosity quietly stirred in her, mixed with reticence.

"The new buildings at the Bayside Village," Randy said, "including Bayside Village Community Housing, are built in the highest standards for green building design. Not only do they conserve as well generate energy. They're also living buildings. You can see here, for instance, that the roofs are alive with grasses and plants." Randy pointed to the roof tops, four stories up, with little tufts of grass poking up over the edge. "It doesn't rain much in California, and we're highly dependent on a few rivers and declining ice pack in the Sierra mountains. So in many of our buildings, we harvest rainfall and even fog from the roofs in bladders inside the walls where it's circulated to heat and cool the buildings, and then used in the dry months to water the plants. You'll see that the bricks in the walls have lips for small plants, fed by rainwater collected in the bladder. The courtyard also has a rich garden, picnic patio, and playground."

Sara was caught for a moment, admiring the ecological design, appreciating the beauty.

"So at this point," Randy said, "let me introduce Bill Chapman, our Director of Residential Community for the Bayside Village. Bill oversees the community living program and serves as a liaison and bridge to other communities across the planet. He brings wisdom to our residential community, and he has a lot to offer." Randy turned to Bill and opened out his hand.

"Thank you Randy," Bill said, standing up and walking casually to the front of the group. Randy stepped back and leaned against the Bridge-Tiled wall where Bill was sitting.

"Some of you might be thinking that it's pretty neat to have an intentional community on campus," Bill started, "and co-housing just north of campus. It makes housing easier for faculty, students, and staff. And it kind of fits with the novelty of everything done here at the Bayside Village. But while these are, indeed, features of community living at Bayside Village Community Housing, residents don't just live here like they live in any other housing, and they don't just get a convenient location on campus. We live differently. And for that reason, it may also be said that some people may chose not to live with us, in fact, since they may not be interested in living this way."

Right, Sara thought.

"The faculty, students, and staff of the Bridge Institute are eligible to live in Community Housing," Bill said. "And a few others in our special projects. Many who wouldn't otherwise have a need of it have chosen, nevertheless, to make a lifestyle adjustment to come and live with us. They come for the experience of community living, and for the educational experience.

"We do the typical things many intentional communities do," Bill said. "Like, we have a consensus-based decision processes. We live together by a set of principles and guidelines called the Bayside Village Community Housing Handbook. We share more resources in common so that each household, or dorm room, doesn't need to procure duplicate resources. We share chores so we all don't need to spend our lives in labor, and we can enjoy more leisure time together or use it, say, for spiritual practice. We offer our lives to each other in deeper ways that are unfortunately quite uncommon in our larger culture. As it is in the Christian tradition, we strive to bear one another's burdens. We talk, share, and inquire. We take an active interest in each other's lives. So we share these many things in common with other intentional communities and some cohousing neighborhoods."

Greg decided he liked Bill. He would have to meet with him, if time permitted on this trip. And he liked the unfolding presentation. The thought, or fantasy, he realized, of living communally once again, stirred in him. This visit stoked a longing for life together. He had let it go years ago, and he still let it go, now—a renunciation without remorse. He simply witnessed, without attachment, the interest now aroused in him.

"Intentional community isn't new," Bill continued. "In fact, I qualify as a Director of Residential Living because I have lived in several other intentional communities in America and Europe. But what we are trying to do here with intentional community, at Bayside Village Community Housing, is new. Our community living is focused on recovering a way of living together that both supports and expresses spiritual practices and lifestyle choices based on sacred sciences, which is the theme of the Bayside Village"

Greg whispered to Sara, "I want to meet with him and ask about that— lifestyle choices based on sacred sciences." Sara smiled and nodded, acknowledging Greg, showing reserve.

"Community living is often associated with creating a better life," Bill said. "We, too, strive to live better. We provide here the seeds of a new civilization—in our case the seeds of new ways to live together."

Greg listened with rapt attention. Living together for this—for sacred science, for the seeds of a new civilization. This pushed his interest beyond fascination into active yearning. He longed for this. His renunciation may require practice now. How to be non-attached to an idea he felt strongly?

"Okay, so that's a high level view," Bill said, as wind gently blew through the tall grasses beyond the courtyard. "Let me now give you a taste of what it might be like to live together here as we do."

Sara felt the afternoon sun shining hot on her neck and shoulders through the crisp California air. She turned her eyes to the famous Bridge Tiles in the wall Randy now leaned on. Half listening to Bill go on, she wondered again about the interior décor. The Bridge Tiles here have a different pattern. What's the pattern inside?

"Residents here set aside an hour every Sunday evening for house meetings, which they lead in turns. In house meetings residents discuss a wide range of topics, from current events and health to politics, society, and the environment. Or sometimes they talk about the quality of community life, and how to live together more effectively. Sometimes they discuss feelings or fears or the deeper things going on in their lives. The residents have also set aside Thursday evening for a common supper here in the Bayside Village Community Housing. Sometimes they have guests, and in this way, too, they are sharing their experience of life together."

Greg leaned to Sara, shielded his eyes from the sun. "We're meeting with Josh and Trish here for dinner Thurs…"

Sara nodded quickly. Okay, Greg thought. I shouldn't push.

"Some residents have set time aside for a meditation group, prayer group, or sharing circle, which they design and lead in turn in the common spaces here. Friends from the larger community are often invited, so that in this way, the space of the Bayside Village Community Housing is used to share our vision of life together.

"In short, many residents here have found community living a very satisfying way to live, a way that meets their values. They participate in each other's lives in a way far beyond what they could do living alone.

"But I should say…" Bill's voice changed, and he paused, marking a warning. "In addition to the lofty, idealistic side of living together, there are quite mundane experiences. Day to day chores are rotated amongst residents, daily conversations are shared in the hall way, people brush their teeth together, parents and other adults play together with the children. Lest our life together be seen as a panacea, many residents find community living challenging. It adds a layer of complexity to student life, married life, family life, in trying to get along together with other residents. For people do sometimes offend one another; lifestyles and values aren't always synchronistic; people don't always have the same mood or interest in being together. Nor are people always kind, supportive or loving, despite their best intentions. And it's sometimes challenging to find the willingness or capacity to live up to the values we espouse as most worthy to live by."

"Hmm," Sara said to herself. That's honest, she thought. She decided she trusted this man, Bill, and felt his integrity. Whatever she might feel about community, about wanting her own space, he was honest.

"When living together challenges us, we must find again those enduring values for which we decided we prefer to live together. So we return to the basic reasons we offer community living, and residents return to their basic motivation for choosing it over living separately in the larger Bay Area."

Sara leaned to Greg, decided to say it now. "That's honest."

Greg nodded, saw that Sara perked up at this.

She said to Greg, "I'd like to see inside."

Greg looked at her, eyebrows raised.

"Not saying I want to move there. Just want to see what it looks like."

"We'll get a tour for Thursday dinner."

26

Roger sat typing at his desk in Avicenna Hall, dashing off a text message to President Steve Bateson.

> Steve, I talked with Chris Mueller this morning about Friday's
> AlignIt Commons board meeting. A few matters arose. Possible
> conflict of interest, possible misuse of influence via gifts. Like to
> discuss. What's your schedule? Cheers, Rog

Roger got up, walked to the Research Access Office, a quarter way around
the Bridge Institute quadrangle.

Jackie sat forward, projected the document in the air above the
conference table in the Research Access Office for Roger and Jeff. She
stabilized the image from her mobile, then picked up the mobile for a laser
pointer and pointed at the projected image. "So it appears these are recent
investments for Mueller," Jackie said, pointing and circling with a thin ray
of red. "And here's his new membership in the Game Network."

"It's very astute of you to check that," Roger said to Mark. He sat
down next to Jackie.

"Thanks," Mark said. "Yeah, and I wondered if you or Jeff have any
professional memberships in gaming associations. We might find more
stuff like this."

"It's a good idea," Jeff said. "I didn't think of those networks. I have
some memberships and I'll check them."

"Okay, so we have two game companies, now," Roger said. "And they
appear to be recent investments. So it's possible Mueller is just responding
to fresh investment opportunities."

"We rechecked his company disclosures," Jackie said. "I don't think
we missed anything before. If these are new game companies, we're
probably not dealing with a failure to disclose."

"Its probably just me that has a conspiracy theory working here," Jeff
said, with a smirk on his face. He sat back against the wall. "It's just—this
is GameIt's first competitive threat. I'm just really uncomfortable. I don't
like not knowing what we're dealing with here."

"I hear you," Roger said. "I think at this point, for me, I'm just trying
to discover the landscape. The next question is what do we do with it."

"Well let me ask you this," Jackie said. She leaned forward toward Jeff.
"Just to get this out on the table. Is there any room for GameIt to delimit
its rights in gaming? Are there other fields of use that don't overlap your
commercialization plans?"

"Maybe," Jeff said. "I'd have to look at this carefully. But we're talking
about Mueller rushing in and grabbing at stuff while we're operating in a
trust-based commons model. That's what bothers me the most right now."

"I understand," Jackie said. "I'm not suggesting we do give any rights.

And I don't know if Mueller is the right person. But just to be clear for ourselves—is there even a discussion here? You've got the exclusive rights in games. If there are other fields of use we could subdivide, and if you're willing to renegotiate, there's a discussion. If not, no discussion. Doesn't matter if Mueller has game companies. I want to understand first if you have any rights to give."

Jeff took a deep inhale, breathed out through tight lips. "I mean, maybe, I don't know. Maybe. He looked up at the ceiling, thought for a minute. "Okay, I'm uncomfortable saying it. But there are probably other areas where GameIt isn't going to exploit AlignIt technology and develop games. Sure."

"So a conversation is possible, at least," Jackie said. "You still hold exclusive rights. And between GameIt and the Bridge Institute, we're not going to ask to renegotiate a license with you that we think would harm you or the technology or us. So the next question is whether Mueller and his companies present the right opportunity."

"That comes back to me again," Roger said. "I need to talk to Mueller before the board meeting to air some of these concerns and find out what he's up to. And how he's approaching this. Because I don't like what happened this morning."

Back at the GameIt office down the hall from Jackie, Jeff called his team together for a quick confab in the meeting room. When everyone settled around the conference table, Jeff said, "I've gotten wind of a possible competitive threat to GameIt."

Jeff delicately explained the situation about Chris Mueller, about game companies he wants to bring into the AlignIt Commons.

"Well can he do that?" asked Cindy, the middle-aged CFO, the business smarts of GameIt. "We're supposed to be the only game company in the Commons."

"That's right," Jeff said. "But it looks like Mueller's trying to push in. I can't say how just yet."

"I'm surprised someone's trying to copycat us," Landon said. He was the wizard of code. The geek brain of GameIt. "We're way out front."

"We are. We were," Jeff said. "But evidently, a VC has now seen the potential of what GameIt is doing and wants to butt in and bump us over and grab up what we're doing. So I'd like us to put on another hat right now. We're not just a bunch of design geeks and coders. We need to do some intelligence gathering. I want each of us now to watch the shop more carefully."

Jeff explained how Mark in the Research Access Office found traces of Mueller's recent membership activity in the Online Games Network, and the implications he drew from it. "So here's what I want us to do. Each of us has networks, memberships, and contacts. So I want each of us to see what we can find about Mueller. I want us to find any game companies he's connected with, any interests or strategies or…whatever you can find. This needs to be quick. And it needs to be discreet. Don't go leaving traces about this. Don't mail on lists or post on blogs. Just find what you can find. And give me what you have tomorrow by mid-morning. Okay?"

27

Randy walked the group out of the enclave of Bayside Village Community Housing townhouses, down a path by an open field of long grasses beside the bay, and down another path leading to the waterfront.

Greg noticed strong memories aroused in him as he left Community Housing. The prospect of community living piqued his interest. How am I going to deal with this in my life, he wondered. Can I live this or not?

Randy turned around to face the group, walking backwards again. "We'll end our tour today with an exploration of our Bayside Village waterfront.

"We're fortunate to live, study, and research right here in the San Francisco Bay Area, one of the world's greatest and most diverse estuaries. The Bay coastline is a sensitive habitat of shorebirds, waterfowl, oysters and salmon. Unfortunately, with the impact of modern Western settlement and civilization—from filling in wetlands for residential and commercial development to shipping and oil spills, to the high impact of industrial pollution, the San Francisco Bay is one of this country's most profoundly altered aquatic ecosystems. At Bayside Village we recognize that our regional problem of overdevelopment is but a small instance of a global crisis of relationship to the earth, water, and ecology. For this reason, we've taken earth, water and ecology as research priorities at the Bridge Institute. We're developing a new relationship to nature. This orientation is critical to our waterfront, docks, and marine science program."

As they walked down the road stretching between housing and the water front, Greg noticed in a field to their right a few thatched roof buildings made of logs and reeds and a round house built into the earth. It looked to him like a reconstructed Native American settlement or a ritual site. Greg pointed it out to Sara. "I wonder what that is."

Sara looked, nodded.

Randy turned, led the group down a path to the wetlands, to an observation platform with a small educational and activity shed. Greg breathed in the Bay aroma. The smell of the mud flats at low tide wafted through the air.

"We call this the Ohlone Observation Deck," Randy said. "From here, you can get a good view of the Siegel Marsh area over there," Randy said pointing, "and the Taylor Slough, in that direction, and the Bay at large."

"The industrialized Bay," a man said. He pointed ahead to the Bay bridge, and a cargo ship hauling refers out of the Port of Oakland.

"This is true," Randy said. "Natural setting plus industrial impact. But even today, the San Francisco Bay estuary is home to a wide array of fish and wildlife. We have crab, salmon, egrets, ducks, seals….If you look farther out, you'll occasionally see the ducks and seals. But closer at hand, the Siegel Marsh here is about nine acres of restored bay land habitat. If you look here, you'll find grebes, egrets, willets, and herons. With the restored salt marshes here, we've seen a return of the endangered harvest mouse and California clapper rail populations. You will see quite a few of them now."

"The Clapper Rail," Sara said to Greg. "That's Clappy, Tara's toy."

"Right," he said.

"It's so cute."

"You'd have to get right up into the mudflats, pickleweed and cordgrass," Randy said, "to see the crabs, mussels, snails, worms and insects. But that's also the diet of the clapper rail, so we want to leave it alone. If you want to come back here after the tour, you can rent binoculars from this station, or bring your own—or just rely on the naked eye. You can look at the pictures on these plaques to get an idea of what you're looking for, and you can read about these wonderful creatures. When you spot them, you'll see them foraging for food, building shelters, or nesting. We're in the Clapper Rail's nesting and mating season now, which runs February to August."

"We should bring Tara here," Sara said to Greg.

"I noticed you called this the Ohlone Observation Deck," a middle aged man said. "And I saw that Ohlone settlement on the walk. There must be a story to this?"

"Yes, thanks," Randy said. "I was coming to it. The Ohlone, Patwin and Miwok peoples have lived here in the Bay Area in balance with nature, some say for ten thousand years. In fact, many still do live in the Bay Area, but obviously not in the way they used to before European settlers arrived. The Ohlone lived here in what we now call the East Bay. So to remember and honor their historical presence here, to honor their ways of living in greater harmony with nature—certainly greater harmony than modern Western civilization has lived here on this land—and to learn more about their old ways, we have named this the Ohlone Observation Deck.

"Here's an Ohlone story that gives us a hint of their ways." He pointed to a wooden display bolted to the railing with the words burnished and painted in black. "Now, consider the Coyote Story as you look out from the deck to our wild friends.

"One day Coyote and his wife went to the ocean. Or I like to say, Coyote and his wife came here to the Bay. And Coyote told his wife all about the mussels, the crabs, the sea lions, and the octopus. He told her not to be afraid of the ocean. Evidently she must have feared the sea animals. He told her that all of those sea creatures were their relatives. The mussels, crabs, and sea lions—they were uncles and aunts, grandmothers and grandfathers, cousins, and so on. Now, there's a little more to the story. But one thing we remember as we work with restoring our natural coastline habitat is that these animals are our relatives, our family.

"So for us, today, standing here on the Ohlone Observation Deck, we remember that these beings in the Siegel Marsh—the crab, salmon, egrets, ducks, seals, grebes, willets, herons, egrets, harvest mouse and clapper rail—we hold these as our relations. They're our uncles and aunts, grandmothers and grandfathers, cousins, and so on. Why is this important? Because at Bayside Village, we do more than honor the memory that Ohlone people were here, and still live around the East Bay. We try also to remember the awareness they held—like seeing these animals as our relations. We tell this story to help us remember not just the story, but the awareness, the consciousness, the view, the cosmology. And just maybe we can sometimes step into that consciousness, too. At the Ohlone Observation Deck, we invite you to try it."

Greg looked out from the Deck to the immediate marshes, the grasses, the birds, the tide. What kind of consciousness would the Ohlone have had? How would they have seen the Bay?

"So," Randy said, "the Ohlone Observation Deck is one piece of our effort. The Bayside Village has also dedicated some land for use by Ohlone people—a recreated round house for community meetings, and a sweat lodge for traditional Ohlone dances and ceremonies..."

"That's what it was," Greg said to Sara. She nodded.

"On our way from Community Housing," Randy said, "we passed the Ohlone Learning Center, which the Bayside Village hosts and the Ohlone operate, for educational and cultural programs about the native California peoples, cultures, and ways of living with nature. And we have spaces for Ohlone, Patwin and Miwok people to sell or trade traditional crafts, or other crafts or works they've created, if they're consistent with our Bayside Village mission."

"Now, another little bit of history—*after* the Ohlone people's land and ways were taken over. We've had nearly two hundred years of adverse human impact on the Bay's biological diversity—everything from filling in wetlands for real estate development, to heavy industrial shipping, intensive agriculture, manufacturing of toxic chemicals, and more. Consequently, the native habitats of the Bay Area have experienced profound devastation.

Presently the Bay Area is home to more than five hundred diverse types of fish, amphibians, reptiles, birds, and mammals. And if you count invertebrates, the number shoots up substantially—to well over a thousand. There may have been many more species, before European settlers accelerated urban development of the Bay Area in about the 1850's, and those species may be forever lost to us now. If we go back to old diaries, letters, and other descriptions of the first European explorers in the San Francisco Bay, we find descriptions of the skies being darkened by birds, so great was their number. The Bay waters were teaming with fish. Sadly we find comparatively few birds and fish today."

"Wow," Greg said to Sara. "Sounds like Puget Sound and Washington's clear-cut forests…"

Sara raised her eyebrows and nodded.

"The California clapper rail—again, its this small hen-like bird right here," Randy said, pointing to one of the plaques, "this bird thrives in these salt and brackish tidal marshes. At one time, these little guys were everywhere in the Bay Area and to a lesser degree, they were up the coast as far north as Humboldt Bay and as far south as Morrow Bay. But just a few years ago there were almost extinct.

"We've done a lot for these little birds at Bayside Village, which is why we take pride in their recovery. You've probably seen images of the clapper rail around campus. We've taken the clapper rail as a sort of mascot of the Bayside Village and an emblem of many efforts toward ecological restoration."

"And for kids," Sara added, "you have the cutest little clapper rail stuffed animal toys. Our daughter got one yesterday."

"Yes, that's right," Randy said. "If you'd like to support the Bayside Village and clapper rail habitat restoration, you can help us spread awareness of the clapper rail by purchasing a clapper rail toy for the kids in your life. A few of the shops here carry them. They're all made locally, of locally sourced organic materials—some parts are made onsite, here, in a worker-owned toy shop. Thanks for bringing that up.

"Now, I know some of you are on this tour as an orientation to our ecological restoration work. So let me just say a few words about industrial pollution and remediation. Before the Richmond Chemical Company owned it, this property was once owned by The California Gun Powder Company, from 1870 to 1950. For some seventy years explosives were manufactured here, leaving behind mercury fulminate. And it got into everything—the ground, the marshes, the Bay. Next door to us, over there," Randy said, pointing to the east of the Bayside Village, "from 1896 to 1961, the Baker Chemical Company, manufactured industrial chemicals including sulfuric acid, and left behind pyrite cinder waste which we've found on our property, here. Even up to 1992, RCC manufactured pesticides over there. Well, of course this is a sad story for our little friends in the tidal marshes and mudflats. As I said, the California clapper rail almost went extinct. Thanks to remediation efforts by several federal, state, and nonprofit agencies and universities beginning in 2002, the Clapper Rail, along with the harvest mouse and many crops and shrubs in the marsh and ecotone habitats, are making a comeback in this area once heavily polluted by industrial waste. At the Bayside Village, we're beneficiaries of a substantial public and private investment in baylands restoration, and it's a very big part of our mission and mandate to maintain and grow this work."

"Well, folks." Randy clapped his hands once, loudly. "It's 5:00, and this ends our tour today. And this ends my tour guide role with you, except for the Raymond Lully Museum tour tomorrow." The group spontaneously clapped and playfully cheered Randy. "Okay, okay. I'll sign autographs now." Then he briefly outlined the remaining orientation schedule through the evening and the next day.

Sara turned to Greg, "We have to get Tara. It's 5:05."

"Yeah," Greg said, turning to leave with her. "It's been a long afternoon. I hope she's had a good day."

Greg and Sara walked briskly up the central path from the marshes to the Bayside Village School and Daycare. At the daycare, Greg and Sara walked into the gate and again found Tara by the picnic table playing with new-found friends.

"Mommy," Tara said, and came running for a hug. Sara embraced her. Indeed, it was a long first day.

28

After taking quiet family time together in the Lodge, Greg, Sara and Tara arrived at the reception hall adjoining the Dining Commons and walked in for the evening's Sacred Science Game Reception. Just inside the door, a booth was positioned with a skirt draping down from the table. A banner with "GameIt" written in large, bold letters hung behind the table. Game products were displayed for sale, and GameIt representatives were stationed for demonstrations.

"Welcome to the GameIt reception," a young woman said at the front door with a pleasant, enthusiastic demeanor. Probably a Bridge Institute student, Greg imagined. Seeing Tara, she said, "We have a children's game section on this side. Please help yourself to the food bar in the middle."

"Thanks," Greg said. He looked around. The crowd was larger than the orientation. Who were the others, Greg wondered. He noticed game stations established about the room, with small crowds gathered around.

To the left, immersive game stations were the site of action and brilliant light. In the middle of the room and separated by dividers, large plant pots and sound barriers, an area was established with tables and board games, couches with parlor games and role playing games. Another area to the right side was set up with both regular and low tables for children's games.

Tara asked, "Daddy, what games are we going to play?"

"I don't know, Sweetie. There are lots of games for everyone—for children and for grown ups. And we also have food like last night."

"Is Sasha here?"

"Who is Sasha?"

"Daddy! She's my friend!"

"Oh. Did you meet Sasha at Bayside Village School today?"

"Yes."

"Maybe she's here. I don't know if she is part of our group."

"Why don't we start out together in the kid's section," Sara said, "and then switch off watching Tara there?"

"Good plan," Greg said. As the family walked to the children's game area, Greg quickly scanned the room for people to speak with. No one recognizable. Then in the children's area, Greg and Sara explored games with Tara until one captured her attention.

Tara sat down and pulled knobs. Greg and Sara sat near her, watching, encouraging, interacting. Sara observed the spread of children's games and took in the whole atmosphere. Tara moved to another game and then another. She settled down again, applied herself.

"These are clever games," Sara said to Greg, watching Tara. "Look at how they form a sense of pattern in the child. These aren't just commercial gimmicks or superficial, single-goal oriented games—they have real educational content." Greg nodded. "And they have aesthetic integrity. I really like that for her."

"She seems to be taking to them," Greg said. "I brought some Bayside Village Dollars. Maybe we could get one or two for her if she stays with it."

"Ooh, but let's be careful about our spending. We don't have much in the bank this month."

"I bet they're not cheap. But this is special."

"Why don't you look around first? I know you want to meet the GameIt guy. I also want to."

"Really?" Greg said.

"Yeah. But I think we should get Tara to bed by 8:00. I'll stay with her if you want to look right now."

"Sure. Why don't I take a half hour and then switch?"

"Okay."

Greg walked the room, explored the stations, surveying the games in broad glances. He went first to the immersive, electronic games, advancing booth to booth, game to game. The console displays and immersive formats were vivid, brilliant. They showcased archetypal themes and stunningly beautiful, strong, and grotesque characters. Game players wore head gear for audio visual immersion. Some wore shoulder pads, gloves, knee pads, and slip-on footies—each having wearable body sensors feeding body position data to the game. The game world and avatar of the suited players were displayed in the flat screen projection in one game, projected in a 3-d hologram in another. Vivid scenes with fabulous creatures shimmered holographically around the gamer, presenting fascinating game tasks, symbols, threats and opportunities. Greg searched displays and projections for underlying patterns, for structures that could be organized ontologically. How does GameIt run on AlignIt, he wondered. But amidst the game scenes, the foundational patterns and relationships were complex, elegant, nonobvious.

Greg moved to the middle section of the room with board games, parlor games, and role playing games. He strode down a crowded aisle of couches and seats arranged around tables. Some games unfolded mathematical patterns. Others featured language challenges. Still others were strategy-oriented. Greg again observed, scanning for underlying patterns susceptible to ontological elaboration. Where is AlignIt implicit in the game design?

One game, The Palace, caught Greg's enduring attention. He stopped there, by two couches with a game table in the middle, and a group of people standing around. The Palace featured two game boards side by side. Two women and two men sat playing, rolling dice and moving pieces around the two boards. One board appeared as a feminine platform with curvilinear patterns. The other appeared to have a masculine theme with square and angular patterns. Here the players advanced on the game boards by the role of dice, moving ahead or behind by taking a card with a task or special condition. Each board had its own card deck. Listening to the players, Greg distinguished that each deck presented the rules and opportunities for its corresponding game board. But landing on certain positions on either board meant the player must jump to a corresponding position on the other game board, changing bodies, changing genders, changing lifetimes. Or was it going into the contrasexual sides of oneself in this lifetime? Greg studied, uncertain about this. Clearly, the masculine and feminine game worlds interacted, with players moving back and forth across the boards as chance may land them or choice may move them. Sometimes the players were affected by affinities or disaffinities, established by the changing positions and qualities of the other players. Greg felt himself enraptured in the fascinating possibilities in game play, rich in organized, complex patterns. He stood absorbed, focusing.

Greg came to himself, then, felt his time running out. He hadn't taken in the whole room. He looked about. He finally spotted GameIt founder Jeff Baker across the room by the immersive games, with a group of gamers huddled around a holographic heroine.

Greg approached him. "Jeff?"

Jeff turned.

"Greg Cobb, University of Washington."

"Greg!" Jeff stepped aside, giving his full attention. "I hoped we'd meet tonight." He extended his hand and shook Greg's.

"Good to meet you in person."

"Roger told me you were here already—the full week, not just Wednesday to Friday."

"Yeah. I have interviews lined up all week, actually—for Bridge Institute and AlignIt."

"Great," Jeff said.

"I also brought my wife and daughter—they're in the kid's section."

"Good. Roger told me." Jeff turned. "We have a great children's section this time."

"Indeed! My daughter Tara's absorbed." Greg paused. "So we just arrived last night, and we've been in the orientation all day."

"Good plan," Jeff said. "That way you see what we're creating here. Although…Roger tells me you already have a sympathy with this vision."

"Yes, I'm tuned in to similar lines of thought."

"Hey, have you eaten yet?"

"No, actually I haven't."

"I haven't either—I've been welcoming and talking all this time. Let's grab a plate. Do you have a few minutes?"

"Sure."

"We can get a jump on our Wednesday meeting."

"Great," Greg said. He turned toward the food buffet in the middle of the room, replete with colorful, exotic dishes. Greg picked up a plate and eyed the dishes. He picked through the buffet offerings with tongs here, spoons there. Casserole, salads, breads. As he picked up Indian pekoras in tongs, he became aware of great affinity with Jeff. He liked him, felt attracted, felt a flow. Then he remembered. "I have just a short spot of time right now, since I'm here with my family. I'm switching off with my wife, Sara, in ten minutes. Then I'm on duty with my five year old, Tara, while Sara explores the room."

"Ah. Been there," Jeff said, picking up an egg role. "I have two boys, eight and ten. Which gives me a little more independence than a five year old. Have your wife and daughter eaten yet?"

"No. We just went right to the children's games."

"Why don't we bring 'em a plate and sit there?"

"Yeah, sure." That's considerate, Greg thought. He circled the table, fetched lasagna. What does Sara like? Eggplant, bean dish, vegetables. "This is an extraordinary reception. I'm really intrigued by your game worlds."

"Thanks. Yeah, it's a lot of fun to do these receptions." Jeff went for lasagna, olives, deviled eggs. "It works out well for the Bayside Village. It's a great evening event for orientations, delegations, and retreats. It gets people talking and connecting. And the games help illustrate what the Bridge Institute is about."

"What sacred science is about," Greg said.

"Yes."

"It's gotta be good for business too," Greg said, scooping up dolmas and sushi.

"It is. And, frankly, it's good for product refinement and market testing since we see what people like and don't like, where they get stuck and where they have fun."

Jeff waited for Greg as he filled another plate for Tara with pasta and a fruit salad. Then Jeff and Greg walked to the children's area.

29

"Sara," Greg said, "this is Jeff Baker, founder of GameIt."

Sara stood up and shook Jeff's hand. "Nice to meet you."

"Pleasure to meet you," Jeff said.

Seeing the food plates, Sara said, "Please, join us." Greg and Jeff pulled up chairs and sat down.

Greg handed a plate to Sara.

"And this is our daughter, Tara," Greg said, "...who has had a very long first day at the Bayside Village School and Daycare." He held a dolma up to her mouth, which she accepted.

"I see," Jeff said. "Hello Tara." She chewed, said hi, and continued with the puzzle before her.

"So you're here for the week?" Jeff asked Sara.

"Yeah. We're looking at the Bayside Village, the Bridge Institute, AlignIt. Greg's looking at AlignIt."

"What do you think so far?"

Sara looked at Greg and then to Jeff, "It's really amazing. We haven't shared our impressions yet. We just arrived yesterday, and we've been on tour all day today. But for me, it's very stimulating overall."

Greg felt Sara reaching out to Jeff. "Yeah," Greg said, "It's a lot to absorb in one day. But I'm really amazed by all we've seen. It's hard to imagine that so many of our shared interests and values can be concentrated in one place."

"Right, that is one feature of this place," Jeff said. "If you like this kind of stuff. Despite our considerable diversity of traditions here, there is a harmony of basic ideas, values, and practices. I'm immersed here every day, so it's easy to forget that."

"I haven't had a chance to look around yet, or read your materials or talk to people," Sara said, "so I hope this isn't an obvious question." She speared a slice of eggplant with her fork. "But did you create all of these games?"

"No, it's a good question," Jeff said. "Just a few. I'm a game developer myself. But only a small part of what's here tonight is my own creation. At this early phase, GameIt has scouted out a collection of games like these, based on certain philosophical and developmental criteria. You could call them sacred science games, though not all of them are. Much of what's here tonight is games we've found and brought together under one roof, so to speak. So we identify and sell these games as a short term path to revenue while we're developing and releasing original titles."

"That's good business savvy," Greg said.

"Which ones did you create?" Sara asked.

"Mainly, the ones there in the electronic, immersive game section."

"What's the other phase?" Greg asked.

"Ah, that's the part that may interest you. The second phase is developing new games on the AlignIt platform. And this is where your knack for sacred science comes in."

"We have quite some common ground," Greg said.

Sara cut small pieces of curry squash for Tara and bade her to take bites as she played.

"It amazes me that building sacred science games doesn't require explanation or warrant for you," Jeff said.

"Well, it's a question of what you mean by sacred science," Greg said. "But no, on the face of it, I'm quite at home. Sacred science requires application. Otherwise its just arm chair philosophy for an esotericist."

"You can't imagine how rare you are!" Jeff said, taking a fork of lasagna.

"Even here?"

"Well, okay—here it's a little oasis. I have discussions, give demonstrations, host game sessions. Most people who come here get it. They come here looking for it. But to take our game platform out into the world…Then it's a question of making connections in the game industry, in education, in other fields where we're building applications."

"Daddy, look!" Tara said. Greg looked at her game, her accomplishment. He affirmed her, stroked her head, watched a few moments, then returned his attention to Jeff, who started again.

"In the game industry, people want the exotic. And there are lots of exotic games—delving into the occult, mystical powers, metaphysical subjects. But it always has some dark element, something to do with lurid sex, power, and violence. It's a very adolescent focus, and one-sidedly masculine. The exotic is used superficially and romantically—to allure, but not to feed the soul. I get started in demonstrations with game companies, and initially people are interested when they hear words like mystical, archetypal, magical. But they want us to cut out the very parts we've developed the games for in the first place—the sacred science. And they want us to add trivial features that stimulate puerile interests. But what I'm after is to restore games for education, human development, even initiation." Greg's eyes lit up. He looked at Sara, then back. "Our games are no less compelling, intriguing, or challenging. But we're having some difficulty selling into big commercial publishers—at least initially. There isn't a ready pathway yet for games based on sacred science."

"I understand this very well," Greg said. "The role sacred science can play in providing a deeper archetypal basis of games."

"For now, at least, it's not what the game industry looks for. It wants entertainment, sensory stimulation, excitement, thrill, addiction. But not education and development, and certainly not spiritual training."

Sara looked up from her plate to Jeff, carefully following the train of his thought, moved by his integrity.

"Interesting," Greg said. "I can well imagine it, but I don't know the game industry."

"I get what you're saying," Sara said. "I work in industrial and graphic design at a boutique design shop in Seattle." Jeff shifted his attention to Sara. "I've had two accounts with game companies. And the design specs, market segmentation, and psychographics they give us....Clearly the games we've worked on are not focused on higher aspirations like they could be—which I guess is what you're targeting. What about bypassing the game industry and going directly to consumers?"

Greg was proud of Sara's capacity in professional meetings, despite her protestations that she's not the best at small talk.

"Well, you've hit on it," Jeff said. "That's just what we do, in fact. It appears the most viable route. Except that I then have to front the capital and pay my own way for development, testing, production and marketing. It's one reason I've become a collector and distributor of sacred science games in addition to doing game development. When I'm selling other people's games, I can subsidize my own game development by revenue from game sales. It's slow-going, though. And I haven't given up on the game industry. I'm still hopeful something could open up."

"What about education?" Sara asked. "What's your experience there?"

"Even more closed than the game industry. Our educational system regards students as blank slates needing to be written on from the outside—by external programs. Education means delivering content, and making kids memorize and spit back. The vision I have of games is that they elicit the person's own recognition of deep archetypal patterns. Games can facilitate self-discovery and self-knowledge as much as deliver content."

"What about alternative schools?" Sara asked.

"That would seem a pathway. But most alternative schools that could be open to this, in terms of affinity with the content, are neo-Luddite—espousing some form of anti-tech romanticism."

"Daddy, what else do you have?" Tara asked, leaving her game. Greg held his plate so Tara could reach it. "Here, these egg roles are good." He pointed. "Try one."

"Anyway, not to bore you with my challenges in market adoption," Jeff said.

"Not at all," Greg said. "It's very interesting."

"Well," Jeff said, "I want to hear your background and what you would bring to AlignIt—and what you might be able to do in games."

"I'll let you two talk," Sara said. "I'm going to look around at the exhibits and see what you've made and collected here."

"Oh, Sara, definitely check out The Palace, in the middle," Greg said.

"That's one of mine, actually," Jeff said.

"Wow, really?" Greg exclaimed. "That's a cool game! I want to talk about that, too."

"Okay, I'll be back in a little while," Sara said.

"Alright," Greg said to Sara.

"It was really nice meeting you," Sara said, and shook Jeff's hand with a darling smile, and then walked off.

Greg turned to Jeff. "So, where to start? You're a member of the AlignIt Commons."

Jeff nodded. "Right."

"What's your experience working with AlignIt?" Greg tapped Tara and pointed to her unfinished egg role. She picked it up and nibbled some more.

"It's a very intimate experience. It's a tight community. We build game worlds on the AlignIt platform and create rich user experiences along the lines of sacred science. Right now, that's the bulk of the technical relationship. AlignIt has that software commons model..."

"Right."

"Which means," Jeff said, "that Commons members get access and grant back use rights to software assets created by using the platform so other members can use them." Greg nodded, his forehead furled as he listened. "GameIt grants back a lot of our models, data sets, and even some art work, for other Commons members to use. But the fact is that AlignIt Commons is still maturing—it doesn't have a diverse enough membership yet. The traffic, shared stuff, and uptake across the Commons is still building."

"Hmm," Greg said.

"What I contribute back isn't taken up by others because there aren't enough other companies for whom our grant backs are useful. Conversely, there aren't a lot of other members whose technical contributions to the AlignIt Commons are useful to GameIt. We need companies across many sectors, not direct competitors. So I like the idea of the commons in principal. But it needs time to mature. I don't think we'll attract more members until AlignIt itself matures. And maybe that's where you come in."

"Maybe. Do you work closely with Roger on any projects?"

Jeff spooned carrot salad into his mouth, nodded, chewed, sat back on a table as another child came into the space. "We work near each other in the Research Park, and that proximity leads to many conversations—and I think that's very important. Roger's also a good friend, so we talk a lot. But aside from the licensed platform, we don't have much technical work together. As a platform technology, AlignIt is upstream from us. GameIt is downstream application development."

Greg nodded. "So AlignIt is a platform for developing applications— at least right now, until Roger comes out with better applications so users can go directly into AlignIt."

"Right," Jeff said. "But where we do work together now is in marketing and outreach. We coordinate our marketing messages since GameIt is obviously part of the AlignIt Commons community trademark family, and since GameIt was the first practical expression of AlignIt. Roger tells people, 'If you want to see AlignIt, look at GameIt'."

"Nice!" Greg said. "Yeah, he told me that, actually. That's a testament to your work, isn't it?" Greg pointed Tara to some steamed vegetables on his plate, and some olives. "What are your main challenges right now as a company, if I can ask?"

"Certainly. Challenges…let's see." Jeff contemplated, forked some asparagus, brought it to his mouth, chewed. "Building our game world developer tools. Building a network of game developers who can build on the AlignIt platform. Yeah, that's the big one. There are a lot of developers out there who can build cool games and create cool effects. But to deliver on the GameIt value proposition, we need developers who understand sacred science and can really build game worlds and gamer challenges intuitively from inside the sacred sciences, so to speak. GameIt can't just give developers libraries of cool images and effects to build the games on standard commercial patterns. The big challenge is to build games that express sacred science and convey players along a pathway that matches their own profile and developmental needs. And that takes a special kind of developer who knows sacred science from study and practice."

"Mmm," Greg said with emphasis. "Okay, so we're back again to what you mean by sacred science."

"Well, this is what we're all about here."

"Yes, but it can mean different things to different people. And various sciences can be categorized under that rubric. So what do you mean by it?"

"Well, I'm not a philosopher or esotericist, so I don't claim a special definition. I guess in the broadest sense, I think of maps of the psyche and cosmos, like the ones in the Raymond Lully Museum or in Roger's office."

"I haven't visited his office yet."

"Oh, wait till you see it!" Jeff said. "I also think of maps that show pathways for human development. And since you're a theurgist like Roger, then it would be development pathways for anything—plants, fish, bugs, whatever. But I'm not developing games for plants, fish or bugs, so I focus on human development. So, you get what I'm saying? The big archetypal themes of human development in myths and tales. So, take the hero's journey, for example. We want to develop gameworlds using, say, states, stages, challenges, and beings in Tibetan Buddhism, or Taoism, or the ancient Greco-Egyptian mysteries. My own practice is Tibetan Buddhism."

"Roger told me. So for you, sacred science in GameIt means figures like the Buddhas and bodhisattvas and great yogis, and the symbols, states, and stages."

"Whatever we get in the AlignIt platform," Jeff said, "we can build into a gameworld. But we need people who can understand that content and create a player avatar and advance that avatar through the gameworld on, say, a hero's journey. Does that make sense?"

"Yeah, I get it," Greg said. "That's what I imagined you were doing, actually."

"And the human development part of it comes into play when the game player recognizes, through active engagement with the game, the echoes of familiar archetypal game motifs in their outer life. Not that the player has encountered every theme in outer life yet. But even then, games can also be preparatory for stages yet to come in life, by laying down a template in the game that may be encountered subsequently in life. Then the pattern established in the game can be recognizable when it is finally met in real life."

"Brilliant!" Greg said. "That's also true of many stories and folk tales, as I understand it. And the great games in human history."

"This is where the anthropologist in me comes out," Jeff said, sitting up enthusiastically. "There are many purposes of games in different times and cultures, and not all of them are consciously recognized by the people playing them. Some games simply serve to acculturate people in the rituals and rites of passage of the tribe—like games on puberty or return to normal time after mourning a death. I think of that as like *participation mystique*, where you wouldn't say there is conscious reflection on what is happening. But then there are games with a complete cosmology in which the forces in the game represent cosmic forces, and the struggle in the game is the struggle of…however you'd like to say it—the soul's return journey home, or the struggle to break free from the prison of worldly existence, or the lover's pursuit of the beloved, to use some ancient Persian metaphors, or the aspirant's struggle to discriminate delusions from essential qualities and original true Buddha nature. I'm most interested in developing games organized on this ultimate concern of the human quest."

"Oh, this inspires me!" Greg said. "This is fabulous work. Hopefully new developments in AlignIt will be very useful for GameIt."

"I think so. Well, I've talked a lot," Jeff said. "Now tell me more about your background and what you would bring to the AlignIt team."

"Sure," Greg said. "So beyond teaching ontology at UW, I also teach a few basic courses in the history of philosophy, primarily in metaphysics, which ontology comes from. That's what I teach at the university. I have many more philosophical interests, like Neoplatonism, and theurgy as you mentioned, but there isn't enough demand to teach it there. I also consult with industry in ontology projects, and that's the piece that connects with AlignIt—doing ontology work on the AlignIt platform—and maybe also for games."

"So help me out," Jeff said, forking through his plate. "I'm an anthropologist, not a philosopher. What exactly is ontology?"

"Okay, so in philosophy, it's a branch of metaphysics and it's formally the study of being, of what exists and how those things exist, including their functions, properties, roles, and relations. In computer science, ontology concerns representing what exists in structures like classes, and how we relate what exists to other things that exist."

"Okay," Jeff said, with a slight laugh. "I get that theoretically, but it's pretty abstract. How do you unpack that?"

Tara left the game, and the food, and began playing with another child nearby, with a mother overseeing. Greg felt freedom to focus, not needing to shuttle his attention back and forth as much.

"Think about AlignIt, as it is now," Greg said. "You'll recognize the current ontology in the structures like the seven traditional planets and the seven chakras, or the corresponding essential triads found in alchemy, Ayurveda, and oriental medicine—Salt, Sulfur, and Mercury, or Kapha, Pitta and Vata, or Jing, Chi and Shen. Or think of the eight Tibetan Buddha families and the eight Taoist Immortals, and the eight trigrams of the I Ching. Or the letters of the Hebrew, Arabic, and Sanskrit alphabets, and all the sounds, colors, physical postures, and other qualities associated with each of them." Jeff nodded his head. "These are archetypal patterns of things or forces that exist, and things related in a class."

"Okay," Jeff said. "That's closer to home."

"For instance, you practice Tibetan Buddhism."

Jeff nodded.

"The class of eight Buddha families is related to the class of eight Taoist Immortals."

"Okay."

"Take one Buddha family of the eight. You can find a corresponding Taoist Immortal in a class of eight. It's not simply that there are eight in each class. The relation is established because the eight in one class have thematic and typological correspondences to the eight in the other class. They match up ontologically, that is, in structure, function, property, role, and relationship. They have a common deep structure even though their expression in one class has a different 'local color,' so to speak, than that of another class—Tibetan rather than Chinese, in this case, but still the same underlying structure. Ontology is very much more than that in the larger world of computer science—you can build ontologies of molecules, legal terms, complex rules for operating equipment, inference engines for artificial intelligence. But this is a picture of ontology as we meet it in AlignIt."

"Okay," Jeff said. "That helps. I get what you're saying—I know those themes in AlignIt, and I recognize the archetypal structures underlying our gameworld creation. I hear it often from Roger, so it's good to hear it from an ontologist."

"Ontology isn't that important for most people to know, in the grand scheme of things," Greg said. "Ontologies are implicit in the things we do, but they operate at a level of abstraction beyond which most of us think. It lies to geeks like me to build ontologies, and there are communities of people who collaborate, critique, annotate and elaborate them. So it's just fine for most people to simply do what they do, with ontologies working implicitly in the background."

"So what does it mean to build an ontology for AlignIt?" Jeff asked.

"AlignIt already has an ontology—accidentally, if you will. Or implicitly. It's there in the traditional frameworks Roger incorporated. It's just a static and simplistic one, and the plan is to upgrade it to a dynamic, open, collaborative system. So ontology becomes a conscious and explicit project for AlignIt."

"Okay, you're upgrading the AlignIt ontology," Jeff confirmed.

Greg nodded. "You could say that. Technically, we're creating an upper ontology, a meta layer above other ontologies."

"What does that mean for GameIt?"

"Do you know what Roger is planning to do next?" Greg asked.

"I'm on the AlignIt board—but go on." Jeff lifted a cut of an avocado sushi roll to his mouth.

"Whether I move to Bayside Village or not, the alignments Roger found in Perennial Philosophy will be graduated to a more variegated system, actually more scientific in orientation, so that quite a number of new patterns, and pathways for traversing those patterns, will be made available. It may turn out that we push the development of Perennial Philosophy as we know it today. That's some of what I could bring if I come. But as I say, Roger is planning this whether I come or not—others could do it, too, and I would be just a small part in the process."

"Well, that's not Roger's view. He's pretty impressed with you."

"I think we have a lot of values and interests in common, but I think other ontologists could probably do this."

"Its your field, you would know. But it's not Roger's view. And hearing you speak, I can't imagine many ontologists have your background."

"Okay," Greg said, shrugging it off. "Anyway, in your case, the addition of new patterns and pathways in AlignIt will mean that GameIt can build far more complex and interesting games—especially if you're going beyond the well-worn paths like the archetypal hero's journey that most people know from general reading. Imagine a game based on a forgotten or suppressed ontology, like one from Iamblichean theurgy."

"Like what?"

"Iamblichus was a Syrian Neoplatonic philosopher marginalized by Western philosophy. And he developed a theurgic philosophy, which Roger would like. So instead of morphing or mashing dominant themes together into tidy grand syntheses, imagine finding new patterns for games, like those based on Iamblichean theurgy."

"Okay," Jeff said, raising his eyebrows. "That's interesting."

"Daddy, I'm tired," Tara said, returning to Greg's side and leaning into his arm. Greg realized he hadn't much time left.

"Okay, Honey. We're going soon," he said, putting his arm around Tara and looking to her. He kissed her on the head. Then turning back to Jeff, Greg said, "I think we've got to get her back now."

"She looks tired. Greg, you're dangling a tantalizing carrot in front of me now. Let's bookmark that conversation for our meeting on Wednesday. I see how GameIt could benefit from your knowledge and expertise."

"Sure. It's a great place to pick up. And now…" Greg said, smiling and putting his hand on Tara's head, "first things first." Looking out to the room Greg said, "I bet Sara has gotten absorbed somewhere."

Jeff and Greg stood, put their plates on a cart, shook hands, and parted ways.

Greg took Tara's hand. "Okay, precious girl. Let's go find Mommy."

Greg maneuvered around clusters of gamers and observers in search of Sara, holding Tara's hand. He almost bumped into a gentleman before him, and then looked up. "Roger," he said. Roger Barnes turned around from a group huddled over a complicated game of Rosicrucian Chess.

"Hey, Greg," Roger said. He held his right hand to his heart and smiled warmly with a slight bow of his head, a gesture familiar to Greg but not one used on his path.

Jenny stood there, too. "Oh, hi Greg." She brightened to see Greg and held her hand to her heart. She looked at Tara. "Hello, Sweetie."

"It's good to see you both," Greg said. It felt like bumping into friends on the path, he realized, more than meeting colleagues at a networking social.

Greg lifted Tara onto his waist. She looked at the faces, familiar from last night, then nestled her head on Greg's shoulder. "This day was amazing! I feel so immensely expanded!" Greg could scarcely contain his thrill. "I'm just...I feel so inspired."

"It's a rich place, Bayside Village," Jenny said with a deep and knowing look, beholding Greg in her gaze.

"It's such a dazzling feast. With every new discovery, I feel tempted to go off into flights of fancy."

"Tempted to go off?" Roger asked curiously.

"On our path, we talk about how the practice can be mundane." Here I am venturing, Greg thought to himself. He had talked with Roger in the past about their common practice, but not with Jenny. And not in public. "Our path brings us down into the routine, commonplace conditions of life. Like being ground down. I often need to surrender enticements to go off and away into mystical states, into philosophical contemplations. I've been told I need to be more grounded here in this world, have my feet on the ground." Greg conveyed his grasp of this teaching, meant for him by his teacher.

"We call it *sobriety*," Roger said firmly, with an uncanny depth of authority.

"Okay, yes," Greg said, recognizing the technical term and feeling well understood.

"There's quite a lot of sobriety here, too," Roger said with a faint grin on his face, as though a trickster winked from behind a mask. "Don't let appearances fool you." He let the words press into Greg the way a smoldering ember burns through surfaces. Roger held a penetrating glance. "Not everyone here follows the sober way, of course. People here are on all kinds of paths—most people, anyway. But sobriety is a most important counterweight against the powerful elevating forces here."

"Really? With all the talk of utopia and social experiments?"

"Talk of utopia is one thing," Jenny said with quiet but unmistakable inner authority. "Many fascinated people come and go. But to stay and actually carry out these projects, you need some real solidity, some weight." Greg noted that Jenny's introverted demeanor often gave way to discriminating and insightful explorations of a theme. He liked this part of her.

"I must admit," Greg said, "I feel giddy like a kid in this atmosphere. I don't have these aspirational currents back home—not outwardly, at least. It's just the daily grind at the university—advancing slowly toward tenure, working on my lectures and publications—just the meat and potatoes of the job. It's only late at night after the family's in bed that I get any time at all for my larger interests. By then, its late and I'm tired. But that's when I do the work that really matters to me."

"That's probably a good thing, for a time, don't you think?" Jenny said. "You're young, you have a family, you have a lovely daughter. Having some weight in a mundane life can help you ground your aspiration."

"That's probably true. Not always fun, but true. One of my shortcomings," Greg confessed, "is getting so focused on my deeper interests—esoteric philosophy, Neoplatonism—that I let other things go. But luckily, I'm finally staying focused on ordinary work, house chores, and family duties. But I sometimes let go my regular spiritual practices and just focus intensely on esoteric philosophy."

"Need they be different?" Roger asked. "That could be made a kind of meditation, depending on your attitude and intention. Depending on how you read a book or a household chore."

"Oh, there you are," Sara said. She came up from the side, her face joyful at seeing Roger and Jenny.

Yet too soon, Greg thought, as the moment felt ripe with Roger and Jenny. How can the study of esoteric philosophy be a meditation? And how to read a book—or a chore? He wanted more.

"And family can be an effective agent for sobriety," Roger advanced, loud and deliberate, as Sara stepped close.

"Ooh, did I miss something good?" Sara asked, her interest piqued, her eyes brightening.

Roger turned. "We were discussing how it's good for a family on a sober path to embrace quotidian life conditions. Otherwise a place like this can carry you away into distraction. Are you enjoying the games?"

A wave of energy and impressions hit Sara and went in, somewhere. Roger added the question so fast and emphatically, with just the right force, that it felt to Sara in a flash like a deliberate addition and shift. Greg felt it too, as a wave, a wind, but too fast to grasp with his mind, and gone.

"As much as I can in a short jaunt," Sara replied immediately, out of prudence to Roger's inquiry and the flow of conversation. But the former impression, whatever it was, went in too fast to work it out. It scrambled her conditioned response, set up a double attention wherein she watched the thread of ordinary conversation and yet felt another action, kind and destined for their evolution. "They're quite amazing. I'm not into games, really, but I'm fascinated. They come from somewhere else, it seems."

Roger nodded. "Indeed. Many things here come from somewhere else. Have you met Jeff yet?"

The two couples discussed Greg's and Sara's first full day at Bayside Village. Sara followed the flow of conversation, watched for more from Roger, and decided that the quick shift itself, the impression made by some words about family and sober path, were the action she was trying to follow and observe. It was working in her already, whatever it was, wherever it went.

"Actually," Greg said, "I was just looking for Sara when I bumped into you. We were going to turn in early on our first full day and get our girl to bed."

"She spent all day at the Bayside Village School and Daycare," Sara said.

"Oh, she's so sweet," Jenny said, putting her hand on Tara's back. "Looks like it's been a long day."

"Okay, we'll see you tomorrow night at our place for dinner," Roger said.

"I'm looking forward to it," Sara said.

Again, Roger and Jenny held their right hand to their chest. To Greg, it felt an intimate gesture, if a foreign one.

30

"What was that about?" Sara asked when they left the Dining Commons, heading back to the Lodge.

"I have no idea," Greg said. "I just bumped into them looking for you."

"But he said something about a family on a sober path?"

"Yeah, I don't know." Greg mused. He reconstructed Roger's words for Sara, filled in what was said before she turned up.

"He was doing something," Sara said.

"Yes, I felt that."

"I trust him implicitly, but I couldn't follow it."

"Nor could I." Greg cogitated. "He means us. But...how to work it out?" Greg trailed off.

Then Sara turned resolutely from perplexity. "He's funny. I like him."

Walking back, Sara noticed the night watch from Village Security. A woman and man walked together mindfully down the path toward them. As they passed, each with clear, shining eyes of presence, each with an air of attentiveness, Sara noticed that slight bow again. She bowed, too. And Greg carefully bowed his head, with Tara in his arms, holding her head on his shoulder with his hand so as not to rock her neck.

Back at the Lodge, Greg and Sara prepared for the night and next day. Tara perked up in the containing confines of the Lodge room. She set about arranging the night stand, pretending to work the registration desk in the lobby. Picking up Greg's mobile, she answered imaginary calls and imitated front desk behavior she had observed on past trips. Then she asked, "Daddy, can I play with the coins?"

"The Bayside Village Dollars? Sure. For just a minute, okay? We need to go to bed soon." Greg looked into his side bag and pulled out a handful of gold colored coins, larger than U.S. federal currency. "Here you go," he said, placing them down on Tara's make-shift reception desk. "What are you going to do with them?"

"You'll see," Tara said. She organized the coins into piles and then talked aloud to imaginary customers about how much the items collected from the room would cost them. Greg smiled as he watched her a moment, and returned to getting ready for tomorrow.

Sara checked work email on her mobile. Shortly after, she said, "Maybe Daddy can read you a book."

"Sure," Greg said. He took off his shoes, emptied his pockets into his side back, and headed for Tara's bag of books and toys. "Let's see. What do we have here?" Holding the bag open, he flipped through the books with his finger and called out loud. "The Monkey King, The Seven Chinese Sisters, Water Babies, The Wonder Flight to the Mushroom Planet…"

"The Seven Chinese Sisters," Tara said.

"You brought Water Babies and The Mushroom Planet?" Sara asked.

"Yeah."

Sara rolled her eyes, unbelieving.

"What?"

Sara smiled and shook her head. "Only you would bring those."

"They're kids books," Greg defended.

"Hardly."

It felt endearing. Greg shrugged his shoulders as he brought The Seven Chinese Sisters to the master bed. "Okay, let's take off your shoes, Honey." Tara was overtired. Greg removed her shoes. "Oh, sandy feet. You've had a big day of play." Greg emptied her shoes into a small trash can by the desk and brushed her socks with his hand. "Okay, up you go," he said, lifting her. Tara crawled on hands and knees to the middle of the pillows at the head of the bed and waited for the story. Greg climbed onto the bed, sat beside Tara, put his arm around her, and opened the book before her. "Sara, are you going to join us?"

"Yeah." Sara grabbed <u>The Beads of Dew from the Source of Life</u> out of her purse and set it on the night stand beside her. She sat beside Tara and kissed her on the head. "Okay, I'm ready," Sara said.

Greg opened the cover, turned the pages, read the story. Tara yawned and leaned her head on Sara's arm. As Greg read, Tara leaned deeper into Sara, eye lids drooping. After the story, Tara drifted to sleep. No protest for reading only one book that night. Sara laid Tara down, and she fell into sounder sleep.

Greg picked up Tara and carried her to the roll-away-bed. Sara got up and lifted back the covers as Greg put Tara in.

Sara returned to the master bed. "Look what I got," she whispered. She pulled a box from her purse. "A Taste Parlor for kids. From the Sensory Parlor Collective." She handed it to Greg. "And I used those coins."

"BV Dollars?"

"Yeah."

"Oh, neat," Greg said. He took the box and studied the packaging. "Looks fun." He turned it over, read the back side, handed it back to Sara. "I'd love to do this with her."

"I thought so." Sara returned the kit to her purse, laid back on the pillows, and rubbed her scalp. "Wow, I'm exhausted. This was quite a day!" she said. Greg nodded. "What's with this Neil Benson guy? Who is he?"

Greg laid back across the bed, put his head down on Sara's thigh, and rubbed his eyes. "Oh, he's a big shot in information science." He yawned. "Service provisioning models." He stretched his arms out, yawned again. "Roger invited him to explore consulting on AlignIt service informatics."

"Hmm," Sara said, thinking. "He sure is full of himself. He has such a contemptuous attitude."

"I guess."

"It makes you wonder why Roger would bring a person like that here."

"What do you mean?" Greg asked, keeping his eyes closed.

"Well, he and Jenny have such deep integrity. I just can't imagine Roger choosing someone like Neil to help develop AlignIt. He doesn't seem to have an affinity for a place like this."

"A place like this?" Greg repeated. He opened his eyes, turned his head toward her. "This weird utopia in this ugly industrial setting?"

"Well, okay, the place does hold something special. And Roger and Jenny hold something special. That's what I mean."

"Mmmm," Greg said, nodding his head on Sara's thigh, looking back to the ceiling. "But Neil does have academic integrity. He's very good in his field."

"But his attitude. I mean, you could just feel his contempt for all this stuff on the tour. He looks kind of like David in your department…"

"Yeah, he does, doesn't he?" Greg snickered at the comparison.

"I feel like we've got some difficult choices to ponder," Sara said, recalling familiar concerns in the weeks leading up to the trip.

"I know. We've seen a lot today. How is it for you?"

"I'm giving it a serious look." Sara rubbed her scalp again, yawned, and then laid her arms down, rested her left hand on Greg's chest. "You know, I feel on the one hand we need to have our feet on the ground and accept our mundane life conditions—being practical and living a grounded, responsible life."

"Roger said 'We call it sobriety.'"

"Hmm," Sara said. "Well, it's kind of unexpected to come to this utopian place when we've had to surrender so many ideals in recent years. Its pretty far out intellectually and culturally. But we have been attentive to the mundane parts of our lives over the last several years, and I feel we've been learning those lessons. It does feel like things have been changing for us."

"Mhmmm, it does seem like that," Greg said. "This is what I was saying in the taxi yesterday. There are contracting and expanding cycles. To me, it feels like things are coming full circle. I feels like things we've had to surrender are now returning to our lives."

"So maybe its time to listen to these longings we share. We could have a community of like-minded people. You could work on AlignIt—I see that that's important to you. I can see how you feel this is meant to be." Sara paused, thinking. "I guess I'm also finding this place interesting. I'm not convinced about it yet. But it's more than I expected."

"Like what?" Greg asked. He turned his head on her leg, looking up at her.

"Well, like the Bayside Village School. I didn't expect it would be so complete. And the Dining Commons reminds me of my college days when I had so many friends and so much community. And…the tour. What an amazing place—just seeing that all of these spiritual groups and classes are concentrated on one small campus. And the Art Center. And the Sensory Parlor Collective…." Sara trailed off. "I've also been thinking about the interview with Karen. I totally didn't expect that. I'm trying to think about what to show her."

"Yeah, that was really unexpected, wasn't it? Are you thinking seriously about that job? You've felt critical of the Village so far."

"I mean, we're still looking. We just arrived, really. It has to be a good fit for all of us. I just didn't think there would be so much here, like the Art Center and this job."

"Don't feel you need to do it for me," Greg said. "I could always come here just to consult with Roger. This place is pretty far out."

"I thought you were really excited about it." Sara sat forward stretching her back into a spinal twist.

Greg moved off her leg, turned up on his side, facing her. "I am. But I don't want to be unrealistic about it, like you were saying. That's weighed on my mind, too. I mean, look at this—an idealistic, utopian village with an alternative graduate school and research institute that doesn't have an established reputation yet. And like you've been saying, it's not necessarily the best move for my career."

"Did something change for you?"

Greg sighed. "I don't know." He stared off to the side wall in reflection. "Seeing Neil does touch off my sensitivities. And you're right," Greg snickered again. "He does look like David. Just meeting him today made me look at the Bridge Institute differently—just a little. He does come off as self-important, but he's also part of an elite academic research culture. And the Bridge Institute doesn't match that profile yet. So it makes me circumspect about whether I should leave UW for the Bridge Institute. It may not be a good career move after all. Clearly I'm interested, but..." Greg left it unfinished.

"But there are a lot of researchers here, and the Bridge Institute has connections to Berkeley, Stanford, and other schools."

"Yes," Greg conceded. "But from a career point of view, academic prestige is important. It may be better for me to simply visit the Bridge Institute on a sabbatical, or just consult with AlignIt. Then I could remain in the respectable university position while I'm advancing toward tenure." Greg laid down on his back, closed his eyes, massaged his face and scalp. "It may be premature to move here before getting tenure." Greg fell silent, rubbed his temples. "What could I do after I came here? I'm not an established professor. It's not easy do this so early in my career." Greg paused, breathed in. "But just in case, I think you should give yourself to this interview with Karen. It may be a great opportunity. And who knows? Maybe it would be a good move for us."

"You baffle me sometimes." She looked at him. "But I understand what you're weighing."

31

"What do you think about Keith and Leah?" Sara asked. She shifted her position, sliding to lay down fully. As she moved, Greg brought his head to the pillow and lay beside her.

"I don't know. They're an interesting couple."

"Leah seems concerned about this Bayside Village thing."

"Yeah, I'm not sure if I see them staying together as a couple. I wonder if they're mismatched. They don't seem to want the same things."

"I wondered about that," Sara said.

"I wonder why Keith is drawn to her. I mean, she's attractive and she's a nice person, but..."

"She does seem afraid of the world," Sara said, "like she lives without her own center of gravity. She seems deferent to others in conversation."

"That's my feeling, too," Greg said. "Keith seems very young spiritually, but you can see a fire in his eyes, a burning wish for spiritual training. It seems he's trying to emerge from the conditioning of his childhood. I don't know if I see that so strongly in Leah. That's why I wonder if they're a match. It seems like Keith has an inner tug of war between his longing and whatever Leah represents to him."

"I don't know," Sara said. "I can also see Leah being grounding for him. She wants a family and roots, and Keith seems really intense and unfocused—that's just my intuition. Leah could be helpful for Keith."

"Mmm." Greg thought. "How do you know that about her?"

"I asked. While you were talking to Keith."

"Mmm. I could see that being good for Keith to a degree—just a wife, any wife. But it seems to me that unless he can share his intense dynamism with another woman who has... not necessarily the same but at least a corresponding yearning and inquiry, I don't see his soul being able to really sing with hers. I mean, he may stick with her, but maybe on account of his conditioning rather than on account of his soul destiny."

"He has a strong longing," Sara reflected.

"Yeah. It's inspiring to see it in someone younger." Greg thought for awhile.

"But she has a simple and pure love for Jesus," Sara said. "I also got that from our one-on-one. Maybe it's just harder to see because she's quieter and more inward."

"Hmm. Yeah, I saw that, too." Greg reflected. "You talked with her a bit, then?"

"A little while."

"Why?"

"I don't know. Same situation as me, maybe. I mean, totally different relationship, different personality, but she's coming here wondering about this place just like I am."

"Hmm." Greg reflected. "Anyway, her simple love for Jesus seems qualitatively different to me from what I feel in Keith, which is more like a burning passion for truth. For Leah, its almost like an unconscious background assumption that she'll always stay in her kind of Christian world without the archetypal pilgrim's journey, so to speak."

"What do you mean?" Sara asked.

"She seems like the kind of person who has Christian parents, wants to marry a Christian man, raise Christian children in a Christian school, listen to the same teachers over the course of her life, and never really subject any of it to inquiry."

"You got all that from our conversation?"

"No. Just guessing."

"You seem critical of her."

"No, I do like her, and I agree—I can see a simple and pure faith." Greg pondered. "Maybe I am a bit critical. It's just that to me, it's a question of whether she's equally matched with Keith, whose faith and life don't seem so simple—nor so pure. I mean, I don't know him, but he seems complex—hungry, angry....maybe longing but afraid. I just feel he would devour her and still be hungry intellectually, sexually, and spiritually."

"Ok," Sara said. "She does seem slower and denser spiritually. I grant you that. But she could also be drawn to him because she has a latent longing that she hasn't become responsible for yet. She projects it onto him, and that's how she'll discover it—it'll get awakened in relationship to him."

"Okay, but what if her attraction to him is not to his spiritual aspiration, but to his darkness—whatever it is that makes him so intense and changeable?"

"Even then," Sara said, "maybe they're attracted to each other to work out their karmas."

"Maybe," Greg said. "Maybe you're right."

"But why should it be one or the other—positive and negative attractions?"

"It could even be both, I suppose."

"And don't you think even a negative attraction could be transformative?" Sara asked.

"Ah, I wonder about that..." Greg sat up on his elbow. "I wonder if a negative attraction could be transformative, a basis of relationship, if there is not also a positive attraction rooted in common aspiration. What if they're just attracted on the basis of familiar conditioning, for instance? Something like Freud's repetition compulsion? What happens as they increasingly discover and live their soul qualities? If they are not deeply aligned, then they'll tend to grow apart even as they become more individuated and whole within themselves. And if they're concerned about their relationship, or if they're married, they may tend to put the living of their destiny aside to preserve their relationship—because authenticity increasingly conflicts with keeping the relationship together. Or else they grow father apart while living like strangers under the same roof. Or split up."

"Something deeper is going on here for you," Sara said. "This seems kind of charged for you."

"I guess. You too, no?"

Sara paused a moment. "I'm more aware of you seeming charged." She thought a moment. "Are you thinking about your own parents, maybe?"

"Maybe, yes. It seems like that dynamic."

"Are you feeling this way about us—about our attraction to each other?"

"No, thankfully." Greg laid down again on his arm and looked deep into Sara's eyes. "I worked very hard to be sure I felt aligned with you in the most important ways, soul to soul, before we married."

"Are you doubting it?"

"No. I mean, I don't think so. I feel very satisfied intellectually, emotionally, socially, and spiritually. I mean, we're not perfect. But I feel deep gratitude for our relationship." Then he realized he didn't say sexually. Why not? Should he have?

"Just checking," Sara said. "Do you think we have a negative attraction and that we'll grow apart as we individuate—is that how you said it?"

"Yeah, that's what I said," Greg confirmed. He thought for a moment, his eyes searching the ceiling. "No, I don't think we'll grow apart the more we individuate. I mean, we have many positive things in common, like our spiritual aspiration, our work with our teacher, Samuel, our appreciation of art and ideas, and...my love for you." Greg paused and thought. He couldn't quite bring himself to say 'our love for each other,' perhaps because he wasn't sure how strong hers was for him. "I guess this is still a raw area for me since my parents lived their whole married lives by suppressing their true selves in order to stay together. Or else they didn't find a creative way to live out their very best together."

"I wonder if this trip and the idea of working here are bringing this up for you now," Sara explored. "Because that question is probably coming up now with an opportunity like this, isn't it—where you can finally work on your subject area in a place that meets your values?"

"It could be. It could be," Greg mused. "I don't have a clear feeling about this place yet. Seems very interesting. It seems possible that this could be a great next step. But I'm not sure yet, either. And I want to make sure it's a good next step for you, too. I know it's a strange place, and I don't want to put you off. I want it to really work for you."

"You're not putting me off, don't worry. And, I love you, too—you know that." He wasn't sure how much, and it was good to hear. "Greg, we'll work it out. I want what's best for both of us just like you do. If this is our next step, we'll feel it. I trust that."

"Mmm, thanks. I know we can work it out together." Greg sat thinking for awhile.

"Do you think we're attracted to each other by our negative qualities?" Sara asked again.

"I don't know. Maybe. But I don't see this as dominant. I feel our positive attractions far more strongly."

Greg sat silently for awhile, and Sara didn't say anything, either. Which negative qualities? he wondered.

After a silence that became uncomfortable for him, Sara said, "Do you think Keith is ready for spiritual training? I wonder if he can stick with anything. He seems capricious. Like maybe he's running from something."

"That's perceptive. How do you see that?" Greg asked.

"In the suddenness and intensity of his interests. It seems like they come fast, and that suggests to me that they could leave fast, too…"

"Or be rapidly substituted with other interests," Greg said.

"Yeah. It's too much affect up front, which suggests something unintegrated in him, or suggests he has powerful, semi-conscious forces driving him that he's compensating for by so much up-front affective display."

"Mmmm," Greg pondered, as if looking in to Keith. "That's insightful. Yeah, I can see what you're saying, especially in terms of affect. But he does seem intent on spiritual interests."

"Yeah, I see that too. But don't you think he might move from group to group, teacher to teacher, unable to stick with something? He seems unstable right now." Sara paused. "I guess in that sense, I can see Leah being good for him—to hold him, to contain him."

"He's also younger than we are—that moving quality kind of goes with his age," Greg said. "But in terms of Leah, he could also end up resenting that containment, especially if she would want it for different aims, not necessarily as a container for the spiritual depth he seeks."

"He does seem like a young man in that sense."

"Anyway, I enjoyed them." Greg said.

Greg opened his eyes, stared at the ceiling, thought for awhile. Then his attention shifted. "Do you want to meditate?"

"Sure." Sara stretched into a forward bend, brought her nose to her shins. She came up, moved into a half-lotus.

Greg grabbed his mobile, flicked screens with his thumb for the room controls, cut off the lights. He sat up, adjusted his clothes, pulled his legs into half-lotus, breathed in deeply, and out.

Sara breathed deeply. Soft breaths beside him. Aspiring, like him.

Greg turned his attention inward, toward a central axis. He called on his teacher, formed an image of him before his mind's eye. Then he called on his Beloved. He concentrated, practicing silent repetition of a great divine name with each breath. His sharp sensory awareness of the room and his own body softened. In time, he moved close to absorption, then away, then close again, never yet all the way. Beloved, bring me near to you. Let me melt in you…He repeated the name on his breaths—his doorway to unseen worlds, to dissolution of worlds, to emptiness. Almost there at times. But the sense of self, while softened, muted, always remained somewhat. He concentrated on the name, longing, calling.

Day 3: Tuesday

32

Sara rose early, grabbed her yoga mat from the closet. She kissed Greg as he sat up to meditate in bed. Then she closed the door gently, went off to yoga.

Greg meditated, let Tara sleep in. Yesterday was long and new. Only when it was time for breakfast did he gently sing an improvised song. Tara's eyes opened to slits. "Good morning, Sweetness," he said.

Tara sat up. "Where's Momma?"

Greg moved his legs out of half-lotus. "Momma went to yoga. She'll meet us at the Dining Hall. Are you hungry for breakfast?"

Greg and Tara walked to the Dining Commons, went through the line, and selected their breakfast foods—mixed grain cereal, banana, nuts, yogurt, chai tea—and then walked out to the tables.

"Daddy, can we sit near Kids Corner?"

"Sure," Greg said, leading the way. Finding a table with some children, Greg pulled out a chair for Tara and then he sat down.

"Hi Tara." An older girl called out from a group of three kids. Greg noticed that Tara recognized them. She said a quick "Hi." But she was shy at first and focused on her breakfast. She gave occasional glances. Interested. Warming up.

Greg looked to a brown-haired, slumping woman. He guessed she was the mother. "Good morning," he said.

"Good morning."

Greg was cheerful. She was expressionless. He cut the banana on Tara's plate. "Looks like our kids met in the Daycare," he said.

"I guess so," the woman said.

Different personalities maybe. "We're visiting this week. Are you a regular there, or visiting?"

"No," she said with a stilted but kindly laugh. "I work in accounting." She sipped her coffee, put the cup down. "These are my girls, Cayce and Susan. Charlie's my co-worker's son. I bring 'em for breakfast and drop 'em off at the Day Care."

Now she had some life, Greg thought. "I see. Must be nice to share a breakfast here."

"Yeah." She dropped the conversation again.

The other three children got up to play in the Kids Corner.

"Daddy, can I go play?"

"Not yet, Honey. I want you to finish your oatmeal and banana first. Then you can get up and play."

Greg focused on Tara, helped her eat.

She took two bites. "Now?"

"Finish your banana."

Greg said to the woman, "I'm visiting for the Orientation."

She nodded. She seemed tired, maybe disillusioned. Greg realized she was the first person he'd met here so far who seemed out of step with the energy, the feel, of Bayside Village. "Accounting is in the main Bayside Village administration building?"

"It's on the Bridge Institute quadrangle."

"Now, Daddy?"

"Yes, now you can play." Tara got up and strode to Kids Corner. Greg continued with the woman. "How do you like Day Care?"

"It's quite good. The school, too." She put down her fork. "They work well with Cayce and Susan." She paused. "We moved a year ago from Boston. The adjustment was difficult for the girls. All of us, actually. But the school works with them. Now they're doing well."

Greg pushed his tray back and picked up his cup of chai, spreading his fingers around its warm surface. "From Boston? For the Bayside Village or other reasons, if I may ask?"

The woman wiped her fingers on a napkin and leaned forward, matching Greg. "I was recruited from MIT by a former colleague who took an administrative post here. He said they're looking for seasoned people from other universities. He said if I'm ready for a change in life, this would be a great place to find something new. I'd just lost my husband in an accident."

"I'm sorry," Greg said.

"It threw all the doors open. So I thought I'd give it a try here."

Greg listened tenderly. Took a moment of pause. Then he reflected. A seasoned administrator recruited from a big name university. He had talked with Roger about the approach to recruitment taken here. And its consequences. An impression of Mrs. Blocke flashed in his mind. Roger had said she was new, too.

"Has it worked out?"

She hesitated, sat back. "Well, there's a lot that's new here, that's for sure! I was ready for a change. But I'm not ready to change this way. It's a lot. It's not for everyone."

Greg nodded at her sober admission. Maybe it isn't for her. Was the place right for him? Meeting Neil yesterday made him circumspect. But Greg did feel in himself a basic affinity for Bayside Village. It was just his gut feeling, but he didn't see a fit for this woman. A place like this must see a lot of people come and go. Her mood didn't rankle him, though. Too many songs of praise would have triggered a warning signal for him. It would have said there's something manufactured here, something forced. If anything, the woman's story made the place more real. She was honest, at least. Indeed, this may not be for everyone.

Sara entered the Dining Commons and caught Greg's eyes. She approached, put her hand on his shoulder, and leaned over to give him a kiss. "Hi Love."

Greg could smell a hint of Sara's perfume and her scent as she bent over. "Hey, how was yoga?"

"It was great. I feel so refreshed. Where's our girl?"

"Kids Corner," Greg said.

She looked there, then back. "Okay. I'm going to get some breakfast." She put her yoga mat down in a chair and left for the line.

When Sara had gone, the woman said, "I need to get going. Nice talking with you." She didn't bother with names. Seemed to prefer anonymity.

"Okay, good talking to you," Greg said.

Greg glanced at Kids Corner. He didn't see Tara. He scanned the room. Maybe she was hidden behind a shelf or chair, he thought. He got up to look. Walked up close. Still didn't see her. He looked at the Dining Commons tables around him. No Tara. He looked back to Kids Corner. Now he grew concerned. He looked at the doors—had she gone outside? In a flash, an image of losing his daughter shot through his mind. His eyes raced along the windows. Where could she have gone? Then reason came. She couldn't have gone far. He looked around the Dining Commons.

A door to a side room stood open nearby—the GameIt demonstration had been there last night. Greg walked up, peered in. There he saw a class on yoga and meditation techniques, and there was Tara sitting in a backjack on the floor with other participants. He took a breath, relieved. A teacher was seated in front with her hands up in the air demonstrating *mudras*, hand positions. Tara's hands were up in the air, too, with everyone else's, following the demonstration. Greg was humored now. He smiled at the sight.

Greg stepped inside the doorway unobtrusively to a position where he could watch for Sara returning to the table. He studied the room. Anatomical charts of the body were posted on tripods around the front. Framed prints of colorful yantras were now hung on the walls. He looked again at the teacher's hands and fingers, moving now into a new gesture.

She commented on the finger positions. "Remember that mudras are like *asans*," she said. "They generate *kundalini shakti*, a current of energy."

Sara walked to the table looking for Greg and didn't see him. Greg stepped out momentarily and waved. When her eyes caught him, he motioned for her to come. Sara put down her tray and joined him at the door.

Greg pointed in to Tara sitting in the backjack. Everyone's hands were down, and then up again with the next mudra. Tara's went up, too.

"What's she doing in there?" Sara whispered, with a mix of shock and delight.

"She wandered in. I thought she was in Kids Corner."

"Look at her!" Sara smiled, turned to Greg. She grinned and shook her head.

Hands came down now. "Okay," the teacher said, "we'll turn now to a demonstration of *tratak*, candle gazing." At her direction, the group got up and repositioned in front of chairs with candles placed on the seats.

Greg walked up quietly. "Momma is here, Honey." He picked up Tara and walked out.

33

Greg and Sara walked Tara to Daycare, left Tara in Claire's competent hands. Back on the path, Greg pulled out his mobile and said, "Before the museum tour, I'm going to try Mrs. Blocke again."

"Has she gotten back to you?"

"No," Greg said, putting the mobile to his ear. The phone rang. No answer. He left another message. "Hi Mrs. Blocke. Greg Cobb here, from University of Washington. As you know, I'm here on campus this week, and I'd really like to meet with you about the faculty position. It's Tuesday now, and we still don't have a date and time nailed down. I'm leaving on Saturday. Please give me a call and let me know which of my available times works for you. Thanks."

Greg ended the call and uttered a groan of frustration.

"Wow," Sara said. "Maybe you should just let Roger know you haven't reached her yet."

"Good idea," Greg said. He called Roger. Left a message.

Greg and Sara walked up the path from the Daycare to the Bridge Institute quad. Walking around the square to the Raymond Lully Museum, Sara said, "I can't wait! I wanted to see this so badly yesterday."

"Me too," Greg said. "And I really like Randy. I could talk a long time with him."

Greg and Sara joined a small group in front of the museum and struck up conversation. Keith and Leah had come back, and Neil was walking across the grass of the quad. Neil's return surprised Greg. When a sizeable group gathered, Randy said, "Welcome back, folks! Good to see you today, and see some new folks. The Raymond Lully Museum is actually one of my favorite classrooms for demonstrating sacred science. So, let's get started." Randy turned and led the group up a step and inside the front double doors to the lobby of the Raymond Lully Museum.

"I'm surprised you're back," Greg said to Neil as they walked in.

Neil stepped up close. "Roger said the museum tour is critical for the consulting. AlignIt is simply a bunch of moving mandalas, or something like that. So if I see the museum, I'll know what he's building." Neil shook his head, rolled his eyes. "Isn't the requirements document good enough?" He shrugged. "Whatever."

Randy stood again in the lobby by the introductory display. "So let's just remember the mural from yesterday, and let's keep these principles in mind as we continue through the museum—1.) chains or threads from the above to the below in successive orders of manifestation, and 2.) horizontal typological correspondences across systems, organized by levels or plains. In its most rudimentary and popular expressions, sacred science can be found in simple charts and diagrams of relationships. Complex relationships can also be charted, including those between planets and physical organs, planets and psychological dynamics, as we'll see."

Randy now walked the group past the lobby and turned to a hall of murals where he stopped. The group looked at a bedazzling array of Medieval and Renaissance diagrams, ranging from the simple to the complex, including wheels with Latin and Hebrew letters, magic squares, and more. Randy introduced a chart showing analogies between planets and minerals, demonstrating the relation *as above, so below*. He paused a few moments.

Neal swooped up by Greg, leaned into him, and whispered: "Ready for pseudoscience? Everything's in sevens. Seven planets, seven chakras, seven of this, seven of that."

Greg acknowledged. It isn't quite right though, he thought, contemplating Neil's repast while he glanced over an Enochian sigil. Once seven planets was science. Sticking to it blindly in the face of new knowledge is bad faith, yes, but new knowledge doesn't reduce the utility of the history of science or make it pseudoscience. There are things to learn here, but critically. Greg took in an impression of himself ruminating, answering Neil in his mind, wondering why he felt the need to do this. Then he came back to himself on the tour.

Randy proceeded to the next set of images. "Here we find relationships between musical scales and days of the week, colors and musical notes." Moving on, Randy said, "And our last mural on this panel links planets, days, and colors.

"Any of these elements could be extended sixty or more columns to the right, linking in more correspondences" Randy said, waving his hand across the entire row of images, "with times of the day, musical notes, internal organs, metals, stones, plants, yogic postures, medicines, holiday festivals, songs….You get the idea."

A woman in the group said, "They could have benefited from a database just to keep track of all those categories!" She laughed.

"Ah," Randy said with keen interest, raising his forefinger. "This is a very important insight. Remember our tour yesterday? One such database we observed is AlignIt—and it does track and operationalize these things. AlignIt is one of the Bridge Institute's foremost technologies, researched and developed right here by Principal Investigator Roger Barnes, and its being incubated here in the Research Park in a software commons called the AlignIt Commons. In fact, Professor Barnes is giving a talk on it in the next period. Let's keep your insight in mind as we move along."

Randy turned. "Let's move to our next exhibit, the history of sacred science." He walked around a corner to another room, and the group followed.

"Now, I'm less an historian of science than a philosopher of it," Randy said. "Or a wanna-be philosopher of science, at least. And we come now to a room of early technologies, or what we can call mundane sciences as compared to sacred sciences—even less my area. While the sacred sciences involve the higher metaphysical and cosmological principles and direct relations between above and below, mundane sciences are considered derivative, secondary, and more applied, explicated, or manifested. On the right side of the room," Randy pointed to shelves, display cases, and murals, "the exhibits show technologies in mathematics, astronomy, geography, and medicine. On the left," again, Randy pointed to displays, "we have pharmacology, optics, alchemy, animal physiology, and plant sciences. All of these technologies were developed within the context of early sacred sciences. They're drawn from civilizations ranging from ancient Greece and the Near East to China, India, and Islamic countries. All before the rise of modern Western sciences."

"In case you wanted a brief early history of the world…," Neil whispered to Greg.

Randy walked the group around the room, making broadstroke comments on each exhibit. He pointed out displays of astronomical observatories, irrigation systems, bridges, water wheels, periodically noting his inadequacy for illuminating the mundane sciences. After circling once, Randy said, "So I'll let you browse the room on your own for a few minutes."

Greg was particularly taken with the exhibit on mathematics—because he knew it too little, he felt. There, the study of numbers, music, equations, and tile patterns intrigued him. But the diagrams of hand reckoning systems for counting—those captured his fancy. How to render it in AlignIt? Could these be related to mudras, the Indian hand movements? Are there cross cultural similarities to hand movements like these? So many questions. He made mental notes.

Neil took special interest in geographical maps and technologies, particularly astrolabes, Greg noticed. He contemplated old world maps and trade route maps. He found something of interest after all, Greg thought.

Sara moved in close to manuscript illustrations of great encyclopedists. The illustrations, the calligraphy. Look at those animals, she thought—do these still exist today?

Greg saw Leah holding Keith's hand as he looked at exhibits on optics, the theory of rays.

Randy reconvened the group. "Now, many people ask us what all of the foregoing ideas, charts, and diagrams have to do with science. This present room demonstrates the many ways the great metaphysical and cosmological principles of the sacred sciences are usefully applied to mundane technical applications. Let me give some context for this point.

"Ultimately sacred sciences are directed toward remembering the divine in all things, taking all created things as mirrors of the divine, even recognizing one's own divine nature. Finally, most traditions agree that the greatest sacred science of all is the science that shows the way back to God. You could say the Divine, or the Absolute or the Tao that cannot be named—however you want to call it. This greatest science showing the way back is the greatest concern of the human being, even of all beings. Yet the vision of most sacred sciences is not just of an isolated soul journey of return to the Divine, casting off the world. Certainly there are many expressions of religion and spiritual practice that approach life this way— life is something to put aside for the soul's return journey home. As most of us study and express it here at Bayside Village, though, sacred science encompasses the whole of existence and non-existence; so even when seen from the highest perspective, sacred science must necessarily encompass the more utilitarian or mundane sciences and technologies. Sacred sciences therefore often lead to applications practical in nature, helping entire societies align daily life with cosmic harmonies so that daily life can be experienced as sacred, brought into alignment with higher forces. People from many walks of life, from priests to physicians to farmers to governors and military strategists, have used these sacred sciences for the development of Eastern and Western civilizations. "

Greg leaned to Sara, whispered, "I have a strong feeling for this view of things. This is why I want to work on AlignIt with Roger—I feel it can support this kind of alignment of daily life with cosmic harmonies."

"I can see that," Sara said.

Randy next led the group into a room on sacred architecture. The group gathered around.

"This captures my interest," Sara said to Greg as they entered and saw displays all around. Greg nodded, smiled deeply at her.

Inside the room, Randy turned to the right. "This exhibit features a diagram of a Buddhist stupa showing its psychological and cosmological correspondences. The stupa is an Asian monument or memorial, often containing relics—the remains of a great saint, or even Buddhist scriptures. Here on the left panel," Randy said, pointing, "we see images of great stupas in…" He leaned forward to read the exhibit, "…Tibet, Nepal, India, Sri Lanka, Indonesia, Malaysia, and Thailand, respectively. These are great devotional structures. Buddhists traditionally circumambulate them while conducting their prayer and mantra recitation. Our interest in the Raymond Lully Museum is in the symbolism in the stupa design. The stupa is a form of mandala, a concentric visual diagram in Hindu and Buddhist traditions. But whereas the mandala is a flat, two dimensional image, the stupa is like a three dimensional mandala, rising up from the flat surface. The stupa has a rich symbolism in its design which is studied and meditated upon by practitioners. As this section shows," Randy said, pointing to a side panel on the mural, "it symbolizes the Buddha himself, sitting in meditation— with his head, spine, body, legs, and throne represented in the structure of the stupa itself. It also represents the five elements in their purified forms—earth, water, fire, air, and space. The stupa has both a psychological and a cosmological significance, and these two aspects are integrally related, flowing into each other, influencing each other."

"Interesting," Sara murmured to Greg, focused intently on the diagram.

Greg walked over to Neil. "There you go, Neil. Never mind AlignIt as moving mandalas. Model that!" He pointed to the diagram before them. "AlignIt as a 3D stupa."

"Jesus!" Neil said, shaking his head. "But I see what Roger's getting at."

Randy moved on slightly to the next exhibit in the sacred architecture section. "Stupas are associated with India and South East Asia. In East

Asia, however, a unique form of the stupa arose in the development of the pagoda. Found in…" Randy rocked forward on his toes to read, "…China, Japan, Korea, Vietnam, and other Asian countries," and leaned back again to resume his talk, "pagoda architecture integrates elements of Buddhist symbolism with Chinese and other oriental iconography. Again, we have a left panel with images from various countries through various dynasties. And here," Randy said, pointing to the right side, "we have a diagram of the pagoda design.

"Now, I've already pointed out the Buddhist symbolism of the stupa. Pagodas may have circular or octagonal shapes. Like the five elements in stupa symbolism, some pagodas have five terraces symbolizing five spaces surrounding Mount Meru, the symbolic mountain of Buddhism. The five again symbolizes five orders of being. Later pagodas have three or even seven, eight, or nine terraces, each with its symbolic associations in Buddhism—but usually pagodas have an odd number of terraces. The terraces may also represent cosmological cycles, or Buddhas living in different time periods. Pagodas may also have geomantic functions; sometimes they're placed to create good influences for the surrounding environment."

Sara leaned to Greg and whispered, "These are really fascinating! The number symbolism, the elements of design….I want to come back and sketch these." Greg nodded, smiling deeply, a sparkle in his eye. He knew Sara's long-time interest in art and design, especially esoteric themes.

Randy moved across the room to the other side and the group followed. "Like many examples of sacred architecture," Randy continued, "mosques in Islam are frequently built on complex number, shape, and color symbolism having psychological and cosmological significance and correspondences. The worshipper's attention is directed, in this space, to higher realities. In this exhibit, for instance, we see a classical mosque dome. This symbolizes the One, or oneness. Below this," Randy said, pointing, "we have an octagonal form, symbolizing, in Islamic cosmology, the Throne, Pedestal, and the angelic realm. Then the four-fold base symbolizes the material world. These *muqurnas*, looking like stalactite, or sometimes people say like a honeycomb, these show the relation of the above and below—they represent the archetypal world descending into our world, or a reflection in our world of the celestial world of archetypes. I won't even begin to explain the sacred geometry expressing outwardly the world of sublime forms, or the number and alphabet symbolism in the Quran, or the color symbolism in the white, black, and green, or the number and spacing of arches and columns. All of these architectural features have a deep significance both to orient the adept meaningfully to our world of physical manifestation, and to prepare the aspiring seeker for the return journey home.

"You studied this, right?" Greg asked Sara.

"Yeah," Sara said, "that class on Islamic Art and Architecture," Sara said.

"So you can begin to see," Randy said, "that through studying sacred architecture, you can study the cosmos. Because sacred architecture embodies the cosmology of the tradition it houses."

Sara put her hand on Greg's forearm, and leaned in to him, whispering, "This is exactly what I'm trying to do in my own art, late at night!" Greg nodded, looking deep into her eyes with a solemn expression. Here was the intimate connection between them.

34

Jeff Baker's staff convened in the GameIt meeting room in the Bayside Village Research Park. Cindy pushed aside a headset and gloves left on the table. "Someone needs to put the gear away after they're done with it," she playfully scolded.

"No, leave it out," Landon said, waving his hand at her, his hair in a tussle, his collar half tucked in, half sticking out. "I'm working on it."

Landon sat down. "I took a game approach to my sleuthing on Mueller."

Jeff seated himself, already impressed with his team's initiative.

The room became serious and eyes and ears focused on Landon. "I figured if we have enough data on him, we could give a little game-like presentation to Roger and Jackie. So I built a gameworld based on what we can learn about Mueller."

A huge, delighted grin shone across Jeff's face. He shook his head incredulously. "Only you would make it into a game." But he liked it.

"It's not a game yet," Landon said. "I only input a few facts. I made the rounds just before the meeting to get everyone's findings. But Alisha, you were out to a meeting, so I didn't get yours."

"Are you going to demo it?" Alisha asked.

"I want to input more data points, then demo it."

Jeff sat forward. "I have some good intel for you. And Jackie has some. It'd be really cool to give back to Roger and Jackie what they've given us, in game form."

"What is it, a simulation?" Mia asked. She was a beautiful, half-Anglo, half Japanese woman in marketing and promotion.

"Kind of, kind of not," Landon said. "It's a tool for visualizing the competitive landscape and showing our due diligence. We represent what we know of Mueller, and we follow his footprint in the gameworld."

"Sweet," Mia said. "We could probably use it for other intelligence gathering."

"Or develop a commercial app for competitive intelligence," Landon said.

"Let's not get ahead of ourselves," Jeff said. "We have an urgent need right now. So what do we have so far? Who wants to start?"

The room was quiet. "I will," Alisha said. "I got word on the street that Mueller's recently hired a few game developers for BlackDog. He's put them on an aggressive schedule to convert a game engine from some tiny little start up in New Jersey called Forq. He has the developers stripping out a bunch of features and layering in a BlackDog feature set. They said the game engine is crap. And he's pushing them hard, working evenings and weekends."

"Wow," Jeff said. "You hit pay dirt."

"You wanted me for my connections," she said with a charming smile.

"BlackDog," Landon said. "So that's San Diego. And he has this start up in New Jersey." He typed notes to himself in an AuthorIt plug in to his gameworld. He seemed to be building the game right there in the meeting.

"Oh, so the start up's not an acquisition," Alisha said. "This is in confidence. He has some kind of intellectual property sharing deal where he gets rights to their game engine. Apparently, he does that a lot—this IP sharing strategy. Like cross licensing."

"Confidential," Landon said to himself. He typed notes.

"So do you know his relationship to BlackDog?" Jeff asked.

"I don't," Alisha said. "Maybe external consultant? Advisor? He's not on their staff or board. But he has rights to their IP."

"Do you know what he's sharing back?" Jeff asked.

Alisha shrugged.

"Probably venture advising, maybe capital," Landon said.

"I don't know," Alisha said. "That's all I know—just what he's getting, and what he's doing with it."

"He's with Hilltop Ventures, right?" Mia asked. Jeff nodded. Mia typed, searched a page of their portfolio companies. She shook her head. "No BlackDog," she said. "They must have some VC backing, though." She searched again.

"Any comments from your connections about what Mueller's like?" Jeff asked. "He has them on an aggressive schedule..."

Alisha scrunched her face, shook her head. "Mmm, no. I guess just that. And my friends thought the game engine was crap, so it probably lacks technical or aesthetic merit. So we don't know why he chose that technology."

"Private equity," Mia blurted. "BlackDog has a few networked equity firms. One in Reno, Nevada, of all places." She laughed. "One in New York. One near Toronto. But nothing in California, none in the Valley."

"Shoot me the link?" Landon said to Mia. She nodded.

Randy led the group to the next room in the Raymond Lully Museum, with a vast set of murals. "Here we have instances of sacred science in Christianity."

"This will be cool!" Keith said to Leah. "I've known this was here, but I haven't seen it yet." Then Keith vaguely wondered why he hadn't come yet, after several months.

Leah nodded, hoping to see something not too remote. She did not wish to feel embarrassed before Keith and now Greg and Sara by knowing so little. She did not want to feel Keith stepping too far away into places she did not know how or whether to follow. Thus far on her trip, very little felt familiar.

"In Late Antiquity," Randy began, "Dionysius the Pseudo Aereopagite expressed a system in a Neoplatonic and theurgic scheme, as we see in this diagram." Randy pointed to the wall before him. "This is his hierarchy of spiritual beings in three categories of three angelic forms in each. It's important for Christian sacred sciences not only as a singular historic example but also because of its continued influence on later thinkers."

Greg recognized Dionysius as Professor Joshua Meade's area. He would meet with Meade tomorrow. He read materials on the plane.

"The first level of the hierarchy, nearest the Divine, has Seraphim, Cherubim, and Thrones; the second is Powers, Virtues and Dominions; and the third is Principalities, Archangels, and Angels."

Randy waited a few moments for the group's contemplation and then proceeded. From his long reading, Greg knew there was more than could be digested quickly.

Randy continued. "In the high Medieval period, Thomas Aquinas may be one of the greatest apologists of sacred sciences in the Christian world— in fact, he used the term *scientia sacra*, from which our own use of the term sacred science comes here at Bayside Village. And for those on the tour yesterday, recall we walked through Avicenna Hall; recall that Aquinas was influenced in part by the philosophy of Avicenna, who himself was regarded as a third Aristotle. Our chart here shows a Thomist scheme of sacred science." Randy again waited some moments and then proceeded to the next mural, walking a few paces.

This is pretty far for Leah, Keith thought, imagining that he himself followed along well enough. He felt, though, an unnamed tension brewing inside himself about the vast distances between his own faith, and this greater unexplored world.

"And here we have Raymond Lully," Randy said, "whose name we've given to this, our beloved museum. In the late medieval period, Raymond Lully was a philosopher in Majorca, off the coast of Spain at a time when Spain had already been under Islamic rule for five or six hundred years. We remember Lully more as an early computationalist, even to the point of being recognized as the first in the West to build a computer."

"It's interesting he says this," Greg whispered to Sara, "because this is one of the historical connections I want to draw for Roger and the AlignIt board—that there is historical precedent for an ontological approach to AlignIt. He probably already knows this."

"Hmm," Sara nodded. She connected Randy's presentation with Greg's work, imagining Greg's drawn relationships.

"In this image from his Ars Magna," Randy continued, "Lully conceived an invention of moving wheels based on Latin letters, representing elemental qualities or philosophical categories. By the contemplation, employment and combination of these letters, a practitioner could study all possibilities of the cosmos."

"Those wheels—those are probably the origins of computer science," Greg whispered to Sara. Now Sara got it. She had seen Greg working at this before.

Greg walked to Neil, pointed this out to him, whispered about its relevance to AlignIt.

"Lully traveled in the Arab world," Randy continued, "and was acquainted with Islamic theology, philosophy, and science. His wheels seem to be based on an Arabic astrological device called a Zairja, which made use of Arabic letters to the same end. In this sense, Lully may not be the first computationalist, and we may have to look back to the medieval Islamic world he traveled in for the inspiration of his invention in Western soil, and for the first conception of a computing device."

"Oh," Greg said humbly to Sara.

"Lully Latinized the originally Arabic alphabet letters of the wheel and recalibrated the corresponding qualities to Western philosophical terms and concepts. While highly influenced by Arab philosophy and science, Lully was, in fact, a Christian, and he wrote his major works as an endeavor to show the heights of Christianity, and to win Muslim converts to Christianity."

Keith picked up on Lully's missionary activity, glanced at Leah, thinking this would impress her.

"In this," Randy said, "Lully was neither successful nor magnanimous. Our museum remembers Lully's philosophical contributions more than his missionary zeal."

"Hmm," Greg said. He didn't know that earlier territory of the Zairja. Would he have time to investigate it and rethink his planned comments to Roger?

"In the Florentine Renaissance," Randy continued, "we have the great works of Pico della Mirandola and Marcilio Ficino." Randy pointed to displays and discussed Ficino's astrological medicine and his harmonious, non-confrontative relation to the church. He then turned to Dominican friar, philosopher, mathematician, and magi Giordano Bruno who further developed the Lullian ideas of the Ars Magna in his Ars Combinatoria. "Influenced by Arab and Neoplatonic ideas and Renaissance Hermeticism, Bruno developed robust cosmological theories beyond those of Copernicus, a qualitative and spatial approach to mathematics, and devices for the arts of memory and imagination. Unlike Ficino, Bruno had a run-in with the church and was burned at the stake during the Roman inquisition."

"These are precedents for AlignIt," Greg whispered to Sara, pointing to Lully's and Bruno's wheels. "Bruno's aren't in AlignIt now, but they should be."

Randy waited as the group studied the charts detailing wheels of qualities and then walked a few more paces. He expounded on the work of Giordano Bruno in its continuation of Lully's wheels.

Much to see, Greg thought; quick impressions must satisfy.

"And in the Protestant Reformation," Randy said, "several scholars and theologians developed elaborate systems, some of them integrating Alchemy and Cabala with Christian theology like these images from Daniel Cramer." An entire mural was devoted to a system of Cramer's Christian visual devotional aids—emblems with their scriptural quotations and alchemical aphorisms.

Keith was fascinated, and he pointed out to Leah the various Bible verses there from Isaiah, Jeremiah, and Daniel. Leah saw those, but she also saw strange drawings and wondered about them.

Again, Randy waited as the group surveyed the images, and then continued to the next exhibit. "Here is the floor plan of a utopian city, Christianopolis, reminding us, in its rather contrived urban plan, of a Renaissance alchemical emblem with its numbers and letters. The image comes from the frontispiece of a book of the same name, Christianopolis, by German Lutheran theologian Johanne Valentine Andreaes, whom some hold to be the author of the Rosicrucian manifestos." Randy made some comments about the inner meaning of the various parts or chambers of the urban plan.

Randy moved on. "In Emmanuel Swedenborg, both scientist, natural philosopher, and spiritualist, we find again the familiar themes of number meanings, a hierarchy of spiritual beings, and correspondence theory." Randy pointed to a display of Swedenborg's discoveries and inventions, another of his philosophical diagrams. He discussed the relation of Swedenborg's spiritual and philosophical investigations and his later mystical visions to his scientific work. The strong Christian character of

Swedenborg's extensive body of work left an impression on Keith.

Again, Randy waited and then continued to the next and last exhibit for Christian sacred science. "Rudolf Steiner is a modern, twentieth century figure who drew upon Goethean science and the Rosicrucian stream of Christianity to develop a number of modern applications, from biodynamic farming to anthroposophical medicine. He is known most widely as the founder of Waldorf education. Steiner's work is also deeply grounded in correspondence theory and a hierarchy of spiritual beings after the work of Pseudo Dionysius, but is decidedly less systematic and computational."

The group studied the images collaged on the mural, some featuring diagrams of Steiner's anthroposophical science, many from drawings and paintings by Steiner himself.

Randy moved forward to the next exhibit—a case of six inch figurines with flowing robes, each demonstrating a different posture or movement. "Here is an alphabet Steiner conceived in dance movements, an art form he called Eurythmy."

Greg and Sara stepped forward, amazed at the art form. They had seen a performance at a Waldorf school Tara could attend in Seattle.

Keith now felt troubled. Religion was his study, and he should know these personages—or at least have heard of them. But this was many steps beyond his knowledge. Maybe this is why he hadn't darkened the door of the museum, he vaguely suspected. This was indeed a challenge for Leah too, he thought. Now came a moment of insight. How could he represent the Bayside Village as a good place to Leah if he didn't feel at home in it himself? No, this material was a stretch almost beyond where he could reach.

A middle-aged woman in the tour group said, "Excuse me, Randy. Perhaps this is an ignorant question. But as I'm listening to you and following through the exhibits, what I'm struck by is how little I know of these systems. I take myself to be a cultured, well-educated, well-traveled world citizen. I recognize Thomas Aquinas, the New Testament, yoga, and pagodas. But there is very much more here, particularly in the West, that I don't recognize."

"Yes," Randy said.

The woman continued. "In this room especially, these systems appear well-developed and I see they have similar patterns. But I haven't seen any of them before."

Leah took comfort in this woman's admission, and she saw now that it wasn't just her who felt surprised by so many new names and ideas.

"Yes, good point," Randy said. "Well, I can offer a few of my own thoughts on this. But there are several opinions on it here at the Bridge Institute. So...as some of you may know, sacred sciences have had a relatively more difficult journey in the West than they have in many other cultures. This difficulty in the West begins with religious suppression of philosophy and science to the point of inquisitions, exiles, bannings, and burnings by official Christendom. During the modern period, modern science shaved off the metaphysics and cosmology of its traditional scientific forebears reducing investigation to only its material aspects, classically called *physis*, as the new foundations of modern science. For example, modern Western chemistry began by stripping alchemy of nearly everything but empirical observations—eschewing psychology, cosmology, and metaphysics, while in Indian, Chinese, and Islamic alchemy, this integral system was preserved."

Neil sauntered over again to Greg and whispered, "Never mind that cultures are conservative by nature and retain only their best attainments, and let their inferior elements die out." Greg snickered. Evidently enjoying his derision, Neil again said, "And never mind evolution, and human societies emerging out of ignorant, pre-rational mythologies into concrete sciences."

Greg smirked, not giving the now expected smile. Then he said, "How about suppression, political motivation, conquest? Evolution isn't always a neat linear progression. What about devolutions, deviations, eclipses in the history of ideas?"

Neil did a quick double-take, wondering at Greg's defense of these silly ideas. Did Greg not share his view or sarcasm?

Greg was aware of this, and struggled inside himself with courage. Was he going to continue pretending he was the mainstream scholar he always passed himself to be?

Emboldened by the woman's question, Keith raised his hand slightly. "Question."

"Yes," Randy said.

"I'm a Christian," Keith said, feeling brave diving into the unknown, surprised at his definitive use of the term Christian, somewhat for Leah's sake. "And I've studied religion in college. But I'm surprised that I don't recognize any of these Christian examples, except maybe Aquinas. But I've never studied Aquinas. Are there Christian sacred sciences based on the Bible?"

"This question is somewhat related to the last," Randy said. "Christianity has certainly interacted with sacred sciences, and within Christendom there have certainly been exponents of sacred sciences. Now, I'm not a scholar in church history or Christian theology, and I'm not sure I'll understand the same thing as you by the term *Christian*. But if you look further into the work of Daniel Cramer in the Protestant Reformation, and others like him, you'll find many biblical references of what I'd consider an evangelical character, and you'll find Christ referred to as the philosopher's stone—in other words, the most important goal of the Christian's quest."

Keith's eyes dilated as he heard these words and recalled the Bible verses engraved above Cramer's woodcut images. Despite the unfamiliar material, Keith felt that Randy intuitively picked up on his more specialized kind of Christianity and the web of questions and needs spun out from it.

Leah began feeling concerned, though not fully grasping why. Hers was a simple faith. She just wanted to love God, she thought. She eschewed great debates. The personal views of Randy about Christendom unsettled her. Though if she were conscious of it, she would have to admit to herself that for all his knowledge and enthusiasm and even his personal edge on these points, she felt no disrespect in him for the gospel of her Lord Jesus Christ.

Randy continued on Keith's question. "Andreaea's Christianopolis portrayed a fully articulated city set on a hill, to use the biblical metaphor—in other words, it showed one vision of what an ideal Christian society could look like. Dionysius also articulates the angelic realm according to angels in the Hebrew scriptures. His work, like that of his period, is filled with biblical references. Also, as we've seen very rapidly just now in the Renaissance and Reformation periods, some Christian systems began including the Hebrew letters as an organizing basis, so that may be a point of interest for you to explore—the so-called Christian Cabala. That may be the extent of my limited knowledge. But I encourage you to talk to others here about this."

Sara was transfixed now by Cramer's Emblem 4, titled "I love," with the image of a flame growing out of a heart. She read the associated scriptural verse from Song of Solomon, 4:16: Blow upon my garden, that the spices thereof may flow out. Then the associated verse of Cramer's pen: Let me be kindled, Jesus, by your incense and breath; I flame, let yours be the love; I am fragrant, let yours be the scent. She was moved.

"From my own limited researches in this area," Randy continued, taking added time for Keith's question, "it has often seemed to me that Western Christianity, at least in its most official expressions, has often defined itself by what it excludes as much as by what it offers. And much of what official Christendom excludes is the sacred sciences and their philosophical frameworks, from the very beginnings of Christianity right up to our day. One of our professors here, Dr. Joshua Meade, studies these matters in greater depth."

"I'm meeting him this week," Greg whispered to Keith.

Keith's eyes widened. It was awe-inspiring to him that Greg moved in the worlds of such people.

"I understand from Meade," Randy said, "that some of the earliest church councils excised the sciences and philosophies, whose exponents often fled Eastward to Syria and Persia, when they weren't outright killed by the church. The great inquisitions also tortured and burned many associated with philosophy and science. Official Christendom also has suppressed and censored the great philosophical schools and sciences, as when the emperor Constantine closed Plato's academy and Aristotle's Lyceum. So, official Christianity in the West has had an uneasy relationship with the sciences, and my own opinion is that I don't think we are yet finished with this strained relationship."

Greg listened to Randy with focused attention, subtly nodding in silent assent. These points were obvious to him and well documented. Keith, too, listened with rapt attention.

A few people began shifting their weight and looking around, apparently less interested in the historical questions of Western civilization and Christendom.

Randy went on. "The fact that many Christians today practice secular modern Western science isn't really the best evidence that Christianity and science are on better terms. The great questions of worldview, cosmology and metaphysics are often left in the dark in the compromise that stands as the foundation of modern Western science—namely, that the church dominates religion while science is free to explore the material world so long as it does not explore the sacred. The relationship of Christian spirituality to scientific inquiry is really one big issue at the heart of this inquiry, at least from a Western perspective."

Keith turned over Randy's words in his mind. The relationship of Christian spirituality to scientific inquiry…How should he understand their relation, he wondered. This was a new question.

A plausible argument, Greg thought, knowing much of this territory from his own research. What would it be to teach and research in this academic climate?

For Keith, the ideas were almost too big; he scrambled for reference points but had nothing in hand. Another reason he avoided the museum tour so far, he vaguely sensed. He thought to himself that he should become more active in his search.

Randy continued. "As Asian traditions have come into the West in the past hundred years, we tend to sever these traditions in this Western-type split, too, just like early modern science was split. Today, we take Taoism as philosophy, but separate its medical and martial arts, we push yoga into aerobics and exercise, severing devotion and knowledge from it." Sara's attention returned from Cramer's Emblem 4 at Randy's mention of yoga and devotion—the heart path, *bhakti*. She herself felt yoga rendered asunder. Images of yoga classes back in Seattle came to her mind. She always wanted the full teaching, with *bhakti* and *gnana* yoga. But it seldom went beyond aerobic workouts.

35

"Okay," Randy said, "let's enter to the next room—music."

Finally, Sara thought, feeling an itch to move.

Randy led the group into an adjoining room in the Raymond Lully Museum replete with visual exhibits on music, musicians and instruments. "Here," he said, "we showcase music designed to express higher laws, and to guide the listener's attention to finer realities. We have audio stations around the room where you can listen on headphones to a variety of musical pieces. But since we're together on this tour, I'll play a few selections on the overhead speakers for everyone to hear. And please feel free to walk around the room while these play and view the exhibits featuring musical instruments, musical traditions, and traditional contexts of this musical activity.

"Our first selection comes from the musical, artistic and poetic masterpiece *Atalanta Fugiens*, by Michael Maier, from 1617. On the wall to my left, we have an astounding collection of images from his alchemical plates. Examples of Maier's sheet music are part of the exhibit here to the right." Randy waited a moment for the group to turn to the images of this extraordinary set of woodcuts. He then unclipped the mobile device from his belt and touched the screen to begin the music. "This piece is called Fugue 18."

Renaissance organ and choral music played through the room as the tour participants moved about viewing mandolins and dulcimers, studying Maier's sheet music and alchemical engravings. Sara studied the sequence of Maier's emblems, making quick sketches in her mind. This was interesting, she felt.

Leah stood close by Keith, utterly perplexed at the lizards, two headed androgynes, and the sun and moon before her. What were these odd images, and how were they connected to the music, or anything spiritual at all? What was Keith doing here at the Bayside Village? She just wanted him to come home.

When Maier's Fugue 18 ended, Randy said, "Now we'll hear a brief excerpt of *Raga Malika*, from the repertoire of classical Indian raga." Randy walked down the room several steps. "On the wall to my right, you'll see portrayals and artifacts of *nada yoga*. This yoga can be understood as the practice of listening to fine sounds or tones, and attuning oneself to its vibratory energies, ultimately to the primary inner, mystical sound, the ultimate, original vibration from which the universe manifested. See if you can feel something like this while listening." Randy again touched the screen of his mobile and the music sounded through the room.

Greg was transfixed by the raga. It brought associations of earlier study of Vedanta, of meals with Sara in various ashrams, of traditional Indian culture and customs embodying higher principles.

Sara, too, was moved, recalling *yantras*, incense-filled practice rooms, teachers.

"Wow, I feel moved!" Greg said to Sara. "It makes me want to sit in contemplation and have my attention elevated to higher realms."

When the excerpt of raga concluded, Randy said, "Now we'll listen to Chinese five element music. This type is based on an understanding of five basic qualities, or phases in time. Each phase has a different feeling quality. Each represents a season, with its corresponding time of day, psychological moods, organs of the body, and so on. We'll listen now to a brief excerpt of Spring." Randy again touched his mobile, and music filled the room.

After Spring, Randy said, "That ends our musical selections."

A murmur of conversation picked up.

"Mhmmm," Sara said to Greg, "that was nice."

"Okay," Randy said, ushering the group onward, "let's move on to our last exhibit for the museum tour." The next room contained images of database charts, user displays, and images of exotic human sexual conduct, portrayed sensitively for a wide public. "This last room features a project in its nascent stages. We don't have a name for it yet, except to call it the sacred sexuality portal. This tool is focused on mapping all possible expressions of optimal human sexuality—in case you thought sacred science is only for ascetics, monks and yogis." A few people in the group chuckled lightly. "Seriously," Randy continued, "it's a cataloging project at this early phase, and it's aimed at investigating the world's vast and diverse expressions of human sexual activity. So everything you've ever imagined may be here—and more. On the walls immediately around us we have historical paintings and other images from India, China, and various indigenous groups, featuring sexual practices, rituals, and implements. In a few of the display stands here, we have actual implements used in various places."

"Where's all the sexy photos?" a young man in the group called out, humorously. Some people laughed. Others gave disapproving grins.

"Right," Randy said. "Well, we don't have sexy photos."

Randy paused, turned to another wall. "While the project aims to cover all of human sexual activity, it's focused on mapping humanity's higher sexual potential. Mainstream academic sexology is largely devoted to sexual pathology and establishing normal, healthy sexual functioning, and together with psychology, it aims to establish sexual intimacy. This project, however, is focused on identifying the higher reaches of human sexual experience, practice, knowledge, and tools. It presumes as a baseline neither pathological nor ordinary human sexual behavior, but the extraordinary."

"What's the extraordinary?" the same young man asked, more earnestly.

"Well," Randy said, "the extraordinary could be highly potent and active people…"

"Like sex superstars? Or sex goddesses?"

"Perhaps. But it may also include expressions of transmutation, asceticism, even mutilation. The selection criteria for these exhibit contents includes the higher development of consciousness, will, and ability, usually in a larger metaphysical and cosmological framework than we find in modernity. The San Francisco Bay Area is well known for its history of the Barbary coast, and its extensive exploration of alternative sexuality, especially in the 1960's and 1970's, like the 1967 Summer of Love in San Francisco. But few of those expressions show up in this project. This isn't a catalog of free sexual expression or sexual libertinism. The sacred sexuality portal unfolds in rich depth the higher reaches of human sexual potential, and its possible benefits for the development of human consciousness. Maybe one end result could be to liven up ordinary sex, or find a partner—but you could say these results, if they occurred, would be byproducts, not intended results. The chief aim of most catalogued practices is the transformation of human consciousness together with the development of increased will and other higher human capacities.

"Hmm," Sara said. Greg heard her, saw her contemplating.

"The next phase of the sacred sex portal which is just now being initiated in our Research Park, is linking the data and images collected in these catalogues with the table structures of AlignIt, the sacred science database we saw yesterday morning."

"And what could we do with this," Sara said to Greg, waxing intimate and playful.

"This will make it the largest resource for sacred sex the world has ever seen. This chart," Randy said, pointing to a nearby wall, "prepared collaboratively by the sacred sex portal project and the AlignIt team, gives an example of such a characterization. The table shows correspondences of symbols, organs, seasons, times of day, positions….These have been used to help guide the cultivation of human sexuality toward its highest peaks. And at these peaks, the project leaders maintain that human sexuality is one powerful engine, not the only, to move human consciousness to its highest realization—of the One, and ultimately beyond the One, to Nothingness."

"Oh," Greg said aloud to himself.

The group took a brief time viewing the art works and diagrams of the sacred sex portal. Sara touched Greg on the shoulder and pointed to a colorful diagram titled Amritkala. It showed a woman's nude body and lunar cycles, and charted the relations between the energy centers of a woman's body and phases of the moon, called Chandrakala. Greg and Sara leaned in together, studying.

Randy called the group together. "Okay, folks. We've seen a lot in the

Raymond Lully Museum in our brief time this morning, and I encourage you to return at your leisure and explore the museum further. And with that, I hope you'll enjoy the rest of day two of our Bayside Village Orientation."

Greg and Sara exited the Raymond Lully Museum with the group. Sara leaned intimately into Greg as they walked, saying, "Hmm, think you'd work on that project?"

"Which one?"

"Which one?" Sara asked.

Greg then realized which one. "Mmm."

"You used to tell me such things," she said discreetly, with people all around.

"Mhmmm," Greg smiled. Memories came to him of things he said, things he did, with the arts of sacred love and sex. That was earlier in their relationship, he realized. "I don't know if Roger has that in mind, too. Maybe I'll find out tomorrow."

"Maybe we'd learn a few things for our own higher reaches in the bedroom."

Greg pondered. Why has that dropped off in our marriage? The demands of family life? The requirements of the path, of its grinding, devastating action in their lives? Or simply that he had lost a certain inspiration, lost hope of returning to ideas that inspired him years before, now brutally ripped away by a harsh path? "What could help us, I think, is finding examples of two working parents with limited resources who figure out how to create intimate time in their busy lives. Just having enough time together would be a great feat. Maybe babysitters or a day care."

That was part of it, Sara thought. She didn't feel all of Greg's resolution. Somehow visiting Bayside Village reminded Sara of parts of Greg that once shined but were now a pale reflection of their earlier beauty. Greg was more balanced now, more mature. Yet something has dimmed in him.

36

Greg and Sara entered the courtyard between the Raymond Lully Museum and the Research Park. Tuesday's Orientation activities were filled with optional break-out sessions, and Roger would soon give an overview of AlignIt for Orientation participants.

By a courtyard fountain between the buildings and opening to the Bridge Institute quad, Greg pulled out his mobile, checked for messages from Mrs. Blocke about meeting to discuss his faculty interviews. Nothing. Again. He double-checked her posted availability and saw that she was listed as "in the office." He placed another call. No answer. What was he going to do about this?

Greg and Sara discussed the Museum briefly with Keith and Leah and another woman, and then entered a small auditorium next door in the Research Park used for business presentations. Greg and Sara socialized with fellow Orientation guests. When President Steve Bateson walked to the lectern on stage, they sat down.

President Bateson looked out to the audience and smiled. "Welcome to Day 2," he said and paused, waiting as people shuffled to their seats. "One of my favorite activities is introducing our illustrious faculty, because they exemplify what we're creating in this grand Bayside Village experiment. And this makes me proud. To give you a taste of our faculty's caliber, then, and a taste of one exciting project which has gotten some real traction here lately, it is my great pleasure to introduce Dr. Roger Barnes."

Greg sat forward, listened attentively.

Bateson paused. "Roger is the developer of the AlignIt software platform at the Bridge Institute and founder of the AlignIt Commons, a commons of applications companies that has grown up around AlignIt here in the Bayside Village Research Park. With all the media buzz, I hardly need to sing AlignIt's praises. But I'll sing Roger's." Bateson looked to Roger in the audience, smiled at him. "Roger is Bridge Institute professor in the History of Religions, Integral Philosophy, and Sacred Science. He's an exemplary Bridge Institute faculty member in many ways. Not only is he a fine colleague and friend. He also embodies the integration of intellectual rigor and practical application with social impact that we strive to achieve here. Roger is also a long time adept in a Sufi school, the fruits of which he brings to bear upon his research, inquiry, and technology development. And he's a successful technologist who has brought his years of research to bear on the creation of a new technology which has become the basis of products and services for AlignIt Commons member companies—several of which are being incubated right here in our Research Park. With that, I'll hand it over to Roger."

President Bateson clapped and stepped beside the lectern, an overhead beam lighting his white hair. Roger Barnes energetically bounded to the stage from the front row, shook Bateson's hand, and cordially patted his shoulder.

Greg leaned to Sara amidst the clapping. "I'm surprised they're so open about affiliations with spiritual schools." Sara nodded, clapping.

Bateson returned to the audience. Roger took the lectern and the clapping subsided. He looked to Bateson with a deep smile. "Thank you, Steve, for those kind words."

To Greg, Roger embodied the academic and the practical. Roger was a man of action, moving swiftly with purpose, will in action. His cultivated social grace in this setting, next to Bateson's, revealed Roger the scholar. The quality of Roger's presence evinced his spiritual training.

"In our brief time this morning," Roger said, "I'll introduce the background and vision of AlignIt. This will serve to illustrate why the Bridge Institute creates marvelous new technologies based on sacred science in the first place. I'll take just a few questions at the end, as our time is short. "So," Roger said, touching his mobile to queue up his slides. The first slide read, The Need. "Long before the advent of modern science, technology, and business, traditional knowledge and sacred science provided norms and guidance in every field of endeavor. In many traditional societies, every domain of life was addressed by traditional knowledge and sacred science, from law, government, and social organization, to medicine, architecture, astronomy, physics, and agriculture."

Now Sara would get an overview directly from Roger, Greg thought. Here was an opportunity, finally, to see it for herself, to be inspired by Roger himself.

"Traditional knowledge and sacred science," Roger said, "have existed for several thousand years. What do I mean by these terms, sacred science and traditional knowledge? You'll hear them used frequently at the Bridge Institute. When we say sacred science, most people here mean scientific knowledge in a given domain that is linked to traditional metaphysical principles. The ultimate sacred science is the science of the heart showing pathways that lead individual beings on a return journey home to the origin from which they came. Related to this are lesser sciences in all domains exploring the full range of things in the world—physics, chemistry, biology, and so on. For instance, Pythagorean mathematics is rooted in a larger tradition of philosophy and human development. When we say traditional knowledge, or TK for short, we mean local, indigenous knowledge in a given area, usually involving plants, medicines, or other practical arts, and usually related to native wisdom, knowledge and teachings. Both are terms of art, and in some instances they overlap. Some TK might be sacred science, but not always. Sacred science is a philosophical term; traditional knowledge, or TK, is a legal one in the domain of intellectual property law. And I'll quiz you at the end."

A few people laughed. Greg leaned to Sara and whispered. "I haven't heard the term traditional knowledge used here."

"Me neither."

Roger touched his mobile, the screen advanced.

Greg noticed now that on his past two slides, Roger had included abundant images and a few data points and stats. But in speaking, Roger extemporized charismatically, aiming far beyond the slides, as if speaking from an internalized outline. The tension between image, data and words made Roger's pitch all the more dynamic and compelling.

Roger glanced at his slide and back to the audience. "Both historical remnants and contemporary expressions of traditional knowledge and sacred science can be found in cultures great and small around the globe. They've given rise to remarkable achievements that, in some cases, continue to evoke wonder and defy modern imagination, like…" and here, Roger flashed a string of images, "…the Egyptian pyramids, Stonehenge, Gothic Cathedrals like Chartres, Mayan and Aztec pyramids, systems of irrigation, astronomical and calendrical devices, musical attainments, and medical discoveries—in some cases beyond what modern Western science has discovered or even knows how to approach. And while we typically focus on progress in the modern West, let us remember it is possible for civilizations to lose knowledge as well—whether through conquest, colonialism, changing fortunes, or changing paradigms of knowledge. Hence we can be left with artefacts without the keys to unlock their mysteries. Today, due to rapid globalization and the exportation of modern Western civilization on a global scale, this remarkable treasury of sacred science and traditional knowledge is being rapidly eroded from human culture and memory—in some cases it is being deliberately undermined to create new markets for commercial products, or erased by political and social forces such as secularism, modern scientific hegemony, religious fundamentalism, revolutions, persecutions, and the like."

This is broader in its scope than just AlignIt, Greg thought. He's on a roll.

Roger clicked, advanced the slide. "At the very same time, the dizzying pace of global innovation shows every sign of continued acceleration. The hastening of innovation is driven not just by commercial interest in disruptive breakthrough technologies with high revenue potential. It is also driven by the increasing destabilization of long-existing cultural, social, ethical, scientific, and organizational norms across the globe and the subsequent need for replacement norms, systems, and innovations. The results of rapidly accelerating innovation, the increasing impact of industrialized societies on the global ecosystem, the erosion and destruction of traditional knowledge and sacred science, and rapidly changing cultures are giving rise to increasing cultural, social, economic, political, and ecological instability. Yet the need for innovation to solve increasing global problems is being met by a new global Westernized culture and science increasingly bereft of a guiding compass, provided previously by metaphysical principles underlying traditional knowledge and sacred science."

Greg listened with rapt attention. His conversations with Roger over the past year had increasingly gotten down in the trenches, in the fine details of the AlignIt discovery engine, its underlying principles, the specifications for an upper ontology. Greg felt inspired by Roger's capacity to step back and discuss the broader context, the need, before a public audience.

Roger moved to the next slide, Integrative Theories and Methods. "Several integrative theories and methods have arisen in the past century. These answer the need of people around the globe to make sense of the meeting of cultures through increased travel and communication, and the joining of previously isolated pockets of traditional knowledge and sacred science. Several of these are listed here, like the integral philosophy of Sri Aurobindo, the perennial philosophy as expressed by figures like Rene Guenon, Fritjoff Schoen and Sayyed Hosein Nasr. However, great syntheses are not a modern phenomenon. You can see on the left that there were many such figures before them, in ancient, medieval and early modern times, and we've seen others in our day. I won't spend time here today. The important point is to see that there exist these systems for meaningfully relating diverse religious and philosophical systems on the basis of their underlying patterns or types. AlignIt is a technological embodiment of integral and perennial philosophies, and a tool that aids in revealing types and aligning objects with these larger patterns."

Greg leaned to Sara and whispered, "Roger told me a few months ago that the Village itself is based on integral philosophy." Sara raised her eyebrows and nodded.

Roger clicked his mobile and advanced to the next slide, Market Demand. "Ironically, while modern Western science and industry are becoming rapidly globalized, the traditional knowledge and practices of many non-Western cultures, such as those from Central and East Asia and indigenous cultures, are being introduced to the West. Experiments in adapting and even mainstreaming traditional teachings in the currents of Western thought and practice have been occurring increasingly since the mid 1800's, with a marked increase since the 1960's. Moreover, interest has grown in the same period in the spiritual and esoteric currents of Western civilization. These have given rise to a growing market of new products and services integrating Western with non-Western knowledge. Thus a new period of integrative theories and methods has arisen in the past century in answer to the need of people around the globe to make sense of this joining of previously isolated pockets of traditional knowledge and sacred science. Yet new technologies exploiting the growing integration of traditional knowledge and science from around the world are few. And those meeting the need in a philosophically robust and soul-satisfying way are fewer still. This is the space AlignIt has taken."

Greg noticed Neil come in late, holding his mobile phone in hand.

"Today," Roger continued, "many people express a need for new solutions to rapidly changing times, a need for crossing language and culture barriers while preserving what is best around the world. A demand exists for technologies like AlignIt, and applications based on it, like PlanIt, AuthorIt, GameIt, and others. These technologies can meaningfully integrate disparate streams of traditional knowledge and sacred science and make them accessible for contemporary science and innovation.

"In our time of rapid change in the global knowledge landscape, individuals, organizations, societies, and governments need a compass to orient and develop knowledge, tools, products and services. AlignIt provides that compass needle for pointing contemporary knowledge creation to the magnetic north, to deep patterns in nature, to metaphysical principles for optimizing existing knowledge, developing the most effective new ideas and making breakthrough discoveries."

Sara leaned to Greg now, and whispered, "This is organized like an investor pitch, like the slide decks I get when we handle start ups. But it's also way different, focused on vision."

"Hmm," Greg said. "Maybe the case in the slides is proven now." He wondered if Sara was inspired by Roger's vision as he himself was, or perhaps unmoved, if this seemed nothing more than the investor pitches she sees back home.

Roger clicked to the next slide. "So let me tell you about some of the significant unmet needs which AlignIt is meeting. It's difficult to speak of 'unmet needs' which we may not recognize we feel. Breakthrough technologies often gamble on opportunities ahead of the market rather than tapping consciously felt needs. To that end, let me identify several opportunities created by the convergence of factors I've mentioned which AlignIt and companies built on it are meeting." Roger turned and used the red laser pointer in his mobile, extemporizing through the bullets on his last slide.

"So there's a brief introduction to AlignIt, and the historical backdrop leading up to it," Roger said. "Hopefully this also provides a window into how the Bayside Village at large is spawning, incubating, scaling, and transferring new technologies grounded in sacred science. There is plenty more to say, but our time here is short."

"Wow!" Sara said to Greg. "It's really good to hear this backstory."

Roger clicked to a screen with an attractive visual portrait of an AlignIt data table, with sections pulsating, fading in and out, and left it up for the remainder of the session. "We have time for a few questions. Yes, in the back?"

"Yeah. This is really fascinating," a man said. Several heads in the audience turned back to see him. "I have two questions. So, the main purpose of AlignIt is search and revealing relationships?"

"AlignIt has many purposes," Roger said. "It's a tech platform, so by itself there isn't a lot that can be done with it without application layers built on top of it. And I'll draw your attention again to application providers among our AlignIt Commons members in our Research Park here, like GameIt, PlanIt, AuthorIt, and more. The main use of AlignIt itself, beyond a tech platform, is as a discovery engine. This is our current research phase at the Bridge Institute. So think about drug discovery, as an example. Or materials science, or chemical engineering. We're developing AlignIt as a tool for identifying new entities, and for the discovery of new properties, structures, functions, and more. So AlignIt is also a discovery engine soon to use an upper ontology and logic engine being developed here."

Greg leaned to Sara and whispered, "Soon to be developed here. That's what Roger wants me to work on." Sara nodded.

"Is it available open source?" the man asked. "So anyone can use it?"

"It's a slightly different model," Roger said. "We've made publicly accessible user interfaces, but the engine itself is not public. The engine is accessible only to members of the AlignIt Commons—a membership-based affiliation of companies developing AlignIt applications. But sure, users accessing AlignIt's public interfaces can do anything with what we've made publicly available."

Roger paused, searching for other hands. "Yes, over here, on the right." Heads turned to see the next questioner.

"I don't want to sound old fashioned," a middle-aged woman said, "but aren't you sort of putting this really powerful stuff potentially into the wrong hands?"

"Possibly," Roger said.

"And doesn't that bother you?"

"If you sell an ax," Roger said, "or give it away, one person chops wood, another may chop off someone's head. Neither action makes the ax good or bad, necessarily. But I think some designs are inherently intended for good or ill."

"Is there anything in AlignIt that mitigates misuse?" the woman asked.

"Oh, good question," Roger said. "Sure, several things. We've tried to release AlignIt in an optimal set of conditions. For instance, we provide training and workshops to create a culture around its use. We hold the technology platform here at the Research Park in the AlignIt Commons and ensure quality in its further development. We set diligence requirements for AlignIt Commons members using AlignIt—in other words, we ensure their diligent and socially responsible development of AlignIt applications. We reserve the right to revoke membership, licenses and ownership shares in the Commons—for misuse as much as for lack of development. Our Research Access Office also incorporates parameters in their diligence requirements to ensure appropriate transfer of technology to further the development of sacred science. Does that help? Good. How about one more question?" Roger said. "Ah, yes, the woman in blue, there?"

"Thank you for your overview," the woman said. "And by the way, I have an AlignIt user account and I find it really fascinating."

"Oh," Roger interjected. "Good to have an actual beta tester in the audience."

"But what I still don't understand is why would you take qualities or essences, like you have, and put them in a database? And just to say where I'm coming from, I'm a programmer and web app developer, and I'm also on a devotional yoga path—so I walk in both worlds like you do, and I kind of get what you're doing. But I'm both fascinated and disturbed. Like, you have different mantras in AlignIt. I really like seeing the convergence of my interests in AlignIt. But the question that keeps bugging me, because its unsolved for me, is why not just pray in your heart? I mean, let's just say that if I'm already using mantras on my own, why would I want to look at them in AlignIt?"

Greg sat riveted. Now he got to see how other users encounter AlignIt. This was priceless. He watched Roger in action in front of an audience, like the first time they met in San Francisco at the semantic web conference last year.

"This is a good question," Roger said, "and it actually gets to the heart of what AlignIt is, and isn't. First of all, I'll say as an aside that AlignIt is not designed primarily for general public use without application layers. It's fine for anyone to register and look around and play. But the place to go to get a great user experience is one of the applications providers here in the Research Park, like GameIt, PlanIt, or AuthorIt. In fact, probably the best front end to give you a picture of AlignIt is an online game created by GameIt. Most of you attended the GameIt reception last night, no doubt. This fact actually illustrates how focused the Bridge Institute is on facilitating technology transfer and development. But let me go back to what I think is your deeper question." Roger paused, thought. "To be clear, AlignIt is not a devotional aid, or some kind of e-reader for data. It's not meant simply to hold and display content. Its more than an index. It's not so easy to do in AlignIt what you can do in your heart. Conversely, it's not so easy to do in your heart, or mind, what AlignIt does. Just considering AlignIt itself as a technology platform, AlignIt's power lies in three areas: the knowledge implicit in its structure, its capacity as a discovery tool using that structure, and the operations possible using that structure. AlignIt encodes the entities, relations and operational rules of these qualities you're talking about in the mantras so you can do things with them. It's a tool. And what we can do by its aid is greater than what we can do unaided."

"Yeah, I get that part," the woman said. "I guess what I'm saying is why do you need a database for this? You have the mantras, or names of God, or whatever. For thousands of years, people have had these precious resources and we haven't computerized them. I guess there's an inner voice in me, like an inner critic, that says it's sacrilegious to do this in a big web-based database—even though I'm a techie and a fan of what you've created. Do you know what I'm saying? Doesn't this desecrate the mantras or the names of God, or the gods and goddesses…?"

"Yes, I hear you," Roger said. "Well, for thousands of years, we have also used tools, including tools in the spiritual arena. So if you're on a yoga path, think *yantras*. Right? Think charts showing correspondences of mantras with other qualities. Think correspondences between the body's energy centers and planetary bodies. Raymond Lully, the namesake of our beloved Raymond Lully Museum, created a technology of two moving wheels of Latin letters in the 1300's for exploring the qualities of creation. Technologies like these have always existed, actually—not everywhere, not in all traditions, but they're found frequently enough over time and across the world. You can do things with these tools. They're aids to understanding, to spiritual exercises, even to scientific investigation. So, why create AlignIt? For the same reasons. But with AlignIt, we can do more. In our day, we have computer and information science at our disposal, and these sciences help us extend the capacity of traditional tools as well as expand its theoretical base. I can understand it feeling sacrilegious. Perhaps at one time, painting a yantra on a rock or a building felt like a violation, or making a stone clock to measure the sun's movements, because then anyone in the town or on the road could walk by and use it. Before it was only known to adepts meeting in secret with a great yogi or sage. Taking anything that was esoteric or private and making it public, or reducing it to a tool, does involve a certain measure of risk, of ceding control, of surrendering exclusivity. Today, when you publish an encyclopedia or a software tool, you trade off certain control over access and use. But here at Bayside Village, we hold the cultivation of a civil society and responsible citizenry as important."

Roger closed his talk. The audience clapped and Roger descended the steps of the stage. While the group filed out of the auditorium, Greg noticed a small crowd gathering around Roger. Greg pointed to him and said to Sara, "It's a good thing I have a connection to Roger. As AlignIt grows, it could get hard to reach him." Sara nodded.

37

Greg and Sara parted from each other after Roger's AlignIt

presentation. Sara had planned on visiting the Art Center, and she started walking there now. But she stopped, turned back, walked instead across the Bridge Institute quadrangle to the Administration building.

Sara entered, stood inside an office on the first floor, studied the marquis. Puzzled, she turned to the receptionist. "Excuse me."

A middle-aged man looked up from the mobile screen projection at his desk. "Yes? Can I help you?" He looked thoughtful, deep, patient and kindly.

"Hi. Sorry to bother you. I'm looking for the archives. I don't see it on the map or marquis of rooms."

The man sat back, his eyes squinted. "What kind of archives?"

"Archives of the Bayside Village and Bridge Institute."

"Hmm. I don't believe we hold such archives. Wouldn't be a bad idea." He thought for a moment. "Are you thinking of the Raymond Lully Museum or Avicenna Hall?"

"Not those. I'm pretty sure its here."

"We don't have a collection like that here. These are administrative offices."

"Well, I asked Randy Seton on the Orientation tour yesterday and he said there are archives in a vault in the Administration building."

"Oh the vault." The man laughed slightly.

"I'm looking for posters and promotional materials of the Bayside Village…"

"Yeah, the vault is off limits," he said firmly. Seeing Sara's disappointment, he added thoughtfully, "It's not what it sounds. It's just an empty storage room with boxes and old files and furniture—even holiday decorations and broken chairs."

"Oh." That stopped Sara, surprised her. What next, she thought.

"There could be a surplus of posters there, too, I guess, if Randy says so. But I'm sorry, there are also confidential documents. It's really just a storage room."

"Isn't there anyone who could take me there and show me the older posters?"

"I'm sorry, Ma'am. The room is only for our facilities people. It's really just storage. Maybe you could check with Karen Mitchell in the External Affairs Office. Their office produces our promotional materials. We also have some displays in our Atrium across the quad."

"I've seen the Atrium already."

"I think that's the best I can offer."

"Okay, thanks a lot for your help," Sara said. She turned and walked out of the building.

Sara stood on the sidewalk in the late morning sun thinking what to do. She looked around the quad, studying the Bridge Institute buildings, taking in a wide view, feeling the place, giving her conscious mind something to do, waiting for a solution to her problem. She mentally retraced her steps on the tour yesterday. Where else could she see the design history of promotional materials? But the vault had what she sought.

Sara pulled out her mobile, searched for Randy's number, clicked on it, placed a call.

Greg and Neil walked from Roger's AlignIt presentation to the Dining Commons. Neil opened the wooden screen door, held it for Greg, and they walked in. Greg got a cup of coffee. Neil ordered something, waited.

Greg sat down at a table, set his coffee down. He pulled out his mobile, turned on keyboard and screen projections, checked messages from University of Washington. Then he checked for messages from Mrs. Blocke. None. She now seemed evasive. Why hadn't she returned his calls and emails? He knew she was in; she knew he was here.

Neil came now, pulled out a chair and set down a small breakfast plate with an egg omelet. "Are you ready for the big disclosure?" He sat down, put down a cup of steaming, hot black coffee.

Greg looked up. "I'm just catching up on email here." He deactivated his screen projections. "Yeah, I'm ready. So, I didn't see you at the GameIt reception last night."

Neil took a bite of his omelet, talked while chewing. "Yeah. I went to dinner with some colleagues I met a few years ago at a conference. Some folks at UC Berkeley's School of Information."

"Ah. Are you well-connected with Berkeley faculty?"

"Of course." That was a confident, almost incredulous voice. "Information science is a tight community. How about you? You brought your family here. How's that working out?"

"It's working pretty well, actually. It didn't seem at first like the most interesting place to bring a family—compared to a conference at a downtown hotel with entertainment and museums." He said this more for Neil's sake, though of course he was delighted to have the Daycare. "The Bay Area has plenty of attractions, but Richmond isn't a great place to be holed up for a week without a car. But it's worked out well. We've put my daughter Tara in the Bayside Village Day Care. And there's enough here to engage my wife, Sara."

"There is, huh? Like what?" Neil asked, chewing.

"Morning yoga, art studios, evening activities. She's taking her sketch pad around the Village and drawing during the day. She's an industrial artist in the IT sector."

"Right," Neil said. "She began to tell me yesterday."

"She's in a design firm in Seattle."

"Huh. She's pretty sharp. I see she keeps up with you." Neil put down his fork, pushed his plate away. "I wouldn't bring my wife here," he said, sitting back and shaking his head. "She wants amenities—pool, spa, doing the hair and nails, dining, dancing."

Out of the corner of his eye, Greg spotted Sara entering the Dining Commons with her sketch book in hand. She didn't see him sitting there with Neil on the side by the windows. Listening to Neil, Greg stole occasional glances at her. He watched her gather up a couple of pastries on a counter by the kitchen and walk to a far corner, facing away, to sit alone and eat. She seemed disturbed again, Greg mused.

"When I'm in session," Neil continued, "she goes to boutiques and buys clothes and jewelry. There's none of that here."

Greg sipped his coffee. He contemplated how different Sara seemed from Neil's description of his wife—her qualities, their shared interests, her disturbances. He put down his cup. "Yeah, its all industrial outside the Bayside Village." He looked out a window. "It's kind of ironic that some of the faculty here teach utopian ideas while the surrounding area seems rather dystopian."

"That's why I stayed in Berkeley."

"Oh, you're not staying on campus here?"

"Here? Hell no," Neil said, chuckling in disbelief. "There's nothing here. No, I've got a nice place."

"Yeah? Where?"

Greg listened with half an ear as Neil prattled about hotel and amenities. Greg's attention kept turning to Sara. Is this daring venture to the Village really bothering her this much, he wondered? Was he driving her to binge? But then she got up swiftly. He watched her pick up the second pastry, uneaten, walk to a trash bin, discard it. She left the Dining Commons, as if with sudden purpose. That was quick. Interesting, he thought. Had she decided against it? What does she need?

"Anyway," he said as Neil reached a logical end, "looks like it's time. You ready for Roger?"

"Yup."

Greg and Neil stood up. Greg fetched his cup and turned to the kitchen. He recognized quickly that Neil hadn't eaten yet at the Dining Commons. "You can put your plate and cup over here," he said, looking back to Neil.

Neil humpfed with a sardonic smile. "They can get it."

Roger picked up his mobile. "Hello?....Hey, Randy....How serious is Greg? Oh, very serious. All the core faculty in my department are interviewing him this week and we're prepared to make a good offer....Why?....Sara? She's not convinced yet. That's the harder piece to put in place....She asked you what?!?....Just now?....No kidding!....Right, I asked Karen if she would consider interviewing her. Karen looked over her portfolio and got pretty excited, actually. So apparently Karen's interviewing her Thursday. Maybe that made a difference for her....Yes, I do think it's worth your time....Yes, please. I appreciate it very much....Thanks. Keep me posted."

"You sure are determined," Randy said. He walked ahead of Sara down a lonely, darkened back hall in the Administration building that lit up as they walked through. "I don't think anyone has gone through these materials yet since we put 'em there. You may be the first." He turned to a door on the left. "This, my dear, is the Vault." There was that funny voice again, like yesterday on the tour. It must be a thing for him—the Vault. In a playful, sing-sing voice of a mystery thriller narrator, he said, "No visitor has entered here before." He pulled out his mobile, held it up to her and grinned. "I worked my connections to get the key download."

"I really appreciate this," Sara said.

Randy clicked around on his mobile. He found the key, clicked it, waved his mobile over the door, and heard it unlock. "I guess that's the one." He opened the door for Sara and followed her in. The light switched on. The room was filled with stacked boxes of the same size on one wall, an assortment of office furniture neatly organized, and a motley assortment of boxes of various shapes in the middle, some opened, some sealed.

"Wow," Sara said. "It's like a treasure store."

"Could be. A lot of it's old legal and financial files. But the archives you're after are somewhere over here." Randy walked to the collection of uneven boxes.

"I was so delighted to get an interview with Karen," Sara said. She stood by Randy while he rummaged. "I just want to be prepared. I want to see what's been done before."

"It's a good idea. I'm impressed." Randy talked into the boxes as he searched. "Like I say, I don't think anyone's sorted through this stuff before. We probably do need a proper archive. There are just so many other things to do to get this campus set up right now. We've only been here six years."

Randy was silent as he stepped over boxes, looked, opened flaps, closed them. "It's in this section somewhere," he said. He opened one box, picked up papers, read a few moments. "Ooh, this is valuable." He turned to Sara. "Not for your quest today. But right here are some of the early vision documents and early discussions before the master plan was fully fleshed out."

Sara felt momentous purpose—the potential for it. But to what end? She felt vaguely that her simple search for early drawings opened now a new vista, whose purpose she could not discern.

Randy looked at the papers again. "We do need an archive." He put them away and kept looking for the art.

Sara looked into the open boxes around her. "Geez, there's a lot of treasure here." She saw office equipment, desk top items, mementos. Then she saw a box with polished metal arcs reaching out the top—silver plated, some gold plating, some copper. "This looks out of place," she said.

Randy looked back, stared, registered it. "That was probably submitted for inclusion to the Raymond Lully Museum. It's a contemporary innovation of…a whatchamacallit. I'm blanking on the name. A time piece. A map of the heavens. Something like that."

"Can I peak?"

"Sure, just don't get yourself hurt." He turned back to his boxes.

Sara opened the top flaps of the box and studied the instrument. The arcs had strange markings and measurements. It was disassembled, with a base at the bottom of the box. Cables were neatly organized in a separate internal box. Some scrawled notes and assembly diagrams were loosely shoved into to an inside pocket. It almost looked ancient, but it was polished and had contemporary assembly diagrams. Curious thing.

"It's funny," Sara said. "Yesterday we did the tour, and we focused on all the things that Bayside Village wants to put out publicly for others to see. Now we're in the Vault looking through all the things that no one sees. It's like integrating the conscious and the unconscious."

Randy laughed. "Very true. It's a good metaphor. Of course there's more to the unconscious of this place than what's here. But you're a very lucky gal to gain entry to the Vault. Most employees haven't even seen it."

Randy continued opening boxes, sorting, reading, closing.

Sara read some handwritten notes inside the instrument box about the inventor, Sergio. Then a letter by him, dated a year before the opening of Bayside Village. She glanced at it. He had appealed to have his instrument included in the Raymond Lully Museum collection. Then she saw a reply by Jenny Barnes. Jenny? Interesting, she thought. Jenny was involved that early? Sara reached down to pick up Jenny's letter.

"Ah," Randy said. "Here it is." Sara looked up. He pulled out a large, poster-sized box. Sara left the instrument and the letter and walked to the box by Randy. "Here, let's move this over to the desk. Then we can pull stuff out and have a look." Together, they dragged the large box and leaned it against a stack of boxes.

Randy pulled out some posters of different sizes and laid them flat across the desk.

"Wow," Sara said as she got her first look at early promotional poster renderings, some transformed into final versions on display in the Auditorium lobby, some rejected. Sara pulled out her sketch book. She looked, studied, made quick sketches, asked questions. Randy answered, commented. Together they explored like this for some time.

38

Greg and Neil walked out of the Dining Commons, the wooden screen door smacking behind them. They walked to Avicenna Hall on the Bridge Institute quadrangle. Inside on the second floor, Roger's door stood open. He sat surrounded by bookshelves in front of a large screen projection working on ontology diagrams, like a crystal web of pulsating light.

"Hey, Roger," Greg called. "You ready?"

Roger turned, stood. "Hey, come on in, guys." He stepped forward and shook hands.

"Roger," Neil greeted in a straightforward voice, eyeing him like an eagle.

Greg and Roger shook hands. They exchanged deep glances with the confidence of fond and familiar friends.

"Here, pull up some chairs," Roger said. He sat down, turned back to the projection. "I'm just lining up a few screens for our walk-through."

Greg and Neil scooted up chairs and sat down.

"You had quite a huddle of questioners at your AlignIt presentation," Greg said.

"Yes," Roger said, "I've just arrived back, just in time for our meeting."

Neil glanced around Roger's office. To the left, he scanned a broad selection of over-sized volumes of alchemical plates, mystical diagrams, Indian yantras, Buddhist paintings, Taoist diagrams. To the right, arcane titles on thick books lined the shelves. Next to those, he had some key texts on software programming and a few works in Greg's field, ontology. "You've got an impressive library here," Neil said.

"Thanks," Roger replied. "Rare books, most of them."

"I suspected. Museum curators would probably salivate."

Greg surveyed Roger's exotic prints hung in the few empty spaces on his walls, beside bookshelves. His eyes scanned, and his mind wondered if Neil really cared about Roger's library, about museums. It was polite banter. Neil couldn't possibly have an interest in Roger's collection. Greg looked up to a large, framed ink print of sixty-four hexagrams in a circle pattern hanging over Roger's computer desk. Then he added, "And impressive images. I like your I Ching."

"One of my favorites," Roger said, opening a table.

"So you already have the history of ontology," Greg said.

"How so?" Roger asked. He looked into the screen, clicked.

"The way you stand in the intellectual lineage of Gottfried Leibniz."
Roger turned now in his swivel chair to Greg. "I don't follow you."
"That's not why you hung it over your computer desk?" Greg asked.
"What, the hexagrams?" Roger said. He looked up. "No."
"No? Leibniz patterned his Characteristica Universalis on the I Ching."
"Really! I had no idea. It's just a gift from a colleague."
"How significant, then!" Greg enthused. "And you've placed it over your work space where you elaborate ontologies! Yeah, this is a perfect image for you, especially in light of Characteristica Universalis. You're definitely standing in his lineage."
"I know nothing about this," Roger said with surprise and a slight laugh. "And I haven't read Leibniz."
"Oh, it's one of the most philosophically robust expressions of the *ars combinatoria*, the art of discovery."
"Well, you've lost us both on that one," Neil said.
"This is the intellectual lineage of AlignIt!" Greg waxed. "This is one stream of sacred science ontology—a system rendering archetypes, if you will, or implicit primary principles, and showing their relation to explicit facts in the world around us. And Leibniz based at least some of his vision of it on the I Ching."
"No kidding," Roger said, his right hand on his chin, his pointer finger on his lips.
"He's also heir to Raymond Lully and Giordano Bruno, so you'd be standing in that lineage, too." At this, Greg felt himself a supreme philosophy nerd, and years of him feeling a loner, an outsider, rushed up in his awareness, except it was balanced by a feeling, especially now with Roger, of being right on the mark, in the flow of what is needed.
Roger gave the I Ching a good look from this new vantage point. "It does look awfully like a computer circuit board or a software diagram."
"Or a semiconductor chip," Neil said.
Roger looked back to Greg and Neil. "We haven't even begun, and we're off to a great start already."
The men chatted over pleasantries. Roger asked about their stay so far, their accommodations, their impressions of Randy's Bayside Village tour yesterday.
"Okay," Roger finally said. "So, you've seen the proposed consulting scopes of work for each of you. I thought we'd go just briefly through the main tasks and milestones and then run through the AlignIt Discovery Engine. And I'd like to pick up the thread of conversation from before your arrival—about what you can bring to AlignIt."
Neil pulled out his dog-eared consulting scope of work, filled with his own hand-written notes and questions, ready to dive in.
Roger continued. "We've taken the most basic, universal patterns and

built AlignIt on that basis. It turned out that the Perennial Philosophy became a sort of compromise for us because it offered a neat and seemingly universal synthesis of the deep structures of all or most spiritual traditions. And it's what many of our constituents know. So again, this served us well when we started out and built the proof of principle, the prototype, and now our beta version and first products."

"Okay," Neil said, "so I have to stop and just ask, What's this Perennial Philosophy?"

Roger sat forward. "Oh, it's an approach to the study of religions from the last century that focuses on dominant, universal themes that all religions are supposed to have in common. It has its merits. Especially when it reveals patterns that really are shared across many religions. That very universalism can tend to obscure some things, too, though."

"It's a term of art in Roger's field, the History of Religion," Greg said, "but it comes with a point of view as well."

"Right," Roger said. He was delighted to see Greg's awareness of his field, his world of thought. "But AlignIt is maturing," Roger said. "We're aiming to build a more differentiated ontology that helps us see better the universal and the unique features of traditions. We're also forming more partnerships with organizations to build out products and services, broadly speaking. Not only commercial products and services, but also academic tools, charitable works, and whatever else our partners build on the platform. And we're coming to the place where we need to release more papers and information artifacts to the public domain about the underlying structure of AlignIt. So we need to expand from the Perennial Philosophy, and that's the work we'd like to do with you."

Neil shifted in his chair, sitting back, assuming his skeptical demeanor. "So let me back up a minute, just to make sure I'm following you. This Perennial Philosophy is what you have now, and you want to replace it?"

"Or expand the Perennial Philosophy itself," Greg said.

Roger nodded. "Yes, expand is probably a better word. Perennial Philosophy makes sense of some data that fall into AlignIt's broad, dominant categories. And this allowed us to build a system and applications, as I wrote in your scope of work. It was good for a proof of concept. What concerns me, as I wrote in section B, is that this system doesn't allow for variances even within the same tradition. And I want to introduce and align other systems that don't match the structures we've already built, based on Perennial Philosophy. What we currently do now is show a single model within a religion. Which means that when variants exist on a given theme within a religion, as they most often do, we have to choose one. In most schemes of a Perennial Philosophy, that choice ends up being one that conforms with what is already mapped, or what corresponds neatly with one's model of world religions. We can do better than that—place variants side by side, dialogically, so to say, and let them interact in more meaningful ways. Also, the presence of one model in a religion that happens to correspond to a similar idea in another religion does not mean that the one model assumes a prominent or central role. There's a mistaken idea that similarity should confer greater importance, should elevate the ideas found in common. But the tendency to make things fit in a system means we occlude certain data that don't line up. AlignIt should help reveal these distinctions and provide tools and operations for working with them. AlignIt will shift these choices from the system builder to the end user."

"This is your big concern," Neil reflected.

"It is," Roger said, "especially as we prepare to open more of our table structure to the public. What began as a useful simple model for building an IT system is now a conceptual limitation as we become more complex, variegated, and broadly representative of a global panoply of spiritual traditions. It's not so neat and tidy in the real world as most schemes of the Perennial Philosophy make it seem."

"Okay," Greg said, focusing the discussion. "First, variances within a system." He scribbled notes and then looked up again. "Second, importing and aligning other ontologies, particularly non-conforming ones. Mapping provisional relations. Does AlignIt require a definitive meta system now, or ever? There are some existing meta systems in the history of religion. Is this your project?"

"This is one of our open questions," Roger said, "and for the sake of rigorous investigation and intellectual honesty, I'd like to suspend that determination at the outset. I'd like to pursue our development inductively. Let's discover the world rather than represent it according to our preexisting notions."

"Works for me," Greg said. "Better for me, in fact."

"That's one of the most respectable things I've heard about this AlignIt project of yours," Neil said. "Whatever else its merits—and I am still dubious about its merits—at least at it appears you're trying to do fundamental research, and you're open."

"Right," Roger said. "We're not just building up technology around a bunch of old wheels and conceptual diagrams."

"I have to say—that's what I thought you were doing."

"No, you're right. AlignIt is investigative from the start," Roger said.

"I like this intellectual honesty, Roger," Neil said. "But pragmatically speaking, if you don't have at least a hypothesis, at least some deduction at the outset, I don't know how you'll ever get to parameters and design specs. This is one of my comments from reading your SOW." Neil pointed his pen on his hand-written comments.

"Okay," Roger said. "Perhaps a modified inductive-deductive

approach, if that works for you. As long as you're willing to surrender your assumptions if you discover something that doesn't fit the pattern. I'd rather accommodate anomalies than force them to fit or exclude them. This is where it's more science than business."

39

Greg and Neil walked out of Avicenna Hall to the quad where students were sitting out on the grass studying, talking. Neil shook hands and parted. Greg pulled out his mobile and clicked on Sara.

"Hi Sweetie….Where?....Oh really?....Good!....Okay, meet you there in a minute." He ended the call and slipped the mobile into his pocket.

Greg walked across the grass to the Bridge Institute Art School complex. He peeked into a few studios until he found Sara. She was in a painting studio, absorbed in a sketch of a painter painting before her at an easel. Greg liked seeing Sara in her creative mood. There she was, his beloved artist.

"Hey beautiful," he said in a half-whisper, respectful of the other painters. He walked up to her chair.

Sara turned and flashed her eyes. "Hi." Then she turned back to her sketch pad, cocking her head to the left for perspective. "Are you ready for lunch?"

"Yeah, if you're ready."

"Yup. Let me just pack up my pencils and erasers." Sara closed her sketch book and put her pencils back in order in her pencil case.

Greg looked around. "It's a nice space. It feels easy to concentrate here."

"It is." Sara stood up and they walked out of the studio, out of the art complex, and down the path to the Bayside Village Day Care to pick up Tara for lunch.

Greg, Sara and Tara entered the wood-paneled screen doors of the Dining Commons. A door clap following behind them as the spring pulled the door in to smack the frame. They walked up to the buffet line, now smaller than Monday or this morning.

After moving through the line, Greg hovered at the end near the condiments. Sara came up behind. "You're getting hot sauce?"

"Yeah," Greg said, looking back with a smile. "I don't know why. I'm just amazed at all the variety."

"You never use hot sauce."

"I know. Just thought I'd try it."

Sara passed by to the desert aisle where she set down her tray and surveyed the options. Vegan Tiramisu. Chocolate Pudding. Peach and Berry Cobbler. She picked up one of each and set them on her tray, then picked up her tray to leave. Then, hesitating a moment, she eyed the tiramisu on the counter top. She put her tray down again, quickly picked up another, and left.

Sara turned around and walked to Tara standing by Greg at the condiments. "Tara, Honey? Do you want to get our silverware and napkins? We need three spoons, three forks, and three knives." Tara strode purposefully to the silverware containers and carefully picked out the correct number of each, with napkins, and returned to Sara. "Good girl. Thank you, Honey. Let's find a table and put our things down. Greg, we're heading over to that side."

"Okay, I'll be there in a second." Greg went to the dessert isle and picked up chocolate pudding. Turning around, he maneuvered through the people free-floating around the buffet and islands of food, and into the table section where Sara pointed.

"Ah, there's my family," Greg said, putting down his tray on the table.

"Oh, you got desert, too," Sara said. "I got this for you." Sara pointed to the tiramisu and chocolate pudding. "Oh well."

Greg raised his eyebrows in surprise at the row of four deserts. "Yeah, I got my own. But thanks."

Greg sat down and moved some dishes on his tray to Tara. He cut her vegetables and manicotti. Sara put the peach and berry cobbler in front of Tara.

Turning back to his tray, Greg dug in to his own food, doused with various hot sauces. "Mmm." He let out a visceral groan. "Wow!" he said, breathing in, fanning his mouth with his hand. As if that would do anything. "I don't know what's up with this spicy thing for me. Just wanted to try it."

"Ever my mysterious husband," Sara said, shaking her head with an ironic smile, lifting a fork full of salad.

"Mysterious?" Greg swallowed, his mouth burning. "You say that a lot about me. Don't I seem plain to you?"

Sara grimaced and shrugged her shoulders. "I don't know."

"I feel that you feel I'm too plain."

"I don't think so," Sara said.

"Anyway, you seem the more mysterious one," Greg said.

"Me? Why?"

"I don't know. Your spiritual aspiration unfolds in ways I don't expect. Your art often has complex, hidden depths. And maybe, I don't know….You have a kind of sweet darkness about you."

"Hmm? What does that mean?"

"I don't know how to explain it. You have tender passions that are just you—too specific to be just anyone's. And you have a kind of delicate, sweet suffering from it that also seems like just you. It's like, amidst your yearning for the Beloved, there are these sweet, delicious thorns that scratch and hurt you. Yet you yearn all the same. It even seems to me that your passions and suffering are also your yearning."

Sara sat listening with a perplexed look on her face, unsure whether to smile at feeling beheld and loved by Greg's keen observation, or to hide from his scrutiny. "No," she said after a long moment, shaking her head subtly, smiling now with a grin. She pointed at him with her fork in a folksy manner, uncommon for her. "When you talk like that, you're definitely more mysterious than I am."

Greg and Sara sat silently a few moments, chewing. That stirred something in her, Greg noted. Sara arranged the food on her plate with her fork. And arranged it again.

"Mommy, can you butter my bread?" Tara asked. Sara sprang into action, and that shifted their attention momentarily. Sara realized this.

But the attention was shifted. Greg and Sara reflected on the morning's activities, interspersed with questions and comments about Tara's experiences at Day Care.

"Oh," Sara said. "Speaking of mysterious, I saw a letter from Jenny this morning in a box in the Vault." She explained to Greg how she had pursued Randy, got into a secured storage area, studied posters and other art works created for the early promotion of the Bayside Village. In that context, she explained finding an unusual art piece in a box, a letter by an artist named Sergio from a year before the opening ceremony, and a reply from Jenny. "She was involved here that early."

But Greg was astounded by the story of Sara getting into this place Randy called the Vault. Sara did have this incredible feature, this quality. She pursued things. She looked underneath the obvious. He admired this part of her. She found loose threads.

Getting into the Vault didn't stand out in Sara's mind, though. Yes, she got in, she made sketches, she would use them somehow. But her imagination was captivated by the memory of that box, the contraption in it, the letter by a certain Sergio, and a reply by Jenny that she was just about to pick up and read before Randy found the gold she had sought—the posters. There was more history, more depth, to Jenny, and Sara wanted to know it.

Tara was ready for play. Greg got up with her and went to Kids Corner, off to the side of the Dining Commons.

Sara sat alone eating one of her two tiramisus. She eyed the other one, considering. She meant it for Greg. Or did she? He likes chocolate pudding. But he got his own. She eyed it again. Resolve quickened in her. She stood up, put the uneaten tiramisu, the uneaten chocolate pudding, onto her tray, and walked to the kitchen. After clearing her plates, she walked to Kids Corner.

40

After lunch, Greg and Sara dropped off Tara at the Bayside Village Day Care. Turning out of the gate, they walked briskly up the path to the Bridge Institute quadrangle, up the steps to the auditorium. Inside, they entered a large, open room adjoining the atrium for President Steve Bateson's creative writing workshop for the Orientation, called, 'Building Your Own Utopia.' The room was filled already with the familiar Orientation participants. Chairs and pillows were arranged in a circle on the warmly colored orange carpet, with a teacher's chair and screen at the front.

Greg and Sara sat down on the left side of the circle. Greg pulled his paper journal out of his side bag, deciding in advance to leave aside his mobile, his keyboard and screen projections, even the AlignIt application AuthorIt.

"Going unplugged?" Sara asked.

"Yeah. I love AuthorIt, and a part of me wants to link up my freewriting exercises to categories. But another part of me just wants to write freely, untagged, unlabeled."

Sara nodded. "Me too." She pulled a journal out of her art bag, and then a sketchbook, pencils, eraser, and pencil sharpener. "I might draw," she said, noticing his attention to her supplies.

Greg smiled. "Good thing you brought it, huh?"

"We'll see."

The tone of her voice reminded Greg of her uncertainty about Bayside Village. They'd shared so many daring ventures, he reflected. This one started off difficult for her. Yet, she's opening to it. Something magical is happening. She's drawing again.

President Steve Bateson walked into the room carrying a blue cloth bag full of actual printed books, his front tuft of white hair flying upward as he moved through the room. He put down his cloth bag by the front chair and sat down. Greg wondered what manner of man the president of a place like this would be. Here was a chance to observe closely, beyond stage presentations.

Bateson took out his mobile device and clicked to send his slides to display on the large screen. The cover slide read 'Building Your Own Utopia: A Creative Writing Workshop. Steve Bateson.' Then he took out his books, dog-eared and filled with bookmarks and paper notes, and stacked them on a small, round table next to his chair. Greg liked books, and he looked with pleasure on the stack Bateson organized there. He wondered about Bateson's choices, his tastes.

With his books in place, Bateson turned and chatted with participants seated near him.

Then it was 1:30. Bateson addressed the workshop. "Let's get started."

Participants adjusted their chairs and pillows and focused on the front.

"Welcome to 'Building Your Own Utopia.' Most of you attended the Orientation yesterday and heard my opening comments about utopias. As many of you know, I specialize in the history of ideas, and utopian literature is one of my research areas.

"Our plan for today's workshop is to explore examples of utopias by both hearing excerpts from utopian classics and viewing images of famous utopias. We'll do creative writing exercises on specific utopian themes. We'll move successively through utopian themes in this way, stopping to write about each of them, and then we'll have small and large group discussion after our writings periods to reflect on our work."

Keith and Leah entered the room and quietly found cushions on the floor near the back. Leah looked visibly embarrassed at the impropriety of arriving late, Greg thought. Keith got out a writing pad from his backpack, and Leah had a small pad and looked ready to take notes.

"This public workshop is a mini version of a regular graduate seminar I teach here," Bateson continued. "This course can be taken for one semester or a full year. For those who are interested, I'll just say that in the graduate seminar, students have individual and group projects to create designs for utopias or a given utopian theme, such as law, government, society, culture, communication, transportation, etc. We work together on a project of creating in the real world—in our world today, here and now— some kind of actual program, structure, product, service, or some real creation, inspired by the better ideas of the utopias we study. I have called this work *utopianizing*—the work of making real-world projects inspired by utopian ideals."

Greg scanned the circle of seated participants for Neil, hoping to catch his response to Bateson's approach, to the idea of utopianizing. He then realized Neil hadn't arrived yet. Either late or not coming, he thought. He recalled Neil's sarcastic comment yesterday—he hadn't come for new age gurus or utopian idealism.

"And now," Bateson said, "let's move on to utopian themes and writing exercises." He led the workshop participants through thought-provoking excerpts drawn from utopian classics. He canvassed a slue of themes: family, housing, education, work, food supply, government, politics, society, law, business, and religion and spiritual practice and their relation to science and research. Bateson took particular care to explore in writing exercises the role of education in forming children, and the role of elders in society—"lost inquiries in this society of ours, yet emphases we take up here at the Bayside Village, with our Day Care and our Academy of Elders."

This point caught Sara's attention, stimulated her imagination.

"Now," Bateson said after a writing exercise, "let us turn to a classic utopia at the beginnings of modern Western science—The New Atlantis, published in 1627 by the famous English statesman and philosopher, Francis Bacon."

"Our story begins as European explorers have gone out on ship from the coast of Peru *en route* to China, Japan, and the south seas. But great winds kick up and their provisions run out. As an answer to prayer, the crew discovers a new and unknown land, which they later learn, on shore, is called Bensalem. Let us suppose ourselves to be in this situation—facing great winds in our culture, the end of the intellectual, cultural and spiritual nourishment in our vessel, and in need of discovering new land.

"The utopia proceeds with the leaders of the advanced civilization of Bensalem graciously and humanely receiving the crew of European explorers and giving the crew's best men a revealing look at their esteemed society. The book ends with one of Bensalem's leaders giving the unnamed protagonist, a European visitor, permission to write what he has seen in Bensalem and publish it back home in Europe. That published work is our utopia, The New Atlantis.

"Now, Bacon's The New Atlantis is often regarded as an inspiration giving rise the modern research university. It is acknowledged as leading directly to creating the British Royal Society. While the formation of modern Western research universities owes much inspiration to The New Atlantis, we have more often read the work with an interpretive gloss that veils very apparent facts. For instance, we put aside the religious origins of Bensalem's society, the religious origins of its scientific enterprise called Salomon's House, the leadership of Salomon's House by esteemed Fathers, the absence of any bifurcation in the work itself between the religious and the scientific—a bifurcation we have introduced in the modern world. We do well to remember that The New Atlantis was a serious spiritual work invoking Salomon, a type of the Hebrew King Solomon, and under the miraculous apostolic mission of one of Jesus' original twelve apostles, St. Bartholomew. Indeed, King Solomon himself, the prototypical wise king, is offered as the very model of scientific inquiry—not as a secular or mundane science, but as a science that holds scientific investigation in a larger metaphysics and cosmology grounded in Hebrew and Christian tradition. Nor is this a merely mainstream warrant for scientific research under the auspices of the church. For any of the four apostles associated with the

canonical gospels—Matthew, Mark, Luke, or John—could have been
invoked for such warrant. But why St. Bartholomew?" Bateson stopped.
He let the question sit, agitate, in his now enraptured audience of workshop
participants. "And why the Turkish type of clothing in Bensalem? What
might St. Bartholomew and the Turks have to do with Solomonic wisdom
and scientific inquiry?" He let these questions work in their imaginations.
"I have published on these details elsewhere. Though the work has seldom
received this kind of treatment, I offer to you that there is, in The New
Atlantis, a necessary relation between these spiritual preceptors of
Bensalem, the regnant spiritual foundations of Bensalem's civilization, and a
kind of ongoing scientific investigation from the early days in that land that
holds together exploration of the entire works of creation with a personal
and social piety deeply embedded in Bensalem's civilization. Holding this
as a model, we will explore, in our creative writing now, the same
integration of spiritual culture and scientific inquiry.

"Now, let us move on to our first exercise with Bacon's New Atlantis.
One of the Fathers of Solomon's House gives the greatest jewel he has to
impart to the visiting unnamed European protagonist. This greatest jewel is
knowledge of the true state of Solomon's House. The Father reveals four
things: the end of the school; its preparations and instruments; its
employments and their functions; and finally, the ordinances and rights
observed there. Of the ordinances and rites, one in particular is easily
overlooked in our day of modern secular science. Yet it is one in which we
at Bayside Village find some agreement as an exemplary model. The Father
says:

> We have certain hymns and services, which we say daily, of Lord
> and thanks to God for his marvelous works: and forms of prayers,
> imploring His aid and blessing for the illumination of our labours,
> and the turning of them into good and holy uses.

"Now let us recall that Solomon's House was an extremely progressive,
innovative scientific research institute for its day. In The New Atlantis,
Bacon anticipated in 1623 much that has transpired over the preceding four
hundred years, and some things which still remain unrealized. Chiefly, he
foresaw prophetically, as it were, a kind of science conducted by people
who had developed all points of humanity, who were mature in spiritual
wisdom, in organizing the state, and in benefiting the public good. Their
knowledge of the world was developed together with, and arose together
with, their overall spiritual, social, economic, and political development. In
other words, science was not unbridled. It was not the result of
overdeveloped brains with underdeveloped hearts and characters. Nor was
the science of Bensalem tethered to a kind of stifling religious orthodoxy

prescribing the official lines on which scientific inquiry must be conducted. No, this was a mature science, as fundamental as the inquiries of King Solomon into nature, and as guided as King Solomon by an awareness that all knowledge comes from the divine realm. In recognition of this, and perhaps in order to cultivate it, one of the rites of Salomon's House was the daily practice of hymns, services, and prayers. Now, Bacon did not have this Father of Salomon's House reveal the content of such hymns, services, and prayers. Perhaps it was because only so much could be told to Strangers, as the Father said, and the rest must remain secret. However it may be, this is where we shall now practice our creative writing.

"Imagine yourself now on the utopian island of Bensalem. You stand in a small company before the wise Father of Salomon's House—which house is the very eye of that kingdom. The Father wears a blue, satin embroidered cloth over his head, a mantle and cape of fine black cloth fastened around him, an under garment of excellent white linen down to the foot, together with gloves and a Spanish montera. The wise Father invites you and your company to a tour of Salomon's House, much as you have taken a tour of Bayside Village and the Bridge Institute these past two days. But I digress; let us stay in the 1600's on the utopian island of Bensalem. Though secret to strangers before, your trustworthiness has been recognized during your stay. Imagine now that you are being conducted about Salomon's House, being shown this greatest jewel the wise Father has to give. You are conducted to laboratories, furnaces, caves, towers, lakes, orchards, and the houses of all the branches of research described in The New Atlantis. You are reminded by the great Father that this great House, instituted by the ancient lawgiver, Salomon, is dedicated to the study of 'the works and creatures of God,' to find 'the true nature of all things,' to discover knowledge of all causes and all motions of things, and to expand the range of human mastery of all things that exist. And how shall these ends be accomplished, you are asked. Not alone by knowledge born of investigation, as has become the lot of that Western science poorly imitating this great example shown it. And herein lies the jewel, the secret of the House of Salomon, which was not rightly copied when the author of The New Atlantis brought back the secrets he was permitted to publish. You are permitted now to see the spirit and inspiration that underlies the conduct of this high science in this great house of learning.

"You stand in a hallway before impressive, heavy wooden doors. The wise Father points out to you the special carving of the hierarchy of spiritual beings upon the doors—the Seraphim, Cherubim and Thrones at the top, the Kyriotetes, Dynamis, and Exusiai in the middle, and the Principalities, Archangels, and Angels at the bottom. These are the doors to the great Temple where the researchers daily conduct their worship, as laid down in the interdicts of the lawgiver twenty-three hundred years ago. The wise Father reminds you that this great investigation, at Salomon's House, is conducted also by a piety of the heart, and a remembrance of God who is creator of all things, all laws, and all knowledge. A great guide and assistance of this science conducted in Bensalem is the rites and ordinances kept by researchers of that House. Taking account of this, you are invited in to the great Temple to witness and partake of their daily worship. The wise Father opens the heavy, wooden doors carved of the hierarchy of spiritual beings, and lets you in, deeper than earlier visitors of Bensalem. You are invited to participate in the hymns, services, and prayers which affirm and aid the researchers, that their research be illuminated, and that it be made practical and of benefit to the people.

"Our company," Bateson said, "that is, those of us in this workshop, is now ushered into a row in the middle of the Temple. The pews about you are largely filled, while a few remaining researchers stream in from various doors in a circumspect state of attention and prayer of the heart. As you look about, you see that the Temple building itself is ancient, made of expertly carved and fitted stone, of large and darkly stained beams, and of the arts of glass, fabric, paint, and carved stone which bear higher vibrations than the arts you know.

"You witness in this great Temple readings from other works of King Solomon which are unfamiliar to you, and you recall now that this community retained those works of natural history which are lost to other nations. You witness now readings from works sounding like those of the New Testament but not familiar to you, but which, you now recall, were bestowed to the people of Bensalem by the very Saint Bartholomew, one of the original twelve Apostles chosen by Jesus of Nazareth. And your heart and mind are stirred upon hearing and contemplating these divine words, for your attention is directed, as was meant by the giving of the Word of God, to divine forms all the way down the Ray of Creation explored in this hallowed House of research, and all the way up through the hierarchy of spiritual beings to the very throne of God the Father, dissolving into the absolute transcendence of Nothingness, God beyond God.

"You witness now the recitation of hymns and prayers, some in Hebrew, some in Syriac, with an inner linguistic structure and cadence barely cognizable to you but felt deeply in body, soul, and spirit. The hymns stir and awaken divine impulses in you, stirring your heart with unfamiliar sensations and longings, illuminating your mind with the true nature of creation beyond the veils of appearances.

"Here you are now, in this place, in this state. What do you see? What do you hear? I'm going to ding the bell, and let's freewrite for ten minutes. Then I'll ding the bell again at the end. So our question is, 'In this illumined state, what do you see in the Temple in the great House at Bensalem?'"

Bateson dinged the small bell on the table beside him. Heads went down as participants turned to freewriting. The resounding tones of the bell rung through the air and subsided.

Sara turned the page in her sketch book and drew pictures. Grand pictures, translating her inner vision by broad strokes on the page, bold here, light there, small marks now, and again broad strokes.

Greg wrote energetically. He walked to the front left corner of the Temple, to an instrument such as the history of Western music has never seen—a kind of harmonium with small keyboard. The carvings on its sides were of mythical beasts, each signifying a divine quality. He depressed a key with his index finger. An ancient song of the soul came beaming out, with glorious and perfect musical accompaniment unfolding elegant sound structures, a material substance, like a carpet unrolling across the empty space of the room, with glorious colored lights shining out and up to the vaulted roof of the cathedral. The solemn air sparkled, and wafts of incense swirled out as if carried aloft by the rushing wind of the Spirit. Greg felt all that transpired from the touch of one key, the divine action tumbling out of the instrument, rushing out to do its work in the sensitive hearts and minds of devoted servants of that hallowed House of research. He mused about the keys—so few, and yet a single note sounded its quality so boldly, carving its sound impression into tracks, channels, passageways of the Spirit, aligning the sensitive souls there to its higher forms. What would happen with the next note, if one was already so grand?

By now, Greg had filled pages in his journal. Sara sketched away madly, turning page after page.

Greg paused, breathed in deeply, and looked around the room. In the back, Keith wrote furiously. Leah sat in a frozen stare at her pages borrowed from Keith's journal, her pen in her mouth, stuck on what to write. Neil hadn't shown up, and by now it was clear he wasn't coming. He must have skipped out on the workshop. Greg mentally compared his own broad engagement at Bayside Village with Neil's focus on checking out AlignIt. Before the eye of Greg's imagination lay the opportunity of moving to Bayside Village. Neil would only consult, if he would deign to do even that.

Bateson called the group back and asked for volunteers to read or share their piece. Some shared. Greg shared, proud of his ideas, fascinated by the connection of his own scholarship and connecting to the world of utopian literature. Sara shared her drawings.

"Let me conclude our New Atlantis exercise," Bateson said, "by making an observation. Just as we have created the Bridge Institute here in the Bayside Village, in acknowledgement of forming a bridge between the old world and the new, between science and spirit, between knowledge and vital piety, so in The New Atlantis we find a similar sort of bridge. Early in the work, the unnamed protagonist calls his fellow men together and says in a speech to them, "for we are beyond, both the old world, and the new." Similarly, the great patriarch and saint Noah is mentioned many times, as is the image of his ark, as a vessel conveying the seeds of something old into something new. We, too, are beyond the dualism of old world and new. This is the opportunity before us in this workshop. You have these seeds and you are here, now, in this world. So take them forth and plant them."

41

Roger walked into Jeff's GameIt gallery and office in the Research Park. He walked around exhibits featuring scenes of game worlds and shimmering holograms of characters on a quest. He walked around a table in an open collaboration space where two interns worked together on a project, walked around them to the door of Jeff Baker's office.

"Hey Jeff. Any updates on Mueller?"

"Yeah, a few."

Roger entered, pulled up his usual chair near Jeff's desk.

Jeff turned. "I called Jack to see if he had any scoop."

"And?"

"I don't have much," Jeff said. "No more than his initial feedback he when we discussed Mueller joining the AlignIt Commons board. He said he'd ask around his VC network. He's also having someone search an information service they subscribe to. So hopefully that will give us something to go on."

"Well thanks. That's a big help. That's some of the intangible value you'd hope from an investor. It's more than we have so far. I've also told Jackie. I asked her to recheck Mueller's file and do further due diligence."

"Good," Jeff said. "Jack also said we should try to find out when Mueller got these game companies in his portfolio. He said it would be pretty stupid to hide them from us on the disclosure form and then go talking to you about signing up game companies. More likely there's an unexplained gap or something amiss."

"Hmm, that's possible," Roger said. "Yeah, I don't like jumping to conclusions about people. I don't feel the rapport with Mueller that I'd like to feel—not like yours with Jack. But I had thought he was giving good counsel and was able to help us move AlignIt and the AlignIt Commons to the next level." Roger paused a moment. "The thing that really bugs me is that Mueller gave me a false impression of having talked with you about his game companies, like somehow you're on board with it. That seems like outright deception, and it's harder to see that as a simple information gap."

"Right, that piece doesn't fit," Jeff said. "It doesn't smell good. Also, Jack mentioned that we should check the pulse on philosophical alignment. He said its concerning to him that Mueller seems to be shifting course on you so soon, and right before the board meeting. Responding to data points in the market or company financials is one thing. But his insistence on inserting discussion on game companies, when the board agenda is already posted, appears driven by Mueller's own interests. So Jack suggested we keep an eye out for basic philosophical misalignment."

"Mmm," Roger said, shaking his head, thinking. "Good points. I agree. I just want to have more to go on before deciding what next." Roger took a deep breath. "You've got a treasure in Jack, especially on philosophical alignment."

"Yeah. Hey," Jeff said, with an uplift of his voice, "I met Greg and Sara last night, speaking of treasure."

"So I heard. He bumped into me after talking with you. What do you think?" Roger sat back.

"I like him. He's a great find. We didn't have a lot of time to talk—maybe a half hour. They had to get their daughter to bed. We'll meet in depth tomorrow, just the two of us. But my quick read? I think he gets what we're doing, I think he's capable, and I think he'd be a great addition."

"Good, I'm glad you think so. Yeah, he get's what we're doing." Roger rubbed his eyes and put his hands down. "I'm really glad he brought the family. I'm working on Sara. I like her, too."

"Yeah, she's sharp," Jeff said. "She'd be a great addition."

Roger nodded. "I'm working on Greg, too. Both of them. It's not a done deal. Consulting is no problem for Greg. That's done, pretty much. But I'll wager it's no better than a sixty percent chance he'd take the academic appointment and they'd relocate. Sara isn't on board. She's unsure of moving here. I'm working to discern her fear. Sometimes she wears it openly for anyone capable of observing; sometimes its hidden. I think she fears she'll be competing with Greg's idealism and get left behind."

"That's perceptive."

"Greg and Sara are coming over for dinner tonight." Roger tapped his fingers on a side table as he contemplated, then looked up to Jeff. "Not sure I want to say much about Mueller yet since we're still unclear about what's happening."

42

In the late afternoon, Greg, Sara and Tara walked down the hall of the Lodge. "It's so nice they have a hot tub here," Sara said. She pulled the straps of the towel-filled bag tighter over her shoulder. Flip flops smacked on her bare heels and echoed in the hall. Greg walked behind, carrying a backpack and towels.

Tara strode between them, pressing forward eagerly. "Mommy did you get my goggles?"

"They're in your backpack, Sweetie," Sara replied.

"Yeah, it's really nice after today's intense activities," Greg said. "I need a little break from focused activities with people."

Sara waved her mobile phone over the door knob and it clicked open. Inside, the far wall was open and faced out to an enclosed, flower-filled garden courtyard. "Wow, this is beautiful," she said. The floor and three walls of the room were set with attractive tile work. The doors and the open wall were made of simple, elegant wood trimming. The right wall had a small wood table with a freshly cut flower placed in a lean ceramic vase. The left wall had an open shower set with Bridge Tiles. Sara and Greg put their bags and towels down on a bench by the door and walked to the open side of the room. Below was a small pool with coy fish surrounded by beautiful rock arrangements, trimmed bushes and small, sculpted trees.

"I love Japanese gardens," Greg said.

Sara returned to the bench and carefully laid out the backpacks, towels, water bottles, and shoes.

"I can't find my goggles," Tara complained.

Greg came to the bench, searched her small backpack. "Here they are." He pulled them out for her by the pink rubber strap.

Greg took off his shirt and stuffed it inside his backpack, tied his trunks tighter, and headed to the shower. Sara removed her shirt, placed it into her bag and joined Greg at the shower, adjusting her new suit.

Greg stepped out and went to the tub where steam rolled off the surface. "Aaahhh," he groaned, going down into the hot water. He drifted to the side of the tub with the best view of the garden, where the afternoon sun shone brightly on it.

Tara adjusted her goggles by the bench.

"Tara, Sweetie," Sara called, "come wash off quickly before going into the tub."

Tara joined Sara, showered, and went to the tub. Standing at the edge, she adjusted the goggles over her head and pulled her long blond bangs around the rubber straps. She sat down on the step and carefully put her feet in.

"Daddy, why are hot tubs always so hot?"

"I don't know. They're made hot so we can relax."

"It's too hot."

"I know. It feels hot at first. But you'll get used to it. Just come in slowly."

Tara stepped onto the first step and squatted into the water.

"Where's my wifey?" Greg called to Sara. She stood above the steps, tied her long hair back in a bun. Descending into the warm waters, she waded slowly over to Greg.

"Come here," Greg called, affectionately pulling her close for a backrub.

"Mhmmm," Sara purred with an affectionate smile, moving into position.

Greg kissed her cheek and neck and started his massage.

As Greg rubbed Sara's neck and back, Tara gradually inched into the tub. Finally, she swam underwater to her parents and came up. "Watch this," she said, blowing the water streaming down her face, and went under again, swimming to the other side. She came up and turned back. "Did you look?"

"Yes," Sara said.

"Great job," Greg affirmed.

"Oh, this is so relaxing," Sara said, closing her eyes.

Greg kneaded her shoulders and back.

Sara melted. "You should have been a masseuse."

Tara swam back and forth. "Are you looking?"

After several times watching and affirming, Greg said, "Sweetie, enjoy your swimming. We see you. Sometimes we're looking, and sometimes we're just relaxing." Tara went under again.

"Oh, right there….Yeah, that spot." Sara's head hung low, eyes closed. Then she lifted up her head. "Thanks." She drifted to Greg's side. "Okay, your turn." Sara pulled Greg in front of her, positioned his torso between her legs. She massaged his back, head and neck, rubbing long, slow, deep. He relaxed into a long, wonderful massage.

Then Greg looked up and moved to the side. "Look at that garden!" he exclaimed in wonder. "Look at those brilliant bougainvillea bushes! I just love how the sunlight filters through and dances on the pink petals."

With hair still wet, Greg and Sara walked from the Lodge, holding hands with Tara on both sides. They headed down the pathway across the Bayside Village campus, to the adjacent neighborhood where Roger and Jenny lived. People streamed around the family in the opposite direction *en route* to the Dining Commons.

As they approached a gate leading out of Bayside Village into the neighborhood beyond, Sara noticed the evening watch from Village Security on their beat, a man and woman standing together mindfully by the gate, looking in opposite directions. No weapons, no badges. Just two ordinary people with a clear and open presence to all that comes and goes. They stood ready, it seemed, to respond skillfully at any moment. As Sara passed them, each seemed to have clear, shining eyes of presence. Sara noticed a nod of acknowledgement. How interesting, she thought, as she observed her response. Their very attentiveness brought her to attention. Perhaps it was all the deterrence needed to diffuse or transform trouble.

Entering the neighborhood beyond the Village, Greg checked the address on his mobile. "62 Bay Street," he confirmed. "Should be on the left." In the middle class planned development, all the houses looked alike, with grey shingles, white trim, and manicured lawns. Hardly the creative setting of Bayside Village.

At 62, Greg, Sara and Tara approached the front door. Tara got to ring the bell. Jenny opened. "Hi," she beamed. "Come in." The family entered, and Jenny ushered them in. They entered the living room, and Sara quickly noticed attractive art pieces, many of them prints of ancient Eastern arts. They sat down on plush couches, Tara sitting between Sara and Jenny.

"Roger will be out in a moment," Jenny said, sitting down. "He's just putting something into the oven."

Jenny and Sara discussed art. Sara wanted to learn Jenny's connections to the Village art scene and began with a series of her most burning questions.

Greg noticed the room's décor looked at once Turkish and Californian. Music, maybe Felix Mendelson, sounded ubiquitously from speakers hidden in the walls.

Momentarily, Roger walked in, smiling. "Hey, there they are. So glad you could come."

Sara had just begun asking Jenny about her board role at the Art Center.

"Hey Roger," Greg said. He stood and shook hands and then the men sat down.

"It's nice to have a home to visit," Sara said. "Greg would rather live in the commune, but I'm glad to see inside these houses in case we move here."

"You want to live in Bayside Village campus housing?" Jenny asked.

"Yeah," Greg said. "I lived communally in college, and after college, and I've always wanted to get back to it."

"But I want to see these houses," Sara said. "Just to explore options."

Roger nodded, eyebrows raised, noting Sara's interest. He offered a tour, and the two couples walked room to room around the house, talking about the neighborhood, its community association, the rules of what can and can't be done to the houses and lawns.

As they returned to the living room at sat down, Greg noticed an oud resting by an oak bookshelf. "Oh, do you play?" he asked Roger, pointing to the instrument.

"No. We have it on loan from a friend, Tosun, a Turkish musician here in the Bay Area much of the year. He had an extra and asked if we'd hold it on one of his travels home. He plays it when he visits."

"I love the oud."

"Do you want to play it?"

"Really? Sure. I don't know how, but I'll give it a try." Roger picked up the oud, walked to Greg on the couch, handed it over, and sat down beside him. Roger reached for his mobile, touched, turned off Mendelson.

The oud caught Tara's attention, fascinated her. She got up and stood near Greg, by his knee, watching.

"I don't even know how to hold it," Greg said.

"Like this." Roger adjusted the instrument on Greg's lap.

Greg stroked the strings. He worked out a melody he knew on guitar. It sounded half descent, he thought. Then he played freestyle a few moments.

"Nice," Sara said.

As Greg played, Sara restarted her question with Jenny. "So again, I was curious about your role at the Art Center. I'm finding myself returning to fine art after several years of straight industrial design and family life. I'm really intrigued by the Art Center. I'm wondering if it might be a way for me to go deeper if we would come here. I thought I'd spend some time there this week."

"It's a wonderful place," Jenny said. "Many fine people are connected with it. It has a prominent role in shaping the future of sacred arts and crafts." Jenny began describing the board, its composition, some decisions it recently took up.

Tara sat down next to Greg now. She watched him strum the oud, watched her mom talking with Jenny, watched social cues.

"I'm sure a master can make this thing sing," Greg said, getting up to replace the instrument by the bookshelf.

"Let me put on Tosun's music," Roger said, scrolling through the playlist on his mobile. He found an album, tapped it. Slow, haunting melodies sounded from the speakers hidden in the walls, touching something, calling the soul, awakening it. Greg listened, enchanted. Roger pointed out Tosun's characteristic techniques.

Jenny invited everyone to the dining room. Conversation broke as everyone stood. Sara wasn't finished. She was fascinated by Jenny as a possible connection to the art world at Bayside Village. What is her role, what is her interest, she wondered. How can this be a way in for me? These questions pressed at her. She approached the dining room with a clear aim of addressing these lingering curiosities.

The table was stocked with breads, cheeses, and pickled condiments, and a salad with nuts, seeds, feta and vinaigrette dressing. Jenny brought Roger's rosemary polenta dish topped with braised vegetables and set it on a hot plate. In the other hand, she brought macaroni and cheese for Tara.

"Oh, thank you," Sara said, seeing the mac and cheese. "That was sweet of you."

Greg and Sara got Tara situated between them, positioned the macaroni and cheese before her, and filled her plate with other foods.

As dishes were passed, Sara asked Roger, "So AlignIt is your brainchild?" She served herself Roger's steaming polenta and passed the dish.

"Yes, it's my baby, my creation, the fruit of my life work."

"How did it come to you?"

"Oh, good question." Roger mused pensively, holding the salad tongs mid-air for a moment. Then a spark of inspired thought arrived and he reached into the bowl with the tongs, and spoke. "Most of my life, I've had a sense of systems. At the very beginning when computers, operating systems, and software were in their infancy, I could imagine databases that hadn't existed yet." He looked to Sara as he returned the tongs. "At the same time, I had a vivid imagination that stretched far beyond physical reality, and I found myself envisioning structures and systems in my mind's eye that had no corresponding material basis in anything I knew. But I also had a knack for organizing what I saw around me. Almost everything I did in the outer world, I turned into a system."

"He still does," Jenny said with an affectionate smile. She speared a fig with a slice of cheese and brought it to her mouth.

Roger smiled, nodded. "In those days, it might have been a bit obsessive-compulsive. My mind worked incessantly at system building. And for what? I don't know…an inner sense of things, an intuition, an ancient memory? In college, I created a massive meditation manual for myself—just to collect the many categories of meditations I knew about."

"You wrote a meditation book?" Greg asked.

Roger nodded. "Yes—quite extensively organized into themes." He paused. "Few of the meditation books I saw had any higher thematic systematization. How could anyone cultivate their interior lives without meditations organized to cultivate different qualities? So I built it up myself, for myself, in my study and meditation. I created it in meditation."

"Your own meditations, or others?" Sara asked.

"Both. But I wrote many of my own."

"Wow. Like what categories? What did you include?" Greg asked.

"Oh, many types. I collected forms, chants, and scriptures for each. I used them as a kind of model. And I found that I was prolific in authoring new meditations as I labored this way."

"That's amazing," Greg said. "That's really amazing. You could probably build an ontology around that, too."

"No doubt," Jenny said.

"I did without knowing it, I think" Roger said. "Like I did with AlignIt."

"Do you still have it?" Sara asked.

"Yes," Roger laughed. "In a box somewhere. I haven't developed it since my college days, years ago. When I began studying religions systematically, I expanded my system-building to organize different practices and images.

"The basic insight for AlignIt came to me years later. It began late one night when I sat at my desk reading a description of esoteric science from Peter Ouspensky, if you know his work."

"Sure," Greg said, chewing.

"Oh," Sara said, "the Gurdjieff Work."

"Right. I discovered that many medieval and renaissance traditions were already organized into systems. Ouspensky's was the first description I found. He outlined a system of traditional typologies showing thematic correspondences between magic, astrology, tarot, and cabala. I saw a coherent structure of correspondences between four separate systems—for the first time. I had never seen anything like it in my graduate study. This discovery left an indelible impression on me."

"So that's where it all came from," Greg said. He buttered broccoli for Tara.

Roger nodded. "I was utterly fascinated. So I sat there that night and drew out a typology of these traditional sciences. I realized that if these traditions had this kind of internal consistency despite their different histories, terminology, and mythologies, there must be more here than I supposed. That led me to old books with astounding tables, charts and illustrations. I discovered that grand syntheses had already been created to reconcile Neoplatonic systems, alchemy, astrology, magic, and cabala. Some of them integrated Hebrew and Christian ideas. This led me to the study of esoteric art, alchemical emblems and the like. Alchemy was entirely unfamiliar to me. I studied those strange pictures, full of archaic symbols. It seemed unexpectedly recognizable, deeply Western, and yet entirely unfamiliar. I ran across names, terms, numbers, Hebrew letters, astrological symbols….and they were organized into charts, tables, schemata….Some pictures were organized into series. I was astounded. What was the meaning of all this, and what were the relationships in these pictures?"

"I remember the first time I came to the same realization," Sara said, swallowing, clearing her mouth with her tongue. "I looked at it from an artistic point of view, mainly, and I wondered how the colors and symbols were related to the numbers. It was a big insight when I suddenly saw archetypal patterns."

"Yes!" Roger said. He held his spoon but hadn't used it yet. "You have more background in art than I do. Actually, you may be interested in this. So, then I recalled one of my favorite theology classes in seminary called 'Religion and the Arts.' The object of the class was to impress upon students that art could be a medium of communication, that art was capable of conveying theological content, and that this theological content could convey the *logos*, the Word of God."

"I've run across that," Sara said.

"Well, the idea compelled me," Roger said. "I sought those seminary classes, in fact, to find a new approach for a yearning in me that had no outlet in ordinary churches. But the best results of those classes, and the approach overall, were largely impressionistic experiences from contemplating a painting related to some theological idea or a pastor's sermon theme for the week. Overall, the effort seemed as significant, or trivial, as your ordinary church sermon, but with a visual rather than verbal medium. It might have been novel, hip, or avant garde for a church. But it satisfied nothing in me. In the esoteric art, however, I found a higher order—or at least the memory of higher systems. Here was a mystical and symbolic depth beyond merely religious art. I remember standing with a book in hand in a small esoteric bookstore, realizing then that this was entirely different. So I bought the book.

"I continued my search through esoteric bookstores, buying many rare books in Alchemy, Hermetic Qabala, Sufi teaching, Yogic art, Taoist cosmology, Buddhist systems and so on. The symbolic languages of these discrete philosophical systems were laid out in tables I had never seen before and aligned with corresponding symbols in the other systems. I hardly knew these systems in themselves, much less that they were capable of analogous relations with other systems. I sat staring night after night at these charts and tables with their strange symbols, terms, numbers, and alphabet letters. Night after night, my eyes raced up and down the columns, across the rows, reading the correspondences and checking in my intuition if I recognized the themes, if I saw anything essentially similar across these otherwise seemingly disparate systems. I understood very quickly that here were entirely new languages, new to me anyway, and that these functioned in ways I had never before learned despite years of theological training. Here were meta systems relating these otherwise separate systems. This whole enterprise seemed a kind of science."

"Very interesting!" Greg said. "I can totally relate to your experience. I've had something like it myself, though probably more formally philosophical and less vast in scope. It's easy to see in ancient Neoplatonic systems, which the university doesn't study much. But anyway, this began your understanding of ontology?"

"Hmm," Roger mused. "I guess you could say that. I wasn't aware of ontology as a field yet. I didn't learn it directly in my religious studies, but of course I met discussions of ontologies in the literature without them jumping out at me. But yes, obviously these were ontologies. So you could say my intuition of categories and relationships really got started then."

"But you also have yoga in there—in AlignIt," Sara said. "How did you come to that?"

"Right. Well, I had also studied yoga, Tantra and Ayurveda, outside seminary, because it didn't really fit in to my seminary studies, and I knew that there were symbol systems there, too."

"You practiced yoga," Jenny said to Roger, setting her plate aside and producing a pad of paper and pen for Tara. She drew Tara's attention and quietly showed her some drawing games while the adults talked.

"Yes, that's right," Roger said. "We practiced together. At a yoga ashram in the Catskills in upstate, New York."

"Really?" Sara said. "We've done yoga together, too."

"Hmmm." Roger nodded, acknowledging. "So that's where we learned about yogic charts, diagrams, and esoteric practices. But these were entirely separate systems to me. I learned the yoga systems in different places from the Western systems, in isolation, so to speak. And no one connected them for me. So I began wondering—were the yoga systems similar to those in Western alchemy, Qabala, and astrology? Were they essentially the same? I wasn't sure if they were historically related. But it seemed clear they had at least some typological similarities. I noticed, for instance, that Alchemy had a three-term system—mercury, sulfur, and salt. Yoga had *sattva*, *rajas*, and *tamas*. Ayurveda had *vata*, *pitta* and *kapha*. Taoism had *jing, chi, shen*. Were these essentially the same, or standing in similar relation, despite their different names? If they were different, how so? The more systems I studied, the more I found correspondences like these—sets of threes, fours, fives, sixes, sevens, eights, nines, it went on and on. Many traditional sciences seemed to have similar deep structures."

Greg shook his head in agreement, resonating with the story. Sara noticed his intense, wide eyes and a faint, knowing smile.

"Over the next several weeks," Roger said, "I sat at my desk drawing out the systems I had seen. I tried linking symbols from different systems to see if the correspondences I could see did, in fact, match up. Many of them did. Some didn't. Why did some fit while others didn't? What made a fit? How to account for non-conforming systems, non-conforming data? The problem to me became how to represent these many other dimensions."

"And this is the beginning of AlignIt?" Greg asked.

"This was the beginning, yes. My early experience with computerized databases—and they were not ubiquitous then like they are today, nor even in the zeitgeist of the general public—my computer experience led me to an unstinting intuition that these esoteric systems could be organized in database tables. A few years later, I discovered that there were not just religions but also sacred sciences, and that these sciences had already been ordered systematically or conceived or revealed systematically."

Jenny looked up from her game with Tara. "Why don't you tell them about your early dreams?" She returned to her drawing game with Tara, which itself looked to Greg like a massive data table of odd symbols.

Sara's eyes widened. "Oh, you have dreams? We do dream work!"

"So I heard," Roger said. "We don't do dream work, as you do. But yes, I've had a few dreams about this."

Roger wiped his mouth with his cloth napkin and sat back.

"About ten years later, I was beginning to create AlignIt—actually developing the initial table structure. Then one night I had an odd dream. It didn't have a narrative as most dreams do. Rather, I felt the image and presence of my teacher's teacher. And it seems I was working during the night. I felt somehow that I was being taught structures of sacred science and how they could be put into computerized tables. I was seeing relations of data previously unrelated. I felt the need to be attentive and alert because so much was being given, and I was given so many tasks. There was a feeling of urgency and a strong demand for attention. I couldn't remember most of the dream the next day—just the impression of having been at work in the night, of somehow being shown or taught something at a soul level. It seemed like something was infused or transmitted, like a big download."

"Wow," Sara said. Greg noticed she had stopped eating, just sat listening.

"Another night, maybe some months later," Roger said, "I had a dream of being in an institute of some type, working on the creation of a large database. The buildings didn't look like this, like the Bayside Village. They looked somewhat like a research institute where I worked at the time. But I knew it was a new building, a new project, an entirely new creation. The database tables had an unearthly, numinous quality."

Greg laughed in delight. "Imagine that—someone who sees data tables in an unearthly light. If anyone is going to build a sacred science database of the future, you'd hope they'd see it with a numinous glow."

"Yes, well…" Roger laughed quietly in humility. "Nothing transpired immediately after these dreams. I had the same mundane, outer-life conditions. But after those dreams, it became easier to map sacred sciences across many places and through many times, over the centuries. I knew I was creating an entirely new type of database that hadn't existed yet—new on account of its completeness on a global and historical scale. But it couldn't simply be an assemblage of static tables showing relations. Otherwise, why computerize it?"

"Well," Greg challenged, "even a static collection of data tables never before connected is better than what existed before AlignIt."

"True, true," Roger said.

Greg threw in quickly, "But that just makes a stronger argument for what you've actually done with AlignIt."

"Yes, I guess I agree on both points. AlignIt could have been simply a collection of digitized historical records. But you're right—I saw more than that. AlignIt would have to perform operations that mere tables on paper, or tables rendered digitally, could not do. It would have to relate new data not yet related, and it would have to perform operations that could only be suggested on paper. So a global sacred science database capable of performing operations slowly emerged from my daily efforts. And one by one I worked out most of the features AlignIt has today."

"Oh, what a fascinating story!" Sara exclaimed. "I've rarely heard stories of the birth of a new technology."

"So there you have it," Roger said. "That's how the idea came to me. And with my background in religious studies, esoteric philosophies, living residentially in various spiritual centers, several with Jenn," he said, looking fondly to her, and she looked back fondly, "I was able to map out table structures on paper. But one might say that was the easy part. Getting the idea—that was easy."

"That was easy?" Sara said. "Who thinks of these things? That's so totally amazing."

"Well," Roger said, "it *was* the easy part."

"You can't imagine!" Jennie said, looking up at Greg and Sara. "The hours and hours of work! We actually had no resources then to pull it off. And no one could really imagine it and share his vision. Computers and spiritual practice didn't really go together. They were different worlds. You know, people interested in spiritual things often set themselves against the collective, often identified themselves on the fringe, often participated, consciously or not, in neo-Luddite assumptive worlds. And scientists were just as often set against spirituality—at that time. It's taken a long time to find a community of people bringing these worlds together. I've lived with Roger over the years. It's truly been a life work." Then she went back to her game with Tara, a spiritual work of a different kind.

Sara looked at Jenny's game scribbles on the paper there before Tara. She wondered if Jenny might herself be an artist. But the games, whatever they were, didn't evidence an artistic touch. Sara intuited Jenny was not an artist herself.

"Everyone has ideas," Roger went on, "and many people hit on great ideas now and then. The much harder part was how to build in outer life what I could see so vividly with the eye of imagination. Even worse, you could say, was that I felt the burden of having been given something—an idea, a vision for it, dreams about it, transmission in the night. I had these dreams, so I felt I had been given a trust, of sorts. But how could I bring it into some kind of form in the 'real world?' I felt in a very bad position."

Roger picked up a glass, drank, breathed. He held the glass, looked into it. "We had no resources, like Jenny said, and we had difficult outer life conditions. And no one reflected it back, outwardly. I built an early sacred science database myself with an off-the-shelf software package. But I needed to do more. And my scholarly training in religion and philosophy hadn't prepared me to write software code and algorithms. And our path offered me very little outer communication at that time, especially of a kind that could help me outwardly. I felt almost crazy at times, wondering if I had delusions about this. But I felt deeply that I was carrying something and that I needed, somehow, to bring it into a form and begin attracting people to this vision."

"I was his only confidant for a long time," Jenny said. "Imagine that."

"It's true," Roger said. "I'm so grateful for Jenn's friendship over the years."

"So I heard all about it," Jenny said. "But he had a lonely period there for awhile, and probably felt rather isolated."

"Did you develop this work in seminary, in your doctoral work?" Greg asked.

"Before seminary initially," Roger said. "In seminary, I really had nowhere to go with it. It didn't match anything they were teaching—even at a big consortium of eleven seminaries. I developed it in my dissertation at the Graduate Theological Union in Berkeley, but I was really on my own. And the more I studied these traditions, the more I realized that they could not be studied only theologically, in the traditional Western sense."

"It's the same in academic philosophy," Greg said. "It makes a farce of philosophy as a way of living. The great schools encompassed everything."

"Right," Roger said. "So I realized religion alone, in a Western sense, wasn't enough; a complete philosophical and scientific education was necessary. For example, think about yoga and Ayurveda. The study of theology might help me bridge to Vedanta or Yoga philosophy. But it's not enough for understanding yoga postures, diet, the cycles of time, medicinal herbs, therapeutic interventions and the like. I needed to be with people who were integrating, or re-integrating, religion, philosophy and science. My inquiry led to the reintegration of these three areas." Roger turned now to Greg with special passion. "So I became increasingly interested in the philosophy of science, scientific integrity, and the capacity to create, invent and develop things that work, and work well, on the basis of sacred science."

"This is a question I set for myself this week, actually," Greg said. "What would a philosophy of sacred science look like? Then I realized that maybe it's already been done."

"Well, you may know better than I do," Roger said. "But from where I sit, more is needed. I did what I could in my doctoral work to document these sciences and their underlying structures. But I found myself frequently walking down from the Graduate Theological Union over to Electrical Engineering and Computer Science at UC Berkeley, going to seminars and lectures, trying to learn how to build what I could only imagine. I felt I needed to acquire the skills to build it. And that's where I found collaborators to help me build the earliest versions of AlignIt."

"Wow," Greg said. "You sought a true university education, but our schools of higher education could only present disciplines standing in isolation, in piecemeal form."

"Exactly my feeling," Roger echoed.

"Even separate schools. So you have to slip out of one and go over to the other," Greg said.

"You know this too, I think—you're employed by two departments to teach what you would rather teach as one inquiry."

"Yes," Greg sighed. "I hadn't thought of it that way." The idea captivated him. "And in grad school I couldn't study my interests openly, and I still can't even teach or publish openly, even in our very liberal day— especially on my tenure track."

"Mhmm," Roger smiled in playful smugness. "All the more reason to move over to a school where you can do it all under one roof! But I digress."

Greg snickered.

"Anyway, I had the scholarly interest and capacity, but I envisioned AlignIt also as applied science, as well as a research tool. I wanted to apply sacred science. I also wanted to improve things already created by others by the application of sacred science—to tune things up, so to speak, using what eventually became AlignIt. I was also motivated by social values—to make or improve things that can help make the world a better place. I feel satisfied that I can finally do these things with AlignIt. This has become a life work."

Greg nodded, contemplating what he could do by a move to Bayside Village—having it all under one roof.

Sara looked at him, stared in thought for a moment, looking at his face from the side, imagining at the same time.

"Why don't we move to the living room?" Jenny said.

Everyone got up from the table, and expressions of pleasant satisfaction were given for a meal well prepared.

As they reentered, Greg noticed the oud music of Tosun playing. It had continued playing, but he had forgotten about it in the dining room, with the engaging conversation. In the movement back to the living room, his awareness returned, and he heard the minor chords, the plucking, and now the singing, in Turkish, of what must be love ballads, calls of Lover to Beloved.

Greg sat on the couch where he had sat earlier, and Roger sat again beside him.

Sara and Jenny also sat in the same positions, and Sara patted the couch beside her, encouraging Tara to sit there. Sara hoped, now, to revisit the art world with Jenny.

Jenny asked, "How was Steve's Utopia workshop?"

"It was fascinating!" Sara said, taking the first opportunity. "It was a writing workshop, but I brought my sketch pad and I drew for several of the exercises. I also wrote a little, too. But yeah, I really went into the exercises. It was deep for me."

"Yeah, it was very inspiring," Greg said. "I hadn't really thought about utopias much. But I found myself wondering if I might connect some of my work in ontologies with utopian literature or work with Bateson collegially."

Roger raised his eyebrows.

Tara became tired and it was time to return to the Lodge.

43

At the Lodge, Greg brought two hot cups of tulsi tea from the bathroom, past Tara who lay fast asleep on her roll-away bed. He set the cups down on the bedside stand and sat down at the table to review his AlignIt Commons Board presentation.

"Thanks," Sara whispered, sitting down on the bed near the table. She took a sip, reflected on her conversations with Jenny. Intriguing but unfinished. She knew Roger better now, but Jenny remained a mystery. Not an artist, but on the Art Center board. An Art Center that aims to guide the future of sacred arts and crafts. What is Jenny's role in all this? What is her background? How could Sara connect with her, she wondered, as part of her own journey back to art?

Sara bent over to pull a book from a backpack filled with art supplies. Blakesley's classic work on aesthetics. She held the book in hand, contemplated its cover, as though it were a magical object. This was the book she poured over some years back when she and Greg were in school, dating. She was a romantic artist and he a philosopher. Blakesley's investigation of esoteric themes in aesthetics had elevated Sara's search, her perception, her work upon her art. Blakesley's lofty scholarship combined with the intuitive insight of a mystic, a scholar-practitioner, made the work a bridge for Sara between her artistic world and the high and noble ideas Greg ever contemplated in their time together. This was the one book, the main book, Sara brought to Bayside Village, hoping to open again to its pages, hoping her life could again expand to include this great work, hoping this book could now be the stimulus to open worlds Sara once explored in her simpler but stormy student days before family, before Tara.

Greg couldn't start yet on his presentation. He noticed that the books he had carefully arranged on the table, one atop the other, the largest on bottom and smallest on top, had become disordered by Tara's morning play. While Sara sipped her tea, he re-arranged his book pile, putting the stack back in order. Sara looked up. He noticed her sipping, watching him. It was a quirky habit, he knew. But Greg liked his universe ordered before he worked. He sat back, then, and opened his AlignIt presentation.

Sara put her tea cup on the night stand, turned back to Blakeley, opened the cover. Its an old book now. She had read it, underlined, and reread many times. It inspired her paintings years ago, before Tara. She hadn't opened it in that long a time. But packing for the trip, something moved her to throw it into her bag. Good choice, she thought. It was the very intellectual substance she needed now, the weight, the gravity, yet the alignment with finer ideas, turning her apprehension to subtle realities. She stared at the worn pages, the passionate underlinings, recollecting those years, those passionate, lofty, inspired years. She used to paint from that ground, that inner attention, that vision. And now something stirred in her to return, to reclaim it. And did she know this stirring, did she suspect it, while resisting Greg's talk with her about Bayside Village the last several months? She turned pages now and reread her underlinings from years ago, evincing great insights she had then, ones she seldom recalled now in her day-to-day life back home. The spiritual path has been so hard, grinding down ego attachments, identifications, destroying everything. Even art, her greatest aspiration—her greatest attachment. The path was crushing. It broke art away from her. And she bore the breaking, the crushing. She bore it, and the path gave her this incredible freedom from her identifications with the art world which had been strong in her—an identity in her youth, and yet a bondage for a woman who seeks real freedom. And she has lived like this, surrendering to a mundane existence of job and family life. But now this impetus to reclaim her art arose in her. Where had it come from? When did it start? Yes, she knew it, she suspected that maybe something here at Bayside Village would get stirred in her, get reawakened. That's why she brought the book. Yes, this was growing in her, like pregnancy, starting already before coming to the Village. Ah, that's it! she thought. That's my resistance—coming here makes me confront this. Yes, that's it! Am I ready to own this again, bring it back into my life? She turned pages in a heightened state of attention, remembering, reintegrating, feeling where all of this wanted to go in her life. Her mind quickly fit together the forces awakening in her life, the doors opening.

Greg sat back from his AlignIt Commons board presentation, now polished. It felt right, and he could see his imagination extending into that future of what AlignIt could be. He felt part of this, and he wanted to be part of it, with a yearning that felt like a slow burning fire. But what about Sara, his soul mate? He sipped his tulsi tea and listened to the silent room, stirred only by the occasional page turning in Sara's fingers, by Tara's deep inhale now and then. How could things work? Sara's not happy here. So he opened files on faculty tenure at University of Washington and reread them—just skimming, imagining staying there. He went back and forth inside himself, feeling the security of tenure at a mainstream university, seeing the image of himself as a respectable university professor, feeling again the uncertainty of work on sacred science ontology at the Bridge Institute. Coming here would be harder for Sara, he imagined. He shuttled between two imagined futures, cogitating, searching for what is truest in himself.

After an hour of inspired reading, Sara down put her book. She closed her eyes, breathed deeply, digested this food. After a short silence, she opened her eyes. "Want to meditate?"

Greg breathed in deeply. "Yeah." He came back to himself, saw himself looking at the screen, witnessed his anxiety over tenure and the decision about Bayside Village. It was time to let go of this, go deeper to an inward peace.

Greg touched his mobile, withdrew his screen projections and climbed onto the bed with Sara. He arranged his pillows behind him, pulled his legs into half-lotus, adjusted his clothes. Sara put her copy of Blakeley on the night stand, switched off her light. She sat up in a half-lotus against her propped pillows. In the dim moon light filtering in from the window, Greg put his hands together at his solar plexus, turned slightly, and bowed to his earthly beloved. Sara did the same, bowing to him. They said Namaste, I bow to the god within you, a practice they had adopted from a yoga ashram years ago, another daring venture together. Resuming his erect spine, Greg breathed in deeply, then out. Sara breathed in, then let the day go in a long exhale.

With the lights off, activity stopped, and talking finished, memories from the day returned to Greg now with force. Images of the meetings, conversations, places, people, the whole trip, paraded now before his witnessing I. Questions called for his attention, beckoned for his energy. Greg witnessed all this in a detached state of mind, identifying himself not with the mind which grasps at thoughts and worries, not with the image of himself as Greg Cobb at Bayside Village doing all these things, but with a vast ground of consciousness, a witnessing awareness in which all these things, images, and energies swim. This practice helped quiet his mind. He found alignment with the longing of his soul for love and set his intention there. This longing in him to be intimate with his Beloved, this longing for home, was stronger than all the noise of the day, and he gave himself to a strong inward pull toward surrender, love, peace, bliss, and, God willing, to Nothing. Yet his attention flitted to this and that, his mind caught by passing thoughts, taken by distractions. He brought himself back to his practice. With conscious will and intention, he inclined toward his heart.

Part 2
Remarkable Meetings

Day 4: Wednesday

44

Before dawn, Greg opened his eyes in bed. He stretched and looked over to Sara who lay asleep beside him on her stomach, her bare shoulders up over her pillow, her long brunette hair fanned over her arms. Greg gently caressed Sara's back to rouse her.

Sara moaned in a half-asleep way. "Okay," she said, stirring.

As dawn broke, the family walked to the Temple Greg and Sara toured on Monday, and down the hall to the Tibetan Buddhist room. A small group of people removed their shoes outside the door and placed them on a rack. Greg, Sara, and Tara did the same, Sara helping with Tara's shoes.

Inside the room, a woman at the front with a shaved head and robes of saffron and maroon was laughing with others who were getting seated on maroon cushions.

Greg approached another woman near the back, also in robes. "Hi, we're visiting for the first time."

"Welcome to our sangha," the nun said with a smile, putting her hands together with her prayer beads in hand, and giving a slight bow.

Greg returned the gesture. "We've been to other Buddhist meetings, including Vajrayana. But we're not familiar with your practice here. Do we just sit anywhere?"

"You can sit anywhere. If you want, you can sit next to me and follow along. I'm sitting right there in the front row." She pointed.

"Oh, okay," Greg said. He looked, saw two rows of cushions.

"I'm Tenzin Jorchu, by the way."

"Oh, I'm Greg, and this is my wife, Sara, and my daughter, Tara." Sara smiled and gave a bow, and the nun returned the gesture.

Greg, Sara, and Tara turned and sat down on the maroon cushions in front, Greg sitting next to Tenzin Jorchu's cushion, Tara on the other side of him, and Sara on the next cushion down. Greg and Sara both sat in meditation for a few silent moments, and Tara sat, imitating the meditation position.

Tara tugged at Greg's shirt. "Daddy?" she whispered. Greg opened his eyes and leaned his shoulder and head toward her. "When is it going to start?"

"In a few minutes."

"Why are you starting already?"

"I try to meditate always and everywhere." As the response satisfied Tara, or mystified her, Greg resumed his posture and closed his eyes again.

Tara tugged on his shirt. "Daddy?"

Greg leaned down again. "Yes?"

"Are those Buddhas?" Tara asked, pointing ahead to a row of Buddha statues arranged directly in front of the cushions, a row of them, each a different color, each holding different items in their hands.

"Yes, those are Buddhas."

"Why are there so many?"

Greg improvised. "Each one has a gift for us."

"And, um, um, why are they different colors?"

"Each Buddha is a different color because each one has a different gift."

"What kind of gift?"

"Oh, like happiness, joy, laughter, love."

"Are they going to give it us?"

"I think so, yes. We're going to sing and chant, and let's see what happens. I think the Buddhas give gifts from their heart, like love."

Just then, Tenzin Jorchu sat down on the cushion next to Greg. She wrapped her robes around her knees ceremoniously, leaned her torso to the right and then to the left, stretched her neck to the right and left, and then stabilized in the middle. When she finished, she leaned to Greg and opened a chant book on the small table before him. "We start here, on page 3 with taking refuge, and the Four Immeasurable Thoughts. When we get to the Bodhisattva and Tantric Vows," she said, flipping pages ahead to show him, "we ask that these are recited only by those who have taken their vows. Have you taken vows?"

"In my heart over the years, yes, but not formally before a sangha."

"Okay. Just follow along with me if you want until we get there. And here's a really fun way for you daughter to participate," she said with a smile. Tenzin Jorchu reached to the other side of her and produced a bell. She turned around again and said to Tara, "Would you like to ring this bell?" Tara nodded her head. "Why don't I give it to your dad, and the two of you can ring it together when we chant. Do you see these symbols on the side of the page?" Tenzin Jorchu pointed to symbols in the margins. "This is the bell, and when you see this by the words, you ring the bell. And this picture stands for the damaru, right here" she said, holding up hers. "When you see the symbols of the damaru in the margin, I will strike this. So why don't you work with your dad to ring the bell at the right time, okay?"

Tara nodded her head. She had a part to play, and this was interesting and important.

The nun at the front sat down in the same row, facing the Buddhas and an empty, raised chair for a Lama who wasn't there. The room quieted, and she spoke aloud. "Become aware of your breath." The room fell silent, and deep breaths could be heard. "Become aware of your motivation, keeping in mind the wish for liberation for yourself and for all sentient beings. Hold the noble thought to practice for your own happiness and the happiness of all sentient beings." After another moment of silence, the pure and sonorous sound of a struck bell rang through the room. "Let's chant the Refuges on page 3."

Tara at first held the bell with Greg when he rang it. But since she did not yet read well and could not follow the chant book, her attention went instead to watching the mudras, or hand movements, of the monks, nuns, and lay people around her, and their wielding of the dorje, bell, and other implements as they chanted.

After 45 minutes, the chant ended. Some people arose and performed full prostrations on their own, depending on their own practice. Some people got up and socialized.

The other nun came to talk to Greg and Sara. She was shorter than the first, seemed a practical, grounded woman. "Have you seen our holographic mandala?"

"No," Greg said. He imagined, by having observed her earlier, that she would be a keeper of the space, a maintenance person, an operations person.

"Let me show you." She walked to one corner of the room with a limp, and the family followed her, to a raised square platform of five feet by five feet, just three feet from the ground. "You've seen sand mandalas created by monks?"

"Yes," Sara said. And Greg nodded.

"This mandala is made by the monks, but it's made of light and projected holographically." She flipped a switch by the wall. An elegant and dazzling show of laser light revealed a high resolution mandala in three dimensions, pulsating and moving, unfolding across the table as if monks were now pouring colored sand in high speed. Its rays of light were so brilliant, so intense, the mandala looked made up of gems.

"Wow," Sara said. "It's beautiful." She paused, enamored. Tara's eyes were transfixed. Greg studied the structure, the symbols, impressed by the brilliance. He traced the outer doors or gates, followed the pathways in toward the center.

Tara asked Greg to pick her up.

"Are they artists?" Sara asked.

"The monks? Some are," the nun said. "Some are computer scientists, some work with visual computing, some work with projection technologies. They apply the same inner effort and work from the same dharma teaching in constructing the mandala."

They stood discussing the brilliant, 3D light mandala. Then the nun said, "and here is the practice of non-attachment to form." She flipped the switch and the projection blinked out.

"Bye bye mandala," Greg said to Tara in his arms.

"Wow," Sara said. "It's amazing that you can create such beauty with light."

"We can create beauty with anything if we know how," the nun said.

"Mmm," Sara said, contemplating. Then the looked to the nun. "Do you mind if we walk around the room and look at the Thanka before we go?"

"Please, be our guest. The room is locked up after this until tonight, so now is a perfect time. And you're welcome to join us every morning. We have special visits from Rinpoches on weekends and our Tuesday night meeting."

"Thanks," Sara said.

Greg and Sara walked slowly around the room, Tara still in Greg's arms, looking at the thankas hanging on the walls, displaying the pantheon of buddhas, bodhisattvas and great yogis in the Nyingma lineage.

"Oh, there's my mirror," Greg said, stopping before a busy thanka. "The Wheel of Life."

"Your mirror?" Sara asked.

"Yeah. It shows suffering in different realms of deluded existence. I don't remember all the realms, but...it's like anger, greed, and delusion, the three poisons. It shows the ignorance of our samsaric existence." Sara contemplated a moment. "There are the hell realms," Greg said, pointing to the bottom of the wheel. "I can't remember all the realms...Animal realm, human realm, devic realm, asuric realm, hungry ghost realm..."

"Hungry ghost?" Tara cut in, obviously attentive, picking up what she could.

"Yes. See here," Greg said, pointing. "See, their bellies are really big, which means they're really hungry. But look at their necks—they're long and really skinny. This means their throats can't swallow very much food. Imagine if you were really, really hungry, but you couldn't swallow because your throat was really, really thin. So these poor hungry ghosts can never eat as much as they want. They never get as much food as they hunger for, and they suffer a lot."

"Mmm," Sara uttered to herself, studying the familiar image. "But why your mirror?"

"I don't know. It reminds me of my more frequent states, I guess, or at least it reminds me that all of these realms are potential places we can go—not just ordinary consensus reality and a simple heaven and hell. It's just a reminder to me to keep me humble."

"Well they're all mirrors, aren't they—all the Buddhas, bodhisattvas, saints, whatever? Aren't we supposed to have Buddha nature already, except that our ignorance clouds the clear light of the sun?"

"Yeah, I guess you're right," Greg said. "Good point." He looked ahead, taking in a visual sweep of other thankas before him. "Maybe I need to let go of what could be an attachment to self-abasement, or a fear of forever being stuck in lower places in my practice."

"Oh look," Sara said, pointing to the next thanka. "Tara, who is this?"

"The Green Tara," she said triumphantly.

"Good for you," Greg said, patting her arm as he held her. He moved up to study the image closely. "Do you see what she's holding in her hands? Do you remember her powers?"

"Is she a protector?" Sara asked. Tara nodded her head up and down in big movements.

"Good," Sara said. They studied the image. Then Sara advanced to the next thanka. "Oh, and who is this one?"

Tara looked as Greg moved up for a closer look. "White Tara."

"Excellent," Sara said. "And what is her quality?" Sara waited, but not too long. "Is she a divine mother?"

Tara nodded.

"And what do you see there on her forehead, hands and feet?" Sara asked.

"Eyes," Tara said.

"Good!" Sara said.

"And why does she have so many eyes?" Greg asked.

"To help everyone."

"Good girl," Greg said. Good enough.

They stood for a moment, contemplating.

"Oh, I like that one," Greg said, and stepped up close to the next thanka to read the caption. "Palden Lhamo: The Dark Goddess." Then he stood back, taking it in. "Oh, that's powerful." Greg fixed his gaze on the flowing, fiery image, the dark black, the deep red.

"That's intense," Sara said.

"I don't like that one," Tara said after a few moments.

"Okay," Greg said, and slowly moved on, yet feeling drawn to stay.

"Wow, look at the Sri Yantra," Sara said. Greg and Sara stopped by the next thanka. Greg stood with Sara as she traced the interlacing upward and downward facing triangles with her eyes.

"Daddy, why does he have so many hands?"

Greg looked at the next image where Tara pointed. He remembered answering this same question before. "Oh, that's, um, Avalokitshvara. He has a thousand hands, and look, each hand has an eye—see that?"

"Why does he have so many hands?"

"I think because he's very helpful—he can do a lot of things for different people. Imagine if you had that many hands. Think of all the people you could help."

45

In his office on the second floor of Avicenna Hall, Roger sat at his desk before his mobile's screen projection, on an early video call with prospective AlignIt Commons board advisor Chris Mueller.

"What kinds of questions?" Chris asked.

"About the game companies you mentioned on Monday."

"Yeah?" Roger saw Chris leaning back confidently in his desk chair against his credenza, his arms up, his hands clasped behind his head.

"We've found some game companies apparently associated with you. We didn't see them in your board application," Roger said.

Chris paused, surprised, put his arms down. "How did those turn up?"

"Just doing our due diligence."

Chris laughed. "What do you guys do—voodoo?" He sat up, pulled his chair closer, leaning on the desk now with his elbows. "That opportunity just came up. Something turned in the funding of a few of my network companies and I seized it. Those deals are in the works. Why?"

"We've licensed game rights exclusively to GameIt, like I said Monday."

"Yeah? I know. So what does that mean?"

"So…I don't know. We may have looked at this differently if we knew you had game companies. We might have had this discussion already about rights in gaming."

"You'd exclude me from advising the board because of the changing flux of my portfolio?"

"I'm talking about discussion," Roger said. "We would have already discussed how we don't have gaming rights to offer."

"I told you—I talked to Jeff, and I said to you on Monday that I simply want to have a frank discussion. That's all. Just a frank discussion. Maybe there are fields of use GameIt isn't pursuing and would be willing to offer. Who knows? That's what frank discussion is for."

"Jeff didn't know about your game companies and he was more than surprised when I said you had talked to him."

"What? I talked to him! We had a very extensive discussion about gaming."

"That was part of your introductory discussions with board members, right? He didn't know you had game companies or that you were interested in gaming rights."

"No one knows—or should know. It all just happened. And I didn't tell him then because it was just the beginning of a discussion in my network. Nothing was decided then. Nothing's decided now. They're not even my companies."

"Not your companies?"

"No. They're just in my network."

"What does that mean, in your network?"

"It means I know people, I make connections, I work deals."

Roger paused a moment, working this out in his mind. "Okay. But you brought it up on Monday, so it must not be so new anymore. Can you say what kind of game companies?"

"What, are you grilling me? I'm bringing opportunities to you."

"What kinds?"

"I can't say yet. These deals are in the works, and I can't say until they're done."

"Okay, how about the fields within gaming?"

"I can't say that either."

"Well what do you expect to discuss at the board meeting that you can't say now? I've told you we don't have rights available in the gaming field. Yet you're coming with game companies."

"Hey! I'm bringing opportunities to you. This is part of what I do, you know? Part advising, part scouting, part introductions. This is what you want. I'm helping you out, here. If you don't want to do a deal, you don't have to do a deal. But these things bubble up, and I'm bringing you opportunities as they arise."

"I appreciate that," Roger said. "You have a lot of connections, and that's what we need at this point in the life cycle of AlignIt and the AlignIt Commons. Maybe I just don't understand well enough how you're going about it. This is my first foray into venture capital advising. I guess I don't understand what you want to put on the agenda for the board meeting."

"I want to save that for a frank discussion on Friday."

"Chris, you want a frank discussion. But you're not able to tell us frankly about your interests. I'm looking for more transparency here."

"My world isn't an open academic environment like yours. Its governed by confidentiality and trade secrecy. There's not a lot of specifics I can give right now. You've got to appreciate that, too."

"I do, Chris. AlignIt Commons has a little of both—openness and confidentiality. But isn't it premature, then, to bring this discussion to the Board? We can't just willy nilly take up a topic without background information. The materials were already posted. We have Greg Cobb and Neil Benson here on campus this week as guests. If it's not the right time for you to give more information, its probably not the right time for a board topic."

"Okay, alright." Chris paused. "I take your point. We can table it for Friday."

Roger was taken aback. That seemed too easy. "Table it? That quickly?"

"Yeah. Hey, I'm just trying to help you out here. If it's not helping, we can table it." Chris looked at Roger and left the discussion open.

"Okay, we'll table it." Roger paused a moment, looked at the agenda before him on an open screen hovering in the air to the right of Chris' image. "Okay. Another question. If you're interested in games, specifically, I'm wondering if the board is the right venue for a preliminary discussion. Usually we would discuss this kind of thing privately first and then raise it at the board meeting. I understand you've spoken with Jeff just once. Maybe a good next step is a frank discussion with him, at the right time."

"Okay, fair enough, fair enough." Mueller paused. "I've also had a good, long conversation with President Bateson. And he's in favor of this kind of advising and connections."

"With Bateson?"

"Of course. Hey, I'm doing my business. I don't just work the Valley."

"Sure, of course. But this isn't Bateson's project."

"He's your chief man."

"Right, but Bateson's head of Bayside Village and the Bridge Institute. The AlignIt Commons is a group of separate legal entities, and Jeff's in charge of GameIt. Bateson's not involved in this."

"*You* don't need to advise *me*, Roger." Chris made himself sound offended and pushed the offense back onto Roger, with an edge. "I *know* how to work in academia. I've negotiated scores of university technology licenses. I'm doing my work, my relationship building. I'm not looking for just a quick transaction."

"I don't doubt that. I'm just saying I think you need to talk to Jeff about this a little more before raising it at a board meeting."

Chris gasped, sounding impatient. "Alright." He left a pause. "I can circle back to Jeff."

"I guess all of this brings the question, for me, why you're focusing on games. You have access to a broad swath of companies, there are lots of available fields of use for AlignIt." Roger left the question in the air. Chris left it there, too, and stared back blankly at Roger, revealing nothing. Roger continued. "Why don't we focus on available fields of use, like, I don't know, digital archives, document management, design tools, discovery tools? One of *my* big interests is discovery tools."

"Yeah. I have feelers out in all of those areas," Chris said. "I'm always talking to companies across my networks. But you have to wait for the right opportunities to bubble up, and then you see one and you seize the moment. I wouldn't have thought of games, per se. But the right opportunity came, and I said to myself, 'Now there's a great play for AlignIt.' So I seized the opportunity. But you know, Roger, I'm always stirring different pots. That's what I do, and that's what I'm doing for AlignIt. Just like these game opportunities shot up and I grabbed 'em, there are plenty of others like it. So I'm definitely looking out for AlignIt, and I'm waiting for the right timing. You don't have to worry about that."

"I have to say, honestly, that you do have me a bit worried. And Jeff too. Maybe a little reassurance is in order."

"Roger, I can't just go spilling the beans on every opportunity that pops up. I have my duties of confidentiality, too, my professional ethics." Chris was silent. Roger now left the space open, not filling it with easy acceptance. "Okay, look. I have my eyes on a digital archive management company. Alright? That's central to AlignIt. It's wide open territory, it's available. Right?"

"Digital archive management?" Roger's voice turned on his interest. Was this a good sign, a good opportunity? "Okay."

"I can't say more about that one, either. But there's some reassurance for you. Just that I have my eyes on a company. It's another company in my network, just like the game companies. It's coming along, but the game companies popped up first. Look, I didn't mean to create a stir on games, alright? So we've tabled it. We can lay it to rest for now. We can focus on digital archive management if you like, except that it's even newer and less certain."

"Digital archive management *is* strategic for AlignIt," Roger said. "That would make a good demonstration of the power of AlignIt."

"Okay, it's probably a better company to put out front. Maybe I should have come to you with that first. But like I said, it's not ready yet. I don't pull stuff out of the cooker before it's ready. So I can't say anything to you about it. But if it inspires you, let's switch gears to digital rights management."

"Okay," Roger said. Something relaxed for him, and he felt easier about this question. Others remained though—his main interest for AlignIt, his passion. "Discovery tools is central to AlignIt," Roger said. "In the informatics space. That's my highest goal for AlignIt."

"I see where you're going with your AlignIt Discovery Engine, Roger. I think it's a noble project. I really do. But you know, I have to make my investors happy. It's not my money. What you're talking about is academic markets, and that's not a great ROI."

"But there are venture-backed informatics companies."

"Okay, sure. It's not big money, but sure, its there. Platform techs are not hot right now. It's a niche market."

"It's not one of your investment areas?"

"No, no, I cover that, too. Alright, look." Chris gasped, exasperated, and spoke slowly, a hint of condescension in his voice. "I know a guy who's in that space. I'll give him a little intro to AlignIt. Alright? I'll see what he has. I'll ask him to keep his eyes open for the right informatics company.

"Okay." It didn't sound as full a commitment, but it satisfied Roger for the moment. "So another question…"

"Geez, what do you guys have, a pre-Board screening? I feel like I'm on trial here."

Roger was silent for a moment. "Chris, I have to say that our conversation Monday threw open a few fundamental questions for me." He was silent again. "It's not just a question about games. What's coming up for me are more basic issues about how you work and how we work as a commons. These are different cultures, and we're trying to open our commons model organically and sustainably to venture backed companies. Forgive me if I'm not a natural at VC. Maybe it's my limitation. But I do have real questions."

"Okay, sure." Chris waved his right hand before the screen, expressing continued openness, if stilted. "Like what?"

"So, we're a commons," Roger said. "We work not only on AlignIt as a common core technology platform. We also work with each other collaboratively by a core set of values inscribed in the AlignIt Commons Membership Agreement, like we've listed in the Board chair application."

"Right. I read it. I get that."

"So we have trust-based relationships. On that basis, Jeff and I have had a lot of discussion since my call with you on Monday. That's part of how we work. I don't know what you're thinking in terms of these game companies. But Jeff is a fellow Commons member and a trusted friend and colleague. He's part of *my* network, you could say."

"Sure." Roger saw Chris sit back again in his chair and put his hands behind his head.

"And I'd like to think he's part of your network, too. But you've had one general, introductory conversation with him, and already you're thinking of…I can't tell exactly, but what he fears is that you'll compete with him." Roger paused, looked at Chris. Chris didn't flinch at the words. "So I've got to look out for him. You see what I'm getting at? Our commons operates in a specific way. And I have to ensure the integrity of our commons in bringing in a venture advisor."

"So what you're saying is I'm playing a little rough?" Chris asked. He lifted his foot casually and rested it on some object outside the screen view.

"I don't know how you're playing, because the situation is not as transparent as I'm accustomed to under our commons model."

"Roger, like I said, I have my duties of confidentiality, trade secrecy…"

"I know. So I don't know how you're playing. I know what I'm feeling, which is that my level of trust was mitigated on Monday, and I felt I needed to check out several things with you to see if this feeling is valid, or if there are some missing pieces. I'd like to think we can work together in the commons in a trusting way."

"Roger, I hear you. What would help you with that? We just tabled games, right? What do you need? I gave you guys all kinds of documents with my board application. I gave you references. I can give you more. What do you need?"

"Mainly disclosure." Roger paused. Chris wasn't forthcoming, and Roger knew he couldn't press for confidential information.

"Okay, look. I can see that the games thing caused a stir. It's an unintended consequence. So I'll make good on that. First, we said we'll table the games and foreground digital rights management, though I don't have anything to offer yet. Second, I'll give my informatics guy a preview of AlignIt and get his take on it as a discovery engine. Third, if mending is needed, I'll reach out to Jeff, like I said, and we'll have another chat. Okay? That's three things. Anything else?"

Roger was silent a moment, thinking fast. Was this all he needed for reassurance? This sounded right. He mentally reviewed his talking points for Chris, scanned Friday's agenda before him. There was still the question of fit—the fit of company and the commons. "Can you tell me what you envision when you have what, in your mind, is the right kind of company for the AlignIt Commons?"

"Well yeah. I mean, we talked about this, right? I bring them in, make the introductions, they get a look at AlignIt, you both evaluate the opportunity, and if it's right, they join the Commons….Then we're in business, and money flows, and AlignIt gets funded."

Roger nodded as he listened. Did Chris really get the big picture, after all?

46

After the Tibetan Buddhist meeting, Greg, Sara and Tara took a before-breakfast stroll on the boardwalk at Taylor Slough over the mudflats. Greg carried Tara, but felt her weight. "Why am I still carrying you, my big girl? Are you ready to get down?" Tara clung to Greg as the cool, fog-filled draft of early morning hugged the marsh before the rising sun.

"I had a dream last night," Sara said. "It feels like a big dream."

"Really?" Greg said with interest. "What was it?"

"We were together, and we were looking for a new home. I don't know where it was. I didn't recognize it. We went driving to a neighborhood with new condominiums. We went in, met a realtor or caretaker there, and looked around. It turns out that this place was owned by a friend, but the dream didn't say who. I remember the image of Matt from our Sufi Center—that man who owns the house he always opens up to parties and gatherings—and Randy, the tour guide here on Monday. These two people were superimposed as one, either as the realtor or as someone who owned the space. It seemed we would get a reasonable deal on the space."

"Wow," Greg said, listening intently.

"I was amazed because the space was much larger inside than it seemed from the outside. I walked around inside and looked at the rooms. The space had a very large living room almost like a hotel lobby and several large rooms adjoining the living room. It had lots of nice chairs, and it seems the chairs would stay with the house if we wanted them. It even had two wet bars for entertaining. One space off to the side was large enough to be our whole house. I was surprised as I kept walking around and seeing other rooms open up. There were enough rooms for me to have an art studio, for you to have a study and library, and enough space to host events, like meditation, study, discussion, and social events. I thought to myself that we couldn't possibly furnish this large place on our own, so we would need to keep the chairs. I came back to the realtor in the foyer but I didn't see how much the rent would be each month."

"Daddy, I want breakfast."

"Just a minute, Honey, Momma's telling a dream," Greg said. "We'll go in just a minute."

Sara continued. "I went outside to look around the back and sides of the condominium. I could see that the space was really big. It wasn't exactly square on the back and side. It had, like, this unexpected angle projecting out farther. It's like the back grew in size the farther back the house went."

"Hmm," Greg said. "That's an interesting detail."

"It seemed that we were being shown this house as our new place, almost like it was being given to us by the path. So it wasn't like just going to another open house with a realtor. It was something special." Sara paused, searching. "And that's the dream."

"Wow, that seems very significant," Greg said, looking at Sara as he walked, contemplating her dream with focus and interest. Then he looked beyond to the pickleweed and cordgrass of the marsh. They carried on a few steps silently. "What do you make of it?"

Tara wriggled. "Do you want to get down?" Greg said. And he let her down to run ahead and poke a reed into the mud.

"It feels like a 'big dream,'" Sara said, reflecting. "It seems to me like it's about a new psychic space. Moving into a new house is like moving to a new phase spiritually."

"It's interesting that you have two wet bars," Greg said.

"Yeah, that's kind of weird. It's like alcohol."

"Could it be the wine of love, or even stronger drinks? Like the intensity of devotional love?"

"Oh, right. Yeah. I didn't think of that. Yeah, the wine of love makes sense. Hmm. That's what it feels like, because it's also in a place where it feels like we would entertain people, and it feels like it has something to do with meditation and fellowship."

"Chairs are places to sit, and it's a way to welcome people to the space," Greg said.

"Yeah, that's what I mean—the wet bars are in that space."

Greg paused, thought. "Chairs or seats also have something to do with authority. Perhaps this is about you or us taking our seat in a place like this."

"Maybe."

"What does it mean that you didn't see the price?" Greg asked.

"I didn't see if we could afford it. Because, you know, in ordinary life, a place like that would be too expensive for us. But in the dream it seemed it would be made affordable for us, somehow." Sara paused a moment, reflecting. "The dream could also be about a literal move to The Bayside Village. Like, on another level, it may be telling me more of what I feel about moving here than I'm aware of, or showing the kinds of opportunities here."

Greg had thought of that, too. "It's interesting that you dreamed of us looking at a new place with a realtor," he said, "and here we are visiting the Bayside Village and asking questions about moving here. Do you think the dream is commenting on this outer situation?"

"Well…" Sara said hesitantly, "I don't know if I should take the dream literally, as if it's about actually moving to the Village. Its probably more about a new psychological state—like maybe a new part of my life is opening up."

Greg didn't push the point, sensitive to Sara's inner struggle over Bayside Village. It probably was psychological. Though he felt the inner and outer were more interactive, he stayed on the psychological level with Sara. "The space is larger on the inside than it first appears on the outside."

"Yeah," Sara said. "New rooms kept opening up. And that detail about the angular extension of the back of the apartment. You know, I was looking at my Islamic art and architecture course books again before we left Seattle, and I was intrigued by one feature of mosque design."

"Ah, I was wondering where that came from."

"Yeah. When medieval mosques were built in large, established urban centers, like Cairo, they were built on existing city lots. But the requirement to face the qibla toward Mecca means that the entire mosque pattern was aligned with the qibla direction, not necessarily with the city streets. From a floor plan view, you can see that the mosque building has the conventional square or rectangular shape, and then extra walls and rooms were added to bring the complex flush with the street. So these structures ended up with quadrilateral or other polygonal shapes. And the apartment in my dream seems to have that kind of shape."

"Hmmm. That's very interesting." Greg was silent a moment, pondering. "Maybe this new apartment or new interior movement in you is aligned with the qibla direction within you—symbolically, a new movement in you is aligned with the center, the most important thing."

"Oh, that's insightful," Sara mused. "I was thinking it was just daytime residue from browsing art and architecture books."

"Well, it's your dream. But that's what comes to me. It's interesting that you dreamed about Randy," Greg added.

"Well, it was two people in one. It was also Matt in our Sufi group. I think Randy's tour made a big impression on me two days ago. I think that was a turning point."

"How so?" Greg asked.

"Well, you know I came here feeling skeptical. I don't usually feel closed to things. But I did think the utopianism would be ungrounding. And the surrounding area felt odd and grungy—not where I'd want to raise Tara. I didn't think it was the best move for your career or mine. But I'm amazed at the people we've met, the opportunities unfolding. It seems like things are lining up and pointing to this place—for both of us."

"Really."

"I mean, the dream shows a new space opening up, at least internally. But it's symbolized as looking for a new apartment and seeing a realtor. And the space is held by Matt from our Center, and Randy who comes from here. So it feels like two worlds are coming together for me."

"Right." Greg contemplated this. "What do these two figures mean to you?"

"Well, both of them have to do with welcoming people to a space. I wonder if it means our lives could shift from being so private, alone, bereft, ground down to nothing on the path, to being in a place of receiving people, even in service of the path. Maybe that's too much to say. But that's what comes to mind."

Greg, Sara and Tara entered the Bayside Village Dining Commons through the front double doors, which stood open as the fog burned off in the morning sun.

"The Orientation table is gone," Sara said as they walked to the breakfast buffet line.

"Yeah, a lot of people left after the utopia workshop. I saw fewer Orientation people staying for dinner."

As they inched closer to the buffet in the food line, Tara grabbed Greg's hands and swayed her body around, side to side, using his support.

"Now that the special food and special treatment are gone," Sara said, "I guess we'll see what Bayside Village is really like."

"Now's your chance to look for big surprises or disappointments."

Moving through the buffet line, Sara found a wicker basket of fortune cookies at the end. 'Organic, all natural,' she read aloud to herself as she leaned over to see the description. She turned back to Greg. "Remember we used to read fortunes to each other in grad school?"

Greg chuckled, smiling. "The oracular fortune cookies," he declared with a sing-song voice.

Sara picked up a few and dashed off to the coffee bar.

"Tara, can you get us some silverware, Honey?" Greg asked. "Three spoons, three forks, and three knives." Tara dutifully applied herself to the silverware dispensary and pulled out the items under Greg's observation.

After getting seated at a table and sipping her coffee, Sara handed out the fortune cookies to Greg and Tara. "Okay, one for you, and one for you."

"You're serious?" Greg said, with an ironic smile.

"Yeah, what does the Beloved have to say to you today?"

Greg laughed to himself, shaking his head, as he took up the cookie. "Okay." He broke it and crumbs fell to his tray. He pulled out the fortune inside. Wiping the cookie dust and straightening the fortune, Greg read with a half-serious air: "New doors will open before you." Greg paused, staring at the fortune with a smirk curling across his lips. "Well, that's non-falsifiable," he said in playful defiance, putting down the fortune on his tray. "New doors open before everyone. Even death is a new door."

"Come on, Mr. Philosophy. What is the Beloved saying to you?"

"Okay," Greg sighed, looking up to the ceiling in a moment of thought, and then down to Sara. "A door to a new life in my academic career will open this week at Bayside Village. On this trip, I put a moratorium on my old identity back home. I am here in this place to experiment with new roles. There. The fortune becomes a projective device, and I have just projected my wish."

"Come on, this was your idea," Sara said.

"Okay, I'll behave. How about you?" Greg asked.

"Let's do Tara next," Sara said.

"Alright," Greg said, "do you want to open your fortune cookie, Sweetie?"

Tara broke open her fortune cookie the same way Greg had done. She pulled out her fortune, looked it, then gave it to Greg. "Can you read it, Daddy?"

Greg took Tara's fortune and held it up, wiping off the crumbs with his thumb and forefinger. "Let's see what Tara's fortune says. You will be surrounded by friends." Greg looked to Tara with a smile and raised eyebrows. You will be surrounded by friends," he said again. "Ooh, that's a good one. Do you think you'll have lots of friends today at Village Day Care?"

"Mhmm," Tara said with a smile matching Greg's, and moving her head in big sweeps up and down."

"That's a good one, Tara," Sara said. "You're lucky."

"How about wifey?" Greg said. "What does the Beloved have in store for you today?"

Sara broke open her fortune cookie. She pulled at the fortune inside, but it was stuck in the cookie. "What's with this thing?" she said. Sara cracked the other end, and the fortune came loose. She held up the fortune and read. "Through creative work you will discover your hidden essence." She looked to Greg with raised eye brows. "Wow!"

"No way," Greg said.

"Seriously."

"Okay," Greg said. "Now I'm a believer in fortune cookies! That one is falsifiable because not everyone is nearly as creative as you are."

Sara smiled at him.

"I predict…" Greg said, squinting his eyes at Sara and waxing a mysterious voice, "that you will go deep in your creative work this week and discover hidden wells of living water."

"You corn ball."

"What?"

"Can't you take this with even a modicum of reverence?"

"Reverence? A freakin' fortune cookie?"

"This was your invention!" Sara said. "Or did you forget your more inspired days when we first met?"

"My more inspired days when we first met? What does that mean? I'm not inspired now?" Sara lifted her shoulders in an 'I don't know' sort of way, which left a kernel of doubt for Greg. "Anyway, it fits you and I affirm it. The Beloved has revealed how he is orchestrating your life this week to bring about a return to your rich creative life after years of mundane work and hardship."

"Come on, you're playing with me."

"Maybe. And in play, deep truths may come tumbling out."

"You really think so?"

"Yeah, I see you yearning. And the universe mirrors this back. And I witness it and mirror it back to you. See, all of life around you is conspiring to bring you deeper into contact with your wish."

Sara smiled at Greg affectionately. "You're such a mystery. Sometimes you're so serious and exacting, and then you break into this mirthful silliness that also seems serious and true."

Greg smiled sheepishly, caught in the act.

"That reminds me," Sara said. "I had a really powerful experience last night before meditation. Remember that aesthetics book I used to read? The esoteric one by Blakely?"

"I remember Blakely."

Sara related her big insight into why she felt resistant to the Bayside Village, and how the book became a focal point for seeing it. She told how a new feeling had been growing in her, how it had to do with reclaiming her art.

Greg listened, feeling Sara's passion, remembering their early years together, those stormy, lofty years—her as artist, him as philosopher. He felt inspired, now, too. He loved this part of her, and while appreciating the transformative and destructive power of the path in her life, he was glad to see this part returning, but differently now.

"Well this is definitely related to your dream last night, don't you think?"

"I do, yeah," Sara said at once.

"A new space is opening up in your life."

"I felt that on waking this morning."

"I see that for you." Greg paused. A smile curled on his lips. "And..." He squinted his eyes again, sported his mysterious voice, "it's also related to your fortune cookie, don't you think? And my intuitive reading of your situation. I did see this, didn't I?"

Sara smirked, rolled her eyes, shook her head. "My mysterious husband, when will I ever understand you?"

47

Roger met with GameIt founder Jeff Baker and with Jackie Schrader, head of the Bridge Institute's Research Access Office, in Jackie's Research Park corner office. Her windows looked out to the Bridge Institute quadrangle in one direction, and to the Raymond Lully Museum in the other—a favorite view of Roger's.

Roger leaned back in his chair. "So I focused the call on clarifying questions. I just asked about the board meeting and his game companies. I also self-disclosed about my concerns—how his approach with game companies raised some fundamental questions for me."

"How did he take it?" Jackie asked.

"Defensively, at first. And he didn't come out and tell me about his interests. He said this opportunity with game companies was in very preliminary discussions when the offer to join the board came. So it was too early to disclose anything."

"Okay," Jackie said. "I mean, that's plausible."

"You can't fault him on that, technically speaking," Roger said.

"So he didn't say anything about his game companies?" Jeff asked.

"No. I asked if he could disclose them now—now that he's told me about it—and he still wouldn't. Then I asked about the fields of the game companies. Nothing."

"That bothers me," Jeff said. "He's being secretive. It's not building my trust in him."

"So we keep confidentiality too, right?" Roger said. "It sort of makes sense when I look at it from his point of view."

"Did something change for you?" Jeff asked. "You seem more positive."

"He was willing to back off the frank discussion at the board meeting."

"Really?" Jeff said.

"Yeah. He backed off completely. I said that if it's premature to disclose his game companies to us now, then its premature for the board meeting."

"And he backed off?" Jeff said.

"Yeah." Roger said. "And I urged him to talk to you about it first, before bringing it to the board. And he said he'd reach out to you and build that trust."

"Oh." Jeff thought about this. "Well it would have made a world of difference if he had started that way," Jeff said.

"Agreed," Roger said.

"So what does that mean?" Jeff asked. "He's going to call me?"

"I don't know. Call you, talk to you at the board meeting."

"Alright," Jeff said. "Let's see what he does. Maybe I can get a little more from him."

"And it could rebuild your confidence," Jackie said.

Jeff nodded, thinking.

"And this also changed things for me," Roger said. "He said he has another company in mind—a digital archive management company. He admitted that maybe he shouldn't have put game companies out front, and he suggested that we focus on digital archive management."

"Really?" Jackie said. "Huh. So it sounds like something shifted."

"Yeah," Roger said. "But if the game companies are too early to talk about, this digital archive management company is even earlier. So he said even less about this. But he did point out that this is central to AlignIt, which is exactly right, and that this field of use is available for commercial licensing, which it is."

"Okay," Jackie said. "So it sounds like he's tracking with our needs."

"I think so," Roger said. "He seemed to recognize at the end that he made a goof in leading out with game companies when GameIt holds those rights. But he's willing to put that behind us and move on."

"Hmm," Jeff said. He sat back, pondering. "Was I overreacting? Maybe I've just been sensitive about a perceived competitive threat."

"I think we did the right thing, though," Jackie said. "Roger came to you right away. And I think you were right to feel what you did. We responded diligently to signals, to a perceived competitive threat. We checked out some concerns with Chris. And we've heard a little more about his game interests—that they arose concurrently with his board application, and together with confidentiality obligations, they didn't rise to the level of disclosure. We know about them now."

"And he's tabled the game company discussion for Friday," Roger said.

"Well, let's see if he calls me," Jeff said.

"And he was responsive to my questions and challenges," Roger said. "I'm pleased that he stayed with it. He admitted he created a scare unnecessarily. He's willing to mend things and call you," Roger said to Jeff. "He gave some important things, too, like telling me about digital archive management. Oh, and I also reiterated the Commons values. He's on board with that—that the companies he brings have to be motivated that way."

"Do you feel he really grasps the Commons ideals?" Jackie asked.

"I'm not sure," Roger said. "But he speaks as though he does. At least he knows the companies he brings have to meet that criteria."

Jeff took a deep breath and leaned back, frowning.

Jackie looked at him. "You're concerned about something."

"I am." Jeff nodded. "I can't put my finger on it. Something feels off." He looked to the ceiling, thought a moment. Then he looked at Roger. "But he wants to cut out the discovery engine, the ontology work with Greg. He wants to just focus on marketing and licensing. And that's not the vision of AlignIt."

"Actually," Roger said, "he's agreed to look further into that area. He's not entirely convinced, but he's willing to explore it further. He knows someone in informatics and he's going to introduce AlignIt and see what this guy thinks, if he has company recommendations."

"Well, that's something," Jackie said.

"That discovery engine is your baby," Jeff said sternly. "I'd watch that closely."

"Yeah," Roger said. "No one who comes to Bayside Village is perfect. This isn't a utopia. It's not a community of exactly matching interests and values. And sometimes people need to be cultivated, to come along for awhile before they see things a new way. I guess what I like in Chris' approach is that he's willing to keep open this line of inquiry. Maybe he said too much on Monday, before investigating fully."

"Well, Friday's coming," Jackie said. "He'll meet Greg and see his ontology presentation. So you'll get a far better sense of where he is on that score by Friday. At least we can go forward until Friday. Why don't we check in after that and share impressions?"

"Right, and he'll probably reach out to you by Friday," Roger said to Jeff.

48

After taking Tara to Day Care, Sara kissed Greg on the path and returned to the Lodge to collect her art materials. Greg walked to Avicenna Hall. He watched students walking across the green grass in the sunny morning. These could be my students, he thought, and he searched their faces, considered their manner. Inside Avicenna Hall, he found the faculty office of Catherine Stone, professor of the Philosophy of Imagination and potential future Bridge Institute faculty colleague.

The door stood open. In a glance, Greg saw wall-to-wall book shelves and a little space left for a desk, guest chair, and a window to the trees and lawn. A beautiful woman in her late sixties with long, white-blond hair and artful dress worked over a manuscript at the desk with pen in hand.

"Catherine?" Greg called.

Catherine turned her head and torso, and looked at Greg powerfully and warmly. "Hi, come in." Her eyes were radiant, her mouth and cheeks drawn into a smile of instant acceptance and joy. She stood up from her desk and went swiftly to the door to greet him. She has power, will, movement, he observed. She held out both hands, receiving Greg's hand with both of hers in a firm shake. She looked deeply into his eyes with her full presence.

"Greg, good to see you," she said. Instantly Greg felt not only seen and recognized, but explored, as though she was looking into him to discover his soul qualities. "Welcome to the Bridge Institute." Her genuine eyes hadn't moved away from his. While trusting her, Greg felt unexpectedly shy from being seen with such powerful presence.

"Thanks. It's great to be here," he said, superficially by comparison, he thought. Yet he felt full acceptance by her and he relaxed into this embrace.

"Please." Catherine motioned to the guest chair near her desk.

Greg sat down in it. Catherine pulled her chair away from the desk and close to Greg's and exchanged pleasantries. Then the two scholars discussed their academic backgrounds, the Bridge Institute, the available faculty position and several faculty interview questions Catherine had waiting for Greg. She was an extraordinary human being, Greg thought, and she'd make a fine colleague. Thoughtful, incisive, penetrating, original, yet methodical—unexpectedly, perhaps, for a scholar of imagination.

Then Greg began, "So I'm interested in your work. I read a few of your papers before visiting. I esteem the role of imagination. But I haven't yet encompassed the whole of your work."

"I think of myself as a professor of imagination," Catherine said with an assuming smile. Then the musculature of her face shifted to a serious demeanor, her brow furled, and purple blood veins on her beautiful, aging forehead came to the fore. "I teach philosophy courses focused on the theory, mechanism and products of the imagination, and the practice of creative imagination as a means of knowledge, work, and service." Catherine unfolded the theoretical basis, the principle figures and the referential corpus of her field.

"This is all very interesting," Greg said. "Judging from my own background in creating computer-based ontologies, I well appreciate the role of imagination, and its necessary relation to observation. Ontologies model things and their relations in the world. So there is a continual need not only to observe the world as it is, but also to imagine relations not yet documented in existing ontologies. In my imagination, for instance, I anticipate entities and relations that should exist in a given system. This can sometimes lead me to look in certain areas, and then I can discover something new, or infer something that should be there but isn't documented. Even in learning ontologies developed by others, it's necessary to retrace those documented ontologies in one's imagination and come back to the concrete world to see how, or if, the documented ontology describes the observable situation."

"I see," Catherine said. "Indeed, an important employment of imagination, especially if undertaken consciously as part of one's method."

"Ah, method. Yes," Greg said. "I have a feeling for method in imagination, but I haven't been formally trained in it. There isn't really a pathway for this kind of training in academia." Catherine smiled and shook her head in knowing recognition. Greg continued. "I also skimmed your papers on the philosophy of the imagination in historical periods—the Renaissance, the Romantic period, what else? Something about Taoist practices and Tantric Indian and Buddhist visualization."

"Right."

"That sounds fun."

"Fun," Catherine laughed to herself, eyes widening, smile returning. "But it's a lot of work." The serious face returned. "You know that philosophies of imagination aren't well developed in modern Western philosophy. And what we do have fails to encompass imagination in Eastern philosophies. And seldom do our modern Western philosophies relate back to practice. These are some of the challenges—bringing back something abandoned for several hundred years, integrating global traditions of imaginal work, and re-linking theory and praxis."

"I see. This is your work."

Catherine nodded, smiled with brightened eyes and raised eyebrows. "We cultivate the imaginative faculty in class, trying out the philosophical frameworks of imagination studied in the course. Creative imagination requires a cultivated will to direct the imagination. And it requires knowledge of a relevant domain in which imagination is to be applied and its products developed, in order to know where and how to direct the imagination. Most students—even those interested in imagination—come to my classes with a lazy, untrained will, with little regard for the relation of imagination and knowledge. Then, of course, students today are well-trained for passive engrossment in fantasy, being taken by someone else's will—like an entertainment producer, or a game producer."

"Yes," Greg said. "It seem to me that what the academy teaches on imagination comes largely from romanticism, emphasizing subjectivity and personal expression, unrelated to the objective world."

Catherine nodded, considering Greg's view, his way of stating it. "Our Western educational systems have produced generations of students accustomed to passive entertainment by movies and computer games. We've stopped cultivating purposeful inner direction. It's a different matter if the student sits alone or in class with few outer props and needs to recall pedagogical aids from memory, and use the will in the imaginal exercise, and formulate corresponding aims in study. Some students expect passive entertainment in my classes and they get discouraged when they discover the individual discipline involved in this work—and how untrained they are for it."

"Interesting," Greg said, shifting his chair unexpectedly. "Yes, I have some experience with this—in a slightly different way. I see students seeking to be passively led along, but unprepared for work. I think this is why I find a special interest in your method. I take an imaginal approach in contemplating ontologies, and I think it will work especially well for AlignIt."

Catherine nodded, acknowledging Greg's words, pausing. She began slowly, with intention. "We use a variety of training exercises at preliminary stages—exercises that train the imagination and direct it toward specific ends. I've created a student training book, in fact." Catherine reached to her book shelf for her reference copy. She handed Greg the spiral-bound workbook. "It's unpublished."

Greg flipped through the pages, looking with interest at training exercises, images, diagrams.

"First," Catherine said, "we exercise the imagination. An atrophied faculty can't do the mature work of creative imagination. So we exercise it. That's the first chapter. We spend a good part of the year working here. We come back to it in each class and on mandatory class retreats."

Greg flipped through pages, thrilled. "Oh, I could use something like this!" he said. "Ancient philosophy is one thing. But I've never seen work like this." He thumbed past entire sections of unexpected exemplars of imagination. Many of them were not academics; most of them were practical, across many fields of endeavor. And exercises—practical exercises. Greg's heart and mind flooded with excitement. Here was a working knowledge of how to do it! Then entire sections on Western esoteric traditions of imagination, and Eastern traditions, too. Greg flipped ahead, looking at reproductions of Indian yantras, flipping ahead further to Tibetan mandalas, and again to Taoist yoga, medical and martial charts, and on to Western Renaissance alchemical plates, theaters of imagination from Giordano Bruno, exercises from the arts of memory. "Oh, this is fascinating!" Greg exclaimed, with an air of rapture. "I love these! I've always been moved by images like these." Then he looked up. "I haven't had the time with my intense focus on ontology, but I've always longed for the opportunity. I also haven't had the training in imaginal work."

"Training like this is hard to come by," Catherine said, "especially in mature expressions. We're building a new foundation for this kind of training. At the same time, it sounds like you've hit on something that works with your students—and I'd like to learn more from you about your approach."

"Mmm," Greg intoned, contemplating these novel ideas, feeling now like a full cup beginning to overflow. "Wow, this is a lot to think about!" He paused, taking it all in. "Catherine, your work is one of the most stimulating new areas for me this week. I hadn't put together imaginal work like this before. I've gone as far as a 'history of ideas' approach to imagination. But you've mastered bringing ideas into form. I need a more solid theory and practice like you've described. If I come to the Bridge Institute, I'd like to explore these opportunities."

"It would be a pleasure to work with you, Greg. We should stay in contact and explore these matters further."

"Yes, I agree," Greg said. "This is fruitful work, and it has a definite relevance to my work, too."

"It was a pleasure meeting you, Greg," Catherine said. She had those same penetrating eyes Greg noticed so distinctly on arriving at her door. Catherine arose from her seat and walked toward the door, and Greg arose and followed. "Best wishes in your further interviews," she said, turning.

"Thanks," Greg said. He stood in the doorway and extended his hand to her. "And thanks again for this time together."

Catherine again took Greg's hand in both of hers and held his soul in a deep gaze. "Let's stay in touch," she said, keeping the gaze for a longer than customary moment, and then released Greg.

49

Greg walked to Roger's other office, his AlignIt office at the Bayside Village Research Park. He checked his mobile along the way. No call from Ms. Blocke. Using his mobile tracker, he searched for Sara. A map displayed, and he recognized the building. She was painting again in the art studio. A slight smile appeared on the musculature of his face. He walked inside the Research Park building and down the hall, finding Roger's office on the left, door open.

Roger sat at his desk before his screen projection, playing with AlignIt views, moving, manipulating. He saw Greg and waived him in.

Greg entered, sat in a black and silver high tech chair with its spine and gears showing, made of steel, rubber and comfortable foam materials. He chatted with Roger and swiveled around looking over his AlignIt office for the first time. Beyond the retrofitted industrial setting of the Research Park building, a table and filing cabinet were the chief differences from his Avicenna Hall office. Otherwise, both had amazing books and unusual art prints displaying traditional sacred science ontologies. Roger's spaces were neat and organized, Greg noticed. Not obsessively so, but one felt a tight economy of space amidst the rare and arcane works filling the room.

When Neil arrived minutes later and sat down, Roger jumped the AlignIt projection from screen view to surround view. Sitting amidst large AlignIt projections, Roger moved tables around by hand, expanding some, minimizing others, dragging columns through the air by his finger. He pointed to various tables now and discussed the algorithms relating them. "The discovery engine is based on these, but it goes farther."

Neil sat back in his chair, ready for the today's onslaught, rubbing his chin with his thumb and forefinger. Neil found Roger often pushing beyond the consulting proposal outline he had provided, which Neil had out, well marked and ready again for discussion. These exploratory pathways Roger took perplexed Neil further.

"We make inferences from known domains to new ones under investigation," Roger said. "We take a set of protein-protein interactions, like this one." Roger pointed, did a quick finger movement, opened it, ran it, displayed results in the air. "Or a set of marine microbes." He closed the protein-protein interaction view and opened the microbes, ran it, displayed results. "And we make inferences based on known patterns already mapped in AlignIt or another application."

"Okay," Neil said, just as skeptical as yesterday. "I know discovery engines. How yours works, though, still baffles me."

"Let's say this is your search. Those known patterns we've identified in AlignIt reside in another knowledge domain than the domain of your investigation, but they're on the same horizontal level," Roger said. "So we have an algorithm to make domain-to-domain inferences, and correct for domain differences, to a degree. Or let's say the known patterns reside at a higher or lower level of a vertical chain of manifestation than the level of your investigation. This algorithm," Roger said, activating it with a quick point of his finger, "makes vertical level-to-level inferences, adjusting for the information differential entailed in changing level."

Neil opened his hands with a gasp on his breath. "Vertical chains of manifestation? Again, we come back to AlignIt being a medieval system."

"Okay," Roger said, "that's my philosophical language."

"Scale," Greg said to Neil. "Just use scale."

"Right," Roger said. "Same idea."

"So how does that work?" Neil asked. He sat forward, pointing his index finger at the mechanism Roger displayed. "This metaphysical vertical chain of yours. I'm not sure that calling it scale does more than mask the fact that it's a medieval system. That's the sticky part for me. But putting that aside, how does it work?"

"Okay," Roger said, "so if we go back to Ayurveda as an example…We can display alignments of known patterns already mapped in sacred sciences, like Ayurveda, along threads running vertically from astrological conditions to conditions in bodily organs, and we can view ideal yoga postures for these conditions, or ideal foods, or mantras, or yantras…. So AlignIt harnesses these already described, and traditionally validated, vertical threads of connection and influence across levels and shows ways of working with their impacts. The AlignIt Discovery Engine does more than display, though; among other things, it's a tool for making analogical inferences from these domains already mapped in various sacred sciences to new domains not traditionally mapped by sacred science but which could be mapped, like protein-protein interactions or marine microbes. We follow along in the same pattern as the traditionally mapped correspondences, but in this case adjusting in various ways for changes in domain and changes in level—or in scale as Greg says."

Neil shook his head, sighed. "I still see the starting point as archaic systems. This is where I get stuck. You're starting from archaic constructs like—what is this in the table by Greg's head—the four lions of the four corners of the earth or some nonsense like that, and you're trying to organize modern scientific knowledge on that archaic basis. Or, you're trying to link archaic constructs to modern theoretical models. And that approach," Neil said pointedly, "is dubious to me. It means you miss categories of modern knowledge that don't fit your archaic knowledge. I just don't see this as a viable scientific project." Neil broke off in a laugh with a sneer. "We've evolved, damn it! I keep coming back to this when I look into AlignIt—you're recapitulating and reinstantiating the junk pile of discarded ideas from scholarly discourse. It's digging up old bones from a grave yard and reifying it as science simply because you can stick it in a database, digitize a few ancient ontologies, and create a few rudimentary algorithms. Big deal!"

"Neil, sure, some of these may be old bones," Roger said, "and that's where these older traditional sciences need updating, where they've been abandoned a few hundred years ago or more—or repeated today by amateurs in their frozen state. But AlignIt isn't about reifying old bones or inflating early science into modern science. There's a big historical gap between the times when sacred sciences were the leading edge of civilization and our time today. So we need to update. And AlignIt is one research tool for investigations that could lead to such updates. Older sacred sciences are a starting point."

"A starting point, okay…" Neil said.

"And on this point," Roger continued, "I can't agree that everything we're digging up with AlignIt was buried on account of good scholarly discourse. Your argument presumes a modern academy not once controlled by the very religious orthodoxies responsible for burying most of these sciences. It's not like we had open discourse in the early modern West, let alone that we have it today. You must admit some social criticism of the modern academic enterprise itself. Surely you wouldn't maintain that even modern science always advances the best ideas even though it most often intends to. You will admit, I hope, that many of our colleagues, if not we ourselves, unwittingly, are beholden to special interests—lobbies, federal funding priorities, ideologically driven agendas."

"Okay, sure." Neil nodded and waved his hand, conceding the obvious, looking impatient.

"Even if modern Western universities don't study most of these traditional systems documented in AlignIt, except in the history of religions, or archeology, several of these systems are still in use in traditional societies, and even in the West through migrations or cultural adaptation. So they're not discarded."

"Well sure," Neil retorted curtly, "people still practice voodoo and witchcraft. So what? Does that make it useful for modern science, just because you can apply an ontology to it? The mere survival of archaic knowledge and primitive practices isn't a warrant for picking it up as science and trying to advance it. Take an ethnological approach if you like. Study primitive societies. But...you're making unwarranted leaps from a descriptive to a normative approach here."

"But that's not our selection criteria—the mere survival of archaic knowledge available for digitizing," Roger said. "AlignIt is a research tool, and with it, researchers can validate as well as discredit traditional claims. But these sacred sciences are at least deserving of our investigation with new tools, new methods, new protocols, new data and advances in theory, to see what claims stand, and if new claims can be conjectured and eventually validated."

"So, Neil," Greg jumped in. "I take your point about archaic constructs. And I agree. This is one of the difficulties of using sacred sciences as we find them today, in their present state of development, including arrested development. This is precisely why we're working toward a robust upper ontology that can open the investigation to non-conforming knowledge—not just historical variances from the dominant historical systems, but indeed even new knowledge. We're not trying to force the discovery of Pluto's existence, for example, into an archaic seven-planet model of astrology. We're actually working toward the evolution of new evidence-based models, but from larger philosophical frameworks, including those found in sacred sciences. That's the key."

"It would help me to see those evidence-based models," Neil said.

"But it's also the larger philosophical frameworks," Greg said. "That's what I mean when I say that's the key. Philosophical frameworks is one of the chief differentiators of sacred sciences from modern sciences."

"So show me that too," Neil said. "What does that mean?"

"It's the assumptive worlds," Greg said, "not necessarily the findings, of traditional cosmologies and metaphysics. These have been frozen in time, as Roger suggested. For my part, at least," Greg said, "what I'll be proposing to the board on Friday is that we make a shift from a simple version of the Perennial Philosophy, which neatly codifies traditional cosmology and metaphysics, and which has served AlignIt well to establish proof of principle for the technology, to a broader, agnostic approach that lays systems side by side with all of their asymmetries, all of their mis-matching evidence and models, and holds them in dialogical relationship. I'm also proposing the decentering of the Perennial Philosophy, or any other system, in AlignIt, without offering a replacement system as the superordinate, dominant, doctrinally orthodox system. I'm proposing to keep and yet evolve the underlying structure of classes, entities, relationships, operations, etc. found in sacred sciences historically, and the algorithms Roger's team has built for these, but to give the user ultimate discretion about where to begin."

"Or end," Roger said.

"Right." Greg continued. "Or end."

"Okay," Neil said. "So you're not instantiating archaic constructs just because they're there to feed into AlignIt."

"Right," Greg said. "In this approach, there's nothing requiring a user to begin with an archaic system, or any particular system, or to take it in some simple original model—presuming there even is one per tradition as is often postulated in Perennial Philosophy, which I can't abide. I'm proposing that AlignIt should reflect the territory, the plurality of existing ontologies, and be inherently agnostic about them. The user can begin with any system. So if you want to conduct historical research, fine. If you want to conduct a medical, biological, botanical, or marine investigation, fine— you can do it in AlignIt if AlignIt has the ontologies and data sets you need, or if you can find some and add them."

"Or," Roger added, "if you have proprietary data sets and want to run them through, or find them in the cloud and port them."

"Well, okay," Neil said, "a postmodern decentering of archaic knowledge as a starting point. That begins to feel like a measure of intellectual integrity to me. But still…Aren't your searches still running along algorithms based on archaic knowledge?"

"Well, not exactly," Greg said. Roger sat back, listening to Greg take the lead, impressed at his precocious but capable leadership. "We're proposing developing an upper ontology which would incorporate many traditional ontologies, but modern ones as well, and eventually a growing library of ontologies modified in the course of contemporary investigations. But again, it depends on where you start, and how you define your scope of work. And, importantly, AlignIt can outgrow its initial algorithms. AlignIt itself shouldn't get frozen in time, either. The tool itself, and its operational machinery, if you will, is subject to evolution and it should have an extensive revision history."

"Suppose I want to start with properties of dark matter from a recent study," Neil said. "You're suggesting I can do that."

"AlignIt can do that," Greg said. "You'd need to add those properties or related data and constructs. And perhaps existing algorithms need to be rewritten, or new ones written. But yes. This is the proposal I'm making to the Board—this decentering."

Roger interjected. "The AlignIt Scientific Advisory Board is backing this proposal. In our Friday meeting, the Trustees will hear your presentations."

"So it's a matter of time to implement," Neil said. Roger nodded. "And do you have an ontology mapping strategy for relating ancient Babylonian astrology to data from supercolliders? Do you have a roll out plan to attract the brightest minds in science to give their careers to building ontology matching protocols and importing and analyzing data sets?"

"One thing at a time," Roger said, shifting in his chair. "We're planning to import and match a number of contemporary ontologies from various disciplines, starting with medical, biological, botanical, and marine. And we plan to make AlignIt accessible for this kind of research. We're also looking at making internal Bayside Village grant funds available for this work—this build out."

"I'll reserve judgment until I see what transpires," Neil said. "But I do wonder how you're going to attract serious scholars and students when you've got this vertical thing going on there with your 'higher realms'— whatever it is, your Neoplatonism or Greek mythology. You've got Greg, here, and he's a bright kid. But how many Greg's can you find? And I gotta tell ya, I couldn't refer my students to this, and I wouldn't advise putting their names on a paper on AlignIt. I mean, what are you going tell people you're discovering there, with that approach? New angels that might exist but weren't known before?"

"Theoretically, that's possible," Roger said, "and relationships between angels and physical correspondences not mapped before."

"Jesus!" Neil shook his head and rolled his eyes.

"I'll ask you to simply respect differences in our metaphysics," Roger said.

Neil sat back, blew out noisily through his lips. "You just go on with this stuff! Just when I think you're serious!" He sat forward. "You really believe in angels?"

"I didn't say so. I'm referring to different a priori assumptions, different metaphysics."

"You think you're going to attract respectable scientific researchers to use a tool that can help them identify new freakin' angels that weren't known before?"

"Remember," Roger said, "it's a research tool. People use research tools to find what they're looking for. We're not prescribing an inquiry or results. The tool has broad applications. It's a platform technology. We're not going to market a biological discovery engine as a means to discover new angels."

"But it's still in there, isn't it?" Neil said, raising his voice. "Sure, someone could publish drug discovery results from using AlignIt, if they get anything worthwhile. And you know what? The first flakey new age conference, book, or popular talk show that mentions AlignIt is going to kill AlignIt for science and discredit any scientist who was dumb enough to use it!'"

"I don't think so." Greg said. "A search engine isn't discredited for scientists because of flakey people, or others, who use it to search for angels. A syringe manufacturer isn't discredited in hospital sales because people use syringes for illicit drug use. I'm not going to avoid a computer, or an operating system, or a software app or a web service simply because someone else uses it in a way that doesn't interest me. Many tools are broad and their uses indeterminate."

Neil sat back, grunting, hating to concede the point.

Roger sat back slightly. "There's also the fact that AlignIt is a trademark for a tech platform, not for applications, like, say a bioinformatics tool built on AlignIt. People will use an AlignIt-based tool if it helps obtain the results they need. I don't think people are going to avoid one application built on AlignIt because other people will use applications built on it that they don't want to use."

"Okay," Neil said, "how about the fact that AlignIt is really a theoretical discovery engine. Or, for God's sake, a metaphysical discovery engine! It doesn't have hard data, or ontologies built on hard data. You're trying to make inferences about marine microbes from archaic systems of astrology that have been debunked for centuries."

"But we've just gone over this," Greg said. "You're restating a view of AlignIt that we've already put behind us as incorrect."

"Neil," Roger said in a patient tone, "remember that we're not taking older sacred sciences wholesale, as fixed doctrines. We're creating a tool precisely to elaborate investigational paths and findings offered by these traditional sciences—for instance to move from an archaic seven planet system to an extensible set of planetary bodies capable of holding new scientific discoveries."

"But why start there, with archaic systems?" Neil said. "This is what I don't understand. Why go back to this dream of sacred sciences hundreds of years old, or thousands for all I know, and try to reconcile it with modern science? There's just no connection there. My God, we have massive, global cloud computing infrastructures generating more data in one day than most civilizations ever produced in the entire span of their historical supremacy. How do you come to terms with the sheer volume of data today? How do you come to terms with the radical disparity between these conventional, simplistic, archaic maps lying at the bedrock of your data structure and the theoretically vigorous, complex, disruptive, and evolutionary nature of modern science, the IT industry, the knowledge economy? They're so disparate, I don't see them meeting."

"AlignIt starts there," Greg said, "because sacred sciences have some principles, some knowledge, some procedures, that merit further investigation but got eclipsed or were actively suppressed. The continuity of research between traditional societies and our modern times has been disrupted, whether by political pressures, religious oppression, loss of resources, or what have you."

"We've taken the gamble," Roger said, "that AlignIt will help bridge those worlds. But not by making simplistic connections that dumb-down either traditional or modern sciences. Historically, sacred sciences were prominent in many places and did attract the best minds, including in the West, and they yielded discoveries, led to technologies. But then those sciences were abandoned, or actively suppressed, or only their empirical methods or results pursued with the rise of the modern scientific method. Sure, there was a lot of junk, bad science, fools gold. Modern science, too, can lead to false positives. But approaches to science using this more expansive set of metaphysical principles could again attract the best minds, as they did in times past. These sciences haven't been able to develop and keep pace with modern science. They've been suppressed or overwhelmed by historical vicissitudes. They haven't been funded. They haven't attracted good minds in the modern West. So they've languished and need some catching up. We start with them and the project of updating them, and not naively, because we maintain they have something to offer us today that we've lost."

"Like what?" Neil asked.

Greg became frustrated at circling around the same territory without Neil seeming to register the essential points.

"Like a rich variety of traditional cosmologies and metaphysics," Roger said, "an understanding of threads of correspondences vertically and horizontally that show relationships between things—knowledge that gets severed in the views taken in modern science and philosophy. On this basis of correspondences and relationships, sacred sciences offer us a variety of operations in which we have practical knowledge about how to work with certain problems and possibilities."

"Okay," Neil said. "I don't know much about that, but I'll grant you that provisionally and reserve my judgment. So guys," Neil glanced at his watch. "I realize we haven't gotten very far through the proposal, but I gotta cut out of here." He stood up. "I'm meeting some colleagues for lunch in Berkeley's Gourmet Ghetto."

"Already?" Roger said, sitting back from his intense posture. He looked at the time display in the projected AlignIt surround view. "Again, time flies in our meetings! Well thanks Neil, this was stimulating. Have a good lunch."

"See you tomorrow, Neil." Greg said.

Neil nodded to Greg, turned to Roger. "Thanks for the run-through. Ciao." He turned and walked out the door, his shoes clacking down the hall of the Research Park corridor.

When Neil had gone, Roger sat back a moment, breathed in, contemplated. "His challenges are helpful."

"Hmm," Greg said. That was half of it, he thought, just half. He laughed to himself. "Maybe he's a test case for mainstream academic adoption of AlignIt."

"I suppose so." Roger smiled. He leaned forward, touched a button in the air to deproject his surround-view of AlignIt, and leaned back again.

Greg started at the ceiling some moments, reflecting. "Neil's a bright guy. I just hope its not always this difficult for people to lock on to essential ideas about AlignIt and its raison d'etre."

"It's often hard to see what's in front of you if you don't have the background," Roger said. "In my experience, many prejudices in the modernist worldview serve as a perceptual set obscuring what may be more obvious to you and me."

"I'm just surprised at his attitude," Greg said, putting his hand up by his jaw, thinking. "He seems so averse to AlignIt that I wonder if he really did his homework before agreeing to come."

"You've got to wonder…" Roger said, sitting back. "I do find his challenges helpful, though. They sharpen me."

"It's a little disharmonious to me," Greg said. "It seems people here at Bayside Village have a larger worldview and are open to the potentials of integrating modern and traditional sciences. And Neil doesn't fit that openness. Maybe I'm still too much of a visitor."

"Well, it may be disharmonious to have the likes of Neil. But we're not trying to create a closed community of sacred science ideologues. Hopefully, Neil keeps us fresh and honest."

"I guess so," Greg said. "AlignIt has a more solid backing philosophically than is often realized—even in the modern philosophy of science. More so than Neil realizes." Greg paused. Roger looked imploringly, expecting more. "Formal ontology works at this level of maps, diagrams and pictures. And Peirce talked about making experiments on diagrams which can replace physical experiments on real things—at least, as I think about it, to get to proof of concept."

"Really? Experimenting on diagrams?" Roger echoed.

"Yes. Peirce, twentieth century, not Raymond Lully, eleventh century, or Giordano Bruno, sixteenth century."

"That's exactly what we're doing—experiments on diagrams."

"I can see that," Greg said. "Well, it's important to know that it's there in the ontology literature."

"I didn't know that," Roger said.

"Not that it should replace experiments on real things. Physical experiments may be a necessary validation step in most cases. But with experiments on diagrams, you don't have to outlay so much time and money up front in exploring every lead. An efficient process like the AlignIt Discovery Engine offers us can help identify new candidates. The key, I think, lies in establishing diagrams that correctly represent reality."

"Hmm," Roger said, cogitating. He clicked on his mobile again, projected AlignIt, switched to surround view. With a few finger movements in the air, he displayed his menu of algorithms, studied them a few long moments. Then his eyes shifted focus from the AlignIt projection to the walls beyond, and he contemplated his idea of using diagrams to make experiments, as he had worked it out previously. That's the best use case for AlignIt, he thought. And Greg has the philosophical backing for this.

"So Neil's right when he called it a theoretical discovery engine," Greg said. "But he meant it as a dismissive comment. I think he's missing the grandeur, elegance, and efficiency of this kind of system. Many great minds, from Lully all the way to Bruno and Leibniz, to Peirce and Freige have been after this kind of system. It's in the literature. And in many ways, computer science itself was born of this quest. I think it could be very powerful to link your work back to the longer historical trajectory and deeper vision of this quest for a theoretical discovery engine."

"Ah, this is a background I don't have," Roger said.

Roger felt himself in a moment suspended in time, a moment promising fulfillment of some clear, palpable sense of destiny. "Greg, this is exactly why I'm hoping you'll join us, because you have this background. This is what AlignIt needs."

Did Greg feel it, too, Roger wondered. It would be of utmost importance to recruit Greg. Roger could see that. Quick memory images from the week's conversations with Chris Mueller who didn't want Greg, and conversations with Jeff and Jackie about Chris, coursed through Roger's mind. For Roger, the choice of Greg for AlignIt was obvious. It wasn't so for Chris. Jeff liked Greg. Jackie liked him. Who else would meet him and like him this week? And for Greg and Sara, the choice for Bayside Village was not an obvious one. Their choice had not yet been made. A quick imagination of Sara interviewing with Karen lit the stage of Roger's mind, and he wondered how that was going, if it was scheduled, if it happened yet, what its result would be.

Greg looked across the menus and tables displayed in the air before them. "This project stimulated me to create a short history to situate AlignIt in this quest for a theoretical discovery engine. Could be a future lecture or course at the Bridge Institute."

"Really?" Roger smiled, impressed. Greg dashed it off so quickly that Roger wondered if Greg knew what a gift he was. "Well, good. I'll wait for a fuller story."

In the Research Park courtyard, Greg checked his mobile's tracker for Sara's location. Still at the Bridge Institute Art Center. So he walked there, across the quad where students sat studying and talking, others playing Frisbee in the sun. He walked into the Art School courtyard with its native flowers, its kiosks of the new sacred arts. He found Sara in a studio, absorbed in a sketch of a sculpture. He turned, walked in. Her long, brunette hair was tied up in a bun on her head, as she used to do when she painted at home years ago.

Greg liked this view of her being in a creative process. He walked up and looked quietly at her sketch pad and then looked in front to the sculpture before her.

"It's a kinetic sculpture," she said after some moments without looking up. She erased and then shaded with her pencil-darkened fingers. "There," she said resolutely, holding her sketch book out in front to study it with Greg. "The parts keep moving, so it's a challenge."

"Wow, that's cool," Greg said. "Kinetic sculpture, huh?"

"Yeah." Sara looked at up at him, closing her sketch pad on her finger as a place-holder. "Sculptures that move. Or they have moving parts. You'll like these." She stood and walked up to a set. "Look at these amazing pieces. They're moving cosmologies! This is fabulous!"

"Wow," Greg said, following Sara and looking closely. "They're precise. They're like ancient Indian or Arabic astronomical instruments. But…they're not ancient. Mmm." He looked at the markings, the measurements. "I've never seen anything like it."

"Me neither. I want to meet the guy who made them, but he's away on travel." Sara looked closely at the one she drew, standing now at a different angle. "You don't see kinetic sculpture today. It was big in the 1950's and 60's. And back then this stuff was all random—parts moved by the wind or viewer interaction. That was the worldview then. But this work is different. It's based on cosmic laws of different kinds. It's elegant. Really precise, orderly movements."

"I don't recognize these laws, actually. But it's compelling." Greg paused, then turned. "I also like what you did, there," he said, pointing to the sketchbook in her hand.

"Thanks." She opened it up again for him to see. "I'm just getting ideas—just quick sketches." She looked at it with him. To Greg, it was more than quick sketches. "Oh," she said. She walked back to the chair, sat, erased, and resketched a detail.

Greg walked behind Sara, watched her with the pencil. His eyes wandered then from her sketchbook to her hair pulled up—with a paint brush, of all things, holding her bun in place. And his eyes traced her neck and the wisps of loose hair rebelling from the bun and dancing on her shoulders as she erased again and flicked the eraser dust with her pinkie.

Greg seldom saw her neck. Sara wore her hair unfashionably, sensuously longer than the short, business-length hair women wore. Ever the artist, the unique individual, defiant against convention. He loved her hair long, and loved her wearing it long for the reasons she did, and the way she put it up when drawing or painting. He loved the artist in her. And he loved her bare neck, exposed now like a lover lifting a veil, secretly available only for him. He longed to plant kisses there. But she was always drawing, or painting, or busy. Why always this intimate exposure when she's busy being creative, he wondered.

"I'm done," Sara said. "Ready?"

"Yeah," Greg said. She's done. Now he let his fingers stray to the back of her neck, and he caressed her ever so gently.

"Mhmm…And I wonder what you're studying." Sara turned and looked at him seductively. She stood up before him flirtatiously, rubbed against him and gave him a delicious kiss with a little bit of tongue, and pulled back. "We have a child to pick up." She picked up her bag. "So…It will just have to wait." She touched the tip of his nose with her pointer finger and turned away.

"Ooh," Greg said, feigning a playful sting of unrequited gratification.

Sara started for the door, pushing her sketchbook in her bag. She looked back at him playfully with a smile.

Greg followed, walked around the sculpture. He held open the studio door for Sara. "So, you've been here all morning?"

"In and out. I did a lot of sketches—a lot with these kinetic sculptures. I talked to some artists."

"You're getting around."

"Yeah. I also went back to Tara's school to sit in. Remember they invited us to do that?"

"Did I hear you say Tara's school?" he repeated with a tease. They turned a corner into the bright noon sun splashing onto the art quad. "Have we enrolled her now?"

"I mean Village Day Care," Sara said, correcting herself.

"Freudian slip?"

"Maybe, I don't know."

Greg teased, repeating, "'Maybe', she says."

"Anyway," Sara emphasized, "it's really amazing what they do there. It's such a loving and containing environment, like an extended family. It's a long day for Tara, but its just amazing to see how well she does with it."

"Hmm. I'd like to see what you've seen. I'm glad she's doing well there this week."

Roger stood behind Jackie Schrader at her desk in the Research Access
Office. She faced her screen projection, moving through data on Chris
Mueller. "I think we're at the end, here," she said.

"Alright." Roger sighed. "Not enough there."

"That's all we have, Roger. It's all of our files plus some public
records. If there's something amiss in Mueller's dealings, it's not showing
up here. Another kind of search may be needed."

"Thanks, Jackie. This is helpful."

Roger walked from Jackie's office down the hall of the Research Park
to Jeff's GameIt office. He entered GameIt's suite, said hi to a few interns,
and knocked on Jeff's open door.

"Hey," Jeff said. He leaned back in his chair, away from the surround
view of his game projections, and turned to Roger. "So what did Jackie
find?"

"Nothing," Roger said. He walked in and leaned against Jeff's
credenza. "Not a single game company."

"So what do you think that means? A failure to disclose?"

"Possibly," Roger said. "But Mueller did say companies in his network.
Whatever that means." He breathed through his nose, shook his head. "Its
possible he doesn't have any direct ties through investment, or advising, or
whatever. He doesn't need to disclose all companies. If he has no financial
interest..." Roger studied Jeff's projected game world in the air, its
landscape, its figures, the unfinished buildings and pathways. "Or maybe
his ties are new. Maybe they came after he submitted his disclosure forms."

"What does he mean companies in his network?" Jeff said. "What does
that mean?"

"I don't know. I'm not sure how that works."

"What if he has a finder's agreement?" Jeff said. Roger shrugged. Jeff
cogitated, working through his idea. "That would be a potential financial
gain. But we ask for current financial interests."

"I guess that could be a loop hole." Roger nodded, adjusted his stance.
"I don't know. I'll ask Jackie."

"Did they do the broader search, too?"

"Yeah. Still, nothing." Roger exhaled through his lips, exasperated.
He looked at his juice bottle and contemplated. Then he got a flash of
inspiration. "Maybe we should do a search." He paused. Jeff shrugged his
shoulders. "What kind of companies do you think Mueller would have in
his network?"

"I don't know," Jeff said. "You know him better. What's his
network?"

"Hilltop Ventures, everything on his CV. I don't know. Law firms.

Banks. Conferences. Obvious things—his investments, his consulting."

"Yeah, let's do it."

Jeff minimized his game world, opened an app called Connection Finder. He dragged his chair to a round table in the corner, took a seat.

Roger sat down at the table.

"Let's see if we can identify other interests," Jeff said aloud to himself. In Connection Finder, he opened the Professional Networks view, typed in Chris Mueller. The tool displayed a range of Chris' advisory board connections, C-level roles in start ups, web biographies, disclosed stock options, and consulting gigs. Jeff looked at parent and subsidiary relationships of those companies, and who funded, who acquired. "We should have done this sooner."

"Shew!" Roger said. "Look at that spread of companies!"

"How are we going to get through a thicket like that?"

"Let's start with patents." Roger said.

"Okay." Jeff clicked patents and brought up a few. "Hmm," he said. "Six. Not bad. Financial algorithms, business methods, video, security….Hmm."

"What about publication attributions?" Roger said.

Jeff clicked that button, hit go.

"Damn, look at that!" Jeff said. "I didn't imagine he'd written so much."

"I was impressed when I saw his CV. But look." Roger pointed to the screen projection. "Media, music, media, media, news, sports….No games."

"How about companies filing, owning, and cross-licensing," Jeff said. He ran that search. Three companies.

"How about parents, subsidiaries, and affiliates."

Jeff ran that search. Two companies. "And trademarks," he said. "We should find something on trademarks. That's important in games." He ran trademarks. "None. Really?"

Roger looked up to the ceiling, cogitating. He tapped his fingers on the table.

"Wait," Roger said, checking Jeff's pathway to this point. "A trademark won't come up in Mueller's name. Rerun those searches against each other. The companies will have the trademarks."

"Right," Jeff said. He ran companies against trademarks, got a few hits, scrolled through the results.

"I'm curious about those two parents of his patent holding companies," Roger said, pointing to the screen projection.

Jeff opened those, scrolled through, searching.

"What's that?" Roger said, pointing to a black, green, and yellow mark. "Game Cult." He slapped the table. "Bingo! There's one at least. A holding company with a game company in its portfolio."

"That wasn't obvious at all," Jeff said. "And it wasn't in his disclosures. Why didn't we think of this earlier?"

Roger leaned forward, straining his eyes. "What's Mueller's tie to it? Looks like no direct tie to the parent....He's named on a patent held by one of its subs."

"Yeah, this is an interesting picture."

Roger pulled back from his laser focus on the screen projection, just freely scanning, looking for nonobvious connections. Then something caught him. He sat up. "What's this company?" He pointed to a spoke radiating farther from the parent.

"I don't know," Jeff said.

"Click it."

Jeff clicked, opened the company profile, looked. "Recruitment firm." Jeff hovered a few moments. "Nothing." He clicked, returned to the prior screen.

But Roger's imagination still poked at that recruitment firm. "Wait. Go back."

Jeff clicked again, reopened the window.

Roger searched more carefully. "Look!" He pointed to a director. "Amelia Blocke!"

Jeff's eyes widened, his senses sharpened. "The same one?"

"It is!" A tingle ran through Roger's skin. "Our Mrs. Blocke."

"No way!" Jeff said. He hovered over images, revealing connections, data views. "Mueller and Blocke are connected?" He turned to Roger, patted him on the shoulder. "Good find, my man!"

Roger scooted up his chair, sat closer, pointed. "So Mueller used this recruitment firm for...these two companies. Or three—is this one connected, too?"

Jeff hovered over the image, revealed the connections. "Yeah." Then he hovered over the other two. "So these two are game companies." Jeff sat back, pondered. "Blocke and Mueller must be connected somehow."

"They are. Look!" Roger said, pointing again. "Through those three companies." He studied the screen, the links, unable at first to believe his own assertion.

"Whoa! This is uncanny." Jeff looked away, thinking, then back. "So is this connection continuing on here at the Bridge Institute? Are they connected here?" He thought a moment. "Weird. This is like some kind of weird infiltration." He studied the screen.

"Oh, but these are older connections," Roger said. "There's a time gap from then to now." Maybe it wasn't so, after all, he thought.

"Time delay, yes, but it's an obvious inference. There must be some connection between them, then and now."

Roger tapped his fingers, cogitating. "You remember I told you we've had trouble with her? And a few faculty have brought this to President Bateson?"

"Yeah."

Roger turned back to the screen projection, shaking his head slightly side to side, looking half way at the display, half way through it to the wall beyond, deep in thought. "What if they are connected?" He changed the pattern of finger tapping to a new rhythm. "What are we going to do with this?" he asked aloud rhetorically, resting his face in his left hand. Then he looked at Jeff. "Greg tells me she's been avoiding him—didn't answer his calls or emails for weeks. And Mueller tells me he's uncertain about Greg. And now Greg is here on campus and still no connection with Blocke, no meeting."

"Weird," Jeff said. "Something's really weird about this."

51

After lunch at the Dining Commons, returning Tara to Daycare and kissing Sara goodbye for the afternoon, Greg walked to the Bridge Institute quadrangle. He walked upstairs to the reception area before President Steve Bateson's office, stood before the receptionist. "I'm here to see President Bateson."

The receptionist looked at Bateson's calendar and then up. "Greg Cobb?"

"Yes."

"Please have a seat," he said in a rich, resonant voice. "I'll let him know you're here."

Greg sat down in a chair by a table and lamp. The reception area was warm and decorous with artifacts from sacred sciences across time, including a few portraits of the great exemplars, but Greg didn't get up to see their names. He saw images of the Bridge Institute's visual communication, delivering impressions of where the Institute would go, how it would play a role in society. Sara would like this, he thought.

The receptionist now came around his desk, conducted Greg to President Bateson's door and opened it.

The corner office was large. Bateson was seated at a large desk. He turned, stood up. "Greg, come in." He got up, walked around his desk. Greg entered and the door was closed behind him. "Let's meet here," Bateson said, extending his opened hand to a large, wooden, mission-style meeting table on one side of the room by the windows. "Thank you for spending time with us this week," he said, walking up to the table. "I'm pleased we have this opportunity to discuss our Institute with someone of your background in metaphysics and ontology."

"Thanks," Greg said, shaking hands. "I'm very happy to visit and learn about what you're creating."

"Let's see if this will be a suitable place for you and your family."

Greg pulled out the solid wooden chair and took a seat. Bateson seated himself. Greg scanned the room quickly, taking in impressions. He spotted the groundplan image of Christianopolis which he recognized from the Raymond Lully Museum, and an exercise in Bateson's Creative Writing with Utopias workshop. "I admire your print collection. Your office is like a mini museum of yesterday's workshop images."

Bateson smiled. "Yes," he mused, surveying the prints, "I think it helps convey a sense of what is possible here at Bayside Village, especially when I entertain guests like you."

"I imagine it inspires," Greg said. "It opened worlds for me yesterday. And I guess these are photographs of universities, like the ones in your papers?" Greg asked, pointing to a separate set of images on the wall.

"Yes," Bateson replied. "Some in ruins. But in a way, they're all present and living for me. And I hope to make them so for others."

"Is that the Suleymaniye in Istanbul?" Greg asked.

"Good image recognition," Bateson replied, impressed. "Yes, I put it close to the table here because I'm writing a paper on it right now—on factors that can hamper a great institution and dim the light of learning."

"Hmm," Greg said. "I'll be interested to read it. My wife Sara has studied it a little," Greg said. "That's how I know. Just its artistic forms. It's a beautiful building!"

"Indeed, it is."

"Oh, and that's elegant calligraphy," Greg said, looking at the wall beside Bateson's desk.

"Yes, those are quotes of Suhrawardi. I found them in Paris."

"Suhrawardi?"

"A Persian illuminationist philosopher after Avicenna."

"Oh, right," Greg recalled vaguely.

"Suhrawardi united streams of ancient Greek philosophy with Persian Zoroastrianism and Islamic philosophy. He's one of my favorites, actually. I prefer him to Avicenna, whom he critiqued extensively. I've even lobbied to change the name of Avicenna Hall," Bateson said, laughing. "Who knows if that will happen. But I've been working with Roger on inscribing Suhrawardi's system of existents and their governing qualities in AlignIt."

"Really?" Greg said. "I'll have to look it up. It sounds Neoplatonic."

"Yes, somewhat," Bateson said. "Mixed with Aristotle's work. Translators then confused the Aristotelian and Neoplatonic streams of philosophy, thinking it was all Aristotle."

"I'll have to look into Suhrawardi. I'm not familiar with his work." Then Greg noticed a small statue standing on Bateson's credenza. "And who is the saint by your desk?" Greg asked.

"Isaac of Nineveh," Bateson said, turning in his chair to face his desk. "He's one of the great mystics of the Syrian church, in its so-called Nestorian branch. A scholar here, Joshua Mead, gave it to me."

"Oh, I'm meeting with him next," Greg said.

"Good, good. Joshua's a very fine scholar-practitioner—the kind we like. Mystically speaking, Meade considers Isaac of Nineveh a point of connection between Eastern Christianity and early Sufism."

"Wow!" Greg said. "Your office is full of such fascinating, eye-catching objects! I could spend hours in here just exploring."

Bateson smiled warmly. "I do that myself."

"I think of these as aids to opening worlds, invoking relationships," Greg said.

"Yes, Roger told me of this interest of yours," Bateson said. "Quite a lot about your background, in fact, and the work you may do on AlignIt. And he's very pleased that you're able to attend the AlignIt Board meeting on Friday."

"Me too," Greg said. "It took a lot of coordinating to pull it off, with my family and teaching schedule."

The men sat for some time discussing academic matters and the position available for Greg at the Bridge Institute.

"So," Bateson said, "You have a solid grasp of our mission and aims. Do you have specific questions about the Bridge Institute?"

"I was deeply impressed by your utopian workshop yesterday," Greg said.

"Thank you. It's one of my most enjoyable studies."

"Am I correct in guessing a connection between your use of utopian art and literature and your keeping the vision of Bayside Village? This seems useful to inspire others to envision. I realize you're not trying to create utopia here, but I imagine it helps to use this literature?"

"How very perceptive," Bateson said. "There are many connections for me between the two—my using utopian literature and my keeping the vision of Bayside Village, as you say. And neither of them has to do with creating a utopia, which you've heard me say. This is not an idealistic, utopian place. Nor a perfect place, certainly. It's a human community, and we have our imperfections and shadowy sides of the organization here like anywhere else. Let's just get that straight from the beginning."

"Of course. Like what?" Greg asked. "If you don't mind my asking."

"Imperfections? For instance, we strive constantly to have open dealings with problems and not devolve into secret conversations. We struggle with academic appointees in administrative leadership who may have little administrative experience—a common problem with universities, of course. We've brought in certain people in management from other prestigious institutions, in order to start the Bayside Village and Bridge Institute with experts in managing, but who may not share our most important views and values, such as commitment to spiritual training, or integration of spirituality and science. I wasn't in favor of bringing experts who don't share this vision. One or two people were brought in as big names but they don't have deep ties or commitments to our own institution—they were concerned about their own fame and prestige no matter what their affiliation, and they were susceptible to being courted by anyone."

"Hmm," Greg said, wondering at the significance.

"We don't have a fantasy world here free from the problems of other institutions. It's not a place with fully idealistic conditions that cannot in fact be realized within the ordinary constraints of other human institutions. We've all tried to learn from our experience of universities and alternative institutions. But we've undoubtedly recreated some of the very problems we aim to redress."

Greg couldn't help wondering if Mrs. Blocke, while not famous, was one of those people from the outside. One of those problems.

"That's good to know, I guess," Greg said. "My wife Sara and I participated in one organization back home in Seattle that focused so much on the light that the people there couldn't really explore or be honest about their own dark side—the hidden and unconscious parts of the organization. Ignoring the dark side doesn't mean it goes silent, of course, except perhaps in our conscious awareness."

"Well," Bateson said, "I wouldn't say we have that problem—luckily. We don't focus on the light to the exclusion of the dark. We do have organizational channels for a full range of discussion, and that helps dissipate built up, potentiated energy in the organizational unconscious. Our town hall meetings and community fora are intended for more than idea exchanges—they're places to explore the tougher inquiries about what we're trying to create here. And things do bubble up. Several organizations within Bayside Village also have their own governance and group process that provide a place for this sort of exploration. And many of the philosophies you'll find people holding here are sufficiently broad to encompass approaches to working with darkness in the world, in our organizations, and in ourselves. Most of us don't get swept away into the light and leave big shadows, luckily."

"I'm glad to hear that," Greg said. "I've probably seen some of those structures the last few days."

"Good," Bateson said. "Going back to your question about what we're trying to become, I should say that we're not just trying not to be perfect.

We're also not trying to be everything. And importantly, we're not trying to be a replacement or substitute university. We don't want to duplicate other efforts in the arts and sciences done superbly well at other fine institutions. We're trying to support the renewal of branches of philosophy, science and art that have been marginalized in modernity—and we can support this renewal here or through collaborations with other institutions. We're trying to restore a needed balance. We hope other great universities will be stimulated to take up this work as well."

Steve and Greg talked at length about the Bridge Institute, Steve's vision for a new kind of academy, the quality of teaching and cultivation he aimed for.

Greg glanced at a clock and found their time nearing its end. "I have just one more question."

"Certainly."

"How do people bring new projects to the Bayside Village? If Sara and I do move here, I imagine us participating in the co-creation of the Bayside Village."

"Yes, this is an important question," Bateson said. He breathed in, looked at the ceiling, considering his approach and looked down. "We look for people who have this deeper interest in bringing something new into civilization." He spoke in measured tones, paused, let the words settle before Greg. "Just as importantly, we seek people who have something to bring." And he let that settle, for he meant to impress upon Greg that he saw in him a potential co-creator of a new civilization.

Bateson gave examples of people who had come, bringing their ideas and growing them into fully supported programs. "But we're not open to anything and everything. The San Francisco Bay Area is rich in resources, and we're not the only place to locate a new project. The Bayside Village has a definite vision, mission, and mandate. Our role is to create demonstration projects for the seeds of a new civilization. We have space for projects like this. If we inspire, educate, provide the proof of concept and necessary starting points...very good. Then we let larger organizations adopt those projects and scale them up to a societal level. But the new ideas and projects we take on must match our broad aims. We're neither open to everything, nor overly restrictive and imposing."

Greg nodded. "Do you have decision criteria for what projects fit?"

"Yes." Bateson nodded. He became reflective now, tuning in to his vision. "Off the top of my head...Sacred science, of course, by which we mean principally reintegrating a complete metaphysics and cosmology in the investigation and enjoyment of the world."

Greg nodded.

"A focus on investigation, inquiry, and research—in other words, we're not a place to house mere beliefs and untested and untestable doctrines."

Bateson paused, searching inwardly, as if reviewing an internal list. "Integrating spirit and matter. Or otherwise embracing a vision of the whole of the cosmos, or at least not shutting out or excluding some parts of the cosmos in favor of other parts. I say this as broadly as possible since the very language integrating spirit and matter is already a metaphysical claim that there are distinct, discrete categories like spirit and matter, that they're separate, that they need integration, and so on."

"Yes," Greg said. "Even in framing our aims we run into diverging intuitions of the nature of existence."

"The important point is that we try not to exclude parts of the whole, such as excluding matter in favor of spirit, as certain periods in Western history have done, or excluding spirit in favor of matter as Western modernity has done." Bateson completed that thought and presently returned to what seemed to Greg an internal list of criteria for suitable projects. "Similarly, a vision of the whole person. Not excluding or shutting out parts of a person, whether the body, the soul, the mind, or the spirit—again, these are claims that there are such ontologically distinct entities, but we have to use some words to get us started."

"Sure," Greg said. "This is the difficulty of framing one's beginning postulates."

Bateson nodded, then paused, looked up to the ceiling, squinted. Then he brought his gaze level again with Greg. "Cultivating and integrating masculine and feminine qualities. Not excluding one for the elevation of the other.

"What else?" Bateson said, returning to his list. "Service to the whole is our primary motivation here. Personal interest and benefit are subsumed in service, and yet, importantly, they are discovered within it. And finally, as you've seen, we focus on transferring the results of our investigations, including our demonstration projects, to others so that all may benefit—in this case, we're consciously creating the seeds of a new civilization.

"But," Bateson sat forward, again almost too fast, as Greg was still taking in the prior words, "our mission and vision are not tied to specific projects or programs, but to the aims of aligning above and below, so to speak, of holding contact, of bringing new things into the world. Our projects and programs aren't meant to be perpetual." He paused, but keeping a tension, allowing no relaxation. "Our role, our principal mission, is to create a space where people can bring new things into the world. We keep contact or connection with something higher. Then people can come here and create what is new for civilization."

"Wow, this is impressive," Greg said. "This is music to my soul!" And he saw that he had no words for this music just now. It was a pure, fine feeling. Palpable, like a substance. It came as light, crystalline water, fine energy. He felt that Bateson had created a pregnant space for him and was holding it in a way not possible in ordinary conversation. In his heart, Greg bowed before such authority. This was sacred time, one of those rare moments in life when a soul stands face to face with destiny and bows, surrenders to its authority.

This time Bateson did not move on swiftly, faster than Greg thought he could digest. Greg knew the action went in, did its work. And he knew why it was done at a higher speed; it demanded attention, and something in him quickened in order to step up a level. The force awakened in Greg had its own life now. And Bateson could now hold Greg in freedom. The severe love of moments ago was no longer needed; if used now, it would be intrusive, a violation.

Greg knew this food would continue for a time now; he trusted it. And it would not do to continue sitting there as if in meditation. Ours is a sober path. Ours, he saw himself thinking. It was time to move on, even if outwardly it would seem to be a step down again to mundane conversation. He knew Bateson could see this, could even see his own thought process about it. Greg surrendered to what he could only call the rightness of the moment.

"I just hope I can identify enough funding to keep me going here," Greg said.

Bateson stepped down in conversation with Greg, without himself stepping down in awareness. He knew Greg could not yet do this, that Greg would inevitably lose something. So he kept a double attention for them both. "Do you have a project in mind?"

"A few, yes. They're ill-formed. I'll have to contemplate this to find which are deepest in me."

Bateson was silent a moment, giving space for Greg's consideration of what moved in his depths. "I think you probably know about Chris Mueller?" Bateson said.

"I just learned about him," Greg said. "I don't have much background, but I looked him up."

"He's given a handsome donation to the Bridge Institute for distribution at my discretion. And his firm, Hilltop Ventures, is planning to make a nice seed investment in AlignIt."

"Really? Roger mentioned Hilltop, but not the investment."

"Yes. And you may know that Roger's next AlignIt project, in ontology, may be funded by Hilltop."

"Wow! Roger didn't mention that yet, either. I assumed the funding was already there."

"We have the funds for a faculty position and for consulting. The Hilltop gift would provide additional funds for R&D grants to distribute at my discretion. If so allocated, they could take AlignIt a level farther. It plays in to how we're planning your compensation package. This prospective gift should be handled with discretion, of course. And Roger will discuss the funding details with you on the consulting side. I just mention it because I'm planning how to use these funds, if we get them."

"Oh. I wonder if I should adjust my presentation on Friday." Greg's mind began to spin with thoughts, hopes, and dreams, of what could be done with additional funding. Bateson could see Greg already losing his tenuous contact with that finer feeling.

"I wouldn't think so," Bateson said. "But I think Roger is particularly keen on this meeting and introducing Mueller to you, because this new funding has suddenly come into the picture."

Greg wondered what else Roger may have in mind? "That sounds promising," he said. "It must help to have resources to develop new technologies based on sacred science. And it must be wonderful to have a funding partner who understands what you're trying to create."

"Roger has spent the time cultivating that relationship. I've met Mueller only once. But as I say, we don't have the money yet. If it comes, I may allocate a large part of it for AlignIt."

"It's good to know investors like that exist."

Bateson smiled. "We attract many people, and life is full of opportunities and hazards."

Greg left President Bateson's office in the administration building, walked down the stairs and out to the Bridge Institute quadrangle. The lawn was empty now, and quiet. Greg had a short time before his next meeting. What to do? Meeting with Bateson stirred Greg's nascent aspirations, and he wanted time alone to feel it.

Greg set off for a walk behind Avicenna Hall, on a path he hadn't taken before. Passing by, he looked up to the building from its back side, wondered what it would mean to rename it Suhrawardi Hall as Bateson wished. He walked by the Bayside Village Animal Farm noted on Monday's tour, stood by the fence, watched animals in a field in the afternoon sun as he contemplated. What would be his contribution to Bayside Village if he and Sara came? What is deepest in him? So many interests had swirled in his mind over the years. Ideas he could not reasonably expect to teach or research in mainstream academia. What could he do at Bayside Village so that he would live something deep in him? What were the most important ideas, the big ideas, the ones that could define the high points of his life contribution?

52

Checking time on his mobile, Greg turned and walked to the Temple to meet with Professor Joshua Meade. He ascended the steps of the veranda from a side he hadn't entered yet, walked in, and proceeded down the hall past the rooms allocated for Tantric Indian, Nyingma Buddhist, Taoist, Sufi, and other groups to a shared office of two Christian communities. He removed his shoes at the door and stepped quietly onto a plush, wine-red carpet filling the room. Pictures of esoteric Christian art covered one wall. Greg recognized some of it from his occasional study of early Rosicrucian work. Others he recognized from the Raymond Lully Museum tour. On another wall, images and implements of Eastern Orthodox traditions were hung. The room was empty of people, but for one man Greg saw reading at a table in the middle.

"Joshua?" Greg asked.

The man looked up, surprised not to hear Greg's entry. "Yes. Greg?"

"Yeah." Greg sized him up quickly. In his early forties, but mostly bald. Short, thin, compact, energetic. A scholar. A leader of seekers.

Joshua stood up as Greg approached, and the men shook hands. "Good to meet you in person," Joshua said.

"Thanks. And thanks for meeting here at the Village." Greg pulled out a chair and the two men sat down.

"It's no problem at all. You're just down the road, here, from the Graduate Theological Union. I come now and then to teach."

The two men discussed Greg's background, his possible move to Bayside Village, his prospective work with Roger on AlignIt, and the next steps of building a robust sacred science ontology.

"So what about you?" Greg asked. "What do you teach at the GTU?"

"Generally, Christian spirituality. But I also have courses in early church history, the lives of the saints, and the use of Eastern church liturgy in prayer."

"The lives of the saints…" Greg mused.

"The lives of the saints because the lines of transmission are very important. Sometimes they're obscured or lost. So we need to remember that the teaching is given by transmission, as Jesus gave it. Also, studying the lives of the saints has always been important in the Eastern church. The saints are more than examples to us; they're also the cloud of witnesses who have gone before, and they're an ever present help in our sojourn in this earthly existence."

"Hmm," Greg mused. "An ever present help. That's not too different from the lineage of masters in many Sufi traditions."

"Probably not—at least for the more eastern of the Christian traditions. Those that stayed in the West, or were subject to the purgings of the Roman and Byzantine empires, have denigrated the lives of the saints to mere examples."

"Mmm," Greg said. He shifted his chair back and spoke emphatically.

"So, I was really moved by the works you sent me. I read Pseudo Dionysius the Aereopagite on the plane from Seattle, and some of the other materials. With my background in Iamblichus, I think I have a good grasp of Dionysius and the hierarchy of spiritual beings. But help me understand what you do with it."

"Sure," Meade said, sitting back in his chair. "Well, we've both read Iamblichus' De Mysteries. And you're a committed scholar-practitioner like me. So you've no doubt seen that De Mysteries gives you a theoretical framework for theurgy, but it doesn't give you enough to practice it. Not in any liturgical sense. It's an apology for theurgy, really. It doesn't outline the practice."

"Yes, right."

"Now, Dionysus was a theurgist in the Christian tradition. In his practice, liturgy is a theurgical rite. Or liturgy is theurgical. So Dionysius shows us how to do in a Christian way what Iamblichus wrote in De Mysteries."

"Interesting," Greg said. "I haven't explored this possibility—of Christian liturgy being a theurgical rite. But this isn't the typical Christian understanding of liturgy."

"No, not across the board," Joshua continued. "It isn't contrary to church teaching, either. You see, the content is Christian, not pagan. But in the theurgical understanding, we are drawn in the liturgy to participate with the angelic world in the worship of the Lord. We raise our thought, and our minds are drawn to heaven and the angelic hierarchy, ultimately to assimilation of the Lord himself. In the liturgy, we make hieratic use of material imagery to reveal the angelic hierarchy and ultimately the Mystery of Christ."

Greg nodded, feeling deeply impressed. This promised to unlock something entirely new for him.

Meade went on. "The material beauties of the liturgy are given as images of hidden beauty. Incense, for instance, is a symbol of spiritual realms. The light of a candle discloses the light of enlightenment. So the liturgy and its images are given as the grace of God, in recognition of the limits of our knowledge and capacity, to aid our illumination. These divine works have a developmental intent. The higher our knowledge, the greater our illumination in the spiritual Mysteries, and therefore the less we need the support of material forms. But material forms should by no means be despised. They come from God as God's grace to us, and they are steps for us, raising us to corresponding spiritual realities."

"So the soul of the worshiper is aligned with divine archetypes in the angelic world, by means of the icons used in the liturgy," Greg said.

"Aligned…Yes, you could say that, I guess. Though it's more than a simple lining up.   Ultimately, it's not just to come into harmony or correspondence, but to evolve, to be raised up in the divine work. The word we use here is assimilated. Assimilated to the higher beings, and ultimately to the Lord."

"Ah, right," Greg said. "So this is the Neoplatonic aspect."

"Well, yes, but Christianized. But you see, inside the tradition, the liturgy is considered not invented by us as some kind of idolatry or attachment to form. The liturgy is revealed, the prayers are revealed, so that humans can be assimilated, or come into alignment or correspondence if you like, with the work of higher beings who themselves are already aligned with the God-ordained order of creation. So yes, you could say we are elevated by coming into alignment with higher worlds. Ultimately in the Holy Mystery of the Eucharist, the soul participates in the Mystery of Christ and so is reconciled and made perfect in the rite, overcoming the duality of above and below, of human and divine, of one and many. This isn't just a human practice—we are participating in and surrendering to the work of God. This last bit is more than Dionysius says—it's how I understand the end result of the divine work of the liturgy."

Greg nodded, trying to find the trace of Joshua's own practice-born understanding, to distinguish what he remembered from reading. "I was interested in his Celestial Hierarchies," Greg said, "because it covers vertical hierarchies and the laws of their relations, like how the superiors include the knowledge and attainments of the juniors. But the juniors, while partaking in the pouring down of the revelation from the superiors, don't share all of their developmental attainments. But then I was surprised that there was no typological schema, horizontally speaking. This would be important for AlignIt."

"No, you're right," Joshua said. "It does end with a sort of dictionary of symbols which may interest you. But this work itself doesn't lay out a horizontal typology on any given hierarchical level."

"Well, this is extraordinary," Greg said. "I'm really delighted to find this practical way of homecoming. And I'm glad to meet you. You seem to have real depth in this area. I'll have to read more of Dionysius."

"And practice this hieratic art in the work of the liturgy," Joshua reminded, "if you want more than ideas about it. Remember that Iamblichus wrote De Mysteries in answer to the overly rational approach of the school of Porphyry. But if you want to practice, I'll suggest Dionysius is your key."

"Okay, yes. This living in the work of the liturgy compels me. But," Greg said, adjusting himself in his seat, "in the work with Roger on AlignIt, I would be trying to map out the ontology of this work of Dionysius."

"Of course," Joshua said. "You can read, and you can make schemata. For instance, there are nine orders of Celestial Beings, bearing three threefold Orders. To map it out, you'll have the first and highest order as the most holy Thrones, Cherubim and Seraphim. In the second you'll have the Powers, Virtues and Dominions. And the lowest of the spiritual Hierarchies are the Angels, Archangels, and Principalities. That may help you. But I think you'll find real insight and enlightenment in the work of the liturgy itself. My own understanding comes out of this liturgical practice. I'll be happy to work with you on AlignIt, as I have time. I'd have to think further with you about ontology, since I haven't studied it as a special subject apart from my other work. But again, I would suggest this study of yours come chiefly from practice, not from mere study of texts."

"Sure, that's how I want to practice," Greg said. "And I'd like to go deeper into Dionysius. Now, Dionysus I can grasp well enough for now, I think—admittedly on a more intellectual level at the moment. What's this other material you sent me—the liturgy of Addai and Mari, the Odes of Solomon..."

"If I understand your work with Roger," Joshua said, "I think the spiritual hierarchy in the liturgy of the Eastern Church may also have what you're looking for. I work with this liturgy as well, even more actively. So I thought I'd offer it."

"I was deeply impressed by the Anaphora."

"The Anaphora of Addai and Mari," Joshua said. "There are other anaphora. According to tradition, The Anaphora of the Blessed Apostles was written by Mar Addai and Mar Mari, direct disciples of the Apostle Thomas."

"Really? The Apostle Thomas?"

"Yes. And the work is about direct spiritual experience. In prayer and liturgy, we meet the Lord—directly, now. In this liturgy we say, 'my eyes have seen the King, the Lord of hosts.' And we say, 'Today I have seen the Lord face to face, and this is nothing if not the house of God, and this is the gate of heaven.'"

"That moves me. 'The gate of heaven...'" Greg repeated.

"The liturgy itself acknowledges the direct, immediate encounter with the Lord. This is the gate of heaven—a gate, an opening in us. The heavens and all the heavenly host are seen, and we can have a face-to-face encounter with the living Lord. We say 'he came and he comes.' And he comes in our prayer and liturgy. Among other things, our liturgy is the gate of heaven. Because in the liturgy itself we presently participate in the whole spiritual hierarchy that He created to worship and glorify Him."

"I didn't see an ontology explicated, but I thoroughly enjoyed the reading."

"It doesn't outline the orders of angels like we see in Dionysius, but there are some important elements in this ancient liturgy. First of all, there is clearly a retention of the angelic world, broadly speaking. One of the sections says:

Thy majesty, O Lord, thousands and thousands of heavenly spirits,
And ten thousand myriads of holy angels,
*   hosts of spirits, ministers of fire and spirit,*
Bless and adore; with the holy cherubim and the spiritual seraphim
They sanctify and celebrate Thy name,
Crying and praising, without ceasing crying unto each other.

Joshua sat forward, his eyes focusing, his energy taut and quick. "There is something theurgic here. The liturgy says, 'For Thou has associated creatures of dust with spiritual beings.'"

Greg repeated, making sure he understood: "'associated creatures of dust with spiritual beings.' Well, there's the above and below of Hermeticism."

"Yes, but it's not just a mirror image of the Emerald Tablet—what is above is like what is below. God has associated, linked, related, what is above and what is below. In other words, there is an association, an alignment, between us and the angelic world. This is the purpose and the work of the liturgy. You could design into AlignIt this association of earthly and spiritual beings. Right here in the ancient liturgy of Mar Addai and Mar Mari, we are acknowledging the order He ordained, and we are working together with spiritual beings in honor of this order."

"Mmm," Greg said, thinking, his eyes squinting as he looked on vaguely to the wall holding Christian art works, his imagination at work with Joshua's words, organizing, displaying, arranging for AlignIt.

"We say 'Before your glorious throne, we your people worship you, together with all the spiritual beings'—and they're named in several places—'thousands of heavenly spirits, ten thousand holy angels, hosts of spirits, ministers of fire and spirit, thousands of cherubim, ten thousands of seraphim and archangels.'"

"I saw that," Greg said. "Although it seemed more a poetic statement than a science of qualities."

"It is poetic, yes. The point is that we, together with these spiritual beings, are before the throne of God. Together, we are bowing down, worshipping, confessing His name, glorifying the Lord at every hour. This isn't a future event—after we die, or in future time or in a future millennium. This is now—we participate NOW," Joshua said, tapping his forefinger on the table, "without ceasing, together with holy angels and spiritual hosts, ministers of fire and spirit. Angels and people together, now, cry out to the Lord. We are in a mysterious communion now with the heavenly host in our worship of the Lord."

"Wow," Greg said. "I'm moved by the immediacy of your presence and your command of the liturgical Word, if you will. Your enthusiasm is like a living witness to the veracity and meaningfulness of the tradition."

"Just as it should be with the living Word of God. We are called, here and now, to participate in the Mystery. This liturgy isn't just a descriptive narrative—it's also said in the form of a practice injunction: 'And with the angles let us cry aloud to him, Holy, Holy, Holy Lord God.' You see? We are crying out with the angels, worshiping with the angels, hymning the Lord with the angels. Christians are called to participate in the spiritual hierarchy because He made us part of it. So we answer this call in the work of the liturgy—not in some intellectual sense, or just in terms of worldview, but practically, at every hour, without ceasing—in prayer and liturgy. This is the injunction, to participate with the angels in worshiping the Lord. It is our prayer to the Lord that He mingle our voices, despite our unclean lips and the weakness of our nature. He mingles our voices with the hallowing of the seraphim and spiritual angels. Why? Because He has associated us with spiritual beings. Why? To raise our worship by joining it to the worship of the angelic beings."

"So this is theurgic, too?" Greg said.

"Well, I'm not a historian, so I won't try to establish an historical link. I just see a similarity of theme between works like these—between the Hebrew worship, this early Thomas liturgy, and the medieval work of Dionysius. I just read what the liturgy says. Praying this over and over again, this is the understanding I have."

Greg nodded, utterly impressed at Joshua's illumination of the liturgy. "I don't think I've heard such a compelling account of Christian liturgy. I'm surprised that I've never run across this type of teaching."

"This is early liturgy, and its Eastern. Even the essential core of the liturgy, the anaphora, has this quality. You may appreciate this—in rhetoric, the Greek term anaphora is a literary device that relates a present word or idea back to an earlier idea in a text. In liturgy, this movement of relating back is the essential dynamic of theurgic liturgy. Like the rhetorical device relating the reader back to an earlier idea, the liturgy and the Holy Mysteries relate the worshipper back to what is prior—to our heavenly counterparts in the angelic realms, and ultimately to the Lord Himself in whom we live. So the Holy Mysteries are like a chain carrying back the symbolic elements to the Logos, the Living Christ, as above, so below."

"Well, this seems like the highest expression of theurgy—a ritual process that accommodates and assimilates the theurgist back into the higher order."

"I suppose so," Joshua said.

Greg continued. "But this is very different from the still mainstream understanding of theurgy; that its lower magic—compelling the gods to come to us and do our work."

"Yes. Theurgy is actually the other way around—we go to the gods, or the names of God, or the angels in Dionysian or Nestorian liturgy, and we do the work of God in redeeming creation. But I don't encounter that older view much these days, happily—probably because I have a circle of colleagues who understand theurgy from knowing the sources rather than looking on from prejudice and the poor ideas encyclopedias perpetuate. What's interesting to me here, in the liturgy of Mar Addai and Mar Mari, is the acknowledgment that the Lord has associated the above and below. This isn't something we are inventing from below, so to speak. This isn't some kind of lower magic of compelling the gods to come to us. No, this liturgy says the Lord has made this association, and we come into alignment with the Lord through the work of the liturgy. The Lord has done this, and does it. Actually, someone in our small community was given a verse in the night, in a dream, that goes like this:

> *We are they*
> *Who achieve*
> *By not doing.*
> *Yet things are done.*
> *Happy are they*
> *Who know the Sun.*

We are not the doers. The Lord does it. We participate in the Mystery, but the Lord Himself associates the above and below, and does the work of redeeming creation. So this little verse acknowledges the grace of God in perfecting our salvation."

"That's beautiful," Greg said. "You even have dreams that open the gates of heaven, so to speak."

Joshua nodded, though hesitating to ponder Greg's way of saying it.

"So tell me," Greg continued. "With your Methodist background, how did you come across all of this work? It seems uncharacteristic...."

"Well, this is an interesting history," Joshua said, sitting back. "I didn't grow up in these traditions. I was born and raised a good American Methodist, and I went to a Methodist seminary. But I was always looking for something deeper. As I studied the works of John Wesley, I became interested in his exploration of the Eastern church fathers, and how he incorporated their theology into Methodism. I began to explore the Eastern church fathers myself, and I became intrigued. I then visited a Greek Orthodox church and then a Russian Orthodox monastery here in California. And I began a series of dialogues with a few monks and an abbot, Father Isaac. I saw that they had a very deep understanding and practice. But the more I explored, the more I suspected there were other teachings lying deeper than the main thrust of practice—though they assured me there were no such esoteric traditions lying deeper. I then encountered the Syrian Orthodox church and the Assyrian Church of the East, and then I discovered what felt to me like a vein of spiritual gold in the mountain beneath the church—the early line of the Apostle Thomas, and his disciples, the Apostles Mar Addai and Mar Mari. I immersed myself in reading and study in that literature…"

"Of the early church lineage of St. Thomas?"

"So it is understood. I could find no easy access to a living lineage, outside of India where that branch of the church is still alive. So I created a study group to read the scriptures and practice the liturgy of Mar Addai and Mar Mari, and the memorials of St. Mary and the holy fathers in the Syriac tradition. I've also tried to reconstruct what we believe the early communities in the apostolic line of Thomas read and practiced. So we use the Peshita, which is the Syriac version of the Bible. We use the Diatessaron of Tatian, one of the earliest gospel harmonies. We also read and pray the Psalms and the Odes of Solomon."

"Ah, the Odes of Solomon," Greg said. "I loved those! I never heard of them before. And you do this work of the liturgy with the Odes of Solomon?" Greg asked. "I'm just trying to get a picture of what you actually do."

Joshua nodded his head once, definitely. "Yes. This work with the hymns, Psalms and Odes—this is our work." As he searched for his next thought Joshua's eyes seemed to trace a distant structure—a window or door in the room. "Ode 16 says something like 'Just as the work of ploughman is to plow, just as the work of the helmsman is to steer the ship, so my occupation, is the psalm of the Lord. My service is His hymns.' So you see, this is our ongoing work. This is what we do."

"Wow, you've really got this down," Greg said, deeply impressed. "I'd love to have my texts so well memorized."

"Well, you see, it's not just mental memorization. I chant the Odes every day. So it's in my heart as a prayer. If it's in my heart, then it's on my lips."

"Nice," Greg said, letting the words settle in his soul. "Wow! So you've recreated an early Christian community!"

"Well, we're continuing a Christian community. We're drinking from the same stream of what we take to be an earlier and authentic line of apostolic Christianity, the Judean Christianity in the Semitic language of Jesus. Much of what we know today in the West is the Pauline version of Christianity which, of course, introduced many other elements—Greek and Hellenistic—and departed from the Judean branches of early Christianity and then suppressed them. Several Christians who have gathered with us feel that the gospel that survives in the Roman, and even Byzantine, versions of Christianity has been extensively tampered with, that much of the original teachings have been suppressed, banned, burned, Hellenized,

Romanized, subject to all manner of so-called ecumenical counsels which subverted the Gospel and the Holy Mysteries and changed their meaning. It isn't an explicit part of our group to critique or amend this situation, or even fuss about it. We just try our best, by the grace of God, to worship and love the Lord, in the light and lineage of our great Father, Saint Thomas."

53

Greg walked to the Dining Commons where he would rendezvous with Sara and Tara in forty five minutes for a dip in the hot tubs before dinner. Outside, he saw Roger sitting on a bench by the path under the trees, grading a stack of papers.

Greg walked up. "Hi Roger."

"What a surprise." Roger put down his stack. "I'm waiting for a student. This is what I call my outdoor office hours. But I'm early. What are you up to right now?"

Greg sat down beside Roger on a portion of the bench shaded by a tree. "Today I had back-to-back meetings. Tibetan Buddhist sangha, Catherine Stone, Steve Bateson, Joshua Meade."

"You're making the rounds!" Roger said.

"Oh, this place is so rich! I feel inspired, and I'm walking on air! I'm amazed at the caliber of folks here. These people are top notch. Just having one of them would be amazing."

Roger nodded.

"But you've got a whole team of people like them for AlignIt. And I found myself wondering how you did it."

Roger laughed. "Just being in the right place at the right time, and then the right people show up. Its just being in a flow, and doors open."

Greg nodded, absorbed the impression. "Hey, by the way, I was going to stop by Mrs. Blocke's office in HR. It's Wednesday afternoon already, and she hasn't returned a single phone call or email."

"Still?" Roger said, surprised. "I've even put in a few calls to her myself to get things moving. Keep me updated on this. I should drop by, too. We need to get you that meeting before you head back to Seattle on Saturday. But you're getting the important part, at least—the meetings with key people."

"Okay, I'll keep you posted," Greg said. "I'll leave you to your papers. I had better get going to Blocke's office so I have a few minutes before meeting Sara."

Greg strode across the Bridge Institute quad feeling larger than life. The rich meetings of the day, Roger's and Steve's encouragement and support, the superb April afternoon. Drawing near the administration building on the Bridge Institute quad, a feeling of thrill shot through Greg's mind from the day's events. All of these impressions elevated Greg with thoughts of a nobler life. So many fine forces at play. So many new connections. What freedom it would be to pursue his ontology work, to pursue his deeper interests, with such astute colleagues. Could the grass smell fresher? Could California's crisp, radiant sky burn bluer?

Inside the administration building, Greg walked down the hall on the first floor, searching for the Bridge Institute's Human Resources office. Then he saw it, there on the right side of the hallway. He knocked on the closed door of Interim Director of Human Resources, Mrs. Blocke. Here he was, finally. Why hadn't it occurred to him to drop in sooner? After a moment, the door opened slightly, and a stocky woman looking in her late fifties, with short graying blond hair, stood in the door way.

"Yes?" she said. Her voice was imposing, monotone. She held the door half open. This caught Greg by surprise.

"Uh, Mrs. Blocke?"

"Yes." It was the same monotone.

"Hi, I'm Greg Cobb, from the University of Washington." She remained in the door. Greg remained in the hall. "I've left a few voicemails, and I've emailed." Mrs. Blocke stared blankly. "About my application for teaching, and the interview process."

"Yes, I have them." Her voice struck Greg as contemptuous. "We don't have your application yet, and we're backlogged processing other applicants."

Backlogged with applicants? With an institute this small? "Well, I've been trying to reach you to meet this week. I haven't heard from you, so I'm stopping by to see when we could talk. Is this a good time?"

"We're rather busy right now. But it's no worse a time than any other." Mrs. Blocke opened the door a bit wider and stood by it, holding it open. Greg walked in and she closed the door behind him and walked back behind her desk, positioned to face outward toward a chair on the other side of it by the door. Odd hierarchical arrangement, Greg thought, comparing it to the open, inviting floor plans of the other offices he visited so far. He waited for her invitation, but it wasn't offered, so he just sat down in the empty chair. He looked around. Piles of stuff was stacked on every surface. Folders, forms, packages. Maybe Roger was right. She could be overwhelmed by a new job.

"So, I'm not sure if you recall my voicemail and email…" Greg left open a pause for her to fill in, but she didn't take it. This behavior threw Greg off, making him feel unexpectedly anxious, triggering some old feelings he couldn't exactly put his finger on. "So I'm visiting this week for the orientation tour and meetings with faculty."

"Yes." She stared blankly but impatiently.

"I have two more documents to submit before my application file is complete, and I'll get those in next week. I was hoping you could help me understand the process from here," Greg said. He hoped for rapport and conviviality with Mrs. Blocke, as from all of his meetings. Would she give him just a plain statement of the process? But how to ask for an enlivened discussion of process from someone who seemed so dreary and mechanical? "I understand from Roger that several faculty members have positively evaluated my credentials…"

Mrs. Blocke laughed oddly to herself and shook her head, either by accident or…deliberately. "Well, consulting for AlignIt is one thing, but Roger needs to understand there's a bit more to the hiring process at the Bridge Institute than just faculty interest and recommendations, and he shouldn't be going around giving people assurances before the process even begins."

"Well, the process has begun. I'm here on campus, I've met with a lot of faculty this week so far, I've…"

"The process begins with me, and with your application, which I don't have yet."

"What?" Greg felt himself surprised at this presumptive contentious behavior. "Uh, okay," Greg staggered at her words. "You have my application. So I'll get the remaining documents to you next week. Anyway, I didn't mean to imply Roger's given me assurances…."

"You don't need to imply it. We've been down this pathway with Roger."

"What do you mean?" Greg asked.

"I mean that there's a process, and your credentials and references will need to be fully checked. Surely you expect background checks from your other university experience. If Roger wants to bring you in to his own business as a consultant, that's his prerogative—he can do that on his own. But interest from a few faculty isn't sufficient for hiring at the Bridge Institute. We're young, but we've established high academic standards. You still have to face a review panel."

"Of course! Sure," Greg said, unexpectedly defending what had seemed obvious moments ago. "Every university has a review process. I don't expect special treatment, and I don't expect coming here is any different."

"No, it isn't different. It might even be more demanding."

"I'm sorry," Greg said incredulously, "but I must say I'm surprised by your approach. Is there some cause for suspicion about my record, or about Roger? I'm not following your implications."

"I'm not insinuating anything. But a faculty member can't just bring in anybody through a side door and expect preferential treatment in the faculty hiring process."

"Um, okay, this is really astonishing me," Greg said. "I'm not expecting any special treatment, and Roger hasn't suggested to me that I can slide into a faculty position through a consulting assignment, if that's what's you're saying. I presently don't have a consulting assignment, although he did put both the faculty and the consulting opportunities before me equally as possibilities. If there's some perceived conflict of interest here that is going to adversely affect my application process, I need to know about it. I'm quite happy to turn down any consulting offer and stand on the merits of my academic and professional record."

"I'm just saying there is a due process, and you will be evaluated on the merits like anyone else."

"But of course!" Greg said, almost indignantly. "I don't expect otherwise." Then he stopped himself, realizing the absurdity of this discussion, that it's going nowhere, quickly thinking through his best path forward in this awkward situation. "Is there anything else I should know about the application process?"

"Everything you need to know about the process is disclosed and fully transparent. We have well-designed application packets. So there is nothing special in your case."

"Again, I understood that much and I don't expect otherwise. But actually you have taken the trouble to say some special things just now about perceived conflicts of interest, and it's probably useful for me to know that. So...if there's anything more I should know, I'd appreciate hearing it."

"I haven't said anything about conflict of interest. And no, I haven't anything special or preferential to say to you. The hiring process is disclosed, public, and transparent. You can see everything that every other candidate can see, and you will get the same review process every other candidate will have. We look forward to reviewing your completed file, Dr. Cobb." The words felt final. And they were ingenuine, unduly formal, and offensive.

"Okay, thanks for your time, Mrs. Blocke," Greg said abruptly, emphasizing formality as a return volley. He stood up and walked out of the office, closing the door behind him.

"Shit!" he breathed to himself in a flurry of rage and fear. He turned, walked fast and stridently down the hall.

Outside the Administration building, Greg walked briskly to the bench where he had seen Roger, feeling desperate to talk. But Roger's student had now arrived and Roger was busy advising. What now?

Greg walked down the path, aimless, passing students, crossing a tram track, thinking what next. He stopped and watched a tram whiz by, almost hovering over the grass. He stood there a moment, watching birds flitting through flowering trees. Then he fetched his mobile from his pocket, clicked on Sara, selected tracker. He saw that she was at the Plaza. He placed a call, asked if she was free to meet. She was. He started for her, already feeling some relief.

On his way, he pulled out his mobile again and clicked on Roger and left a message. "Hi Roger. This is Greg. I'd like to talk to you when you have a chance. I just met with Mrs. Blocke, and I had a really, really weird experience. I just want to talk to you about what's going on. If you have some time this afternoon or evening, can we talk? Cheers."

Greg spotted Sara sitting in the sculpture garden in the Bayside Village Plaza. He approached her, feeling affected and tense. She was sipping tea and leafing through her sketchbook. "Hi Sara," he said, and sat down.

"Hi." Sara instantly felt Greg in a different world from her.

"I just popped in to see Mrs. Blocke. I finally met her."

Putting her sketch book aside, Sara turned to Greg. "Hey, are you alright?"

"Yeah, I'm alright," Greg said. Then he said quietly, "Actually, no." Greg shook his head to himself, breathing out and looking across the Plaza. "She's the only person here who uses the formality of her last name. And she's the only person who has called me 'Dr. Cobb.' She used it to create distance. She never answered my calls or emails, and then she was astoundingly rude to me when I arrived at her office. And she cast suspicion on my academic merits and suggested Roger was trafficking in conflicts of interest by bringing me here."

"What?" Sara said, surprised. "That's bizarre."

"Yeah. I'm still trying to figure out what just happened. She even said he was trying to slide me in through the side door of consulting, and implying that that's how I'm trying to get in, and implying that otherwise I couldn't stand on the merits. And she said 'We've been down this pathway with Roger before.' I asked her what she meant and she gave me these bullshit formal replies like 'Everything is disclosed and transparent,' and 'You haven't begun the process yet; the process begins with me.' And she said, 'We will evaluate your application on its merits.'" Greg lowered his voice, but not his intensity. "I'm like, what the fuck is that! I just lost my cool, and I probably blew it."

Sara lowered her voice, too. "What do you mean you probably blew it?" She stayed calm and listened with focused attention.

"I don't know." Greg shook his head with an intense look on his face and got louder again, as emotion blew like gusty winds. "Like who is this woman? How does this rude, bureaucratic woman get into a gate-keeping position in a place like the Bridge Institute? No one here has been like that so far. I've met with lots of people this week already. No one prepared me for someone like her. I'm just totally shocked. Like I just got hit by a truck I didn't see coming. Something feels weird about what just happened, but I don't know what."

Sara took in a deep breath and blew it out through her lips. "Wow, that doesn't make sense. But you said you probably blew it?"

"Oh, I didn't answer you. Well, I probably didn't say anything out of turn. But after so many of her offensive words and calling me 'Dr. Cobb,' I said back to her in her own tone of voice and formality, 'Thank you for your time, Mrs. Blocke.' And I got up abruptly and left."

"What?" Sara laughed. "So that's blowing it?"

"Well, outwardly, no. But on a feeling level, on an energy level, I was going there to build a bridge, and I came away burning it."

"No, she burned it," Sara said.

Greg stopped himself, thought about Sara's words. "Yeah, you're probably right." Greg paused, felt himself breathe in and out. "But if the process really does start with her, and she's giving me all this bullshit, with no basis in fact that I can trace, and no relationship or rapport, and she doesn't even have my completed file—what does that say about beginning the process here, formally?"

"Mmm." Sara winced and put her hand on Greg's shoulder. "I'm sorry, Greg. It does sound strange." Sara drew her hand back and thought for a moment. "But you've met with Roger and you're meeting a bunch of faculty. And you just met with President Bateson, didn't you?" Greg nodded. "He seems very affirming. And I'm meeting with Karen tomorrow. I mean, the process can't really start with Mrs. Blocke. It's got to be just a step in the process. And…she has to be an anomaly."

"Yeah, I guess so. I hope so. I think it just disturbed me."

"Did you talk to Roger about it?"

"Not yet. He's actually outside on a bench, but he's with a student. I'll tell him when I get a chance. Anyway, you're probably right that it's just a step in the process. I'm just feeling really weird about being blindsided like this and wondering what that says about this place. I need to put it aside for now." He paused, breathed in deeply, then out, looked sideways at her. "Well, thanks for listening."

"Of course."

Greg's mobile rang. He pulled it out. "Hello?…Roger…Yeah…4:00. Avicenna? Okay, great, thanks. Bye."

"Good," Sara said. "Maybe he'll help clear things up. Hey. Do you still want to do a family hot tub at the Lodge?"

"Yeah, of course. Might help me unwind a little."

At 4:00, Greg appeared at Roger's door on the second floor of

Avicenna Hall.

Roger felt the concern in Greg's call. "How about a walk?" he invited. He stood up.

"Okay," Greg said.

They walked together down the hall, down the stairs, and out of the building. Until they were alone, Roger shared light tidbits of his meetings and how Friday's Scientific Advisory Board meeting was shaping up. Out on a far side of the Bayside Village campus, when they were away from people, Roger asked, "So, what's up?"

"I just met Mrs. Blocke."

"Right. Finally."

"I had a really weird experience with her." Greg recounted the meeting in detail. Roger listened, showed concern in the musculature of his forehead. "She also said some pretty deprecating things about you. I wondered what she's getting at."

"Like what?" Roger wondered if any details would turn up that could reveal a connection between Blocke and Mueller, any details that could illumine the strange events unfolding.

"She suggested you try to slip things by informally, like holding out two positions before me and trying to slide me through the HR process by consulting. She said she's been down this road with you before."

"That surprises me," Roger said. "I've had only one other encounter with her before talking to her about you. I helped my colleague, Professor Catherine Stone, with her new hire process."

"Hmm." Greg trusted Roger's integrity. He never doubted that Mrs. Blocke's insinuations must be groundless.

"That got difficult," Roger said, "because Mrs. Blocke—actually, her name is Amelia—was strongly attached to a process she brought with her from industry. She doesn't have a university background. Her whole song and dance is avoiding litigation or something, which doesn't happen in academia the same way it does in business."

"Hmm."

"She's taken onto herself a burden to defend her HR process. In part, it's a different philosophy than the faculty hold. Several faculty members including myself are looking into it."

"What do you mean by a different philosophy?"

"The faculty here play a strong role in recruiting and hiring new faculty. We feel this is of utmost importance for the integrity of this institution. And she's one of those people brought in by the Institute's Board of Trustees who was successful in managing HR functions in a variety of companies and a few nonprofits. So she struggles against faculty as though she carries the authority of a Board mandate. Whereas we see her as a playing a role that should support faculty selection. We clearly need someone to help with all the necessary HR tasks. But she's over-stepping her bounds in trying to drive faculty hiring. And she creates road blocks in the hiring process. Anyway, this is an internal struggle. It doesn't have anything to do with me or you. She's being unduly scrupulous."

Greg took a deep breath. "That helps me feel a lot better."

Roger wasn't sure, though, if that was the root problem, or if it masked something else. If Blocke and Mueller are connected now as they were in the past, if the troubles Roger experienced with both of them this week are related, then how are they related? Did Blocke come in randomly and then reconnect with Mueller? Did Mueller place her here? One insight came to Roger just then. Blocke had come to Bridge shortly after Mueller expressed interest in AlignIt. Could Mueller have orchestrated her coming? But why would he? That seems like overkill just to get access to AlignIt.

"I'm meeting with Bateson about it, probably tomorrow," Roger said. "So don't worry about this part of getting here, Greg. Just give her what she needs. But if it feels right to you to come here, the doors are open. You have the right advocates in the right places. Mrs. Blocke's hiring process is incidental."

54

Greg returned to Sara at her bench in the garden. He felt relief now from his walk with Roger. They picked up Tara from Bayside Village Daycare, returned to the Lodge, and got ready for the hot tub in the Lodge complex.

Walking down the hall to the hot tub room, Sara said, "I think I could willingly suffer a daily dip in the hot tub."

"Yeah?" Greg said. "Good reason to move here, no?"

"You're still working that angle, are you?" She turned and grinned playfully at him.

"Of course. It's a good one, ay? Anyway, I sure need a dip right now to unwind from that crazy meeting with Mrs. Blocke. From the whole day actually! Wow, the meetings I've had. And it's a good way to unwind and have some family time."

"And a good way to get this girl to shower."

As they approached the door, Tara asked, "Can I do it, Daddy?" Greg took out his mobile and handed it to Tara who waved it before the door. Tara opened it and rushed in.

"Tara, Honey, I need my mobile," Greg reminded. Tara stopped, returned. She handed it back to him.

Greg and Sara put down their towels and bags and went to the showers. Sara took Tara.

Greg showered and then stepped out, went to the tub. "Oooh," he groaned, going down into the hot water. "I need this!" He drifted to one side of the tub, then moved around for a view of the private garden courtyard, visible only by two hot tub rooms, separated by a wall. The late afternoon sun angled in brightly, lighting up a side of the pond and flowering bushes before them.

"Where's my beloved?" Greg called to Sara. She came to the steps, descended into the warm waters, waded slowly over to Greg. She stood, waist deep, tying her long hair back in a bun.

"You owe me, you know," he said.

"How is that?"

"You exposed that gorgeous neck of yours in the studio, and I was attracted like a bee to honey. And you said not right now. And then you walked off like you know you've got what I want."

Sara looked flirtatiously at him. "It's true, isn't it?"

"Oh, she does it again!"

Sara smiled, turning her torso directly toward him, looking down seductively as she finished the bun.

Greg rolled his eyes. "Sit down, already!"

Sara had a big smile now. She turned and sat down in front of Greg, moving up against him.

Greg put his arms around her.

Tara waded, got in, and swam up to her parents. "Watch this," she said, and went under to swim to the other side. Coming up and turning back, she asked, "Did you look?"

"Yes, Sweetie," Sara said. "Good job holding your breath! Can you do it again?"

"Uhu." Tara dove under.

Greg kissed Sara's neck gently now, brushing aside her wisps of dangling hair falling out of the bun.

"Mmm," she purred. She leaned her head back, resting it on him.

Roger visited Jeff's GameIt office again in the Research Park, leaning on his credenza. "So Greg showed up at Mrs. Blocke's office unannounced, and she was rude and off-putting."

"Doesn't surprise me, from what I've heard," Jeff said.

"She cast suspicion on his academic record—saying he can't just slide in on the side by consulting, that he has to undergo a due process, as if he wasn't planning to…"

"Really? That's offensive."

Roger repeated Greg's details of the encounter.

"And then there's Blocke's possible connection with Mueller," Jeff said. "But the thing I can't put together is that I just can't imagine Mueller's interests extending to the Bridge Institute as a whole. AlignIt I can understand. But the Bridge Institute?"

"Oh, Mueller said something to me this morning. He said he gave Bateson a gift."

"A gift?" Jeff looked surprised.

"So there may indeed be something he wants from the Bridge."

"Hmm." Jeff contemplated. "Well, that could explain his connection to Blocke, because she's Bridge HR."

"She's difficult," Roger said. "I've told you that. Stalling faculty recruitments, difficult to talk to, not fully transparent and accountable."

"But why the Bridge Institute? I can't get a feeling for his interest."

"I don't know."

"Well, I'm not sure how much to extrapolate, here," Jeff said. "But putting two and two together, at least we can see that both Blocke and Mueller have a relationship to each other, at least in the past, and both have some connection to game companies, and both independently were overtly discouraging about Greg."

"Very bizarre," Roger said. "Something's going on here. I need to meet with Steve and raise these matters—Blocke and Mueller's gift."

With their hair still wet from the hot tub, Greg and Sara walked from the Lodge down a pathway to the Dining Commons holding Tara's hands, swinging her as she jumped forward, then falling back and swinging her forward again. People streamed around them on their way to dinner.

"Wow, that was a busy day," Greg said. "I feel so relaxed now."

Greg spotted Keith on a bench outside before the Dining Commons, sitting directly in the 6:00 sun slitting through the trees. "Hey, Keith," he called as they approached his bench.

"Oh, hey, I didn't see you coming," Keith said, looking up from a book he held in his hands. "How's it going?"

"Good," Greg said, stopping with Sara and Tara. "We've had a full day of meetings around the Village. I'm ready for dinner and a break!"

"Where's Leah?" Sara asked.

"She's right over there, calling her parents." Keith pointed to Leah, sitting with her back turned on a bench beneath a stand of eucalyptus trees several yards away from the Dining Commons—just out of earshot. "She calls home every night." Keith paused, looking disappointed, and then laughed to himself. "They want to know where she is and what she's doing—in case she's gotten wound up in a weird cult or something. I don't know," he said. "Ever feel like you were dating someone's parents?"

"Hmmm," Greg said, nodding and smiling sympathetically. "Can't say

I have. But I hear you."

"How's your time together been?" Sara asked.

"Up and down," Keith said, putting his book on the bench beside him and leaning back.

Greg tried to see the title—the jacket was gone, and the print on the spine was upside down and thin. But he saw it—Herman Hesse's Narcissus and Goldmund. And he remembered reading that book years ago—a struggle between the containment of conditioning and the adventurous journey of youth into the wider world.

"We've done a lot of talking," Keith said. "You know, about what next, our future, my future here....Oh, guess what?" Keith interrupted himself in a burst of energy. "I just had an interview with Roger today!"

"An interview?" Greg replied, surprised. Sara's face brightened, too.

"Yeah. For being a research assistant. We really connected! He's really cool. That would be a really, really cool job—working with someone like him. I mean, I don't know what'll come of it, but I have a good feeling. Anyway, I think we had a great interview."

Greg mused, felt it significant somehow that Keith would connect with Roger. Was it significant that he himself connected with Keith? Was there more here?

"He's really something," Sara said. "We had dinner with Roger and his wife Jenny, last night, actually. Lot's of rich, long discussion."

"Wow, you had dinner with him?" Keith asked, surprised. Despite their feeling of immediate affinity, it was the kind of comment that defined the social difference between them—the worlds of students and faculty.

"Yeah," Greg said. "Working with Roger would be good exposure for you. It would open a lot of doors..." Greg noticed Keith's attention suddenly drawn beyond him to someone approaching.

"Hi, Keith," a young woman said. Greg turned and saw a petite woman with curly, shoulder-length brown hair walking up and looking to see if she was welcome to step in.

"Oh, hi Emily," Keith said with a voice that bade special welcome. "This is my friend Emily," Keith said to Greg and Sara. "Emily, this is Greg and Sara and Tara. I met them in the Orientation Monday."

"Hi, nice to meet you," Emily said, beaming and effulgent at Keith's welcome.

Turning back to Greg and Sara, Keith continued. "Emily works here, too, like me. We've kind of hit it off and become really good friends the past few months. We've spent a lot of late nights talking about, like, everything in the universe."

Emily laughed. "Yeah, we do. I miss our walks and talks," she said, turning her attention toward Keith. "You've been busy this week."

"Yeah, I know. I have a friend visiting from college this week." Keith had a hesitatant look. "Girl friend, actually." He said it shyly. "I think I told you about her? Leah?"

"Oh, right," Emily recalled, her light dimming, trying not to look shocked.

Tara hung from Greg's and Sara's hands, swinging her torso back and forth, pulling her two pillars off-center now and again.

"She's actually right there, talking with her folks on the phone." Keith pointed toward the eucalyptus trees, hoping she wouldn't come back yet. "She'll be leaving for home on Friday, so I'll have time again soon."

"Okay," Emily said. "No rush. I just hadn't seen you around." An awkward moment of what to say next after the girlfriend news seized Emily, especially in the presence of Greg and Sara. But she recovered quickly. "Well, I'm heading to dinner, so I guess I'll see you around."

"Okay Emily," Keith said, making sure to say her name. "I'll call Friday when I'm free again."

"Alright. Bye, and nice meeting you" she said to Greg and Sara.

"Nice meeting you, Emily," Sara said, smiling somewhat somberly in recognition of the awkwardness.

"Nice meeting you," Greg followed.

"Well, I guess we should get Tara some dinner, too" Sara said. "Will you be out here a little while?" she asked Keith.

"Not sure. Probably ten to fifteen minutes."

"Why don't we head in," Greg urged Sara. "Maybe we'll see you inside. I'd like to hear more about Roger if you're up for it."

"Yeah, I am. Alright," Keith said. "Have a good dinner."

"Bye, bye" Tara said.

"Bye," Keith returned, smiling again.

Opening the Dining Commons doors and joining the food line, Sara turned to Greg with raised eyebrows. Greg returned the glance.

"Okay," she said. "I change my wager from Monday night."

"We were betting?"

"I thought they'd stay together and Keith would return to college, or where ever. You thought he wasn't compatible with Leah. But now my prediction is that Keith will stay here, and my gut feeling is that things won't work out with Leah. Just a guess."

Greg laughed and shook his head. "You're a real people watcher."

Sara smiled, shrugging her shoulders.

"I wonder how things will work out with Roger," Greg said. "If that works out, I bet he'll stay. But you're focused on the Leah question."

"Well, you could tell from his face that he was really into Emily," Sara said. "I haven't seen him that way with Leah."

"His face?" Greg asked.

"Yeah, his face was radiant. Didn't you see him light up when she came?"

"No."

"No? He totally changed. He gave his full attention to her."

Greg shrugged. "I wouldn't bank on things developing with Emily, necessarily. She's cute, but I think he's more inclined to follow his career and his longing for truth at this stage." He paused, thinking. "But I could tell from her lighting up that there's something between them."

"From her lighting up?"

"Yeah."

Sara paused a moment with squinted eyes, thinking. "You were looking at her." She elbowed him playfully.

"Come on!" Greg said. "You were looking at him."

"I like him. He's a nice guy."

After dinner, Greg and Sara took Tara on a stroll over the raised boardwalk sensitively coursing through salt marshes and mudflats. The tide was rolling in. Despite the sight of industrial tankers and barges in the Bay, the buzz of late rush hour traffic on the distant highway 80, the energy of San Francisco city and bridge traffic, the immediate marsh bubbled up with little critters and wading birds. The family ambled along as Tara pointed variously to one plant, bird, animal or trail marker after another. Greg and Sara fell silent, periodically reflecting, minimally, on one matter, leaving it, and another, and leaving it. Alternately, they focused attention on Tara, refocused on the day, and back to Tara. Their attention was free and ranging as they strolled, their busy minds unwinding the day's events.

The raised marsh pathway circled back to a connecting path across campus. At the juncture, Sara saw Roger and Jenny sitting on a bench with a marsh view. As the family approached leisurely, Sara made eye contact with Roger and Jenny.

"How's the marsh?" Roger called out.

"Lovely," Sara said, approaching. "It's great for Tara. There's so many little creatures scampering around there. It's a beautiful nature sanctuary."

"It really is a sanctuary, isn't it?" Jenny said, looking up and out to the marshes, then back to Sara. "And how has your day been?"

"Good. Busy." Sara described her explorations in the Art Center, the Day Care. "Tomorrow, we're looking at the Bayside Village Community Housing."

"Oh, you are?" Roger said.

Tara found a beetle in the grass near the bench and squatted down to watch it, pulling Greg's hand to look.

"They're very nice accommodations," Jenny said, "if you like living communally."

"Yeah, they seem nice from the outside," Sara said. "We're thinking about where we would live if we moved here. Earlier in the day I was looking at maps while Greg was in meetings. I looked at Berkeley, Albany, Point Richmond—just in case it doesn't work right here in Community Housing."

Maps? Greg hadn't heard that bit of news yet.

"We'd like a yard. Well, I'd like a yard," Sara said, pointing to herself and smiling.

"A yard is good—for making great discoveries," Roger said, looking momentarily at Tara following the beetle. "Of course, the whole campus is your yard."

"We have our first yard right now, in Seattle," Sara said. "Before that, it was always apartments. I'm planting a garden with Tara this spring, and we're arranging flower pots and an outdoor pond filled with little fish and water plants. Tara can romp around busy with toys, mixing bowls and experiments. Having a yard is nourishing for all of us. We don't want to give that up. I don't want to."

"No, I don't want to, either," Greg said, turning around from his squatting over the beetle with Tara. "But the community housing did look nice, to me, and it has a playground and other parents and kids around for Tara."

"It's important to Greg," Sara said.

Greg stood. "I lived in an intentional community in college and we had a few children around. I've always wanted to do that again, and I've wondered how it would be to raise Tara in a community like that."

"Daddy, look! It's moving," Tara called gleefully. Greg turned back to the bug and kneeled.

"We'll have to talk more about it," Sara said, "because we'd have to make sacrifices to live like that. We'd also like enough room for me to have an art studio and for Greg to have an office, and we may not get that if we moved to the Community Housing. From the floor plans, it seems the units are kind of small."

Floor plans? Greg wondered. When did Sara look at floor plans? He turned again and stood up, taking a few steps next to Jenny. "An art studio for Sara would be great. Our house benefits from her good eye and fine touch in the decorative arts. She has a knack for placement. Things just feel right to me after she's done. And sometimes her painting expands to a mother-daughter activity—recently, at least, as Tara dons the smock and rolls up her sleeves right next to Mom." Greg smiled at Sara, looked at Tara. "She also has a way with crafts and has worked with Tara on many craft projects over the past year, like…What did you make? A puppet theater, hand-made slippers, a princess outfit."

"How nice," Jenny said.

"We don't want to give up that kind of space," Greg said.

"Mmm," Jenny said. "Its evident you both have a deep love for Tara and do a lot to cultivate special qualities in her."

Sara smiled and nodded. "She's our magnum opus right now."

Roger nodded.

Jenny smiled. "And will be for years to come."

Tara kneeled, tracked the beetle on its journey through the grass. She turned to report each latest development to Greg.

"Well," Roger said, "if you chose Community Housing, keep in mind that they also have co-housing opportunities in part of the complex. Your resources extend to the whole complex, and to The Bayside Village itself. While you may give up some things in taking a smaller space, you'd share many resources that you might not have in a single family house. You'd share some activities, and those become communal activities."

"Hmm," Sara said. "I'm not used to family planning that accounts for the resources of a whole campus. I like the idea of community, and I know it's important to Greg. But there's something about having your own home, your own yard, and for me, my own art studio. That's a big one— the studio."

"Have you looked into studio space at the Art Center?" Jenny asked.

Sara's eyes lit up. Here was a connection with Jenny and the Art Center. "No, I haven't. I could do that?"

Jenny nodded.

Sara raised her eyebrows. "Hmm." She pondered, thinking of next questions to ask Jenny.

"It looks like you've explored Bayside Village quite in depth," Roger said to Sara. "Dining Commons, Day Care, Community Housing…"

"We have," Sara said. "If this is serious for Greg, we want to cover all the bases."

"It's a daring venture just to visit here," Greg said, "to interview, to meet with so many gurus and sages, even to explore living here."

55

Greg, Sara and Tara stopped briefly at their guest room at the Lodge. Greg picked up Tara's stuffed Clappy, a blanket, and some jackets for the cool San Francisco Bay evening. Then they set out for the Temple, the building on the Bridge Institute quad housing many paths of spiritual practice and realization.

"So the Swami is talking with you before the meeting?" Sara asked as they walked down the path.

"With us."

"Me too? Okay. About AlignIt?"

"About Tantra. And what he's doing with Roger to bring this material into AlignIt."

"Okay." They passed by a tram stopped by a sidewalk with people boarding. Sara looked at the colors, the designs, now familiar. "Did you get the coloring book and crayons?" she asked.

"Yeah, it's in my bag." He turned to Tara. "Sweetie, we're going to do some singing and dancing tonight. And we're going to talk with the yoga teacher. We got a coloring book for you to color in while Mommy and Daddy talk to the teacher, okay? And then we'll sing and have some yummy snacks at the end."

"What kind of coloring book?" Tara asked.

"It's a book with stories of gods and goddesses from yoga. Remember the Mahabharata? Remember Krishna?"

"Mhmm," Tara said.

"It's like that."

"Are we going to have ice cream?"

Greg laughed. Every occasion with food raised the prospect of ice cream. "I don't think so, Sweetie."

Arriving at the Temple door, Greg, Sara and Tara removed their shoes to a beautiful, wooden rack on the veranda. They stepped inside the main Temple room, which had been empty on Monday's tour. The emptiness still impressed Greg. Now the big space would be used for a Path of Ananda meeting, and devotees stirred about the main hall setting up. Musicians rehearsed at the front, with their guitars and sitars, tabla and cymbals, starting up the music, stopping to discuss the song, tuning an instrument, starting again.

Greg looked for a man who could be the Swami. He and Tara stepped aside as two men rolled out a Persian carpet across the polished hardwood floor leaving an elegant sea of floral patterns in red, gold, white, beige, and green. Two young women laid out small rugs, cushions and pillows on the newly laid carpet for seating.

An elder woman with long, grey-black hair, glasses, and artful dress appeared. "Welcome. Are you here for satsang?"

"Yes, and we're here early to meet with the Swami," Greg said.

"Swami-ji hasn't arrived yet, but he should be here soon," the woman said. "Is this your first time?"

"Yes. We've visited satsangs before, but not Path of Ananda."

"I'll be happy to orient you once we're set up."

"Oh, thanks," Greg said. "I think the Swami will."

The woman smiled. "Okay. Let me know if I can answer any questions." Greg nodded and she walked away.

Sara glanced at images of Shakti and Siva being carried to the front and placed there. Indian mother goddesses in paintings and statues were being moved into the room from Path of Ananda's office down the hall. "Beautiful," Sara breathed to Greg as the figures paraded by.

"Yeah. I love this—music, art, devotion." After a moment, Greg bent down to Tara. "That's a harmonium," he said, pointing to an instrument at the front. Tara looked. "That's a guitar. That's a sitar. That's a mandolin, and a hammer dulcimer. Those drums are called tabla—and you see, he's playing with his fingers and thumbs. And those are cymbals." Greg knelt for a few moments, looking with Tara. "And there is the altar," Greg said again. "There is a symbol of Shiva and Shakti—the god and goddess celebrated by this group. And the altar has candles, and incense, and a picture of the Mother—she's the master teacher."

"Daddy, are they going to light the candles?"

Two women crossed in front of Greg and Tara with a profusion a tiger lilies and orchids.

"Yes, soon," Greg said. "We're early."

A man with a commanding presence appeared at the door holding a small side bag and Greg knew it must be the Swami. He was a radiant older American man with a long beard, dressed in ordinary clothes, but looking different nonetheless, like he moved with finer energy, with light. He slipped out of his sandals and bent over to put them into the shoe rack. He entered the room simply yet powerfully, recognized and acknowledged Greg and Sara with a nod, and motioned to wait. He walked swiftly to the front and spoke with the devotees arranging the room. Then he returned to Greg and Sara.

"Welcome to our satsang," the Swami said with a glowing face and deep, warm eyes. "I'm glad you could come. Let's meet in our office," he said waving with his hand. He walked towards the hall lined with offices of all the spiritual groups at the Temple—Buddhist, Christian, Sufi, Jewish, Taoist, and more. Turning back, he said, "We have a nice little room where I meet one-on-one with students." The Swami walked into the Path of Ananda office, where devotees where gathering up ritual items for the main hall, and he went into a small side room inside, with a skylight but no windows. Greg, Sara and Tara followed. The evening sun still gave a little light from above. Swami turned on the overhead lights, put down his bag, and lit a candle on a small altar. The room had a soft, off-white carpet, pillows, and a few yantras hung on the walls, with a picture of the guru, the Mother, straight ahead opposite the door. "Please, have a seat." Swami-ji sat down on a pillow on the carpet at the far side, just under the Mother, and facing the family.

Greg and Sara sat down on pillows facing the Swami. Sara called Tara, patting the carpet beside her, and Tara sat down. Sara retrieved the Siva-

Shakti coloring book and crayons. "Okay, Honey. You can draw in here while Mommy and Daddy talk to the teacher. Okay? Here are some crayons."

"Oh, the Siva-Shakti coloring book," the Swami said, glancing at it, then at Tara. "You know? A few children in our center here color in this book. I think it has a few nice stories, too." Tara was shy. The Swami smiled deeply and then withdrew his attention to Greg and Sara.

"So, husband and wife come together," he said. "Good."

Sara smiled. "Thanks for inviting me, too."

Swami-ji nodded and smiled again. "It helps when two eyes look in the same direction."

"Hmm," Greg said, not meaning to vocalize it. "Well, thanks for meeting before satsang. It fits Tara's bedtime schedule better."

"Before satsang is good. After satsang, we let the heart rest in devotion. And we have fellowship and food." Swami-ji paused. "So, what would you like to discuss?"

"I was just hoping to get a preliminary understanding of how you work with Roger. If we move to the Village, I may be working with you."

"Yes, we've spoken of you," Swami-ji said.

"And maybe for Sara's sake," Greg said, "if you could give a brief explanation of how you practice Tantra Yoga. We're familiar with yoga and devotional singing. But I was explaining to her about your focus on Siva and Shakti here, your scientific orientation, and your work with mantras, sound, and color…And I understand that in Tantra, there is a right hand and a left hand path," Greg said. "I didn't know which kind this is."

"This is the no hand path," the Swami said swiftly, instantaneously, almost before Greg finished, before having time to reflect. He let the words settle into Greg and Sara. A subtle smile slipped across his lips. "It's the pathless path of no hands—no right, no left." Greg nodded, thinking he understood this non-dual, attachment-breaking reply. Swami-ji continued. "People have made such a mess of these distinctions. The meaning is lost—not just in the West, but also in India."

"So," Greg clarified, "you take a centrist posture—neither the right nor the left, but in the middle? Or do you integrate the two paths somehow?"

"We work with each individual according to their need," Swami-ji said. "You could say Path of Ananda has a common set of teachings and practices, adapted for the West, even for Northern California. We draw from the ancient Tantric traditions and many others, because Tantra is syncretistic like many Indian traditions. And from these many traditions, with the Mother's guidance and grace, I give to each person what I see he or she needs. Let me introduce it like this—I brought this to show you."

The Swami turned to his side bag and produced an object wrapped in a beautiful Indian fabric with hand-stitched patterns. Placing it before him, the Swami unfolded the covering revealing not an object but a deck of cards, cut larger than ordinary playing cards.

"You may recognize these."

"Yantras," Sara said with interest.

"Yes." Swami-ji looked up, confirmed Sara's words with dazzling eyes, and then turned down to the deck. "Each card is a different yantra." Swami-ji spread the cards slightly with his right hand, then again with his left. "You may know the Sri Yantra—it's widespread in Indian and Buddhist art. And here's the Nava-Yoni yantra. The Kali yantra. The Syama yantra..."

"Wow," Sara said, "that one's structurally uncentered. Isn't that unusual?"

"Yes, the Syama yantra is asymmetrical." Swami-ji left an opening for her

"I'm an artist and I have a Master of Fine Arts degree," Sara said, "so I'm familiar with Indian art."

"Good. Okay," Swami-ji said. "We use this one to represent the iconoclastic nature of some aspects of Tantra. Of course, it stands out because yantras are generally symmetrical. And most of our teaching is not iconoclastic, except in subtle ways that move the heart but don't make the headlines. So, each yantra here is an energy pattern, a structure of consciousness, a psycho-cosmic form. With concentration, they're very potent under right conditions of practice. These yantras have existed in Tantric art, science, and ritual for several thousand years and they've come down through transmission from teacher to teacher. This may be different from the formal study of art," Swami-ji said, looking up to Sara, "since these are technologies used in the science of Tantra by students under the guidance of a teacher."

"My guess," Sara said, "is that you're not studying the form of the art object, per se. You're studying the very nature of our own consciousness—in practice."

"Mommy, look," Tara said in loud and obvious whispers. Her drawing was vibrant and chaotic, with crayon marks jutting out beyond the outlines of the Goddess.

"Shhh," Sara said. "Remember, Mommy and Daddy are talking with Swami-ji. You can color now and we will talk after this."

"Yes," Swami-ji said to Sara. "This is a good understanding. It helps to know something about the form of art, of course. But as you say, we are studying ourselves. And the universe. Not the technology for its own sake."

"So this is what you work on with Roger—the yantras?" Greg asked.

"Yes," Swami-ji said. "Tantric science, generally. But we've started with yantras. I specialize in them, actually."

"Really," Greg said.

"With Roger, I'm working on the structural elements, number symbolism, colors, and their associations with mantras, texts, stories, and so on. I don't use these with every student, however—it depends on what the student needs. Because these are very potent symbols. I give these to my students as meditation practices—to visualize the unfolding of the energies in the mantras, to experience them in motion, and then to dissolve them. Ultimately this is instruction in how to create and uncreate the entire world we project in order that we may come to full knowledge, unobstructed by ignorance."

Greg nodded with keen attention and interest. Sara listened with focused concentration.

"In my case," Swami-ji said, "usually I only give these practices to students who practice yoga asanas, vegetarian diet and fasting, and the pancha karmas, the five processes for purification. So when they take these yantras, it's already a very concentrated practice. Its powerful and efficacious. Not everyone who comes here works with yantras.

"Now, even though I'm working with Roger," Swami-ji said, "I should say—because we're talking about AlignIt—that I do have a concern about reducing these potent forms to AlignIt. I haven't entirely reconciled this in myself. Roger knows this, but I say it for your sake since we may work together on this. It isn't a concern with technology; I have all these images on my mobile and my tablet as well. My concern with AlignIt is that we simply encode these potent forces in some web-based database where what people really want is to find lovers who match their astrological profile, or something like that. And then people run off with the yantras and either they never get the real effect, or they get the real effect without preparation. But this will be my growing edge, you see? I think AlignIt is a marvelous tool, and Roger is a very fine steward of a new idea. Maybe I'm still catching up with these things going out in web applications."

"Yes, I see," Greg said, looking to Sara and then back. "I think we share your sentiment. Putting this material into AlignIt makes it available for everyone. But isn't it just like a library? We don't hold back an encyclopedia, or even books on yantras, to control how people are going to use it. People use it however they will, at whatever level they can."

"We used to hold these things secret—disclosing only to advanced adepts," Swami-ji said. "Maybe I'm just traditional in this way. I admit that I have a deep imprint of the student-teacher dyad, and this is the stuff of transmission. Yet Tantra also has a democratic and egalitarian element. And the Mother tells me this needs to happen now."

Greg nodded and left a space. "I guess…my sense is that people can easily find yantras in books if they want. And they'll look at yantras according to their own level, their interest, their preparation. I'm certainly not a teacher, but does it really matter if people get access? I would think most people don't know how to get the real effect anyway. Some people will come to you and they'll get a deeper experience of yantras because of your instruction. Making this available in AlignIt doesn't necessarily bring down the teaching or practice."

"This is my hope."

Greg continued. "It's simply a tool made publicly available, and people use it at the level of their capability. I mean, the way I think about it is—just imagine what your students can do if they have the benefit of AlignIt as they're working under your instruction."

"That possibility is worth something," Swami-ji said, nodding. "Tantrikas use tools. I understand tools. So, you can see I am working with Roger. I trust Roger's integrity and depth of practice. Anyway," Swami-ji said, making a shift, "explain your role to me again—in AlignIt."

"I would work on the ontology," Greg said, "which means working on the structure, properties and relationships of entities in a given system."

"And what does that mean with AlignIt?"

Sara, having heard Greg's articulation of AlignIt many times already, looked below the conversation to the yantras fanned out on the fabric. The Syama yantra especially caught her eye, with its irregular, asymmetric structure. She peered with such focus until it almost seemed to move.

Greg continued. "It means helping formalize the representation of objects in terms of structure, properties and relationships so they can be mapped in AlignIt. For instance, the yantras used in Tantra—I want to know the qualities, structures, functions, relations, operational rules, conditions, etc. I study how these determine the existence, transformations, and relations of yantras. Tantra has traditional ontologies—probably many. I don't know what they are, but I would study them and organize them into the upper ontology we'll be developing for AlignIt. And I help make these entities and rules machine readable so AlignIt can run operations. There's another part of my work with the upper ontology in AlignIt which is helping to meaningfully relate the Tantric ontologies to the ontologies of other traditions, like those in Taoism, Buddhism, Sufism, Christianity, Judaism, and so on."

"I see," Swami-ji said. "Well, I will need to brush up on Tantric ontologies myself. It's the kind of thing that's implicit in texts, songs, art, and practices, but it isn't lifted out for examination in traditional practice as it may be for you in Western philosophy."

"Right," Greg said. "It's particularly in Western philosophy that this inquiry is lifted out, as you say. And I have another question. You sit on AlignIt's Scientific Advisory Board?"

"Yes."

"What's that like?"

"I advise on dominant patterns and principles. But as I see it, I just play with AlignIt and I show Roger what I'm doing. So I help shape AlignIt, perhaps more by accident than by intention. He tells me I give valuable feedback. I don't know exactly how he uses what I say, what I show, or the ways we use AlignIt. I just talk about how I use AlignIt in practice."

"What practice?" Greg asked.

"For instance, I've played with using AlignIt in unfolding Tantric teachings, working with my students, and organizing our community life. AlignIt, or rather PlanIt, helps me find auspicious times for festivals, rituals, diets, fasts, purifications, and so on. So my work with Roger is not only adding and listing these yantras and their attributes, but also, like you were saying, linking them to corresponding Sanskrit letters, mantras, yoga asanas, times of the day, and so on."

"How do you use AlignIt in your teaching?"

"I'm not entirely sure yet," Swami-ji said. He turned his head slightly and squinted his eyes. "I was trained in working with the shastras, or traditional texts, and technologies like yantras and mantras, and in studying students to see their needs and their obstacles. I'm still finding ways to use AlignIt. But the ways I've tried to use it so far include searching for new information to amplify my understanding of an object or entity, either by its similarity with corresponding objects, or its relationship one way or another. So I can move beyond simply teaching about an entity in traditional ways. Now I can amplify my understanding of these rich, multivalent images by studying their correspondences. I can also find the relationships of one object to others near it. And I can find what comes before it and after it in time—that's useful for getting a picture of how a person's practice could develop, like seeing possible next steps. There are a lot of interesting ways to use AlignIt that extend the scope of my traditional training. Who knows? Maybe someday AlignIt will be encompassed in the Tantric training of the future in the same way that working with yantras was an innovation compared to traditional Brahmanic practice according to the Vedas."

Swami-ji looked at his watch. "Satsang will begin soon." He reached down before him, organized the yantra cards back into a pile. Sara's concentration on the cards broke. But she wasn't finished yet with something that stirred in her now in response to her gaze. She watched Swami-ji wrap the fabric around the deck.

Sara's attention broke again and she came back to herself. "Tara, Honey, can you finish up what you're doing there? We're going out to the main room for singing." Then turning back to Swami-ji, Sara said, "Can I ask how you came here to the Village?"

"Sure," Swami-ji said, removing the covered deck to his side bag. "I came here to work with Roger. Since I specialize in yantras, this was a precious opportunity. Working with Roger is truly amazing, and AlignIt is a unique tool for my specialty. And since I decided to relocate here in Bayside Village for this work, I brought the Path of Ananda here under the Mother's direction. And Mother soon came, too. Now we have a growing community of Tantric adepts right here at Bayside Village."

56

Swami-ji held the door open, and Greg, Sara, and Tara walked through it, down the hallway, and back into the main Temple room. It was almost dark outside now, and the room was almost filled with people. Many devotees were seated on small rugs and cushions arranged on the Persian carpets covering the floor for meditation. The music practice they heard on arrival had now stopped. To the right, more people entered the room bringing covered pots wafting the aromas of Indian food, delivering them to a side table already set with pots and bowls of food.

Swami-ji greeted some people at the entry way and held light conversation.

Looking about the room for a place to sit together, Greg observed that the audience was mixed with American and Indian people, some sitting quietly in meditation, some talking lightly or jubilantly with others, some practicing Sanskrit verses. "How about there?" Greg said, pointing to a spot on the left side.

"Yeah," Sara answered in a half whisper, and walked up the side aisle between the wall and the cushions to enter a row near the front. Sara brought Tara to the cushion next to her, and Greg sat down on Tara's other side.

When they were all seated, Sara leaned over to Tara. "So in this satsang, most people sit like this." She demonstrated a half-lotus, and then pulled her feet with a little effort into a full lotus.

"Daddy, can you do what Mommy does?" Tara asked, turning to Greg.

"Hardly." Greg moved into half-Lotus position, with his right foot over his left thigh. "This is comfortable. But this..." Greg lifted his left foot over his right leg with difficulty, and then up to his right thigh and fitted it there gently. "This is quite uncomfortable for me," he said to Tara. "I didn't start this when I was young like you, and I don't practice it every day. I can't keep it this way very long. Can you do it?"

Tara put her legs into position, as Sara and Greg had done, with relative ease, though her balance was untrained. She looked up as if to say, 'See what I can do?'

"Good, Tara," Sara praised. "That's a good lotus position."

"Can I take them out now?"

"You can sit any way you like," Sara said, "as long as you keep your quiet voice during the meeting. Okay? Or you can sing, too. If you get tired, you can put your head down on my lap."

Musicians now returned to their instruments in the front—the tabla, bass drum, sitar, and harmonium, together with a mandolin, hammer dulcimer and guitar, and began playing informally, growing slowly into a formal rhythm and melody. "Look," Greg said to Tara, pointing to the front, while gently lifting his left leg off his right thigh and returning to half lotus. Tara looked forward and watched the musicians.

Swami-ji walked to the front and took a seat on a cushion on the floor in the center before a low microphone a foot off the ground. He moved into lotus asana and moved the bass drum up beside him, and then flipped through a song book. He talked with fellow musicians.

"This is called Bhakti yoga," Greg said to Tara. "We sing from our heart to the Lord, feeling love in our heart." Greg put his hand to his heart.

Swami-ji looked up to the gathered group and took a deep breath. He looked around the room at everyone gathered, with his hands together at his solar plexus, seeming to smile at each person. "Namaste. Let's begin with the Devi Bhava."

The harmonium began, and the singing.

In song after song, Greg sang deeply from his heart, feeling joy in the music, the song, the high energy in the room. It carried him, with his heart of devotion, away into a liminal state. After several songs he came back suddenly to his usual sense of self. Tara's head was now rested on his open right thigh where earlier he could not bear to hold his right foot in the lotus asana, and her knees and lower legs rested up against Sara's fair posture, still in full lotus. He glanced at Sara whose head and chin were poised, eyes closed, singing with a joyful expression. The intense energy of devotion exuding from her—it was all hers, genuinely hers, her unique expression; and his wish to bring her to Bayside Village did not dim her light with any air of compulsion. The words of Swami-ji came back to him just then: 'Husband and wife come together, like two eyes looking in the same direction.' Turning again to the front of the room, and closing his eyes again, he felt something sublime and ineffable about how precious this bond is with Sara—two eyes looking in the same direction, whether at home in their Sufi group or here visiting the Path of Ananda, in the Buddhist sangha early this morning, at dinner with Roger and Jenny last night. She was truly a partner in the work, the path, the journey. Here they were in the middle of a week's visit, and this single activity, this single glance, this single expression of joy on her lovely, compelling face, stood as a signature of all that mattered to him in his marriage to her. What a blessing, he thought, and his attention went out like a fragrance into the wide air of devotion to the Beloved, to Devi, his intuition reaching forms now thinner than air and receiving impressions of Nothingness, even if he could not realize it fully yet.

After much ecstatic singing and chanting, the group now rose for a late potluck meal. Greg and Sara roused Tara from sleep. "Tara, it's time for a yummy snack," Greg said, rubbing her warm back. Tara rose, her eyes distant in sleepy worlds, her cheek red where it rested on Greg's lap. The family joined the group as it gathered around the table, holding hands. When all had gathered, Swami-ji initiated the meal chant:

> *Om Brahmaarpanam brahmahavir*
> *Bramaagnau brahmanaa hutam*
> *Brahmaiva tena gantavyam*
> *Bramakarmasamaadhinaa Om Shanti Shanti Shanti*

Hands released, a line formed around the table, and the room filled with the hum of discussion. Sara and Tara joined the line, and Greg followed behind them.

Reaching the table, Sara's attention turned to plates, serving dishes, serving spoons, and wonderful smells of vegetarian Indian cuisine, where hot plates had been turned on just prior to kirtan ending. After moving down the line, Greg, Sara and Tara took three chairs arranged loosely against the wall. After a few minutes, Swami-ji came to sit next to them. A few others gathered around, sitting near Swami-ji, drinking in his presence. While eating, they shared life stories, discussed Swami-ji's teachers and the Mother.

Sara wiped her fingers on a napkin, put her plate under her chair, and turned to Swami-ji. "I love the feeling of Indian devotional singing," she said. "I read the Bhagavad Gita several times a few years ago—actually, we read it together, didn't we?" Sara said, turning to Greg, who nodded, his mouth full and chewing Tara's left-overs.

"Yes, the Gita is a lovely book." Swami-ji said.

"Doesn't Tantra use non-Vedic texts and traditions?" Greg asked.

"It is true—the Gita is based on the Vedas," Swami-ji said. "Some of Tantra is non-Vedic, and there are also Vedic Tantric traditions. We use both. In our group, we use the Upanishads and the Gita now and then. We have a slightly different mix of cultural factors here in American than in India where these things might matter a bit more. We use a mix of literature and ritual, but all for the same ends."

A woman sitting next to Tara turned toward her as the man on the other side got up. The woman showed Tara her prayer beads. "Do you want to see these? This is called a mala." Tara looked, touched the beads.

"I hold it in my hand like this, and I use my thumb to count, like this. Do you want to try?"

"Do you want to try it, Tara?" Greg asked. "Those are prayer beads."

Tara took the beads in hand, and the woman showed her how to use them.

Greg continued with Swami-ji. "So you aren't restricted, per se, to one line of Tantric tradition?"

"We say people need to make full use of whatever truth and tools they can find," Swami-ji said. "This is our Tantric attitude. We say people should look for tools from every people, every culture, and every period of history. Wherever truth is found, in whatever form it is found, we should not shrink back but feel free to use it, respectfully, if it suits the higher purpose we are serving. We should not say, 'Oh, that's a different path—we don't practice like they do.' That is not the attitude we take. We recognize truth wherever it exists. In universities, scientific laboratories, great religions, great philosophies, mystical paths, indigenous cultures, folk stories, great art. We use whatever truth and whatever tools we find, if it meets the need of the moment, and if it suits our higher self."

"I like that universal, integral attitude," Greg said. He wiped his fingers with a napkin, wiped his lips.

"So what exactly is Tantra as you practice it here?" Sara asked.

"Tantra is an ancient science of self-realization," Swami-ji said. "By it, we come to insight into the appearance of the world outside and inside ourselves, ultimately knowing the nondual Truth or Reality behind appearances."

"So, you're not wearing the orange robes," Sara said to Swami-ji.

"That's right," Swami-ji said. "I'm not a sanyassi. Some men and women here have taken sanyassi vows. But I'm married, like you. I'm also married to Mother," Swami-ji said with a smile.

"Isn't Tantra also about sex?" Sara asked.

Greg was taken aback, embarrassed.

"Yes and no," Swami-ji said. "Tantra is about realizing who you really are—awakening to your Atman, your higher Self or Soul. Discovering that Atman is none other than Brahman." Swami-ji turned to Greg. "To put it in Vendantic terms." He turned back to Sara. "Tantra uses many methods. So in one way, Tantra includes everything, rejects nothing. One of our operative principles is the employment of shock—traditionally using things which in traditional Indian society were taboo. For a saddhu, sex can be shocking."

"Oh yeah, there is also this aspect of shock," Greg said. "This is also used on the Sufi path by some teachers, like the Malamatis."

"But taboo is culturally relative," Swami-ji said, somewhat ignoring Greg's comment. "An Indian of the ninth century had attachments and identifications very different from yours, sitting here tonight. After the sexual revolution of the 1960's and 1970's, how shocking is sex today, really? In American culture, sex is glorified; its ubiquitous. It's expected and allowed everywhere, from movies, magazines, and music to advertising. It fills everything. Pop culture is addicted to sex. What shocks people today is when sex is not part of the program. Right? Even Tantra is supposed to have sex in it, people think. Many people come here expecting yogic sex. And when sex is not part of the program, then they are shocked." Swami-ji laughed. He leaned down to put his plate under his seat and came up. "Then you see their attachments. But then Tantra is working, right? They were shocked, and an opportunity for insight opens up. But maybe they didn't want that shock. They don't want Tantra. They want sex. You see? Tantra was just another exotic kind of sex. Is that what they want? God bless. We don't judge. Sex is out there everywhere. They can find it. But here, we work with people who want to awake, to attain Self-Realization."

"But aren't you suggesting sex is only for shock?" Sara asked. "It's also used to awaken energy, isn't it?"

Greg squirmed. This is someone I could work with on AlignIt, he thought. Why is she pressing him on sex?

Swami-ji laughed and looked down to the floor, humbly, with a smile. "Yes, maybe I have," he said, turning his head away from her to the side and shrugging his shoulders. He looked up again, and straight ahead into the room. "Yes, sexual energy may also be used—except that in Sanskrit, there is nothing called sexual energy, per se. It is just energy—shakti. But we always use discernment. You see? It is not so straight-forward. Sex, where it is used, is used in service of the higher goal of joining Shakti, or energy, with Shiva, consciousness. This is a divine marriage, a union which brings ecstasy. And we can awaken shakti in many ways. Sex may be one way. Though for many people, sex awakens nothing higher than ordinary desire—even among my students!" He gave out a laugh and slapped his hand down on his knee. "Our shakti typically follows along the deep grooves, or vasanas, of our conditioning. Its often easier to awaken shakti in other ways than sex, because our sexual longings also take our shakti down familiar vasanas. We use many methods here, but we usually focus on devotion in the heart—to Shiva, or Krishna, or Devi. Or you can say Jesus. Or you...for Sufis, you can say our Beloved one. We worship our Beloved."

Swami-ji's eyes seemed to flow like rivers of light, energy, fire. Yet they drew attention like magnets. "You can raise energy in many ways, change consciousness in many ways. Ananda is so tender, so delicious, and it takes us right into the heart of our Beloved." Swami-ji paused, momentarily enraptured. "Ahh," he exclaimed, looking up to the ceiling, and then he looked down again to Sara and Greg. "Done the right way, and with the right attitude and wish, sex can change consciousness." He let the words hang in the air for an intense moment, as if waiting with a net for fish close to the surface. "But so can many things. And who really wants to raise energy? Who knows what it is for? Even more, who is capable? Eh?" Swami-ji smiled and almost broke into a laugh. "See, so many people use Tantra as justification. What do they really want?"

"In California, it seems everyone wants a good couples workshop," Greg said, trying to follow along with Swami-ji's social criticism.

"In America," Swami-ji said, "you can't sell a gun to a child, but you can sell Tantra….Of course what people get usually isn't a loaded gun. It's just a toy. That's what people want. Okay. Fine. People can find it if that's what they want. But then they come here and want it. But we don't deal in toys."

"You deal in loaded guns," Sara said.

Yikes, Greg thought. Leave it alone!

"We deal in people," Swami-ji emphasized, "and sound methods, using what is needed for their awakening—with the seeker's consent, at the right time, in the right conditions. Every person is unique. So a person who comes here and takes this path seriously should be clear what they really want, and be careful what they ask for."

"So you don't teach Tantric sex?" Greg said.

Swami-ji let out a deliberate sigh and groan. "What have I been saying? We do what is needed for awakening. But it is what you need that counts—your real, ultimate need. If you come with that aim, and you work with a teacher, then you are the student and you graciously receive what is given. If you want to teach yourself, there are books. We don't recommend it. We recommend working with the instruction given by one who sees. Why? Because a real teacher can see your qualities, see what you need, and just as importantly, see what you don't need. If you come thinking you already know the methods you need, the teachings you want, you are like a cup already filled to the rim. You know this Zen teaching story? What can a teacher give you when your cup is already full? But if your cup is empty…"

Swami-ji looked keenly at Greg, then at Sara, looking in, looking at more than their eyes. "Alright," he said. "I never say so, but I will say to you—technically, if a person, or a couple, are capable, if they meet the criteria for a prepared student, I could teach it." Swami-ji paused. It felt like a moment of truth, but without any practical import, for Greg or Sara at any rate. Then Swami-ji quirked his head suddenly. "But I haven't taught it yet," he said with force. It was like a little shock. "You know this saying, When the student is ready, the teacher appears?" Greg and Sara nodded at the familiar aphorism. "Consider it this way: The teacher is ready when the student appears."

"The teacher is ready when the student appears," Sara echoed. "Wow, that's a neat saying."

"Where is it from?" Greg asked.

"From this moment," Swami-ji said. "It comes to me just now." Swamiji looked, paused. "Maybe it isn't always so. I can teach things for which I have no students. If it is needed, I can teach. But I have never taught it yet. I have no students for this. So I do not teach it. We practice ritual, worship, diet, lifestyle. This I teach. Who knows? Maybe I am not ready. But there are many things I don't teach—and for just the same reason. A room full of people and no prepared students. Everyone is a student, of course. But you speak of special methods."

Greg's mind returned to the Zen image of the full cup that can't receive what a teacher gives. Circumspectly he reviewed his manner this week, his approach to teachers like Swami-ji. He saw himself filled with questions about ontology and AlignIt as a frame for his meetings. He replayed impressions of his encounters with Swamiji tonight. He found himself too intellectual, and to that extent he realized he missed Swamiji who was always going around or beneath the snares of the intellect for something more direct and vital. Greg wondered if he had opened himself enough to these pregnant encounters with teachers here at Bayside Village. Probably not enough, he thought.

People began leaving, and soon, conversation with Swami-ji wound to a close. Greg and Sara said good bye to Swami-ji and to others around the food table. They walked out of the room, with Tara in hand, to put on their shoes at the rack on the veranda.

"Carry me," Tara said, looking up to Greg with her hands in the air.

After putting on his shoes, Greg bent down and picked up Tara. The couple walked out of the Temple, onto the walkway leading back to the Lodge. The moon shone brightly over the campus, lighting up the ground with a pale glow.

On the way, Greg hummed aloud a tune he remembered from kirtan as Tara put her head down on his shoulder. Greg's hum broke into soft words: "Siva Om, Siva Om, Siva Om."

In between, Sara said, "I love the music and the joy in their worship. And the food and fellowship is really nice. I love the food!"

"Mmm," Greg said, feeling so full in his heart that he had no words to speak. The night air was quiet, still and brisk. The two walked along quietly and then Greg returned to humming.

Back at the Lodge, Greg and Sara tucked Tara into her roll-away bed. Greg sat on the bedside. Sara dimmed the room lights with her mobile and then sat quietly in the master bed, reading by a bedside light.

"How about if I tell you a story before Leah comes?" Greg said.

"When is she coming?" Tara asked.

"Soon. In about fifteen minutes."

"How long is that?"

"Soon."

"When are you coming back?"

"After we go into the hot tubs. It won't be long. Leah will be here, and she'll read you a story and stay with you until we get back. Okay? How about I tell you a story now?"

"Can you tell The Pearl?"

"Okay." Greg closed his eyes, waited for inspiration, and then began extemporizing on the basic structure of an ancient text, a favorite of his, the Hymn of the Pearl. Greg's became poetic and animated as he entered the story world.

> Once upon a time there was a beautiful princess named Princess Tara. Princess Tara lived with her parents, the King and Queen, in a beautiful castle in the far away land of Persia. It was a beautiful land with gardens, flowers, and birds. Princess Tara loved to walk in the garden every day and see the flowers.
>
> One morning, her parents, the King and Queen, told her they were going to send her on a special journey to a land called Egypt. "We want you to go there and fetch *a very special pearl* and bring it back with you," they told her.
>
> The next morning as the sun was rising, Tara and her friends packed their suitcases and some yummy snacks. They climbed onto their camels, and they left for Egypt, waving goodbye to the King and Queen. They rode their camels all day across the desert. Finally, when it was getting dark, Princess Tara and her friends arrived in Egypt.
>
> When they arrived in the city in the land of Egypt, Princess Tara and her friends were fascinated by the many new and strange things they saw. They wandered through the market place and looked at all the booths with colorful clothes and beautiful jewels. Everything was new and exciting. They found wonderful, tasty foods, and they ate everything they wanted. They heard enchanting music and they danced, and they danced, and they

danced.

This went on for days. Tara and her friends explored *all* the marvels of this new land. But after many days, Princess Tara's Mom and Dad, the King and Queen, became concerned. Princess Tara hadn't returned home yet with the pearl. They could see through the eyes of their hearts that Princess Tara was getting distracted. She forgot that she was a Princess. She forgot why she was sent to Egypt. She forgot all about getting the pearl. "We must remind her," the Queen said to the King.

Princess Tara's father, the King, wrote a note to her. He tied the note to the foot of a dove. Then the King went to a window of the palace and sent the dove away through the window to find Princess Tara in Egypt. The dove flew up and away into the sky, and it flew all day toward Egypt. When the sky was getting dark, the dove crossed into the land of Egypt. Soon the dove saw Princess Tara from way up in the sky, and it flew down to her with the note written by the King.

At once, Princess Tara saw the dove. Then she saw the note tied to its foot. She knew at once that the dove was sent by her father, the King, from her very own palace. "It must have been sent for me," she said. So Princess Tara untied the note and read it. The note said,

> My precious daughter Tara, remember that you are a Princess from a Royal Palace in the land of Persia. Your father and mother, the King and Queen, have sent you on a journey to Egypt with one task—to *find your precious pearl* and bring it back home. Please remember, now, to get your pearl and come home.

Princess Tara suddenly remembered everything. She remembered where she came from, and how she was sent to Egypt to get her very own precious pearl, and where she must bring it. She realized that she had become distracted on her journey. So she went immediately to tell her friends about her task. They all said to her, "Oh no, then you must face a dragon that guards the pearl....That will be scary!" Princess Tara thought about the dragon. Now the task felt scary to her. But Princess Tara had courage, and she decided she would face the dragon in order to get her pearl.

Princess Tara walked around town that night, asking everyone she saw if they knew where to find the dragon's cave. Many people were afraid of the dragon and would not speak to her.

Finally when Princess Tara was at the edge of town, she walked up to the last house and she asked an old woman there. And the old woman knew about the dragon. The old woman knew because she had visited the dragon's cave once before, and she had found her very own pearl. The old woman invited Princess Tara into her house for a cup of tea, and she told her all about the ways of the dragon and how to fetch a pearl.

Princess Tara then set off on a lonely road out to the desert, all alone. Finally, she arrived at the dragon's cave in the dark. As she approached the cave on the dusty path, Princess Tara could smell the dragon's fiery breath and she felt scared. She stopped behind a big rock and looked around it into the dragon's cave.

The dragon sat in the opening of the cave, guarding the pearl inside. Princess Tara wondered how she would get past the dragon. She decided she would have to wait until the dragon fell asleep. As she waited there behind the big rock, she saw the dragon walk around the cave, and then sit down again. The big dragon put its head down on its front legs, just like a dog would do. And she watched the dragon fall asleep. And soon she heard the dragon snoring in loud snorting sounds.

Princess Tara stepped quietly, carefully, out from behind the big rock, and she sneaked into the cave. She walked quietly on her tip toes so she wouldn't wake up the big dragon. She stepped carefully over it's long tail, which lay across the mouth of the cave.

Then Princess Tara walked all the way in, to the back of the cave. She looked around. Where is that pearl? she thought. Then she saw a soft glow lighting up the back walls of the cave. She walked toward the glow. There, on a shelf made of rock, she saw a pearl. How beautiful, she thought as she approached it.

Princess Tara picked up the pearl and held it in her hands. It was the most beautiful thing she had ever seen. "Oh, it is so precious! Here it is. This is my own pearl, my very own pearl!"

After looking at the pearl a long time, Princess Tara turned around and slowly tip-toed out of the cave. At the mouth of the cave, she again stepped carefully over the dragon's long tail. The dragon made a sudden snort and rolled its sleepy head to the side. Princess Tara stopped and held her breath. She didn't make a move. She waited until she heard the dragon snoring again, and then she continued on her way. She walked out of the cave, into the desert that was lit up by the light of the moon.

When Princess Tara reached the dusty path again, she held the pearl tight in her hand and she ran as fast as she could back to the safety of the town. When she finally reached the edge of town, she passed by the house of the old woman who had advised her, and she bowed to the house.

Princess Tara then returned to the Inn where she was staying with her friends. "Wake up," she said, "and let us return home! I have done what I came here to do." Her friends were surprised. It was still the middle of the night. But they got up, packed their bags, and mounted their camels. Then Princess Tara and her friends set out by the light of the moon for the journey back to their home in the land of Persia.

Finally, as the morning sun was dawning, Princess Tara and her friends arrived back home at the Royal Palace. The King and Queen were just sitting down for breakfast, and they welcomed the returning party. Everyone shared in a big breakfast while Princess Tara and her friends told tales of their journey. Privately, Princess Tara showed her precious pearl to her mom and dad, the Queen and King.

"Now that you have found *your very own precious pearl*," her father, the King, said, "your new task is to learn to live with your pearl every day. Now you shall learn what it means to live with a precious, shining pearl, the most beautiful thing in the whole world."

58

At 9:30, Leah knocked at the Lodge door. Tara was already tucked into bed and ready for her next story, with Leah, before sleep.

Leaving Tara with Leah, Greg and Sara walked to the Bath House Cooperative in the Plaza, the public one which they hadn't visited yet. "Wow, we've had a full evening already," Sara said. "This should be relaxing."

They opened the door and walked into the dimly lit, dark-wood-paneled entry way. Sara noticed pictures on the walls. "Look," she said.

Greg looked. They stopped and perused images of Japanese baths, and Greg pointed to small poetic stanzas underneath. Candles threw flickering light across the walls. "Oh, these are gathas," Greg said about the caligraphed poetry.

"Turkish baths," Sara said, moving to the next set of images. "It's a gallery of traditional bath illustrations. Oh, I want to come back and see this."

"Yeah, the lights are dim now," Greg said.

Greg and Sara walked to a desk with an attendant—a woman in her thirties, with a male friend about the same age sitting close by, talking quietly.

"Hi," Sara said, hovering her mobile over a sensor until she heard a confirming beep. "We're Lodge guests. Do we just enter here?"

"Um, sure," the woman said with an instantly charming smile. "Are you familiar with how our bath house works?" She took a few moments to explain bath house etiquette, the respectful atmosphere, and tips on health and wellness. "We're one of the Bayside Village's worker-owned cooperatives," the woman explained, "so collective responsibility for the baths is a really important value."

"Oh, right," Greg said. "I remember reading your charter."

"So you're an owner?" Sara asked.

"Mhmm," the woman said. "Both of us, actually," she said, opening her hand to her friend. "About fifteen of us. I'm Jan, this is Ray."

"How you doin'?" Ray said. Greg nodded.

"That's so interesting," Sara said. "So how does that work? Can anybody join as a worker/owner?"

"Well, if there's an opening," Jan said, "like with any organization. But Ray might actually be looking for someone to do enzyme research. So if you know anyone…"

"Really? Enzymes for hot tubs?" Greg said.

"Well," Ray said, sitting up, "microbes that digest plant material at high temperatures. Not sure if it's going to be a worker/owner position in the co-op or a grant-funded research project. More likely the latter. But yeah, I'm spearheading a project to green the hot tub business using our baths here as a mini lab—an extension of my lab research at the Bridge Institute."

"No kidding?" Greg said. "So you're also a Bridge Institute researcher?"

"Yeah. I don't really put stuff in the tubs here. Don't worry! People don't come out all green and hairy. But I do take samples from our tubs up to my Bridge lab. I'm testing hyperthermophilic microbes to see how efficiently they digest gunk from our tubs."

"Not that you'll see gunk in the baths," Jan said to Greg and Sara with keen business savvy, jabbing Ray gently with an elbow. "Right Ray?"

"Of course," Ray said.

Sara and Greg laughed lightly.

"Maybe we can talk about this another time," Greg said to Sara. He turned to Jan and Ray. "We have a babysitter back at our lodge, so we have just a short time."

"Sure, no, I understand," Jan said. "So, the hot pool is really hot, so just be careful. We keep it at 110°F to 115°F."

"Wow. Okay, thanks," Sara said.

Greg and Sara walked through a doorway to the dimly lit bath area to a bench under an eave partially filled with backpacks, clothes, shoes, and towels. Putting down their towels, undressing, and dropping their clothes on to the bench, they went for the shower near a wall artfully covered with the famous Bridge Tile pattern, turned on the showers, and entered their streams, rinsing hair and body before entering the pool.

The main tub was dimly lit underneath, and steam could be seen gently swirling away from the surface. Inside the pool, people stood in the middle or sat on built-in benches, some whispering, some quiet. The walls of the room opened up to the starry night sky, with tree tops above and bushes inside the pool area waving in the gentle night breeze. The trees were lit with strings of small white lights, and light from dim underwater pool lights shimmered in wave patterns on the trees.

Greg walked naked, dripping and cold to the pool-side railing and stepped slowly down the steps into the warm water, wading toward a built-in pool bench. Sara came presently from the shower, stood fully naked at the steps, and gave Greg a sweet smile.

Sara descended the steps and waded toward Greg. When she reached him, Sara drifted forward into him, put her arms around his neck, embraced him and kissed him on his lips. She hung there, floating, her arms around his neck, feeling the warm water all around her. "Mmmm," she whispered into his ear, "I can melt into your arms." After long moments of an intimate hug, her body against his, he motioned for Sara to turn her back toward him and sit down, which she did. Greg applied his hands gently, firmly, intuitively, and worked his thumbs around the contours of her back muscles, shoulder blades, spine, and thighs. Closing her eyes, Sara sunk into the massage, lowering her head forward so that her chin entered the warm water. Her wet hair draped over her shoulders and spread out like an oriental fan in the water.

After a long massage, Sara turned to Greg and whispered, "Okay, your turn." Greg switched positions with her and leaned in to her firm but gentle massage. Sara's fingers and thumbs worked magic in his neck and shoulders, tense, he thought, from mental exertion in his meetings. Working her way down his spine she massaged his waist and thighs and opened new awareness of his being in the tub.

When she had finished, Greg said, "I want to go into the really hot tub. Want to come?"

"Okay," she said. "Oh." Sara touched Greg's arm and pointed ahead to artfully painted signs reading "Meditation Area – Please Practice Silence." Greg nodded.

Greg and Sara stepped out of the main tub. The night air was cold, now, and their bodies steamed in it. They walked to a small room with a roof. Inside, a candle flickered in a small, artistic candelabra suspended from the ceiling, and votive candles flickered by the tub. The room was filled with heat, and steam rolled off the surface of the water. Greg and Sara stepped slowly down the stairs. The water was shockingly hot. A groan of pain and pleasure went out from Sara's throat. Greg let out a deep, guttural breath as he went down in. When they had gotten down into the tub, and the water was up to their necks, Greg and Sara silently waded around other bathers toward a wall and settled there. It took some moments to adjust, when the scalding heat turned to pleasure.

Greg closed his eyes and went deep inside. The heat enveloped his body and consciousness in a snug, womb-like embrace.

Sara studied the room. In front of the tub was a small altar with flowers, candles, and a central image of two sculpted swans. A fish between the swans, with open mouth, gushed steaming water into the tub. The only sound came from the water pouring in from the fish, and painful gasps of pleasure at the heat as new people entered.

Greg practiced remembrance, with his tongue touching the roof of his mouth, and a word given him by his teacher repeated on his in-breath and out-breath. The tub was a perfect container, and whether his eyes opened slightly to the flickering candle or closed again, the whole scene was felt in a state of oneness.

After several minutes, Sara touched Greg and roused him from contemplation. She pointed to the steps. Greg nodded, consenting. Together they moved forward, around other naked bathers immersed in their own worlds of heat, and ascended to the entry way.

"Let's do the cold pool," Sara whispered when they were out. Greg followed as Sara led the way behind the small building with the hot tub. "Wow, that was 115°F," she whispered on the way around the corner as other bathers passed.

A small enclosed area with a cold pool was filled with flowering bushes, potted plants and flowers. Two women were seated on a bench facing a statue of Durga, the Indian goddess, the Great Mother, and a man walked by, bowing to her. All about her were blossoming flowers, and a candle and incense were lit, the incense rising, filling the air with sweetness.

Sara and Greg stepped into the cold pool, where a man and woman were sitting and two men leaving. Greg let out a gasp—"Aaah!" Sara went in and plunged underneath. Greg went in slowly, trying to get used to the cold. When Sara came up, Greg looked at his timid approach and then plunged in resolutely—up to his shoulders, at least. The two stood there momentarily.

"I have to get out," Greg said. Sara followed, though she could have stayed longer.

At the top, Sara stood briefly before Durga. Greg stood by her quietly observing, feeling heat, still, from the hot tub even after the cold plunge. Bringing her hands together by her breast in prayer position, Sara made a brief bow to the Mother. Greg followed, hands together, with a bow.

The two walked back toward the hot tub. Greg felt a numbing chill from the cold tub deep in his chest, felt goose bumps on his skin. "I want to go back into the hot tub," he said, as they approached the entrance.

"Okay, I'll meet you back there," Sara said, pointing to the main pool.

Greg entered the hut with the very hot tub, descended again into the cauldron of heat. He soaked there in the thick steam, feeling cold and hot at once, regaining a sense of warmth. He stood awhile as the heat penetrated his body.

Greg returned to Sara who was now sitting alone in a small, intimate heart-shaped pool near the main one. It was empty but for Sara. Greg descended the steps slowly and waded in front of her.

"My fingers are shriveling like raisins," Sara whispered, raising her hands out of the water to show Greg in the dim glow of pool light.

Greg smiled, brought his hands to hers, interlaced his fingers with hers. He looked into her eyes, and she returned his intimate gaze. "After the hot tub, I went back to the cold pool again," he whispered. "This time, I stayed in there a minute and then went back to the hot tub."

"How was that for you?"

"I love the really hot tub. The cold one is hard for me."

"The hot one feels too hot for me," Sara whispered, "but I love the decor in there."

"I like the hot one because I feel like I can go deep. I feel I can go into a very deep space." Greg paused and whispered again, "The water is so relaxing. It slows down every wish to do something. I feel reduced to a simple state of being."

"We should do this more often," Sara said. "This is good for you." She touched his nose playfully with her wet forefinger. "It slows down your mind."

Greg smiled. He now lowered his gaze to her neck, her shoulders, her breasts under water, her nipples, her belly, her pubic hair. He let go his fingers and playfully massaged her arms.

"Well, you're affectionate tonight."

Eventually, Greg pulled Sara toward him and massaged her back. After a long time massaging, Sara turned around to him, looked affectionately into his eyes, and said, "Okay, I can move here. Take me where you want, my mystery man."

Greg smiled. He fixed his eyes on hers in a visual embrace, eye to eye. Playful smiles relaxed into something deeper. Greg searched Sara's eyes. Under water, he searched again for her hands, found them, grasped them, interlaced his fingers again with hers. Sara's eyes shone with an unearthly light, as though singing a haunting melody of love and longing and sorrow. What is she thinking? What is this longing in her? His gaze turned to an inquiry, searching her eyes for hints of her soul purpose. He searched his own heart, too.

As if speaking to her aloud, Greg thought words across the bridge of their gaze to her witnessing soul, projected words across the space between them, looking eye to eye, soul to soul. Here we are, together, he thought-transferred. Why have we found each other? What have we to do in our brief years together in this life? Do you hear me? Now and then her gaze darted from his left eye to his right, and back. Then she would blink. Can you read my eyes, hear my thoughts? Greg could feel his heart strangely warm, felt sensations he seldom felt there. Bigger, grander than romance. Bigger than awe at the beauty of nature. Bigger than daily meditation—his own, at least. Greg faintly felt as if he looked into Sara, into her soul, and reached beauty so sublime, reached the very Goddess herself, including Sara in her being but infinitely larger.

Sara saw the man she loved and married, and more. Do I know you from somewhere? she thought. Here is this feeling again, like an ancient memory, like a veil pulled away. Her heart fluttered, her breath all but stopped. Very profound, this stillness. I see you. You see me. You see right into me. I know you, and yet more. What is this knowing, now, greater and greater the longer we gaze? I belong to you. I have waited a long time for you.

Sara's defenses came up. Doubt tainted her beholding. Do you accept me fully as I am? What if you really saw me? You see me now, I see myself now, and am I okay? Sara shuddered. A veil came over the bright, intimate, warm, tender feeling of the heart that was too loud and raw and primal to sustain, for the moment. She could feel the veil coming, feel the loss of intimacy. And she wished not to lose it. She tried to stay present This eye contact. We haven't looked like this in a long time. Have we ever done this before, this much, this long? This is more than before. Stay, my heart. You can bear it. She opened her heart, returned open presence to her gaze, rejoined Greg.

"I can hardly bear the feeling," Greg whispered. He blinked and returned his fleeting gaze into Sara's eyes, struggling to sustain eye contact.

Have I caused this, Sara thought? I contracted, then he did. "Me too," Sara admitted. Bear it, my heart. She redoubled her effort and felt the brightness returning. Stay with me, my beloved. I'll do my best to stay with you. I want to see you, Sara thought. I want you to see me. I want you to go down into your heart and melt with me.

Greg kept eye contact. It's hard for me to stay in the heart, he thought. But I want to and need to. His ordinary thought forms were so trivial, he felt, so far away like muffled echoes. Her eyes, his eyes, windows, portals to their souls, or one soul, something so palpable, filling, expanding, almost too much to bear.

"It feels like soul love," Greg said. Something between them was precious, ancient. The soul gazing was powerful, magical, like true witnessing, deep affirmation. Something was clearly moving in her, he thought, and in him.

"Do you remember what you wrote in our wedding ceremony?" Sara asked. "From the Gospel of Thomas, or something."

"Yeah." Greg shifted now to his intellect, but gently, oh so gently, to keep that tender feeling. "Gospel of Thomas 2:22. I used to know it by heart. I might have forgotten it." Greg paused, broke eye contact, looked up to the strings of tiny white lights in the canopy of braches above the pools. He remembered, looked back to her eyes, then recited while keeping eye contact:

> *Jesus said to them,*
> *"When you make the two one,*
> *and when you make*
> *the inside like the outside*
> *and the outside like the inside,*
> *and the above like the below,*
> *and when you make the male and the female*
> *one and the same,*
> *so that the male not be male*
> *nor the female female…*
> *then you will enter the kingdom."*

Greg breathed in deeply, and out.

"It's amazing you remember that," Sara said.

"I memorized the entire Gospel long ago."

"I remember."

"Why did that come to you now?" he asked.

"That's the bridal chamber language."

Greg nodded, confirmed. "Heiros gamos." He always brought in other terms, he observed—Greek, Latin. Trivial habit.

"It's like we have this container right now," Sara said. "It feels uncanny, like something is unfolding." She gently squeezed Greg's fingers, interlaced with hers under water. It reminded Greg they were standing there in warm water in the heart pool.

"I've had this feeling recently," Greg said, "like we're playing a role in the unfolding of each other's souls. But it feels more intimate now than we've experienced before."

Sara nodded, and it felt to Greg that she knew this, too. They waited a long time, gazed more, talked lightly, and then, feeling the time and remembering Tara, they released fingers, stepped out of the heart pool.

Returning to the bench with their clothes, they dried off and dressed again in the day's clothes. They didn't have all night. Tara was waiting at the Lodge, after all. Tomorrow was another full day.

In the lobby, a plaque caught Sara's attention as they walked by. She stopped for a moment. Greg stopped. She read it. Then, turning back and continuing with Greg, she said, "It's about the worker-owned co-op."

"Mmm."

Greg and Sara left the Bath House Cooperative in the Plaza, walked in the crisp and fragrant night air back toward the Lodge.

"Wow, everything feels alive and fresh," Greg said. Something from that soul-gazing experience stayed with him, like the tenderest flower not to be crushed by ordinary talk, by the mind, by worldly cares. He lightly hummed a kirtan from earlier at Path of Ananda. "Devi, Devi, oh my Devi."

Greg found Sara's hand in the dark. They held hands like young lovers, walking back to the Lodge.

Sara noticed the night watch from Village Security, a woman and man together, on a mindful walk down the path toward them, passing with clear, shining eyes of presence and a bow, and away. It reminded Sara of one of the eleven principles of their path, to watch every step attentively.

Sara waved her mobile before the door knob, opened the door to their guest room. Leah had a single light on by the round table where Greg usually sat with his computer and books. She had her Bible opened on her lap and looked up from it when Greg and Sara entered. Then she stood, put it down on the table with a leather bookmark in its gold-tipped pages."

"Hi," Sara whispered, walking to Leah. "How was she?"

"Good. She woke up again. I told her a Bible story. She asked for you a few times, and I said you were in the pool."

"She went to sleep easily?" Sara asked.

"After the story. I sang her a song gently and then she went off to sleep."

"Good. Well, thanks for watching her for us. Here's some babysitting money."

"Thank you," Leah said, taking it and putting it in her pocket.

"Thanks," Greg echoed. "It was good for us to have some time alone together as a couple without some formal activity."

"Okay, well, I'll probably see you tomorrow," Leah said, a little awkwardly, not knowing how to relate to Greg and Sara.

"Have a good evening," Greg said.

Sara walked Leah to the door. "Good night," she said. Sara closed the door gently behind her.

Greg went to the table and rearranged his stack of books, which Leah had moved. He restacked them into his familiar pyramid, with the largest on bottom and the smallest on top, each exactly in the middle of the one below it.

Sara watched this little ritual again tonight, but now with amusement and incredulity. Casually, romantically, she sauntered up close to Greg, stood before him, inside the bubble of his personal space, looked him in the eyes expectantly. With her left hand she playfully pushed his book pile off center, out of its careful alignment with the table.

Greg looked at her ironically, saw her playful grin. He broke into a quiet laugh. Sara laughed too. "You're a very observant woman," he said in a voice mirroring her romantic glances.

"Why don't you just come and align yourself with me," she said, tugging on his shirt. And they cuddled in bed with light caresses and sublime gazes, making a meditation of their intimacy.

Day 5: Thursday

59

Greg arose early for Qigong practice, dressed in the loose-fitting clothes he had packed. Sara lay sleeping on her stomach. Greg leaned over the bed and kissed her right shoulder blade, exposed in the tussle of covers. Sara stirred enough to say a sleepy goodbye. Closing the guest room door quietly behind him, Greg walked briskly across campus in the morning fog to Village Security.

Stepping inside the training room, Greg saw a man he guessed was Master Chao Pi Ch'en standing in front, with his white cloth zhi fu outfit. Chao Pi Ch'en stood before a wall covered by a large mirror from which he could see the whole studio behind him. A few people were spaced throughout the room, engaged in warm-up practices.

Greg removed his shoes and placed them in a rack inside the door. Turning, he noticed to his right a large poster with aphorisms calligraphed in black brush-strokes. The room faded from his awareness as he stood, contemplating.

1. Practice in peaceful times; be ready for crisis
2. Keep equipment primed; in crisis it is ready
3. Be attentive always; distracted minds miss the way
4. Put aside self-interest; make service your aim
5. Forget the heroic; embrace the mundane
6. Think without thinking; act in this moment

7.   Restore harmony; leave no traces

Greg approached a middle-aged man by a desk who looked like he worked for the studio, wearing a dojo uniform, handling some business. "Where are those taken from?" he asked, pointing to the wall.

"From right here," the man said plainly, no expression. He shuffled some forms.

"From right here?"

The man looked up. "We wrote them, we teach them. They're a guide in remembering teachings from the manuals. And we use them in training outside organizations." The man bent down to the desk, signed some papers.

"Hmm." Greg reread the aphorisms, imagined what kind of training. Qigong or something else? Must be a martial art. Then he turned, found a spot on the mat and began stretching, watching people beside him for warm-up cues. Still groggy, he reached into unfamiliar Qigong positions, felt his body in new ways.

Master Chao Pi Ch'en touched the screen of his mobile. Classical Chinese Qigong music played around the room, instantly elevating the space with beautiful sounds. He turned to face the room, stood a long moment, a stoic expression on his face, attention concentrated inwardly. Then he spoke. "To begin Qigong practice," he said in a firm but resonant, accented voice, "we take the basic standing posture, Wu chi." Chao Pi Ch'en moved into position, demonstrating the pose with archetypal solidity. Greg took the pose in the best way he could, watching the teacher keenly for hints of how to stand.

"In Wu Chi, the first meditation is to find your posture." Chao Pi Ch'en spoke in unhurried words. "This is not mechanical moving. It is study." Greg wobbled. "You study your basic points of posture. Focus your eyes forward and slightly down. Bring your chin in toward your chest. Let your arms hang loosely." Effortlessly Chao Pi Ch'en ran through the practice injunctions, and Greg made clumsy adjustments in his stance. "Drop your shoulders and elbows. Your knees should be loose and unlocked. Your heels shoulder length apart. Keep the breathing through your nose. Your fingers should be lightly and naturally curled."

Greg wobbled again, feeling his morning tiredness before his coffee. He redoubled his effort to stand just right.

"Explore each point of posture," Chao Pi Ch'en said, "like a dialogue between you and each postural point. Ask yourself like this: 'How is it going here, with my eyes? Are they forward and slightly down? Are they soft? How is my chin?' And so on. Eventually, you will discover that your moving mind, your tan tien or energy center below your naval, will find the postures. Then it will be unnecessary to say to yourself where your eyes should be, where your chin should be, and so on. You discover your body's wisdom. It knows how it should flow into each posture. You just do what is necessary in each position. You do it without thinking. This is the way in Qigong." Master Chao Pi Ch'en fell silent a few long moments.

"Wu chi is the basic standing position," he continued. "In Taoism, we say wu chi is the void, the original emptiness, the primal energy. The universe is born from wu chi, from emptiness and void. From Wu Chi comes Tai Chi. This means, before any moving, training begins in wu chi." Greg wobbled again, feeling even more his wish for his usual morning coffee—always his first ritual. Chao Pi Ch'en continued, "In wu chi, we are just right here. No need. No wish. No thought. No movement. Just the void.' There is no yin and no yang. No five elements. No ten thousand things. Just this still, quiet, motionless space."

Master Chao Pi Ch'en returned to silence. Greg admired him standing perfectly still in his zhi fu, in a posture it seemed only a master could find and sustain.

"Next," Chao Pi Ch'en finally said, "after checking each point of posture in wu chi, now visualize yourself 'standing like a tree.'" He was silent for some moments. "Be firm, yet flexible—as a tree is firm and flexible. Wind comes, the tree is firm. Yet it gently sways." Greg's stance was lax, he thought, not firm, definite, solid, and supple like the students around him. "People pass by, the tree is firm yet gently sways. Be firm and flexible, standing like a tree."

Images of Greg's reaction to Mrs. Block yesterday invaded his mind as he tried to stand still, focused, alert. His use of the word fuck came back to his mind. Where had his presence gone yesterday? He had become gross, dense, reactive. He could have used this Qigong training with her, he thought—firm and flexible like a tree.

Chao Pi Ch'en was silent again for a long minute. Then, "In standing like a tree, draw up Qi, or energy, from the earth. Imagine the potent energy, or Qi, rising up through the wells of your feet and up your legs to your tan tien, the energy center just below your naval. Collect energy rising up from the earth and hold it in your tan tien."

Greg stood still and firm, or tried to. His attention sharpened. So many things to see. The slightest shift forward on the toes, or back on the heels. The slightest movements of the left hand or the pelvis. The slightest modulations of breathing—too hard on the out breath, or forgetting to breath, or breathing too much from the mind or will, instead of letting the breath flow naturally in and out.

Chao Pi Ch'en just stood and looked forward, his words flowing out of a timeless abyss. "When we use this image, standing like a tree," he said, "study yourself—does it help you stand still?" He stood silently. "Images are a powerful part of Qigong practice. You take the image in mind and you study what happens." Chao Pi Ch'en waited.

With all these preliminaries simply focused on standing, Greg thought, what will movement be like?

"Now picture yourself as a hibernating dragon." Chao Pi Ch'en's voice was deep and firm with intention. Greg imagined himself a dragon, hibernating. "Your energy rests now in stillness—as the potential of a hibernating dragon before it wakes. But it is there, resting in you. Picture the dragon. You are the dragon, resting." Chao Pi Ch'en took long pauses. Greg felt only the hibernating. "Standing still, you feel your great power— the full power of a dragon. When your muscles tremble or twitch, this is your dragon power." Chao Pi Ch'en was silent, with a stillness more powerful than movement. Greg pictured himself as a dragon, feeling his energy ready and waiting—waiting too long—to spring into action.

"You may think," Chao Pi Ch'en said, "that standing still is doing nothing. But remember—standing still is the practice. Do you see reactions in your standing? Reactions signal that your energy is disordered, not flowing in its natural pathways. What does this say to you?"

Chao Pi Ch'en was silent a few endless minutes, giving practitioners time to discover their reactions. Like impatience to begin Qigong movements, Greg thought as he witnessed it in himself.

"Pay attention in stillness. You will discover many things happening in stillness. The Tao Te Ching says:

> *Standing alone and unchanging,*
> *one can observe every mystery,*
> *present at every moment and ceaselessly continuing—*
> *This is the gateway to indescribable marvels.*

Pay attention. A vast world opens before you in stillness. Cultivate this fine awareness of the subtle, and you will see more. Pay attention to sensations in your body and see how they change in the practice. Watch sensations arise and fall away. Study the tension, stiffness, tightness, and pleasure. Observe it. *Observe every mystery*. This is the gateway to *indescribable marvels*."

For a long time, Chao Pi Ch'en seemed to disappear into a silence as silent as his posture was still. He stood like a potent power source before the class, like radiant light waiting to race across the room from a lamp about to be switched on. Greg admired Ch'en's command over his will and body. To Greg it seemed Chao Pi Ch'en must know these indescribable marvels, as if calling a band of travelers in the wilderness from far ahead on the trail.

"Now," Chao Pi Ch'en said, "the hibernating dragon awakes. Now we move."

After practice, Greg walked slowly to Master Chao Pi Ch'en at the front. "Excuse me," he said. Chao Pi Ch'en turned around like the earth rotating half way in a split second, and the impression flashed in Greg's mind of an exceedingly powerful man.

"I'm Greg Cobb from the University of Washington." Greg now felt pedestrian before him. "I called you a few weeks ago and we spoke about your Taoist Yoga meeting tonight."

"Yes, I remember," Chao Pi Ch'en said, his eyes like oncoming headlights that made Greg circumspect about not wasting his words.

"I just wanted to introduce myself in person, and thank you for meeting with me. I'll bring my wife and daughter. And if my daughter makes too much noise, my wife can bring her out."

"Yes, this is good. You want to study Taoist alchemy?"

Greg felt like a beginner. "I'm working with Roger Barnes at the Bridge Institute on AlignIt—so I wanted to understand what you've done so far in AlignIt. I'm helping Roger on the next step in AlignIt's development, which is building an ontology."

"Yes. It's good that you come to Qigong practice. Now I see how you stand." Chao Pi Ch'en's eyes flashed a limitless gaze that reduced Greg to nothing. "You will understand more this way. Otherwise it is just ideas—but not living in you, not from your practice, not tai chi coming from wu chi. In Qigong, we stand in wu chi. From wu chi, we move in tai chi, that is, in Taoist ontology—the ten thousand things. In this way you learn the teaching. Then your work on AlignIt will be in accord with the Tao."

Greg hadn't expected this. Has the work begun now? "Good," he said nervously. He felt things stirring in him, things mysteriously beyond his grasp. "Well, I look forward to the meeting tonight." He felt his words were shallow.

"Yes. Good to see you in practice today."

Greg left the martial arts dojo at Village Security and headed to the Dining Commons. He replayed the impressions registered there. Chao Pi Ch'en's eyes, the impact of that glance in his own being. The utter silence of the master, and the noise in his own yearning but distracted mind. The solid stance of Chao Pi Ch'en, and his own trembling stance. Chao Pi Ch'en's words burned in Greg: 'Now I see how you stand.' How do I stand? he wondered.

60

After breakfast and taking Tara to the Bayside Village Daycare, Greg and Sara went on a walk behind the Day Care to the Bayside Village

Gardens and the Animal Farm.

"So do you have any more thoughts on your big dream?" Greg asked.

"Which one?"

"The new apartment—yesterday."

"Oh. Not yet. Geez, our days are so full! I guess I am thinking about how much a dream is guidance, and how much it shows a wish, or a potential..."

"Or a conscious anticipation?" Greg interjected.

"In a dream? Aren't they supposed to be unconscious contents?"

"According to Jung they can also reflect a conscious attitude or a conscious anticipation."

"Really?"

"Yeah, that nuance is often forgotten."

"Well, I don't know. I'm just thinking about how to take dreams in general. When are they guidance? When are they prospective? When do they simply reflect my own wishes, unconscious or conscious?"

"What about this one?"

Sara and Greg found a new path and followed it around the Village.

"On Sunday, when we just arrived," Sara said, "I would have said unconscious, but...the last few days...We've seen so many interesting people....Like, what in the world was Swami-ji getting at in his comments on sex yesterday?"

"I don't know," Greg said. "I was actually surprised you asked about it."

"Why?"

"Because, its not something we've asked teachers we've just met, and it felt rather bold—a little embarrassing to me."

"I'm sorry. I didn't mean to embarrass you."

"It's just that I could work here, and I could work with him."

"I hear you," Sara said. "But also, I could live here, and I could work with him, too."

"So you're feeling this more strongly now?"

"I don't know. It goes back and forth. Anyway, I thought he was saying one thing, and then it seemed he was saying the opposite. I feel left hanging."

"Well, we just met him. He's not our teacher. We're not his students. And he's not advising us."

"How do you know? What if we were? What is he saying?"

"What if we were his students?" Greg laughed and shook his head. "I don't get it. You don't want to be here, and yet you say 'What if we were his students'. Where is that coming from? We have a teacher."

"He doesn't address sexuality."

"So? We're married. We have a sex life. I mean, I like Swami-ji, and I like singing. But what's the need?"

"Well," Sara said more quietly, "we hardly have a sex life."

"Really?" Greg asked. "Why do you say that?"

"Greg, come on…," Sara said, looking at him disappointingly. "I'm always wondering how I can…draw you and thaw you."

"Draw me and thaw me? What's that supposed to mean?"

"You're like, not open or interested. And it's kind of boring. Don't you feel that?"

"I'm open and interested. I'm often pursuing you….You want a Tantric teacher to spice up our sex life?"

"No…Well….I want to feel you're more interested. It's like you're always off somewhere. I feel like I'm always initiating. And its always just ordinary, conventional. It's like you don't show any interest or life or passion."

"Really?" Greg was surprised. He reflected on their history together. Then he looked around. He hoped no one was walking down the path, hoped no one would hear this. No one he was meeting with. "It sounds like this is about me, not a teacher. Like Swami-ji is a proxy for me."

"Maybe. I guess since you're so focused on philosophy and spiritual practice, maybe Tantra could be a way in to your sexual interest. I can't seem to find any other way to it."

"Hmm." Greg took a breath. "I mean, I feel I am interested and I pursue you. But I guess I see what you're getting at. About the degree of my passion."

"I think that's one of my greatest fears of moving here, actually. You go off into philosophy and spiritual practice, and you're not here, not present. You've become a lot more grounded since we came to our path. But…imagine if we move here. All of that groundedness could get unhinged. There are so many big ideas here, and I could totally see you going off."

"I see. Is that what's going on for you in your resistance to Bayside Village? You feel you'd lose me?"

"That's some of it. I don't want to lose you. I feel like you'd get so lost in all this stuff, like you'd have another lover."

Greg looked at Sara tenderly as she spoke. "Mmm. I didn't realize you felt that. Now I get it." Greg paused, looking down the road. "Yet it could also work like last night in the hot tubs. We were so present to each other, beholding each other. That intimacy happened because we're here."

"It could. But we're also on vacation. Everything is new and special right now. This week isn't our daily life. Day to day life here could take you away into ten thousand important meetings and projects."

"It is intoxicating to me now, this week, compared to UW. But then remember that Roger and Jenny talked about sobriety. Theirs is a sober path like ours. And if they're senior students on the path, and they're here…that would be a great reminder."

True, but Sara didn't look satisfied.

"I guess I feel my own unfulfilled sexual interest," Sara said, "and if I can't do something with it, I want to take care of it somehow. I don't know. Maybe we should have an ascetic life. Married life doesn't necessarily mean a sex life. We could be married and ascetic. It's just that it doesn't feel right for me. I mean, do you want an ascetic life? Sometimes it seems that way to me."

"I guess sometimes I can imagine an ascetic life so sex doesn't get in the way," Greg said, "so I don't expend my vital force."

"But you did marry me, and we've been doing spiritual practice since before we met. When we married, asceticism never came up. And our path doesn't require it."

"You know, I don't feel this is about asceticism." Greg said.

"What do you mean?"

"It's also not about you, because I'm deeply attracted to you, and I love you with all my heart. And I feel like I do fully participate in our marriage."

"Yeah, you do, I know. And I'm grateful. Except in bed."

"But then I enjoy it when we have it. And like I said, I do pursue you. Don't you remember when we first arrived here and I waltzed over and kissed your bare back while you were getting dressed? And in the Art Studio I caressed your neck when your hair was tied up? And it was really romantic last night in the hot tub—I thought so, anyway."

"I know. I guess, it feels like you don't fully participate in bed or put your whole self into it."

"Okay, I do hold back sometimes," Greg said. "I'm not sure why. I'm willing to explore that." He walked silently some moments. "I don't know why I hold back. It could be a growing edge for me, so I see it's something I should explore."

"Okay."

Greg looked at his mobile for the time.

"I know you have to go," Sara said.

"Yeah. But I hear you. I'm willing to explore that."

"Okay."

61

Greg walked to the Dining Commons, entered through the screen door. He went to the tea bar, fixed himself a steaming Darjeeling, and turned around. He looked for Marty Blumstein, a Jewish Kabbalistic adept.

He scanned the Commons and spotted a middle-aged man with curly black hair, graying on the sides. He was reading alone. Greg walked up to the table.

"Marty?"

The man looked up. "Yes. Greg?"

"Yeah."

Marty stood up and the men shook hands. "Good to meet you," Marty said. "Is this a good place," he asked, pointing to a seat.

"Sure." Greg took the seat. "Thanks for meeting here."

Marty sat down again. "No problem. It gives me an opportunity to get out of San Francisco and visit a few friends. I don't get over here to the East Bay often enough these days. But Roger's a good friend, and I've been fascinated by his project for several years."

The men broke the ice discussing their backgrounds.

"So tell me again, now," Greg said, adjusting his chair, "you're a psychotherapist?"

"Yep. That's my official training, in Jungian and transpersonal orientations. I see clients in my private practice most of the week, supervise interns on Fridays, and then I offer weekend workshops."

"And you weave Kabala into your private practice and workshops?"

Marty nodded.

"And how do you integrate Kabala?"

"Ah," Marty said. "The Kabala provides a framework for theory and practice. I take an East-West integral approach to bringing together Kabbalistic resources with my Jungian analytical theory and practice. For instance, I work a lot with stories, especially in workshops. Are you familiar with Jung?"

"Somewhat," Greg said.

"He talks about stories and folktales. So I'll take stories about the Bel Shem Tov in the Hassidic Jewish tradition, or stories of Rabbi Nachman of Bratslav, one of my favorites. And I use the stories to amplify themes in human development. And then I do dream work. Jung, of course, has a whole approach to dreamwork."

"So as I said, our Sufi path also works with dreams." Greg picked up his tea cup. "From a Jungian point of view."

"Right, right," Marty said. "And the Jews historically did a lot with dreams—like Joseph."

Greg nodded, smiled. "And we have Joseph in common. There's a little Sufi classic, Yusuf and Zulaikah."

"I've heard of it, actually. Haven't read it. So we have the Kabbalistic book, the Zohar, which has a lot to say about dreams. I use little gems of wisdom here and there gathered from readings in Kabbalah, mainly the Zohar. In a nutshell, that's how I integrate Kabbalah into my practice."

Stories, dreams, little gems. I don't know if that helps. I know you're doing that philosophy structure thing with Roger…"

Greg smiled, put down his cup. "Ontology."

"Ontology, right. So I don't really know a lot about that. And you mentioned the Sefer Yetzira?"

"Right," Greg said.

"Yeah. Of course I work with it. But I'm more of a heart-centered guy, and the Sefer Yetzira is really terse, mathematical, and enigmatic. But what I do know about it could interest you. I teach meditation on the Hebrew letters and other Jewish meditation practices and working with symbols. But that mathematical thing, that's another area." Marty stopped himself. "Well…" He looked into the distance, thought to himself. "Maybe I can introduce you to a Rabbi who's into that. Meditating on the Hebrew letters is as close as I get to it."

"Fair enough," Greg said. "Who's the Rabbi?"

"Oh, Rabbi Geller. He lives in Jerusalem, and he comes to the Bay Area now and then. He's steeped in the traditions, and he's like a walking encyclopedia of esoteric Judaica. But he's also a spiritual advisor. I mean, he's one of those people who you can just tell that he's got it. When the Rabbi comes, he meets informally with a bunch of us Jungian folks, and a few colleagues of a Freudian bent, and he systematically unfolds the Kabbalah. He actually gets into the Sefer Yetzira. That's why I mention him. He talks about the Hebrew alphabet letters being like the elements of creation. He knows the kinds of things you and Roger would be interested in—like how to use the Hebrew letters in mathematical practices like gematria, or how to use the word initials in the practice of notarikon, or the permutation of Hebrew letters like temurah. Do you know those practices?"

"I've read a little, but I haven't seen examples."

"Yeah, see? That's outside my reach. I do some of them. But I'd defer to someone like Rabbi Geller for those sacred sciences, you know, using the Hebrew alphabet. He's way beyond me. Now, the Rabbi doesn't really apply it to psychology or clinical practice. And I couldn't tell you if he knows about ontology. So in my case, we put on a follow-up seminar after the Rabbi leaves where we work through the implications of his teaching and try to port it over to our psychotherapy practice. He's kind of eccentric, but you can just tell he's got the teaching. This guy's the real thing—or the closest I've come to the real thing. I could probably invite you next time he's in town—I'd have to ask him, and tell him what you're doing."

"That would be fine," Greg said. "You could forward to him the summary of my research interests—the one I sent you. Even just to get a better taste of Kabbalah would be good for me. What would help is if you could ask him if I could interview him as a subject expert. As I wrote to you, I'm interested in more than just delineating and executing operations. I also want to get a feeling sense of each tradition we're drawing on in AlignIt. Otherwise, AlignIt is just a web-based tool mechanically matching qualities and running operations."

"Yeah, you want to go deeper. I don't know how much you can do with a web service. But I do know Roger has real integrity and I expect he'll keep it all at a high level. And then he gets good people like you who approach it from the inside as well as the outside. But I know from my own work that it's one thing to spout mystical ideas—and a lot of people want to claim knowledge of Kabbalah, whether they're Jewish, Christian, Hermetic, Pagan, New Age, or God only knows what else. Kabbalah has a lot of mystique. But you know, Kabbalah's been around a long time. And it's another thing to be steeped in prayer and meditation, in study of Torah and Talmud, in the stories and symbols, and—you may laugh, but even in the traditions and high holy days."

"No, I don't laugh."

"Well, you know? It all makes up a part of the tradition. And there's something that makes the Rabbi, eccentric though he is, different from other people who just want to add the Kabbalah to their bag of tricks. So I see someone like him, and I hold a healthy respect for the man. And hopefully some of what I get from working with him carries over into my clinical work."

62

After the meeting with Marty, Greg walked vigorously to the garden by the Plaza. He checked his mobile for the time. Slowing to a saunter, he turned to enter under the arbor into a garden pavilion. There he walked around raised garden beds, walls with pockets filled with soil and plants, and planter bricks with lips for soil and plants—all arranged in elegant patterns. Not seeing Sheikh Chadlee, the gardener, yet, Greg stopped to investigate a pocket wall, searching for an internal watering system. He moved on to walls made of planter bricks, wondering how water was fed to their lips.

"We can't plant in the ground yet," a voice behind him said. Greg turned to a man dressed in a colorful robe and green turban.

"Sheikh Chadlee," Greg said, stepping forward and stretching out his hand. "Thanks for meeting today."

"It's my pleasure," Chadlee said, shaking hands. His face was tender and timeless, his posture unassuming yet mysteriously commanding.

He looked of Arab or North African origin. Good English, slightly accented.

"What do you think of them?" Chadlee waved his hand to the pocket walls and planter bricks.

"My first impression is of their beauty. I think of landscape art. But these are beds and walls."

"Beauty and pattern are very important—they hold something for the people who pass by. But they're functional, too." Chadlee shifted his posture. Greg pivoted slightly toward him. "As I say, we cannot plant in the ground yet. Too contaminated, still, from industrial waste."

"This is from the chemical dumping, before the Bayside Village?"

"Yes, we're remediating the soil. In the mean time, we create these raised beds with liners underneath. We build the pocket walls and lay planter bricks with these lips. Now, this way, we keep the compost-rich garden soil from the toxic chemicals in the ground. Even now, while we're transforming the ground soil, we can still create a rich ecology here. At least we can grow a little edible food for our Dining Commons."

"Really? The garden supplies the Dining Commons?"

"A little." Chadlee walked around the pocket walls and Greg followed. "But for now we are mostly recreating a rich, local ecology, bringing back butterflies, bugs, and birds. And the contaminated land here is a learning lab."

"A learning lab."

"You could say we study transformation." The sheikh emphasized the word. "We study bugs, microbes, and plants. It's a social responsibility and a love for the earth. But our goal is to open a full kitchen garden here in five years, provided the soil gets healthy."

"So your work with plants is your…what, your inner and outer study?" Greg asked.

Chadlee nodded with glowing eyes, hinting a smile. "Yes. Inner, too. You see that."

Greg nodded. "What's that like?"

"I care for these lovely beings," Chadlee said, waving his hand to plants around the semi-circle enclave with a table, to which he now moved. "For me, this is like having children. It's a long investment. And you have to stick with it. You know this with your students, yes? A freshman comes to you and boldly proclaims he wants to study philosophy. And mid-semester, what does he do? He is already looking for another major. Just like that, a lot of people come to me and they want to work with gardening. They want to do it for a summer or a semester. And I never see them again. This work with plants and with soil is long work. It takes dedication."

Greg nodded, looked again to the gardens. "Plants as lovely beings, as children."

"Yes."

"It's too bad the land here is polluted. You can't grow on it."

"We offer grants for remediation," Chadlee said. "This partially overlaps my work, but it's mainly the work of a faculty colleague, Joe Graham, in microremediation."

"Oh, I've seen those little plots of land roped off."

"Yes. Hopefully it looks artful enough. There is a whole world of mushrooms under those brown tarps." Chadlee walked to a tarp at the edge of the garden and Greg followed. He bent down, held his colorful robe back with one hand, unfastened one end of the tarp, pulled it back. There, Greg saw a host of mushrooms in the moist ground. "Their job is to suck toxins out of the soil."

"These aren't your gardening clothes, I take it."

"No." He looked back with a laugh. "These are my meeting clothes, my teaching clothes. I'm telling a story to the school children."

"Ah." Greg bent down, looked closely. "Look at all the bugs and centipedes and worms."

"There's a whole ecosystem right there." Chadlee stood up, then Greg. "We're investigating how to put this little operation into small kits packed with local mushroom varieties for different bioregions. If we can get this figured out on our own land, we increase our property value here so we can do more with the land. This is our demonstration. Then we can license the intellectual property rights in the kit design to a company or nonprofit, maybe start one up here in the Research Park, and bring revenue back to the Bridge Institute. If kits are available, then other people can develop their own land as well."

"That's ingenious," Greg said. "And you have a role in that, too?"

"A small one, yes. The trouble is, there isn't much motivation for this R&D in our society. There is no market for it. Remediation is driven by regulation, which isn't very efficient. So R&D doesn't lead to revenue-generating activity."

"But you're researching it. What's your secret?"

"Our market is home owners and small businesses. Remediation on a smaller scale. People care about the land they live on and work on, at a scale where they can act. We have a system for identifying mushrooms suitable for different bioregions. We can scale it up to industrial scale eventually. But we're starting with concerned citizens and cheap and local materials. This is part of an overall solution that can be coupled with air and water purification."

"Hmm," Greg said. "And what's your role in this work?"

"I'm the gardener. And the botanist. Graham is the mycologist. And we're working with teams in business and law, and with the Academy of

Elders, to find optimal modeling of small scale kits."

Chadlee bent down. Holding his colorful robe back again, he pulled the tarp back to its former position, clipped it into place, careful not to dirty himself.

"I must say, the juxtaposition of your robes and your work with the earth is striking."

Chadlee stood up, looked at Greg knowingly. "Solitude in the crowd, my friend." He turned, walked to a flowering arbor with chairs underneath.

Greg knew that aphorism. He was surprised to share it in common with someone wearing robes and turbin, as for him, it also meant being with the people, in the same outer activity, not standing apart outwardly. Like, When in Rome, do as the Romans do. Of course, it meant more to him than that; it meant outwardly with the people, inwardly with God. It must have layers upon layers of meaning. He turned, walked beside Chadlee, who sat down in the shade.

"I have gardening clothes," Chadlee said. He looked to Greg when he sat down. "These are teaching clothes. Now, let's come to the Abjad system, which you asked about." He adjusted his robe and then looked to Greg beside him with radiant eyes. "So you know the Abjad system of Arabic letters?"

"I know it in passing, but I don't really know it."

"This is part of my work with Roger. This is what you wanted to hear, no? I am training him in the Abjad system, consulting on its employment in AlignIt. It is one of the baseline structures undergirding the knowledge AlignIt holds. There is probably a better way to say it, but I am a sheikh, not a software guru."

"Sure. So the Abjad system," Greg said, "is…a system of correspondences between Arabic letters and numbers."

"Yes, this is true. It is a science of numbers and letters. And it is more. There are other systems of letter-number correspondence. Like Hebrew— most people in the West know of that. The Hebrew alphabet has 22 letters, like the Aramaic, Phoenician, and Canaanite alphabets. The Arabic system has 28 letters—which means it has additional number correspondences, additional possibilities. And it is important to understand why, what it gives us, why use it this way." Chadlee let that question sit like a gestalt in the open space of their conversation. "The words we use in Arabic to disclose certain inner teachings have more meaning than the simple way they are stated."

"To disclose teachings? I was thinking of it mainly as a system of qualities."

"Yes, but a system of qualities for what purpose? For people to study themselves and study the universe. For instance, you know the word heart."

"Yes."

"In Arabic we say Qalb. Qalb has a trilateral root, QLB. The word for heart, QaLB, comes from this root. But so do other words come from the root QLB, which have a relationship to heart. These can be easily found in a dictionary. But it is important to know, from the standpoint of inner teaching, that there are these word groups. The connections between the words in a word group play an important role in conveying teachings."

"Okay," Greg said, following along the unfolding of a science new to him.

"For instance, QaLaB means to turn a thing upside-down. On a path of transformation, can you imagine how this may be related to the heart, or to one's life overall? QaLaB also means to extract the marrow of a palm tree. The word marrow concerns the essence of a thing. Can you see the similarity to heart?"

Greg nodded, impressed, listening attentively.

"Not only that, but palm has a range of esoteric meanings. QaLaB also means becoming red—an image of transformation on the path. The heart becoming red. The fruit of a date palm becoming red—or ripening. Ripening is maturation, you see? This is why alchemists used the term red elixir, because the reddening is the transmutation into gold and the philosopher's stone."

"Interesting," Greg said in wonder. "So this has connections with alchemy."

"There are many connections, when you go under the surface to the structure of it." Chadlee paused in response to Greg's point, then continued. "AQLaB means to be baked on one side, like bread, which again means transformation on the path, like turning dough into bread. TaqaLLaB means being restless, like someone tossing and turning in sleep. In the path of transformation, we say this is like the sleeping person, which is ordinary humanity or people not on the path—feeling a certain dull anxiety, uneasiness and uncertainty about life. Do you see what I mean? We say ordinary people are asleep. And to feel drawn to a path—this comes from the yearning in us to wake from the sleep of our ordinary consciousness."

Greg nodded affirmatively. "Yes, to wake up from the sleep of ordinary existence to...the clear light of reality."

"Okay, yes. That is Buddhist, maybe, but okay. Then QaLB means the reverse, inverse, wrong side. In the great work of awakening from our sleep, we relate this to the ordinary mind, or you could say lower thinking. You could also call it automatic thinking, habitual thinking. A certain wakefulness, attentiveness, and sensitivity are missing in the thinking. QaLB also means the heart, the mind, the soul. It means intimate thought. It also means the marrow, the pith, the best part of something. For instance, in Arabic, we use the term qalb el-muqaddas, the sacred heart—the best part of us, the part that participates in divine essence. So with all of these permutations, you can see there is a wide range of meanings of just this one trilateral root, QLB. Like this, we introduce words associated with groups of root letters. This helps a student contemplate a range of concepts and practices."

"Wow, this is very impressive," Greg said, exulting. "I can see that the Arabic language is very flexible. I did, actually, have a sense of this—how Arabic could unfold like this, almost like geometric patterns in Islamic architecture."

Sheikh Chadlee smiled, nodded. "Yes, this is true. You could say it is like geometric patterns."

"But I don't know it myself, and I wouldn't know how to encode or decode it."

"The language has pattern—this is what people miss, especially in the West where there is no deep structure under the surface of languages. Western people forget entirely that language has pattern—everyone has tried to break up language and say that it is a pitiful, surface thing only that has no meaningfulness in itself, even that there is no meaning in the cosmos anywhere."

"In contemporary linguistics," Greg said, "there's the idea that words are only so many signifiers attached arbitrarily to signifieds. Just signs pointing to things by human convention. This is what intrigues me about Sanskrit, Hebrew, Arabic, and other natural languages—the letters are like basic building blocks of reality, and all their relations are laws of reality. "

"Yes. Now," Chadlee said, "let me just give you a taste of numbers." Greg sat back in the bench, listening. "What about the numbers? Each letter has a numerical value. If we add up Q, L, and B, we get the number 132. This is equal to the root M, H, M, M, D, which is the name Mohammed—the essence of Mohammed. Do you see how these ideas are linked, not by superficial associations, not by mere human convention as you say, but by their deep structures? Thirty-two plus one hundred, Q, make up one third of the total of divinity, the ninety-nine names of Allah."

"Wow! This is most impressive." Greg's eyes were bright, intense, as he sat forward again, looking at Chadlee, affirming his intuition but realizing he had little else to build on. "I had a sense of this but didn't know how it worked. So…" Greg paused, trying to think of the implications, and looking off into the garden beyond Chadlee, "…what does this mean in terms of AlignIt? What are you trying to do?"

"Roger is trying to do," Chadlee said with a tilt of his head to the right side, and a tender smile. "I keep the garden." He was silent for a moment. The words couldn't settle in Greg who sought for some further connection, some larger purpose. Then Chadlee picked up the thread. "I just water the flowers. Roger expounds the science."

"The letters, numbers, and words," Greg confirmed.

Chadlee nodded. "When you know how, these numbers and letters can be computated, combined and recombined in many ways, to discover new meanings. Roger is interested in this—the discovery of new possibilities. The Abjad system provides a mathematical pathway to this discovery."

62

After lunch with Sara and Tara at the Dining Hall, Greg walked toward Roger's office in Avicenna Hall. On his way, he passed the Art Center with its craftsman yet postmodern architectural style, imagined what Sara might do there if they moved to the Village. He walked across the Bridge Institute quadrangle with the early afternoon sunlight splashing down and students all about, talking, studying, playing ball. Greg walked up to Avicenna Hall, in through the front door, up the steps to the second floor. It was just a minute longer when Roger came, waved his mobile before the door and opened it, with the lights going on. The two men sat talking, waiting for Neil. This would be their third and final consulting meeting before the board meeting. They waited some minutes before Neil texted Roger to say he wouldn't be coming; he had a schedule conflict with a call on one of his federal grants.

At this change in plans, the men went out from Avicenna Hall, walked behind a new academic building under construction, back to the gardens and the Bayside Village Animal Farm. They walked along a path studded with tall eucalyptus trees planted in an earlier era. Their sweet fragrance filled the air as they walked.

"Neil's a funny guy," Greg said. "I guess I'm still working on some of his points from the last few days." He left space, walking on. "He's very sharp, and he doggedly pursues a point of view. He's helpful in sharpening dull blades. But he gets attached to views." Greg reflected. "On the other hand, he does concede a point when he sees it doesn't hold."

"It was valuable to have these discussions," Roger said. "He has brought an acid doubt, skepticism, and criticism. But I find that his acid helps me separate the course from the fine. So I'm happy to have these conversations with him. Up to a point. Then it begins to consume time we don't have."

Greg sighed, looked ahead on the path. "It's a curious thing that he's come here and spends his time and energy with us." Greg paused, reflecting. "This way of talking does have its limits. I guess AlignIt is big enough to hold his view of things, too."

"Ultimately I think we can't go very far with Neil on account of limitations he puts in the way. But I'm glad to have him here for this short period."

Greg laughed to himself in a moment of self-reflection, a moment of truth. He looked to Roger as he walked. "When I first met Neil, I felt intimidated. I felt he was some big wig academic, some mighty giant. He's tenured, he's successful, he's an information guru and well respected in his field—everything I seek. Whereas I'm just getting established." Roger nodded. "My experience here the first few days was colored by my imagination of what Neil must be thinking. Is this a robust enough place academically, is it respectable enough to a big mainstream academic like Neil, what does he think about this technology or that one?"

"Interesting," Roger said. "That really concerned you."

"Yeah. I'm on a tenure track. I'm still getting established. These things matter to me."

"Neil works from another assumptive world."

"You know," Greg said, "I do understand Neil's world. It's my world too, to some degree. But it's my world by necessity—it's what I have to contend with by being in my position."

"I see what you're saying."

"But something has changed over the week," Greg said. "I can see Neil's limitations, even if he is respected and well-established. But I've also met a lot of bright people here. I can see how I fit here. I think I've been answering many of my own questions about the Bridge Institute through these meetings."

Roger turned to Greg. "So, I noticed when we last spoke with Neil that you're using the term 'we' when you're talking about AlignIt. And you just talked about Neil joining us."

"Hmm," Greg said, reflecting. "That's right, I am speaking like that."

"Despite your proposal," Roger said, "I can see your larger vision for AlignIt. It keeps growing as we meet."

"Mmm. It does. It can't help but come out, I guess." Greg mused, looking now to the Marsh on their right as they came around a turn in the path. "What you're creating here is of much greater interest to me on a deep level. Your creation of AlignIt is a daring venture. And I feel aligned with your venture." Greg paused, thought. "Aligned with AlignIt." He snickered at the pun.

Roger smiled briefly in response. "You're already joining the team, on some level."

"Yeah, I guess. At the very least, it's clear that you and I are working more or less from a similar world of ideas. And I do feel an affinity with you and AlignIt, and the Bridge Institute overall."

"Well, I'm glad to hear it, of course," Roger said. He walked some steps and turned his head toward Greg. "So how is it going for you and Sara?"

"We're taking about it very seriously," Greg said. "It's a big question for us."

"How so, if you don't mind my asking?" Roger asked.

"Not at all. So I've worked hard to get to the highly competitive teaching and research position I have now at UW. It's not a great position, I'll admit. But it took me forever to get there. The value in moving here, of course, is that I would get to teach and conduct research in areas close to my heart, areas rarely offered at most universities. The trade off is that I'd lose my progress to date on the tenure track."

"Yes, I can feel what you're saying. And Sara?" Roger inquired.

"Sara wants what's best for me. She'd be willing to come if it felt right for us. She doesn't have any attachment to me teaching in mainstream academia, per se. She just wants what's best. And she wants me to be practical about my career. And she wants a good place for our family. She actually would like to be here more than she lets on, I think."

"I thought so," Roger said. "I can feel it in her. I see it in her eyes."

"She's shielding me from the imposition of her wish, which I think she's feeling more strongly just being here. She could more easily work in either place than I can. The stakes of moving here are higher for me, though, because of what I'd lose in walking away from tenure at UW. So she's kindly holding back so that I can feel for myself."

"Ah," Roger said. "Yes, I can see that, now that you say it. It's very thoughtful of her."

"It's an incredible gift. And you know, we have this conversation about accepting the mundane, ordinary conditions of our lives. This is some of the teachings on our path—not pursuing high minded, idealistic visions, not chasing dreams. Just living an ordinary life. Most of the path unfolds subtly in ways we can't easily see, behind the scenes."

"Well, yes, that's our path, too—sobriety. We aren't taken by intoxication, in mystical states, in ideas, in idealism. Even here at Bayside Village."

"Its tempting to rush into big, exciting projects. I've been encouraged to have my feet on the ground, not go off chasing big projects."

"Well sure," Roger said, "if you have your feet on the ground you can reach further to the stars, so to speak. I know the predicament very well, believe me. I've been beaten down from my spiritual states and visions. I even had them taken away for some ten years, until I became well-anchored in life."

"Really? You?"

Roger nodded.

"Well obviously it helped. Look at all that you've created," Greg said.

"Creating," Roger said, emphasizing the present tense of the word. "And being watched, no doubt, to see how I do. It's a work in progress, an experiment, a test, like the Bayside Village itself. But you'll have to feel in your heart if coming here is right for you. Mundane conditions are instrumental, not an end. One purpose is to stabilize the person so the higher reach of the heart, imagination, and intellect don't cause instability. Then, of course, our potential, our capacities, are often introverted by this path as we're ground down and learn that we're nothing: I am not some great person who can see this, imagine that, create this, get recognized for that. I am not the doer. But then amazing things get done."

"Yes," Greg said with a sigh. "That's where I've been for several years—in that grinding down phase. Sara too."

"Okay, so there are lessons to learn there," Roger said. "I can't say for you. Often the path gives us wide scope for individual discretion. But being ground down is a stage, and we should be as free and unattached to contracting phases as we become to the exciting, enthralling, intoxicating states and stages. We don't stop at anything."

"Right, okay."

"There are contracting and expanding stages, you know? And there are times to let go and move on—from either contracting or expanding phases. Ultimately we come out of contraction. Ultimately, we're here to be in service. We're here to live what we are, to live our destiny. And this is an opportunity for service."

"Well said." Greg felt that Roger had articulated his nascent, unspoken feelings, his sense of the opportunity before him. As though Roger could see many steps farther down Greg's path than he could see himself.

Roger turned his head to Greg and smiled warmly and knowingly. He then looked humbly down to his feet as he walked, watching his steps, then ahead on the path. "Consult your heart, Greg. I know what you can see and do. If you can work here without attachment to your knowledge, experiences and states, this could be a place for the right work of your true self. You'll be a great complement to the Institute. And we need what you can do."

63

Sara found the Bridge Institute's Development office on the second floor of the Administration Building on the Bridge Institute quad. She stopped in the hallway, drew a deep breath. She felt primed and ready for her interview with Karen, wherever it would lead. The receptionist conducted Sara into Karen's office and left. Sara stepped in, bumped her purse on the door frame. "Hi Karen."

Karen looked up from her desk. "Hi Sara. We'll actually meet in the conference room next door. Let me just get my things." Karen wrapped up her project. In quick glances, Sara examined Karen's artful office, organized to a tee as one would expect for someone in a public, visible role. Large, framed art pieces hung on the walls. Karen stood up and reached for her mobile, and then picked up a folder as she walked by the door. "Let's meet over here," she said, gesturing for Sara to enter the room next door.

"Thanks," Sara said as she entered. The meeting room had large windows on one wall looking out above the Bridge Institute quadrangle to the other buildings, the temple, the auditorium, the atrium. A credenza against the wall adjoining Karen's office featured displays of the Village's visual vocabulary, which caught Sara's eye. The other walls sported large photographs of the Bayside Village at various stages of construction up to its present state—views fit for a development director entertaining prospective donors.

Karen walked to the small conference table. "How has your week been so far?" she asked, pulling out a chair.

"Oh," Sara said, turning around to the table and pulling out a chair, "Its a tour de force. We've seen so much!" Sara sat down when Karen did. "My husband Greg calls it a daring venture."

"Good. Yes, it's quite a place, isn't it? We're not so large in terms of campus size, or the number of students, employees or businesses here. But if you look at it from the number of programs and the breadth of disciplines, we have quite a robust program. And Greg is getting around with his interviews?"

"Yeah, his days are packed this week. It's more than faculty interviews in philosophy. He's also meeting with companies, like AlignIt, GameIt, and PlanIt. And then we're making the rounds together to meet people—not just on the Village tour itself, but also Community Housing, the Village Day Care..."

"I guess it is a tour de force."

"We're covering the bases, just in case."

"And how about you? You've had almost a week. Have you seen our brochures and other collateral?"

"Yeah," Sara said. "Since we met Sunday, I've gotten hold of everything I could find. I've also sketched a few themes and logos—just playing."

"Oh really? Like what?"

"Well, I noticed that the California Clapper Rail was like a mascot for the Village, so I drew a few Clapper Rail logo ideas. And the Plaza gate is a theme, so I played with that, too. Actually, I brought my sketch book—can

I show you?"

"Sure. Let's see it."

Sara reached into her side bag, rustled around, and fetched her sketchbook. Opening it, a few brochures and pictures tumbled onto the table. Sara scooped them up, returned them to her side bag. Then she turned to a page filled with Clapper Rail images and set it before Karen. "So, here are some images. And again, it's just playing, without the benefit of any directives or specs."

"Sure, I understand," Karen said, surveying the work, and turning journal pages. "And I have a few documents I can give you for specs," she said, looking up to Sara momentarily and putting her hand on the folder she had put down on the table. "A strategic communications plan, some survey findings. But um..." Karen returned her eyes to the sketch book and fell silent a moment. "Oh, these are nice," she said, stopping before images of the California Clapper Rail. "You're good with pencil."

"Thanks. That was yesterday on the boardwalk with my daughter, Tara."

"I'm not an artist myself," Karen said. "I actually got into communication through journalism, and I've just overseen the hiring of artists under contract. And now I'm doing development, too. Too many hats."

"Mmm," Sara said, as she watched Karen flipping backward, now, to retrace the pages she had seen. Then Karen flipped forward again.

"And these are images of the Plaza gate," Sara said, naming the obvious to fill the empty space and appear active in the interview.

"Nice," Karen said.

"I've also done some studies of your earlier promotional materials, from the opening ceremonies forward."

"Really?" Surprised, Karen raised her head, her eyebrows.

"That's a few pages ahead."

Karen flipped forward. There, she saw versions of posters hanging in the Atrium, and variations Sara conceived. Flipping further ahead, she saw versions of early brochures and web designs, and Sara's variations. Karen nodded her head as she looked, turned pages, studied, turned again. "Nice," she said. "You've done quite a thorough study. You did all this since we met Sunday?"

"Yes," Sara said.

"Impressive." Karen turned the next page and stopped. Her brow furled, head cocked forward, eyes concentrated. She stayed there a moment. "We never used this one. Where did you find it?"

"In the Vault."

"The Vault?"

"In the Administration building."

"What's the Vault?"

"It's a storage room of old Bayside Village documents, posters, surplus furniture…"

"Really? How did you find that?"

"On the Orientation tour Monday, when we passed through the Atrium, I asked Randy Seton if there were any more posters like those hanging there. He said yes, in the archives. I asked where the archives were. He said in the Vault in the Administration building. So I came here the next day. When I asked the man downstairs for the Vault, he said it's just a storage room. There's no public access. So I called Randy and begged him to take me there. And later that day, we met and went in and rummaged around for the promotional posters I was looking for. We studied them for an hour or so."

"You're kidding!" Karen's eyes widened. She looked surprised, dumbfounded, unsure what to say. She shook her head, opened her hand, as if about to say something. But for a moment she was speechless. "That's quite some initiative! I didn't even know such a room existed. I thought I had all the extant originals." She stopped again, searching for words. "The fact that you found such a room, went there, and studied these materials…I'm very impressed by that story!"

Sara nodded her head. "There are a few more."

Karen looked down, turned the page. More familiar pieces. "Nice renditions." Then another drawing of an image that was not used for the opening ceremonies. Then a surprise. "Is this your own design?"

"No, that's from the Vault, too."

"Really?" Karen said. "I've never seen this one." Karen studied it closely. "It's not one I commissioned….Hmm." She looked up. "I thought I'd seen everything." She took a deep breath. "You've done quite some research!"

Karen closed the sketch book and handed it back to Sara. "We haven't even begun yet! Wow."

Sara smiled. She put the book back into her bag.

Karen now wasn't sure where to begin. How to digest this experience of Sara? What questions did this already answer?

Sara put her bag back on the floor.

"So," Karen said, "we've only retained artists under contract. And the result is that we haven't had a unified visual identity. The situation now is that we have some new funding in our communications budget to retain someone full time. And I actually want to hand off the artistic direction to someone. My objective is to hire someone capable of not just doing one-off jobs, but creating and managing the Village's visual identity and ensuring that our visual communications consistently follow a well-articulated strategy. So, I've seen your work online—and now this, too." Karen pointed to Sara's side bag. "I don't have any questions about your artistic abilities, which are really amazing."

"Oh, thank you," Sara said.

"So, thanks for shooting me your resume." Karen pulled it out, ran through some questions about Sara's past positions. "So tell me about managing larger strategic projects like a visual communications plan."

"Sure. This is a big part of working in a firm. We don't just do one-off pieces. We have accounts with companies, and we work with the company's communication strategy, or we develop one with the company, which is actually more fun. So beyond simply receiving specs, we also recommend and develop corporate communications strategies. So it's not just fulfilling a one-time job request. We look at the big picture, the long-term relationship, the organization, or the product as a whole."

"Can you give me an example of how you've managed a project involving strategy?"

Sara passionately related several high profile projects with her favorite clients, describing the market sector, audience psychographics, visual communications problems, media of choice, communications strategy, and resulting pieces. Sara was animated, and the conversation flowed richly. The women struck a compelling resonance.

"As you may guess," Karen said, "we're looking for at least a little experience in a nonprofit like Bayside Village or an academic institution like the Bridge Institute. So tell me about your experience with the Seattle Alternative Arts Guild."

Sara hesitated, fiddled with a pen she forgot she held in her hand. How did Karen find that, she wondered. It wasn't in the portfolio. "Uh, that was a little bit of pro bono work."

"And what was that like?"

Sara was unexpectedly tongue-tied. Her mouth suddenly felt dry, as if she needed to swallow but couldn't. "Well, its probably one of the few jobs that didn't turn out so well." That's something one doesn't say in an interview, Sara thought. Now out of her mouth, she worked to justify it. "It was early in my career. And it was a small nonprofit. It took awhile to complete the project, and they didn't use the designs."

"Do you have a sense of what didn't go well?"

Sara felt exposed, surprisingly unprepared. She recognized in a flash of insight that she hadn't applied for a job in a nonprofit organization—since that one experience. "Yeah," she said, thinking fast. "I wasn't focused enough on the needs of the organization. And the Guild didn't have a clear plan. It was a small organization, you know—and I worked with just one man. A young man. And I was young. Anyway, I've since learned to capture an organization's mission, strategy, and market in a communications plan, and I pick my clients carefully."

Sara recovered quickly. But a feeling remained of coming unzipped.

Karen picked up on the recovery, not sure what unsettled Sara. "Not every project works, of course. And I'm sure much depends on the choice of client."

64

Greg walked briskly up the path from the Animal Farm, where he had walked with Roger, to the Bayside Village Research Park for his in-depth meeting with Jeff Baker, Founder and CEO of GameIt, a member of the AlignIt Commons. He gripped his backpack tightly over his right shoulder, taking big strides. He saw the Bayside Village Tram, with its complex mathematical designs and images of local wildlife, rolling blithely by on its almost hidden track, carrying passengers. Approaching the two-story professional office buildings making up the Research Park on the Bridge Institute campus, Greg found the door marked 'GameIt' and entered. Jeff leaned over a large drafting table working with a younger man and woman.

Seeing Greg at the door, Jeff stood up, erect. "Greg. Come on in." Greg approached. "This is Melanie and Phil, two of our animators."

"How do you do?" Greg said, shaking hands.

"We're looking over a near final game world design," Jeff said, "for a module in our soon-to-be released Mastery Series. You saw some of it Monday night at the game reception." Melanie and Phil stood beside the table quietly as Jeff led the conversation.

Greg raised his eyebrows, nodded, and looked visibly impressed as he surveyed the table. "So this is where it all comes together."

"This is where worlds come into being," Jeff said. "So guys," Jeff said, turning back from Greg, "let's finish up the desert section and we'll run a quality check tomorrow morning."

Melanie and Phil nodded. "Will do," Melanie said.

Returning to Greg and walking away from the review monitor, Jeff waved his hand forward. "Let's meet in our conference room."

Jeff and Greg walked into a small but well-appointed, high tech conference room.

"Impressive facility," Greg said, entering.

"Cool, huh? The walls double as projective screens and white boards. And we have 3D projectors positioned around the room." Jeff pointed to ceiling-mounted units. "We have surround-sound speakers positioned around the room as well. And over there is our rack of head gear, gloves, slippers and body suits, just behind the door, all with wearable sensors."

"Huh," Greg said, nodding, his eyes wide as he curiously surveyed the room. "So I get to test-drive a game?"

"That what's I thought we'd do." Jeff sat down. "But let's chat first, then go immersive."

Greg sat too, putting his backpack on the floor. "Sure."

"So, you've been here now—what, three days?"

"Four."

"Four." Jeff leaned back in a black leather swivel chair. "And what do you think so far of our weird and wonderful experiment?"

"Most impressive," Greg said, echoing Jeff's relaxed posture. "I think I'm chiefly impressed by the absence of any apparent bifurcation here between the metaphysical and the technological. Many alternative, counter-cultural experiments are split between the two. You know—being communitarian somehow gets associated with separatism and neo-Luddite resistance to technology. Maybe its true often enough. But so far, I find a mature philosophical balance here."

"Yeah, I suppose," Jeff said, his eye lids thinning as he looked thoughtfully at Greg, contemplating this point. "You said that Monday night. I'm in it every day, so I sometimes forget. But yeah, I guess that integration is a more explicit part of the Bayside Village mission. The Village tends to encourage discourse, projects, and events born of that explicit integration of...what did you say—the metaphysical and the technological."

"Right," Greg said. "So that must make a very nice development environment for GameIt, which brings together the sacred with the technical."

"Yeah," Jeff said. "I think it helps us raise gaming to a higher pitch. And we're fortunate that sacred science games have caught on at the Bayside Village. Not only is it nice to have great entertainment value for social bonding. It's also nice to have people in this environment of rigorous inquiry take it seriously as a training tool. We use the games as training tools. You probably saw the security training games at Bayside Village Security?"

"Hmm. I don't recall that. We saw a lot Monday. Maybe I missed it. I do remember hearing about it."

"Well, we have ample opportunities to create game test beds for Bayside Village, and integrate gaming into the creation of a new culture here."

"The creation of a new culture," Greg echoed. "I like that. I keep hearing that from different people."

"That's my passion, creating a new culture. And gaming is my vehicle."

"Hmm. Um, you said being here helps you raise gaming to a higher pitch?" Greg asked.

"Well, the Bayside Village is an experimental environment, right? It's not a commercial game shop. It's not exactly a university. It's a different atmosphere for game development. We're not working at entertainment, per se, at least not as an end. Our games have human developmental objectives. We're creating tools for training and development of higher human capacities. And it helps to have an institutional environment like the Bayside Village where people around us keep a rigorous educational and spiritual atmosphere. The user base here, the opportunity to test and deploy prototypes at the Village—it all works together to elevate our game development."

"I see."

65

When Roger returned to Avicenna Hall from his walk with Greg, he walked down the hallway to the office of his colleague, Catherine Stone. He knocked on the open door. Catherine turned her head, white wisps of her long hair falling over papers she was grading. "Hi Rog."

"Hey, Catherine." Roger walked in slowly, took a seat near her desk. "I've come for a consult," he said in a tired, playful voice, leaning back in his chair.

"A consult, eh?" Catherine put her grading pen down on the stack of papers. She turned and gave Roger her full presence. Roger saw the light purple blood veins in her forehead, on her hands.

"Yup. On your complaint about Amelia Blocke."

"Ah. You're having trouble with Greg?"

"Yup." Roger put his right leg over his left. "She hasn't returned his calls, nor mine about him. Greg's been on campus all week, and she hasn't made any time for him. So Greg showed up at her office yesterday, unannounced. He surprised her. She was rude, condescending, and intimidating."

"That's trouble we don't need."

"You lost your recruit. I don't want to lose Greg."

"No, you don't! He's a keeper. For all of us. This behavior needs to stop."

"I dug out your complaint to the academic senate and reread it. Did you find background on her?"

"On her? No. I just documented my experience of her stalling and rude behavior."

"I'm asking because Jeff and I made a surprising discovery. We're also having trouble with the prospective AlignIt Commons board chair, Chris Mueller."

"The guy who's given the big research gift to Bateson?"

"Exactly," Roger said. "So the plot thickens. He may be dealing dishonestly with us about his interests in game companies that overlap Jeff Baker's exclusive game rights in AlignIt. So Jeff and I were doing some further due diligence. We found that Mueller has a few connections to Amelia Blocke, of all people."

"Wow," Catherine said.

"So I need both your hats on this one—faculty colleague and AlignIt Board member."

"Okay."

"We discovered Amelia Blocke's been a recruiter for Mueller's companies." Roger explained the matter in as much detail as he could, going through the search results. "Now Mueller is trying to make inroads to the Bridge Institute, trying to get access to AlignIt by a number of avenues, and he has this older connection with Amelia Block. I don't know if anything is happening between them now. But it's awfully uncanny"

"I would urge you to talk to Steve Bateson about this—sooner rather than later," Catherine said. "Not only is Amelia presenting complications for all of us in hiring. If this connection between them is real, it may be that Mueller's giving us tainted gifts. And of course, if what you're saying is true, Mueller won't help the AlignIt Commons. Having your specific account on record will help with Amelia Blocke at least, and it may unravel more as well."

"Tell me more about the GameIt technology itself," Greg said. "What are you up to here?"

Jeff paused, considering the best angle. Then he sat up and leaned toward the table. "We're building most of our games on the AlignIt platform. Our animations are linked to entities and relations mapped in AlignIt."

"Fascinating!" Greg said. "How does that part work?"

"The user enters a game world and performs game tasks. The tasks and characters prompted by game play activate entities in the GameIt engine. Animated game figures arise in the game world as the outer clothing of a corresponding entity in the GameIt engine."

"Ah, that's beautiful," Greg said, following closely. "So…game worlds and their creatures arise and dance and struggle in a coordinated choreography. And the AlignIt ontology specifies their relations and what transpires when one entity operates on another."

Jeff paused. "That's interesting. I hadn't thought of it that way."

"Or, in the game environment," Greg said, "AlignIt determines what transpires when one character acts on another."

"Yes, you're right. It's funny, I just hadn't thought of it ontologically.

Anyway, It's a very elegant experience when you're in the game play, especially if you can recognize the archetypal correspondences implicit in our game worlds and characters."

"Ah! I understand your concern, now, about migrating to a new ontology," Greg said, working intuitively. "GameIt animations are directly linked to AlignIt entities. That means my work with Roger will directly affect the elegance of your game worlds. A mistake in AlignIt modifications will immediately affect GameIt displays."

"I've had a vague sense of this, but I couldn't articulate it," Jeff said. "Yes, you've hit on it exactly!"

"Which also means if the ontology accurately describes reality, your game worlds may become even more elegant."

"Well, yes," Jeff laughed. "That's a positive way to spin it. That would be an ideal outcome. But my fear lies in the opposite direction. I don't know if I really get ontology, so my fear is that as you go in and mess around with the ontology, while our GameIt figures are tied to Roger's old system, then my game worlds can get pretty messed up."

"Mis-aligned," Greg said.

"Right. You know, when organizations migrate legacy systems to new systems, everything gets messed up."

"Yup, been there," Greg said.

"Yeah. So that's my concern. So I want to make sure I'm part of these migration discussions. If you move here and work with Roger, I think we'll want to work with you, too."

"You want to make sure the games still work, the game figures are still properly matched with entities, and they still invoke the right corresponding relations and actions."

"Exactly. I want to ensure a seamless migration."

"Sure. I hear you. It's a valid concern. I think all members of the AlignIt Commons would have similar concerns, and I think Roger has that in view. So—you know this—we create a test environment first, do the migration, see what happens, and then roll out the new system definitively..."

"I know," Jeff said, with a knowing look. "I know that it can be done successfully. I want to make sure it is done successfully. Because I have a lot of grant money and a lot of angel funding invested in GameIt. A lot of my own money and sweat equity, too. And I really care about bringing this new gaming approach into our culture and collective consciousness. This is my service to recreating our civilization. And I've got to make sure it comes out well."

"Yeah, I understand your concern," Greg said, recognizing Jeff's need for confirmation. "We have methods for introducing ontologies and validating performance. Keep in mind that it's potentially a creative time, too, if you have a mind for it—for making new discoveries. My own approach is that its important to look at it in a larger way than just managing risk. There may be some unexpected blips, and we have methods for this. But the shift to a new ontology is also about enhancing AlignIt, and I think those enhancements will translate to GameIt, especially if you're strategically poised to seize and exploit them. And it may open new technical vistas for the Commons."

"You're an optimist, and I like that," Jeff said. "I am too, and that's my Achilles heel—which is why I'm cautious. Anyway, you get my concern, and you have migration protocols. So how about a demonstration?"

"Alight."

Jeff reached for his mobile. "Do you want GameIt Lite, or do you want to try out the in-depth personalized version? If the latter, you'll have to go through the long interview—which means you'll have to consent to our using your personal information for the game."

"Let's do the in-depth, personalized version."

"And you have an AlignIt Profile account?"

"Yeah."

"Okay," Jeff said, touching the screen of his mobile, pressing on the screen and keyboard projections. "You'll need the keyboard for some of the screen entries, then you can de-project it. Why don't you log in to your profile on this page, click through the acceptance and permissions, and then go through the interview questions," he said, and waved the screen and keyboard projections over to Greg. "I'll get up and do a few things and then come back in fifteen minutes."

"Okay," Greg said, adjusting the screen and keyboard projections before him.

Jeff got up, pushed in his chair, and left the room. Greg logged in to his AlignIt Profile and ran through a battery of proprietary GameIt personality, cognitive, and learning inventories. In the process, Greg articulated his typological make up, anima images, sex and gender issues, spiritual preferences, meaningful mythic and religious images, and obstacles on the path.

In fifteen minutes, Jeff opened the door and returned. Greg was finishing up the final questions. On his way to the table, Jeff quietly picked up some gear for Greg—gloves, slippers, a vest, a helmet—and then sat down.

"Alright, finished," Greg reported. "That was intense already! I hadn't thought of my life in those ways before. I didn't expect this, but I'm a little unsure, now, about what GameIt will do with all of that collected information."

"Okay." Jeff waved the mobile peripheral projections back in front of him. "Well, give us your best feedback, and we'll have an interesting discussion. Why don't you put this on," he said, handing Greg the gear. "All the gear is outfitted with flexible sensors, of course, to track your movements, pulse, blood pressure, brain waves, eye movements…You know the drill."

"Okay." Greg suited up.

"First, let's run a little introductory demo, and then we'll fire up one of the games."

Jeff projected a game console on the table. He touched a button to turn on the room, select options, and set up the game demo. The room lights dimmed. Symphonic music arose and flowed through the room. The ceiling projectors turned on and images were projected ubiquitously throughout the room. Scenes appeared and faded in quick succession— gardens, deserts, mountains, palaces, cities. Planets from star systems rotated above the table. Stunningly beautiful, strong, and grotesque characters paraded around the walls. The displays were vivid, brilliant. Then, in 3-D holographic images, warriors suddenly appeared at the doors—first Roman Centurions, then Japanese Shogun, and on it went, one type of soldier morphing into another. Fabulous beasts appeared, flying, running, swimming above the chairs and across the room. Human figures of all kinds, male and female, donning all manner of costumes, appeared about the room—standing, running, laughing, fighting, loving. Plants shot up from the carpet. Earthquakes appeared to open up the floor, and a tsunami appeared to come at Greg and Jeff from a far wall.

Then the room quieted. A woman's voice spoke, while images shimmered faintly and quieter symphonic music supported her voice.

"Prepare to enter The Egyptian Palace, part of the GameIt Mastery Series, a suite of immersive archetypal training games, with electrifyingly stunning game worlds and figures. GameIt will draw you into challenging episodes where you'll confront the knottiest mysteries of human existence. You will execute fascinating game tasks, follow opportunities, avoid threats, and contend with dangerous seductions. Beware, for you will meet magicians, tricksters, heroes, charlatans, and fabulous beasts. You'll meet engineers, titans of industry, and captains of starships and their crews. You will be helped and tricked, challenged and tested, loved and maybe harmed. Who are your real friends, and who are your foes? Can you discern one from the next? You may run. You may hide. But you cannot run from yourself. They can seduce you, or help you; hurt you or heal you. Just like you deceive yourself, harm yourself, or seek a pathway out of the prison of your deluded life. Turn to confront these figures as projections of your own self, as actors in the dream of your own life. Every move of yours changes their stance, intent, and ability. A wrong move invites harm, but a right move could open the next door. Can you recognize these figures as projections of *your own self?* Discover the key to unlock the mystery of each alluring and frightening figure on your journey. Get ready for the greatest game—the game of your life. When you have resolved each figure and incorporated its power and secret, the game resolves itself. And you arise, O Divine Child, as one who remembers and sees the way clear. Gear up, now. And begin your quest.

The room went dark and quiet.

"Wow!" Greg exclaimed. "That's intense. I like your intro pitch."

"Okay," Jeff said from the dark. "I chose The Egyptian Palace because it's recommended for what you just fed into your profile. But I'm going to explain some preliminary aspects of the game so we can move quickly and give you a taste."

"Okay," Greg said.

Images of the Nile River projected onto the walls. Jeff explained the game scenario. "So, if you're a guy, you go down the Nile river to the Palace to encounter the princess. If you're a woman, you get the prince. Your profile determines this."

"She's nice," Greg said.

"Good. You can actually fine-tune your anima figure in the game world by working more with images of women you're attracted to, inputting images of Sara…if she's a soul mate to you, or if you just want to work with her."

"Images of Sara? Wow." Greg contemplated the possiblities.

"You could get very detailed. And she could allow you to see some or all of her profile. This option isn't released yet."

"Wow," Greg said, unsure where to file that idea. It hadn't occurred to him that he could do this kind of assisted work with her. "She is my soul mate, actually."

"It can get pretty intense for a couple working together on psychological issues. Or soul destiny. That can be intense. A few of us have done it. I'll just put that bug in your ear. Anyway, on your way down the Nile, you hear Arabic langauge. You see signs of Ottoman and Egyptian culture. And here," Jeff pointed to ubiquitous scenery in the room, "you encounter ordeals along the river journey—keyed off of your AlignIt Profile. You get the opportunity to observe how you get distracted by different ordeals."

Jeff fast-forwarded the game play and controlled movements by running his finger along the table where the game console was projected. "At the palace, there's a patio, and a stone bed or bath there in the patio courtyard where you encounter the princess. You see three of her other suiters. You watch these three men and see each one approaching her. You witness the qualities in them involved in meeting the princess. These are displaced parts of you, of course, drawn from your interview process."

"Wow," Greg said, reflecting back on the questions, recalling what he had answered. How much of this would be revealed in the room with Jeff there watching?

"And you have to bring forth new qualities in yourself to win her."

"Okay."

Jeff tapped his finger on the table to change the room projections. "The palace has different levels. We're on the ground floor. As we move through it, we see that the princess takes you into a room in the palace through a door in the courtyard. So she takes you deeper. She takes you into the palace. You move beyond the outer court where you first encountered her.

"She takes you into a black room, a bed chamber, with a large bed in the center in a sunken section of the floor. There are black curtains surrounding the room. Next to the bed there's a three foot luminous golden pyramid sitting on a base."

Greg fell silent, becoming more engaged.

Jeff let the game run at a higher speed for the overview. The princess went to the side of the bed, sat down. A servant girl approached, gathered perfumed oil from a little stand at the bedside, rubed the oils onto the skin of the Princess.

Another door appeared behind the pyramid. It opened to a hidden chamber farther inside the palace.

"So you have choices here," Jeff said. "Do you go into every door you see? Do you enter every opening? Which figures do you follow and which do you avoid? You have to decide which doors, figures, and objects to engage. You can ask the princess about the different rooms, figures and objects. Sometimes she'll answer you plainly, sometimes enigmatically. So let's ask her…." Jeff said, tapping controls projected onto the table. "And, she takes you there."

The princess figure spoke to Greg aloud, telling him about the first room, "That's where I take other men." She took him by the hand and led him to the threshold of the next chamber.

Jeff intervened. "So, you get the idea of how she takes you through the Palace?"

"Yeah," Greg answered, engrossed in the gameworld.

"Okay, I'm going to switch the game control to you, and you run the rest of the game. Like we discussed a few weeks ago, I'll sit quietly without impinging. I'll just witness, and we can reflect at the end." Jeff switched the game controls to Greg. "It's running now from your movements."

Greg fell deep into a personal engagement with The Egyptian Palace, discovering how the game world changed as he moved, pointed, or spoke.

Greg walked slowly and reflectively out of the Research Park, across the Bridge Institute quad, toward the Dining Commons to wait for Sara who would be picking up Tara at the Bayside Village Day Care. Contemplatively, he retraced the game scenarios in his mind, the way the Princess engaged him, the feelings stirred in him. He felt some vague awareness at the edge of his consciousness about the potential of deepening his relation to the feminine, and to Sara.

Coming to the Dining Commons, Greg found a bench and sat for several minutes. Images of the game kept coming back to him. And the prospect of a game with Sara. Imagine a more intimate game with her as game character. Romantic. What scenarios would that bring up? What karmas could be encountered and possibly unwound, if he and Sara were insightful?

66

Finally Sara walked down the path to the Dining Commons with Tara in hand. When Tara saw Greg, she left Sara and came running to him. "Daddy," she said, in a whinny voice, almost breaking into tears. Greg opened his arms and Tara ran into them.

"Hi Tara. What's the matter?" Greg hugged her. Then he looked up and read Sara's eyes, which didn't give a happy report. He looked at her inquisitively. She looked back, frazzled—not wanting to say in front of Tara. Greg surmised some conflict between them. Then he realized there had been no parent-child conflict since they arrived at Bayside Village. That was amazing. But now, Sara simply mouthed the word "Moody" without saying it. Greg nodded.

"How was Day Care?" he asked Tara.

She didn't answer.

"Did you play with Cayce and Susan?" He had heard her say those names through the week.

No answer.

Greg just hugged her. "Why don't we head over to the Community Housing and get some dinner?" Greg suggested, standing up and picking up Tara in his arms. Sara seemed to consent with a nod, though Greg noticed she seemed distant as they set off down the path.

When they walked away from people streaming to the Dining Commons for dinner, Greg asked, "How was your interview with Karen?"

He wanted to hear all about it.

"So so. It was good for the most part." Sara didn't bring much to her answer.

"You okay?" Greg asked quietly, looking at her. Maybe this wasn't the best time to discuss it. But clearly something was bothering Sara.

"Yeah," Sara said, not quite looking back.

She didn't seem okay. She walked quietly. Greg was struck by the juxtaposition of the Egyptian Palace game he had just finished at GameIt, the thought of working deeply on a game with Sara, and the actual experience, now, of Sara. Interesting, he thought to himself. Here is the game of life—I'm in it.

Greg rubbed Tara's back as he held her, making a connection, establishing presence and rapport, soothing her.

"I think we're doing too much," Sara finally said. "I think we need some down time as a family."

"Okay," Greg said. He felt conscientious now about his ambitious schedule so far. "What does that mean? We're meeting with Trish and Josh for dinner at Community Housing right now." Here was their chance at community, Greg thought. This was Greg's big wish. But he sensed it could be too much for Sara right now. She wasn't in the best mood to experience it. He longed for it, and he hoped she would be open enough to gain a good impression. How would she feel it in this mood? "Do you want to reschedule, or just skip it?"

"No, that's fine.

This surprised Greg. "Okay."

"But I feel we need something."

Greg nodded. He waited for Sara to name that something as they walked.

Greg, Sara and Tara walked in silence a long while down a quiet lane with a large open field on one side and marshes on the other until the Bayside Village Community Housing complex came into view. Community Housing lay at the edge of campus, by the north entrance leading to Roger and Jenny's house in the neighborhood beyond the gate. The land out here was close to the wetlands by the Bay—open, wild, uncultivated. Buildings were sparse, except the two octagonal structures of Community Housing, each three stories high, built in Craftsman style, with Berkeley brown shingle siding. The wild grass was high, giving the land a rustic, untouched feeling. Yet approaching the complex, Sara pointed out the subtle but elegant landscaping in native Bay Area plants, the artful walkways and bike storage, and again, the Bridge Tiles on sidewalks and patios.

Nearing the door, Sara piped up. "Can we discuss it later?" It rather surprised Greg, as he had already moved on to other thoughts.

"Sure." Greg heard a new attitude in her voice. A shift, perhaps. Maybe this, whatever it was, would blow over or resolve itself.

They stepped up to the porch of the first building, the main one, and Greg knocked. A youngish man in his thirties, with a ponytail and goatee, opened the door. "Hi, guys. Come on in." The family entered a large foyer opening to a living room. "I'm Josh," he said, welcoming them in warm tones. He was an easy-going, friendly personality. Then Josh called. "Trish? They're here."

Trish came around the corner. "Hi, welcome to Community Housing." She was about Josh's age, had brunette hair midway down her back, looked sharp and practical. The family made introductions. This was the couple that had corresponded with Greg, making arrangements for the community dinner and interview. They seemed decent, responsible, hospitable.

Standing in the foyer and living room a few minutes talking, Josh made introductions to other house guests already gathered and waiting for dinner. Many were student-age, some were older—faculty, researchers, employees at the Village's projects. Some were short-term researchers, visiting fellows, or guests involved in some project or other. Greg noticed a few more women than men, but not many.

Sara noticed the same type of mathematical wall paper, textiles, and tile work used in the interior decoration as was found in the Art Center and the Lodge where they were staying. This was a nice feature, she thought.

"Well, let's take you on a brief tour before dinner," Trish said, "and then we can sit and talk about community." Josh and Trish lead the family around the open sections of main buildings, making introductions as they went around. They toured the living room, play room, study rooms, laundry room, supply room, storage, food pantry, and kitchen, which was busy with dinner preparation by the residents.

The place is neat, Sara noted. Well-organized. Everything has a place. The furniture and décor are decent enough. The place has visual integrity. It wasn't the dorm of crazy freshmen she imagined and feared. Could a family live here? The space was artful enough, quaint, intimate, spacious.

Josh led into a common study room. A few couches, chairs and tables filled the room. Before dinner, only one young woman was still seated there on a stuffy couch near large picture windows looking out to a back yard of high grasses and a Bay view beyond.

Josh then led the group to a side room. Entering, he said, "This is our resource room." The sides were lined with labeled bins. Contents were neat and orderly, Sara noticed. "We have a check-out, check-in system for community resources," he said. "It works kind of like a library. We have an online resource system with check-out features, reservations, repair and maintenance scheduling, requests for early return, clean up, and even booking items for discussion at house meetings. We have a great sense of shared responsibility for our common resources here. Each resident co-owns these resources, and each of us is co-responsible for upkeep and repair."

"Like, one of the things we're reading right now as a community," Trish said, "is the Tenzo Kyokun, or Instructions to the Head Cook. It talks about resources in the kitchen being like the eyes of the community. So how careful would you be if you were handling someone else's eyes? This is how we treat our common resources."

Greg was impressed. This was the kind of life he lived in college and afterwards, in his commune, but not as highly articulated. This was the life he wanted now. And this was better than he imagined.

"We'll show you our apartment here, since we know it's neat," Josh said with a chuckle. "It helps to know when you'll have guests." He lead them up a set of stairs to the second floor, around the octagonal hallway to apartment number 5. Opening the door, he walked in. The apartment was small, but adequate. Small because many spaces were shared in common on the first floor and didn't need to be held privately in individual apartments. Small because storage was in the resource room on the first floor. Small because the residents mainly ate in the Bayside Village Dining Commons, and on Thursdays they ate in the Community Housing community kitchen. Trish explained all this. And it seemed to reassure Sara, Greg imagined. But he feared she would be shocked at the small space.

"And you could have your art studio at the Bayside Village Art Center," Greg said to Sara, out of turn, because the thought flowed naturally from his own machinations about Sara's concerns with communal living. "Remember what Roger was saying last night?" She nodded.

Josh walked the group back downstairs to one last stop before the dining room. He turned right, into the children's play room. Sara noted it was a quaint, warm, space well appointed with toys and crafts. Not the commercial toys you'd find at any mall across the country. But wooden toys requiring the child's imagination. It had well-stocked drawing and painting areas. It had a doll house. The room was spacious enough, well-lit, and had a few adult-sized chairs, too, for adults to sit in and watch or moderate if needed.

"Look Tara," Greg said. "A playroom."

"How many families live here?" Sara asked.

"Four right now," Josh said. "Soon to be five." He placed his hand intimately on Trish's shoulder.

"Oh?" Sara said.

"I'm a month and a half," Trish said.

"How nice," Sara said. "That's one of my concerns. Or interests," Sara said, correcting herself. "If Community Housing is good for family."

"We think so," Josh said. "We're planning on it. It has everything we need, and it's like a big extended family."

Josh slowly walked into the dining room as the couples discussed family and communal living. Trish and Josh approached a table, pulled out chairs and sat down. Greg, Sara and Tara sat on the other side.

Josh picked up a book he had evidently left there before and handed it to Greg and Sara. "This is our Community Handbook," he said.

Greg leafed through it first. "Wow—meals, common space, personal and common property, privacy...you've considered a lot!"

"We started with some common reference points in the handbooks of other communities," Trish said. "But many things grew out of our own unique experience here at Bayside Village."

After Greg browsed, he handed it to Sara, who flipped through it.

A man with an apron walked out of the kitchen and rang a hand bell. Dinner was served. Residents poured into the dining room, fetched plates, and headed to a bar before the kitchen where food was set out in attractive displays. All carried out by residents rotating kitchen jobs, Trish explained as they stood up and moved through the line. As they advanced in the line, Sara scooped vegetables, pasta, and casserole onto a plate which Tara held deftly, giving assurances that she could hold it without spilling it. Greg spotted his favorite mozzarella cheese with basil and tomato.

The couples returned to their table and settled in for the meal. Over food, they shared their backgrounds, talked generally about the campus and housing, and discussed the opportunity for Greg and Sara to move to the Bayside Village. Greg noticed that Sara perked up a bit in talking with others, as if a momentary diversion allowed something in her to rest from whatever disturbed her before dinner. He still felt off balance, since he could not see a particular light in her glances to him, and the glances were fewer than usual. But in her responses to Josh and Trish she had not let the problem bothering her get in the way.

After dinner, Tara noticed other children running to the play room. "Daddy, can I go play?" she asked.

Greg looked at her plate. It was mostly finished. "Is that okay with you?" Greg asked Sara.

"Is it okay with you?" Sara asked Josh and Trish.

"There's other kids in there," Trish said. "So if you kind of keep an eye on her."

"Okay," Greg said. He got up and walked Tara to the play room, introducing her to other children, getting her oriented. "We'll be in the dining room, Tara."

Greg returned to the table and the two couples talked awhile longer about community life. Then Trish turned to Josh. "We've got to go." She turned back to Greg and Sara. "We have our house meeting, as we mentioned earlier."

They exchanged greetings, and Trish and Josh stood up to get their plates. Greg stood up as well, and then Sara, picking up their plates. They walked to the kitchen, cleared scraps and napkins into compost bins, put silverware and plates into tubs of soapy water to soak. Two residents were busy receiving, washing, and chatting with other residents as they passed through.

On the other side of the kitchen, Trish said, "You're welcome to stay as long as you'd like, and Tara can stay with the kids. There's an adult there now. Anyway, it was a pleasure meeting with you over dinner."

"Yeah, and take a look through the Handbook," Josh said. "If you have any questions, just contact us."

Sara tugged Greg's shirt inconspicuously. Greg looked to Sara who motioned with her hands and eyes that she wanted to stay longer. Greg returned confirmation with a nod.

"I think we'll hang out a bit longer here before we go," Greg said. "I really appreciate your taking the time." Everyone shook hands, and Trish and Josh walked to the house meeting in the living room.

67

Greg and Sara got cups of tea at a side table in the dining room, returned to their seats at the table, and sat down. When the last resident had gone into the living room for house meeting and the door was shut, Greg turned to Sara. "What's up?"

"Greg, I think we need some time together as a family tonight."

"The Taoist group meeting is in a half hour, with Master Chao Pi Ch'en. Remember?"

"Greg, another meeting?" Greg was surprised at her protest. He had been willing to discuss this earlier. He had been willing to forgo dinner at Community Housing.

"Do you see the state Tara's in?" Sara said. "She's fussy and impatient. Can't we just have some family time together?"

Not having seen Tara fussy, Greg considered that Sara herself was in an unhappy state.

"We can all go as a family," he said. "I checked this out with Chao Pi Ch'en in advance. It's like the meeting last night with Swami-ji."

"What's the meeting about?" Sara asked.

"Taoist meditation, maybe some teaching with question and answer. Maybe the meeting can help shift something."

"Greg, we've been out every night this week. We need some time together, too—without meetings. We can't just do all meetings."

"Sara, that's why we're here. This is like a professional conference for me. I planned to meet with Chao Pi Ch'en tonight like we met with Swami-ji last night. I could have come here by myself to do meetings back to back. But I wanted to bring the family so we could all check it out."

"But Greg, you have done meetings back to back. Everything is meetings. We haven't done anything together as a family that doesn't involve a meeting of some kind. I mean, you want the family here, but everything is about AlignIt."

"We could have cancelled this community dinner meeting and done the Taoist meeting instead..."

"What?" Sara said in surprise. "This meeting felt more important to me—this is community, possible new friends, possible babysitting."

"Really?" Greg was surprised again. In this mood, she preferred Community Housing, which she seemed to resist in prior days.

"Yeah. These are people we could live with or at least connect with. And look—now Tara is playing with other kids."

"You're feeling that positive about this community, about moving here? Community has always been my wish."

"I don't know. I like the community feeling, the meals together, the child-friendly environment. I think this was actually good, because at least we're relating. But another meeting focused on AlignIt, or someone else's spiritual practice, or more philosophy...I guess I feel tapped out. I feel like we need time together as a family. Can we can just cancel the Taoist meeting and spend family time together tonight?"

Greg sat back, feeling frustrated, letting out a groan of exasperation. "Augh! Of course we need family time. But I didn't feel it was lacking all this time, like you're suggesting. I felt like we've connecting very well up until tonight. And I've already scheduled with Chao Pi Ch'en. He's expecting us tonight." Greg sat thinking for a moment, looking at the floor. Then he looked up. "How about spending time together tomorrow?"

"When? Your schedule tomorrow is booked solid! And you have your big AlignIt board meeting!"

Greg observed that he felt attached to his schedule. He felt himself getting angry and took a deep breath, bringing his attention to his breath in this present moment.

"Can you reschedule with Chao Pi Ch'en?" Sara asked.

"It took a long time to reach him just so I could ask if we could come early tonight."

"Can you try? I feel like you really need to give attention to Tara."

Greg snarled his lips and nose, looking exasperated. He suspected Sara wanted the time, not Tara. But so far, he didn't feel Sara's need deeply enough yet to repeal his schedule for her sake. "What's really bothering you?"

"Greg, just stop and look at this situation. You have meetings, meetings, meetings. What was your plan for me and Tara this week?"

"What? I've included you in everything! Even tonight—I asked Chao Pi Ch'en if we could all come together."

"Greg, we can't just go to everything you're doing. Tara can't just be dragged along to everything. We need some family time, too. Quality family time, with your presence."

"Sara....I just feel like we're here, and this is a special opportunity. It's been hard to coordinate all of this—our work schedules, my teaching schedule, Tara's needs. It's hard to line-up all these meetings...." Greg felt his voice getting louder, more tense. He quieted himself in order not to be heard in the living room or children's room.

Sara became exasperated. "How many special meetings do you need just to make a decision about consulting or moving here?" Her words now carried an emotional undercurrent like they could blast off and take flight. "You've had plenty of special meetings, and you have more scheduled for tomorrow and Saturday morning. But it's evening now. Do you really need to meet with every last person at Bayside Village?" Sara paused a moment to breathe, and her words landed again. "Life has limits. You just can't do everything." Now her careful voice of reason returned and recalled Greg to the needs of the moment, as so often before. "And practically speaking, you don't need to do everything in order to make a decision about consulting. You're not here yet. Work hasn't started yet."

"Okay," Greg said. "Damn."

"Don't say that in front of Tara, please."

"She's in the other room."

"But still."

Greg took another deep breath. He sat back with a sigh, looking at the floor and tried to shift his perspective. "Okay. I guess this is one of those times I can accept limits."

Sara took her cup of tea and cupped it in her hands. Though still lukewarm, it provided little reassuring warmth to her fingers that she now realized were cold. She sat back as she felt Greg slowly, but uneasily, changing his mind.

"You're right." Greg reached for a dry napkin and wiped some drops of tea Sara left on the table, and then sat back, unobtrusively frittering with it in his fingers. "Maybe I've over-booked. I don't know why.... I guess I don't feel good enough if I just do a few meetings. I admit that I do feel the need to do it all. Maybe I'm over-doing it. Like I'm binging on meetings..."

Sara dropped her cup on the floor at that word. It bounced and the remaining tea splashed out. "Shit!" she exclaimed. She reactively scooted her chair back and reached for a napkin to wipe up the tea. Greg reached for a few napkins and joined her on the floor to help mop up her spill. "Lucky this didn't break," she said, popping up to set the cup on the table and going back down again to wipe up. Greg witnessed the two of them wiping up spilled tea together and found it significant, somehow, even emblematic. Wiping up a spill together, on more levels than one. Sometimes his, sometimes hers.

Greg sat up and put his dirty napkins in his empty cup.

Sara sat up, too, wiping up the table in front of her.

Greg sat back in his chair again, breathed deeply and then resumed the discussion. "Are you feeling alright? You've seemed distant since I met up with you before dinner."

Sara stared at her cup, breathed in, hesitated some long moments. "I just feel a little upset by my interview today." A tear came to her eye. "It went well, I think. But it stirred up some things." Her eyes teared up some more. "I guess I just wanted to talk about it."

Greg put his arm on Sara's back and rubbed her shoulders. At his touch, his reassurance, she let out a cry, brought her hand over her eyes. As he suspected, Sara was the issue, and Tara was a screen for seeing it. He sat and thought as he rubbed her back up and down. Saying the word binging touched off something in her, and he realized he probably chose the word unconsciously to constellate something and get it out on the table, or the floor. He reflected, sitting back again. What could arise in the interview to bother her so? He pondered. This warranted taking restorative time together, he thought.

"Okay. I'll call Chao Pi Ch'en to say we're not coming. I'll try to reschedule. And if I can't..." Greg breathed in and out, "well, then I can't, and I'll just accept it and let it go."

Sara wiped her eyes.

68

After retrieving Tara from the play room, Greg, Sara and Tara walked out the front doors of Community Housing onto the porch. "How about a walk by the water?" Greg offered.

"I feel like we've done that a lot this week," Sara said. "Do you mind if we do something else?"

"How about a walk the other way, through the neighborhood where Roger and Jenny live?"

"Mmmm," Sara said hesitantly, unsatisfied. "I guess I can do the boardwalk."

"Daddy, can you carry me?" Tara asked.

"Okay, where's my girl? How about up on my shoulders?"

"Yeah." Tara lifted up her arms.

Greg hoisted her up, seated her, and put his hands on her legs to steady her. "Okay, you have to steer me, alright? Because I forgot how to get to the waterfront."

Tara played at steering Greg's head this way and that, and Greg made occasional wrong turns on purpose which made Tara laugh.

Sara walked along quietly, enthralled in her own world of thoughts, memories, and anxieties.

"If she wants to be carried the whole way," Greg said, "this walk may not last long, anyhow. She's getting rather big for this." Greg walked along without playing for a minute, trying to balance Tara's need with Sara's. Otherwise, Tara would interfere to get more attention.

"So what's going on?" Greg asked. "Do you want to talk?"

"Yeah. Well, I did have a good interview, I think," Sara began. "Karen had seen my work online, as I told you. And I brought some of my sketches in—like logo studies, just playful stuff. And I showed her the sketches I did of the opening ceremony. She liked it. She was surprised, actually. And it seems I can do all the things she needs. I've done all of that for my clients in Seattle. It actually sounds kind of fun." Sara perked up, turning a corner on the path to the waterfront.

"Like what?" Greg asked. "What sounds fun?"

"Well, like they've outsourced everything to vendors so far. And I don't know if you've noticed, but the Village's visual communications and messaging are kind of piece meal. They're not unified. Karen wants to bring it in-house and hire someone to hold the big picture—to canvass interests across the Village, to approach stakeholders, and create a coordinated strategic communications plan for all visual and verbal messages. I think that's exciting. It's never been done here before, which surprises me. But I know how to do that. I do it all day long." Sara seemed to pull out of her funk. "I think it would be fun to do it on this scale—to kick off something like a first-ever communications strategy for a new organization like this."

"So, that sounds good," Greg said. "In fact, it sounds great. It sounds perfect for you."

Sara nodded and continued walking.

"So, what else?" Greg said after a pause. "We're not even talking yet about whether you want to come to the Village or whether you're qualified. It seems you liked the interview, you feel it went well, but...I feel you're withdrawn."

"Daddy, I want to get down."

Greg lifted Tara up and off his shoulders and brought her feet down to the boardwalk. Tara ran ahead toward a favorite spot with stationary binoculars for looking out to the wetlands. "Stay on the boardwalk, okay?"

"Okay," Tara called, running and carefree.

The sun was descending toward the mountains in Marin County, across the Bay. Greg smelled the earthy aroma of Bay air blowing off the mud flats. A cool feeling rolled in from the West, and a bank of fog seemed perched on the mountains across the Bay. Greg inhaled deeply. "Ah, smells wonderful." He could feel Sara's attention was focused inward. "Do you want to sit?"

"No, can we keep walking?" So they walked on silently a few moments.

"Sara, I'm not pushing the Village on you, alright? I can just consult here. I mean, if something is really disturbing you, I don't even need to consult here. But I do really like it here, and…"

"It's not that. It's not the Village. Well, it is. Kind of."

"I'm not following you."

"Karen asked about my experience with nonprofits. I told her I didn't have very much. And she wants to check my references."

"Yeah? That's normal. You have great references."

"But only one nonprofit. And I don't want Karen to call him."

"Oh," Greg said, his face turning circumspect. It was that old bone not easily buried. "Oh yeah."

"I'm sorry. I thought that was over, and here it surfaces again."

"Mmmm," Greg mused. Karmas do follow us, he thought, well aware of his own.

Sara became angry at herself. "If that one damn thing is going to stand in the way…. I mean, if coming here is what you really want to do…"

"Okay," Greg said, "that's done. We've been through a lot together."

Greg noticed Sara was jittery and nervous. Had she binged after so long? He became correspondingly clear-minded to compensate. "But Sara, you're sinking into your emotions and getting kind of shaken up over it. Just try to think about it clearly: a.) we haven't had time yet to discuss moving and changing jobs; b.) I can also consult here—we don't need to move; c.) there are jobs all over the Bay Area for industrial design in the IT sector; d.) we don't even know if this nonprofit thing with him is going to surface; and e.) if it does surface, we don't know that it's going to be a big issue for Karen. There's a lot of room here. This interview with Karen came out of nowhere. I was glad to see you throw yourself into it—just in case. But neither of us expected it."

"But I don't want history to get in the way for us—for you, or me, or us. And I don't want to be running from something," Sara said. "And I'm tired of fearing this is going to come up again some day."

"You've been feeling this over the years?"

"Yeah, I guess."

Greg saw tears in Sara's eyes.

"It feels like my life is serving this up for me to deal with, or else it's my unresolved karma that comes up again when I try to move forward." A few more tears came, and Sara wiped her eyes. Greg put his hand on her shoulder. "I wish I never did that. Why doesn't the path just destroy me and wipe away my karmas?"

"Mmmm. You and me, both," Greg said, acknowledging his own weaknesses. "Well, you know? Maybe this is the action of the path, using life to bring up and resolve things." Sara and Greg were silent a few moments, and Greg felt this point of view was common ground, common language for them. "And maybe it won't become a big deal. Are you thinking he'll give a bad report to Karen this many years later?"

"I don't know. Why wouldn't he?"

"Why would he? It's been a long time. Don't you think he'd want to move on, too? I mean, I don't know him, but…Well, I don't know what I'd do in your shoes."

"I just feel like the path grinds us down, and it never stops."

Tara came back. "Daddy, can you play with me?"

"How about we go back to Community Housing? They said they were taking the kids out to the playground," Greg said.

"Yeah," Tara exclaimed.

"Is that okay with you?" Greg asked Sara.

"Yeah."

Greg and Sara walked back to the playground at Community Housing with Tara running ahead. Somehow, the family-oriented space felt comforting to Sara, at a time when she felt the forces of her past actions pulling against the seams of her family life, which she now felt as comforting against the possible future changes. As they reached the sandy area, Tara ran ahead to the play structure, and soon acclimated herself with other children playing there. Greg and Sara stood back, hovering over the boundary between the grass and the sand in the play area so their conversation wouldn't be overheard by the babysitter.

"I just feel kind of raw right now," Sara said.

Greg guessed she had binged. She hadn't for a long time. The trip here, the interview with Karen, that man in Seattle that Karen could call— these things seemed to have pushed her.

"I guess I wanted time together with you, too."

"With me?" Greg looked surprised.

"Yeah. I feel your attention is out there with other people, and I just want to feel you closer."

Greg stood next to Sara. This he couldn't understand. He had given her so much attention, so much consideration. The issue bothering her now began to stir in him. "It seems you're more often drawn to other men."

Sara gaped in exasperated surprise at the comment. "Can we just not talk about that right now?"

"Yeah, sorry."

Sara chewed on her lower lip. She put her hands in her pockets and fiddled with a barrette in her left one. "I'm doing my best here this week, alright? I've done so many things with you. I even went to an interview I didn't expect to have."

"Okay, sorry. I know….I meant to emphasize that you haven't seemed awfully drawn to me. It often seems to me that I'm more drawn to you. I guess I'm surprised you'd wish to be with me as a comfort."

"Can we just not talk about it now?" Sara asked again with more emphasis.

Greg nodded. He didn't mean to go there again. He stood there awkwardly, watching Tara play, feeling a stranger beside Sara. The moment was open and raw for him, now, too. He wasn't sure why. What to say next, he wondered. What needed to happen to move things forward? His mind searched, examining any hint of the need of the moment.

"Well, you could spice it up," Sara said quietly, not really expecting Greg to take the prompt. "Maybe I should accept that there's just no more flame there, and maybe that time of our life is over now."

"What? No flame there?" Greg said. Sara apparently did want to talk about it, he thought. Or else she couldn't help herself.

"Yeah—your flame burns in other worlds. But not here. It even burns with other people, but not with me."

"With other people? What? Sara, I love you so much, and I often feel afraid that you'll leave me. I just don't see it the way you're saying it. I feel I'm really tuned in to you, and I feel I'm trying to do everything together as a family."

"God, Greg, don't you get it after all these years? You leave me all the time—not for other women, but…for ideas, for projects, for career. Don't you get that something is missing? I know I fucked up, alright? But…"

"Sara, that doesn't bother me anymore. It's long gone."

"But why do you think I feel drawn elsewhere?"

"What do you want from me that I'm not giving?"

"You! Just you! Not ideas, not philosophical conversations, not career treadmill, not meditation and spiritual practice….Just, where is your flame for me? I want some kind of passion in our lives, not just duty and laundry and struggle."

Greg recognized the theme from last night's discussion after Path of Ananda. He looked down and twisted his right foot in the playground sand for no particular reason, and then carved a little ravine in the sand. "I know what you're saying. I feel there's a bigger pattern here, like a dance we're dancing together, but I don't see what it is or how to change it."

"I'm craving for physical attention, and I want that with you, and I feel you're always looking away. And I feel I want to look somewhere else to get it."

"Are you sure you're really looking elsewhere because you don't have me? Are you sure you're not afraid of intimacy? I feel like I'm here and I love you, and maybe that scares you."

"Well, maybe you're scared too, and run away into other pursuits."

Greg paused, thought about this. "Yeah, I see that. I guess I feel anxious about other things—acceptance, the opinions of others, getting established in my career. I guess I also want the path so badly, and I sometimes feel that worldly affections pull me down."

"But Greg, why don't you see me as the path?"

"I do see you as the path. I was really moved yesterday when Swami-ji said 'Good, two eyes looking together in the same direction.'"

"But you were uncomfortable when I asked him questions."

Greg hesitated, raising his eyebrows at the thought.

"Don't you remember years ago when we were just dating? We were making love in my bed, in my apartment—I even remember the sheets I had, with orange and pink stripes…"

"Oh yeah," Greg recalled. How is this getting stirred by being here at Bayside Village?

"And you said in some enraptured state that I am the path and the practice, the altar and the Goddess of the altar. You totally gave yourself to me. We merged into each other. And I remember that we both had an intense orgasm that night. I mean, what happened to that?"

Greg felt transported from the playground, the sand below his feet, and Tara on the playstructure ahead, to those early days. "I was more free then, wasn't I?" Greg broke a light smile at the reminiscence. "I had a more antinomian view, then. Yeah. I don't know. Maybe with family life, and with all the things said to us about duty—everything has become so heavy and grave. But also more stable. Our lives were also pretty rocky then."

Sara nodded.

"I don't know. Maybe the path has changed, too, being in America longer. Or the general cultural attitude has changed. Maybe I also fear losing the path now, or being kicked off the path…I mean, I know that the body ultimately doesn't satisfy. And so many spiritual texts and traditions discourage attention to life in the body. And the individual person doesn't satisfy…"

"So when did you start to care about those things? God, I'm the one with the Catholic history. I feel like I'm reminding you of things you've said to me."

"Well, I have a Protestant history. Some denominations fare no better when it comes to the body. Think of all the fire and damnation preaching and Jonathan Edwards' 'Sinners in the hands of an angry God.'"

"But don't you remember telling me all of that non-dual stuff about how the individual is the point of access to the universal? And the body is a gateway to divine light? And about spiritualizing the material, and materializing the spiritual?"

"Yeah, I do."

"I was so impressed. My God, I thought you were so different from other boyfriends. You seemed to have these parts integrated. Or at least you were striving for it. You opened up my mind and gave me permission to let go into love with you. Where is that for you now? You're a theurgist. But it's like you've forgotten me as your earthly point of access to the divine hierarchies."

"Wow, you're bringing up a lot here," Greg said. The truth of Sara's words came rushing down like a land slide. "You're right. I don't know where that's gone. I need to…"

"Mommy," Tara said, running up to Greg and Sara from the play structure. "I'm hungry."

"Already? Okay, Honey." Switching back to responsible mother in present time, Sara pulled her mobile from her right pocket, checked the time display. "Yep, its time for a snack. Greg, do you want to try something in the Plaza? And then maybe we could head back to the room."

"Yeah, okay. The Plaza it is."

"Daddy, carry me," Tara said again.

"Again? My, you're getting a lot of rides today." Greg lifted her up again. "Are you going to steer me? I don't remember how to get to the Plaza."

"Daddy! Yes you do."

69

Walking into the Bayside Village Plaza, Greg lifted Tara off his shoulders and set her feet down on the walk. Sara noticed a small gathering of people on a far end in a shop she hadn't seen before, where a buzz of conversation filled the Plaza.

"What's that?" Sara asked.

The family sauntered over to explore.

"Wow," Greg said. "It's a tea bar."

"Tea Emporium," Sara said, reading the sign overhead. "Want to check it out?"

"Sure."

Greg, Sara and Tara walked into a warmly lit room painted the color of green tea leaves. Tara wanted to get up again, and Greg picked her up and walked ahead. On the right side, a tea tasting bar ran the length of the room. On the left side small, intimate tables were arranged. An attendant sat behind one, facing a man and woman on the other side. She poured steaming tea from a small cast iron pot into two tiny porcelain cups. Strolling by, Greg overheard the attendant saying, "This one has a grassy flavor. It has good benefits for relaxation and sleep."

"Look at all these teas," Greg said inconspicuously to Sara. Further back along the right wall long shelves held jars of tea rolled into balls. Greg read the labels as he walked by: Pu-her Tea, Red Tea, White Tea, Yellow Tea. Some jars held flower petals and ginseng. Greg read: Chrysanthemum, Jasmine, Lavender, Osmanthus, Red Rose.

"Mmmm, its so aromatic," Sara said.

"Can I help you?" an elder Chinese woman asked, standing in the main aisle.

"Oh, we're just looking," Greg said. "We've been here all week and didn't see this Tea Emporium before."

"Special event tonight—all finished now. We're still open now if you want tea. Usually we're open in mornings and afternoons—usually on weekends and holidays, and for Bayside Village special events. We can also do special event for you."

"We're actually looking for a bedtime snack for our daughter," Sara said. "Do you have snacks?"

"Oh, she look tired. Hello, little girl. You looking for snack?" Tara put her head on Greg's other shoulder. "Heh heh, she's shy. What we have? Uh, like fortune cookie. But too sweet. She like rice cake? We have rice cake. I give you tea."

"Tea would be nice," Greg said. "I can't sleep if I have caffeine, though."

"No, no. We have many kind. You see?" she said, pointing to the walls. "Many kind." The woman turned around and called out in Mandarin to a younger Chinese man who presently came.

"Explain them what we do," the woman said.

The man turned and smiled to Greg, Sara and Tara. "Hi. In the Tea Salon we draw from an ancient Chinese tradition of tea drinking." Greg and Sara noticed his English was impeccable, yet with a hint of accent. "But we've modeled the Emporium after the wine bar, with our complimentary 'Try before you buy' tastings. We have loose leaf teas. We have hand-rolled flowering tea balls. We have flowers and herbs. We also have tea accessories," he said, pointing to a wall—"tea pots and tea sets, made of porcelain, glass, and clay."

"Wow," Sara said. The young man's sales savvy impressed her.

"Do you know about creating an AlignIt profile?" the young man asked, pointing to a promotional chart on the wall.

"Yes, we have profiles," Greg said.

"Good," the young man said. "When you come for a tasting, we help you select teas based on your AlignIt profile. We personalize the flavors and health benefits to meet your constitution, your personal medical information, the time of year, time of day, and global position. Most teas have benefits good for everyone, like increasing your antioxidants and blood circulation, sharpening your mental clarity, and improving your skin tone. Beyond these, we recommend teas to help you study, reduce anxiety, or sleep soundly. Of course, if you just want to come and enjoy a warm and satisfying cup of tea, you are always welcome to come and be with us. Our teas are high quality, and we offer an intimate and comfortable setting to just relax."

"Wow," Sara said. "How did we miss this?"

"Now you know we are here," the young man said. "Here's our price list." The man picked up a colorful promotional brochure, from one of several piles on the counter, up and down the left side of the Tea Emporium. He held it up before them and pointed to different spots. "Here is our regular schedule. We're open now for only a little while, so you are fortunate. But if you want to come back, here are the usual hours. And here we list benefits of different teas, herbs and flowers. You'll find a lot of information here. Okay? Now Mrs. Chong is going to serve you something."

Already? Greg thought. She just left us.

The young man handed the brochure to Sara and escorted the family to an open table where the older woman had laid out a spread of what looked like bean paste cakes and some candies or confections. Three elegant empty cups and one small iron kettle were on the table. The woman carried two more small pots to the table and put them on a shelf behind her on a serving tray. Greg sat Tara down on one stool and then sat beside her, while Sara took the other side.

"I give you each different tea, okay?" the woman said. "This one for little girl. It help with good night sleep, so you wake up happy in morning." She poured from the kettle on the table into Tara's cup and then removed the kettle to the tray behind her, and picked up another kettle.

"This one for mother," the woman said. "It help restore harmony, bring mood into balance." She poured from the second kettle into Sara's cup, and then returned it to the tray behind, and picked up the third kettle.

Bring mood into balance? Sara wondered how Mrs. Chong picked that tea for her. The Emporium seemed special, even fantastic, magical.

"This one for father," the woman said. "It help with calm mental clarity, and boost stamina and sexual function."

What? Greg thought. How did she pick that?

Mrs. Chong poured from the third kettle into Greg's cup, and returned the kettle to the tray behind her. She then picked up an ice cube with chopsticks in a small dish on the tray and turned around, placing it gently into Tara's cup. "Tea is hot. This cool it down for you to drink." The elder woman lay down the chopsticks on the table top and sat squarely and masterfully in the back of the table. "This is bean paste cake. This is fortune cookie—you like fortune cookie? These are candies—licorice, ginger, and ginseng. For little girl, licorice is good. For parents, all three. Try. It good for health."

Sara took a sip of Tara's tea to feel its temperature. "Mmm, that's remarkable," she said unexpectedly, hesitating and looking into the rich brown color of the tea. Then she put it down before Tara. "It's fine now, Honey. Sip it slowly."

Tara picked up the cup and took a sip. Greg and Sara took up their cups and sipped, each expressing amazement at the unfamiliar taste and aroma of the teas chosen for them.

Before they could talk, Mrs. Chong said to Tara, "He tell you story, okay?" An older man, possibly a Mr. Chong, pulled up a chair and sat down at the corner of the table. An incredible human presence. "This story I choose for family," Mrs. Chong said, and the man looked at her. "Tell them Mr. and Mrs. Tea Master Frog."

The elder man smiled, turned slowly, and spoke in a measured way, to Greg and Sara and then to Tara.

"One day, far, far away in a forest, there was a pond." The man spoke poetically, with good English and a noticeable and delightful Chinese accent. "And in that pond there was an island. And on that island, there was a little cottage. And in that cottage, there was a bedroom where two little froggies, Burpy and Grog Frog, were just waking up to start their day. When the first light of the morning sun shone into their bedroom window, Burpy and Grog Frog hopped up out of bed and they jumped around the room, jumping this way and that way, up and down, hippity hop, hippity hop.

"Burpy and Grog Frog hippity hopped out of the bedroom and into the kitchen where Momma Frog and Poppa Frog were sitting at the table and drinking their morning swamp water. Burpy and Grog Frog sat down for their breakfast. And do you know what they ate for breakfast? Why, they ate what all frogs from that pond like to eat—turtle eggs, topped with dried flies and spider legs, just like salt and pepper."

"Ew!" Tara said, scrunching up her nose and laughing, looking to Greg and Sara to see their response.

"Burpy and Grog Frog ate their breakfast, and then they got up and hippity-hopped around the cottage, bouncing here, and bouncing there. 'Okay, Burpy and Grog Frog,' Momma Frog called. 'Don't bounce so high, or you might break something.' But Burpy and Grog Frog had so much fun that they just kept on jumping. They jumped high, and they jumped low. They jumped fast, and they jumped slow. But most of all they liked to jump high and fast. And that is what they did. Until they both jumped at the same time, and in the same direction, and Burpy and Grog Frog bumped their heads into each other and fell down. And that didn't feel very good. In fact, Burpy and Grog Frog got some bumps and some scrapes, and they felt sad, and each of them got a headache.

"'What should we get Burpy and Grog Frog for a headache, Poppa Frog?' asked Momma Frog. Then Momma Frog said, 'I know just the thing we need. We will swim across the pond to the Redwood Forest, and visit Mr. and Mrs. Tea Master Frog.' They are called Tea Master frogs because they knew how to make special teas for everything that happens.

"When Burpy and Grog Frog heard about Mr. and Mrs. Tea Master Frog they felt better already. And do you know why the two little froggies already felt better?" the man asked Tara. "Because every time they visited Mr. and Mrs. Tea Master Frog, they would have good tea—good for playing, and good for hopping. And they always got a cookie and a candy."

"So out they went—Momma and Poppa Frog, and Burpy and Grog Frog. They went hippity-hoppity, hippity-hoppity all the way out the front door to the edge of their little island in the pond. And then they took big, long jumps into the pond. Splash, splash, they went, as they dove into the water. And they swam and they swam under the water to the other side.

"When the frogs got out of the water on the other side, they shook their front legs and they shook their back legs, until they were no longer wet. Then the whole family hopped up onto the bank and over to the giant trees in the Redwood Forest. They hopped to Mr. and Mrs. Tea Master Frog's tea hut, in a pod of redwoods standing by the bank.

"When they hippity hopped into the tea hut, Mr. and Mrs. Tea

Master Frog said, 'Why, hello Burpy and Grog Frog! We haven't seen you in a long time. We're so glad you have come.'"

"Momma Frog, who had the idea to come, said to Mr. and Mrs. Tea Master Frog, "We've come for your medicine tea. Your special tea is always good medicine for our bumps and scrapes."

And Poppa Frog said, "Sometimes we feel sad, and sometimes upset, and we know that your special tea is always good medicine for turning unhappy feelings into happy ones again."

"'Oh, I see,' said Mr. and Mrs. Tea Master Frog. They listened carefully and nodded their heads. 'Yes, we will make you just the right kind of tea for your bumps and scrapes, and your sadness and upset. Please, won't you have a seat on our mushroom stools?'"

"So Poppa and Momma Frog, and Burpy and Grog Frog, sat down on the mushroom stools. Mr. Tea Master Frog put wood in the old stove and heated up the water. Mrs. Tea Master Frog fetched jars of tea on the tea hut shelf, and she brought them down to the table and opened them up. And do you know what was in those jars? She had every kind of flower in the forest. And she had special leaves in all shapes and sizes. And she had magical roots of every kind. And each one had a special purpose. And Mrs. Tea Master Frog knew every purpose of every plant, and which ones were good for this and good for that. So she took a little of this and a little of that, something special from each jar, as each guest needed, and she made a wonderful tea for each tea cup.

"Then Mrs. Tea Master Frog brought her tray of tea cups to the stove for Mr. Tea Master Frog to fill with hot water. And soon enough, the kettle on the stove began to sing, because that's what a tea kettle does when the water gets hot. Mr. Tea Master Frog took the kettle handle in his hand, and he lifted up the kettle, and he poured steaming water into each cup that Mrs. Tea Master Frog had set on the tray. Steam rose up from the cups, and the tea hut filled with the wonderful smells of the flowers in the tea cups.

"Mr. Tea Master Frog picked up the tray of tea cups and carried it to the mushroom table where the Frog family sat. He placed it down before them. And Mrs. Tea Master Frog brought special sweet candies with magic medicine inside.

"Each sweet candy had a special surprise. And do you know what was inside the candy?" Mr. Chong paused, waiting for Tara to answer. "What do you think frogs like to eat? Do you know how frogs stick out their tongues to catch things? Do you know what frogs like to eat?"

"Peanut butter and jelly sandwiches?" Tara answered.

Sara looked to Greg and smiled.

369

"Maybe," the man said. "And what else do you think frogs might like to eat with their long tongues?"

Tara didn't have an answer.

"What about flies?" the man suggested. "Do you think frogs like to catch flies with their tongues?" Tara shook her head. "That's right," the man said.

"And each special sweet candy, with its magic medicine, had a surprise fly in the middle. And if you were a frog, you might think that a fly inside your candy was the best surprise in the world."

"So Burpy and Grog Frog, and Momma and Poppa Frog, sipped their special tea, made by Mr. and Mrs. Tea Master Frog with a little of this and a little of that in it. And they could taste the love and joy that were put in it, too. And when Burpy and Grog Frog were finished with their tea, they picked up their special sweet candies and put them into their mouths. And they sucked on their special sweet candies with the fly in the middle.

"In no time at all, Burpy and Grog Frog, and Momma and Poppa Frog, were all better. They felt happiness from the tea, and the candies. Their bumps and their scrapes didn't hurt them anymore. And Burpy and Grog Frog were ready to go out and play again."

"And here is a piece of licorice for you," the man said, giving a piece of it to Tara. "But I promise you—there is no fly in the middle." The man smiled as he put a piece of licorice on small plate near Tara.

"Thank you," Sara said to Mr. and Mrs. Chong. "That was really sweet."

"In America, there is habit of quick tea and coffee," Mrs. Chong said to the adults. "We say this not good. Our mood not so good. We don't see beauty. When we drink tea, we need to take time. Appreciate taste, smell, color, vessel, decoration of room. Feel the tea. Follow the tea in your body as you drink. This is how we do it."

70

In the hallway at the Lodge, Greg reached for his mobile as he neared the room.

"Can I do it?" Tara asked.

"Sure." Greg gave her mobile and she waved it in front of the door to unlock it.

"Here, Daddy," Tara said, returning the mobile and opening the unlocked door. Greg entered behind Tara and Sara, removed his shoes, emptied his pockets on the dresser, and put on a sweater. He felt the week passing by rapidly now, and soon it would be time to leave, to return to their ordinary life in Seattle. He then remembered that the Taoist meeting was happening right now, and they were missing it. It's okay to surrender that, he thought. Sara needed him, and time together was nourishing, after all.

Sara put down her purse, removed her shoes, and headed for Tara's bag of books and toys. "Why don't we read a story before bed?" she suggested. "Let's see. What do we have here?" Holding the bag open, she flipped through the books with her finger and called out loud. "The Tibetan Boy and the Deer, the Seven Chinese Sisters, Suzie the Fox..."

"Seven Chinese Sisters," Tara said.

Sara brought the book to the master bed. "Okay, let's take off your shoes, Honey." As Tara was overtired now, and relaxed from the tea, no doubt, Sara helped her remove her shoes. "Up you go," she said, lifting her. "Daddy, are you going to join us?"

"Yeah." Greg grabbed his copy of The Beads of Dew from the Source of Life from the table where he usually sat, this time forgoing the ritual reorganizing of his books into an exact pyramid, and set Beads of Dew on the night stand at his bedside. He sat beside Tara, who was seated in the middle of the pillows and ready for a story, and put his arm around her affectionately. "I'm ready," Greg said.

Sara read in a remarkably warmer mood than Greg felt from her earlier in the evening. After the story, Tara dozed off peacefully between Sara and Greg.

"You know," Greg said softly, when Tara was sleeping. "It's kind of funny. I let go of our time with Chao Pi Ch'en, and yet we ran into a Chinese tea shop and had that magical encounter with that elder couple. Something unexpected unfolded there."

"Yeah, that's funny. What do you make of that?"

"I don't know," Greg said. "Well, we had time together as a family tonight, and it seems it helped Tara get off to a good night of sleep. How about you? Was this helpful?"

"Yeah," Sara said. "Thanks. I just felt I needed a deeper connection as a family, and a deeper connection with you. It feels like something is coming up in my life right now, and I feel I need this."

Waiting for the moment beyond which Tara would not wake again, Greg finally stepped off the bed, slid his arms underneath her, and gently picked her up, carrying her to the roll-away bed in the corner. "Can you help me?" he whispered. Sara dashed up and pulled back the covers. Greg put Tara down and Sara gently brought the blankets up to her neck.

Returning to the bed with a question mark hanging in the air, Greg and Sara climbed in, rearranged the pillows set up earlier for Tara. "So you want more of me?" Greg asked affectionately. He clicked his mobile, turned off the lights. Then he leaned toward Sara and put his hand on her shoulder, gliding it slowly down her back, over the folds of her shirt.

Sara turned to him with her magical brown eyes, which seemed always longing and calling—for the path, for creative expression, for sensory experience, for him. These eyes, this glance of hers, like a trance. He remembered the first time ever seeing her at a work day years ago, at the center where they first met, when she carried a tray of cups from the kitchen to the dining area, and he went in. That first glance was a decade ago, he recalled. That first impression burned its powerful form into his heart—and now again, this glance of hers, like an echo of some deep ritual of call and response between them, burned again into his heart, tenderly, sorrowfully, sweetly. The thought of soul mate often crossed his mind in moments like these, and a feeling of gratitude and brief uttering of thanks in his heart, passed like a mist before the screen of his observing 'I' with little need of conscious help from his will. And now, without books, without conversations, without activities, with Tara asleep, they were together.

Sara turned over onto her back under Greg, available, open.

"My beloved," Greg said, putting his hand on her face in the dark, "indeed you are the path and the practice."

"Now you're talkin'," Sara grinned.

Greg ran his fingers around her ear, through her hair, around to the side of her head and down her neck to her collar bone. "You are the altar and the Goddess of the altar." It sounded playful because it was just spoken earlier, on the playground. But she felt he meant it, felt he meant to recover the seeds of that earlier way and find its authentic expression now. He moved his torso closer as he ran his hand down her shirt to her left breast and caressed it gently, finding her nipple through her shirt with his finger. He knew she liked that. He lingered there, then found her other breast. Sara reached her left hand and caressed Greg's side. They glanced into each other's eyes expectantly. Like last night in the hot tubs, they gazed deeply soul to soul, caressing each other. He soon glided his left hand down to her pajama pants, in, under the elastic, over her underwear, where he could feel her pubic hair through the delicate fabric. He curved his hand around her form. He kept the loving gaze into her eyes, and she sustained it, too.

"Let's be a gateway for each other," he said, "to the intoxicating love of our Beloved. Let us be earthly points of access for each other to all the divine hierarchies." Greg was adding now, he realized, to what he would have said years ago. Through study and practice, through observation and presence, the years since had deepened his understanding. And he brought that to bear on this moment with Sara. "Let us move through each other into every plane and ultimately to non-dual consciousness."

Sara felt it, too. She felt his eyes, present and burning with some ancient longing of the soul. She felt his aspiration for authentic being, beyond habitual moves and speech filled with clichés. She felt his hand between her legs, his finger wandering. She didn't feel him especially passionate just now. No, it was her request, and he was meeting her. But he was there, as solid in friendship as the organ was now stiff that pushed against her hip. In body and soul, in a balanced attention to different parts of themselves, he was there and he met her.

Sara felt herself relax from earlier anxieties. She released old identities like the husk of something now emptied. Here was love, tender passion, a friendship of souls. And she surrendered as when the Beloved fills the heart.

Leaning over to kiss her, falling into a lush embrace, Greg let go of everything Bayside Village, everything AlignIt, everything else, and gave himself utterly to Sara.

Greg and Sara lay asleep, expended, locked in a delicious, sleepy embrace. Greg awoke, reflected awhile on his early, stormy days, his passions, his longings, as his eyes studied lights and shadows on the ceiling. Then he sat up in bed.

Sara roused, whispered. "Where are you going?"

"Nowhere," he said softly. "I'm going to meditate."

She awoke further. "After that?"

"Yeah."

"You're mixing sex and meditation?"

"That was meditation." He sat silently. "Everything is included."

"Mmm. I know," Sara said, pondering. Then in a playful challenge, she said, "Are you going to confess your sins?"

"What sins?"

"What you just did, you wild man," she said in a romantic voice.

He chuckled, surprised. "What sins?"

"No, that's my issue," she whispered circumspectly.

Greg looked straight ahead in the darkness. "I just want to penetrate my ignorance to know what is real."

"See? My mysterious husband."

"So that's what you mean."

"That's part of it." She turned on her side toward Greg, put her hand tenderly on his leg. "Mystery is multivalent, like you."

Greg sat for a moment in the dark. "You know what I mean—how everything is included. This isn't really mysterious to you."

"I know. I think part of the interview with Karen just hit me and threw me off." She pondered some moments. "Its hard to trace the thread of our karmas." She was silent, reflecting. "Its hard to find and follow our true longings. Whether in sex, meditation or anywhere in life."

"Mmm. Yesterday with Mrs. Blocke, I hit a weakness, and it threw me off. I wonder where does that vulnerability come from in me and how do I transform it so that I can have a stable practice and awareness?"

"I appreciate how we support each other in seeking the truth, doing the work."

"Indeed." Greg put his hand tenderly on Sara's, smiled in the dark, breathed deeply. "Want to join me?"

"Sure," Sara said, sitting up. She propped up her pillows. "I always wonder how you meditate in sex, or after it."

"I don't know." Greg adjusted himself as Sara sat up. "The face of the Beloved is everywhere."

When Sara lay back down to sleep, Greg got up from the bed. He quietly slipped over to the corner table, set down his mobile, and activated the screen and keyboard projections. He set the projection on a low brightness, careful not to disturb Sara. He opened his ontology presentation for tomorrow's board meeting and got to work. He advanced through the slides—traditional science, modern science, the need for a bridge, ontology as bridge, open ontology architecture. Feeling satisfied with the overall presentation, Greg zoomed in for the remaining challenging points, imagining the attendee list, anticipating questions about ontology and scientific integrity, searching for better wording and positioning. An hour later, he felt tapped out, his eye lids sticking as he blinked, his back now tired in the chair. One slide still didn't feel right, like an unreachable itch. But enough for now. Tomorrow he would have a fresh mind. But as he stood up and stretched, he remembered he had rescheduled for Chao Pi Ch'en in the morning. So, less time for work on the presentation.

Part 3
Mysterious Wrinkle

Day 6: Friday

71

"Okay, I'm going," Sara whispered, picking up her yoga mat from the closet. Tara was still sleeping. Greg turned from the corner table where he worked on the final touches of his ontology presentation for today's AlignIt board meeting. Sara came over to him. "Good luck on your slides." She put her hand tenderly on his shoulder and bent over to kiss him on the forehead. He made a guttural sound of satisfaction at the sensation. Sara left the room, closing the door gently.

In time, Tara rose, alert and perky, and sat up in bed. "Where's Momma?"

Greg turned from his screen projection. "Good morning, Honey. Momma's at yoga."

Tara stretched and yawned and then jumped out of bed. "Is Momma going to meet us at breakfast?"

"Yup. We'll meet her there in a little while."

Tara picked up her new stuffed toy, Clappy the California clapper rail. She arranged pillows and clothes on the bed into a nest, and moved Clappy about the bed, into the nest, out of it, onto the floor and back to the bed. Soon, she was talking and making bird noises as she moved Clappy about in a story she made up. A story, Greg realized, made of new impressions from walks together at Bayside Village. Greg redoubled his concentration on his slides, especially the difficult one that gnawed at his inner sense of elegance.

"Daddy, look!" Tara showed him a new bird nest made out of his sweater.

He looked. "That's nice, Honey." He turned back to his presentation, trying to get the words right. This slide, how to say it just right?

"Daddy, look. Look at Clappy now." The bird was tucked in. There was nothing impressive in this beyond the last view.

"Tara, can you let Daddy focus for just a minute? I'm trying to write something."

A minute went by. "Daddy," Tara said, leaving Clappy hanging upside down on the edge of the bed. "Can we go to breakfast? I'm hungry."

Greg looked at the time display on his screen projection. "In a minute, Honey. Let me just finish what I'm working on here." Greg tried finishing a few last thoughts on that difficult slide. Tara's requests for help and need for attention tugged at him, distracted him. Tara played some more, and her bird calls seemed louder and sharper to Greg than her earlier play, moments ago. He knew the slide was good enough. It was time to move on. Feeling Tara's need for attention, Greg deprojected his screen and keyboard and slipped the mobile into his pocket. He felt unfinished despite hours of work. The transition from traditional to modern science didn't satisfy him yet. Nor the instrumental role of ontology as a bridge and expansion.

Greg got up and let go of the presentation entirely. He turned and walked to the bed. "Here are your clothes for today, Honey." He pointed to the bed where Sara had laid them out neatly. "Why don't you get dressed, and then we'll go. Okay?"

When Tara had dressed, Greg turned to her. "You're feeling better today, huh?" Tara didn't answer. Greg realized 'feeling better today' makes little sense in a five year old world. Comparison is nothing where today's mood is the world itself forever and always. He smiled to himself and bent down to the floor where she sat, helped put on her socks and shoes. "Are you ready, my precious girl?" Greg said, with a kiss on the crown of her head.

Sara entered the Dining Commons with her yoga mat and walked towards the line. She saw Greg and Tara eating, and Tara saw her.

"Hi Mommy!" Tara called.

Sara walked over and gave Tara a hug from behind and a kiss on her cheek. "Good morning, my beautiful!" she said. Then she smiled at Greg and rubbed his back.

"You look good," Greg said, smiling at her, admiring her beauty and vigor, her hair loose and wild, with strands swept into her face.

"Thanks, I feel good." Sara put her arm around Greg's shoulder and planted a kiss on his cheek. Greg smelled the fresh, intimate scent of her sweat, mixed with a bit of perfume, expelled like a warm breath from her shirt as she pressed in to him. "Yoga's great in the morning. Did you finish your presentation?"

"More or less," Greg said. "It's as good as I can make it. I began obsessing, so I let it go."

"I think you'll do fine. I know you will."

"Thanks," Greg said with a grateful heart, appreciating her constant support of his work.

"I'm going to get breakfast. I'll be right back."

Sara returned soon with a plate of grain cereal, banana and yogurt and sat across the table where chairs remained open. She scooted up her chair. "I need yoga." She looked into Greg's eyes. "It makes such a difference in my health—mental health, too."

Greg lifted a piece of toast and held it. "Mmm. I should do yoga, too," he said.

"Yeah, we should do it together, especially since you like Path of Ananda."

"Mommy? Are we going to move here?" Tara asked.

"I don't know, Honey. We're exploring."

"Can I get down and go to Kids Corner?"

"Yes, but I want you to finish your banana first," Sara said. "Greg, can you cut it for her?"

Greg cut it. Tara finished it. And Tara got down and ran off to Kids Corner. Sara looked to Greg. From across the table, she playfully grabbed his right leg between hers. Greg looked at her with a surprised and romantic grin. She then moved her left foot up the inside of his leg.

"Are you flirting with me?" he asked with a squint and a curling smile.

"Maybe."

"There are karmic consequences for that, you know."

"Like what?" She raised her her foot still higher.

Greg squeezed his legs together, caught her foot. "Not here."

After dropping off Tara at the Day Care, Sara asked, "What time is your meeting with Chao Pi Ch'en?"

Greg pulled out his mobile, looked. "About ten minutes."

"Do you have enough time for a quick..." and she trailed off, not intending to finish.

Greg hesitated, his mind racing hot between options. "Damn. I'd have to shower. I need to be clear-minded."

"Okay," she said, looking playfully disappointed. "I don't want to distract you." She looked tantalizingly still open.

"Fuck," Greg said under his breath, aroused, torn. He didn't want to mess up his concentration. "You get me all wound up."

She smiled.

He breathed in deeply. "I need a rain check."

"Okay." She let it go. "I'm going to run off to the Art Center."

Greg raised his eyebrows. "Again, huh?" He smiled. "That sounds good."

He leaned over and kissed her on the lips. He put his arms around her, grabbed her buttocks from both sides and subtly pulled himself up against her there on the sidewalk. "Some karmas are fun to repay," he said.

"I will wait for you, my love," Sara waxed poetically. She turned and started down the path, her sketch book sticking out of her purse.

Greg turned and walked briskly to the Plaza, shifting attention swiftly away from his pants toward Taoist ontology.

72

In the plaza square, Greg walked to the Philosophy Salon. He entered the French style door, looked about. Master Chao Pi Ch'en was seated at a booth by the window facing the plaza, lifting a bamboo tea strainer out of his cup and setting it in a dish.

Greg approached him. "Good morning."
Chao Pi Ch'en looked up at him and nodded. "Good morning."

"I'll get a tea and join you." Chao Pi Ch'en nodded. Greg walked to the food line and waited to order. He glanced back at Chao Pi Ch'en, who easily appeared just an ordinary man. He was dressed in plain clothes. He sat there quietly, unassuming, sipping his tea. His face seemed ordinary, his eyes looked somewhere else. Was this just another discussion in his busy days? But the impressions from yesterday stayed with Greg—his presence, his eyes, his words: "Now I see how you stand."

Greg moved ahead in line. He looked at the tea choices, then trailed off in reflection, retracing his steps with Sara. What did she need from him? Where are things going in the big question of moving to Bayside Village? How to align his love of Sara with his own sense of his life purpose?

Greg ordered Chai tea and croissant. He laid down a few shiny Bayside Village Dollars on the counter with a clink and walked back to Chao Pi Ch'en at the table.

Greg sat down. "Thanks for meeting me like this," he said, sipping his tea and then putting it down. He sat close to the table, upright. "I'm sorry to have called you a few times to rearrange my schedule. My family is here all week, and we needed some time last night."

"This is okay." Chao Pi Ch'en looked stoic. "Family duty is the first obligation."

"We brought our daughter to the Path of Ananda Wednesday night, and that worked out well. So I fully expected we could come to your Taoist meeting."

"It's okay," Chao Pi Ch'en said, with an intention that rested the matter. His eyes were powerful. "What do you want to discuss?"

Greg shifted, his attention now on the task. "Well, you know I may work with Roger on AlignIt. I'll reduce teachings, like those in Taoism, to a set of entities with relations and rules in a traditional framework, so these can be built in AlignIt and operated."

Greg noticed himself formal, intimidated perhaps by a man in full possession of his power. Greg hadn't returned to himself yet, he observed. He came back to himself now as he spoke. "Then we can map entities from Taoism to those from other traditions as we work toward an upper ontology of sacred sciences. So I wanted to get a sense of Taoist ontology."

"Yes. Yes." Chao Pi Ch'en said. He took a deep breath and closed his eyes inconspicuously for a moment and then opened slightly. He peered down at his tea cup, now empty. He looked up at Greg with full presence that put Greg in a state of attention. "We start with practice. We study theory in the practice. Qigong practice embodies our investigation of the Taoist Chinese view, the cosmology, the ontology. We do this in our exercises every morning at the Village Security dojo."

"Yes, this is what I'd like to discuss." Greg's mind quickened eagerly, but some stiffness remained, making him mentally race ahead of his experience.

"But you see, we don't just talk theory and list the basic elements of Taoism. I ask you to stand like a tree. And you stand like a tree for a long time. If you keep asking 'What does this mean?' or 'What is a tree?' or 'How is a tree connected with this symbol or that one,' you may miss the Tao. But if you just stand like a tree and pay attention to your experience, you may see. And if you are ready to stand and work like this, I may explain something. Or you may find it without words. But you need to study this inside your body, in your experience—not using your mind alone."

The pure force of Master Chao Pi Ch'en's intention penetrated Greg, who opened before him. He sat back and drew a breath, trying to absorb Chao Pi Ch'en's influence.

"Taoism has a view, it has cosmology, metaphysics, ontology," Chao Pi Ch'en continued. "It has what Roger calls entities and relations. It has all these things. But the key is to learn the view in practice. If you get the view—the entities, the relations, the forces—then you can study it systematically in practice. In standing and moving, you study and confirm the view. You see? The view isn't separated from the standing, moving, sitting, breathing, and visualizing. We cultivate by keeping view linked to practice."

Greg nodded. This is the real thing, he thought. He sat with rapt attention, remembering himself, aware of his breath.

"You teach by lectures and readings," Chao Pi Ch'en said. "You want to know ideas, texts, traditions, arguments." How did Chao Pi Ch'en see all of this, Greg wondered. "But here, we study Taoist cosmology and psychology by observing sensations, feelings, intuitions, noticing what arises now in practice. First in ourselves. Then in forces around us. You can study ontology this way. Taoists have a written canon of sacred texts. You may have it already. We have charts and descriptions. Maybe this comes from Buddhist influence in China. So Taoists developed their own canon, too, since the Buddhists placed more emphasis on rational study and contemplation. But we seek the heart of Taoism in practice. The kernel of Taoist cosmology, psychology and ontology is not in the written canon, but in practice of Qi Gong, or Tai Chi, or Kung Fu. It can take any form. Do you understand?"

"Yes," Greg said. "Yes, I understand this. It's very important to me, actually. I get distracted from it more than I wish."

"Work on AlignIt from seeing, and see from practice. Even better, see from life. Life is practice. Always practice. If you want to work with yin and yang, discover yin and yang in things, and most intimately in your own body as you practice. Yin therefore is not only attributes like female, earth, stillness, darkness, down, and in. Yang is not only male, heaven, activity, light, up, and out. Yin is now this sensation, and yang is that one—in your own body, here and now. This is how we practice."

"Hmmm. Interesting," Greg said, feeling his confidence again, noticing these things in himself, as he breathed, as he felt his weight on the seat. "Yes, I understand this. I don't have a physical practice like this. But I readily grasp how a physical practice embodies a view of the world."

"All practice has a cosmology and psychology, implicitly, whether practitioners—or even teachers—recognize it or not."

"Yes," Greg said. He quickly scanned his experience for examples. Yoga. Martial arts. Sufi dances. He dug behind mere exercise. In his memory, only the finer expressions of these practices connected physical movement deeply, intimately, with a view. Could he study ontology this way?

"It helps to have something, if you can—some kind of practice. Then you don't go off or space out. A physical practice helps ground you."

The suggestion of Greg going off made an impression in him. Was Chao Pi Ch'en saying this from seeing it in him yesterday morning at the dojo? 'Now I see how you stand,' he had said. Greg felt his postures and poses there were wobbly. He recalled that impression, saw himself back in that moment.

"And you used music in class," Greg said. "It's more than background music to create a nice atmosphere." Chao Pi Ch'en nodded. "What's the relation between music and Qigong practice?"

"It is more than atmosphere, yes." Chao Pi Ch'en looked down to his cup, put his fingers around it, and then looked back to Greg. "I use traditional Qigong music based on five element theory. Music creates associations, and we feel the 'spirit' or sensibility of Qigong. Music is sound energy, and it sends auditory signals to the brain. This stimulates the flow of Qi in the body. Qigong music creates calm and concentration. It soothes your body and invigorates your spirit. The music is non-trivial; it influences physiology and entrains energy. So music creates a right environment for the mind and energy during Qigong practice." Master Chao Pi Ch'en contemplated, looking into his tea cup. "Music also embodies a view," he said. "If you listen carefully, you can hear Qigong in music. Some Qigong is merely Chinese culture." He looked up. "But listen carefully to good music. If it comes from the right place, it can take your attention to definite states and help you embody the Tao."

"Yes, I can see that in some of my Chinese music. It makes a big difference for me when it comes from a higher place. And Qigong uses imagination," Greg said. "You have visualization practices."

"Yes. Visualization is very important in Qigong. When you visualize, observe how images extend your understanding, feeling, and embodiment of the posture. Images invite a response from the body, heart and mind. When you imagine yourself as a tree, you feel solid, strong, and still."

Greg nodded eagerly. Chao Pi Ch'en's words were sinking in. Practice is a way to study. Practice is a way to work with AlignIt. This would be different from his typical university work. He knew this. But he always knew this way and longed for it. His academic mentors never mirrored this back to him. But here a teacher reflected it back to him. This would be different at Bayside Village.

Master Chao Pi Ch'en sat eternally silent for a moment. "Is this enough for now?"

Greg quickly returned from contemplation of the vast Taoist cosmology to his seat at the table, with a quick and appreciative nod to Master Chao Pi Ch'en.

"Be careful not to fix these ideas too tightly," Chao Pi Ch'en advised. "These are poetic and symbolic ideas, and one has to respect their fluidity. One principle evokes one set of meanings now, but later, from a different point of view or a different stage, it can point you to other meanings. Now I see that fire thaws; later I see that fire burns and reduces to ashes. So do not attach fixedly to one view, but see with a wide vision. Every element is dynamic and has many qualities depending on how you see it. Depending on the context in which you find it, or it finds you. Depending on your state. Depending on your maturity. This is enough for now. Okay?"

"Wow, thanks!" Greg said. "This is enough for a long time."

"Yes. I have told you preliminary exercises. The possibilities of this practice are great. Don't race ahead to what you imagine are advanced stages. There is great subtlety in basic practice. This is more than enough to slow down your fast-moving mind so you can relax into these postures."

My fast moving mind? Greg felt that Chao Pi Ch'en saw him as he really is, better than Greg saw himself most of the time. Chao Pi Ch'en's view was more honest, more real. "I'm sure I could spend a long time just learning the basics," Greg said.

"You have the capacity to discover 'indescribable marvels' like the Tao Te Ching says."

"Oh, I have one more question for you, if it's alright."

"Yes?" Master Chao Pi Ch'en had the face of an ancient mountain.

"Do you know about Gottfried Leibniz' use of the I Ching in his Characteristica Universalis?"

Chao Pi Ch'en thought for a moment with a furl of his brow. "I've heard of Leibniz, but I don't know about this. I'm sure many Europeans and Americans have incorporated Chinese wisdom and systems."

"Okay, thank you very much," Greg said, instinctively bowing his head slightly, for some reason.

"Stay with practice when you work," Chao Pi Ch'en said. "You will see more."

73

Sara sat in a vacant studio in the Art Center. The morning sun peered in through the window, lit the floor with the pattern of the window pains. This was her last full day at Bayside Village, she reflected. This would be her big day for art, her big day for self-discovery, a reversal of her turn away from art for the sake of the path. Was there a chance, now, of turning back—for the path, with the path, as the path? But she sat there unable to get started, finding it hard to concentrate. The opportunity was there. The space was there and she sat in it. And she had the morning to herself. Yet something gnawed at her. Another unfinished possibility. She recalled the Sensory Parlor Collective and the online form that she had filled out but hadn't submitted. She hadn't scheduled a time with Elizabeth. It was her last day for this, too. Would she ever return to Bayside Village? This was the rarer opportunity. She could do art on her own. But there was no other Sensory Parlor Collective.

Sara pulled our her mobile, touched on her screen projection, opened the form. She scrolled down, quickly reviewed what she had written so far. Good enough, she thought. At the bottom, she found the submit button, and she moved her finger through the air to touch the button in the projection. The form was submitted. Then she touched a phone number on the submission confirmation page, picked up her mobile, the screen projection muting automatically. She held the phone to her face.

Lucky day. Elizabeth picked up. Sara asked if she had any time today for a session, apologizing for the last minute call. Indeed, lucky day. Elizabeth had an open morning and invited her right now. Sara agreed, put down her phone. She packed up her art supplies—sketch book, pencils, erasers, charcoal—and headed out the door.

Sara walked down the path from the Art Center on the Bridge Institute quadrangle to the Sensory Parlor Collective in the Bayside Village plaza. As she approached, she had a different impression than Monday when she approached with the tour. The building seemed odd for something so revolutionary—just an old industrial building from the period when Richmond Chemical owned the site that is now Bayside Village. It was an old building, now adapted and reused, now artfully garlanded with eaves and flowering bushes.

Sara passed by the sign in the small lawn out front, opened the door and went in. She saw Elizabeth sitting in a front office with her reading glasses, looking over a screen projection she guessed was her newly submitted form.

Elizabeth turned on seeing Sara enter, removed her glasses.

"Hi Elizabeth. Is this still a good time?"

"Indeed, it is. Welcome back." Elizabeth stood. She wore a stunning black dress today with artful wisps of radiant blue. Her fingernails were painted dark blue or black, and her jewelry all matched the theme. A sharp contrast to the pattern of white and gold found in the Parlor overall, the chaise lounge chairs, the signage. She was a stunningly fashionable woman at her age, Sara thought. "Let me see, now," Elizabeth said, scrolling, reading.

Sara noticed faint sounds in the building as she waited by the desk. The hall itself was noticeably empty, and she heard only the faint sounds of steps and quiet voices from a parlor down the hall. Otherwise the building seemed silent.

"Taste Parlor," Elizabeth said. "Okay." She looked up. "That's a fine place to begin."

Elizabeth came around the front desk and walked Sara down the hall. "I guess we'll start at the beginning," she said, turning, walking in. "It's our first parlor." Elizabeth stood before the first of several sensory stations lining the walls inside the parlor.

"Okay, so let's have a seat here," Elizabeth motioned, pointing to the white chaise lounge chairs in the center of the circular parlor area. "Let's get comfortable, relax, and then we can go deep into your sensory experience."

Sara sat down, pulled her feet up, reclined, and got herself comfortable.

Elizabeth sat down on a Chaise lounge chair next to Sara's and reviewed her questionnaire again on a screen projection she called up by the seat. She glanced at Sara's AlignIt profile for typology, for constitution. Then she looked over to Sara. "I don't know how much you recall from Monday's tour," she said. "Essentially, each sensory parlor is a tribute to our embodiment in physical existence. What we want to do in each parlor is expand our sensory awareness through the parlor experience. We aim for shifts in consciousness."

"That's what I'm looking for, actually," Sara said, sitting up a little, tensing her muscles. "On Monday's tour, you said something about moving beyond our limited set of familiar habits. That stuck with me. Like, discovering our own conditioned embodiments and trying to expand beyond them."

"Yes," Elizabeth said. "Just relax your body. This is the beginning of stepping outside the familiar world of physical habits."

"Oh, right." Sara released, laid back a bit, breathed in and let go. She looked at the ceiling across the parlor and started again in a more relaxed state. "I wanted to start with taste because I want to explore my psychological conditioning around taste and eating, and see if I can have a shift of consciousness."

"Ah," Elizabeth said. "Food issues. You're very focused."

Sara nodded, an apologetic smile on her face. Embarrassed to affirm it out loud.

"Okay, yes," Elizabeth said. "You mention this in the questionnaire." She looked to Sara in a kindly way. "Many women struggle with this. You're a brave gal to bring it to us." She paused, thinking. "We haven't quite developed the parlor for therapeutic uses like this. Maybe we should. Are you okay if we try some things out? Okay if we don't have a well-tested road map?"

Sara nodded. "I don't have much else to work with. It's okay with me if it's okay with you."

Elizabeth interviewed Sara further on her taste preferences. In a moment, she stood up to collect taste samples from the various stations. She returned momentarily, placing the samples on a tray by her chair.

"Now, I'd like you to relax your body." Elizabeth took Sara through an awareness exercise to recognize and release her muscle tensions, become aware of her breathing, and turn attention to her pallet.

"This flavor is vanilla," she said, handing a swath to Sara. "Keeping your eyes closed, put this on your tongue, and observe your attention as you become aware of the flavor."

Sara took the swath, placed it on her tongue. She became aware of sensations inside her mouth—the watering of certain glands. She saw images associated with the sensation. She followed the sensory-imaginal experience, seeing how it transformed in her awareness.

Elizabeth led Sara in this way, flavor by flavor, taking time with each, interspersed with occasional discussion on what arose in Sara's experience.

After many flavors, Sara sat up for a break. "Wow, that was deep!" She looked around the room, got her bearings, as if she had awakened from far-off states of consciousness. Then she trained her eyes on Elizabeth. "Can I ask you a question?"

"Yes." Elizabeth put down her pallet of flavors on a side table and gave Sara her presence.

Sara brushed her hair behind her left ear. "As I understand it, most spiritual traditions we know today are concerned with subduing the senses. I'm thinking of yoga, mainly. Yet isn't the Sensory Parlor Collective indulging the senses in a way that works contrary to spiritual practices?"

"Yes, this is a good question," Elizabeth said. She breathed in and out deeply. "It gets to the heart of what we do."

Sara focused on Elizabeth with keen attention.

"I would say that indulging versus subduing the senses is a familiar polarity in our Western world, uneasy as we are with the senses. In that kind of framework, in that polarity, you either fight against the senses or surrender to them. And in our contemporary indulgence of sensory experience we are witness to a Western reaction formation against subduing the senses for many centuries."

"Hmm," Sara said.

"What we're after here in the Sensory Parlor Collective is neither subduing nor surrendering, but training the senses, harnessing them in our exploration of the world in and outside ourselves. We are training our awareness of ourselves and the world. Indulging the senses is often driven by unconscious motivations and desires. But training the senses is conscious work. Training the senses, and the will, is another way to overcome unconscious impulses to indulge the senses."

"Hmm," Sara said louder than she expected to, and then became self-conscious. Sara recalled her motivation, her awareness of how food, maybe sexual appetite as well, drove her from some hidden place inside herself. Too hidden to see its full working, but not hidden enough from coming out unexpectedly at times. She observed something stirring in herself that yearned to hear this.

Sara turned to Elizabeth. "In the work you do with people, do you ever work on stopping or transforming habits?"

Elizabeth gave Sara a solid and deeply human look, years of warmth behind her eyes. "Say more," she encouraged.

Sara confided. "Sometimes I wonder if I'll ever be able to get out my bad habits enough to stop creating bad karmas. I have such a deep and abiding aspiration on the Sufi path, but I don't remember it or feel it strongly enough all the time to sustain through periods of relapse into old habits."

"What do you mean by relapse?" Elizabeth asked, curious about Sara's use of the word.

"Well, that's addiction language, I guess. Which is what I feel sometimes. I struggle with food cravings, especially for potent foods like chocolate, caffeine, and sweets. I used to binge and purge. I did it a few times in college and early in grad school. I recognized it was unhealthy, so I got therapy. And that helped a lot. But not completely. I sometimes come back to old habits when I get stressed out—at least eating more sweets than I need to. And right now, I can feel myself drawn to eating sweet and strong foods as a way of coping with the stress of being here."

"You mean Bayside Village?"

Sara nodded.

"You feel stressed about being here?"

"Yeah, I do, I guess. I'm concerned that all this utopian idealism could pull our lives apart—mine and Greg's. We have a pretty solid, workable, practical life right now. And it wasn't easy to get to this place." Elizabeth listened, nodding. "We're both so idealistic, and if I'm not careful, I can be a crazy romantic." Sara hadn't referred to herself that way in years, not since her stormy student years when she identified strongly with being an artist—a limitation ground down in her by the Sufi path. "When we eat at the Dining Commons, or the evening receptions, I can feel urges to eat more than I normally would. Or to eat intense foods without rounding out my diet. But I feel awful seeing this arise in myself, especially since I'm on a spiritual path, and it seems I should have gotten beyond all of this by now. Or it seems that the path would be able to heal a pattern like this, but it hasn't—not yet anyway."

Elizabeth listened pensively, looking at Sara, nodding, taking in everything she said. She looked to the white fabric of Sara's lounge chair, reflecting. Then looking back to Sara, she said, "Maybe more can be given if your penitence finds concrete expression."

"Hmm," Sara said, not expecting this. The words touched something inside her, for Sara sat, looking at the posh carpet, nodding her head slightly as she considered the words. Then she looked up, "Say it again? More can be given…"

"Maybe more could be given if your penitence finds concrete expression." Elizabeth paused. "I don't know if it fits for you. It just came to me as I heard you."

"Yes, it fits, actually. I'm just reflecting on it." The two women sat silently in a pregnant pause for a moment. "I'm an artist," Sara said. "I could draw some of my struggles. Drawing would be concrete."

"Or give a gift," Elizabeth said.

"A gift?"

"Yes, give a gift."

"Why a gift?"

"Again, it just comes to me. I don't know if it fits for you. A gift has to do with relating to another person in a selfless way. Its one form of antidote to the behaviors you've described, which center around yourself and your cravings. A gift given in the right way changes attention from yourself to another."

"Hmm. Interesting. I see what you're saying."

"See what that does," Elizabeth said. "Or take it as a practice with observation. You may be contracting against new things coming into your life. And it seems that a lot of new possibilities stand open before you and your family right now. If so, see if you can catch this contracting pattern and just witness it." She paused. "See what happens when you meet new possibilities in your life by opening your hand and making some kind of concrete offering instead." Elizabeth paused again. Sara nodded, listening. "This doesn't come to me in the same way, but just my common sense tells me it's important to accept yourself and not cycle round and round in mental habits of judgment. Just stop, witness, breathe, and accept what is going on for you. Consciousness itself has an incredible transforming power. Then try something different. See what happens if you open yourself to the wonders life holds for you instead of contracting against them. What happens if you instead draw from the great ocean of boundless love as a resource to meet what arises in your life?"

"Hmm," Sara said.

"I can talk with you like this, yes?"

Sara smiled, nodded. "Yes."

"And drawing from the ocean of infinite love, see what happens if you open your hand with a gesture of offering something toward life, offering something concrete to the people in your life."

"Mmm. Yeah. Somewhere I know what you're saying. Okay, next time I feel an urge, I'll try what you're saying. Stop, breathe, witness, and try to offer a gift."

74

Roger walked down the steps of Avicenna Hall, onto the sidewalk, and a quarter way around the quad to the Bridge Institute Administration Building. Inside, in the Development office, he knocked on Karen Mitchell's door.

"Roger," she said, looking up from her screen projection.

"Hi. Do you have a minute?"

"Sure." She stayed at her desk, held up her finger. "Just a second, let me finish the sentence and hit send."

Roger took a chair at a side table and faced the desk. He looked at the new items around her office—the chart of Bayside Village fund raising, a banner rolled up in the corner, framed promotional pieces across the short history of Bayside Village. Karen got up, came around and sat with Roger at the table.

"So I was curious to hear about your interview with Sara Cobb." He uncrossed his legs and turned slightly toward her.

"Oh, it was promising. We met yesterday. I'm impressed." Karen sat forward. "The first thing I liked is how responsive she was, even from our first meeting at the reception Sunday. I didn't have time to call her before that—I'm sorry. Deadlines got me."

"Oh," Roger said. He squinted, wrinkled his nose, felt a bit disappointed.

"Yeah, I'm sorry Roger. I surprised her at the reception, and I think that put her at a disadvantage. But she was right there with me, very professional." Karen made a firm hand gesture. "And she followed up immediately that same evening to schedule a meeting. And what really impressed me was that by the time we met, she had made a thorough study of our visual communications. She spoke intelligently about our design strategy, even spotting some of the holes because of a consultant here, a consultant there. So, she's very perceptive. And then—get this." Karen's eyes widened. "She brought in a sketch book filled with design ideas she drew between Sunday and yesterday. And they were really good!"

"Really."

"We could use those! I wanted to hire her right there! I tried not to reveal too much."

"Wow."

"Yeah. And get this. She even got Randy to take her into this place called the Vault to dig up visual images from before I got here."

"Oh, right. He called me to ask if this was okay."

"Really? You knew about this?"

"Yeah, he called me. Just to ask if Greg and Sara were serious, if it was worth his time. But I didn't know what she would do with it. So I said 'go for it.'"

"Have you ever heard of the Vault?"

"No, not the word," Roger said. "I think it's just Randy's funny term. But I had an inkling about the place. It's just storage, right?"

"It is, I think. I want to see it, now. I'm curious." Karen's eyes flared a moment. "So anyway, Sara sketched early images of the Bayside Village. Images I'd never seen. And that," Karen said with emphasis, "is how Sara does her background research!"

"I'm impressed," Roger said. "Good. So you think you could work with her, train her?"

"I'm pretty sure I could hand off director-level duties for all visual and verbal communications. Then I can focus just on fundraising like I've wanted to do all this time. It's her combination of initiative, strategic sense, and design sense. And she has the background to lead and manage. So yeah. If Greg works out for you, I'll take Sara."

"Good, good. I hope we can get Greg. I'm deeply impressed with him. He's met with a lot of people this week, and I have good reports from everyone. I'm not sure if we can get him, though, or Sara." Roger paused thoughtfully. "He's moved by what he sees here. I think Sara is, too. But a change like this has to be big enough for both their career ambitions. Greg's close to getting tenure, and that's not easy to walk away from."

"Oh, I see," Karen said.

"And we're still a small and young institute. But I'm working hard to get him. By the way. Have you worked with Mrs. Blocke in HR yet?"

"She's new there?"

Roger nodded.

"No."

"A few of us have found her difficult. I just wondered about your experience."

"I haven't even seen her yet," Karen said. "And she's been here, what, six months now?"

"About. I've tried to get Greg in to see her while he's here, and she's been virtually unreachable, and off-putting. I'm meeting with Bateson tomorrow on some issues that arose with her. Well, maybe I'll just wanted to give you an early alert to watch for anything unusual so you can be on top of it. Because if Greg and Sara say yes, we'll need to move quickly to get them here by August."

75

Greg met up briefly with Sara and Tara in front of the Dining Hall for lunch. "Hi Sweety," he said, bending down to kiss Tara on the forehead. He stood up, turned to Sara. "So I have my big luncheon now with Roger, Neil, and Chris Mueller, the venture capitalist. This is the big opportunity. I'll meet with them a little while just to schmooze. It's in a side room in the Dining Commons. Then I'll come out and eat with you."

"You're sure that's alright?" Sara asked. "You don't have to be there for lunch?"

"Yeah, I talked to Roger. I'll rejoin them for the board meeting."

"Okay," Sara said. "We'll go through the line, and we'll sit by Kid's Corner."

Greg walked in to the front door of the Dining Commons and found the side room for the AlignIt board luncheon—the room where Tara wandered into a Mudra class on Tuesday. He saw Roger standing, talking with a small group. He saw Neil standing in a corner and approached him, striking up conversation, finding common cause with the other man there as a consultant.

Roger turned, approached. "Greg, Neil. I'd like to introduce you to our prospective board member, Chris Mueller, who will chair the meeting this afternoon."

"Sure," Neil said, nonchalantly.

Here is the big opportunity, Greg thought.

Roger walked Greg and Neil over to a man in his fifties. He was smartly dressed in casual business wear, an expensive watch, mala beads around his wrist, talking gregariously with a woman. Greg noticed the mala beads. Interesting detail. "Chris," Roger interrupted. Chris turned to Roger and the two men standing by him. "I'd like you to meet our two prospective consultants, Neil Benson from University of Maryland, and Greg Cobb from UW."

"Oh yes," Chris said, looking at Neil, "Roger told me about you." Chris shook hands with Neil and then Greg with a quick glance. "You've worked with BKG," Chris said.

"Yeah," Neil perked up. "I was their CTO through series B and C right up to IPO, before returning to academia. I'm surprise you've heard of it."

"They made a sweet acquisition deal a few years back."

"I made out well," Neil said smugly.

The conversation went on between Chris and Neil, with Chris' frequent glances to Roger. Greg watched Chris chatting up Neil's industry experience, consulting, and prestigious academic publications and recognitions. Greg shifted his position to his other foot, and then back again, waiting for Chris, feeling an outsider, barely catching an eye of Chris' recognition.

Roger observed closely, seeing Chris gloat over Neil. Maybe it's not getting better, he thought.

After some five minutes, Chris turned to Greg. "And you're an assistant professor now?"

"Associate Professor," Greg clarified, feeling slighted by the light shed on his pre-tenure status. It rubbed that vulnerable spot he struggled with on this trip.

"Right, right," Chris said. "And what are they doing in the philosophy department these days?"

"Oh, I have a joint appointment in computer science, too."

"Of course, right. Well, touching into philosophy is great for bright young students." Chris seemed to suddenly light up with Greg. "You know? One of my favorite undergrad courses was in philosophy. I think everyone should take a philosophy course. It was that time to step back from engineering and contemplate those grand questions. Like Descartes in his arm chair contemplating who he is."

"Descartes," Greg almost laughed, surprised. "That would be a survey course. Most of my teaching is graduate seminars in theoretical and applied ontology." Greg wondered at his defensive, knee-jerk reaction. It was an unintended return volley to Chris' undergrad comment. He didn't mean to do that.

"Ontology, well, a philosopher must bring an interesting perspective to a computer science class room," Chris said, coolly. "I guess we'll hear about its usefulness to industry after lunch, then?"

"I'll show a number of possibilities that can open up for AlignIt with a migration to an upper ontology." Not a great elevator pitch, Greg thought. Must be nervous, thrown off by Chris' strange behavior. Greg saw that Roger saw this, too. What is this looking like to Roger, Greg wondered. Here is the big guy, the guy with the money, and Greg couldn't strike a resonance with him. Things just didn't connect. This didn't feel good. And it couldn't have looked good to Roger, either

"I look forward to your ontology lecture," Chris said. "You're not joining us for lunch?"

Greg contracted, felt conspicuous. Fear seized him, and he almost felt himself trembling. "Yeah, I brought my family this week." As if this was a crime. "And I'm meeting them for lunch." Then he noticed his legs wet with sweat inside his dress slacks. "I have a young daughter whose been in day care all week."

"That's okay, we'll see you at the board meeting."

Chris turned back to Neil. Greg felt Chris was finished with him. Greg nodded to the men, searching Roger's face for a quick read on the conversation. In Roger's eyes, he read Roger's witnessing of this exchange. Was it supportive or disappointed? In a flash, he also read concern in Roger, but for what? He could hardly bear the glance, the uncertainty in it, the uncertainty and discomfort in himself. He nodded to Roger, then, and turned.

Greg left the room, feeling suddenly very awkward. He walked outside the doors of the Dining Commons. Sara and Tara were seated, but he needed to unravel a knot of stress pent up in him. Chris' sudden flare of interest felt rather like a knife stab turned in his gut with a friendly smile. Chris tried to shove him into a smaller place, he thought, to make him feel insignificant and small, young and academic. And Chris focused on Neil.

What was Roger thinking of all this?

Greg walked toward the Plaza, just to walk somewhere and sort things out. First Mrs. Blocke. And Roger confirmed something was strange about that, but it still felt to him like an unsolved puzzle. Now Chris marginalized him, put him down. What had happened? The whole week had seemed to be unfolding like an increasing confirmation of his wish to move to Bayside Village. But now everything seemed to turn with the coming board meeting. Here were two new people—Mrs. Blocke and Chris Mueller. The impressions of both encounters lodged in him, compelling his attention. His breaths were short as he walked, his stomach tense. Greg became aware of himself and took deep breaths as he walked briskly in a broad sweep around the campus and then back to the Dining Commons.

Greg spotted Sara and Tara seated by Kids Corner. He breathed deeply, then approached and sat down next to Tara.

"Hi Honey." Greg kissed her on the forehead.

"Hi, Daddy," Tara said.

Greg saw that Sara had gotten him some food. He was glad for that. He wasn't sure he otherwise could have focused enough on what he wanted to eat. But Sara already selected foods she knew he liked, and that felt like a blessing.

In the best way he could, Greg asked Tara about her morning, cut her food, gave her his presence. He turned to Sara. "It's just gotten more weird." He shook his head, feeling deep stress and fear.

Sara looked to him with concern, gave her full attention to him. She had wanted to tell him about her morning with Elizabeth in the Sensory Parlor Collective. But this lunch, this coming board meeting, these were crucial for him, and now something had become a problem. She decided to wait for a time when Greg could give his full attention. And right now, she gave her full attention to him.

Greg took a few things Sara got for him, pulled them closer—a salad, some casserole. He took a fork, sorted through the food, more attentive to his inner machinations than the food. He explained it all to Sara, as he could understand it, in between words to Tara and bites of casserole. Greg felt himself inwardly pulled away to Blocke and Mueller, and yet pulled by the family's need for his presence as father and husband.

Greg simply recounted the prior events, tried to make sense of them. Sara listened, commented, asked insightful questions. Nothing shifted for Greg. No insight. Hardly any relief. Although he was grateful for Sara's thoughtfulness.

After eating, Greg, Sara and Tara took their trays to the kitchen window. Tara carefully carried two soup bowls on her tray all the way to the kitchen. At the window, she triumphantly declared her success—no spills. Greg praised her.

They came out of the wash area. Greg looked around, and he didn't see anyone from the pre board meeting luncheon. He was glad to have some mental space. Yet he felt even more estranged, afraid that his absence from the luncheon would be counted against him. What created this great fear?

Greg and Sara took Tara to the Bayside Village Community Housing playground for some family time. The minutes stretched to unbearable aeons as Greg pushed Tara on a swing and tried to loosen up and connect with Sara. He still felt disturbed by meeting Chris. In between Sara's words, he distractedly went through his forthcoming presentation in his mind, contemplating modifications to address Chris Mueller. But what would he change, in any case? Greg saw himself less present than he wished.

Sara said to Greg, "Cheer up. Roger is behind you. And you've had so many good interactions this week. Just focus on those." She smiled at him, put her hand on his arm. "You really do know your stuff. Just do your best and offer it to the Beloved."

Greg took a deep breath, stood up taller. She was right. He had somehow gotten contracted into smaller states. He had let himself be pushed to the side, made small and insignificant. Indeed, he observed that he had accepted the small view that Chris intended him to take on. How had he been so susceptible? Sara now reminded him of other views of himself, other states, other postures. Greg straightened, held his head higher, breathed in and lifted his chest. He exhaled, regained contact with his inner being, came back to a state of presence. "Thanks, Love." He nodded. "You're right. I'm getting caught in petty things. Okay," he breathed again. He remembered Roger. He refocused on why he wanted to come to Bayside Village. "I'm going to go into that meeting and shine."

After finally dropping off Tara at Daycare, Greg stopped in the pathway outside with Sara. "Where will you be this afternoon?"

"I'm heading to the Art Center. I thought I'd use my last bit of free time here to go back and feel this part of myself, sit in the studio….I haven't done that in a long time."

"Mmm," Greg said, feeling lifted out of himself and drawn into Sara's world of feeling. "I hope you find something there about how to get in touch with that part of you. Its beautiful." He paused. "I love that artistic part of you."

Sara nodded with a sparkle in her eye. "Okay, I'll do my part. Now, you go in there and shine!" She kissed him, turned, and walked away.

76

Greg looked at his watch. It was almost time for the board meeting. He headed instead for the Administration building. Walking up the main path, he saw Neil exiting the Dining commons.

"Neil," he called.

Neil turned.

"How was the lunch?" Greg asked, catching up with him. The two men walked a few paces, talked. Greg resumed his confidence, feeling comfortable in Neil's presence.

"Where are you headed?" Neil asked, as they stopped.

"We have a few minutes, so I'm going to swing by Mrs. Blocke's office and drop off my application—since the process begins with her, as she told me." Greg bantered, appealing to Neil's sarcastic side. "So I'll meet up with you at the board meeting."

"Hey, good luck with that," Neil said. He stopped, turned to Greg. "I know this means something to you." Neil's eyes shone with a depth of humanity.

Here was that longed-for collegial connection. After the disappointing luncheon, the lack of rapport with Chris, this was most unexpected. "Thanks, Neil."

"I think if you're really into this, you should go for it. Just thought I'd say so."

"Thanks. It means a lot to me."

"Okay, Kiddo. See you at the board meeting." And Neil turned away.

Greg strode across the Bridge Institute quad feeling larger than life at Neil's good will. The afternoon sun was bright, the grass was green, the sky was blue. Must take a lot to induce Neil's support, he thought. And 'okay Kiddo?' An affirmation like this from the likes of Neil is one of those precious jewels Greg always seemed to weave his life around attaining. And here—unexpectedly, gratuitously. From Neil. What is the worth of that?

For a quick instant, two impressions flashed in Greg's imagination. Mueller with his mala beads, displaying outward spiritual apparel, yet undermining him. Ironically, Neil who is obviously antagonistic to the Village seems to affirm and support him.

Such encouragement from Neil calmed his anxieties, Greg reflected. It relaxed something, at least. What irony, Greg thought—me, a spiritual adept, and yet concerned for Neil's approval. I'm supposed to be unattached to the opinions of others, unconcerned for approval. Behold my human weakness, Greg thought. Neil has a good mind, he's well-known, and I hanker for his approval. Help me, Beloved.

Greg walked to the Administration building, his Bridge Institute application folder in hand. He had carried it in his backpack the entire trip, just in case. He hadn't felt ready. But now, resolve quickened. If the process really does start with Mrs. Blocke, then she'll have everything she needs to start the process.

But the light was dimmer in the hallway approaching the formal Interim Director of Human Resources Mrs. Blocke with no first name. Maybe things will sort out with her, Greg hoped. What more could he do but his best?

Greg turned the corner to her hallway. He spotted a water fountain there and dove down into it, turning the handle. It's no good meeting a tough person with a dry throat. Then, in his peripheral vision, over the arc of spouting water, he saw Mrs. Blocke's door open, saw a sharply dressed man leaving, saw him close the door quietly behind him as if secretly, saw him walk down the hall, as if conscientiously. Greg sipped, observed. The sport jacket, the hair. Chris Mueller. Greg breathed deeply, but quietly, to offset the rush of adrenaline. His heart beat fast as he sipped. Greg's intuition reached out, registered the events, followed Mueller down the hall with his eyes. He swallowed. He breathed, his attention roused and alert. He released the handle, stood up. Steps sounded down the hall. And Mueller didn't notice him, didn't turn to look. Must be that I was quiet, wasn't walking, Greg thought. The details burned fast, sharp. Mueller's head balding in the back. His tweed suit coat. His confident swagger, yet cautious steps. Mueller turned the corner.

What was this all about, Greg wondered. But that question is for later, and he pushed it aside. Mrs. Blocke is in. Now, minutes before the board meeting, it's time to deliver the application.

Greg strode to Mrs. Blocke's closed door, knocked. Blocke opened with a face he hadn't seen before. Expectant, upbeat. For an instant, her attention reached out boldly, until she saw Greg. In a flash her eyes bulged wide. She contracted sharply. He had caught her off guard. She must have expected someone else—Mueller. He felt her resistance, a resistance she tried quickly to hide. Just as quickly, she recovered, normalized her affect.

"Yes?" she said. He guessed now the monotone was more contrived than natural.

"I brought my application packet."

She looked at his folder, stunned. He gave it to her. She took it.

"You said the process begins with you," Greg said. "So I'm giving you everything you need to begin."

She stood blankly.

"All of the documents are there. Please let me know if you need anything further."

Some clumsy words of acceptance passed her lips and she nodded and closed the door.

Greg walked away. Good. That was done. What a shock it must have been to expect Mueller and get me, with my full application packet, he thought. He felt a small triumph from her surprise. He managed to shift his fear to a positive drive as he walked, resuming a confident gait.

Greg quickly fit impressions together in his mind now as he exited the building and walked back to the Dining Commons. There must be some connection between Mueller and Blocke. And he's had troubles with both of them. Could that trouble be connected, too? He felt clearly now that something is amiss in his connections with Blocke and Mueller, whatever it is. The way Mueller left, surreptitiously. Surely Roger doesn't endorse this. He recalled Roger's words about Mueller on Sunday, something like, "I hope we've got the right man." And Greg pictured again the look in Roger's eyes before lunch, standing there witnessing Mueller's differing treatments of him and Neil. He saw in Roger some knowing look of recognizing Greg, yet some concern—about Mueller? His adrenalin was primed now as he approached the Dining Commons. He walked with his chest up, head high, feeling renewed strength by returning to his purpose.

77

Greg pushed open the wooden screen doors to the Dining Commons. He saw Roger, Jeff and Catherine seated at a table in the main hall, talking quietly. As he approached, he noticed that the conversation stopped. Judging from body language, Greg felt welcomed and he sat down to join them, yet he felt something else from their sudden silence. Roger turned, looked at Greg knowingly, confidently. In a quiet voice, Roger said, "We'll have some things to discuss. But now's not a good time." This was said in Jeff's and Catherine's presence, Greg noted. "In the mean time, just give it your all. Don't get thrown off." Greg nodded. He corroborated this with impressions formed through the week. We're getting down to something here, he thought.

"Just one more thing," Roger said to Jeff. "Has Mueller called you yet about gaming?"

"Not a word."

Roger smirked, looked disappointed. Then he shifted the conversation, chatted casually with Greg. Greg turned chatty too, part of him taking the queue from Roger to relax and focus on doing his best, and part of him still piecing together impressions recorded—Mueller's visit to Blocke, now Roger's conversation with Jeff and Catherine about Mueller. And what is Jeff's role in this? And Catherine's?

Roger spotted a late-middle-aged man walking into the Commons. He spoke aloud. "Ah, there he is—Saint Thomas of Finnegan himself."

The man turned. "Roger the Capitalist!" He walked up to the table, exchanged warm greetings with Jeff and Catherine. He leaned down to hug Catherine, gave her a kiss on the cheek.

"Thomas, I'd like you to meet Greg Cobb," Roger said, "our guest consultant for the board meeting, also here to interview for our illustrious faculty position and to work with us on AlignIt. So you're not allowed to dissuade him."

Good, Greg thought. Roger is still wooing him. Despite Chris Mueller, nothing has changed for Roger.

"The poor fellow," Thomas said to Roger, shaking his head. "You're already corrupting the youth. Nice to meet you Greg. Thomas Finnegan," he said, shaking Greg's hand with a warm smile. Thomas pulled out a chair and sat down, placing Plato's Phaedrus on the table. Playfully confiding in Greg, Thomas warned in a loud whisper, "You'll have to watch Roger. He plans to commercialize the intermediate realm of qualities between heaven and earth. He's already amassed substantial holdings there and he wants to extort value for human access rights."

"Now Thomas, there you go again," Roger said.

Thomas turned in playful defense. "Roger, if he's joining the team, he should understand your mission."

"Don't mind Thomas," Roger said to Greg. "He must be jet-lagged from a long trip to guide us with his wise counsel."

"No, I'm fine, actually. I've been in San Francisco the past few days visiting old friends."

Jeff stood up. "Tea, Thomas?"

Thomas looked up. "If you would, please, thanks."

"The usual?"

"With a wee bit of honey.

Jeff walked off.

"You see, Greg," Roger said, "when they teach you about negative externalities in business boot camp, they don't train you in dealing with obstinate board members."

"Board?" Thomas said in feigned surprise. "I'm just here to make sure you're reading good books and keep you out of trouble."

"That's why I need you on the board," Roger said. "Just keep me out of trouble."

"That will take all of my time!" Thomas turned to Greg. "So you're the ontologist? You hail from Seattle?"

"Yup, University of Washington."

"You teach in philosophy and computer science?"

"Right."

"Then you need no further warnings." Thomas put up his hands, palms out. "You're fully responsible for your collegial associations." He put down his hands. "Anyway, you're another soul from the North West. I'm from Bainbridge Island, though I lived in San Francisco for many years. And you're thinking of moving here, too?"

"We're considering. It has to work for all of us—for our careers, for family."

"How old is your daughter?"

"Oh you know I have a daughter?"

"Of course."

Of course? "Tara is 5. We're also exploring the Bayside Village School here this week as well."

"You're serious about this."

"We'll see. I'm quite intrigued so far."

"Well, it sounds like the Bayside Village School is shaping up well," Thomas said, looking to Catherine who nodded. "I'm sure it'll be a good school for your daughter if you decide to move here

"I guess you know it's a Rudolf Steiner school," Catherine said. "Steiner worked extensively with the imagination, as well."

Greg nodded. "Yes, I'm aware. I'm amazed to see how it reaches something essential in her. She's there with the Day Care this week."

Roger leaned forward on the table toward Thomas. "And his wife Sara actually interviewed yesterday with our Bayside Village development director, Karen."

Greg wondered at Roger. How did he know that? Then Greg intuited that Roger may have staged it. And how many other things?

"Good," Thomas said. "Despite my allergy to business," he said to Greg, "I will say you're in good hands with Roger, here. Aside from his wayward economics, he does know his Neoplatonism. Which means he'll be a good match for you. And he has a good heart."

"You know my interest in theurgy?" Greg said.

"Roger keeps me apprised."

"And you're a former curator of the archetypal image collection?" Greg asked.

"Ah, he's briefed you, too. Yes, that was my past life. I mostly have leisure time now in my humble life to read, write, and lecture."

"Now he curates the *mundus imaginalis* directly," Roger said. "He beats drums and shakes rattles to call the gods and bid them reveal their mysteries."

"I do precious little shamanism, but I do take the occasional journey."

"Curating an archetypal image collection sounds fascinating," Greg said. "I'd love to learn what you did, how the collection was organized."

"I think Sara would be interested as well, with her artistic bent," Roger added.

"Yes," Greg said. He noticed again Roger's mention of Sara. Deliberate, he thought. "She has quite a library of archetypal images and folk art pattern books." He turned to Catherine. "We have a nice connection this way—work with the imaginal realm. Sara the artist, me the philosopher." Greg raised that older pattern, trying it out again after many years in the closet, feeling how it fit here at Bayside Village.

Catherine nodded, smiled.

"I'll be happy to share what I know," Thomas said. "I'm sure you could improve on the classification system with your ontology background. That's probably what Roger wants to do next—organize archetypal images by your ontologies."

"Yes, archetypal images," Roger cut in. He patted Thomas on the back. "That's why we need your expertise, most gracious St. Thomas. Ah, it's splendid to come together again around a grand project of epic proportions. I'm glad you've reconsidered being our Archetypal Advisory Board member to bring help bring wisdom back to our collective zeitgeist."

"As for your advisory board membership," Thomas said, "I have to laugh since you are always mentioning it without my ever understanding what you are asking."

"But Thomas, here you are in this very capacity. Don't you understand your advisory role for today?"

"You need a credible name and a title?"

"Of course."

"And you thought of me, how very endearing."

"A credible name, yes," Catherine said, "like someone who lectures on symbols and mandalas. Like someone who formerly curated images and now interacts with them directly."

Roger cut in again. "I won't get more funding until my slide for the AlignIt management team says: 'Dr. Thomas Finnegan, Archetypal Image Advisor, Curator at large of the Mundus Imaginalis, Critic of Capitalism and Social Entrepreneurship, Liaison to Intermediary World Helpers, Advisor on Western Esoteric Tradition."

"Charming. Are you sure the risk isn't greater for having me on board?"

"It's probably well and good that you deliberate about this since I can only offer a complimentary cookie in return for your pro bono service to the world's need for the development of a new and robust metaphysics and cosmology grounded in sacred science." Thomas shook his head side to side in disbelief as Roger went on. "It's hard enough to get you to sign up for the AlignIt Profile."

"I need to be taken in hand and such computer realities explained to me explicitly," Thomas said. "I have just barely, and recently, mastered social media. I am not entirely reconciled to the mobile, even. I did upgrade it before coming. At least we can be in the same century together."

Jeff returned with two teas in travel cups. "We should head up, guys."

Roger, Greg, Catherine and Thomas stood up with Jeff, exited the Dining Hall and began walking to the Research Park. The sun was bright, the sky a brilliant blue, the grass a blazing green. Greg realized his mood had changed. The boyish banter between Roger and Thomas had shifted his attention. Had Roger done that on purpose?

"Okay," Roger said. He turned to Thomas. "Let's get back to familiar ground before we wear you out on business matters. What are you reading these days?" Turning to Greg, Roger said, "This Spring, Thomas is reading the entire corpus of Western esoteric literature."

"Rereading," Catherine said.

There is something older, larger and wiser here than Chris Mueller, Greg reflected. This place has deeper roots. Roger has stronger ties. Thomas lives in the same world of ideas as Roger, Catherine and Jeff. This is my kind of place, he thought. Something here will work out if this is meant to be. But then how could Mueller get his foot in the door like this? How could he get in so deep? How could Mrs. Blocke get in, behave as she does? Surely this many sensitive, intuitive, gifted people could see something in Mueller and Blocke.

78

Roger, Greg, Jeff, Catherine and Thomas arrived early to the meeting room in the Bridge Institute's Research Park. Thomas sat down at the conference table. Catherine and Greg were talking, and Greg followed Catherine into the Research Park office kitchenette to fetch a tray of pastries freshly baked and delivered by the Philosophy Salon.

In the meeting room, Roger walked to a credenza and then to the conference table, holding a file in his hand. Walking up to Thomas, Roger pulled out a contract from the file and placed it before Thomas with a pen. "To ink the deal for our new Archetypal Image Advisor, we'll need to take down some information."

Thomas turned around, surprised. "Information? This is preposterous! I have already taken the trouble to bring myself to your capitalist meeting, in full physical embodiment, but you want information! Probably for some Big Data super computer project to mine with your

AlignIt thingy and resell at a profit."

"You've got to be the most cantankerous Archetypal Image Advisor I've ever seen."

"How many do you have?"

"You're the only one, I admit."

"Well how much blood do you want?"

"We'll need to know the nature of your existence, the level of your manifestation, your rank, stage and state…

"Geez, why not my governing planet, rock, fish, algae, plankton, and microbe?"

"All of it, yes. We need the full disclosure of your coordinates, on every scale, up and down the chain of being."

"Honestly! Do I have to hit you over the head with the obvious?"

"Saint Thomas," Roger said, sighing, "I do, indeed, recognize your governing qualities, but we need it on record."

"You bureaucrats are all the same. Where do I sign?"

"Here and here," Roger said, pointing.

Thomas signed the Board agreement and pushed it away to Roger like it was a dirty thing he wanted taken away in haste. Roger put the document in a folder on the credenza and rejoined the table, setting down his mobile and activating his keyboard and screen projection.

"What, not feeling eluscent today?" Thomas chided. "Your response is somewhat sabricious."

"What are you reading to get vocabulary like that?" Roger asked. He paused, typed, scanned. He flipped through screens. "I give up. I can't find it."

"What?" Thomas asked.

"Eluscent."

"I made it up."

"No you didn't."

"I did."

"It may be in a dictionary accessible only to people of higher evolution like you. But I'll find it."

Catherine returned with Greg carrying trays of refreshments, placing them on the table and taking seats near each other.

"Eluscent," Thomas extemporized, "Adjective: the quality of charm that radiates through a person's character when he or she is continually stimulated by creative inspiration."

Roger returned the volley, extemporizing in full stream of consciousness:

From the Dictionary of Thomas of the Inframundo, 3rd Edition, Revised, channeled from Archon 3 on May 2,

2022 in the Gregorian calendrical system of Earth, a planet orbiting the Sun in the Milky Way Galaxy."

"Just so you know," Thomas said, "even with my severe technological handicap, I can see that the conference phone was unmuted and your clever intergalactic speech was heard by anyone who has already called in."

"It's too early, St. Thomas," Roger said, arranging his mid-air screen projections for the meeting. "No one's on."

"Hello?" Thomas called. "Is anyone on the phone?"

"Have any humans joined us yet?" Roger asked defiantly, moving his screen projections.

"Hello Thomas of the Inframundo," a woman's voice called from the phone speaker. "It's Jackie Schrader. Very amusing, Roger."

79

Chris Mueller walked into the room boldly with Neil. An entrance made to capture attention. He laughed and made a show of his rapport with Neil. Three board members followed behind and joined the table, now filled.

Jeff waited for Mueller to approach him, talk with him about the game companies. But nothing. No eye contact. This bothered Jeff and he began to doubt in earnest Mueller's intention to make amends or build his trust. Finally, though, Mueller made his way over to Jeff and struck up conversation. He apologized for creating a scare. He explained how the game companies were new to him, and how he just wanted to act quickly and seize the opportunity, how he agreed with Roger not to advance the game agenda item in this meeting. Mueller said he'll try to shoot Jeff some information in the coming days on the new game companies he found and see what Jeff thinks about it.

The effort was lame, Jeff thought, and too late. He already had a mind full of reservations about Chris, and this did nothing to change it.

Randy Seton walked in and mingled. Then he made his way over to Greg, shook his hand. "I'm looking forward to your talk," he said with genuine rapport, and seated himself close by.

Roger brought the meeting to order, and everyone took seats. He reminded the board that Chris Mueller, who had now attended two meetings as prospective board member, would guest chair today's meeting.

"Okay folks," Mueller said with a strong command. "Let's get started. Before jumping into the business for today, let me welcome our guests. As you know, Neil Benson and Greg Cobbs are joining us today in partial fulfillment of two board tasks from our last meeting—to extend our user interface and services, and to explore ontologies and see if they fit with AlignIt."

Cobbs? Greg said to himself. He glanced at the agenda, noticed that it correctly said Cobb. And explore ontologies? Weren't they beyond exploring by now?

Roger noticed Mueller's slip immediately, and his slight. He glanced at Greg to read his response. Greg looked quickly to Roger to see if he noticed, and he saw Roger looking back at him. Greg averted his eyes. But he knew now that Roger was on to Mueller's antagonism. And Greg wondered if this behavior was partially unconscious on Mueller's part. To slight him in small talk is one thing. But before a board? Why here, where Mueller wanted board membership, wanted AlignIt? Could he simply not realize what he's doing?

"So let's do quick introductions. I'll start. I'm Chris Mueller, prospective AlignIt Board Chairman, web media veteran, and industry consultant."

Greg noticed Roger exchanging subtle glances with Jeff, then Catherine. Curious, he thought. There's a larger discussion going on about something. Maybe me? Maybe Mueller?

The group went around the table making introductions. After board reports from each board committee, Mueller went to the first and only agenda item before coming to Neil's and Greg's presentations—Accelerating AlignIt Development. Greg noticed Chris' name by the agenda topic, and he imagined by the way Chris launched into it that Chris brought the topic into the agenda.

Chris started in boldly. "To help me attract more AlignIt Commons members in the Valley, I need a list of what discoveries and inventions have come out of AlignIt. What companies have signed on? Who are the partners? Who are the universities?"

Greg mused. Here were tough new questions from the Silicon Valley serial entrepreneur who knew start up culture and pitching to investors. Was this the value added Chris brought to AlignIt? Was this the future of the AlignIt Commons? Seems helpful. But there's an edge to it. And how does it reconcile with Chris' strange behavior, and Roger's response to it?

"We can't list universities," Randy said, "because these individual faculty are acting on their own behalf."

"Okay, list faculty with their affiliations," Chris said. "Also list faculty by expertise, by where they commented or contributed. But the main thing is inventions. What goes into AlignIt?"

"How about a discovery tracker?" Roger suggested. "Discoveries and inventions created to date by the use of AlignIt."

"You need to drill down into that," Chris replied. "If we're saying

AlignIt is about science and technology, more than just organizing historical maps, then I need to show the inventions, the technology, developed from using it."

"I'm not sure AlignIt Commons is ready to list inventions at this stage," Jackie said from the phone. "The technologies are still early. It takes time from proof of concept. It takes time to incubate"

"Then AlignIt's development has got to be accelerated," Chris said. "If you can't show me that AlignIt has led to specific discoveries, then I can't go out and raise funds and bring new members to the Commons. I'm sorry to put it to you bluntly. But you're not going to get any traction to mainstream this platform until we can show results in the Valley. Discoveries made, inventions, new technologies, new products. So I'm going to give you a challenge. Accelerate your development. You've got to push this faster out of the lab, into the market."

He's really pushing against the development of AlignIt as a discovery engine, Greg thought. I wonder if he has other interests.

Roger sat forward. "As a stopgap measure, what about showing discoveries made in the history of science using earlier sacred science tools similar to AlignIt, and related to specific categories? At least it shows what we're trying to achieve"

"Ok, that's something. But it's not what this tool can do. It's what other tools did, what sacred sciences of the past have done. We need to show what AlignIt can do."

It's helpful, Greg thought, giving Chris the benefit of a doubt. Pushy, insistent, but helpful. To a point.

"Now," Chris said, "let's move on to our guest presentations." Neil was introduced by Sandy Meeger, VP of AlignIt Commons Marketing, a well-dressed, mid-sized woman, with warm eyes and engaging smile. She read Neil's impressive credentials, awards, honors, and distinctions. Which he must have provided in his bio for the meeting. She told how Neil was brought in to see how to expand AlignIt's market interface for its broad constituency by a broader web-based service orientation. Greg felt himself small before Neil's bio, then caught himself in the midst of negative self-talk, stood up straight in his mind, sat up in his chair.

Neil stood, walked to the front, and spoke formally, more formally than the small audience required, Greg thought. He spoke eloquently of the need for a service science infrastructure, the principal challenges in the way, and the design and costing models for creating a service science platform. Along the way, Greg noticed Neil using examples from his many years of consulting clients, citing his own journal articles, and dropping names with many noteworthy people in the IT industry.

"Thanks, Neil," Mueller said at the end. "That was a brilliant presentation. Thanks for underscoring for us the crucial need for a robust service architecture if we're going to scale up AlignIt and sign on more companies."

Greg again observed Roger, Jeff and Catherine making glances. To what end, he wondered. Roger had the two of them seated at the Dining Commons to walk up to the meeting with him. And Greg now recollected noticing something subtle between Roger, Jeff, and Catherine there, too.

"Now we have some time for questions," Mueller said.

The room was silent.

"Alright, any questions for Neil on service science?" Mueller asked again.

Jackie Schrader spoke from the conference phone line. "Neil, thanks. This gives me a clear picture of service science and its benefits. Your presentation focused on business to business services for government agencies and large corporations in defense, telecom, and utilities…"

"Those are the clients I work with," Neil interrupted.

"So my question is, how would you adapt that system to our situation here at AlignIt Commons? As a commons of small companies, our constituency differs from government and global corporations. For where we are now, can you relate how the AlignIt Commons might design, create, and implement a service infrastructure?"

"For my clients," Neil said, "I begin with interviews of their key constituents to see how they interface with the industry sector now, what they need, how they acquire services. Then we'd build requirements for a service platform and deliver the specs to your IT group."

It still didn't address the question, Greg thought. It didn't address AlignIt or AlignIt Commons members.

"So let me just summarize what I'm hearing, Neil," Chris said, looking to Neil and then very obviously to Roger, and back to Neil. Greg caught Mueller's directed attention. "What I'm hearing is that a dynamic, robust service science infrastructure will help us do three things: one, fully deploy AlignIt," Chris stuck his thumb up in the air to count, and then he shot up his pointer finger, "two, attract new AlignIt Commons members, and three" and he flung out his third finger, his middle finger, toward Greg, "maximize member revenue. And we have to do it right from the start. What I'm hearing you recommend is that we should get a complete service science infrastructure designed and built from people who really know what they're doing. Is that right?" Neil confirmed and made a few more comments. "Okay, thanks Neil," Mueller said. "This has been a very helpful presentation, and I can see it helps move us closer to our board mandate from the last meeting."

Greg saw that Chris tried to appear as reflecting a consensus. But there was no consensus. There was almost a silence. In reframing it this way, Chris seemed to have advanced an agenda of his own.

"Now," Mueller said, "I think Greg Cobbs is going to tell us about why some companies may choose ontologies, and discuss if they add any value in attracting new members to build AlignIt Commons revenue."

He reframed the question put to me, Greg thought. He slanted it. Whether ontologies have any value in raising revenue. That's not what I put in my bio. It's not in the invitation I got. And there he is again, saying Cobbs.

"Roger is going to refresh us again on why we agreed last meeting to explore ontologies, and to introduce Greg Cobbs from the Philosophy Department at University of Washington."

He's emphasizing philosophy again, Greg noted. Even after discussing this.

"Thanks, Chris," Roger said. Greg noted Roger's confidence. "As discussed in our last meeting, we're on schedule in the development of ontology tools for AlignIt. We've developed AlignIt so far on the basis of Perennial Philosophy. We've worked with our partners, like GameIt, PlanIt, Author It, and others, to develop applications. As I've noted in the past, however, the Perennial Philosophy on which AlignIt is presently built is ahistorical. It fails to account for a wide body of evidence. It has served us well as a provisional system, a proof of concept. With it, we've validated AlignIt's model.

"Now, in order to take the next step scientifically and to broadly expand to other scholars and partners, we'll need a more robust technology platform. We discussed building a robust upper ontology for AlignIt to boost scholarly research, particularly in the history of religions and the history and philosophy of science. We're hoping to recruit Greg Cobb, a specialist in theoretical and applied ontology, from the University of Washington's Computer Science and Philosophy departments. I met Greg last year at a semantic web conference and we've been discussing AlignIt ever since. Under an access agreement six months ago, I confidentially provided Greg the table structure, algorithms, and some strategic plans for AlignIt. Greg joins us now to lay out some of his recommendations for using ontology to enrich AlignIt's scientific appeal and build a sophisticated tech platform beyond proof of principle. So, let's welcome Greg," Roger said.

That came off well, Greg thought. That was the question put to me by the board.

"Great, thanks Roger," Greg said, standing, walking to the front of the table and facing the group. In a flash, he remembered Sara's pep talk. He shined, feeling soul purpose. He looked especially to Roger, Jeff, Catherine, Randy, and Thomas. People he felt were interested in his work. Even Neil had been collegial with him. "It's a pleasure to join your Board meeting today, and it has been a pleasure to work with Roger over the past year in scholar-to-scholar dialogue. I'm impressed by what you've developed to date. Hopefully our discussion of ontology now will shed some light on possible future directions of AlignIt."

Greg picked up his mobile and clicked to advance his slides on the screen. "So far," Greg said, "AlignIt has used a singular meta system based on Perennial Philosophy. This has served to organize a number of sacred science traditions. You've had relatively simple operations so that you can select from a table and execute. You can perform searches and execute operations keyed off of the deep structure, or the implicit ontology, of the Perennial Philosophy. And you get decent results, consistent results. The question is, can AlignIt do more?

"The next phase, if implemented, will be substantially more complex. The Board has put forth the following challenges, which I'll summarize, and then I'll relate some proposals I have. Here are the challenges.

1. First of all, the new upper ontology implies a jump to a variegated pluralism, opening the platform to rich scholarly discussion and debate.
2. Second, rather than simply having buttons for automated operations, the operator will have, with the new upper ontology, the option to build complex operations. The operator should have the ability to make educated choices about which ontologies to use in running operations, which data sets to use in the operation, how to display reports, how to manage gaps in the ontologies operated on.
3. Third, new upper ontology tools will be available for comparison, analytics, and inferential gap filling.

Greg then laid out, in careful steps, with simple schemas on his slides, what would be involved in creating such an upper ontology, and what he himself could bring to the task. His points were clearly tied to the Board's mandate: handling variances within systems; importation of new, non-conforming systems; and applying operations from one system to another. His proposed plan for design, creation, implementation and migration to an ontology-based system with an upper ontology related knowledgably and intimately to the current AlignIt environment. Greg also shared, and addressed, specific concerns of AlignIt Commons members he had met with during the week.

The room was full of questions, and Roger stepped in to facilitate where Chris foreclosed discussion.

After the meeting, Neil stepped outside on a back patio under the stand of Eucalyptus trees in the grassy field beyond. Roger followed him. "Well, what do you think, Neil?" Roger asked.

Neil turned around and leaned against the half wall. "Well, you've got a decent platform technology and a solid development plan. But I still don't know about the content," Neil said, shaking his head side to side.

"Okay," Roger said.

"Look, Roger, maybe you can find someone else who can help you structure your products and services. Valid or not, I just don't have a taste for this kind of thing."

Roger paused. That was definitive. "Okay, Neil. Thanks for letting me know. Thanks for taking the time to visit us and explore the opportunity."

"Yeah," Neil said, surprised that Roger acknowledged and accepted his decline.

Roger talked with Neil casually, ending on a good note.

"Best of luck," Neil said, and he turned and walked back inside. Roger watched him through the door as he collected his things and left the board room.

In the hallway beyond the meeting room, Greg entered the men's bathroom, walked up to the urinal.

Neil stood at the sink starting at himself in the mirror. His facial skin looked looser to him than before. He put his hand to his face, touched his skin, pulled on it to feel how loose it is now. With his finger tips, he tugged at his skin, checking if it was looser here or there. He scanned his eyes in the mirror, saw bags there. He studied wrinkles around his mouth. He frowned, relaxed, frowned again, studying how the lines formed.

Greg came to the sink beside Neil and washed his hands.

"I'm getting old," Neil grumbled, exaggerating in self-deprecation.

Greg snickered, shook his head.

"Hey, I told Roger he'll need to look for someone else on service science. This isn't my kind of work."

"Yeah? Okay," Greg said, waiting for more from Neil.

The two men walked out of the men's room together, and out of the Research Park building to the courtyard. But Neil said nothing more about it.

Hesitating in the outside walkway, Greg said, "I appreciate your mapping of the service science space. I hadn't seen that work in detail, and I think the AlignIt Commons needs something like it. But I didn't see as much affinity as I'd expect between you and most of the board."

"I consult for multinational corporations, international organizations, federal programs—large, well-funded initiatives. I don't work with bootstrap entrepreneurs, start ups and small non-profits, and I don't work on the fringe. VC-funded start ups, yes. So Chris Mueller's role motivated me at first. But I told you, I came here as a courtesy to a former student who's intrigued by Roger's work, and I thought there might be something in it. I know you're a sharp and careful scholar, but to me, this place is just too far out for my comfort."

"Well, I'm sure the board appreciated your contribution to the meeting today," Greg said politely. "It seemed Chris was quite interested in your work."

"Chris? Yeah, he was interested alright," Neil agreed. He quickly scanned his surroundings for Chris, didn't see him. He turned to Greg, lowered his voice. "But he's a player, and he's after something. I wouldn't trust him. Let me give you a piece of advice, Kiddo." Neil leaned in closer to Greg, eyed him sharply. "He said too much to me at lunch, and he said it too soon. I don't keep the confidence of a jackass like that. I'd watch my back if I were you. He's got an agenda, and I don't know what it is, but you're not part of it—I can tell you that."

"Can you say more?"

"I don't know more. He didn't give specifics. But he's got his own big ideas for AlignIt, and I can tell you it has precious little to do with Roger's vision or yours. My guess is he has some commercial interests and he wants to grab up AlignIt and exploit it for his own interests."

"Hmm." Greg's mind worked at piecing impressions together.

"Anyway, even if I was interested in Chris, I can't work with Roger. I told him I just don't have a taste for this stuff. And the rest of the board? You saw it—it's not a match. I'm not what they're looking for. And this isn't the kind of project I want on my CV, either."

"I'm sorry to hear that," Greg said, "but it doesn't surprise me. I'm really glad you were here this week, and I think you've given a lot of sharp critique." Greg paused. "I am disturbed, though, by what you said about Chris. I trust your judgment. I also felt quite uncomfortable with him."

"I don't know who wants to make him chairman, but…maybe you could do me a favor. Maybe you could tell Roger what I said about Chris. If I were Roger, I'd be careful about what he's giving away to Chris. I think he should look into Chris a little more."

Greg nodded. "Okay, I'll tell him."

"So, uh, I'm going to see if I can catch an early flight. Look me up next time you're in D.C."

"Alright, take care, Neil. Good meeting you." Greg extended his hand.

Neil shook with genuine collegial rapport, yet a characteristically cool persona. "Ciao," he said, and turned and left.

Jeff walked out into the research park courtyard and ran into Greg. "Hey, that was a great presentation! That was dead on what we asked for."

"Thanks! I put a lot into it. I'm glad you think it hit the mark. Not sure it's what Mueller wanted to hear."

"Eh. Mueller's new and he's not on the board. I wouldn't worry about that. For most people, it takes a little time to get what we're doing. And some people don't get it. We've seen both cases."

They stood for a few minutes reflecting on the meeting.

"Hey," Jeff said. "Are you coming to the Floricanto tonight?"

"Yeah."

"Check out my booth. We're debuting a Mayan Ball Game."

The board room door was closed. Everyone had gone but Roger and Chris.

"Hey," Chris said defensively, sitting on the table facing Roger, "you wanted me on the board to fast-track innovation, right? I know what I'm doing! I've managed hundreds of innovation projects, budgets, and timelines."

"Right," Roger said, "but the high point of this meeting was to gain board approval for developing and migrating to the new ontology. We'd gone over this. I thought I had your buy in."

"I told you. I just question the return on investment of bringing someone like Greg here. I think it'll consume a lot of resource while adding very little value. Look, Roger, you already have commercial licensees— Game It, PlanIt, AuthorIt—and they've created product on the AlignIt platform. Right? So it's already working. And if you spend more time developing the tech platform, you'll miss the revenue opportunities. I think we should spend your limited funds in marketing and licensing. More companies can come on right now. But if you keep tinkering with AlignIt, your current companies will have to retool, and you'll make it harder for new companies to join."

"I don't think incubating a technology on campus means companies have to retool more than the would otherwise. Chris, the point of AlignIt isn't just creating products on the current technology. The ultimate end goal of AlignIt is creating a new scientific discovery engine. And our ultimate social goal is creating the seeds of a new civilization. And pushing philosophy, science, and technology."

"I agree, a discovery engine is a good future target, for one embodiment of AlignIt. But you don't have any validation of that embodiment, or any expression of interest from companies or VC. It's pie-in-the-sky right now, Roger. But right now, AlignIt works, and it works very well for games. You can expedite signing on more game companies right now."

Roger nodded his head. He'd heard this before, and it didn't wear well any more. And Chris didn't respond at all to his greater aims beyond the technology itself.

81

Greg returned to the room at the Lodge, exhausted. It was just after 4:00. He put down his backpack and mobile, let out a gasp and then flopped down on the bed for a few minutes. He moved Tara's stuffed toy, Clappy, to the side.

Greg let go completely and cleared his mind. He brought attention to his breath, gave attention to his heart and felt a warm contact.

Minutes later, Greg got up, rubbed his eyes, put on a casual shirt and shoes. He picked up his mobile, clicked location tracker and found Sara. Art Center. He dialed her. "Hey beautiful...Yeah, I'm done....Yeah, already....The Art Institute? Okay. You want company?....Be there in a few minutes."

Greg walked to the Art Center on the Bridge Institute quad, found Sara in a studio. "Oh, you're painting!" he said, spotting her with a smock, her hair tied in a bun on her head. "Wow, this is more than pencils."

"Yeah, come in." Sara's attention followed her brush on the canvas. Greg entered the studio, with an all but empty mind.

"Look," Sara said, stepping back from the easel, paint brush in hand. Before her stood a canvas with brilliantly shimmering colors, flowing vertical lines like electric hair, and emerging feminine forms.

Greg stood wordless, entranced. "Wow, that's deep. Mesmerizing."

"I'm having fun!"

"I can tell. Where'd you get the supplies?"

"Oh, the purchasing and exchange coop. It was in the free box. It's Friday, and I guess some people have taken off for the weekend. They just left stuff for anyone to use. They always do this. And someone just gave me this canvas. Isn't that cool? The frame is a little broken, but it works. And this woman let me use her space and her brushes if I clean them out."

"Wow, its a reservoir of shared resources."

"Oh, I love it here!" Sara said in a rapture, holding out her hands. Anyway, I'm done. I just need to clean the brushes and tidy up the space."

"Okay." Greg stood contemplating Sara's painting while she cleaned up, returned paints to the free box in the coop window. His mind was tired. His soul thirsted for expansion and release. He gazed into the painting there on the easel and felt glimmers of Sara's soul seeking expression. And he witnessed it. "It's like your odyssey this week," he mused suddenly when she returned.

"Mmm. I guess so. Do you want to look around at the other easels with me?"

Greg paused. "Wow, I'm on overload, Love. I can't drink in anything new right now. I just need to unwind. I can wait here or outside if…"

"No, that's okay. I'm ready. Are you?"

"Yeah," Greg said, turning toward the door. "So, you've been here most of the day?"

"The afternoon, yeah," Sara said. She stepped out. Greg followed. "I also went back to Tara's school to sit in."

"You said 'Tara's school' again."

"I did, didn't I?" Sara said.

"I'd like to see what you've seen," he said. "It seems to me that Tara's done well this week."

They turned down a path and strolled around the Bayside Village. "I also want to tell you about my morning," Sara said. "I went to the Sensory Parlor Collective."

"Wow, really?" Greg said.

"Yeah, but I first want to hear about your meeting. You seem in a better state than at lunch time. How was it?"

"Wow," Greg said, letting out a sigh. "Really good, I think. Big day. A lot of mysterious things. I need this walk." Greg ran through all the impressions from the day—how he shifted his perspective after Sara's encouragement at lunch time, his return to Mrs. Blocke with his full application for the faculty position, his catching Chris at Blocke's door and suspecting their collusion in some way, Roger saying he has some things to tell him, the board meeting, Neil's words to him after his break with Roger, and Neil's warning about Chris. Greg knitted strands together into a coherent fabric, making as much sense of things as he could. He felt now the urgency to tell Roger and to pass on Neil's warning about Chris.

"Well how did your presentation go?" Sara asked.

"Oh, it went well, after all." Greg discussed his impression of it, the feedback he got from others. "And I'm still digesting my meeting with Master Chao Pi Ch'en this morning."

"Oh yeah, how did that go?"

"It was rich. He's an amazing teacher. His presence is strong, yet he also seems so ordinary. He knows a lot about Taoist teachings and I think I could learn a lot from him for my work on AlignIt. But he challenged me to study entities, attributes and relations in Qigong practice. He suggested I use practice to study and confirm what is in the literature and historical evidence. Makes sense. But how to do it—it's a big stretch. I don't even have a practice like that, except just sitting and trying to go into emptiness."

"You should do yoga with me," Sara said.

"Maybe I should. Yoga is intimately tied to Samkhya philosophy, which I should know better for AlignIt. I haven't read the Yoga Sutras in several years."

"Just do it with me."

"Okay." Greg laughed, catching himself intellectualizing. "So, you went to the Sensory Parlor Collective?"

"Yeah. Oh, it was amazing!" Sara described the inner struggle she felt in the morning between drawing in the Art Center and going to visit Elizabeth. She related how she hadn't submitted the intake form, and then decided at the last minute to do it. Luckily Elizabeth was available. Then she related the experience, how Elizabeth led her, how they went through the different tastes.

Greg listened intently as they walked by the marshes, taking in all that Sara shared.

"It feels like a turning point," Sara said. "Like I finally found something that could shift some deep patterns in me. It's not really meant to be therapeutic; it's really more like a spiritual practice. But Elizabeth is a really intuitive woman, and we got to a healing place." Sara described their exchange, how she opened up about food cravings and binging, how Elizabeth's intuitive insights felt on the mark. "I'm just amazed at the kinds of people drawn here," she said. "I felt like I could continue doing that work for a long time. I like Elizabeth and I feel like I could work with her more."

82

"He wanted you on the call, too," Jeff said, sitting down at his GameIt office table.

Roger took a seat beside Jeff. "Did he say why?"

"No." Jeff set his mobile on the table, touched on the screen projection and camera. "Just his findings on Mueller. Must be something important for both of us."

Jeff initiated the call. It rang and Jack answered. "Jack?"

"Hi guys," Jack said. "Good, you're both there. How are you doing, Roger? Sounds like you've got a situation."

"We do," Roger said. "We just had our AlignIt Commons board meeting, and Chris is driving hard to accelerate AlignIt's development. But it's our feeling that he's got some other interests that he's not being up front about."

"Well, I have some intel to add to your mix. You ready for this?"

"Yeah. Let's have it," Roger said.

"Okay. This comes from staff research and insider scoop." Jack opened up a side window in the conference call view. "This is the document I just emailed you. So Mueller's an entrepreneur-in-residence at Hilltop. And he's new in the Valley, by the way. Been here just under a year."

"Interesting," Roger said, "because…his CV tells me he has a lot of experience in the Valley."

"He may have," Jack said. "Some of his companies were here. But his base of operations has been elsewhere." Jack used an in-screen laser pointer to indicate his place. "A year ago, he was an entrepreneur in residence at Clearview Venture Partners in Reno, Nevada. Kind of a quirky organization with an unlikely cast of characters. Worked there for two years. He was brought in to run their portfolio companies. Here's the list," he said, highlighting with the pointer. "Most of those are startups with licenses from universities."

"So it looks like he's familiar with that kind of deal," Roger said.

"But he's a pretty aggressive CEO," Jack said. "Word is he's a brutal negotiator and squeezes his collaborators. He's had his share of successes, but he's also run these companies into the ground—the ones starred here." Jack pointed. "More than a traditional VC wants to see. And in those two years, he was sued twice by founders."

"Wow," Roger said. "Sued twice?"

"In two years," Jack emphasized. "One case is available, and I sent you the link. The other isn't yet; it looks to be still in litigation or it may settle out of court."

"That looks risky," Jeff said.

"I'll leave it to you to read it. I've skimmed it. Looks like he went like a shark after the profit center and squeezed the company dry. The university also has a claim in this one because he failed to diligently develop the technology."

"Hmm," Roger said. "Failed to develop the technology. That sounds consistent with what he told me on Monday. He wants to focus on marketing and licensing the AlignIt platform and abandon ontology development. But he eventually moved off that position when we talked the other day—or so it seemed."

"Jeff told me," Jack said. "It might be his modus operendi, though. Before Reno, he worked in New York for a questionable outfit called Heritage Holdings that's changed its name several times. Over about nine years, he purchased a lot of distressed companies, did a lot of risky deals with debt and assets, brought in unusual technology and people and management practices. He did this in Reno, too, by the way. Shedding the people, infrastructure, and company culture, changing out everything with resources from his other holdings. In New York, too, a lot of his companies failed." Jack pointed to the starred ones on the list.

"Wow," Roger said.

"More than a VC wants to see," Jack said. "They were distressed already, so it's hard to say he ruined them single-handedly. But you can see that its a colorful picture, and it leaves an odd impression. It gets hard to track because he's worked under so many DBAs, many off shore."

"Hmm," Roger said, pondering. His eyebrows crowded together into a frown. "That doesn't match his CV."

"Have you found anything on game companies?" Jeff asked.

"No," Jack said. "It's only recently that he's gotten into high tech investments. He's really been all over the map in terms of industry sectors. Utilities, shipping, chemicals, real estate, consumer electronics, health food. Even a yoga studio franchise. It's a very odd investment history. Many of these holdings were brief. So he buys low and sells high. Many of them, like I said, he completely gutted, filled with new technology and management, rebranded, and sold."

"So Jack, what do you make of this?" Roger asked.

"Based on this history," Jack said, "I'd be very, very cautious. He looks like an opportunist. And my read would be that he's identified AlignIt as a tech platform to snatch up, inject into a company, rebrand, and flip for a profit."

"Wow," Roger said. "I can see this. Now that you've pointed it out like this. I'm rethinking many of our conversations, and I can see this pattern." He breathed out loudly through his lips, shook his head. "I can't believe I didn't see this before. I feel like I got suckered by a crook."

"I can't find anything overtly shady here," Jack said, "but let's say it's a very unusual history and bizarre behavior for your typical VC. He knows how to make good money, but he deals in very risky approaches, and it's caught up with him several times, including the two law suits. And it looks like he shifts a lot, so you can't really tell where he is or what he's doing. But my biggest concern for you both is that his investment philosophy is inconsistent with what you're trying to do with the AlignIt Commons."

Roger sat back. "Well, he's certainly not into optimizing intellectual assets, let alone commonly held assets, like we're advocating through the ejido and usufruct principles of the Commons."

"And it looks like he just burns through people and companies," Jeff said. "I don't feel at all comfortable working with a character like this."

"This is a very different picture than what we've had of him," Roger said. "From what we have on file, it looks like he's been in the Valley for several years, handled lots of successful high tech companies, knows the big names."

"You can spin a story many ways," Jack said. "But my intel is good. It's from veterans in the VC community who've had dealings with him. You have to sift through a lot of noise which very often he himself created—constant name changes and companies holding companies holding companies."

"I'm just shocked at this picture," Roger said. "I feel dumbfounded."

"Yeah, it's like meeting someone entirely new, or like a split personality," Jeff said.

"So is this the kind of person we want to have on board as a guide?" Roger asked.

"Why is it, actually, that you've taken to him?" Jack asked.

"Initially, it was just because he approached me with interest and offers of assistance. This was at the semantic web conference in San Francisco last summer." Roger paused, pondering what drew him to Chris. Then an insight came to him. "Only two angel investors had been interested before that, and they gave small investments. It surprised me when Chris came with money, expertise, and connections. So we talked over coffee, and it seemed he understood and valued what I was trying to do with AlignIt. He said he was a meditator and he was interested in yoga. He seemed to know something about it. It felt uncanny to me. Here was someone apparently well connected, with access to capital, who understood what I was trying to do. But come to think of it, I didn't really know much about his background except the names he dropped—the investors, entrepreneurs, the companies he's worked in, the people he knows."

"You may be a magnet for a certain kind of predatory VC-entrepreneur, even a spiritual one," Jack said. "You may have to be more circumspect about who you let in."

Roger nodded and thought. "This is a big lesson in discernment." He was silent a moment. "This is humbling."

After the call, Jeff walked into Landon's sandbox, as he called it—his creative workspace. "Are you still working on that Chris Mueller game?"

Landon looked up. "You asked me to put it aside."

"But you're still working on it?"

"Well yeah. New tips came from friends. So I updated it some more. Why?"

Jeff remained standing. "Why don't you pull it up again. Roger and I just got off the phone with Jack and we have a whole lot of new stuff on Mueller. I just moved a file into that work folder."

"What did he say?"

Jeff summarized, explained the document. "So we're back to high priority on this. Can you work it up quickly? Roger's trying to schedule a meeting with Jackie right now."

83

Roger and Jeff brought Landon with his mock up intelligence game on Mueller into the Research Access Office. They waved at the receptionist, walked back to Jackie's office.

"I invited Rachel Ho, too," Jackie said, "just to have legal counsel in the room."

Roger's eyes brightened to see her there. "Hey, Rachel. It's a good thing."

Rachel nodded, chatted.

"Okay, I have something that's going to knock your socks off," Jeff said when they sat. He put his mobile on the table top. "Landon built a game out of our intel on Mueller."

"Really?" Jackie said. It stopped her, eyes wide.

"I just learned of this, too," Roger said. "So this may help us put the pieces together."

"And Landon integrated Jack's notes from our call," Jeff said to Roger.

"Already?" Roger asked, surprised.

"Yup," Landon said.

"The guy's a wizard," Jeff said.

Landon touched on the screen projection, directed it to the wall. Jackie stood up, walked to the windows. She turned the blinds to darken the room.

"Just so I'm up to date," Rachel said, "Mueller's not yet on the board, correct?"

"Right," Roger said. "We should have nothing binding us, and I can't foresee any ramifications."

"I pulled up the AlignIt Commons bylaws, just in case," Rachel said. "But I think you're in a good position."

"He can't pull back the gifts to me and Bateson?" Roger asked, even though he knew the answer.

"No," Rachel said. "They're gifts, no strings attached. Once given, they're yours. I wouldn't expect any more gifts from him, though."

"Okay, ready?" Landon asked. Everyone nodded. He touched play. Stunning visuals displayed onto the wall, and a slew of information about Chris Mueller appeared, including a few photos.

"Here's a geo map of companies he's been involved with," Landon said.

"They're all over," Jackie said. "Palo Alto, Reno, New York, Toronto, Tel Aviv, Johannesburg. It's interesting to see your data visualization."

"If I touch here," Landon said, "the primary companies fade, and we get a look at related but secondary companies." One view faded to another, revealing those companies. "I touch here, and we see that some of the people, technologies, and IP he has access to cross between primary and secondary companies."

"You did all this in just the last few days?" Roger asked.

"Yeah," Landon said. "Now check this out." He turned to Jackie and Rachel. "Jack, our VC, uncovered two law suits." Landon touched another button in the projection. All the companies were muted except two, which got highlighted. "If we look at lists of plaintiffs from news and public records, you'll see that they're not only in these two companies, but," Landon clicked again, "Mark Johnson is a director of a holding company who has assets connected with Mueller. Pete Schlissel is on an advisory board for a bunch of companies that Mueller's also an advisor on…this is a web of tightly connected business transactions. It's very strange. A bunch of these people are on each other's boards, invest in each other's companies. Some of these investors and advisors use the same consultants over and over again in their portfolio companies."

Roger's jaw dropped, seeing the visualization of the loose threads of facts compiled by disparate people over several days. Fact patterns he hadn't seen yet himself.

"That makes Mueller a highly conflicted individual," Jackie said. "Even if it didn't show up in our search. Because he has financial conflicts, and conflicts of obligations, yet he's right in the middle of these transactions. And sure enough, he has two law suits on his hands." She paused. "Wow, this is amazing work." She turned to Jeff. "My office could use this game of Landon's for our due diligence on other companies and technologies."

"I think he's had ideas about that," Jeff said, chuckling.

"This is astounding," Rachel said. "If Mueller has conflicts like this, and if he engages in the kind of risky business behavior you've uncovered, this is obviously not the kind of advisor we want for AlignIt."

"Okay, but here's the kicker," Jeff said. "Mueller said he has game companies in his network?" He looked to Roger for a confirming nod. "So far, we've turned up very few direct ties, right? Like direct investments, direct employment, board roles. But look at all of these weak ties." Jeff pointed to Landon's screens views. "If you follow this cluster right here, bingo, here are the game companies he's not telling us about. This holding company has invested in a whole bunch of distressed game start ups that got jettisoned by their investors after series A. And these guys on the board have ties to Mueller."

"So he's flipping companies," Jackie said.

"That's what Jack said, too." Jeff said.

Jackie turned from the screen to Roger and Jeff. "We've spotted four cases of some pretty brutal shredding and recoupling of technologies in his companies. Like the example Cindy gave of the New York start up, Q4."

"Right," Jeff said. "Mueller got access through an IP sharing agreement, and he stripped it and built in BlackDog features. Jack says this appears to be his modus operendi."

"I told you I met with Mueller here about six months ago," Jackie said. "He was scouting for available Bridge Institute technologies. He kept telling me he gets access to a lot of nascent technologies and plugs them into companies in his network. I remember he name-dropped a lot, so yesterday I went back over the high profile roles on his CV. I checked several, and it turns out most of them are volunteer, self-interested no less, and they're very short term. In one case where Mueller said he worked with Dmitri Popovich at InfoMundo, I discovered that it was a panel Mueller himself created and invited Popovich to join. Popovich apparently had only expressed willingness to consider the invitation. When he saw his name listed, he was pretty upset. So this seems to be Mueller's drill. He talks big and creates the impression he rubs shoulders with big, mainstream companies. But he has this other network going on behind the scenes of the big names he drops. Anyway, Mueller wanted a special access agreement, an exclusive subscription agreement, to everything that comes out of the Bridge Institute."

"What?" Rachel laughed, surprised. "That's absurd."

Jackie nodded. "So he could do the same thing here that he's done elsewhere."

"Suck up technologies and run them into companies to resell," Jeff said.

Jackie sat back. "I told him we couldn't do that; we'd need to see his business plan in each case."

"Ready for a grand finale?" Landon said.

Rachel and Jackie looked at him, surprised. "There's more?" Jackie said.

Landon raised his eyebrows with a triumphant smile. "You know your valued Bridge Institute employee, Mrs. Amelia Blocke?"

"The mysterious woman no one seems to have met yet," Roger said.

"Here's your Bridge Institute HR director, Mrs. Blocke." Landon clicked a button, revealing ties Blocke had to numerous primary and secondary companies on the map. "HR for all these companies."

Rachel's eyes opened wide. "What?"

"Look at them all," Landon said. "And look at this." He touched another button in the air. "Blocke's ties with Mueller."

"Wow!" Rachel said in a breathy voice, staring at the screen projection.

"Sixteen companies!" Landon said.

"No doubt the reason Blocke has put off Greg this week," Roger said.

Jackie shook her head, staring at the screen projection, following the connections. She took a breath, reflected. Then she turned around in her chair, faced Roger. "Why don't you talk to Bateson? I know there are other complaints about her."

"I'm going to." Roger leaned back on the wall. "Catherine Stone tried to hire someone recently. She was stalled a long time and ultimately lost the candidate."

"She told me," Jackie said. "It doesn't sound good."

"I don't want to lose Greg."

"I think this is important," Jackie said. "Bateson is the only one over Blocke. That's one of the problems right there, if you ask me. But if an investigation is needed, he's the one to authorize it. And it looks like there are things to discover."

Roger nodded. "Okay," he said. "So I said to Jack and Jeff that I feel pretty humbled by all of this. I got suckered by Mueller. I was too eager to have someone of his stature, or what I thought was his stature, take an interest in AlignIt. I think his interest really surprised me. And I implicitly trusted him where it's clear I shouldn't have."

"I wouldn't take it too personally, Roger," Jackie said. "Other universities went for it, too. He talks a good talk, he's confident, and what he says is so plausible it's easy not to investigate it sufficiently. He had all of us fooled. Even Bateson."

"He's a con artist," Rachel said. "He's set up a false screen of business activities. And he's deceptively concealed the real trail of his dealings."

"I feel responsibility," Roger said, "because I created AlignIt, and the AlignIt Commons, and I brought this guy in."

"Well, you acted in the best interest of everyone with the knowledge you had," Jackie said, "with all the systems we have for checks and balances. There are lessons to learn here, for all of us. But again, I wouldn't be hard on yourself."

"And it's really been a group effort to surface this history of Mueller's," Jeff said. "So yeah, I'd give yourself a break on this one. I think we're all learning a lesson here, like Jackie says, in being on guard against opportunists coming to scoop or subvert what we're trying to do here at the Bayside Village."

"Fair enough," Roger said. "So we need a plan of action. I want to take back his invitation to the AlignIt Commons board. And I want to freeze any transactions we may have with him."

"We don't have any," Jackie said. "We're very lucky to have caught this early. Nothing to terminate, no financial headaches, nothing to work out."

"Roger, from what I see," Rachel said, "all you need is a formal letter rescinding your offer of board membership. I'll draft one for you."

"And no one here could have anticipated this connection between Mueller and Blocke," Jackie said. "That's central administration. And that needs to be addressed, too."

"Right. I have my meeting with Bateson tomorrow morning," Roger said. "He's scheduled a call with the Board of Trustees."

84

Greg, Sara and Tara walked through the Dining Commons and out to the reception patio where they had met for their first Bayside Village event Sunday evening. And tonight was their final night, for the Friday evening Floricanto, their last Bayside Village event.

The patio was fully transformed into a festive Latino atmosphere. Booths were set up where attendants cooked food, demonstrated traditional crafts, offered games, sold books and media, and promoted events and organizations. Decorative artisanas were strung about overhead, and piñatas were hung. Most impressive to Sara was a series of mini sculptures and statues, including small scale replicas of Mayan, Aztec and Incan palaces and temples, like those at the Ateneo de la Scientia Sacra. A stage was decorated, and a band had just begun Peruvian pipe music.

"Let's make a quick circle around the patio just to see what's here first, okay?" Sara said. "Then we'll get some food."

"Okay," Greg said.

The family walked amidst the smoky air, smelling of corn cooked in the husk, yucca, plantain, beans and rice. At one booth, a group of onlookers watched tortillas being made by hand. Greg and Sara stopped, and Greg held up Tara to see over the adults. Tara watched as tortillas flipped back and forth between women's palms.

Greg stopped by Jeff's booth with the Mayan Ball Game. It had a large projection screen under a tarp shielding the early evening sunlight, and many people were huddled around. Sara and Tara stopped with Greg and watched amidst the crowd. Two players stood before the game projection on the screen. They wore suits with body sensors wirelessly feeding player movement data to the game system. A Mayan ball field was vividly portrayed in graphic images, with small rubber balls hit from the hips of players, aimed for small portals high above the game field.

"Hey, Greg and Sara," Jeff called, walking over. "Good to see you again."

"Jeff, long time, no see," Greg said.

"Hi Jeff," Sara said. "And you remember Tara?"

"Yes I do, hello Tara." Tara smiled at Jeff and said hi.

Tara reached for Sara, wanted up to see the game over the heads of adults.

"Your husband gave a great presentation today," Jeff said.

"I'm glad to hear it," Sara said.

"So Greg, you haven't seen this one yet—the Mayan ball game. You want cosmology? We've got cosmology!" Jeff beamed proudly. "The game of creation, life and death—right here."

"This is vivid," Greg exclaimed, studying the screen. The ball moved quickly up and down the field and ricocheted off the ball field walls. One player in front of the screen finally hit the ball into the other team's portal. The crowd standing around the screen went wild with excitement. The game played on, as the ball went up and down the field. The game scenes featured the ritual costumes of the projected Mayan audience in the bleachers, the king and queen, and the royal court. Then, all at once, the hard rubber ball impaled a player in the chest and unleashed a blood bath on the field.

"Ooh," Sara exclaimed, turning Tara away.

"Yeah," Jeff said, "you might avert her eyes on some parts. It's a violent game, traditionally. No Hollywood embellishing here—this is how it was. Quite a bit more dangerous than soccer."

"I'll say," Greg said.

"So, if we can get an ontologist on board," Jeff said, elbowing Greg and smiling, "we might get to some depth about the traditional layered symbols and meanings of the ball game—blood, death, sacrifice, field, ball, and two teams. Right?"

"Yeah, there's a lot here. I'll need to study up..." Greg trailed off, his attention captivated again by swift and skillful game plays. He felt a rush of adrenalin. "Wow," he said, with sudden enthusiasm at a pass of the ball.

"Greg, I'm going to take Tara to the temple replicas. Can you meet me there in a few minutes?"

"Sure, Love," Greg said, turning to Sara, and then back to the screen. His eyes shuttled between the suited players standing on a mat, and their representations on the screen. He stood closer to Jeff. "It's amazing that they can get so deep into the game just standing here and making all of these moves in place."

"Yeah, it's challenging, actually," Jeff said, "because there isn't a lot of space to move around, and we haven't arranged it for running up and down the field. But my hope in this game is to recreate something of the historical game beyond pictures—to help people get a feeling for Mayan roots and how something of this can be lived today—the right things. It's great when people get physically involved in something with a whole world of meaning like this."

"Yeah. Jeff, this is amazing!" Greg watched several moments. "Hey, I want to catch up with Sara and get some food for Tara. We were going to do a quick go-round, eat, and then spend more time at each booth. So will you be around later?"

"Yup, all night. Oh, before you go…" Jeff turned in closer to Greg. "Just so you know, you did a great job today. Your Q&A was awesome!"

"Thanks."

"I know you're scheduled to debrief with Roger tomorrow." He paused. "A lot happened in the luncheon and board meeting today, as I'm sure you picked up. And we're handling it. I know you're still evaluating us. But we want to be sure you take away the right message. A lot of us want you here, if you decide to come." Jeff spoke deliberately. "Just make sure you get the scoop from Roger before you head out." Jeff looked carefully at Greg. "Okay?"

"Okay. I figured something was going on, and I've observed some odd things myself."

"I'm sure. You should discuss it with Roger. But I just wanted to make sure you didn't take on Mueller's approach to you as representative."

"Thanks."

Greg walked over to Sara and Tara who were now standing again by the Tortilla making. They stood watching for a moment.

"They sell tortillas here, with a variety of fillings," Sara said, pointing to a display. Artful bowls of cut tomatillos, peppers, cactus, rice, and beans were on display. "I think Tara's hungry."

"Mmm," Greg said. "Maybe something small until we go around?"

"Yeah." Sara walked up to the counter and asked for a burrito with mild fillings.

"Do you want to watch them make it?" Greg asked Tara, and he picked her up to watch the man on the other side taking a hot tortilla, adding cubed cactus, beans, tomatillo and rice, and folding it up. Sara took the burrito.

"What's on the mango, there?" Greg asked the man, pointing to a bowl of yellow-orange cubes.

"Chilies and salt," the man said. "Its very spicy. If you like spicy, it's good."

"I'll try it," Greg said. The man scooped up mango chunks into a cup, put in a spoon, and handed it over the counter. Greg took it. He reached into his pocket, about to pay.

"Do you take Bayside Village Dollars?" Sara asked the man.

Greg turned, squinted, surprised at this turn in Sara.

"Yes. We prefer them, actually," the man said.

"Do you have any, Love?" Sara asked Greg.

"No."

Sara dug into her purse, found some, paid the man.

They turned from the vendor and Sara handed the burrito to Tara. "Hold it carefully, Honey, so the vegetables don't fall out." Tara took it and began eating.

They walked on, around the patio. Greg looked at Sara. "You're using them. The coins."

"I've been using them, slowly. They're almost gone."

Greg nodded. "Really?" He took a bite of his mango and chili. "Whoa!" He breathed fire.

"What's that like," Sara asked.

"Hot. But really tasty. Want some?"

"Okay, I'll try it."

Greg spooned up mango cubes speckled in red peppers and salt and held it up to Sara's mouth. She opened and received the spoon.

"Ooh," she said, "Wow. That's hot." She smiled. "Oh, that's different."

"Can I have some, Daddy?"

"It's too hot, Honey. It'll burn your mouth. We'll get you a treat after we have dinner, okay?"

85

The family walked around the stalls, looking. Then Greg pointed. "There's Roger."

Roger was seated at a table eating and talking with another man. Greg realized then that he hadn't seen Roger after the board meeting. Roger had shut the board room door with Chris. Greg felt that he had presented well, but a seed of self-doubt lingered in him. What did Roger and Chris discuss in private? What's going on under the surface here? These questions need answering sometime, he thought. Yet Jeff just gave encouraging feedback. So Greg took heart and walked bravely to Roger with Sara and Tara.

"Roger," Greg said.

Roger stood up. "Hey, Greg and Sara, I'd like you to meet Jorge Gonzales. He founded our Floricanto events."

Jorge stood and turned. Greg and Sara shook hands with him.

"This is the philosophy guy?" Jorge asked.

"Yep, he's the one." Roger said.

"Ah, very important work, it sounds like. Maybe you can help Floricanto as well. Roger says you can help to find patterns, to lift out things hidden."

"Well I guess so. That's one outcome," Greg said. He noted briefly that Roger was still promoting him, and Roger had stood up when they approached. Greg searched but found no hints of change in Roger's rapport. "And Sara is an artist," Greg said, shifting attention to her. "She can bring decorative flair."

"So he said." Jorge waived to Roger.

Sara nodded. "I do industrial design in the high tech industry. But on my own time, I also paint and draw."

"You don't say." Jorge turned his shoulders and torso to face her.

"I've done a few sketches of Mayan ruins, actually—like Chichen Itza on the Yucatan Peninsula near Cancun."

"Chichen Itza! That is the best."

"Yeah. We were there—what Greg—maybe six months ago now?" Greg nodded. "Just visiting for a week-long vacation with friends, mostly exploring ruins."

"One of our friends has a pensione in Merida," Greg said, lifting a last, uneaten bit of Tara's burrito to his mouth.

Sara continued. "We've visited a few times, actually. Each time, we visit the ruins. Especially on the Yucatan Peninsula—some on the coast, some inland. I'm always amazed to see these awesome structures, the apartments, the ancient ball fields, the temples and ritual areas. I could almost feel what it would be like if the whole thing was alive and vital now. I imagined I felt the ancestors."

Greg turned to Jorge. "She enjoyed studying the structures and symbolism so much that she deeply imagined her way into the mythic fabric of Mayan life."

Sara nodded.

"Yes, yes. This is a good way," Jorge said, surprised, delighted.

"And you always sit and draw them," Greg said to Sara, prodding her. "And several years ago you took your easel, remember?"

"Oh yeah," Sara said, recalling a distant memory. "Yeah, the architecture and the artistic motifs really fascinate me."

"You have a feeling for this," Jorge said.

"I think so, yeah," Sara said, smiling beautifully from his attention. "I can feel something deeper in it, and I tried to capture the spirit in it."

"This is good. This is what we try to do with Floricanto here, too—to bring the spirit of our old traditions alive today, and to make ways to live this today, in our world, in our time. Do you have them here—these art works?"

"No, I wish I did," Sara said. "Maybe next time we come I can bring some of my work."

There it is again, Greg noted—next time we come.

"Yes, I would like to see it," Jorge said. "Especially your feeling, how you feel the ancestors."

Randy and Elizabeth Seton walked up behind Roger. Randy put his hands firmly on Roger's shoulders and squeezed. "Has he been good to you this week," Randy asked Greg.

Roger turned around. "Hey Randy, Elizabeth."

"Hello Roger," Elizabeth said. "Hello Sara." She lingered with a kindly and penetrating look to Sara.

Sara nodded to Elizabeth, smiled deeply. "Hello again."

Greg noted the connection.

"Really nice talk today," Randy said to Greg. "I look forward to hearing more."

"Thanks," Greg said.

Jorge turned. "Hola Senorita, como estas?"

"Muy bien, Senor Gonzales." Elizabeth stepped forward and they gave kisses on the cheek. "Y tu?"

"La vida es buena," Jorge said, raising his hands, gesturing to the surroundings, the Floricanto event.

"Hola, Jorge," Randy said, "que pasa?"

"Randall, this time you should try Rosa's chicken mole," Jorge said. "It is the best mole, I tell you."

"We will, Senor Gonzales." Randy turned. "So," he said again to Greg, "how is this man treating you this week?"

"He's been a gracious host and colleague," Greg said.

"Good," Randy said. "We like to hear that."

"And so have you," Sara said to Randy.

Elizabeth turned to Sara, a commanding yet unbelieving look on her face. "I heard he took you into our storage room."

"He did," Sara said, feeling center stage again. "I was interviewing with Karen Mitchell, the Development Director, and I wanted to find everything I could on the Village's visual communications. Randy told me there were other collections in a vault somewhere. So I asked him where."

"Randy, Randy," Elizabeth said, turning, rolling her eyes. "Opening up our closets and bone yards."

"It was fun," Sara said, with a twinkle in her eyes. "It's like another side of the Bayside Village. Like another tour."

"It is," Randy said. "We found some treasures there, like you said." Randy then squinted his eyes, spoke with a humorous air. "And who knows what else may lie hidden in the Vault?"

Elizabeth shook her head incredulously. "You read too much."

Randy grabbed Roger's shoulders tightly and slapped him on the right one. "We'll see you around." And they continued walking around the patio.

"Will you join us?" Roger asked Greg and Sara, pointing to the table and benches where he and Jorge had been sitting.

Greg looked to Sara who nodded, and back to Roger. "Sure."

Everyone sat down, and HowHGreg turned to Jorge. "So, we heard about Floricanto on Monday's tour at the Ateneo de la Scientia Sacra. And now we've met you. I've been wanting to ask about Floricanto."

"Ah," Jorge said, taking a sip of horchata and putting it down. He cleared his throat. "The word floricanto means…a form of poetry, a form of cultural narrative. It is used traditionally in Mexico—by the Aztecas. And in 1960's in the U.S., this was reclaimed by the Chicano movement. Floricanto was the new approach in Chicano poetry. It brings together prayer and poetry, as they were combined originally in Aztec culture."

"Prayer and poetry," Greg said, reflectively.

Roger sat back. Having introduced the two men, he let them get on together.

"It derives from the Nahautl language of the Aztecs," Jorge said. "It comes from the Nahuatl phrase 'xochitl in cuicatl,' which translates to the Spanish 'flor y canto,' and the English 'flower and song,'"

"Flower and song," Greg echoed. "Oh, that's nice."

"So we've reclaimed floricanto here at Bayside Village," Jorge said. "It's our regular celebration. We reclaimed it for sacred science. We put it on through the Ateneo de la Scientia Sacra on festival days in the Mayan calendar. We do a whole evening celebrating the sacred traditions in Latino culture. This includes the readings by poets, art works like you see all around, like this dancing with the live Latino bands playing, and rituals like we will see with the Mayan dances—and this good food. And let me tell you a secret," Jorge said. He narrowed his eyes, bent closer to the table, and leaned to Greg and Sara. "See that booth over there?" he said, pointing, yet holding his hand close to his chest. "You should go there and ask for the Chili Relleno. It is the best," he said, sitting back again after divulging the secret. "And their Chicken Mole is also the best, because of how they cook the chocolate and the peppers. You should go there. My wife Rosa is there." Jorge winked, and a faint, ironic smile rippled across the musculature of his face. He sat back, raise his voice again. "But also, look at the lines. I am telling you, it is the best food."

"Okay," Greg said, smiling. "Maybe we'll do that." He looked at Sara who nodded, shrugged her shoulders.

"What makes Floricanto special here," Roger interjected, "besides the food, of course," he said, nodding and waiving his hand to Jorge, "is the historical, cultural, and spiritual depth Jorge and Rosa bring to it. It's focused on the deep, sacred roots of cultural impulses that Jorge and Rosa are trying to carry forward today and synergize with American and Western culture, without letting it get co-opted by dominant cultures."

Sara took another spoon of pepper-spiced mango cubes from Greg's cup and let the hot, sweet and salty taste burn in her mouth. She thought of Elizabeth. This night itself, indeed the whole week, was a sort of taste parlor. "Excuse me, Jorge," she said, "I want to get us some food. Where is Rosa's booth—that one?"

"Of course, the family needs to eat," Jorge said, turning his body around as Sara got up with Tara. "Yes, that one right there. Ask for the Chili Relleno and the Chicken Mole. It gives you a taste of Floricanto. Tell them Jorge sent you," he said. "Rosa will give something special to this beautiful girl."

"Okay, thanks. Come with me, Tara." Sara and Tara walked to a long line for more food.

Jorge turned back around. Greg asked many questions about floricanto, imagined what he could do with it if he came to Bayside Village.

After a time, Sara returned with Tara from Rosa's booth. She put down a tray with several dishes. "I got this to share," she said to Roger and Jorge. "Plantain chips," she said, taking a bowl from the tray, "and yucca fries with guacamole," she said, putting the bowls in the center of the table.

"Oh, thanks," Roger said.

Then Sara put down Chicken Mole to share with Tara, and Chili Relleno for Greg, and sat down.

"Thanks, Love," Greg said. "And what do you have, Tara? You have chocolate on your chicken?"

Tara looked at Greg, unsure of the juxtaposition. "It's not chocolate, Daddy, it's mole."

Greg smiled. "It's made with chocolate. Can I taste it?" Tara nodded. Greg put his spoon in the mole and tasted. "Mmm, that is good! Taste it."

Jenny came to the table with a tray of horchatas and spiced cocoa.

"Hi Jenny," Greg said.

"Hello Greg. Good to see you again," Jenny had a grand and gracious smile. She put her hand on Roger's shoulder as she seated herself on the bench.

Sara offered Jenny the treats she had brought. And she realized, with disappointment, that Jenny missed Jorge's questions to her about her art, the discussion with Roger and Elizabeth about the Vault and the interview with Karen. She wished Jenny had heard those things.

Greg and Jorge continued. Roger listened, held the space.

Sara turned to Jenny. "I still want to talk with you about art."

Jenny turned to Sara, gave her full presence. "Yes, you have some lingering questions about the artist community here."

Sara's eyes lit up. She felt recognized, remembered. She saw that she had now the opportunity she had been waiting for. "I do. Yeah, I'm beginning to turn back to fine art after some years. Our path has been hard on us, breaking old things away. And it feels like art is starting to come around again for me."

Jenny nodded, giving Sara deep, concentrated eye contact. "Yes, some things can be given back at a higher level, if they're the right things for us. We've seen this in our group, too. And in ourselves, of course, years ago."

"And with the Art Center here," Sara said, "I guess I'm wondering what kind of community of like-minded people there might be here."

"Ah. You know, I'm not an artist myself. But I have some good friends, long time artists. They use the studio and help guide it along a higher course." Jenny named three friends, described their teachers, their training, what they do at the Art Center. "When you come back for a visit, or if you move here, I'll introduce you."

"I'd like to meet them," Sara said. The image of artists able to guide the Art Center, like elders perhaps, stayed with her. She turned to Tara for a moment, cut the chicken substitute into small pieces. Tara was almost old enough to do this herself, now. But parental involvement itself was just as important as the cutting. She turned back to Jenny. "What actually is your role, then?"

"I don't speak of it much," Jenny said. "I'm on several boards here, including the Art Center and the Raymond Lully Museum, where I help steer program development, faculty and staff recruitment, exhibit selection, curation. I help guide the way we're establishing sacred sciences and arts."

"Wow," Sara said. The thought of such a lofty role struck her, and she realized she didn't have a clear picture of what kind of person, what education, what qualifications, went into such a role. Or how Jenny got there. "What kind of...I mean, how do you...What criteria do you use, say, for exhibit selection? I can't picture what you do, what your role looks like. Or your background. I mean, how do you decide what fits and what doesn't?"

Jenny gave a faint grin, but it seemed to hold back more than it revealed. For the first time, Sara observed Jenny in a reserved attitude.

"Not everything fits here," Jenny said gravely, as if Sara should understand and appreciate it. Jenny raised her spiced cocoa to her lips, sipped.

Sara had noticed Jenny's introversion, but this was something different, something more. Was it a matter of propriety? Was there something sacred here, some line not to cross? Was something too subtle, too fine, to say so casually? Sara was new, after all, merely a visitor, and Jenny had been involved from the beginning, or earlier—she didn't know how long, really. The Bayside Village seems transparent overall, but now Sara was touching a vein of executive leadership, of boards, of first principles, of the power to hire and select and exclude. Maybe this was different. Jenny showed a new face, a new expression. And Sara wasn't sure how to regard it.

Jenny put down the glass, kept it in her fingers, turned it around with her fingers while still looking at it. "It takes a lot to keep this place on course." She let go of the glass, looked back to Sara. "You can't imagine, or maybe you can, all the crazy things people want to bring here. We could easily become a playground for weak, inferior arts and sciences. Just a venue for the fringe elements we already see around the Bay Area. Then we're simply a mirror of what already exists, and we're no longer creating a new civilization, creating new sacred sciences, arts and crafts."

Sara nodded, felt the weight of some burden Jenny carried, felt the truth of it herself, even. Maybe this was why Jenny had seemed to elude her, had been circumspect. Sara had not been down pathways like this before, had not been close to leadership at her Sufi Center, had not been involved in decisions and guiding the course of things. She saw Jenny now as a more capable, more quietly powerful, yet more nuanced woman than she first supposed.

The music on stage now changed as the sky turned a dusky blue. A reader now took the stage, and a guitar player, bass player, drummer, and flutist accompanied.

Jenny gave Sara an intricate smile with shades of warm depths, receptive understanding, severity, and a sense of carrying something portentous, all in one glance. Then she turned to the stage for the reading she knew was coming. The impression bewildered Sara, and she turned to the stage, too, still working out what this all could mean.

The reader introduced the classic Floricanto poem, 'I Am Joachin,' with a brief description of its role in the Chicano movement, and then commenced a dramatic reading of the epic work. A collage of images, videos, and animations paraded on the screen and in holographic images projected into the dance area. Greg, Sara, and Tara watched, mesmerized by compelling images, some disturbing to Tara. The poem, the images, moved Sara with a political consciousness she seldom met in her industrial art world.

Then a new band took the stage, playing Cubanismo. With their food settled somewhat, Sara said to Tara, "Let's dance!" Sara rose, taking Tara's hand. "Greg, come dance with us!"

"I'll be there in a minute," Greg replied. "I just want to talk with Jorge a bit more about floricanto."

Sara gave a playful look of disappointment, but she went out with Tara to the center of the patio. She danced and Greg watched her elegant, sensual moves.

"Greg," Roger said, "You should go dance. We'll be here."

"Augh," Greg said. "I wanted to ask about the qualities in the Mayan system, the ontology...."

"Why don't you go dance the ontology?" Roger encouraged. "I see a beautiful goddess with child out there. Go study ontology on your feet and come back with a report."

Dance the ontology? Greg was halted in his tracks, put off from the chase of his mind after the prey of ideas. He shook his head with a sigh in recognition of this familiar pattern of his, and he brightened to a knowing smile. He looked to Sara, gliding and smiling with Tara to the rhythm of Cubanismo. "You're right. Here I am, Mr. Ideas. And there she is, my Beloved, my earthly consort."

"Yes, go dance," Jorge encouraged. "We will talk later."

"Okay," Greg said, surrendering. And he left the table and went out into the sea of dancing colors on a new hunt.

"Anyway, where is my wife?" Jorge said to Roger.

Greg found Sara holding hands with Tara and dancing.

"There you are," Sara said looking up, desirous.

"I wanted to talk with Jorge. I just met him," Greg said. "But here I am."

"Daddy, up." Tara said.

"Up? My, you're a big girl now. You're getting heavy for Daddy."

"She might be getting tired," Sara said with a jumpy, breathy voice as her body moved back and forth to the bongos, the brass, the passion of Cubanismo.

"Okay, let's see if Daddy can hold you." Greg picked up Tara and awkwardly worked out a shuffle back and forth next to Sara. At first stiff, he soon fell into a natural rhythm, and the family emerged into a new pattern.

Greg saw Randy and Elizabeth dancing behind Sara. He liked the thought of seeing them, an older couple, enjoying the Floricanto. Everything was included, everyone part of it.

When the song changed, Roger and Jenny, and Jorge and Rosa, came out to the floor with Greg, Sara and Tara. After some moments, Jenny asked if she could dance with Tara. Greg asked Tara who nodded and wiggled to get down. Greg put her down and Roger and Jenny danced with her beside Greg and Sara.

Now unburdened, Greg's awkwardness resumed. Just being there, himself, with no child, gave him a freedom to dance he hadn't especially sought.

Greg found security by keeping step with Sara, who danced blithely. He shared tender glances and watched her graceful movements. She was natural; he was not. She was beautiful.

Sara pointed to the side. "I guess Leah's gone."

Greg looked. Across the floor, Keith was dancing with Emily. They both were dressed nicely, he noticed, and he watched them a moment. Keith seemed happier. "I wonder what she's like for him."

The music changed. The last piece morphed slowly from Cubanismo to native, tribal drumming. It began first from the stage, and was joined soon by drumming sounding from behind the crowds, invisibly, in a call-and-response with the stage. The dancing changed, like ripples on a pond surface intersected by new ones from another stone plunging.

Tara tugged on Greg's sleeve, wanting up. He hoisted her to his waist again. Tara looked on at the fascinating, frightful scene. Dancers dressed in traditional, Mayan ritual outfits, with skeleton-patterned tights, slowly entered the patio from all corners. Some bore torches; others carried drums. A man on stage in Mayan dress took the microphone and thanked the band playing the last set. The brass musicians, guitarist, bass player and others now exited the stage. A new musician in traditional dress began with a haunting reed flute melody invoking the sounds of animals. Attention shifted to the middle of the patio, where a space opened up as the Mayan dancers moved slowly, rhythmically, into the center. A space cleared and people gathered around the dancers, clapping, swaying to the new Mayan beat.

Tara held tightly, unsure of the drums, fire and dancing. The music pulsated, entrancing Greg and Sara and all around. Greg spoke to Tara in low, reassuring tones about what unfolded before them. The mood turned shamanic. He relished the worlds invoked in Mayan sound and figures.

86

Greg and Sara returned to the Lodge and put Tara to bed in the roll-away. Sara removed her dancing dress and slipped into her pajamas. She sat down on the bed. Greg undressed, put on sweat pants and sweat shirt, and sat beside Sara. They lounged on the bed and fell into free-form reflection on the week. Now the events were over. It was a grand week, Greg felt as he looked back. Impressions from all the events bubbled up before them.

Sara ran through the arc of her turn toward Bayside Village. She retraced the tour, her trip to the secret Vault with Randy, dinner with Roger and Jennie, her interview with Karen, her meeting with Elizabeth at the Sensory Parlor Collective. She still pondered, but didn't yet share, her exchange with Jenny at the Floricanto. Through it all, she felt the significance of her return to painting and drawing this week and the place this return might have in their lives together.

Greg reflected on the fascinating opportunities before him, his meetings with masterful teachers, the puzzling encounters with Mrs. Blocke and Chris Mueller, the ups and downs in his moods as various fears tugged at him, threatened to overtake his reason.

One theme rose up above the rest right for Greg now. He turned. "It's interesting. Roger said 'Why don't you dance the ontology?' The image captures what many teachers have said to me this week. I felt it in yoga, in Qigong, in meeting that Sufi teacher."

"Exactly!" Sara said. "Roger's so insightful. That's your growing edge, I think." She paused. "I can see that this is no ordinary academic place. You can't succeed here just by delivering lectures on mental models. Something more is needed. They want more from you. If we come here, we'll be eating with people, dancing with people, meditating with people. And I want more with you, too. You're going to have to meditate and dance and…whatever. Dance the ontology. That should be your mantra."

"To take that seriously…" Greg said, trailing off in thought. "It's a departure from everything I've worked so hard for."

"Greg, have you really worked all these years to end up like the senior faculty in your field? Or like Neil? Are you really only after tenure in that kind of system? When I met you, you had a passion to teach certain ideas. It wasn't about maintaining the status quo or fitting in. You've wanted to study and teach things that you can't at UW. Or anywhere, really. And here you could." Sara paused. "I think you should be careful not to apply the success criteria of mainstream academia to being here. This works differently."

"You already see us here."

"Yeah, I guess. I'm just saying that if this is what you want, then why are you trying to carefully protect the tenure route, or some image you have of professorship in mainstream academia?"

"Because I have that in hand, or almost," Greg said. "I don't have this in hand. This is uncertain."

"Tenure is uncertain."

"True."

"Conventional criteria won't serve you here." Sara sat back on the bed. "I think you're torn inside, and you're not sure about what you want."

Greg looked at the wall ahead of him and nodded. This thought obviously put the finger on the big issue. Greg was silent, pensive, turning over Sara's challenge in his mind.

"It's true," Sara said reflectively, "I do see us here. I like the Bayside Village School for Tara. I like the people here. I like Roger and Jenny, and Randy and Elizabeth. I like the spiritual practice here. I see that you're happy, even if you're unsure what you want—I still see glimmers of excitement and hope shine in you when you talk to people here. And I had an interview yesterday—I really like the idea of creating a unified communications strategy here. I guess that's focusing me on how this place could look for us, and for me."

"I see that. It's interesting that things have shifted for you."

"It feels to me—it's a growing feeling—that we actually could have a larger purpose here, a purpose that meets us both at a deeper level. It's coming from more than my job interview. I'm starting to feel like we could really connect deeply with people here."

"Interesting," Greg said, listening. He trailed off in thought, a bit of concern written on the lines of his forehead.

"Do you feel what I'm saying? Isn't this your feeling, too, when you're talking to people, seeing the museum and Temple and all the strange things here, thinking about how you could work on AlignIt with Roger?"

Greg thought deeply a few moments. "You know, I admit I've been in my head a lot here—maybe as a defense."

"Against what?"

"Suppose I give everything to AlignIt. Suppose we uproot ourselves from our friends, our meditation group, our jobs, the life we have in Seattle. Even though our lives are seldom easy, we do have a life that works. Say we move here, and things work out for awhile. But maybe things don't work out as we hoped."

"So?" Sara said. "That could happen in Seattle, too."

"But we're already there," Greg said. "We wouldn't be going to some utopia to pursue a dream. But if we move here, to me it feels like this is the ultimate. And maybe AlignIt doesn't succeed as a technology, or as a business. I mean, there's weird people like Mrs. Blocke who control things, or Chris Mueller could take over AlignIt and boot me out. I have no idea what is going on with them or how they could get into a place like this. What if AlignIt isn't very stable? Or maybe the Bridge Institute has more unexpected weird people . Maybe your communications job doesn't work out. Maybe the Bayside Village runs into problems and falls apart. I mean, where would we go after this? What kind of career path could I have after working on AlignIt, if it fails?"

"What if it succeeds?" Sara said. "What if you give yourself to AlignIt and it opens doors with people and places we haven't dreamed of? What if I get that communications job and it takes off?"

"True," Greg said. "Maybe I'm defending against the brightness of that possibility."

"You're contracting against the fear of losing something so precious."

"Mmm."

"Greg, sometimes you surprise me. Since when have you become so conventional? This was your crazy idea to come here. What happened to your craziness? Think about how we met—in an esoteric school. Think about how we're raising Tara. Think about what we've pursued together— the things we study and practice together. Why are you now focused on fear of loss, on sticking with the familiar?"

"No, you're right. You're right. This is what I want. And this is crazy.

And that makes it a big step. It's a really big step in our lives. And maybe I need to rise up to the opportunity with courage and boldness. If this is what I want," he said, looking off to the wall in the front, his eyes teasing apart the structures in the mathematical wallpaper, "I need to pursue it with all my heart—an open heart. I am defensively contracted and intellectualizing everything, and that isn't living fully. I want to embrace something new with an open heart."

"Of course it can fail—but so what? If you've given it everything you've got, then you've lived with integrity, dignity, and self-respect." Sara paused, looked at Greg. "I know you know this—I'm just challenging you."

"I know. Thanks. This is really helpful. And you're right—Roger can see it too. The next step for me has to be opening my heart to some of these things I haven't lived fully yet—games, dancing, just being with people in direct, immediate experiences. I'm uncomfortable dancing, you know," he said, looking sideways to Sara beside him. "That's a bigger issue than just being here and interviewing." Greg returned his gaze to the wall before him. "I have to face that, too. I won't be effective here if I just stay in my head."

"I think you should dance ontology."

Greg laughed. He reflected on that line. Then he looked Sara in the eyes and she gave him a knowing, loving look back. "Thanks." He reached over and hugged her, and they rested for some moments in a tender embrace.

Then Sara laid down romantically under Greg and pulled him closer. "Starting now," she said. "Dance with me."

"Dance?"

"Horizontally." She stroked him between his legs, gazed seductively into his eyes. He came closer, moved against her. She rubbed gently till he became hard. "Come explore my structure and function, Mr. Ontology." She unsnapped her pajama pants, exposed her underwear. "Come verify my objects and their properties." Greg smirked, shook his head at her silliness. She smiled, continued in it. "Let's investigate inputs and outputs."

Greg laughed. "You know just enough ontology gibberish to be funny. And dangerous." He crawled on top of her, leaned down for a kiss, dug the stiffness poking through his sweat pants gently into her half-unbuttoned pajamas. "Yes," he mused, "its a good way to study the mysteries of being."

Greg spent a long time making slow love to his Beloved, with long meditative, prayerful movements, ascending in lightening-flashing exhilaration and resting. Greg and Sara collapsed into a lovely embrace. Sara drifted off to sleep, blissfully intoxicated, her body exercised, pounded, spent. Greg drifted off too, refracting.

Then Greg woke in the dark. He lay there, reflecting on experiences through the week. His anxiety about Blocke, his panic about Mueller. He reflected on his fear of dancing in public, his reticence to get up and join Sara on the dance floor. He recollected his hankering for Neil's approval, his concern for tenure, his attachment to intellectual discussion. Turning things over like this, he came to a big realization. Fear and anxiety had plagued him during the week. They guided his life. He got up, sat at the table in the corner, touched his mobile, activated his screen and keyboard projections.

Opening the AlignIt application AuthorIt, Greg wrote some notes to himself about fear and courage. Then he opened the Advanced Search. He explored the quality of courage. He went through everything—dictionary terms, synonyms, antonyms, spiritual teachings, spiritual exercises, psychological exercises, poetry, quotes, mythology and folklore, gods and goddesses, saints, saint stories, animal fables, divine names, I Ching hexagrams, mandalas, yantras, physical exercises, diet. He sat reading, contemplating. What is courage, he thought? Do I see the seeds of it in myself? How do I cultivate it? He selected a few poems on courage and meditated upon them.

His eyes heavy and drooping, he returned to bed with new insight, new seed thoughts on courage working in the background of his mind. He turned toward Sara, put his head on the pillow, lifted the covers over his shoulders. He brought his attention to his breath, his awareness to his heart, until he came to a dim state of present awareness. How can I grow this, make it permanent, he thought.

Day 7: Saturday

87

Greg arose early and put on the coffee maker by the sink. He sat down at the round table in the corner. Touching his mobile, he projected the keyboard and screen, opened an entry in AuthorIt, and began to write his night dreams.

When the coffee finished percolating and aroma filled the room, Greg arose to pour himself a cup.

"Can you pour me one?" Sara called quietly from the bed.

"Sure."

Greg poured a second cup, added milk from a carton in the small refrigerator. He got out a packet of powder and poured it into his own coffee. He brought the cups to the table in the corner by the window. The first glimmers of morning light now peaked through the window shades.

Sara stood up, stretched, yawned, and pulled up a chair. Her eyes were sleepy and watery, her hair a beautiful jumble. "Thanks," she said, adjusting her chair next to Greg and taking the cup.

"Sure," Greg answered quietly.

"What did you put in yours?"

"Hingvastak."

Sara nodded. "For what?" She blew steam, sipped.

"Calms excess vata."

"Mmm," Sara said.

Greg sipped, swallowed. "How did you sleep?"

"I slept well." Sara took a few sips with a purr of enjoyment at the heat, and sat in silence a few minutes. Then she said, "Did you have a dream?"

"Yeah. Two. Can I tell you?"

"Sure."

"Let me just tag them. I'm using AuthorIt." Greg finished tagging by the locations, people, numbers, colors, and themes.

"Okay," Greg said, sitting back. "The first one was a visual and auditory dream. Someone called me on the phone. I picked up the receiver and said 'Hello,' expecting it would be a man. It was a woman. I could see her even though she was on the line in another location. She was not very beautiful. She was trying to say hello and communicate, but she lost her voice and was having a hard time expressing herself."

"Hmm," Sara said quietly, reflecting on the dream. She took another sip of coffee.

"Then I had another dream. A woman and a man were inferring a code from another pattern I knew. They were in a large university room. It was dark, and the woman was working near a wall with some lab equipment. Lights mysteriously appeared in mid air and on the wall. The lights appeared in a pattern, but the full pattern wasn't shown. This was an esoteric secret.

"Wow," Sara whispered.

"The man was somewhere else, inside the machine, or a different dimension. He wasn't really in the room. But somehow the man and woman were working together like a team, though they were in different dimensions. He was helping her see the hidden parts of the pattern.

"I said to the woman that I was surprised. I had seen these lights, too. But I would never have come to this method of discerning the whole pattern on my own.

"Then I knew that because I saw these two examples, I had now seen the method and the whole code."

"Wow," Sara said.

"Then I saw another woman. She was a conventional, mainstream university scientist. And there were some other lights in the room, less luminous, less mysterious. She had the old scientific method for investigating a pattern.

"Compared to this conventional scientist, I saw that I had a cipher. And I deciphered something." Greg paused. "And that's the dream."

After a silent pause holding and considering the dreams, Sara said, "Hmmm. Both seem significant."

"They feel important."

"What do you make of them?"

Greg took a sip of his coffee and held the cup close, breathing in the spiced aroma of Hingvastak. Then he put it down. "I have a sense that the first one was an aspect of my own feminine side. It wasn't anyone I know, and she didn't remind me of anyone. It seems significant that I was called."

"Yeah," Sara said. "I thought that, too. And significant that you answered."

"Mmm." Greg nodded. "It also seems significant that the feminine had lost her voice. She knew what she wanted to say. She could form the words, but she couldn't produce sound and project her voice. I had a sense that she needed help." Greg paused, taking another sip of coffee. "So, what is she trying to say to me? And what is my response?" Greg thought a few moments. "The dream doesn't develop to a point where I respond. It ends when I hear her trying to communicate and she can't get the words out. The fact that she calls me, that I pick up the phone and communicate, that she tries to speak, and presumably I will try to listen and respond— these things say I have a connection with her, at least. But the next step is to help her to speak."

"Seems you don't find her beautiful. Maybe you have a hard time valuing her."

"Yes."

"Do you think the two dreams are related?" Sara asked.

"Seems so. They're both about inner feminine figures. Both are about listening."

"Maybe listening to this woman calling you is a key to the second dream," Sara said, "about being shown the method and the pattern. You have a man and woman working together on a common task, from two dimensions."

Tara woke up. She sat up in bed.

"Good morning Tara," Greg said softly.

Sara turned around. "There she is," she said in an intimate, welcoming voice.

Tara rubbed her eyes and stretched. "Good morning." She got up out of bed and went to sit on Sara's lap. Sara welcomed her and put her arms around her.

"Good morning, Sweetness," Greg said, leaning over to kiss Tara on the forehead.

Sara held Tara and gave Greg a few further comments on the dream. Tara often sat with her parents in the midst of morning dream reflection. She was accustomed to the dream world being read, felt and contemplated as real and important.

"Greg, we should pack up our things before breakfast."

"Okay." Greg got up and began packing while Sara held Tara as she slowly woke up.

"This is our last breakfast here," Sara said to Tara as they entered the Dining Commons. "We'll have breakfast, and then we're going bye bye—back home."

The idea of leaving didn't seem real yet to Tara, who didn't answer.

Greg and Sara picked up trays and plates when they reached the buffet, with Tara walking along between them. Greg turned back to the walls, studying the tile work accenting the wood frames, as if for one last time.

Greg, Sara and Tara moved through the line, picking out foods. "We've had some pretty good food here, even after the orientation ended," Greg said.

"We have, haven't we?" Sara said. "It feels nourishing. I like that it's already made for us—that alone feels nourishing. Although I do love to bake."

They found a table and sat down.

"Ah, my last meal to spice up my food."

"What do you have there?" Sara asked, surprised, an ironic smile on her lips.

Greg gave a personally satisfied grin. "Little cups with each of the hot sauces and mustards." Sara smiled and shook her head left and right. "What's the matter?" Greg asked playfully. "We've been to the Sensory Parlor Collective and the Tea Emporium. And now, this is my little Taste Parlor." Greg arranged the cups around his tray. "I don't know what I'm going to do when we get home!"

"You're so funny. You see? You are mysterious!"

"You want me to be mysterious, don't you?"

"You are! And maybe I want you to be, too. Anyway, back home you can spice up your life, too," Sara said.

"Yeah, I guess so. I feel ready for something new and different."

"I have some ideas," Sara said, grabbing his leg under the table with her legs.

"Ah, a love parlor."

Sara made a quiet "shhh" sound and tipped her head toward Tara.

As the family sat eating, Greg looked around the Dining Commons, fixing impressions in his memory. He heard the buzz of conversation, the banging of meal trays, the clinking of dishes being collected and washed in the kitchen. The architectural features of the room caught his attention again—craftsman style, with open, exposed ceiling beams. He loved the large picture windows punctuating wood-paneled walls bounded by wooden window frames. He liked the art works displayed on the walls, the idea that these come from creative work done on campus. Most of all, he loved the feeling of community. This main room of the Bayside Village, a community center of sorts, was a priceless experience. He would miss it.

88

Greg walked to a bench outside the Dining Commons where he met Roger. The two men went for a final walk around the Bayside Village. They started on a different path than Greg had taken so far, winding around behind the Village Plaza.

"So Neil's out of the picture," Roger said. "He told me yesterday that this isn't his kind of thing—he doesn't have a taste for it."

"He told me. I saw him in the men's room after the board meeting. That's too bad." Greg walked a bit, watched his steps. "I understand why. He has a sharp mind, but you really do need to have a taste for this, I guess, or it's just not going to work."

"Maybe more than a taste for it," Roger said. "I think you have to see it. At least I want people to see it. Pretty early on in the week, I didn't think it was going to work with Neil."

"You know," Greg said, "for all of his seeming obstinacy, he was actually very gracious to me yesterday."

"How so?"

"He encouraged me to pursue teaching here and work with you on AlignIt, even though he recognized it wasn't for him."

"Hmm," Roger said. "That's big of him."

"He also wanted me to pass on to you a word of warning about Chris Mueller."

"Really? About what?"

"Remember they sat together at the board luncheon yesterday?"

"Yes."

"Neil said Mueller told him things in confidence that he shouldn't have told him. It was too soon. Neil told me, 'I don't keep the confidence of a jackass like that.'"

"Really?" Roger said. "What did he say?"

"Not a lot, I guess. Most of what he told me came from inferences he drew from Mueller. He said that basically Mueller has different ideas about AlignIt than you do. He doesn't share your vision. He wants to take it in a different direction. He wants to kill the ontology and he wants me out of the picture."

"Wow," Roger said.

"Neil doesn't trust Mueller. He said Mueller revealed his interest too quickly and showed him favoritism. And I have to say, I was really impressed with Neil. Because he wanted me to pass on something to you—even though he didn't feel he could tell you himself. He said you should watch your back. Mueller has other interests."

"I appreciate that." Roger took in a deep breath. "Yeah. I've been seeing that." Roger pierced his lips, sighed, looked to a grassy lawn ahead. "Actually, I have some things to tell you about Mueller." Roger breathed in. "It seemed too soon to tell you earlier this week. And we still don't have enough facts yet." Roger paused. "But I have enough to make a decision."

Greg looked at Roger seriously. Here would be moments of truth about what he had been feeling and wondering.

Roger turned reflective, looking off into the distant path ahead, trailing off in the marshes. "I felt a lot of trust in Mueller when I first met him. He was interested in AlignIt. He gave me good ideas about how to prime AlignIt for commercial deployment. And I had a good feeling about him. While I didn't feel the deep affinity I share with others here, and with you, it felt like enough. And it seemed we had enough rapport since he had an interest." Roger paused. "In hindsight, I see that more was needed."

Greg looked at Roger expectantly.

"On Sunday evening, Mueller gave me a call. We were at the reception. You were standing there. He said he wanted to add an item to the Board agenda. He wanted to talk about two things, and we had a follow-up call the next morning to go in depth. First, he wanted to talk about games. You don't know this, but GameIt holds exclusive, field-of-use license rights to AlignIt in gaming. Mueller knew this. But he wanted to bring other game companies into AlignIt. And the secretive, indirect way he approached it didn't feel good to any of us. So this already felt like it was not in good faith."

"Wow," Greg said, looking at Roger as he walked, squinting in the morning sunlight.

"Then he said he wanted to halt further development of AlignIt itself, especially ontology, and he wanted to drop you out of the picture as a consultant. Not a good ROI."

"Wow. Really?"

"He wanted to focus instead on signing on new companies right now and boosting revenue. None of this felt right to me, and I told him so immediately. He insisted that I should consider this strategy. He's brought several fledgling companies to IPO. He knows what he's doing, he said. So on Monday, I went to Jeff right away and told him about the conversation. In fact, I've had a lot of conversations this week, behind the scenes. Anyway, Jeff and I did some research and discovered a very interesting fact. Using Connection Finder, we discovered that Mueller has a connection with Amelia Blocke in HR."

"Really?" Greg's eyes widened, and he felt something like the awe of revelation. His mind worked to piece together details from Roger's report and his own observations.

"We discovered that they've worked together in the past, and she's placed people in some of his portfolio companies. So we were very surprised to find this."

"Well I have an interesting story for you."

Roger's eyes widened, eyebrows raised. "Okay."

"Yesterday before the board meeting, I went to drop off my full application to Mrs. Blocke. As I approached, I saw Mueller leaving her office."

"Hmm."

"He didn't see me. He walked down the hall in the other direction. But I saw something very interesting. I told you my awful experience with her on Thursday. So I had a feeling for what she was like. Well, after Mueller turned the corner, I knocked on Ms. Blocke's door. She opened with a smile and an expectant look in her eyes. Until she saw it was me. Then she contracted, shocked to see me. When she recovered, she gave me her stodgy old face that I saw the day before. I figured she expected Mueller but got me. So, I saw a different side of her."

"Okay. So there's a picture emerging here," Roger said. "Some of this I could tell you as a consultant, because Chris Mueller relates to the AlignIt Commons. Some I can tell you as a trusted friend and colleague. But some is Institute business because Ms. Blocke is on Institute staff, and she's HR which relates to your faculty recruitment. So you understand that this is also sensitive information and I have to be discrete."

Greg nodded.

"Yet Mueller and Blocke are connected, and I can't help but mention at least a bit of this to you. You'll understand when I say there may be other reasons you've met obstacles with Ms. Blocke. And I hope you know, from the great reception we've given you and Sara this week, that these events with Mueller and Blocke are unexpected, anomalous, and don't represent the Bridge Institute. We've just discovered it this week, and we're still gathering facts and working through our response."

This did bother Greg. Indeed, Mueller and Blocke didn't seem to represent the Institute. But was this problem an anomaly? Was it rather a warning sign? But he continued with Roger. "You think Mueller's leading her to put me off? Maybe they're in kohutz?"

"We don't have all the facts," Roger said. "And it's early to be saying some of these things. I'll just ask you to hold this and keep up with your application process. We have some further investigating to do."

"You know? After I saw Mueller sneaking out of Blocke's office— that's what it looked like, like he was sneaking—I reasoned that this can't be above-ground, that you wouldn't endorse this if you knew of it. I figured, then, that something was amiss. I also saw your glances yesterday before and during the board meeting, and I could read that you weren't okay with Mueller. So I went into the board meeting confidently. I just gave it my all."

"Good, good. It was the right thing to do. I'll ask you to keep it up. So there are two parts to this. Mueller is related to AlignIt, hence to your consulting. But we haven't accepted him as a board member yet. So very much remains in my power to act. And I'll tell you in confidence that I'm going to rescind our offer of board membership. But Blocke is related to the Institute, and hence your recruitment. And when it comes to Blocke, things are less certain right now about her position. We're looking into it, and I'm meeting with President Bateson after this walk to discuss what we're going to do about her. But it's obviously more complicated since she's employed. I can't say more right now. But if you're still interested…"

"I am," Greg said.

"Good, then I'll ask you to hold two things—one, that you have a strong application and we want you here, and two, that something strange is going on in HR, possibly linked to Mueller, and it needs sorting out."

Greg nodded, reflected. They walked up two steps to the raised platform of the Ohlone Observation Deck, looking out on the marsh. Greg found it beautiful taking in the whole marsh in a glance. He spoke, looking out to crabs, muscles, and cordgrass. "One thing I don't understand is why would such a conscious, intentional place as this bring in someone like Block, and Mueller for that matter?" Greg asked.

Roger sighed. "I know. It's perplexing, isn't it? We're trying to create the very best container for this type of school in the West. It's hard to do because the best people in academic administration don't necessarily have the spiritual background we seek. Nor do spiritual adepts who may share our vision necessarily have the best administrative skills, unless they've been working in the world. Not every path has a principle like 'Solitude in the Crowd,' or work in the market place, like ours does. Or that Shaker saying, 'hand at work, heart with God.' So for many Bridge Institute applicants for senior admin posts, we've had to make some tough choices about experience, credentials and network connections. It was a board-level decision to take this approach. Maybe we'll need to revisit the Trustees' decision as we investigate matters with Blocke."

Roger paused. Greg watched the marsh grasses blowing in the gentle wind. He pondered what kind of place Bayside Village was, with institutional hiring subject to a board decision like that.

"And then there's my own connection with Mueller," Roger said, "and there lie some hard lessons for me. Some humbling lessons I've been learning this week, interestingly. Like how I opened myself in a more trusting way than I should have. You know that old hadith, 'Trust God, but tie up your camel'?"

"I've heard it, yes."

Roger sighed. "We're not a utopia or a perfectly realized ideal." He turned, stepped off the Ohlone Observation Dock, headed down a new path Greg hadn't seen yet. "We're a human community with all its hazards, uncertainties, and dark sides. But we try to hold and bring in something from a higher plane. That's what makes us different."

"I appreciate your honesty and self-reflexivity," Greg said. "It inspires hope in me, greater than a facade of perfection would." He paused, thinking. "It does have me wondering a bit, though."

"How so?"

Greg thought a moment as he walked, studied with his eyes some new feature of the landscape he hadn't seen yet on campus—some sort of dug out pit near the water that continued up through campus beside the path they had taken. He turned to Roger. "It makes AlignIt and the Bridge Institute seem vulnerable. It's been a wonderful experience this week, and yet a strange one. It has me wondering—how many more people are there here like Blocke and Mueller?" Greg paused. It wasn't comfortable to raise this. "If I'm thinking of giving up everything I have in Seattle, at University of Washington, and moving here, I want to feel it's secure. I don't want to move here and then everything falls apart. Then I've walked away from tenure, job security, support for my family...and career prospects. I don't know what I'd do next if I moved here and things went south."

"I hear you," Roger said. "It's a real concern and a fair question. This is a strange wrinkle, indeed." This was hard for Roger, too. For AlignIt was his dream, and in Greg he found someone who could fit into it, work with it, help realize it. This was, indeed, a vulnerable time, with this Mueller and Blocke fiasco surfacing, with Greg here at the same time, with the three of them related somehow. If Greg was the next step for AlignIt, Mueller and Blocke posed an immediate threat. For here Greg was wavering not over AlignIt itself, but over its stability, its security, the prospect of its being thwarted. Roger walked silently a few moments. "This isn't a perfect place, for all our study of utopias." He looked to Greg. "It's a human community, with all the hazards of any undertaking." He looked again at the path ahead, at the dug out pit trailing the path they walked on. "We dare to do something bold. With our limited resources, with many countervailing forces, with all our individual and collective failings, we dare to do something bold. And God willing, something bold and beautiful will come about. And by the grace of God, it will be spared from our own failings. One of mine is not seeing Mueller clearly enough. Trusting too much, perhaps. Where I should have tied my camel. I've had many conversations behind the scenes this week to flush out this problem, and I've had some hard lessons to learn."

Greg nodded, considered these words. He felt Roger a sincere and humble man, a man of utmost integrity. "I've often heard from VCs that you bet on the people, not the technology." Greg paused. "It's a little hard to say this. But Bayside Village or the Bridge Institute could fail. AlignIt could fail. I could come here and these could fail. But somehow I feel confident placing my bet with you. Even if you might fail at something…the way you live, the way you work, is so utterly admirable. I feel like I want to be part of whatever you're doing. Even if AlignIt succeeds, things still move on, and AlignIt could move on beyond this place. And whatever is next for you, it seems like it will be something good."

That struck a note deep in Roger's soul. They were negotiating of one of life's deepest relationships. Roger stopped, turned to Greg. "You don't know how much I value the growing friendship between us." Greg stopped, turned, put his hands in his pockets as Roger talked. "I feel a deep sense of scholarly rapport with you, but also a sense of soul work or life work together. Everything would have to fit together in the right way, of course. But if things line up just right, I think we could have a remarkable time together here. And your words to me just now are the greatest honor I could have at this point in my life and career."

The two men stood there, with this moment of truth, this feeling of destiny, hanging palpably in the air. Greg nodded, smiled, looked to his feet humbly. He felt it too. He felt it deeply. This was exactly the daring venture he set out upon—not just to visit or move here, not just to sample experiences and exposures, but to live this, to have this bond, to share this sense of destiny, vision, purpose, and meaning. What a precious opportunity, so fine, so rare. So fine that Greg wasn't sure now what to do next.

Then Greg looked up. His eyes turned to the landscape behind Roger. "Can I just ask…What is this monstrous pit snaking its way up through campus?"

"Yes, speaking of hazards…." Roger turned to look at it. "We're

445

building a canal."

"A canal?" Greg was incredulous, befuddled. It looked that big. The depth of it, the piles of dirt on the side. But words got stuck in his mind as he tried piecing it together.

"A canal," Roger said. "It will start at the marsh—but that's the last part we'll complete. It will run up to mid campus, turn and run across campus, and turn back down to another part of the marsh. It's a giant 'U' shape."

"How could you build a canal here? You have an historic site, endangered species, ground contamination...."

"It's precisely because of the environment, actually. It's an experiment related to sea-level rise resulting from the polar ice caps melting. And we're planning about ten to fifteen experiments related to it, from desalination to water purification to cultivating aquatic life. We'll use it as a grand laboratory. And get this—we'll also have canal boats to make it scenic and accessible."

Greg's eyes popped out. "What? How could you get zoning rights to do this? Isn't California crawling with radical environmentalists who would shut that down in no time?"

"We have some extraordinary advocates for our projects, including environmentalists. Not only that. We have it on an aggressive schedule. They say it will be completed by August—which is when you could move here, if things work out that way."

"Wow!" Greg said. He looked up and down the length of the pit dug so far, saw platforms with supplies, heavy equipment. "This totally surprises me. This is over the top. This is more than just retrofitting an old industrial building and filling it with some utopian people and ideas."

"This is the scale of project we aim for at Bayside Village. We've only been here six years, don't forget. This is a sign of what is to come."

Greg shook his head, stared in silence at the canal a few long moments, then looked to Roger. "Shall we continue?"

"Sure." Roger turned, walked again. "So, aside from Neil, Mueller and Blocke," Roger said, "how are other things looking to you now, at the end of your week?"

"I'll definitely do consulting on AlignIt—at least that. And probably Sara and Tara will join me periodically if we decide only on consulting, because I think Sara has found a place for herself here over the week. And Tara seems to like it here. But the big question is the faculty position and whether we leave Seattle, leave our jobs, and move here. I'm ready to say I want to move here. I'm ready to take on this work with you and AlignIt, and teaching at the Bridge Institute. It would be the greatest daring venture of my life, and I think I'm ready to risk my tenure standing at UW to teach here. Sara has really struggled with this whole thing, too. She had that interview with Karen on Thursday—which you must have set up, right?"

Roger smiled subtly, turned his head to Greg. "I may have thought ahead about some things."

Greg smiled, too. "I thought so. Knowing you better now, it doesn't surprise me. Anyway, she said it went well, for the most part. But she also felt mixed about it. I guess one of the interview questions stirred up some things for her."

"Hmm," Roger said. It didn't seem so to him after talking with Karen. "I know it's a lot to be surprised by an offer to interview."

"I guess." Greg thought through other concerns Sara might have. "And moving to Community Housing, or even near where you live. And the school. And her job. Aside from the interview, we haven't really looked for jobs for her yet. We have a lot of digesting yet to do. And I think Sara is waiting to see how strongly I feel about this opportunity before she runs off investing time in a job search."

"Sure."

"But I know that she really enjoyed meeting you and Jenny. We both did. So I think we'll want to nurture this relationship with you as a couple."

"Jenny and I were talking, too. We're very glad to have made this connection. We'd like to stay in touch and get together again." Roger's face exuded a fond look of rapport, his eyes beaming in a deep feeling of connection.

Almost unable to bear the strength of Roger's fondness, and his own similar feelings, Greg broke the gaze. Roger noticed this and pulled back the intensity of his presence for Greg's sake.

They walked silently a moment, reflecting. Then Greg said wistfully, "I feel sad winding things down for the week and returning home. I feel moved by everything we've done here. It feels like the whole world stands open before us. This was a wonderful week of new possibilities. Yet it's uncertain. Things may go this way, or not."

"If I could give you one piece of advice?" Roger looked into Greg's eyes, felt his implicit consent. "Care about it so fully that you give it your full effort. And don't care at all about it so that you're completely free, so that anything can happen. Have no attachments either way."

Greg laughed. "If only I was that mature."

"Of course you are," Roger said.

"Well, I know what you're saying. I do try to practice like that."

"Alright," Roger said with a deep smile in his eyes. "Its about time I see Steve Bateson. And then I'll see you before you leave."

89

Roger walked to the Administration Building on the Bridge Institute quadrangle. He went up the stairs to President Steve Bateson's office on the second floor. The door was open, and Roger entered. He sat down at the big mission-style meeting table and chatted with Steve who was seated there, still reviewing the files on Chris Mueller and Amelia Blocke Roger had sent him. Steve turned back to finish and Roger sat, gazing ahead. Before them on the walls hung Steve's many prints of famous utopias, actual and imagined, where he often gave them a look in the midst of his meetings, refreshing himself by their inspiration. And he changed them periodically, Roger noticed; some were removed, and new images were hung now.

Steve turned to Roger. "So this file shows the connections you've traced between Amelia and Chris." He sat forward and scrolled back again through the shared file.

"Right. These are images Jeff and I drew from Connection Finder, and then my notes. See," Roger said, sitting forward, "go back to that one. There. You can see Amelia was hiring for these companies, which are Chris'."

"Mhmm," Steve said, studying the images. "These connections are verified?"

"Jackie had her staff check them against Chris' file, at least. In Amelia's case, however, she herself keeps all of Bayside Village's HR files, so…that's why we're approaching you about a formal investigation."

Steve glanced sideways at Roger, baffled. A glint of morning sunlight shafted from the window, lighting his white hair. "Do you have any idea at all what they might be up to? Simple influence peddling? Unfair dealing? Or do we have just a wild coincidence?"

"Its hard for me to come to this. You know the hopes I've had for Chris. But the best we've been able to surmise since Sunday, from Jeff's VC, Jack, and others, is that Chris's a bit of a con artist, creating a large smoke screen of apparent connections. He doesn't have a good reputation in the Valley, it turns out. He moves in on technologies, plays hard ball, acquires low, strips them down, integrates portfolio company technologies, and flips them. And we're assuming now that this is what he's after with AlignIt. This connection with Amelia is suggestive in light of the other things emerging this week. "

"That's serious. And Jackie's investigating this, too?"

"I started with her on Monday, and Rachel Ho, and Jeff, and Jack. So it's been a team effort all week. Chris, at least, has something going on, and probably Amelia as well. He's also very opinionated about not hiring Greg. I just don't know how Amelia's involved, except that she's been very obstinate about meeting Greg and processing his paperwork, and she hasn't returned my calls."

Steve returned his eyes to the screen and continued scanning Roger's file. "And Amelia and Chris both have rebuffed Greg this week." Steve pulled back his hand from the keyboard projection and sat back in his chair. He brought his elbows back to the arms of his chair and raised his hands up close by his chin where he interlaced his fingers, contemplating. He turned his head to Roger. "Does Greg know any of this?"

"We spoke frankly about it just now. He's also spoken to me about his treatment from both Amelia and Chris. He just told me he witnessed Chris leaving Amelia's office yesterday, tip toeing." Roger told the story to Steve.

"This is rather complicated now, because of the gifts Steve's pledged to the Institute," Steve said. "Has Chris approached anyone else? Anyone in AlignIt? GameIt? Jackie's group?"

"Not that we're aware of. Jackie said we have no contracts with Chris."

"And we have no smoking gun with Amelia."

"Just her delay and rude behavior," Roger said, "and Greg seeing Chris leaving her office."

Steve was silent for some long moments, chewing gently on his pointer fingers. He looked up to the wall before him, his eyes moving between images of utopias there—New Harmony, Oneida. "But this has been a trend, and you're not the first faculty member. Catherine's had difficulty with her."

"Yes, we've talked," Roger said.

"And Greg wouldn't be the first casualty—and we don't want that to happen."

Roger sat forward. "Chris made quite a connection with Neil Benson, the other consultant I had in this week for the AlignIt Commons board meeting. Chris was unambiguously courting Neil and marginalizing Greg. If Chris' mention of game companies hadn't triggered our search, Jeff and I wouldn't have found his connection to Amelia. There could be more than what we've found. But this much is already substantial—their prior employment connection, and her subsequent hiring for his companies. I think it warrants an investigation."

"Why do you think Chris would be courting Neil and rejecting Greg?" Steve asked.

"He wants near-term revenue from AlignIt, and he sees Neil as a player with the credentials his investors seek. Greg is a burn on cash. Chris came out and said as much, and his social behavior says as much."

"Hmm. Has Neil spoken of this?"

"Not to me. But to Greg, he gave warnings to watch our backs. Chris put the shine on Neil, and Neil didn't like what he saw. He asked Greg to pass along a warning to me."

"What do you think we should do with Chris?"

"He's not under contract yet, so its low risk for me and the Commons to simply rescind the offer of board membership. But a parallel investigation of Amelia at the Bridge Institute authorized by you would help us both."

Steve sat silently a moment, contemplating, frowning as he focused forward across the table, pondering prints of utopias built, utopias failed. "You do know Mueller could pull his gift from the Bridge Institute. We should factor that into the picture here."

Roger stared a moment, perplexed. "What do you mean pull the gift?"

Steve looked piercingly at Roger. "He has pledged to give, but he's only given the first of four parts. He could renege on the pledge and cancel the remaining three."

"Oh," Roger said. He hadn't known that. The new information hit him unexpectedly. His face looked pained. He suddenly felt the weight of that gift money to the Institute bearing down on him. He realized now that his decision could impact not only him, not only AlignIt, but the whole Bridge Institute.

"Gifts are tricky things," Steve said in a thoughtful voice. "Even though there should be no quid pro quo, people do find ways of attaching strings to achieve the purpose they seek."

The truth of this hit Roger. Yes, a gift in four parts is a tricky thing. Roger didn't mean to sit so long in silence. But it took some moments to digest, to rethink. This was now much more than simply rescinding the board contract. It would affect other programs Steve had in mind. It might reach to funding for Greg. "How do you think of factoring in that Chris could pull the gift?"

"To a large extent, I already have," Steve said. "I kept to myself my suspicion of his interest in AlignIt, and his gift to the Institute, especially broken into four parts. It's a nice bit of leverage on his part, don't you think? His interest lies in AlignIt. He doesn't have an interest in the Institute, per se, nor in me. I felt this immediately when I met him. But I had not enough information to act on my suspicion." Steve paused. Roger listened. "He knows you and I are connected. Maybe he imagines I could exert pressure on you to accommodate his interests. At the right time, if he needs it, he could play that card."

It was immediately apparent to Roger. He nodded, paused. "How would that impact the Institute if Chris reneged on his pledge?"

"It's always good to receive funding, of course. But at the Bridge Institute we have a sensitivity to special interests. It's why we've set up our own funding mechanisms under the Bayside Village Charitable Trust. Not that our approach is infallible, either. But we know well the special interests that come with funding." Steve paused, breathed deeply. "I intuited Chris had a special interest with his pledge to the Institute, connected with his interest in AlignIt. Accordingly, after acknowledging his pledge, I said to Karen that we should not include the remaining three portions in our financial projections. Then if we lose the funds, we're not put out."

Roger was stunned at Steve's calm, wisdom, and foresight. "Well, Chris' guidance is out of step with my vision for AlignIt, the way we do business in the Commons, and my wish to bring in Greg both as faculty and consultant."

"I think we can afford to walk away from Chris' pledge to the Bridge Institute," Steve said. He glanced again at the prints of utopias on the wall ahead, a constant reference for him, an ideal, a compass needle pointing north. "We have other funds for Greg's compensation." He turned and looked confidently into Roger's eyes. "And even if we couldn't walk away easily—if he had gotten us into a dependency situation—I would still urge that we take courage in standing on principles and bear the loss in the short run for the long-term integrity of the Institute and its research, technologies and demonstration projects. I'll let you adjudge his guidance for the AlignIt board. For my part, if Mueller plays that card and reneges on his pledge, it won't move me. I stand by you."

Roger took a deep breath, nodded slowly. He looked genuinely into Steve's eyes. "Here is the real test of friendship, trust and partnership. In this courage and integrity lie the seeds of rebuilding a sacred civilization."

Steve nodded, paused thoughtfully.

"So, back to Amelia," Roger said.

"Right." Steve tapped his lips with his finger, contemplating. "This is another challenge." He sat forward in his chair, bringing his hands before him on the table, his fingers in the same interlaced position. He sighed and glanced at the framed photos of the Suleymaniye complex in Istanbul, the subject of his current paper with its critique of institutional compromises that dim the light of learning. "I was not in favor of opening up our administrative leadership positions so easily, so broadly, simply to attract top talent....Not that Amelia has proven to be top talent. But I'll want to stress this point to the Trustees. We've created vulnerabilities by seeking some top talent regardless of commitment to vision, and now we have this problem on our hands."

"There's also a performance issue with Amelia," Roger said. "She's been unresponsive not only to Greg but to me as well."

"Yes, I've had other complaints" Steve said, pointing to a folder on his screen projection. "I authorize an investigation. We'll need Blocke's files."

Roger checked the time on his mobile and set it down on the table. "Can I ask your thoughts on Greg before the call?"

Steve adjusted his chair toward Roger and sat back, smiling hopefully. "And Sara, too, I suppose?"

"Yes. You met them both." Roger adjusted his chair.

"It's one of those experiences where I feel right time, right place, right people, and things line up."

"Yes," Roger said. "I have that feeling."

"Credentials aside—I have no concerns there," Steve said, interrupting himself, "...I watched his attention as we spoke, and Sara's too. I saw them Sunday night and in my Tuesday workshop. They're both astute and sensitive. I could see their connection not only to ideas but to our vision. Greg is thinking not about what a big sensation he can make as a top faculty recruit. He's contemplating contribution. Sara, too, would make substantial contributions to our community."

"Karen likes her," Roger said. "I spoke with her yesterday The interview went well. I'm doing everything within my means to win their hearts. I'm looking for the right note to strike in each of them, in accord with their soul and their destiny. They're young, still. I see fears and other emotions veiling their fleeting contact with their soul's purpose."

Steve nodded. "Yes, I've seen that. All you can do is call that part in them. How they respond is their business."

Roger looked at the table, thinking. "That's hard enough business."

"Like we've discussed many times," Steve said, "there are hazards in bringing something new into being. We can anticipate and arrange, somewhat. And we can call forth soul to soul. And then we have to surrender our work."

Roger nodded, digesting the impression of Steve's counsel. A moment of unitary consciousness encompassed the two men, and Roger felt deep rapport. Then the memory of time registered in his awareness. "It's 10:30."

Steve nodded and reached forward to dial in to the Trustee call.

90

After lunch, their last meal at Bayside Village, Greg said, "Let's do a final walk around the Village."

The family walked out of the Dining Commons, the wooden screen door clapping behind them. "Down to the waterfront?" Greg suggested.

"Sure," Sara said.

They walked mostly in silence down to the Siegel Marsh, over the board walks extending across the mudflats. Looking out over the Bay, Greg reflected on the week, digesting all that he had seen. He turned around to look back at the Bayside Village campus behind them as a balmy breeze tossed his hair. Feelings mixed in him: thrill about living so many values at once, tiredness from meetings and interviews, sadness about leaving today, thrill about coming back, concern about Blocke and Mueller getting in the way yet confidence that Roger was dealing with them, excitement and noble purpose in working on sacred science and ontology with Roger.

Tara looked through the binoculars on the Ohlone observation deck to the sea lions one last time.

Sara stood beside Tara looking out to the Bay. Greg leaned on the railing next to Sara, looking back to campus. He pondered aloud, "What would a philosophy of science look like that took on recovery of sacred science?" That was his question, he thought, his definitive question, his parting question. Sara was pondering her own thoughts. But she gave Greg her attention, which he felt. "If we come here," he said, "I feel inspired to take on big questions in the history and philosophy of science. I might work on that—a philosophy of science focused on recovery of sacred science. Not just showing evidence that some sciences can work, and have worked. But also why they work, how they relate to modern sciences, and how to extend them."

Sara listened, nodded.

It wasn't her interest or question. Greg knew that. But she could hold Greg's interests, and he could hold hers.

"I want to pass through the quadrangle and Art Center before we leave," she said.

"Sure," Greg said, turning. They started back. "How about you? Parting thoughts?"

Tara ran ahead on the path, knowing the way back, but knowing to stay within eyesight.

"Mmm," Sara said, and she breathed deeply. "A clear feeling of returning to art. That got awakened in me this week. I did a lot of drawing. But this new feeling got galvanized by returning to Blakesly's book and his esoteric aesthetics." Greg listened as they walked up the campus, past the Plaza and Dining Commons to the Bridge Institute quadrangle. He remembered the early days of their relationship, her intuitive reach into esoteric ideas through art, Blakesley's work serving for her as a finger pointing to the moon of her artistry. "I'm thinking about the art program here, the mathematically patterned work at the Art Center, the yantras Swami-ji showed us."

"What about the job interview with Karen?"

"I don't know where that will go. I still feel concerned about my nonprofit reference. I don't know if I should be. But it's fun to imagine being art director and creating a unified communications plan. Maybe I shouldn't care what happens."

Greg listened, nodding. "That would be great for your career."

They entered the Art Center courtyard and walked casually through it, exploring the exhibits, peeking into the open studios. Sara needed this one last taste of the arts before departing.

They walked past the Temple, and Greg looked across the quad to Avicenna Hall, recalling the epithet inscribed on the cornerstone there:

Unite the pair so long disjoined,
knowledge and vital piety

Returning to the Lodge to pick up luggage, Sara said, "I guess I'd like to explore a yogic diet, or maybe an ayurvedic diet. I might want to work with the PlanIt meal planner. It looks pretty interesting."

Greg, Sara, and Tara wheeled their luggage out of the Lodge concierge office to the driveway where a taxi would meet them. Cut stones lined the driveway, and planters and half-walls were attractively inlaid with Bridge Tiles. Wheeling their luggage to a bench, Greg pulled his mobile from his pocket and called Roger.

Minutes later, Roger arrived. "Hey, there they are."

"Hey Roger," Greg said. "So this is it."

"Indeed—day 7, and they haven't run away yet," he said playfully. "Thomas Finegan told me, 'They're brave souls.'"

"It's been a very rich week," Greg said.

Roger looked down to Tara with a container and spoon in hand. "You really like that yogurt, don't you?"

"Mhmmm," Tara said as she applied herself.

"So what's next for you folks?" Roger asked, looking to Sara.

"Back to the daily grind," Sara said. "Work, school, housework. But I'm going to miss the community and commons here. It sure made life easier for a week."

Back to the grind, Greg thought. That had been their common language as a couple the last few years. Could it change now? Could their lives shift from a contracting to an expanding phase? He felt something opening in Sara.

"So do we have a verdict yet, or is too early to tell?" Roger asked.

"We need time to digest the week," Sara said. "But I think we both feel positive about the opportunity. I think we agree," Sara said, looking to Greg, "that we both want an integrated spiritual and family life like we've found here. It's pretty hard to find that elsewhere."

Greg nodded. "Just speaking for myself, I feel my heart opened and my mind expanded by everything I've experienced. Coming for AlignIt isn't the only question, now, though it prompted the visit. There's much more to consider. The community, the school, the practice, what we could live here. We have a lot to reflect on."

"I'll say, for your sake," Sara said to Roger, "that I'm pleasantly surprised. I was closed at first. But it seems this could be a great place for our family, a great next step for Greg. And I'm surprised, but I think it could be a great next step for me, too."

"For you, too?" Roger mirrored.

"You know I met with Karen Mitchell about the art director position. It would be a good step forward in my career. If I got the job, I'd create a unified Bayside Village communications strategy. So if that opened up for me, I think it could be a great experience."

"What do you think, Tara?" Roger asked. "Do you like the Bayside Village Day Care?"

Tara nodded her head up and down as she ate her yogurt and granola. "Ms. Alpine is my favorite teacher. And Hannah is my best friend. And I like the sea lions."

The taxi rolled in and drove around the circle to the benches and planters. Greg turned, flagged it.

"Well, here's our ride," Greg said. He shook hands and then gave a hug to Roger. Sara hugged him too.

The driver lifted the luggage into the trunk, and Greg, Sara, and Tara boarded the car. They waved to Roger as the taxi took off, out the drive way and down the road for the Oakland airport.

In the back seat, Greg took Sara's hand in his and smiled at her. She returned a warm smile.

"Bye bye sea lions," Tara said.

"Bye bye sea lions," Greg echoed.

"Daddy, are we coming back?"

ABOUT RICK WHITNEY

Born on Earth in the late 1960's (Gregorian calendar) and living there all his life so far, Rick Whitney has settled in the northern hemisphere, not far from the Golden Gate Bridge.   He works by day at a world class research university helping important things happen; by night he steals away in the side room of his California bungalow with the dog and laptop to bang out his second novel.

www.ingramcontent.com/pod-product-compliance
Lightning Source LLC
Chambersburg PA
CBHW051432260626
47162CB00001B/62